Fugitive Prince

Janny Wurts is the author of numerous successful fantasy novels including the acclaimed Cycle of Fire trilogy. She is also co-author, with Raymond E. Feist, of the worldwide bestselling Empire series. Her skill as a horsewoman, offshore sailor and musician is reflected in her novels. She is also a talented artist and illustrates many of her own covers. She lives in Florida, USA.

Voyager

Janny Wurts

FUGITIVE PRINCE

The Wars of Light and Shadows

VOLUME 4

FIRST BOOK OF
THE ALLIANCE OF LIGHT

HarperCollins*Publishers*

Voyager
An Imprint of HarperCollins*Publishers*
77–85 Fulham Palace Road,
Hammersmith, London W6 8JB

The *Voyager* website address is
www.voyager-books.com

This paperback edition 1998
5 7 9 8 6 4

First published in Great Britain by
Voyager 1997

Copyright © Janny Wurts 1997

The Author asserts the moral right to
be identified as the author of this work

ISBN 0 00 648299 6

Set in Palatino

Printed and bound in Great Britain by
Omnia Books Limited, Glasgow

For Beth Gray,
who opened the first door
that has led to so many
others.

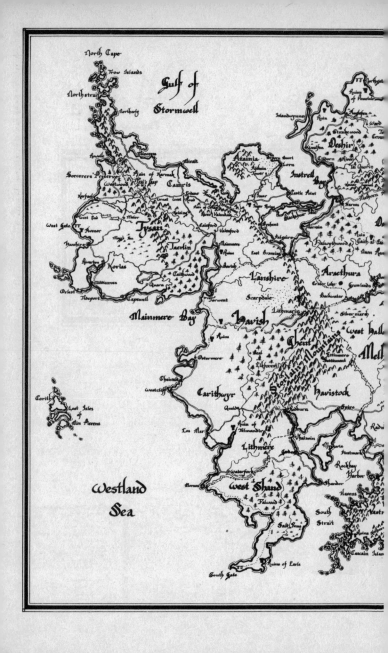

Athera
Continent of Paravia
Age of the Mistwraithe

Fallowmere

North Ward • Brimwood
East Ward
Plain of Araithe
Jaelot
Lithmere
Etarra
Lattorn Mountains
Perlorn
Riverpoint
Crescent Isle

Rathain
Ithilt Rocks
Minderl Bay
Ithilt
Eastwaal
Minderl Ruin
Minderl Strait
Saint's Point
Last Gate

iamon
Narms River
the way
ion Barrens
Shand Pass
Shamon
Tornir Peaks

Bay of Eltair

Vastmark

Ghurdir
Whitehold
Torwent
Varens
Kiens
Ladlair

East Halla
Atwood
Ailan
Tiriac's Ruins

Ardiih

Cildein Ocean

Midhalla
Thaldein Mountains
Mirthlvain Swamp

Kelsing
Kalesh
Adruin

Orvandir
Iveth
methuin
Methisle Isle
Quanlh
Silver
Six Towers

Shand
Arthen
River Ippash
Forthmark
Sebryll
Daveth
Sanpashir
Ruins

Alland
Selkwood
Sanshevas

Lsetmo
Telesin
Scimlade Tip
Merior
Sickle Bay
Shaddorn
Alestron

South Sea

Los Lier

Scale in Leagues
0   10   25   50   100

KEY
Sorcerers' Preserve
Cities
Second Age ruins
City that did not fall in uprising
Worldsend Gates
Standing Stones
Kingdom Borders
Rivers
Forests
Marshes or Mires
Wastelands
Second Age Roads
Trade Roads
Mountains

Acknowledgments

This book would not be in material form
without the help of so many, who gave: Jeff Watson,
Mickey Zucker Reichert, Jonathan Matson, John Silbersack,
Caitlin Blasdell & Jane Johnson, Sara & Bob Schwager, Pieta Pentram,
Lazaris; Don Maitz, my long-suffering husband—and not least,
many hundreds of trees.

Contents

First Book

Thirty-five thousand marched to war.
Their weeping widows all died poor.
Swords against Darkness, reap for Light
Fell Shadow's Prince and rend false night.

—verse of a marching song from the
campaign of Dier Kenton Vale
Third Age 5647

I. Fionn Areth

Strong arms closed and locked around Elaira's slim shoulders. Fingers strengthened by the sword and sensitized to a master-bard's arts tightened against her back. The dark-haired, driven man who cradled her surrendered at last to his blazing crest of passion. His lips softened against hers, the restraint, the control, the terrible doubts which bound him consumed all at once in a rush of tender need. She responded, melted. Her being exploded into sensation like fire and flight. At one with the prince who had captured her heart, her spirit knew again that single, suspended moment, with its promise of inexpressible joy.

Then the fulfillment of union snapped shy of release, doomed ever to fall short of consummation by the rough intervention of fate. This time, a harried, insistent pounding snapped the dream into fragmented memory.

The small-boned enchantress entangled in threadbare quilts jerked out of her fretful sleep. A muted cry escaped her. Chilled in the drafts which flowed over the sill of an unglazed croft window, she fought to regain full awareness. Once again, she grappled the irreversible reality: Merior's mild sea winds and the Prince of Rathain lay two years removed in her past.

Elaira squeezed her eyes shut against the ache. Instead of the muffled boom of breakers creaming against stainless sands, the ferocious,

1

clawing breath of winter whined over the white-mantled dales of Araethura.

Yesterday's blizzard had delivered a biting, cold night.

Over the open glens, through stands of scrub oak and across the rustling flats of frozen marsh, the ice whipped in driven bursts, to rattle the ill-fitted shutters of her cottage at the fringe of the moor. Crystals found the cracks, tapped at the lintels, and fanned a frosted arc of silver across the leaked bit of moonlight admitted through the same chink. While the eddies moaned and clawed past the beams of the eaves, and the spent tang of ash commingled with the fragrance of cut cedar and frost-damp miasma of moldered thatch, Elaira exhaled a deep breath. Given time, the runaway pound of her heart would subside.

She untangled the fist still clenched through a coil of auburn hair. Too many times she awakened like this, struggling against the blind urge to weep, while the ripping, slow agony of Arithon's memory threatened to stop her will to live. In desperation, against the vows of the Koriani Order which tied her lifelong to a celibate service, her refuge from despair became the fiercely guarded shelter of her solitude.

Tonight, even that grace was forfeit. The disturbance which had torn her from lacerating dreams came again, the insistent hammer of a fist on wood.

There would be some emergency, of course. Elaira grumbled a filthy phrase in the gutter vernacular of her childhood and kicked off her tatty layers of quilts. "Fatemaster's two-eyed vigilance! Do they all think I'm deaf as a post?"

Whoever pounded for admittance, the abuse threatened to burst the tacked strips of leather that hung her rickety door.

Sped by awareness that she lacked any tools for small carpentry, Elaira heaved up from her hoarded nest of warmth amid the bedclothes. The shock of cold planks against her bare soles dissolved her invective to a gasp. She had retired unclothed, since yesterday's storm had soaked through to her shift. Through forced delay as she fumbled past the clammy folds of her cloak to snatch the first suitable garment from its peg, the hammering gained a fresh urgency.

"Fiends plague!" The dank cloak would just have to serve. "Whoever you are, I don't dispense remedies naked!"

Elaira bundled the soggy wool over her shoulders. She closed shivering fingers to secure the cloth under her chin, then shot the bar and stepped back as the door swung inward.

A dazzle of moonlight flooded through. The collapse of the drift left pocketed across her threshold doused her bare ankles in snow. Elaira yelped and leaped back. Her cloak caught in an eddy of wind, snagged the latch, and tugged itself free of her grasp.

The herder boy outside froze in startlement, saucer eyes pinned to the slide of the wool down the firm, naked swell of her breast.

Elaira managed the grace not to laugh at his expression. She caught the errant wool and snugged it back up to her collarbones. "Are you going to come in?" she asked with mild acerbity. "Or will you just stand 'til you freeze with your mouth hanging open?"

The shepherd boy shut his baby-skinned jaw with a click. Too young for subterfuge, still innocent enough to flush to the roots of his tangled hair, he ventured a slurred apology behind the snagged hem of his sleeve.

"Of course there's trouble," Elaira said more gently. "You've a year yet to grow before you start calling on ladies for that sort of randy interest, yes?"

The boy shrank and turned redder. Since he was also frightened enough to bolt back into the night, the enchantress caught his arm in a grip like fixed shackles. She bundled him inside, wise enough to slam the door before she plonked him on the stool by the hearth and let him go.

"Who's fallen sick?" she demanded, brisk enough to shock through his stunned silence. She groped meantime across darkness to sort through the pile of last night's discarded clothing. The fire had done its usual and gone out. Gusts hissed down the cottage's flue and scattered ash across the stone apron where her herbal still rested, a dismantled glint of burnished copper and glass reflecting a meticulous upkeep. Seized through by a shiver, Elaira drew on the icy linen layers of her underthings, then laced the stiffened leather of her leggings overtop.

The herdboy huddled under mufflers on her stool and could not seem to find his tongue.

"Don't say no one's sick," Elaira murmured through chattering teeth as she turned her back, cast off the cloak, and wormed into the dank, frowsty cloth of her shift. The hem which had been dripping as she drifted off to sleep now crackled with thin, crusted ice.

"My aunt," mumbled the boy. He stared at his toes, unaware of the stockyard pungency of goat carried inside on his clothing. "She's in childbed. The midwife sent me to fetch you."

Burrowed into her tunic and struggling with numbed hands to hook the looped leather fastenings, Elaira said, "How long since her labor pains started?"

"Since just after midday," the boy replied, miserable. "I couldn't run. Snow's piled too deep." He worried his chapped lip with small teeth. "Will she die, do you think?"

"I'll try not to let her." By reflex, Elaira stilled her thoughts and used the trained edge of her talents to sound the night for the time. Past midnight, she sensed. The tidal pull of the full moon just dipped past the arc of the zenith. She crouched to retrieve the fleece boots she had kicked off and left where they fell. One hid in deep shadow under the worktable, scattered still with oddments of tin stamped with the sigils for fiend bane. The mate perversely eluded her. "Do you know if her water had broken when you left?"

"Aye, so," the boy affirmed in his broad-voweled grasslands dialect. "That's why the midwife would have ye. The birthing's gone hard, and the caul broke and let forth an unlucky color, so she said."

Elaira caught a half breath in foreboding. "What color was the fluid, do you remember? Was there blood?"

"No blood." The boy paused to trace a symbol across his left breast, to avert the eye of ill fortune. "The stream was thickened and greenish. That's bad, yes? My aunt's going to pass beneath the Wheel?"

"No. She's unlikely to die." Sure of that much, Elaira blew on her fingers, reached, found her other boot, the one she had dunked at the ford when she slipped on a stone and the ice broke. The fleeces were still clogged and soggy. "It's the babe trying to come who's in trouble."

She gritted her teeth and thrust her toe in the cuff before her nerve snapped. No time could she spare to warm the wet out, even were the fire still alight. Every second counted, if in harsh fact the boy's call for help had not already reached her too late. She scrambled up off her knees and snatched her satchel from the table. Another minute strayed as she struck light to a candle stub and gathered up the specialized herbs she might need, ones the midwife was least apt to carry. More minutes fled, as she groped amid the disassembled coils of her still to twist the curved segment of glass tubing from the cork which capped the collection flask. She could only pray it would be the right size as she stowed it amid her remedies, to chinking complaint from the crockery and small flasks that held her stock of alcohol and tinctures.

"Come on," she urged the boy. "I'd make you some tea to warm up if I dared, but truly, your aunt's babe can't wait."

No coals lingered in the hearth to be doused. That lapse in comfort became a twisted sort of blessing as she rammed out the door and

plowed knee-high tracks through the dunescape of drifts to the shed.
A rumbling nicker greeted her from inside. Then a white-blazed face
peered out from the dimness, hopeful.

"You idiot butterball," Elaira replied. "You won't be begging more
grain."

The slab-sided roan gelding had come with the croft, no replacement in her heart for the spry little bay who had died of old age the
past spring. Some frivolous initiate had named the beast Tassel, for
reason outside of all logic. Elaira unhooked the rope hackamore that
served as his bridle and looped his whiskered nose through the
cavesson. He butted her, snuffling in quest of a carrot as she flicked
his ears through the headstall, then blew a resigned sigh as she bent
to raise his forehoof and treat the cleft with goose grease to keep snow
from balling up against his soles.

"Wise one," said the boy in whispered diffidence, "I don't ride."

"You will. If your aunt's to have help, you must." Elaira stepped to
the gelding's quarters and grasped a feathered fetlock, not without
heart to spare sympathy. "I'll see you don't fall off." In belated,
breathless courtesy, she asked his name.

"Kaid, wise one." From the corner of the eye, she caught the
clumsy, mittened gesture he made with intent to ward off spells.

Her stifled smile of irony was lost as the wind flogged her hair
against her cheek. "You'll do fine, Kaid. Not to worry." The odd con-
tradictions of countryfolk, to summon her for the magics that refined
the craft of healing, then to trace out a hedge witch's symbols to avert
the dread effects they feared from the selfsame mysteries.

Elaira had never known the reverent respect once offered to initiates of the Koriani sisterhood. The arts of her order had been viewed
with trepidation for as long as she could remember. The ignorant
intolerance arisen since the uprising that upset the rule of the old high
kings had not lessened with defeat of the Mistwraith's fell fogs,
which had masked Athera's skies for five centuries. Quite the contrary, the entrenched distrust the townborn folk held for sorceries had
been inflamed to root deeper since the hour the vanished sunlight
had been restored.

The Koriani Prime Enchantress held adamant opinion on the reason: the new strife arisen through the Mistwraith's curse of enmity,
laid upon the two princes whose gifts had brought its captivity, just
provoked such misguided beliefs. Blame was not shared equally
upon the shoulders of Lysaer s'Ilessid, birth-born to wield the powers
of light. Only the Master of Shadow, Arithon s'Ffalenn, was raised
mage-wise. The Prime and her Senior Circle were swift to point out

his shortcomings. Unlike the royal half brother set against him, he had spurned the strictures of his training and invoked the high arts without scruple.

Few would deny that across four kingdoms, Arithon's name was now linked to destruction and unconscionable acts of bloodshed.

Elaira stamped back that distressed line of thought. The Shadow Master's part in the ruin of Lysaer's war host on the field at Dier Kenton Vale must never become her concern. She knew his heart; had once shared his deepest fears, and knew of the visceral horror of killing that tormented him, mind and spirit. As sharply as she longed to know whether the affray had unstrung his grip on integrity, the unruly emotions burned into her heart lent iron to her resolve. Her order must never be offered a second opening to use the attraction shared between them. Shamed to rage that her love had ever come to be tested as a tool to set Koriani ties on Arithon's destiny, the enchantress applied herself to the crisis of the moment. She slapped grease in the roan's last hoof, straightened up, and wiped her hands on a scrap of old burlap.

"Out, you." She gave a suggestive tug at the roan's headstall, too pressed to delay for the saddle. "We've a hard night ahead. You're going to have to do a generous bit more than shamble."

Another gust screamed past the corner of the shed. Gossamer veils of snow unraveled from the lip of the drifts. The eddy streamed Elaira's hair across her eyes. She clawed back the tangles, impatient. "Come, boy." A swift touch adjusted the hang of her satchel. "You'll need to show me where to go." She raised her wet boot in quest of a foothold in the buried logs of the woodpile, vaulted astride the roan's back, then extended her arm to haul the herder child up before her.

He was shaking through his furs, mostly from fear since he shrank as her arms clasped around him.

Elaira sucked in a breath musked with wool and the rancid tang of goat. "Which way?"

The tilt of Kaid's chin said north. Elaira faced the gelding around into the teeth of the wind. Its cold pierced her clothes like honed steel. The stars overhead were like flecks of chipped ice, and moonlight sheared the hillcrests in razor-cut brilliance against the streaming, knotted shadows sliced by trees.

"Hup!" Elaira cried. She gathered the roan's reins and thumped him with her heels. The gelding shook his mane, grunted back as she drummed another thud against his ribs. His steaming warmth penetrated the damp layers of her leggings, and a breathy snort smoked from his nostrils. Too lazy to show displeasure beyond a flick of his tail, he roused into a short-strided walk.

Elaira shook her cuffs down to muffle her exposed hands. "How long did it take you to reach me?"

"I left our steading before nightfall. Snow fell too thick to know the time." The boy clenched his jaw to still chattering teeth.

Questions remained, over details the midwife might have shared that would tell how far the aunt's labor had progressed. Yet as the gelding breasted through chest-high drifts, or plowed a crumpled trail across the pristine vales carved trackless by the scouring winds, Elaira held her silence. Nothing but hurry could improve the babe's threatened chances. If she failed to arrive at the steading before the moment of birth, the infant might already be lost. Rather than pass her distress to the boy, she reined alongside a thin stand of alder and picked off a branch for use as a switch to force the placid gelding to trot.

The night engulfed her in its landscape of silver and black. Amid the wind-tortured swirls of dry snow, the horse underneath her seemed all that moved in the world. If hare ventured out to gnaw bark and dry grasses, or if owls flew hunting mice, she saw no sign of anything alive. The tattered plumes of the gelding's breath embroidered hoarfrost on her patched leggings. His hooves stitched the hillcrests to avoid the soft drifts, and the boy sent as guide lolled against her shoulder and slept. Where the ground was swept bare, she flicked the gelding to a canter, the glassy chink of snapped ice compacted under the thud of his passage. The gentle, rolling downlands stretched ahead and behind, sere under unrumpled snow, the rippled ink of oak copse and the grayed trunks of alders snagged through by tinseled skeins of moonlight. Over marshes herringboned in storm-trampled cattails, and past the treacherous, inky wells of sinkpools, Elaira forged ahead in relentless urgency.

The fugitive hours were her enemy. The sensitivity of her talent let her feel them, slipping inexorably by as sand would sieve through a net. She drew rein at the crest of a dale, confronted below by the steep flanks of a gully, and the snake black outlines of iced-over current. Araethura's downs were famed for such, obstructions to any traveler unfamiliar with the lay of the valleys. Elaira cursed, remiss with herself. She ought to have wakened the boy sooner to ask guidance, for the narrow, swift-flowing streams which fed the River Arwent ran in treacherous, deep beds, too wide to jump over in snowy footing, and unsafe to attempt a crossing without a known ford. The same had been true of Daon Ramon, long ago, before the diversion of the mighty Severnir's flood by Etarran townsmen had rendered that golden land barren.

7

Elaira gave Kaid's shoulder a shake before the cold let her thoughts stray further. He said as she roused him, "No need to cross over. Our steading's beyond that stand of alders."

Shadows obscured the building's outline, a patched, oblate pattern where drifts had silted over the mosaic outline of roof shakes against the vale beyond. From some hidden byre, the bleat of confined goats breathed in snatched fragments between gusts. Elaira shook up the tired roan, pressed his laboring step downslope. The pricked gleam of stars came and went as the alders closed around her, branches wind racked against the zenith. Two hours until dawn, her tuned awareness told her. That time of night when death was most apt to be welcomed by a body and spirit in distress.

She slid off the gelding's back, left the reins to the boy, to dismount as he could and see it stabled. She wasted more seconds, fumbling to close the iron latch of an unfamiliar gate. Finally arrived in the sheltered space between hay byre and cottage, she thought for a second she heard the pained groans of a woman. Whether the sound was born of labor, or grief, or just a last, cruel trick of the wind, the weight of the moment crushed hope.

Stiff, stumbling across the rutted yard, Elaira tripped the door latch and shouldered her way across the threshold into the cottage of Kaid's aunt. Darkness swallowed her. Cut off from the clean bite of winter, the closed-in smells of lavender and birch coals and the ingrained musk of grease left from simmering a thick mutton stew made the air seem stagnant and dead.

Then, muffled through board walls, the midwife's voice arose in terse encouragement, "Bear ye down, dearie. The time's come upon us, and naught can help now by delay."

A brittle, third voice made shrill with the quaver of old age remarked, "Let the babe come. The *fferedon'li's* here at last." The chosen term was a bygone word for healer, corrupted from the Paravian phrase which meant 'bringer of light.'

Elaira moved on, tense and sharply uneasy, unsure she merited the confidence and trust implied by the use of the ancient title. The room she crossed seemed too still, too close, its eaves sealed tight against the weather, as if the vast, rolling moorlands of Araethura were an adversary worthy of a barricade. The cottage held its carven chairs and furnishings the way a miser might grasp a hoard of coins. A close-fisted family, Elaira sensed through observation; not the sort to ask outsiders for favors. The trained perception of her gift allowed her to pass their cherished clutter without tripping, to avoid the spinning wheel and stool jutted between the wool press and a tub of

8

drawn water arrayed on the flagstones by the hearth. Boards creaked beneath her hurried tread. This steading was prosperous, to have glazed and shuttered windows, and better than a packed earthen floor. Her next step fell softened by a throw rug. The byre and fenced pastures should have prepared her for comforts. Those Araethurian herdsmen less well off let their stock graze at large on the moors.

A paneled door creaked open. Raw, orange light spilled out in a swathe to guide her through to the cottage's back room, a walled-off chamber beneath the beams of the loft, where a row of younger children peered down, their expressions all dread and curiosity. Elaira caught another flurried gesture to avert spells before she gained her refuge in the bedchamber.

A tallow dip in a crockery bowl rinsed the broad shoulders of the midwife, a middle-aged matron of competent presence, sleeves rolled back over rawboned wrists where she knelt to administer to Kaid's aunt. The woman she attended was small as a deer, dark haired and wrung limp, far beyond fear or caring whether an enchantress or a demon had entered. She crouched on the birthing stool, her face lined with sweat, a plait wisped into tangles draped over the wet shine of her collarbones. Her feet were bare. The rest of her torso was swathed in a crushed mass of down quilts, her shift of undyed linen rucked into bunches above her thighs.

As though sensitive to censure, the midwife said, "It's hot enough she is, but the husband insisted." Past a sound of disgust through her nose, she added, "Matter of her modesty, *he* claims. It's all foolishness. No wisdom in it, but the man wasn't born in these downs who isn't bullheaded useless over the propriety of his wife."

The girl on the stool convulsed in another contraction, long since too tired to scream.

"Steady," murmured the midwife in a striking change of tone. Her beefy fingers closed over the straining woman's in comfort. "Don't falter now, dearie. Just bear down." She held on, encouraging, thick wrists gouged in crescents where suffering fingernails had dug through the violent cramping pains, weathering the terrible, fraught minutes of waiting, holding, resisting nature's overpowering drive to push out a babe long since ready to be born.

Over the girl's exhausted grunting, from the corner by a clothes chest, a mass first mistaken for a bundle of old rags stirred to scratch. Attenuated, white-boned fingers went on to sketch out a blessing sign in welcome. Behind the gesture, faint in the gloom, a withered face surveyed the enchantress who came as healer.

The traditional seeress, Elaira identified, grateful at least for one courtesy. A matriarch gifted with Sight attended every birth, death, and wedding held in these isolate downlands, her place to interpret the omens and deliver a guiding augury appropriate to the occasion. Elaira made her response in accentless Paravian. "May the future be blessed with good fortune."

Then she knelt on the boards beside the midwife, and caught the laboring woman's other, clammy hand in reassurance. The wavering glow of the tallow dips threw a sultry gleam off the crown of the babe's head, just emerged and cupped within the midwife's other, guiding hand, which pressed gently downward to ease the child's shoulder past the bone beneath the pelvic girdle.

"Ath preserve," Elaira murmured. "I'm not too late to try and help."

The laboring woman gasped a question.

"Lie easy," Elaira told her. "Let the midwife instruct you. If all goes well, your babe will stay living and healthy."

She straightened, unslung her satchel from her shoulder, and shed her snow-dampened mantle. While she struggled to unfasten the thong knots with chilled fingers, she added quick, low instructions to the midwife. "Now the birth is accomplished, cut and tie the cord as usual. But do not stimulate the child. It must take no first breath, nor rouse itself and cry before I can clear the fluid from its air passage."

The midwife raised no question in protest. Quietly busy with towels and knife, she knew best of any which complications lay beyond reach of her knowledge; had seen warning enough when the mother's water had broken, clogged and discolored. The trauma of birthing had stressed the unborn babe and caused it to void its bowels before it could be pushed from the womb. The fluid which had cushioned its growing had become fouled by its own excrement. If it chanced to draw such taint into its lungs, the newborn would perish of suffocation. No herbal remedy in her store of experience would change the outcome. The child would die within minutes.

If the Koriani witches knew a spell to avert tragedy, the midwife was too practical to spurn the aid of the one who had recently taken residence amid the fells.

But Elaira did not reach to free the chain at her neck from which hung the crystal her order used to refine magics. She rummaged instead through her satchel, found the thin, curved tube borrowed from the apparatus of her still, then warmed the cruel, outside cold of it away between her shaking hands. Methodical, she rinsed it clean of contaminants in a dish filled with her precious store of alcohol.

The laboring woman moaned through locked teeth at the weakened spasm of another contraction.

"No need to push further, dearie," soothed the midwife. Her practiced fingers knotted the slippery cord, last tie to be severed from the mother. "Work's all done. Ye've naught beyond the afterbirth left to drop now."

Through the frantic few moments remaining, Elaira shut her eyes, wrapped a hold on her nerves to force controlled calm over screaming uncertainty. These were fells herders, distrustful of her kind, and knit close with unbreakable ties of kinship. Should she fail in her effort to help this child, she well understood its death might be taken as a bloodletting offense.

To the woman's soft query, the midwife said, "Well-done, girl. By Ath's grace, ye've delivered a fine son."

Elaira steeled herself, turned, received from the midwife's competent, broad grasp the sticky, warm bundle of the child. His blood-smeared skin was pale gray, his limbs unmoving, not yet quickened by the first breath of life. She laid him head toward her on the table, aware through the crawling, unsteady light that his wet, whorled hair was coal black. She pried open the tiny, slack mouth, arranged the skull and neck, and with a hurried prayer to Ath, inserted the tube from the still down the throat and into the infant's airway. She must not tremble. The curved glass was thin, very fragile. Any pressure at an angle might snap it. Where a straw reed might have offered less peril, no interval could be spared to search one out. Need drove her. She must not miss the opening, nor tear the newborn's tender flesh in her haste. All the while the awareness skittered shivers down her spine, that she had but seconds to complete what must be done.

If the child were to die now, it would be of her own, rank clumsiness.

She felt the tube slide in. A sixth sense, born of her talents and training, told her the insertion was successful. She bent, set her lips to the glass, sucked, and spat the juices into the bowl she used to mix remedies. Against the white porcelain, the secretion was greenish, foul. She sipped at the tube again. Another mouthful, and still the drawn fluid was discolored. She repeated the procedure, was rewarded with a slight change in hue. The fourth mouthful came out clean.

"Ath bless," she gasped. She eased the tube free. The hot, close room seemed formless around her, the pinpoint focus of her concentration the lynchpin of her whole being. She slapped the infant's feet. "Breathe," she said fiercely, the exultation of success at last tearing

11

loose, to burst from her heart in searing joy. "Breathe, new spirit. It's safe for you to join the living."

The child's fingers spasmed. His tiny chest shuddered. Small mouth still opened, he sucked in clear air and screeched as lusty a first cry in outrage for expulsion from the dark, wet safety of the womb.

Elaira bundled the squalling infant back into the care of the midwife, then found the nearest chair and let her knees give way. She sat, head bent, her face in her hands, while emotion and relief shuddered through her. The cries of the child grew louder, more energetic. His flesh would be blushing to pink, now, as exertion flushed life through his tissues. Elaira pushed straight, scarcely aware of the commotion which swirled through the outer room, then the blast of changed air as the door opened. Feeling every aching bone, and all the weight of a night without sleep, she looked up.

Then froze, jolted through her whole being as her eyes met and locked with a man's.

He had black hair, green eyes. A face of lean angles bent toward her, the rage in each tautened muscle burnished by the hot flare of the tallow dips. The rest of him was muffled beneath a caped cloak, tied with cord, and woven in the fine, colored stripes preferred by the herders of Araethura.

Rocked out of balance, Elaira felt a cry lock fast in her throat. For a moment fractured from the slipstream of time, she could not move or think. Then the nuance of observation she was trained to interpret showed her the subtle differences: the fist, clamped in rough wool, with thick fingers too clumsy to strike song from a lyranthe string. This man was larger, coarser in build; not Arithon s'Ffalenn, Prince and Masterbard. The rough-edged male who loomed over her was the husband of this house, and the newborn child's father.

"Daelion avert!" His fury bored into the enchantress. "*What's her kind doing here!*"

"Never mind," Elaira said quickly. She had expected hostility in some form or other, since Kaid had appeared on her doorstep. "I'll be on my way directly." She arose, tipped the filth in the basin into the slop jar beside the birthing stool, then turned her back, stepped over the pile of wadded, bloody towels, to repack her things in her satchel. Her part was done. The child's danger was past. If the man was ill-mannered enough to dare set his hand on her, he would regret the presumption.

Like the whine of a whip, the seeress protested. "The *fferedon'li* will not go just yet. Not until the child's augury is spoken." Across the irate glower of the husband, the trembling, diffident anxiety of the mother, the crone arose from her corner, moved, an animate bundle of shawls, to present her appeal last to the midwife. "Tempt no ill luck. There's a sacrifice owed by this babe. He would have gained no firm foothold in this world at all, if not for the hand of the *fferedon'li*."

The husband swore with expressive, fresh venom, his glare still locked on the enchantress.

Comprehension dawned late, like a douse of chill water, or a sudden fall through thin ice. Elaira understood where the brittle, steel tension had sprung from. Her heart leaped at once to deny her own part. "I wish nothing, no tie for my service!" Through the longer, louder wails of the newborn, her voice clashed in rising dissent. "Let the boy's life hold to its own course, with no interference from me."

"Ye know better, gifted lady!" the seeress said, tart. "The debt against this young spirit is a fair one, and to refuse his given charge, a sign of ill favor and disrespect."

The father spun about, his bellow of rebuttal cut short by more withering reprimand. "Foolish man! Were ye raised by a nanny goat? Here's a strong son ye'll have, perhaps to beget other living children of your line! Now let the augury say what he's to grow and become. He may bear your blood. Yet the fate he'll be asked in payment for his birth is nothing else but his own!"

Silent, even mollified, for it had been her summons which had brought Elaira to the steading, the midwife lifted the naked, newborn babe, wiped clean of the fluids of birthing. A rutched comb of dark hair arched in a cowlick over the vulnerable crown of his skull. His face was rosy, suffused with crying, and his miniature feet lashed the air in what seemed an impotent echo of the father's outrage.

At the dry, cool touch of the seeress's hands his wails missed their rhythm and silenced. The crone raised the boy's small body. Her eyes were dark brown, clear-sighted and deep, schooled to reflect the infinite whole, from which grand source came the spark to animate all that held shape in creation. Watching the finespun aura of spirit light flare up as the woman tapped into her prescience, Elaira experienced both relief and sharp dread. The old woman's Sight was no sham, but an untrammeled channel attuned to the resonance of true mystery.

Then the words came, sonorous and full, to augur the coil of the future; they were directed, not to the babe's kin, but to Elaira.

"One child, four possible fates, looped through the thread of his life span. He will grow to reach manhood. Should he die in fire, none suffers but he. Yours to choose when that time comes, *Fferedon'li*. Should he die on salt water, the one ye love most falls beside him.

13

Should he die landbound, in crossed steel and smoke, the same one ye cherish survives, but betrayed. Yet should this child's days extend to old age, first the five kingdoms, then the whole world will plunge into darkness, never to see sunlight or redemption. Your burden to choose in the hour of trial, *Fferedon'li*, and this child's to give, the natural death or the sacrifice. Let him be called Fionn Areth Caid-an." The ancient seeress lowered the babe, the hard spark fading from her eyes as she closed her final line. "Let his training be for the sword, for his path takes him far from Araethura."

Elaira stared transfixed at the child just born and Named. She wished, beyond recourse, that her hand had slipped in its office, or that the dull-witted roan had mired in some drifted-over streamlet and fallen. Better, surely, if she had arrived too late, and this herder's son had gained no saving help to survive his transition into life. As her wits shuddered free of paralysis, the enchantress could not shake off a terrible, pending burden of remorse. The feeling which harrowed her lay far removed from the soft, stifled sobs of the mother. Elaira could not react to the rattling slam of the door, as the father stormed out in mute rage, nor to the midwife, murmuring phrases of helpless consolation for the destiny forewarned by the seeress.

The enchantress felt the trained powers of her focus drawn and strained in a web of disbelief. The babe had such tiny, unformed fingers, to have tangled the destiny of the Shadow Master between them, and all he entailed, the misled fears which had raised marching war hosts; the bloodshed and sorrows of an age.

Crown Council

Far distant from Araethura's wind-raked downs, in a wainscoted anteroom trimmed in gilt and agleam with pristine wax candles, an immaculate steward in blue-and-gold livery bowed to King Eldir's ambassador. "His Grace, the Prince of the Light, will see you now."

The visiting dignitary on the cushioned bench arose at the royal summons. A middle-aged man of spare bones and blunt demeanor, he seemed unremarkable for his post. Nor did he display the stylish, warm manner which trademarked the gifted statesman. Clad still in the travel-splashed broadcloth he had worn from the mired winter harborside, he followed the servant through the massive, carved doors, then down the echoing corridor which led to Avenor's hall of state. Cold light, reflected off a late snowfall, streamed through the lancet windows. Here, no stray sound intruded beyond the measured tap of footsteps upon satin-polished marble.

The palace sanctum where Prince Lysaer s'Ilessid plied the reins of his government lay far removed from the chopped mud of the practice yard, where the handful of veterans returned from campaign drilled their surviving field troops.

No secretaries murmured behind closed doors. A lone drudge polished rows of brass latches, her labors methodically silent. The hush felt inert as the vault of a tomb. Three weeks was too soon for the city to assimilate the impact of a fresh and unalloyed tragedy. The burgeoning industry of Avenor, so magnificently restored, seemed stalled; as if even the very resonance of power stood mute, stricken numb by the news that even now rocked the five kingdoms.

Of the forty thousand dedicated men sent to war in the rocky scarps of Vastmark, all but ten thousand had died of the strategy unleashed by the Master of Shadow.

The declared neutrality of King Eldir's realm made those casualties no easier to grapple. The ambassador sent by his liege to shoulder today's dicey audience was a man appointed for patience, and valued for his skeptical outlook. The outraged grief and shocked nerves he encountered made even simple needs difficult. Since the hour of his arrival, he had weathered a brangle with the seneschal's undersecretary, and before that, a harbormaster's flash-point temper, to secure his state galley a close anchorage. He chafed at the pressure. To miscall any small point of diplomacy could spark an unforgiving train of consequence.

For the stakes ran beyond mere potential for bloodshed. The deadlocked struggle between the Prince of the Light and his enigmatic, sworn enemy had widened. Arithon's works now polarized loyalties, and compromised trade in four kingdoms. Folk named him Spinner of Darkness since Vastmark. Fear of his shadows and rumors of fell sorcery attached to his secretive nature.

Sensitive to the pitfalls in the tidings he carried, the High King's ambassador reviewed his firm orders. Then his sovereign lord's entreaty, unequivocal and clear, given upon his departure: *"Your loyalty may come to be tested, and sorely. Lysaer s'Ilessid can be disarmingly persuasive in pursuit of his hatred of Arithon. But the Fellowship Sorcerers grant no credence to his war to destroy the Crown Prince of Rathain. Your errand may well be received in disfavor. Should you find yourself compromised, even imprisoned under wrongful charges, you must keep my realm of Havish uninvolved."*

If the ambassador regretted the burden of his mission, the moment was lost to back down. The steward escorted him through the arched portals which led to Avenor's state chambers. Masking unease behind a lift of dark eyebrows, for the credentials from his king had been public and formal, the dignitary found himself admitted through a less imposing side door.

In the smaller room used for closed hearings, Prince Lysaer s'Ilessid awaited. He was alone. A less imposing man, unattended, might have been overlooked on the dais, with its massive oak table, hedged by tall chairs with their carved and gilded finials, then these dwarfed in turn by the star and crown tapestry, device of Tysan's past high kings. The woven device masked the east wall, gold on blue beneath the spooled rail of the second-floor gallery.

Limned by a flood of cold, winter sunlight, this sovereign's presence filled that lofty well of space as a jewel might rest in a reliquary.

The dignitary from Havish discovered himself staring, forgetful of protocol or the ingrained polish of court ceremony.

Fair, gold hair seemed tipped in leaf silver. The eyes were direct, the clear, unflawed blue of matched aquamarine. Where Lysaer s'Ilessid had always owned a powerful, charismatic male beauty, the Vastmark campaign left him changed. Now, his majesty went beyond poise. As steel smelted down and reforged could emerge from the punishment of hammer and anvil to carry a keener edge, the pain of a massive defeat had tautened his flesh over its framework of bone. Less given to smiling platitudes, he wore the tempered, private stillness of the veteran who has squinted too long over hostile terrain. The strong southland sun, the cruel weather, the indelible grief imprinted by the loss of thirty thousand lives had but rekindled this prince's resolve; like a lamp set burning on a fuel of sheer faith, to illuminate where a lesser flame would fail.

The ambassador shook off stunned paralysis. He tendered the bow that acknowledged royal bloodline, but implied no stature of rank. The detail struck him as curious: the prince had eschewed to display the sovereign colors of Tysan. Instead he wore a tabard of white silk, trimmed with gold cord, and fastened at the neck with stud diamonds.

Lysaer s'Ilessid began in a brisk form quite altered from the effortless courtesy which trademarked his single, past visit to Havish. "You may sit. I will make no apology. This meeting must be short and private. A gathering of kingdom officials and outside delegates is scheduled to take place after this one. Those who attend have been discreetly handpicked. I hope you'll consent to be present, both as an independent witness, and as King Eldir's representative."

"It is to his Grace of Havish such apology is due." Blunt features immersed in shrewd thought, the ambassador wondered whether his equerry might have talked over beer in a tavern. Had word of his business reached Lysaer beforetime, today's air of secrecy boded ill. He perched on a bench, a touch on edge, his words like thin acid before the autocratic whims of royal privilege. "In fact, my appointment concerns an errand for the Fellowship Sorcerers, entrusted to Havish's keeping."

"Indeed?" An unexpected irony raised Lysaer's eyebrows. "That being the case, all the better if our discussion is kept close." He stepped around his state chair and settled. The stillness in him now went deeper than patience, went past mere endurance, or the blustering confidence a beaten man raised in game effort to shrug off defeat.

About Lysaer s'Ilessid lay a quiet that towered. His immutable, restrained force made the glare through the casement seem displaced, the hard scintillance of his gold trim and diamonds jarring as a master painter's slipped brushstroke.

He said, "I make no secret of my bias. The doings of Fellowship mages are no longer welcomed in Tysan."

The ambassador rejected political wrangling. "Any tie to the Sorcerers is indirect, you shall see. My case concerns the first ransom in gold, raised to free your lady wife. The one which vanished during transit across Mainmere Bay this past summer."

"Five hundred thousand coin weight," Lysaer mused with unswerving mildness. "My merchants, who raised the bullion, remember that setback too well." In phrases wiped clean of residual anger, he added, "That sum was purloined by the Master of Shadow. You bring me word of the contraband? I'm amazed. The Fellowship Sorcerers were nothing if not in cahoots with that blatant act of piracy. Go on."

The ambassador folded stiff fingers inside the lace of his cuffs. Too circumspect to pass judgment on the doings of mages, he picked his way cautiously. "Your lost gold was returned by Prince Arithon's hand, and surrendered under Fellowship auspices. By appointment as neutral executor, the crown of Havish will restore the full sum to your Grace's treasury. The incident, as you claim, went beyond simple theft. The Master of Shadow waylaid your lady's ransom as a tactic to stall your war host from invasion of Vastmark."

"Five hundred thousand coin weight in exchange for the time to arrange for thirty thousand deaths." Lysaer never moved, his seamless detachment enough to raise frost on hot iron. "What price, for the blood that was spilled in Dier Kenton Vale?"

The ambassador sidestepped that baiting insinuation. "The treasure is guarded aboard my state galley, counted and bound under seal by his lordship, the Seneschal of Havish. Upon my receipt of signed documents of discharge, the gold can be consigned to the care of Avenor's state council."

No need to prolong the particulars; a writ of acceptance could be drawn up and sent to the harbor by courier. Avenor's strained resource could scarcely spurn funds, however embarrassing their origin. Havish's envoy straightened, in haste to exchange due courtesy and depart. He had no authority to stay on as witness to the afternoon's clandestine council.

Yet before he could draw the audience to an end, the royal steward flung wide the door. A tightly bunched cadre of trade ministers filed in, their clothes trimmed in furs and jewelled braids. Costly, dyed plumes cascaded from their hat brims; their hands flashed, expressive with rings.

The prince had staged his private meeting to converge with the ambassador's presence. Eldir's delegate settled back on his seat, out-maneuvered by the forms of diplomacy. While the trade worthies vied like rustling peacocks for the places close to the dais, he waited in guarded resignation for the play of Lysaer's strategy.

This would be a volatile, partisan gathering to judge by the seals of high office displayed by the men who attended. Trade background let the ambassador identify at least a dozen of Tysan's ruling mayors, united in their distrust of Arithon. Other delegates with complaints against the Shadow Master had been summoned from extreme long distance, as shown by the black-and-gold lion of Jaelot emblazoned on a dignitary's tabard.

Another who wore plain broadcloth and boots seemed displaced, all fidgety with nerves as he moved through the trappings of wealth and the suave, mannered men of high power. The table filled, then the seats arranged by the side walls. The liverish governor of the Western League of Headhunters hunched uncommunicative beside two stolid commanders at arms with the broad, southcoast vowels of Shand. These would have suffered direct losses on the field, or borne firsthand witness to the devastating sorceries wrought from illusion and shadow.

Rathain's foremost headhunter, Skannt, sauntered in with his gleaming collection of knives. He chose to stay standing, arms folded, in the cranny by the gallery landing. At his shoulder, companionable and stout chested, Lord Commander Harradene chuckled over some pleasantry. To him fell the captaincy of the disheartened remnants of Etarra's decimated field troops. The chair left vacant by Lord Die-gan's death stayed unclaimed to Lysaer's right hand. As yet no replacement had been named to command Avenor's elite garrison. Nearest to the prince, faced bristling across four feet of oak table, a muscled, tight-lipped mercenary traded glares with Mearn s'Brydion, youngest brother of a clanborn duke from the eastshore kingdom of Melhalla. The scruffy little cleric in scholar's robes placed between them stared through the window, oblivious to the smoldering hatreds entrenched through five centuries of bloodshed.

The men Lysaer s'Ilessid had drawn to his cause were of disparate backgrounds and loyalties, too fresh in alliance to mingle in comfort, and too volatile a mix to leave standing too long without war to harness their interests. They crowded the small chamber like rival wolves, the martial devices of the field captains' surcoats bold as game pieces beside the padded silk pourpoints of city ministers.

Lysaer called the meeting to order. He might wear no coronet of royal office, yet the absent trappings of rank stole no force at all from his majesty. His opening phrase slashed the crosscurrents of ambition and froze them forcefully silent. "We are gathered this hour to resolve my claim to the powers of crown rule, offered to me by legitimate blood descent, and sealed into edict by Tysan's independent city councils." His hand, bare of rings, moved, reached, and lifted a heavy document weighted with state seals and ribbons.

All eyes in the room swung and trained on the parchment. Against the expectant, stalled quiet, something creaked in the gallery, behind and above the seated audience.

A snap of air flicked across a taut bowstring, then the whine of an arrow, descending.

Its humming flight scored through Captain Skannt's scream of warning, and above these, the shout of the archer, in sheared, clanborn accents, "Such claim is unlawful!"

A sharp crack of impact; the four-bladed point impaled the parchment and skewered it to the table. The chink of shattered wax became lost in the noise as the dignitaries chorused in panic, "Barbarian! Assassin!"

Pandemonium rocked through the room. Scribes bolted for cover. Overdressed trade magnates and timid mayors ducked, trembling and frightened to paralysis. Entangled and cursing, war-hardened commanders surged erect and charged, bowling over spilled hats and cowering figures. They heaved empty benches before them as shields and pounded for the stair to the gallery.

"I want him alive!" Lysaer cried through the clamor. Uncowed and looking upward, he wrested the arrow from the tabletop. The lacquered red shaft gleamed like a line of new blood against his stainless white tabard. The hen fletching also was scarlet, the cock feather alone left the muted, barred browns of a raptor's primary.

"That's a clan signal arrow. Its colors are symbolic, a formal declaration of protest." The speaker was Skannt, the headhunter from Etarra, his lidded eyes bright in his weasel-thin face, and his interest dispassionate as ice water. "In my opinion, the archer struck what he aimed at."

Lysaer fingered the mangled parchment, slit through its ribbons and the artful, inked lines of state language. He said nothing to

Skannt's observation. Motionless before his rumpled courtiers who crowded beneath the shelter of tables and chairs, he awaited the outcome of the fracas in the gallery. Five heavyset war captains rushed the archer, who stood, his weapon still strung. He wore nondescript leathers, a belt with no scabbard, and soft-soled deerhide shoes. In fact, he was unarmed beyond the recurve, which was useless. He carried no second arrow in reserve. As his attackers closed in to take him, he fought.

He was clanborn, and insolent, and knew those combatants who brandished knives bore small scruple against drawing blood to subdue him.

Fast as he was, and clever when cornered, sheer numbers at length prevailed. A vindictive, brief struggle saw him crushed flat and pinioned.

"Bring him down," Lysaer said, the incriminating arrow fisted between his stilled hands.

Scuffed, bleeding, his sturdy leathers dragged awry, the clansman was bundled down the stairs. He was of middle years, whipcord fit, and athletic enough not to miss his footing. Space cleared for the men who frog-marched him up to the dais. He stayed nonplussed. Through swelling and bruises, and the twist of fallen hair ripped loose from his braid, his forthright gaze fixed on the prince. He seemed careless, unimpressed. Before that overwhelming, sovereign presence, his indifference felt like contempt.

Through the interval while rumpled dignitaries unbent from their panic, to primp their bent hats and mussed cuffs and jewelled collars, his captors lashed his wrists with a leather cincture borrowed from somebody's surcoat. The clansman never blinked. He behaved as though the indignity of bonds was too slight to merit his attention.

"Slinking barbarian," a man muttered from one side.

Another snapped a snide comment concerning the habits of clan women in rut.

No reaction; the offender held quiet, his breath fast but even. His patience was granite. The royalty he had affronted was forced to be first to respond.

"If you wanted a hearing, you have leave to speak," Lysaer s'Ilessid said, forthright. "Consider yourself privileged to be given such liberty." A tilt of his head signaled a scribe to snap straight, find his pens, and smooth a fresh parchment in readiness for dictation. "Set this on record," Lysaer resumed. "To bear arms in the presence of royal authority carries a charge of treason."

"Your authority, royal or otherwise, does not exist," the clansman replied in his clear, antique phrasing, too incisive to be mistaken for town dialect. "Since my arrow isn't struck through your heart, you have proof. I haven't come for your death." He lifted his grazed chin. "Instead I bring formal protest. This writ signed by townsmen to grant sovereign power in Tysan is invalid by first kingdom law. The tenets of this realm's founding charter hold my act as no crime. Your claim to crown rule is in flagrant breach of due process."

"I need no sanction from Fellowship Sorcerers." Lysaer laid down the arrow, unruffled. Winter sun through the casement spanned the stilled air and exposed him; even so, he gave back no shadow of duplicity. For a prince who had lost untold lives to clan tactics, then his best friend and commander to covert barbarian marksmen, this unconditional equilibrium seemed inspired. His reproof held a sorrow to raise shame as he qualified, "I must point out, your complaint as it stands is presumptuous and premature. This writ from Tysan's mayors has not been sealed into law. I have not yet accepted the mantle of kingship."

To the stir of surprise from disparate city mayors, the murmured dismay from trade factions, and the outright, riveted astonishment of King Eldir's ambassador, Lysaer gave scant attention. "As for treason, let this be your trial." He gestured past the clansman bound before him. "The men assembled here will act as your jurors. No worthier circle could be asked to pass judgment. You stand before the highest officials of this realm, and the uninvolved delegates from five kingdoms. Nor are we without a strong voice from the clans. Mearn s'Brydion, youngest brother of Alestron's reigning duke, may serve as your voice in defense."

"I speak for myself!" the barbarian insisted over the scraping disturbance as upset chairs were rearranged, and the attendant men of government refocused their interest through the rustle of settling velvets. "Let there be no mistake. Since the murder of Maenalle s'Gannley, *caithdein* and steward of Tysan, her successor, Maenol, has appointed me spokesman before witnesses. Upon false grounds of sovereignty, *for the act by which you mustered armed force to make war for a wrongful claim of injustice,* hear warning, Lysaer s'Ilessid. Forsake your pursuit of Arithon s'Ffalenn. Or no choice remains for the good of this realm. The response from my kind must open a clan declaration of civil war."

"I think not." Lysaer set down the arrow. A small move, made with unemotional force; barely enough to stem the explosive outrage from the merchants who had lost profits to the Shadow Master's wiles, and from veteran captains his tactics had broken and bloodied on the field. Lysaer's blue eyes remained stainless, still saddened. His regard upon the captive never wavered. "Rather, I believe your clan chieftain would resist me as an act of insurrection. His grandmother died a convicted thief on the scaffold. He will see worse, I can promise, if he persists in rash overtures of violence. Woe betide your people, should you let your clans be bound in support of a proven criminal. To abet the Master of Shadow against me is to threaten the safety of our cities."

"This is a strict issue of sovereignty!" the clansman pealed back through the sawn and inimical silence. "Your royal inheritance has been disbarred by the Fellowship of Seven because your fitness to rule has been compromised. We serve no cause outside of our land's founding charter! This war you pursue against Arithon of Rathain is engendered by the curse laid on you both by the Mistwraith."

The Lady Maenalle s'Gannley had said the same words in the hour of her execution. The heavyset Mayor of Isaer might have borne witness, since she had been tried and condemned in his city, under his justiciar's tribunal.

Havish's ambassador himself could confirm that the statement held more than a grain of hard truth. But his king's will kept him silent, even as the other dignitaries expressed their searing disbelief. Ill feeling already ran hot on both sides. However the thundering crosscurrents of hatred bent truth to imperil the prisoner, Havish's representative could do naught but observe.

Lysaer's control was not absolute. Despite his impressive majesty, no matter how staunch his self-command, distrust of old blood royalty made his claim to the throne controversial; more telling still, the question just raised against the morality of his dedicated conflict. Fresh losses still stung. Inside one year, the campaign he pursued against the Master of Shadow had seen the eastshore trade fleet sundered and burned at Minderl Bay, then the clash as the armed might of four kingdoms ended in an abattoir of spilled blood at Vastmark.

As new uncertainty threaded tension through the gathering, all eyes fixed on the prince in his tabard of flawless white and gold.

His stance held straight as an arrow nocked to the drawn bow. He perused the assembled dignitaries, nestled like plumed birds in roped pearls and winter velvets; acknowledged the military captains with their muscled impatience; then diverted, to touch last on the single man in the chamber born to a laborer's status. One whose stiff, uneasy stillness stood apart from languid courtiers like a stake hammered upright in a lily bed.

"How I wish the threat posed by the Master of Shadow were due only to the meddling of Desh-thiere." A disarming regret rode Lysaer's pause. Then, as if weariness cast a pall over desperate strength, he relinquished his advantage of height, sat down, and plunged on in bald-faced resolve. "But far worse has come to bear on this conflict than rumors of an aberrant curse. This goes beyond any issue of enmity between the Shadow Master and myself. Hard evidence lies on record in the cities of Jaelot and Alestron. Twice, unprovoked, Arithon s'Ffalenn wielded sorcery against innocents with destructive result. Now, in the course of the late war in Vastmark, a more dire accusation came to light. Since it may touch on the case here at hand, I ask this gathering's indulgence."

The prince beckoned for the plain-clad man to mount the stair to the dais. "Your moment has come to speak."

The fellow arose to a scrape of rough boots, his occupation plain in his seaman's gait and hands horned in callus from a lifetime spent hauling nets. Too diffident to ascend to the level of royalty, he chose a stance alongside the accused clansman. His embarrassed gaze remained fixed on his toes, unscuffed and shiny from a recent refurbishing at the cobbler's.

"I was born a fisherman at Merior by the Sea," he opened. "When Arithon's brigantine, the *Khetienn*, was launched, I left my father's lugger to sign on as one of her crewmen. Under command of the Master of Shadow, I bore witness to an atrocity no sane man could sanction. For that reason, I deserted, and stand here today. Word of his monstrous act at the Havens inlet must be told, that justice may come to be served."

Then the words poured from him, often halting, tremulous with remembered horror. Too desperately, he wished to forget what had happened on the summer afternoon as the *Khetienn* put into one of the deep, fissured channels, where the high crags of Vastmark plunged in weather-stepped stone to the shoreline of Rockbay Harbor. Today, pallid under the window's thin sunshine, the seaman recounted the affray, when two hundred archers under Arithon s'Ffalenn had dispatched, without mercy, a company five hundred and thirty men strong.

"They were murdered!" the sailhand pealed in distress. "The vanguard were cut down in ruthless waves as they scrambled, exposed on the cliff trails. More fell while launching boats in retreat. They were dropped in their tracks by volleys of arrows shot out of cover from above." The long-sighted seaman's eyes were raised now, locked to a horrified memory. As if they yet viewed the steep, shadowed cliffs; the wave-fretted channel of the inlet; the still-running blood of men broken like toys in the brazen, uncaring sunlight. As though, beyond time, living flesh could still cringe from the screams of the maimed and the dying, scythed down in full flight, then tumbled still quick in their agony into the thrash of the breakers.

"Such slaughter went on, unrelenting." Before listeners strangled into shocked quiet, the damning account unfolded. Impelled now by passionate outrage, scene after scene of inhumane practice were described in the fisherman's slow, southcoast accent. "Those wretches who fled were killed from behind. Any who survived to launch longboats did so by shielding their bodies behind corpses. Their valor and desperation made no difference. They were cut off as they sought to make sail. Every galley turned in flight was run down and fired at the mouth of the inlet. No vessel was spared. Even a fishing lugger burdened with wounded was razed and burned to her waterline. Mercy was forbidden, at Arithon's strict order. By my life, as I stand here, and Dharkaron as my judge, the killing went on until no man who tried landfall was left standing."

The fisherman stirred, came back to himself, and shifted his feet in self-consciousness. "All that I saw took place before the great rout at Dier Kenton Vale."

The last line trailed into appalled, awkward stillness. City officials sat in their numbed state of pride, pricked down the spine by an incomprehensible fear. Their poise like struck marble, every veteran commander sweated inwardly, forced to accept that the wretched, slaughtered companies could as easily have been their own men.

The moment hung and then passed. Deep breaths were drawn into stopped lungs. Bodies shifted and hat feathers quivered, and humid hands fumbled through scrips and pockets in quest of comforting handkerchiefs.

Then the floor loosened into talk all at once.

"Ath show us all mercy!" The minister of the weaver's guild fanned a suety face with the brim of his unwieldy bonnet. "What sickness of mind would drive a human being to command such a letting of blood?"

"The killing appears to have been done for no reason," the *Khetienn*'s deserter stressed mournfully. "No one who landed at the Havens survived. The wyverns there scavenged the corpses."

But the ambassador from Havish weighed the sailor's lidded gaze, that darted and shied from direct contact. Instinct suggested this witness had withheld some telling fact from his speech. For malice, perhaps, or personal rancor against his former captain, he might slant his account to spark vengeful impetus to Lysaer's ongoing feud.

"But Arithon s'Ffalenn never acts without design." The passionate impact of Lysaer's rebuttal spun electrifying tension in contrast. "No man alive is more clever, or sane. This Spinner of Darkness would have his reason, cold-blooded, even vicious, to have timed and effected such slaughter."

Lysaer stood, fired now by conviction which no longer let him keep still. The light shimmered across his collar yoke of diamonds, template to his distress. "We know the scarps above Dier Kenton Vale were splintered into a rock fall. Earth itself was suborned as a weapon to break the proud ranks of our war host. If the rim walls in that territory are prone to slides, the ruin rained down on our troops was a feat beyond all bounds of credibility. What if more than exploitation of a natural disaster were the cause? Could sorcery in fact have been used to cleave a new fault line? Even weaken the structure of the shale?"

Disturbed murmurs swept the benches. Feathers rippled and velvet hats tipped, as men shared their fears with their neighbors.

"Arithon s'Ffalenn was born to mage training!" Prince Lysaer exhorted above the noise. "Through his seemingly wanton slaughter at the Havens, could he not have tapped the arcane power to rend the very fabric of the earth?"

On orchestrated cue, the shriveled little man in scholar's robes started up from his unobtrusive dreaming. "The premise is not without precedent," he affirmed in a drilling, treble quaver. "There are proscribed practices that herb witches use to tap forces of animal magnetism."

A stunning truth. Every common man-at-arms who ever bought an illicit love philter had observed the filthy practice.

"These distasteful creatures will slay a live animal, then cast binding spells from the spilled effervescence of its life essence. How much more potent the power to be gained, if the sacrificial victims were human?" The scholar cast his accusation above an uneasy, incredulous anger. "Be sure, the massed deaths of *five hundred spirits* would be enough to cleave the very mountains in twain to wreak that unconscionable destruction on our troops!"

"The question is raised," Avenor's deep-voiced justiciar sliced through the uproar. He nodded in respect to his prince, then addressed the bound clansman. "If the Master of Shadow engages dark magecraft, the preeminent arcane order on this continent has not stepped forth to denounce him. The Fellowship Sorcerers have not spoken. Nor have they acted to curb his vile deeds. The Warden of Althain himself is said to feel each drop of blood spilled in Athera.

26

Every death at the Havens would be known to him. Why should he let this atrocity pass?"

A mayor in the front row raised an imperious fist. "The opposite has happened, in practice!"

A scathing point; more than once, the Sorcerers had stood as Arithon's spokesmen.

Havish's royal ambassador stiffened, then stamped down his urgent protest. In even-handed fairness, hard against their better judgment, the Fellowship Sorcerers had also endorsed today's return of the princess's purloined ransom. Lysaer's avoidance of that truth was duplicitous. Pained by the loyalty due his own king, the ambassador endured through the unjust malignment, while Avenor's justiciar widened the charges in his sonorous, gravelly bass.

"What is the Fellowship's silence, if not evidence of collaboration? By this lack of intervention, events would suggest that the Sorcerers may support all of Arithon's actions against us."

"They gave their vaunted sanction to Rathain's crown prince," Etarra's Lord Harradene allowed. "If the Fellowship stands together as the Shadow Master's ally, the consequence can't be dismissed. They may have become corrupted. If they deem the use of dark magecraft as no crime, Prince Lysaer, as the public defender of the innocent, would naturally be obstructed in his legitimate claim to rule Tysan."

The clan prisoner's sharp protest became shouted down by another voice as accented as his own. "Now there's a braw, canting spiel, well fitted for a mealymouthed lawyer!"

Mute on the benches, the ambassador from Havish shut his eyes in relief.

Volatile as spilled flame in the red-and-gold surcoat of Alestron's unvanquished clan dukes, Mearn s'Brydion, appointed delegate of his brother, sprang up in pacing agitation. "While you bandy conjecture in mincing, neat words, let us pay strict attention to procedure! If this slaughter at the Havens ever happened, where's hard proof?" He cast suspicious gray eyes toward the sailhand, impervious himself to the looks turned his way by townsmen distrustful of his breeding. "Or will you sheep dressed in velvets let yourselves be gulled by the word of a man disaffected?"

As the deckhand surged forward, flushed into outrage, Mearn raised a finger like a blade. "I've not *said* you're a liar! Not outright. Arithon's a known killer, that much I grant. I witnessed the debacle he caused in our armory. But whether his slaughter of these companies at the Havens took place as a blood crime, or some cruel but expedient act of war, the killing was done on the soil of Shand. Can't mix your legalities for convenience. Town law won't apply to a kingdom. Under sovereignty of Shand's founding charter, as written by the Fellowship of Seven, Prince Arithon's offense is against Lord Erlien, High Earl of Alland. As *caithdein* of that realm, the Teir s'Taleyn is charged to uphold justice in the absence of his high king. The question of Prince Arithon's guilt falls under his province to determine."

"What is the old law to our city councils?" cried the plump, ribboned spokesman from Isaer. "Just hot wind and words! The *caithdeins'* authority was broken when the uprising threw down crown rule. And even if our mayors cared to bow to dead precedents, has this new evidence against Arithon not tainted the clans' legal claim? What if the Fellowship's morals are debased? Shall we wait and watch our cities become victimized?"

Talk rose, scored through by a treble run of panic. Even the sallow, bored Seneschal of Avenor thumped his stick fist to be heard. "Should we risk being deceived, or stay willfully blind, then suffer the same ruin that leveled whole buildings in Jaelot?"

From all quarters of the chamber, heads turned. Ones bare and close cropped to accommodate mail, and others fashionably coifed. Earrings swung, and jewelry chinked, as every face trained on the Prince of the Light. He alone could speak for both factions, through hard-won respect and ties to an old blood inheritance.

Yet it was Lord Shien, joint captain of Avenor's field troops, whose remark stormed the floor into quiet. "If the barbarian before this council was sent as an envoy to declare his chieftain's enmity, we have sure trouble here at home!" A large man, with meaty, chapped knuckles and a frown that seemed stitched in place, he raised the bull bellow he used to cow recruits. "And whether or not the Master of Shadow has embraced wickedness, or sacrificed lives to buy power, dissent from the clans will give him a free foothold here to exploit. We dare not allow such a weakness. Not before such dire threat."

Attention swung back. Like blood in the water amidst schooling sharks, men fastened their outrage upon the offender held bound within reach. "Sentence the archer! Condemn him for treason! Let him die as example to his brethren!"

"Do that," interceded the long-faced justiciar, "and according to town edict, he dies on the scaffold, broken one limb at a time."

"He was sent to contest a legitimate point of law!" Mearn s'Brydion warned. "Take his life in dishonor, and your clans here will never be reconciled."

"A child knows better than to break into state chambers bearing arms!" a southcoast mayor bristled back.

Inexorably, sentiment aligned. The delivery of the chieftain's message had been insolent, a mockery of civilized practice. No townsman remembered the bygone tradition, when a ceremonial arrow gave symbolic exchange of a high king's censure from his liegemen. Where those old ways once forestalled needless bloodshed, now, they were seen as provocation. The trade guilds had suffered too many losses in clan raids to trifle with forgotten forms of etiquette. Nor was Lord Shien inclined toward forgiveness. Not when his divisions had been held home in Tysan, guarding the roads from the spree of vengeful ambushes launched after Lady Maenalle's execution. His blood burned in balked rage for those companies marched south, every comrade in arms to perish untimely of a sorcerer's fell tactics in Vast- mark.

Only the ambassador from Havish regarded the clan prisoner with pity. The man waited, his stance easy. His attention never shifted from the face of the prince on the dais.

Lysaer s'Ilessid withheld intervention. Serene as smoothed marble, his form touched in light like the finished planes of a masterpiece, he allowed the dissonant chaos of argument to roll and rebound and gain force. He listened for the moment when his disparate factions became unified, their imprecations a shouted resonance of passion, crying for blood in redress.

Then he held up one hand. A spark snapped from his palm, the smallest manifestation of his gift. But the flare of illumination cracked like a whip through raw noise and engendered immediate silence.

Before venomous animosity, he stayed detached, his diamonds like frost on a snowfield. Then he inclined his head to the captive before him. "You're fully aware, a vote cast now will condemn you. Town law has small mercy. You could suffer a brutal public maiming before death."

The clansman said nothing.

Lysaer used the pause. While the atmosphere simmered in fierce anticipation, his study encompassed every minister, hard breathing in velvets and furs. The officers of war endured his regard, unflinching, then the mayors, with their gnawing, hidden fear. The prince they had signed into power was royal, closer in ties to clan ancestry than they wished. The price of their protection from the Spinner of Darkness might come at the cost of their coveted autonomy.

Yet to refute the traditions of city law outright, Lysaer had to know, he would flaw the amity of their support. Foremost a statesman, he showed no hesitation. "The case of your clans might have fared best by waiting. Before you shot down your colorful ultimatum, you could have heard out my answer to this document." He fingered the torn scroll of parchment in unfeigned regret, as he added, "For you see, I have no intent to accept the burden of crown rule at this time."

After the first, indrawn gasp of surprise, a stunned stillness, as if the overheated air had hardened to glue, with every man gaping at the prince.

Lysaer showed long-suffering equanimity. "There are truths to this conflict against the Master of Shadow even I have withheld from general knowledge. I wish above all to avoid seeding panic. After the failure of our late campaign, we need order more than ever to rebuild."

He had his factions riveted, the ambassador saw, struck by a surge of admiration.

"Arithon s'Ffalenn may have been born a man, but he has foregone his humanity," Prince Lysaer resumed. "His birth gift presents an unspeakable threat. This, paired with his use of unprincipled magic, redoubles our peril before him." Lest the quiet give way to fresh altercation, Lysaer delivered his solution. "I sit before you as this criminal's opposite, my gift of light our best counterforce to offset his shadow. For this reason, I must decline Tysan's kingship. My purpose against Arithon must stay undivided for the sake of the safety of our people."

The logic was unassailable. Defeat on a grand scale had shown the futility of choosing one battlefield for confrontation. The inevitable striving to forge new alliances, to restore shaken trust after broadscale ruin, then the wide-ranging effort to buy a mage-trained enemy's downfall, must draw this prince far afield from Avenor.

He said, "For the stability of this realm, I suggest that a regency be appointed in my name, answerable to a council of city mayors. This will serve the crown's justice and bind Tysan into unity until the day I have an heir, grown and trained and fit beyond question for the inheritance of s'Ilessid birthright."

The stroke was brilliant. Havish's ambassador noted a spark of comprehension hood the eyes of Mearn s'Brydion.

Though the prisoner pointed out in acerbity that the realm's *caithdein* held an earlier appointment to the selfsame office, but without formal ties to city government, his case was passed over. Old hatreds lay too long entrenched. Throughout the chamber came a squeaking of benches, a nodding of hats, as guarded interest eased the tensions of mayors and guild magnates. The most hardened eye for intrigue, the most shrewd mind for statecraft, must appreciate that Lysaer gave up nothing beyond the trappings of crown and title. Sovereign power would largely reside in his hands. Except townborn pride would be salved. The uneasy transition back into monarchy could proceed with grace and restraint.

City mayors would keep their veneer of independence. By the time they left office, their successors would wear the yoke of consolidated rule as comfortably as an old shoe.

"We shall have a new order, tailored for this time of need. Past charter law forbids the cruelty of maiming. And this is Avenor, where my dominion is not in dispute." Lysaer stepped to the edge of the dais, pale as lit flame against oncoming storm as clouds choked the sky past the casement. Whether his gifted powers of light touched his aura, or whether his gold trim and diamonds shimmered in unquiet reflection, the effect was magnificence unveiled.

The ambassador from Havish forced himself to look away from the brilliance, the drawing pull of a gifted man's charisma, as the prince's fired, clear diction pronounced final sentence upon the clan archer.

"Here is your fate, by my word as s'Ilessid. Your hand shed no blood. But an ultimatum against me was tendered by your *caithdein*, Lord Maenol s'Gannley. For that, you go free as my spokesman. My safe conduct will see you outside the city gates. Tell Maenol this: he may come to Avenor before the spring equinox and present himself before me on bent knee to beg pardon. Let him swear fealty in behalf of his clan chieftains, and no one suffers redress. But if he refuses, should he declare open war, I will enact sanctions in reprisal for treason against all the people of your clans."

A murmur swelled from the benches, slammed still by Lysaer's brisk shout. "Hear the rest! I have funds at hand to rebuild the eastshore trade fleet. Every galley and vessel which burned in my service at Minderl Bay will be replaced at Avenor's expense. I promise that every merchant who receives restitution will suffer no more raids at sea. The Master of Shadow and his minions will think twice about attacking with fire, since the newly launched ships shall be manned at the oar by chained convicts. Condemned men fairly sentenced as Arithon's collaborators, and as of this hour, take warning: Maenol's own people, if he fails to bind his clansmen under my banner to take arms against Arithon of Rathain."

To the headhunters' stiff-backed dismay, Lysaer granted swift reassurance. "Bounties will not be repealed for renegade clan scalps. But if Maenol s'Gannley refuses his allegiance, double coin will be tendered for each male barbarian captured and brought in alive."

For a moment, as if deafened by a thunderclap, the clan archer did not move. Then he drew breath like a rip through strained cloth and gave answer in blazing contempt. "If any small blessing can be prised out of tragedy, I thank Ath my Lady Maenalle never lived to see this. I will return to her grandson, *caithdein* of this realm, and tell him you threaten us with slavery."

Nothing more did he say as his bonds were released, and guardsmen were dispatched to see him on his way through the gates.

The ambassador from Havish used the confusion to slip through the ranks of halberdiers. Outside in the corridor, he ducked into a window niche, while the sweat dewed his temples and curled the short hairs of his beard. This was not his fight. And yet, even still, his mind seemed loath to relinquish the pull of Lysaer's seductive delivery.

The prince owned a terrifying power of conviction. Thirty thousand lives gone and wasted in Vastmark had left his dedication unshaken. Nor would his adherents awaken and see sense, tied to his need as they were through inherited blinders of prejudice.

The tramp of the men-at-arms and the clansman they escorted dwindled, then faded away beyond hearing. Outside, white on gray, new snow dusted downward. The wind's biting cold seemed to seep through the casement and strike an unmerciful ache in the heart. The ambassador shook off the memory of Mearn s'Brydion's thin features, seething in stifled restraint, his clanborn outrage no doubt throttled silent by some stricture from his brother, the duke.

Worn from the effort of leashing his own temper, the ambassador from Havish shook out his linen cuff and blotted his dampened face. The word he must bear home to his liege boded ill.

On both sides, the corridor was deserted, its white marble arches bathed chilly silver by stormlight. Lysaer's voice carried through the opened door in fiery address to his council. "We are gathered here today to begin the long work of uniting all kingdoms against the Master of Shadow. Given his acts of evil, there exists no moral compromise. Our task will not ease until no dwelling remains on this continent where ignorance will lend him shelter. We are come, in this hour, to found an alliance to act against terror and darkness."

Steps pattered across the council room as someone inside moved to remedy the door left ajar. Sickened, tired, afraid for the future and anxious to embark on his downcoast run back to Havish, King Eldir's ambassador hastened away, too burdened to risk hearing more.

Stag Hunt

Two months after Lysaer s'Ilessid leveled charges of dark sorcery against Arithon s'Ffalenn, the horror instilled by the ruin of the war host had magnified itself into rumors and uneasy fear. Households in mourning for those fallen on the field did not celebrate the festivals. Avenor seemed engrossed by industry, as men of war paid in gold for new swords and laid avid plans to sign on recruits to bolster their decimated garrison.

At least one free spirit inside city walls chafed at the endless, long councils. Mearn s'Brydion, the rakish youngest brother of the clan-born Duke of Alestron, slammed the door from his quarters and strode into the ice melt which pooled the cobblestone street. Today, the state garments laid out by his servants had been ditched for a briar-scarred set of worn leathers. In wild joy gloved over simmering temper, he snapped in the disapproving faces of his servants, "Let Prince Lysaer's stool-sitting councilmen share their pompous hot wind amongst themselves."

This morning, he would fare out hunting for pleasure, and bedamned to his current assignment as the douce representative of his family.

The gray, weeping mists wadded over the battlements failed to dampen his fired mood. Draped on Mearn's shoulder like a desert-man's blanket, the scarlet horsecloth with the s'Brydion blazon threw a splash of sharp color against the drab dress of guild craftsmen who hurried, sleepy-eyed, to their shops. The pair of brindle staghounds just liberated from the kennel yapped at his feet, muddied to the belly from their bowling play through the puddles.

Mearn's laconic, off-key whistles scarcely checked their exuberance. His hounds charged amok, tails slashing, to disgruntle what lay in their path. The racket raised Avenor's rich matrons from sleep. Not a few howled complaint from cracked shutters. Mearn laughed. While geese honked, and chickens flapped in squawking flight, and alley cats fluffed tails and bolted, the carters loosed fist-shaking curses above the manes of their shying teams. Mearn met each onslaught of outrage with bright-eyed, impervious humor.

He was clanblood enough to relish the upset his antics caused any man townborn. No one was brash enough to hinder him. Though his clipped accent turned heads and roused threats, Lysaer s'Illessid decreed that any old blood family bound to his alliance might walk Avenor's streets with impunity. The duke's youngest brother brought his happy tumult into the royal stable yard and shouted for a boy to bring his horse.

Patience sat ill with Mearn. He slapped his riding whip against his boot in brisk tempo while the grooms fetched and bridled his mount. He paced. The horsecloth hooked over his shoulder flapped in the breeze each time he spun on his heel. Restlessness rode his thin frame like hot sparks, while the deer hounds bounded in frenzied gyrations around him.

At last, infected past discipline, they bayed their uncontained joy. Their deep belling note spooked the highbred charger, who sidled and upset the rake the new horseboy had forgotten to tidy.

Milling, shod hooves crushed the handle to splinters. The horse flung back, snapped its head tie, and added its thunderous commotion by galloping loose through the stable yard.

Mearn cursed the groom for his inept hands, then tossed him a copper for his trials. In his bitten clan dialect he added language which raised the eyebrows of the drayman who idled beside his harnessed team. Then he insisted to all inside earshot that he should saddle his mount for himself.

"Please, no lord! I dare not allow you," the groom stammered, red-faced. The rest of the yard boys had wisely made themselves scarce. "Our Master of Horse would see me thrashed bloody if he catches me slacking my duties."

"He'll thrash you anyway," Mearn argued. "Or does he not care if your charges fly loose?" He pursed his narrow lips in disgust and emitted a piercing, high whistle. His bitch hound howled in chorus with the noise, but the charger, obedient, stopped its clattering flight.

It poised blowing, its high neck arched and its ears swiveled back, listening to its master's approach.

Mearn's grumbling irritation changed to endearments. He stroked the bay's glossy shoulder. Then he laughed and spoke a command through the redoubled yaps of his hounds.

The horse turned, dealt him a companionable shove, then trailed him like a puppy as he recrossed the stable yard.

"Fetch out my saddle, and then get you gone!" Mearn called to the fidgety groom. "This gelding never did like a town-whelped runt. Likely you'd just find your skinny butt nipped as you tried to fasten his girth." Suddenly all pared efficiency, he tossed his blazoned saddlecloth over the horse's back. As the boy still hovered, he added, "Hurry on! Do you think the deer will wait while you stand there?"

Minutes later, Mearn vaulted astride, shouted his hounds to heel, and wheeled his mount through the gate. A razor-edged irony whetted his smile.

As his three older brothers would laugh themselves prostrate to explain, he held stag hunts in passionate contempt. His purpose in plying the wilds alone was for game and stakes far larger, dangerous enough that he risked his life as forfeit.

Belying even the semblance of secrecy, Mearn made his racketing, flamboyant departure through the moil of the early-spring market. Chaos surged in his wake. Curs barked, and carriages swerved, and crated sows squealed in their wagon beds. Even the bored guards on Avenor's inland battlement were relieved to see his turmoil pass the gates.

He reined off the muddy road into the shrinking, gray mounds of old snowdrifts. The bare, tangled boughs of the oak forests engulfed his whipping scarlet horsecloth and his laughing whoops to his horse. The baying of his hounds rode the land breeze, until distance mellowed that also. The s'Brydion line was clanbred, barbaric to the bone. Lysaer's captains agreed that their envoy from Alestron was unlikely to be troubled by his murdering, woodland kindred, even had any of Tysan's blood chieftains dared to skulk in the bogs within reach of Avenor's armed might.

The spring was too new for greenery. Ice still scabbed the north sides of the dales, and the air held its chill like a miser. What warmth kissed Mearn's shoulders was borrowed from the sun, half-mantled in streamers of cloud. Their shadows flowed like blown soot across the valleys, and rinsed the bright glints from the streamlets. Mearn gave on his reins, let his horse and his hounds drink the wind at a

35

run, as man and beast might to celebrate life as frost loosed its hold on black earth.

He carved further inland, his horse settled to a trot, through deeper thickets and trackless mires, beyond range of Lysaer's royal foresters. His hounds coursed ahead. If their quarry was not always a swift-running deer, their master scarcely cared. The hound couple badgered any game they could flush. Wild lynx, or red fox, no boon to their training, they were left to track as they pleased, and only whipped off the scent if their hunt veered them northward or south.

Due east, Mearn was bound, his brother's ducal blazon now mantled beneath the drab folds of his cloak.

By noon, under pallid gold sunlight, he reached a bare hillock, scattered with wind-stripped, buff grass. He drew rein there, dismounted, loosened his girth. His stag hounds flopped, panting, to snap at the tickle of dried seed heads as though they were bothered by flies. The bitch whined. The horse shook its mane and rubbed its sweated headstall against Mearn's leather-clad hip.

He shoved back the gelding's nose with a gently spoken epithet, all trace of roguish pleasure erased from his taut, narrow features. One year and events had changed him. His quick mind and observant eye were bent now toward other pursuits than tumbling loose ladies and gambling. The breath of the breeze fanned a chill on his neck, the lovelock he had worn since his first growth of beard shorn off in cold purpose since Vastmark.

A dove called, mournful, from a thicket.

Mearn swung about at the sound, raised the corner of his cloak, and unveiled the ducal blazon. Then he found himself a dry, flat rock in a cranny, and sat out of the wind while his horse grazed.

A slow interval passed, with Mearn touched to prickles by the certain awareness that he was being watched from all angles. Then, with no ceremony, a young man moved upslope to meet him. His approach scarcely woke any sound from dry grasses. He wore undyed leathers and a vest with dark lacing. He carried bow, knife, and sword as if weapons were natural as flesh. Large framed, deliberate, he had a step like a wary king stag's. His light eyes, never still, swept the hillock behind, then Mearn, and measured him down to his boot soles. On that day, the high chieftain of Tysan's outlawed clansmen was nineteen, one year shy as the old law still reckoned manhood.

"Lord Maenol, Teir s'Gannley, *caithdein* of Tysan," Mearn greeted. He arose, inclined his head in respect, and shared grief for the grandson, whose titles and inheritance now burdened his young shoulders through Lysaer's murder of his predecessor.

Unlike the deceased Lady Maenalle, the heir returned neither welcome nor greeting. He stood, chin tilted, silent, while the gusts flicked the laces on his clothing.

No whit less stubborn, Mearn met that challenge with a sheared, bright-edged smile. If the s'Brydion ancestral stronghold had withstood the wars of the uprising; if his family owed fealty to another kingdom and another chieftain on the farthest shore of the continent, the ways of charter law and the old codes of honor were still held in common with Tysan's clans in Tysan. Shared trust ran deep beyond words.

"You have taken an unmentionable risk to come here," the boy said at last in his startling, mellow baritone.

"I bear unmentionable tidings," Mearn countered. "And a packet, bound for Arithon, sewn in the lining of my saddlecloth. I went through Sithaer itself to keep *that* from the handling of Lysaer's overzealous pack of grooms." He added, "You'll want to read the contents before you send them on. Your clans are the ones most threatened."

Tysan's young *caithdein* took that ominous statement in stride; such troubles were scarcely new. His own parents had fallen to headhunters. "It's risky to be sending late dispatches across," he pointed out, vexed more for the snags in the timing. "Arithon plans to sail as soon as the weather settles."

Small need to dwell on the risk of disaster, if their covert crossings to his island haven at Corith were sighted. The fair, warming weather would see the first trade galleys nosing their way from snug harbors, the earliest at sea always manned by the keenest, most vigilant captains.

"I leave that decision in your hands, then." Mearn strode to his grazing horse, removed girth and saddle, and sat down with the redolent, damp horsecloth. He used his knife to pick out the hem stitching. The packet inside was wrapped in cerecloth, by its weight and thickness no less than purloined copies of state documents.

"Oh, well-done," murmured Maenol. Still standing, stiff backed, against a sky that now threatened fine drizzle, he nipped through the twine ties with his teeth, then flipped through the pressed, folded parchments. The dark arch of his eyebrows turned grim as he read. Documents recording rightful claim to clan prisoners to be bound over into slavery; documents of arraignment without trial for acts of dark sorcery, attested and signed, which named Prince Arithon criminal and renegade. Maenol's sharp features, never animated, stilled to pale quartz as he perused the signatures and seals.

"Merciful Ath," the words torn through his reserve as if jerked by the barbed bite of steel. "Is there no end? How can so many mayors bind these acts into law, upon no proof or surety beyond Lysaer's spoken word? It's not canny!"

"It's happened," Mearn said. "I've seen. Lysaer has a tongue like pure honey. Fiends plague, my own family once fell for his trumped-up cause before we discovered any better. I'll need a courier sent to warn my brother Bransian."

Maenol looked up. "That you'll have." He paused, squared fingers gripping the first lists and requisitions appointed for the planned royal shipyard; for the galleys where his people might come to suffer at the oar, under the whip and in chains. He took a moment, seemed to gather himself, then asked, "Is this truth, the accusation Lysaer s'Ilessid has laid against Prince Arithon at the Havens?"

Mearn looked back, intent, his mouth turned glass hard. "I don't know." He could not stay seated, but pushed to his feet, pressured to vent his raw nerves. "But there's one proven fact every charge so far has omitted. Arithon lost his mage powers years ago, in defense of his own by the river Tal Quorin. If the slaughter at the Havens was committed to enable an act of dark sorcery, his hand could not shape the spells."

"The deaths could be his," Maenol said, blunt. "He could have used an accomplice."

Mearn stopped. As his gaze bore into the younger man, relentlessly direct, Tysan's *caithdein* raised his chin and would neither bend nor stand down. "I'm this realm's steward, in the absence of its king. I must ask, since our fate's been entangled with Arithon's. As a mage whose talents were blinded and broken, who knows to what lengths desperation might drive him to wrest back his gift for grand conjury?"

"You never met him," Mearn said, implacable.

"Once." Maenol all of a sudden seemed heartsore. He stared toward the wood where a pheasant pair called, while the breeze framed the unrestrained joy of a lark. "I was eleven. Arithon seemed retiring, unimportant at the time. All my devotion was for our fair s'Ilessid prince, just arrived. I couldn't imagine he'd betray us."

Mearn at last looked away, his sigh a soundless exhalation. "Arithon's nothing like his half brother. Trust me in this. As for his guilt, there's no guessing, given the nature of the man. He's determined, and beyond any doubt, the most dangerous creature my family has ever chanced to cross." Attuned to his master's distress, one of the brindle hounds roused and whined; the horse stamped, and clouds lowered, dimming the earth beneath their soft-footed shrouding. The sky threatened torrents before nightfall.

"This much I can say," Mearn added finally, his arms folded as if the chill of the wetting to come later bit through his leathers beforetime. "I have never yet known Arithon to lie. He received the Fellowship's sanction as Crown Prince. Since his oathswearing to Rathain, his integrity has been tested, once in life trial by the *caithdein* of Shand, and again, by my blood family. His morals were not found wanting. No act he undertook had been done without reason. Before I dared judge on those deaths at the Havens, I would ask in his presence to hear out his sworn explanation."

The breeze hissed through the grasses, rich with the bearing promise of thawed soil.

"Well," Maenol shrugged in that steely light fatalism better suited to a man years older, "the tangle won't be yours or mine to unravel, but Earl Jieret's, as Rathain's sworn *caithdein*. If a boat can be sent, your dispatches will go across. Given luck, Arithon can be reached before he sails. Rest assured, my runner to your kin in Melhalla will leave my camp before nightfall."

"One last thing," Mearn said as he offered his forearms for a formal clasp in parting. "Lysaer has set scholars to work. They'll comb the old archives until they've recovered the past arts of navigation."

"So Arithon expected," said Maenol. The practice of star sights, disused and forgotten through the centuries while Desh-thiere's mists had smothered Athera's skies, could not stay lost for much longer. For each day his *Khetienn* delayed her departure, the risk of discovery increased. Ancient charts might be found, or a rutter, to recall the location of the offshore Isles of Min Pierens. Arithon held neither the resources nor the men to repel an assault from the tumbledown fortress at Corith.

To be caught there would drive him to flight.

Aware like cold death that time was Lysaer's ally, the two clansmen went separate ways. In birdsong, the day waned, while the gentle rain fell and pattered chill tears through the dark, blurred brakes of the oak forest.

Three Warnings

The day after Mearn's duplicitous stag hunt, couriers bearing the same copied dispatches ride outbound from Avenor, their horse trappings emblazoned with the sunwheel on gold, new device of the Prince of the Light; and they pass another messenger inbound from the south, who delivers King Eldir's ultimatum, that slave-bearing galleys henceforward shall be barred from all ports in his Kingdom of Havish. . . .

While dawn mists mantle the oak forests of Avenor, a black arrow screams over the city walls, shot from a clan messenger's bowstring; affixed to its shaft, sealed in Maenol s'Gannley's blood, a letter pronounces a forfeit of life against the s'Ilessid pretender who has dared break the freedom of the first kingdom charter. . . .

Far eastward, in the greenwood of yet another kingdom, the clanblood chieftain named Earl of the North cries out in torment from his dreams; and the warning delivered by his gift of Sight shows a packed city square with a scaffold, cordoned about with white banners and a dazzle of sunwheel blazons, and chained there for the blade of a public execution is his sworn liege, the Prince of Rathain. . . .

II. Fugitive Prince

The prophetic dream broke on a scream of sheer rage, torn from the throat of a doomed prince.

A second, real cry became its live echo, wrung in drawn agony from the *caithdein* sworn to life service of liege and realm.

Jieret, Teir's'Valerient, and Earl of the North snapped awake in Rathain with the vision's cruel vista seared into indelible memory. Unmindful of peace, deaf to the birdsong which layered the spring dawn in the woodland outside his lodge tent, he eased himself free of his wife's tangled limbs and arose from the blankets to stand shivering. Unsettled, naked, he sucked down breath after breath of chill air. The close, familiar smells of tanned deer hide and oiled steel, and the pitchy bite of cut balsam failed to restore him to balance.

"Ath keep our sons!" he gasped through locked teeth.

He could not shed his Sight of the last s'Ffalenn prince, crumpled and still in the swift, welling spurt of his life's blood.

"Another augury?" The bedding rustled. A lavish fall of hair stroked his back, then a cheek, laid against his taut shoulder; his wife, arisen behind him, to link calming hands at his waist.

His tension would tell her the portent was ugly. Too often, in sleep, the prescient vision he inherited from his father warned him of death and trouble.

Jieret raked long fingers through his ginger beard. He braced his nerve, spun, and enfolded his lady into his possessive embrace. "I'm sorry, dove." The soft, misted peace of the greenwood seemed suddenly, desperately precious. "I shall have to travel very far, very fast. The life of our prince is at stake."

She would not question his judgment, not for that. Arithon s'Ffalenn was the last of Rathain's royal line. Should he die with no heir, his feal clansmen would forfeit all hope to reclaim their birthright.

Feithan's fingers unclasped, brushed down Jieret's flanks, and withdrew. "How much spare clothing will you carry?" She caught up the blanket, still warm from their sleeping, and spread it to pack his necessities.

Jieret bent, caught her wrists, and marveled as always. The strength in her was a subtle thing, her bones like a sparrow's in his hands, which were broad and corded beyond his youthful years from relentless seasons of fighting. Their eyes met and shared mute appeal. "I'll take weapons and the leathers on my back, and you, first of all." A smile turned his lips. The expression softened the fierce planes of his face, and offset the hawk bridge of his nose. "Leave the blanket."

He rocked her against his chest, his touch tender. An urgency he could scarcely contain spoke of the perils he must weather on the solitary trek that would take him to Tysan's western shore. Bounties were still paid for captured clansmen. Headhunters plied the wilds in bands, their tracking dogs combing the thickets. Towns and trade roads were no less a hazard, choked with informers and guardsmen sent out recruiting to replenish the troops lost in Vastmark.

The wife in Jieret's arms would not speak of the risks. Strong as the generations of survivors who had bred her, she absorbed his need, then massaged to ease his old scars with skilled hands, until he kissed her and slipped free to dress.

Jieret s'Valerient, called Red-beard, was in that hour twenty-one years of age. Supple, self-reliant, clean limbed as the deer he ran down in the hunt, he was rangy and tall, a being tanned out of oak bark. War and early losses had lent his hazel eyes more than a touch of gray flint. Jieret's inheritance of the *caithdein*'s title had fallen to him during childhood, both his parents and four sisters slain in one day by town troops on the banks of Tal Quorin. On his wrist, even then, his first badge of achievement: the straight, fine scar from the knife cut which bound him lifelong to the honor of blood pact with his prince.

Proud of his rugged courage, too shrewd to voice fear, Feithan reached beneath their mattress of spruce boughs and tossed him his worn, quilloned knife.

She smiled, a nip of white teeth. "The sooner you go, the better the chance you'll be back to my lodge before autumn."

Then she folded slim knees behind her crossed arms and watched him bind on sheath and sword belt. If she wept, her tears were well masked behind tangles of ebony hair. Not on her last breath would she voice her disappointment. If her young husband did not return, his line must live on in the child she knew to be growing within her. She would endure, no less than any other clan woman widowed in a sudden, bloody raid.

Her husband was the oathsworn *caithdein* of Rathain, his birthright an iron bond of trust. The needs of kingdom and prince must come first, ahead of survival and family.

Feithan held no rancor. If the Teir's'Ffalenn died, no clanborn babe in Rathain could have peace. The future would be kingless, while the townsmen continued their centuries-old practice of extirpation. Headhunters would keep sewing scalps of clan victims as trophy fringe on their saddlecloths, until at last the survivors dwindled, their irreplaceable old bloodlines too thinned by loss to sustain.

"Go in grace, my lord husband," were the last words she said, as her man kissed her lips and stepped out.

Three days on foot through his native glens in Strakewood saw Lord Jieret to the shores of Instrell Bay. There, a bribe to a Westfen fisherman secured his safe crossing to Atainia. From landfall just north of the trade port of Lorn, Jieret faced an overland journey of a hundred and fifty leagues. Anviled, rocky ridges arose off the coast, the country between summits guttered in dry gulches, and the scrub thorn which clawed stunted footholds in the sands of the Bittern Desert.

Here, where a man made a target against the luminous sky, Jieret kept to the gullies. Sweat painted tracks through his coat of rimed dust. He jogged, walked, jogged on again, refusing to measure the odds that his errand was already futile.

The winter storms had abated. Any day, the Master of Shadow would raise sail to ply the world's uncharted waters. He would seek the fabled continent beyond the Westland Sea, and finally know if Athera held a refuge beyond reach of the Mistwraith's curse.

The Sorcerer, Sethvir, Warden of Althain could have named Prince Arithon's location. Yet at dusk on spring equinox, when Jieret passed his tower, the Fellowship held convocation. Where Sorcerers worked, the elements paid uncanny homage. The night air seemed charged to crystalline clarity, the land lidded under a transparent sky with its winds preternaturally silenced. Ozone tinged the silvered glow which speared in beams from the keep's topmost arrow slits, and earth itself seemed to ring to the dance of ancient arcane rhythms. Though the clans did not share the widespread fear in the towns toward the powers called from natural forces, the man was a fool who held no mortal dread of disrupting the Sorcerers' conjury.

Dawn saw Jieret on his way. His lanky stride ate the distance, through the rocky, slabbed washes bedded with black sand, puddled still from the snowmelt off the lava crags to the north. Before the ford, he veered west, to give the trade roads to Isaer wide berth. He kept to ditches and hedgerows through the flax bogs and farmlands, and moved softly by night where the headhunters scoured the flats. A stolen horse saw him to cover in the tangled stands of spruce which patchworked the Thaldein foothills.

There, better mounted by clansmen from Tysan, he galloped south with the relays who carried news between their fugitive enclaves in Camris.

The first scouts insisted the Master of Shadow would have left his winter haven at Corith.

Flanked by a campfire, the first cooked meat in his belly since the desert, and his undone braid fanned in hanks upon shoulders still glazed from a wash in a freshet, Jieret said, "I know that." The bronze bristle of his jaw thrust out and hardened. "I have to try anyway."

The scout who lounged across from him spat out the stem of sweetgrass he had meticulously used to scrub his teeth. "Fiends plague, then. Keep your bad news to yourself. We've heard enough already from Avenor to turn our hearts sore with grief."

Every restive sinew in Jieret's body coiled tense. "What's happened?" A late-singing mockingbird caroled through the gloom with a sweet and incongruous tranquillity. "What has Lysaer s'Ilessid done now?"

The scout spat into the embers and spoke, and amid the fragrant, piney gloom beneath the Thaldeins, Jieret Red-beard first heard of the edict which endorsed live capture and slavery.

"Spring equinox has passed, with the ultimatum given," the scout finished off in bitten rage. "Our Lord Maenol would never swear, but sent the false prince his black arrow proclaiming no quarter."

Lysaer's life, among the clans who by right should grant him fealty, was now irrevocably called forfeit. Jieret had no words. The event posed a vicious and unnatural tragedy, a warping of tradition provoked at its root by the evil of the Mistwraith's curse.

The breeze carried the odd chill, breathed down from the snow-fields, bathed pristine white under starlight. Jieret felt as if the cold inside had closed stealthy knuckles around the heart. He sat, eyes shut, and his knees clamped behind his clasped hands. "Events have turned grim in ways even Ath could scarce believe. How are you set when the headhunters start the spring forays?"

"Well enough." The scout shrugged. "Troops and supplies are depleted since Vastmark. We'll have a year, maybe two, before Lysaer's Alliance regroups, but mark me. Then we'll see sorrows."

For a moment, like the drawn-out whisper of old grief, the wind stroked through the greening briar. Then the scout tipped his graying head. "You'll need to go back," he urged, gentle. "Our people will carry your message from here. No better can be done. The *Khetienn* will have sailed. If she has, your wait for your prince could be lengthy."

The stiff pause came freighted with facts left unspoken: that whether or not the Master of Shadow had passed beyond reach, the headhunters' leagues in Rathain were ever in Lysaer's close confidence. The defeats freshly suffered at Arithon's hand, then the loss of their late captain Pesquil by Jieret's own arrow, had fanned their clamor for vengeance to fresh fervor.

"You see what must happen," the scout said in staid logic. "Skannt's going to claim sanction from Etarra's fat mayor to harrow Rathain's feal clans the same way."

"I know that." Jieret erupted in strung nerves, reached his feet, and resisted the blind urge to slam his fist into a tree. "Ath, for chained slavery? The guild merchants will cheer and donate the coin to forge manacles. Morality's no deterrent. For years now, Etarrans have used our child captives as forced labor." His back to the fire, he seemed a man racked, the passage of each breath made difficult. "I have to go on. What I know must not wait. Nor should my liege hear my word at second hand."

By the embers, the scout swore in sympathy.

Forced to the crux of a terrible decision, Jieret summed up troubled thoughts. "My clans are more to me than the spirit in my body, but I am not irreplaceable. The Fellowship can appoint a new *caithdein* for Rathain if my liege is not at hand to make his choice. My spokesman, Deshir's former war captain, Caolle, would agree. He knows the warning I bring is an augury which bears on Prince Arithon's life."

The last of his line, this fugitive Teir's'Ffalenn; threat to him ended all argument.

"Ath guard your way, then," the scout said, blunt as hammered metal. "May the clans in the south speed your journey."

Jieret crossed the Thaldein passes, dismissed his friendly escort, and grew lean and browned from hiding in ditches through the Valendale's sun-drenched, plowed farmsteads. He took no careless step. But headhunters picked up his trail west of Cainford. He left five hounds dead, and two men, and limped on with bound ribs and a calf with a festering dog bite. The hedge witch he challenged at knifepoint for healing cursed his barbarian tongue, then tried to sell him an amulet snagged together from squirrel skin and the strung vertebra of a grouse.

Jieret refused her the price of a cut lock of his bronze hair.

"'Twould be useful for bird snares," the crone muttered. She sniffled over her sticky decoction, then knotted a bandage over an ill-smelling poultice with vindictive and sharp ferocity.

"I like the birds free, and myself most of all." Jieret wanted to flinch at her handling, but dared not, with his dagger point pressed to her back. The crone's hovel had nesting sparrows in its eaves, and the pot on her brazier leaked. Poverty and townborn contempt for her simples had leached all her pride in her trade. Jieret harbored the cynical suspicion that any offering from his person would be sold back to headhunters by nightfall, twined into a tracking spell to trace him.

Despite his need, the crone put a grudge in her remedies. His leg swelled and ached. Through curses of agony, he tore the dressing away and soaked off the salves in a stream. Feverish, limping, he thrashed his way south through the brush. A second pack of tracking dogs winded his scent and burst into yammering tongue. Freshly mounted, their masters tried to run him to earth against the guard spells of a grimward, which no man living might cross. There, he might have perished, inadvertently killed by Fellowship defenses set to keep trespassers from harm.

But clan hunters from Taerlin heard the commotion and spirited him downstream in a boat. Safe at last under Caithwood's dense cover, cosseted by a girl with cool hands, he slept off his lingering wound sickness.

Six weeks, since he had left his wife in Deshir. Early spring exchanged lace-worked blossom and bud for the sumptuous mantle of summer. On the sandy neck of Mainmere Bay, Jieret was met by the clan chief whose ancestral seat lay in ruins across silvered waters. She had ridden hard to bear him a message, the scout in her company said.

The hour was dusk, the sky, cloudless azure. Jieret crouched by her campfire under the eaves of scrub maples and spat out the bones of the rock bass netted for supper. While thrushes fluted clear notes through the boughs, and the deer emerged to nibble the verge of the bogs, he regarded the wizened little duchess who bore ancient title to Mainmere. She watched him eat, her gnarled hands folded. Along with age, she wore callus from sword and from bridle rein. The leathers belted to her waist were a man's, and shaded under the fans of white lashes, her eyes met his own with stark pity.

"What's wrong?" Against the soft, sustained lisp of the breeze, sounded Jieret sounded boisterous and unseasoned.

Lady Kellis touched the battered satchel by her knee. "A documented accusation by Avenor, made against your sanctioned prince." She resumed in her husked, worn alto. "My lord Maenol withheld this one writ from the packet, for your hand alone, he insisted. By your sworn duty, this becomes your legal charge as *caithdein* of Rathain."

Her fingers trembled as she loosened the strings of her parcel. "For this, we risk another passage to see you safe into Corith. There's a chance the *Khetienn*'s departure was delayed. In the month when the ice broke, the Shadow Master heard of Lysaer's proclamation of slavery. Word came back that he intended to make disposition on behalf of our clans."

"What's the charge?" Jieret's appetite fled. He rinsed his hands in the leather bucket used earlier to sluice down his whetstone, in no hurry to accept the offered document.

But Lady Kellis had no reassurance to steady him. "I leave you to read," she said in blank reserve. "Then you must act as your oath to your kingdom demands."

At first touch, the heavy, state parchment filled Jieret with trepidation. He unfolded its leaves, braced as though handed the news of a recent fatality. Then he perused the first lines of official script, and his fists knotted from helpless rage. "But there was never a trial to affirm this arraignment!"

The Duchess of Mainmere gave a dry laugh. "Be thankful. If there had been, the towns would have seen your prince burn."

By the time Jieret finished, he was shaking. Traced bronze by the flame light, he bent his rangy shoulders and dammed silent misery behind the locked palms of his hands.

A *caithdein*'s given charge was the testing of princes, if the Fellowship Sorcerers were preoccupied. The clans of Tysan were lawfully correct. Any accusation of dark sorcery against his liege belonged nowhere else but with him.

Heavy of heart, Jieret tucked the document into his shirt. "I will go on to Corith. Find a boat quickly to bear me."

The grandame arose, touched his arm in mute sympathy, then left him to a comfortless night. While the stars shimmered through the puzzle-cut shapes of black leaves, the ugly duty before him at Corith lent spin to his chafing fear. Rathain's sworn *caithdein* could not shake his dread, that his prescient dream of a city execution and Avenor's sealed writ of arraignment might share a fatal connection.

Passage to the Isles of Min Pierens in a patched-up fishing smack took three weeks, beating against the season's prevailing westerlies, and bouts of calm between squall lines. As the little craft wore through the islands off the headland, Jieret crouched on the deck, stripped down to his sun-scorched skin. Between his knees, he braced a bucket of damp sand against the wallowing roll of the deck. A monologue of curses marked his ongoing effort to scrub the green bloom of mold from his leathers.

"Man, lend it mercy," drawled the craft's only deckhand, perched like a limpet halfway up the mast with orders to watch out for shoals. "Keep on that, and just weep when yer bollocks tumble out and dangle right pretty through the holes."

Jieret looked up, a squint to one eye as he took vengeful aim with the holystone.

But the sailhand's snide interest had swung toward the land, where the high, russet rock notched the sky in crazed patterns. Tumbled walls crowned the summit, bleached with sun, and the broken, eggshell rims of the keeps which remained of a Second Age fortress. Beyond, unveiled by the sliding shift of vantage as the fishing smack nosed downwind, there arose a trim set of masts stripped of canvas, and a dark, lean hull, rocking serene at her anchorage.

"Swamp me for a half-wit!" cried the sailhand. "Who'd have risked coin to wager? The *Khetienn* hasn't sailed after all."

Jieret reached his feet in a rushed, thoughtless movement, and the bucket overset; a wet sludge of sand flooded over the offending set of leathers. "Fiends plague!"

The language loosed next won a laugh from the boat's swarthy captain. "Ach, let her go, lad! The deck won't see harm. For your stripped buttocks, we'll scrounge a loan from our slop chest."

"My naked arse isn't like to be burned for dark sorcery," Jieret groused, his distress not at all for soaked garments. He glowered

48

across the closing gap of water. The brigantine's satin brightwork mocked him back, insolent, unmarred by the damage rough weather might cause to drive her back into shelter. Nor did her decks hold industrious crewmen, but languished untenanted in the heat. Jieret's foreboding deepened. His liege should be long away from known waters, with no trouble too dire to stay him.

The hard-run little fishing smack put in and launched her dory over the side. "We'll hold off for your signal," said the captain from his squint-eyed perch at the rail.

Jieret settled into the tender's stern seat, still damp, but presentable. He brooded throughout the approach to the strand, limned in the flat glare of noon, the shade like slopped ink beneath the cedars. As the craft neared the shore, a figure built plump and round as a partridge bobbed amid the rocks, craned a short neck, then erupted into spectacular strings of epithets.

The oarsman listened, awestruck. "D'ye suppose yon one caught a hornet in his breeks?" He reversed his stroke, and the dory spun about in the wash of a slack tide breaker. "A collection like that's a rare masterpiece. Never heard the like, not in any cutthroat dive the length of the westshore dockside."

His speculation foundered against a peculiar, chilly reticence as, boots gripped in hand, his profile like the anviled rim of a thundercloud, the muscled young chieftain from Strakewood splashed thigh deep in the shallows.

"Well then," the crewman said, stoic. "I'll be off. Show us a light from the point if ye want passage back to the mainland."

Oars creaked. The dory reversed direction, leaving Jieret to wade through the surf.

The diatribe from the headland hiccuped through a pause, then switched key to outraged recognition. "Ath! It's yourself!"

Jieret forbore to glance shoreward.

"He's not with you!" The fat man on the beach hopped the last steps to the tidemark, shook his lard fist, and erupted, "Damn his lice-brained, sow-eared, rutting stubborn mind! He's bent on getting himself killed."

Jieret arrived on dry shingle. "Not with me?" he echoed. Stopped erect in noon glare while salt droplets sluiced runnels down his ankles, he gazed from full height into an unkempt, round face and smoldering, cinnamon eyes.

"Turd-stupid, string-plucking goose," said Dakar, erstwhile spellbinder to a Fellowship Sorcerer, and known far and wide as the Mad Prophet. He licked bearded lips, then clapped his mouth closed,

49

belatedly aware that the clansman who loomed over him brimmed like dammed acid with temper. Dakar's layers of mismatched clothing heaved as he dredged up an ingratiating shrug. "Well, maybe not a goose, exactly."

"You refer to my liege, Prince Arithon?" Jieret tossed a clipped nod past his shoulder. Behind him, a wing-folded raptor on the settled arc of the sea, the brigantine seemed juxtaposed on the view, a wild thing imprisoned by the natural stone revetments which bordered the harbor basin. "Don't you dare claim he isn't here."

The Mad Prophet screwed his eyes shut. Wheezing like a martyr from his headlong rush to the beachhead, he raised chubby, exasperated hands and tugged at his fox brush beard.

Since on their last meeting, Dakar had been the Master of Shadow's implacable enemy, Jieret added, "We *are* speaking of the same man?"

Dakar flounced stiff. "Nobody else drives me to fits of sick fury, and anyway, you should know best. This isn't the first time he's had you come chasing his shirttails the length of the continent."

Too wary to mind insults, Jieret kept his fierce glower. Dakar for a miracle was not wallowing drunk. Though the clownish, suffused features were still slack from loose living, the spirit inside his dissipated flesh seemed transformed into change. The pouched eyes held a glint of shrewd purpose. A queer incongruity, and one at sharp odds with the Mad Prophet's scapegrace reputation.

The silence extended too long.

"What's amiss?" pestered Dakar. "Something's turned wrong. Or Ath's own Avenger couldn't have dragged you to sea."

"Oh, there's trouble, well enough." Jieret parked his hip against a boulder and jammed on his boots to mask his outright anxiety. "Perhaps you'd best say where Prince Arithon went."

"Ashore," Dakar said. Sweating in his seamy, worn clothes, he looked all at once beaten down, just another bit of flotsam cast up by storm to wilt on the waterworn rocks. "His Grace is alone, back on the mainland."

Jieret confronted the Mad Prophet's moon features like a swordsman stunned silly by a mace. "The mainland," he echoed in stark disbelief. "Please Ath, not now. He can't be."

"Best come up." Sly eyes swiveled askance; Dakar surveyed Rathain's tall *caithdein*, bitter himself with shared sympathy. "You look like you need to be out of the sun, and besides, there's a risk. We oughtn't discuss his royal affairs so freely here in the open."

Jieret looked blank. "What?"

"Koriani," said Dakar. "Damn prying witches and their bothersome spells." Then he rolled his gaze skyward, remiss. "I forgot. You wouldn't know how far things went wrong last autumn in Vastmark. The Koriani Prime Enchantress tried her level best to have Arithon s'Ffalenn assassinated."

Jieret shot tense, hand clasped on his knife, his color gone shatteringly white. "On my oath as *caithdein*, is every living faction on Athera dead set to end my liege lord's life?"

"Damned near." Dakar closed his moist grip on the larger man's elbow and tugged. "You haven't brought dispatches in with the sloop? Just yourself? Best move along, then." He nodded toward the cliff path. "I've got quarters up in the old fortress."

Cicadas buzzed amid the crumbled rock stair that jagged up the flank of the headland. The dry air scarcely stirred, thick with the resin taint of cedar. Gray lichens silted like ash in the crannies, and the only visible inhabitants were the finches, flitting in startled bursts through the vines netted over bent limbs and black needles.

From the heights, the isle was a fissured, clenched fist, the fretted shoreline worried by tides, and seamed in jagged grottos, hazed over in lavender shade. Here, in the First Age, Paravian seers had held council with dragons, who flew the world's skies no more. Against the vicious aberrations spawned by the drakes' wild magic, defenders from four races had languished, besieged, in the cramped, ragged bounds of the curtain wall. Now strewn like kicked block, the last ridge of foundation housed basking, gold lizards which skittered away into cracks.

The eldest living dragons had spun their dream of desperation and appeal within these baked, cratered keeps, to draw to Athera the aid of the Fellowship Sorcerers. But if any ghost presence from that past remained to haunt Corith's ruin, the land retained no thread of dissonance. Just bare stone, tuned shrill by the blaze of summer noon, and loomed on the untrammeled song of bundled energies which underpinned all the substance of creation. Centuries of wind and battering storms had swept even the deepest, layered bedrock clean of the imprint of violent vibration.

"Through here," Dakar puffed. He beckoned into gloom and reappeared beyond a crumbling archway.

Jieret followed, but saw no sign of tenancy. The temporary, safe haven for a Third Age fugitive felt abandoned, as if the site had been owned for all time by naught but the wind and the seabirds.

The stillness sawed at Jieret's suspicion. "Where are my liege's people? The crew of the *Khetienn*? Daelion, Master of Fate, save his Grace, has he kept none but you to stand by him?"

Suddenly exposed before dangerous antipathy, Dakar stopped, sliding, to chinks in complaint from loose stone. "I'm not your prince's enemy, not anymore. And he's kept the *Khetienn*'s crew, her full complement. They're all here, and safe, masked under my ward of concealment." A note of plaintive unhappiness crept through. "That's why, Ath forgive me, I had to stay. Given the choice, I wouldn't be here."

Jieret regarded Dakar's sweating tension. "I know the s'Ffalenn temper, none better. You were told to hide the brigantine, if galleys happened on her?"

Dakar nodded, miserable. "Or fire her, should my spells of illusion fall short." He shuffled breathlessly on. "Man, I couldn't stop him from going. His Grace has a will to stand down the Avenger's Five Horses, and no mercy on the fool who interferes. If he gets himself butchered on some mayor's scaffold, I can't argue his right to tempt fate."

At Jieret's worried start, Dakar raised his hands. "No, rest assured. Arithon's not taunting a death wish. He couldn't if he wanted. The Fellowship of Seven forced him to take blood oath last winter. He's bound and sworn to life, whatever the cost, against future threat from the Mistwraith."

"Mercy on him," Jieret whispered, shocked. In all Athera's history, so strict a measure had never been asked of a crown prince. "I didn't know."

"That happened after you parted at Minderl Bay." Dakar reached a gap in the masonry. Beyond him, the hazed jointure of sea and sky dimmed into distance, snagged with fluffs of white cloud. Innocent now, those scattered fleeces would mass into towers by late afternoon, and anvil into a squall line. Just as untrustworthy, Dakar turned right and vanished into clear space.

Jieret's startled shout entangled with a prosaic reassurance, flung backward. "Pay no mind to the wards. They're illusion. The footing's quite safe."

Faced by a jagged opening, then a yawning gap into air, the clan chieftain muttered imprecations against the spellbinder's feckless character. A clutch of fractured boulders overhung the drop, ready to launch from their settings at the first wrong breath of the wind. No coward, Jieret stepped down.

Chills roiled and rippled across his flesh. His senses upended. A fierce, hot tingle sang through his nerves, then stopped with a bracing jolt.

The Earl of the North bit back a yelp, the steel hilts of his weapons turned hot to his hand. He blinked, wits recovered, to find himself standing in a dusty, flat compound, scattered with tents sewn from sailcloth. Nor was Corith any longer untenanted. A circle of sailhands hunkered in the shade of a gnarled cedar. The ones near at hand looked aside at him, bored, then resumed quarreling over a dice throw, the winning stakes a collection of sticks notched with tally marks. The crescent knife used to keep count flashed in the fist of a prune-skinned little desertman, who stabbed air and hurled his scathing invective at a ship's boy for rigging the odds.

"The defense spell is spliced reflection," Dakar said, smug. "Those cliff rocks, and that span of ocean were borrowed intact from a site halfway down the north slope." As the fracas erupted into knee-slapping mirth over the ship's boy's scurrilous rejoinder, the spellbinder admitted, "Of course, the noise was more difficult to mask."

Case in point, a shout pealed out like steel put to the hammer.

The urchin shot erect from amid the pack of dicers. All coltish brown limbs and angular grace, the creature had blond hair tied in a glistening, long braid. The end was cross-laced with a frippery of ribbon bleached to rust. A second glance at a body clad in scruffy sailhand's cottons showed the first, shy curves of a girl at the threshold of maturity.

"Arithon wasn't on that fishing craft?" she shrilled across the brassy wash of sunlight.

At Dakar's headshake, she crowed her wild triumph. "Well then you owe me six royals! He wasn't to embark 'til the winds changed, and the weather's stayed contrary this season."

"There are still three days left before solstice," Dakar hurled back. "Your silver's not won before then." Soured by the prospect of forfeited coin, he confided to Jieret, "That's Feylind, the pest. I misspoke myself teaching that girl to wager. She attached herself to Arithon at Merior by the Sea, and for her talent, your liege thought to train her. She's gifted at navigation and seamanship when she isn't cheating numbers on the dice."

"She has spirit, give her that." Jieret watched her spin back to defend her hoarded spoils, then realized: this girl must be one of the twins that Arithon had spoken of granting his oath of protection. Years passed. Feylind had grown beyond childhood; nor would her brother Fiark remain beardless much longer, wherever his own fate had sent him.

"Come on," Dakar urged. "If the heat isn't making you die for a drink, I want all your rumors from the mainland."

* * *

53

Dusk softened over the broken spires at Corith. The sea beyond the breakwater spread a flat, purple disk. The seasonal squall line rumbled off the coast, stalled through afternoon by the chancy, winnowing breezes. Cloud ramparts loomed off the islands, their sulfurous rims stained by the afterglow. When Jièret refused outright to say what drew him from Rathain, Dakar parked his bulk upon the creaking rope pallet he had strung in the shelter of a tumbledown drum tower. The furnishings consisted of axe-cut fir, lashed at the jointures with twine. A water jug, a basin, and a clump of holed socks lay cached in the niche of an arrow slit. Beneath this, a sea chest in use as a table held a spellbinder's clutter of bundled herbs, and an edged pair of shearwater's flight feathers. Jieret chose to sit on the stone floor through the exchange of desultory small news.

They suffered but one interruption; the desertman burst in without word or apology, and left a meal of smoked fish and greens. The last of the day slowly fled. The ragged old walls were roofed with a haphazard patchwork of sailcloth, worried to threads and gaps by the wind until stars could be counted in constellations. Outside, the sailhands had laid off their dicing. Someone returned from trapping, and coals were laid in to roast conies. No stranger to the nuance of leading men, Jieret listened. Through spirited slangs and the odd burst of laughter he noticed the underlying worry.

Arithon's absence weighed on them all, though the subject stayed scrupulously unmentioned. Even the Mad Prophet's prying, sly talk circled to evade the sore topic.

The temperature cooled. Jieret cracked his knuckles and suddenly ran out of patience. "Why should my liege be alone on the mainland?"

Silence; the fallen summer darkness cut by a yelp as a sailhand burned careless fingers at the spit. Dakar against custom had not touched his food. He regarded his laced fingers, as if he just realized his soft, dimpled knuckles were wearing a stranger's rough callus. He was not drunk. His clothing was mended, and his beard, trimmed neat, as if dogged grooming might suppress the misery that impelled his anguished admission. "His Grace sought Cattrick. That huge master joiner he used to employ back in Merior."

"Dharkaron avenge!" Jieret cried. "His Grace went to *Shand*?"

"I already know," Dakar supplied. "Official books of grievances have been opened on the southcoast. Lord Erlien's clansmen sent warning. Any town citizen can make claim of injury against Arithon. No proof is required. Just a sealed statement from the plaintiff. Those women left widowed at Vastmark have wasted no time recording all manner of spurious spite. The pages are filled to the margins, and the mayors have promised to appeal for redress at Avenor."

"This Cattrick," Jieret snapped. "Is his loyalty secure?"

"Arithon believed he'd be able to win back the craftsman's trust." As this fueled a more alarming shift into fury, the Mad Prophet cringed, and cried out, "You *know* your liege!"

Jieret showed the fat spellbinder no quarter, but drew up his legs and busied his hands working the ringed salt from his buckskins. No need to reiterate the plain fact: that Dakar's intent was equally well suspect, outspoken as he had been in the past concerning the Shadow Master's ethics.

A thunderclap boomed over the ocean. Echoes shook the ominous flat air, and growled through the Mad Prophet's explanation. "Once Arithon heard that his half brother had signed formal sanction for slave labor, his temper lit off like fell sparks. No reason moved him. He would go ashore, use his Masterbard's talent and ply the southshore taverns. He meant to recall his craftsmen and recruit those who dared on some devious scheme to stall Avenor's injustice."

Jieret glanced up, his eyes chill hazel. He asked to borrow an oiled rag and a whetstone, then deliberately tended the steel of his quilloned dagger. Dakar, who had once known the *caithdein*'s father, knew better than to interrupt. The clan chieftain took his time, then stabbed the blade upright in the rush seat of a footstool. He gave his considered opinion. "Had I been here, I would have fought my liege bloody, even bundled him in irons to hold him."

"Oh, you could have tried," Dakar rebutted. "His Grace knows the tricks of his Masterbard's title. Even if he couldn't sing triplets to turn steel, the problem's not simple or straightforward. Arithon has changed. The campaign brought to ruin at Dier Kenton Vale left him marked, sometimes too deeply to reach. You don't want to tangle with his temper."

But that had been true far and long before the devastating war in Vastmark. Every one of Jieret's ancestors had lived with the peril of challenging s'Ffalenn royalty head-on. The clan chief probed, "You haven't mentioned the Havens."

A sudden, fierce gust slapped the sailcloth overhead. Dakar flinched. Brown eyes slid away in discomfort. "Your war captain, Caolle, saw everything."

Jieret stared back in rancorous bitterness. "My war captain? Who came back to us changed? He resigned his post, did you know that? Said he would lift a sword for nothing else except to train our young scouts sharper skills. But no more to kill. He won't say what took

place." Jieret paused, snorted through the high bridge of his nose in mixed admiration and disgust. "For stubborn, close secrets, a clam's less lockjawed than Caolle."

Beyond stiff disquiet, the wind raked the night, deepened by clouds until the stars at the zenith were blackened. Dakar raised no smile as, in boisterous consternation, the sailhands scurried for shelter. His gaze tracked the broken, white line of the breakers creaming the reefs far below. Each crest came unraveled in driven, wild splendor against shores nothing like another blood-soaked shingle he wished he could raze out of memory.

He said softly, "If Caolle can't speak, then neither will I. Trust my word. What went wrong between the Havens and the clash with Lysaer's war host lies beyond spoken words to explain. Hear advice from a friend. Don't ask your prince. I beg you, keep clear and don't pry. Let Arithon explain if he chooses."

"If he's still alive, and not roasted for sorcery on some mayor's pile of lit faggots." Jieret shot out a fist and grabbed the stout spellbinder by the collar. "By Ath, prophet! Where my prince is concerned, I'm more than a friend. We're bloodbond! I've twice risked my life to guard his mind from Desh-thiere's curse." Pain, naked and deep as a canker burst through. "Dharkaron avenge!" cried Jieret. "I've drawn his very *blood* to spare his sanity. What happened on that shoreline, in his right mind or not, could scarcely come to surprise me."

Strangely uncowed by the clansman's fierce strength, Dakar tore away. "It's not what you could bear, nor what I could!" Just anguish blazed through and reclothed his rumpled dignity. "Nor do you question a man's conscience alone, but a masterbard's empathy turned under siege by the Fellowship's imposed royal gift of compassion. Let Arithon be, if you have any mercy."

Hemmed in by the howling descent of the squall line, Earl Jieret went obstinate to the bone. "That one thing I can't do. In this, I am not my own master, but the oathsworn *caithdein* of Rathain. I *am* the realm's conscience in matters of the law! And Lysaer's charges of dark sorcery are too weighty to drop without question or inquiry."

The tempest broke over the cliff top. Wind screamed, and the billowed, dry dust became trampled under the cloudburst. The sky above Corith split apart in actinic tangles of lightning. For a drawn span of minutes, thunder slammed through the old fortress. Jieret hung waiting, racked to naked appeal; he first presumed Dakar had left him. Against the white gush of the leaks through the sailcloth, his agonized words had only the storm's voice for answer.

Then from the tempestuous wail of the elements, the Mad Prophet served his opinion. "Well thank Ath, it's going to be you. Your liege would mangle anyone else who challenged his integrity this time."

"How nicely opportune," a silvery, smooth voice issued unbidden from the rain. "I can see I've returned just in time to play my own part in the satire."

Dakar gasped an oath, and Jieret, spun in one surge to his feet, faced the doorway.

Lightning flared like a rip in black silk, to limn the arrival standing there. The man was slight boned, soaked as a seal in plain cotton. Temper smoked through each stabbing vowel as he added, "I'm back from the mainland, blown in with a spate of foul weather. Don't cheer," said Arithon s'Ffalenn. He stepped forward, reduced once again to a voice clothed over in darkness. "Cattrick didn't sell my killed carcass to the mayors, though assuredly, he had to be wooed."

Dakar's stupor unlocked all at once. He splashed sliding through a puddle, and rummaged after oiled rags and a wet length of kindling. Nerves interfered. When his hands dropped the flints, he resorted to a cantrip, spell driven. A spark erupted in a ripe flare of sulfur. New flame snagged the torch, fought into tormented brilliance by the gusts. Its flittering glow bronzed the first thing to hand, the bent crown of Jieret's head.

He had knelt. Taller than his sovereign, a muscled tiger before a wraith, he stumbled through the ritual greeting, *caithdein* to his sworn prince.

Black haired, green eyed, pale as if chipped from veined quartz, the Master of Shadow poised on braced feet with his crossed arms wrapped to his chest. He was shivering. Shed droplets rocked off the plastered folds of his shirt and scribed rubied flecks through the torchlight. "There's a parchment," he prompted, succinct. "Let me see it."

At Jieret's upflung glance of distress, the prince's brows angled higher. "You can hear? Good. Than arise and stop looking amazed. Your mission's no secret. Every forest scout I met crossing Falwood said a writ had been passed to my *caithdein*'s charge. If I'm not overjoyed to find Rathain's left stewardless, at least I'll see why no clansman in Havish seemed eager to look me in the face."

Jieret stood erect, his every movement cautious. That his prince was unarmed made no difference. The royal presence framed warning like the gleam on a lake of black ice. The pair of them were bloodbond, and yet, here stood a stranger masked in the features of a friend. This diamond-edged malice held a febrile, strung focus more volatile than Jieret remembered. While thunder boomed and shook the ancient foundations, and the rain thrashed in demented torrents, he became aware of Dakar's tense stillness, as if even the whisper of a wrongly drawn breath might trigger the spring of a predator.

Jieret's hand did not shake in its office as he said, "I would soften this, liege, if I could." In the uncanny, grave style inherited from his father, he drew the bundled document from the breast of his leathers and passed it across to his prince.

Arithon stiffened at first sight of the seals: the crown and star blazon of the purloined s'Ilessid device, and another, stamped in a lozenge of champagne wax, the rayed sunwheel adopted since Vastmark. The Shadow Master flipped open the folded leaves, then tipped them to capture the torchlight.

He read. His skin went from pale to transparent, and his very heart seemed to stop. Then he stirred. A word passed his lips, the staccato lilt of consonants framed in the grace of old Paravian. He hurled down the indictment as though its mere touch burned his flesh. Then he whirled, bent, and in a move of pure fury, plucked Jieret's quilloned knife from the stool seat.

"*Caithdein* of Rathain," he intoned in chiseled, formal language. "The truth, on my word as your crown prince. If that's not sufficient, you'll have your sure proof through a death seal set into the lifeblood spilled from my body."

From the corner, Dakar gasped. Before Jieret could decry the necessity, Arithon closed an unsteady hand on the blade, over steel just meticulously sharpened. Scarlet welled from his palm, spilled through lean fingers, and ribboned slick tracks down his wrist. He inclined his head to the spellbinder.

"You have my consent. Lay down the binding, my life as surety that nothing I speak is a falsehood."

Dakar arose. Raised to a grave majesty sprung from stark fear, he clasped Arithon's wet fist. The spell rune he framed burned in lines of cold light, then twined like barbed ribbon through the rich flood flowing from the knife cut. "Beware," he cautioned. "What you ask is done. One word of deceit will destroy you."

By ancient custom, the last scion of s'Ffalenn then knelt before his *caithdein*.

The Shadow Master said in metallic distaste, "The deaths at the Havens are all mine, every one. But this charge of dark sorcery has no ground. No spell was spun, light or dark at that inlet. There were no fell tricks. No engagement occurred beyond arrows and steel, nor even the use of my birth-born mastery of shadow." Still trembling, he regarded the spreading, red stain on his shirt cuff and finished his venomous delivery. "What happened was simple, cold murder."

He laughed then, wide-eyed, and spun the slicked blade. The point now angled against his own breast, its chased silver pommel a reckless invitation to serve judgment. "Are you horrified? Caolle thought treason and threatened to spit me with bared steel."

Jieret swallowed, stunned blank and sickened. Five hundred forty lives had been taken in cold blood: the truth forced out in a naked confession that asked neither quarter nor pity.

"You can't find the gall to ask why?" pressured Arithon, still venting pain into anger. "Or are you waiting for a Fellowship Sorcerer to gainsay a testimony made under truthseals?"

"Almighty Ath, that's enough!" Dakar launched himself across his clutter of belongings and with a competence few would have credited, snatched the knife from Arithon's grasp. He discarded the blade and clutched the prince's soaked shirt in both hands. To Jieret, caught aback as the Shadow Master swayed on his feet, the Mad Prophet cried in rebuke, "What more must you have? Kingdom law has been satisfied. Daelion himself! A crown prince's blood oath alone should have satisfied that the charge of dark sorcery was false. Your duty could have demanded far less, since Caolle himself stood as witness."

With no gap for reply, he turned his invective toward the prince braced upright in his hands. "By Sithaer, you're freezing! Where's Cattrick? Wasn't anyone aboard to share the watch on your sloop? How long were you out there, manning the helm in the storm?"

"Galleys," said Arithon, abruptly too worn to fuel his own manic fury. "Seven, with registry flags out of Capewell. I lost them six days ago, off the shoals of Carithwyr." Against every precedent, he failed to resist as Dakar pressed him to sit. The drum of the rain nearly canceled his speech. "Cattrick's still on the mainland. I meant him to stay. He's agreed to return to my employ."

"He's a fool, then." Dakar shoved past Jieret, who felt awkward and in the way. Displaced wing feathers fluttered helter-skelter as the spellbinder cleared the trunk and flung up the rickety lid. "I won't ask what you promised him."

Folded on the pallet, Arithon said nothing. His face did not show, his head being bent and resting on his knees. The fire in its makeshift bracket across the drum tower had finally ignited the oiled rags. Golden light limned his appalling exhaustion. His loose, sailhand's cottons hung off his gaunt frame, except where heavy wet had slicked the cloth to his flanks. His wrists showed each ridge of old scars and taut sinew, and the cut on his hand bled too freely.

"Liege, let me help," Jieret begged.

"Find him a blanket," Dakar ordered, terse, then rummaged through his things, and snatched out linen strips and tied a pressure wrap over Arithon's gashed hand. "Idiot," he murmured. "You used that damned blade like a butcher. Got tendons laid bare. When the bleeding's controlled, you'll need to be sewn, or risk scarring that may mar your music."

"My throat isn't cut. I can sing." Arithon lilted a slurred line of doggerel taken from a dockside ballad. Then, as Jieret bent down to swaddle him in wool, his maundering humor fled before desperate focus. "Why are you here?" he demanded. A deep tremor racked him. He locked his teeth through the spasm, then ground on in unswerving logic, "Had that parchment reached your hand in Rathain, Dakar's right. Caolle could have refuted those charges."

"My liege, not now." Jieret scarcely noticed the tug as Dakar snatched the blanket from his fist. "The other news that brought me can wait."

"Ah, no!" Arithon shoved off the wool the Mad Prophet sought to drape over him. His eyes raked up, fever bright. "I won't have that sleep spell you've slipped through the weave." He shot to his feet, restored to command through animate, blistering irritation. "By your oath as *caithdein*, Jieret, speak."

The moment hung, its tension spun out in maniacal wind and the distanced percussion of thunder. Leaked droplets pattered under the sailcloth. The torch spat and hissed, fingered by drafts until every shadow seemed crawlingly alive. Black haired, baleful, Arithon waited, his presence stillness incarnate. He was not a patient man. The fretted, willful energy he used to avert collapse seemed nursed from a leashed spark of violence, as if his heart's peace had been razed off in Vastmark, to leave a core of acid-etched steel.

Jieret quailed before apprehension. This was no stranger he confronted, but his crown prince, scarred and haunted by the trials brought down by the Mistwraith's dire curse. The spring's prophetic dream lodged too vividly in recall, with its wrenching potential for tragedy. The vision was terrifying, final: the wide square paved in brick, centered by its cordon of guardsmen and the unpainted rise of the scaffold, pennoned in the dazzling glitter of gold cord and sunwheel banners. His very pulse seemed to throb to the chant of packed onlookers. He shook off the mesmerizing hold of remembrance, in thought or utterance unwilling to grapple the silver-bright length of the executioner's sword, then the scream of this same prince, fallen.

"I had an augury on your Grace's life," he rasped, torn by his need to be finished.

"Oh, how merry!" Arithon exclaimed, sardonic. "My fate's already wound in auguries like tripping strings. No. Don't plod through the hysterical details. Let me have just the bare facts."

"You must listen!" cried Jieret, frightened by the dismissal. "After the slaughter at Tal Quorin, would you take my gifted dreams lightly?"

"But I don't." Unrepentant, Arithon accepted a blanket from Dakar that was combed free of furtive seals to bring sleep. He flicked the wool across his wet frame, winced as he fumbled a one-handed clasp, then stepped back to forestall more assistance. "I can manage. Am doing so, in fact. Your Sight does run true, more's the pity. But for the sake of Rathain, I'd have preferred to be spared the unnecessary favor. As my oathsworn *caithdein*, your presence here can't improve my wretched odds of surviving." He spun, tripped over the stool in a startling turn of spoiled grace. "Now give me the details without any melodrama."

"The time seemed high summer," Jieret resumed, ferociously bland. "A public execution, under town auspice, with every appropriate trapping."

"How splendid and trite. *How predictable!*" Arithon gasped back shrilling laughter. Perhaps goaded on by his *caithdein's* sharp recoil, he bit back like salt in a sore, "All right, my sworn lord, your duty's been met to the last grasping letter of the law. By kingdom charter, I've been properly tried and warned. Now for love of the realm, you are free. Return to Rathain. The fishing sloop that brought you sails tomorrow for Carithwyr on my personal orders. Her captain was told to expect you on board. You will cross High King Eldir's *neutral* realm of Havish to reach your homeland, and avoid another tangle with Tysan's headhunters."

"Go," Dakar urged, cued by a mix of dread and epiphany, since every shred of bad news out of Tysan would have emerged through that prior exchange with the fishermen. Arithon was not sanguine for very good reason, beside being too spent to cope. The Mad Prophet grabbed Jieret's elbow, wide-eyed and imploring. "Come away. What you're seeing's not temper, but a mannerless plea to be alone."

The clansman stayed fixed, his bleak, considered gaze upon the motionless form of his prince. He looked as if he might speak.

The Mad Prophet plugged his ears, shut his eyes, and cringed like a dog that expected a kick.

Yet Jieret held silent. When no explosion came from the figure under the blanket, the spellbinder cracked one eye open.

"For mercy's sake, Dakar, just get him out," Arithon stated in hoarse, deadened misery.

Like an obedient, fat ninepin bowling down a young oak, the Mad Prophet plowed Rathain's young *caithdein* into prudent retreat through the doorway.

Close Confidence

The squall passed. Above the swept rocks of the fortress at Corith, stars emerged from the cloud cover. Sea winds combed the headland and slapped through the sailcloth roofed over the ruined north drum keep. Bronzed by the smoking stub of the oil cresset lit to treat Arithon's hand, Dakar sat awake, keeping watch. Long since, the spooled silk and needles used to close up the gash had been tidied and put away. On the pallet, stone quiet, the Teir's'Ffalenn lay sprawled in exhausted sleep.

The Mad Prophet listened to the call of the night-flying owl, mournful between the irregular tap of twine lacings. He waited, alert for the moment of inevitable aftermath. No man mentioned the Havens inlet in the Shadow Master's hearing that dreams did not come and goad the prince screaming from sleep. Grateful that foresight had seen Lord Jieret dismissed before the inevitable backlash, Dakar settled his chin on plump wrists.

An hour passed, uneventful. The night smelled of puddled rock, mingled near at hand with the astringent bite of medicinal herbs. Gusts thrummed sighing through the cedars down the slope, cut by the whistle of a sentry, come back from the headland to roust his relief watch. Dakar traced out a fine rune. His trained talent as spellbinder raised an appeal to the air, then bent the element's given consent to work a small construct of deflection. When the sailor just wakened in the compound raised a noisy string of complaint, no ripple of disturbance crossed the line of soft conjury to upset Arithon's rest.

Somewhere in the thickets a fox barked. The midsummer stars arced across the black zenith, their dance unchanged through the centuries since man first inhabited Athera. Against their seasonal harmony, a whispered rustle of discord: on the pallet, one fine-boned hand spasmed closed. The Master of Shadow curled into a locked huddle and loosed a harsh breath through his teeth.

Dakar crossed to the pallet. He murmured a cantrip to ground his inner strength in the ageless stone of the headland. Then, as Arithon moaned, twisted sidewards, and thrashed, he grasped the slighter man's shoulder. He caught the fist that snapped up toward his chin, winced for the abuse to new bandages, then pressed down in firm restraint. The prince he resisted might be sorrowfully thin, but his struggles were inventive and difficult. Dakar required main force to prevail. He turned the sharp s'Ffalenn features into the blankets and stifled the rising, agonized groan into the muddle of bedding.

"Wake," he murmured. "Arithon, throw off the dream and come back." He barbed each word in spell-turned clarity. "This is Corith, and everyone is safe."

Dakar waited, spoke again. He absorbed the next onslaught of redoubled, blind fight as the Shadow Master tried to bludgeon free. Against his undignified need to cry out, the Mad Prophet held steadfast, until the corded tension under his hands dissolved through a spasm of transition. The Teir's'Ffalenn in his care passed from nightmare into living remembrance of a horror no passage of time might erase. Then, as often happened, Dakar waited, silent, while the Master of Shadow softly wept.

The cresset by then had dwindled to a coal. Rinsed by ruby light, the Mad Prophet stayed his sympathy, while Rathain's crown prince cocked an elbow and pushed himself upright. The single-handed sail to slip pursuit from the mainland had worn him. The resilience never recovered since Vastmark had abraded further in the months spent ashore. Terrors of guilt and conscience dulled the green eyes that regarded Dakar through the gloom, left them lusterless as sea-battered glass. The expressive, fine bones of the Masterbard's hand rested slack on the coverlet, bundled flesh sapped of small grace.

"Daelion Fatemaster forgive me for the way I treated Jieret," were the first words the Shadow Master said. He looked fevered. Minutes passed as he steadied his breathing, and his high, sweating flush subsided back into pallor. "He is Rathain's true *caithdein*, courage and honor to his core. So like his father, he's become. Does he know even yet what he means to me? Should he take harm from Lysaer's miscalled judgments, I don't think I could stand it. Let Dharkaron Avenger redress his wronged feelings. *I had to send him back to his people.*"

"You did right," Dakar soothed. "Lord Jieret will go, and soon after, the *Khetienn* will sail."

An interval passed without speech. Arithon tipped back his tangled head and rested against the worn stone of the bastion. The steep, angled features of his ancestry carved sharper in the uncertain scrawl of deep shadows. "If Cattrick succeeds, we'll have ships," he murmured, his ongoing effort to control his fraught nerves sketched in pained creases around his eyes. "The clans can be taken to safety. We only have to find the Paravians." His hope was a refuge from the drive of Desh-thiere's curse behind the strong wardspells that masked them.

In the dimness, Dakar averted his face. Ill practiced at patience, he fiddled with his sleeve cuffs, then launched on a sharp change in subject. "What will you do about Jieret's new augury?"

"Ignore it, unless the *Khetienn*'s search fails." Arithon's bitterness scraped through like old rust. "What can I do anyway? My magesight's still blind. Given your help, I couldn't even scry through to find a sane outcome in Vastmark. Ath knows, since that blunder, naught's changed."

"Stop," Dakar snapped. "You can't let your past write the future." Like ill omen, the fading last flame in the torch dipped to an ember and died. This moment, Dakar found no comfort in darkness. "Right now you would do best by sleeping," he advised.

An oath ripped back in sharp, precise syllables. Bedding rustled. Arithon settled prostrate on the cot. His limbs did not move, but through mage-sight, Dakar sensed his eyes were still open. When an hour passed, and his needling conscience kept him wakeful, he loosed a soft word in resignation.

The spidered threads of the spell already prepared between Dakar's hands enfolded his consent on a thought. The wide, tortured gaze became masked by the sweep of black lashes. Tight breathing steadied. Arithon s'Ffalenn relaxed fully at last, the unquiet gnaw of his lacerated spirit eased back into dreamless rest.

Weary, aching, the Mad Prophet arose from long vigil. He shuffled his way to the keep's narrow doorway, and in the drawing pull of the earth through his bone marrow, measured the interval before dawn. Another figure bulked dark alongside the drum tower's threshold. Lord Jieret lay curled there, his great sword at hand, and his hawk features set in repose. A contradictory tautness knit through his body

65

warned of the fact he was wakeful. Dakar chose not to speak, but stepped out, his intent to seek solitude and settle drawn nerves on the heights overlooking the sea.

A grip like fixed iron trapped his ankle. He tripped, crashed flat, and bit back an outraged howl as his cheek slapped into a mud puddle. Then outcry became moot. Rathain's *caithdein* rolled over his felled form and pinned him facedown in the dirt. A predatory hand vised his nape and a knife bit a slanting, cold line across the pouched skin of his throat. Dakar gasped. Contact with the blade shot a dull jolt of misery through his mage-sense. The kept steel of its edge still shrilled with the strung resonance of despair, dark imprint of a crown prince's blood oath.

"Jieret," he grunted. "For pity, let up."

"Ath, you've a fine sense of arrogance to try and keep me from my liege's confidence!" But the hold loosened. The ugly touch of the knife blade lifted. Lord Jieret backed off and squatted on his haunches while his victim rolled upright and swiped a slurry of grime from his beard.

"You were eavesdropping," the Mad Prophet accused, plaintive.

"Aye, and where else does any *caithdein* sleep, but across his sworn prince's threshold?" Met by affront, the clan chieftain muffled a cough of laughter behind his wrist. "Dharkaron's immortal bollocks, you forget. My forefathers were standing down testy s'Ffalenn princes while yours were still pissing in swaddling bands."

Dakar blotted his moist face with napped cuffs, spat something gritty, and forcibly noosed back his temper. "You couldn't have helped. And your suspicions are wasted. I'm no longer Arithon's enemy."

"Does that even signify?" Jieret snicked his knife back home in its sheath, careful to damp the steel silent. "I sat with my liege through the night when my people died for him at Tal Quorin. Again, the time he was forced to burn the trade fleet at Minderl Bay. I've seen how he weeps for the nightmares. I know his fear, that the ones he's come to love will lose their lives." All purpose, he finished, "My place is to stand at his side. *Caith d'ein*, shadow behind the throne."

"I'm unlikely to test his given will on that matter," said Dakar. "He wants you safely back in Rathain. And he's right. You can't steward his realm from the uncharted sea aboard his brigantine."

Jieret looked away through a tigerish pause, the jut of his profile outthrust against the film of fine mist. "What do you know that you aren't saying, prophet?"

"Fiends plague, your whole line was bred to be difficult!" Dakar plowed mulishly erect. "Before you flattened me, I'd planned to take a long walk. The rocks here are practiced at minding themselves, and your liege is secure. I set wards."

The clan chief rose also, his oiled stride shortened to pace the Mad Prophet's bobbling progress. The unlikely pair crossed the compound, captured in mismatched reflection through the silver-plate scattering of puddles. Beyond the gapped walls, the cliff path lay fogbound, shadowed in the refrain of wild surf hewing the obdurate shoreline.

When the sailhand huddled wakeful by the notch to the harbor failed to challenge their passage, Jieret raised gingery eyebrows. "You've set spells of concealment? What do you fear? Or do you already know from the Fellowship Sorcerers that Arithon's course carries risk?"

"Damn you for being your mother's son after all. She always guessed far too much." Dakar snatched an irritable swat at his nape where a bloodsucking insect had bitten. "I share some wider knowledge from Sethvir of Althain, and Arithon as well, since the Paravian charts he was given to steer by were lent for his use by the Sorcerer."

The Mad Prophet stalled, hopeful, while the grate of his tread over chipped rock and gravel silenced crickets, and the mist silted droplets in his hair. Jieret ranged beside him, his panther's stride soundless, and his expectancy taut as strung wire.

"Shark," Dakar ripped out. "One taste of blood, you keep circling." He swiped past the dripping boughs of a cedar and resumed without apology for his companion's adroit duck to avoid a slap in the chest. "Very well, yes, there's more danger than you know, even granted your heritage as clanblood." The Mad Prophet found a boulder, damp but sheltered from the wind. He sat to explain the gift of the grand earth link ceded to the Sorcerer Sethvir by Athera's last guardian centaur.

"The network ties the Sorcerer's consciousness to everything on Athera, animate life or still matter. But the Seven have postulated the connection may hold selective blind spots. Its weave could be subject to guarding wards set by the old races themselves." Dakar stabbed fleshy fingers toward the masked edge of the horizon. "The evidence lies in default. The Paravians appear to have vanished from Ath's creation. And yet, though diminished, through strands and deep auguries, their presence still figures in the weave of Athera's life pattern."

Simple words, to frame this world's penultimate mystery. Dakar paused in sorrowful reflection, his brows snarled down above his pug

67

nose, and his chin bristled out beneath his beard. What eluded the arcane acts of scrying might yet be uncovered by a manned expedition. The oceans girdled the far side of the world, immensely vast and wide. If an isle existed, wrapped under wards, or some hidden, green haven lurked on the shores of the far continent, Arithon would set sail in the *Khetienn* to seek.

"Your prince hopes to beg sanctuary from the Mistwraith's fell curse," Dakar ended. "That scarcely offers much hope for your clans, but the Fellowship Sorcerers agree, Paravian protection offers his surest possibility of reprieve."

Broad-shouldered as a sentinel against drifting mist, Jieret stared out to sea. "The Fellowship Sorcerer, Ciladis, set off on that quest almost two centuries past. He has never come back."

"Nobody argues the choice harbors peril!" Dakar snapped. "The old races have no desire to be found, else their presence would be known to Sethvir." He paused, choked silent by memories very few left alive could understand: of the awesome, pure grace of the unicorns dancing, that could sear sight to blindness from too terrible a surfeit of ecstasy. His very marrow ached for the deep, drowning peace of a centaur's presence, or the lyrical harmonies in a sunchild's song. These mysteries, once experienced, could draw mortal minds to forget food and drink, and waste away, lost, until the spirit forsook the body, lured beyond all common things of earth.

Aggrieved beyond words for the loss done the world by the Paravians' passing, Dakar was jerked back to the trials of the present by Jieret's harsh grip on his wrists. "Take care of my liege. By my charge as *caithdein*, see him happy and secure, or bring him back whole. Else by Dharkaron's bleak vengeance, I will scour the world's four quarters to find you, and make you suffer my judgment."

Dakar gave a raw, hooting chuckle. "That threat cuts both ways, you barbarian wolf. To harry me for my failures, you must first stay alive, and free of a galley slave's coffle." He shrugged, disengaged from the clan chieftain's hold, and heaved his short bulk off the boulder. Around them, the last of the dark was fast fading. Gulls screamed above the jumbled, gray crags, and the knifing wind wore the smells of seawrack and salt. Dakar clasped his arms to ward off the chill, while the charcoal sky brightened and limned his stout form against a lucent pearl backdrop. "Go where your heart calls. The sleep spell I left won't hold in full sunlight. Your liege will wake and feel rested. He'll want to see your face and be sure you are well before the hour comes to sail. Give him that much, for the journey he embarks on could easily span the next decade."

Between a breath and a heartbeat, the Mad Prophet was gone, vanished into the raw cotton mist as if his presence had been knit out of dreams. Jieret was left to the desolate splendor of the cliff head, consumed by worried thoughts, while the throaty crash of flood tide slammed white torrents over the seamed rocks below. Suspicion remained. The Mad Prophet had not disclosed all he knew. A shiver touched Jieret as he measured how subtly the spellbinder had changed.

While playing the drunkard, Dakar made it easy to forget his five centuries of study under Fellowship auspices.

Disarmingly masked behind vexed words and bother, the fat prophet scored his clear point: he could have exerted his trained will at any moment, used powers of sorcery to set one blustering, young clan chief firmly into his place.

Jieret flushed, then loosed a chagrined shout of laughter. He checked the hang of his weapons out of habit and started back toward the ruined fortress.

For Arithon's sake, Dakar had indulged him. Whatever reason underlay the vicious slaughter at the Havens, the shifty little spellbinder had entrusted Rathain's prince with the dubious benefits of his loyalty. From that, the realm's *caithdein* must salvage what peace of mind he could; his liege would not sail westward into peril without an ally to guard his left shoulder.

"Though Ath Creator," Jieret ripped out, as if air itself would carry his balked temper back to the Mad Prophet's ears, "I'd rather be boarding the *Khetienn* myself than turning tail back to Rathain."

Checkrein

For Morriel Prime, Matriarch of the Koriani Order, the rage still burned white-hot, even eight months after her failed attempt to assassinate the Master of Shadow. Due to the intervention of a bungling, fat prophet, Arithon s'Ffalenn still breathed. Morriel shut her eyes. As if by cutting off the daylight which flooded her quilted chair by the casement, she could deny the thorny fact the prince still walked on this side of Fate's Wheel. Old, withered, reduced by years and longevity spells to a husk of sagged flesh wrapped over porcelain bones, she endured the weary pulse of blood through her veins; each heartbeat a throb of endlessly unquiet pain.

More than anything she wished the oblivion of death.

Yet the haven of final rest lay beyond reach. First she must unyoke the chains of command and transfer the massive burden of prime power to the hands of a proven successor.

Forty-three women before this had perished attempting the trials of succession. Fear remained, to poison all pretense of patience. The years spent training the current candidate might be wasted, despite all her promising talent.

Morriel breathed in the humid sea air of the southcoast. Decades of handling critically potent forces had chafed her senses to unwonted sensitivity, until the ceaseless barrage of sound, form and smell besieged the desperately held order of her mind. Even removed to this high tower, confined in isolation above the sleepy commerce of Thirdmark's narrow streets, Morriel battled the distractions. The

70

moldered damp of age-rotted stone, even the salt crystal scour of the breeze through the casement flushed her thoughts to patternless noise. Her cognizance at times felt strung thin as cobwebs, until the air currents themselves seemed to separate into voices. Each passing second tapped a pulsebeat against her dry flesh.

Moment to moment, she denied the seductive lie. Inanimate matter *could not* quicken in sentient vibration. She would not permit inert reality to rock off reason's track, slip the boundaries of discipline, and seduce her to embrace dreaming madness.

She had handled too many sigils of power in the course of her unnatural, long life. The very currents of her aura had been sealed into containment, to interrupt, then deny nature's cyclic rhythm of death. Attrition thinned the veil between senses and perception. The spin of bridled power eroded Morriel's control, until one day no bulwark would remain upon which to snag the purling thread of insanity.

The Koriani Prime endured with the dangerous knowledge that her age was now more than ten centuries. She had clung to breathing flesh far too long. None of her predecessors had dared test the limits so far beyond earthly balance.

Her will on the matter had been gainsaid by fate; and now, yet again, Arithon's persistent survival reduced all her works to futility. The augury she held as fair warning galled most for its absolute, ruthless simplicity: this last living scion of Rathain's royal line would disrupt the Koriani destiny, destroy a body of knowledge that stretched back into history to the time before catastrophe and war had driven humanity to seek refuge on Athera.

Morriel listened to the cries of the gulls skimming the breeze above the tideflats. She had never felt so wretchedly helpless. Her acquired depth of vision only mocked her. Earth turned, day to night, careless, herself a mote on its skin no more significant than any other unsettled speck of dust.

While the Master of Shadow plied the ocean aboard his brigantine, his unformed destiny hung over her sisterhood's affairs. One malignant chain of latent events would snap a succession unbroken for thousands of years.

Morriel endured, her frustration contained. As the *Khetienn* embarked into unknown waters, Rathain's prince would lie vulnerable to any bout of mischance water and gale could mete out. Her opening arose to spin a new plot over the wreckage of the old. A dry smile crimped the Matriarch's pale lips. No step would be wasted. No other enchantress in the order need share in the fabric of her design.

The first move in play could be masked to advance the training of Lirenda, First Senior, selected and groomed, but as of this hour, unprepared to survive the rigors of the accession.

On the eve of summer solstice, while the Fellowship Sorcerers worked in concert to complete an arduous conjury that had immersed them for over a year, the Warden of Althain would be least inclined to take meddling notice of accidents. The Koriani Prime snatched her moment.

The bar of warm sunlight slanted through the casement and cooled to a soft flush of red. Morriel soon heard the rustle of silk she anticipated in the stairwell. Her chosen First Senior arrived on the moment appointed. Such precise obedience was not petty. For a candidate to show less than perfection in all things carried the risk of ill consequence. One woman alone could wield the full might of the Koriani Order. A small lapse of discipline on that scale of power could deflect the course of history, even harrow and scorch the green earth.

The latch grated, gave, and the door swung open. A gush of sea air displaced the miasma of dank stone. Then the shuffled step of the deaf steward who had replaced witless Quen, but who admitted the arrival with the same simpleminded devotion.

First Senior Lirenda presented a regal figure, slender, tall, and purposeful. Groomed and graceful as a panther, she wore hair like dark satin sleeked into a single, coiled braid. Her feet kept a dancer's light tread on stone floors. The fine, sculptured bones of her wrists were set off by the gold-banded sleeves denoting her high office, and her violet silk mantle flowed off her lithe form like water poured from a vase.

She bowed before her Matriarch. Even in obeisance, her manner maintained innate breeding.

Morriel recalled the same trait in the child. Lirenda had always owned an elegant self-possession, that bone-deep assurance lent by wealth and background that touched servants to instinctive deference. This morning, the drifting perfume of the rose petals she used to sweeten her clothes chests came tanged with a trace scent of brimstone. Apparently the crates which sealed the new fiend banes had been troublesome to pack off to market.

Yet if the oversight arose from the duty novice's instructions, or a boy ward had shirked his assigned labor, Lirenda showed no irritation. Her oval features stayed smooth as a cameo as she murmured the ritual greeting. "Your will, matriarch."

That metallic, alto voice betrayed no curiosity, which was well. Morriel prolonged her survey of the prime candidate, her eyes like

72

probing black quartz. Power forgave no shortcoming. Distrust of arcane practice within the walled towns had redoubled since Lysaer's charge of dark sorcery against the Master of Shadow. The Koriani Order could ill afford to risk becoming mired in the backlash of frightened reaction.

"Sit," Morriel commanded in a brevity that stabbed.

Lirenda settled to a rustle of skirts on the bare stone ledge of the window seat. Against failing light, her body affected a cat's aloof poise; her expression settled to waiting. But beneath that unapproachable, aristocratic polish, her mind seethed with ambition. The predatory spark in those pale almond eyes never slept.

Morriel opened at due length, "The time has come for the first trial to prepare you for mastery of our Great Waystone."

Watchful eyes smoldered into full flame. "At last," Lirenda murmured.

"You'll use every minute before nightfall to prepare," said the Prime, and waved her peremptory dismissal.

The massive, polished sphere of the Koriani Waystone stood unveiled under starlight, planed filaments of captured reflection spiked deep in its shadowy heart. Even seated, eyes shut, a full span away, First Senior Lirenda felt the amethyst's aura soak into her stilled senses. With her mind diamond clear from an exhaustive course of ritual, the dark crystal's presence chilled like the breath of a predator: lethal, unforgiving, and charged in pitiless peril. The stone was as ancient as the order itself. Over a thousand prime matriarchs had wielded its dire focus since the cataclysm and war which had cast an uprooted humanity from its homeworlds. The jewel's deep lattice was said to encompass them all; their unquiet memories; the imprint of each departed prime's experience mazed like etched knotwork beneath its stilled facets.

At times in past history such knowledge meant survival. The records in the crystal could not be replaced. Nor could they be transferred. Stones mined in Athera fell under the Fellowship's compact with the Paravians. The knowledge from outside worlds was proscribed. Limited to those crystals brought in by the order, every Matriarch since had no choice but to adopt the fixed practice, that its original set of jewel matrixes must be maintained without cleansing.

No stranger to the contrary properties of first focus stones, Lirenda required firm discipline to stamp down her apprehension. Her gnawing unease was no phantom. The Great Waystone's secrets were held at perilous cost. Twined through the stored experience of the former matriarchs' collective memories ran vicious, ingrained crosscurrents: the coiling, sullen residue left layered by centuries of arcane bindings, crammed together and entangled into dissonant, unquiet knots.

One day, these must become the prime candidate's trial to master.

The protections Morriel laid down for this first exposure were forbidding enough to intimidate. Lirenda resisted the urge to break discipline and steal a glance through cracked eyelids. Against the mild fabric of summer night, she felt the formed lattice of wards stab her flesh like the prick of a thousand fine needles. The passes the Prime completed to frame each new sigil raised dire cold, and the salty damp that freshened the sea breeze came whetted by a bitter taint of ozone.

Minutes passed. Through the still blaze of stars and the tidal draw of the moon on the western horizon, Lirenda followed the pained shuffle of the Prime's steps, circling, tirelessly circling. The low, flinty whisper as the Matriarch chanted in rhythm to align each intricate, chained set of runes. Perception itself drowned. Sensed impressions strung out to elastic proportions, as if moving time and the rustle of dune grass had slowed to congealment in amber.

Elsewhere, the world turned untouched. From the tide pools beyond Thirdmark's harbor, a curlew called. A kicked cur yelped in the fish market alley, and the martial jink of steel as the wall watch changed guard reechoed off the city's gabled roofs. Sounds reached Lirenda as if muffled through gauze, and then not at all, as her awareness submersed, ringed about by ambient power.

When Lirenda's consciousness became a joined circle, sealed into relentless isolation, the Prime Enchantress said, "We are ready to begin."

Instructions followed, the husk of each syllable sandpaper sharp amid that enforced web of stillness. "Do not look upon the Waystone as I raise its grand focus. To try is to beg for destruction. My set protections cannot shield you from direct interaction with the event unless you maintain perfect balance. No matter what happens, through temptation or disaster, remember you follow as observer. Stay passive. On pain of annihilation, however much you feel traumatized, do not exert your conscious will outside the bounds of my ward ring."

One second passed in unbearable suspension. Lirenda fought down the dizzy pound of her pulse. Then in shared resonance, the plunge snatched her up in a rocketing, exhilarated rush, as Morriel Prime bent her will and invoked the Great Waystone's focus.

Stark silence descended. Wide as old darkness, deep as the floor of

Ath's oceans, the stillness reigned absolute. Lirenda felt walled in unbreakable black glass, reduced to a dust speck captured and prisoned in jet. Of her Prime's guiding presence, no sign remained, as if her aged flesh had succumbed to blank death, then faded to final oblivion.

Panic raked through, a blind, clawing terror of abandonment. Lirenda could be left here, forever entombed beyond reach of life and movement. She wrestled to breathe slowly as she had been trained. All of her pride and practiced control seemed trampled and torn into shreds. She had no dignity. In gasping, sweaty struggle, she fought herself steady. The need to leap up, to flee headlong without heed for safeguards became almost too overpowering to deny.

Then abrupt change overset even terror.

The eruption was cyclonic, an invisible whirlwind of force barbed in malice. The vicious, leading edge had a thousand voices, cursing, crying, tearing with words and far worse: the scything, bitter edges of passionate hatreds all stabbing to flay and draw blood. Even sealed beyond harm, Lirenda felt her mind become milled into fragments, her thoughts consumed by unadulterated violence.

No prior experience prepared her, although every other ancient focus she had handled harbored such coils of trapped rancor. By nature, all crystals absorbed the essence of spells raised to resonance through their mineral lattice. If the patterns were not cleared, the vibrations over time and usage thrummed into rank dissidence, a resentful moil of caged energies. A stone pressed to heel by the will of many mistresses was wont to reflect twisted spite, or worse, become warped into hideous subterfuge, to turn on new wielders and seek domination in turn. Greatest of all matrixes, the Waystone's stored patterns spewed forth in unparalleled viciousness.

Lirenda felt the blast as an obdurate, scorching tide of hatred that strove to unravel her being. Never had she witnessed such forceful malevolence. Her own strength was inadequate. Before such a flux, her deepest defenses would snap like so many dry twigs. She shrank inside the Prime's warded circle, cowed to a whimpering huddle.

She was not alone in her terror. The screams of Koriani predecessors who had failed to overmaster the Waystone's maze of trickery roiled through the crystal's depths also. Their despair charged the mind, shrank the flesh, and became a scourge defined unto itself; as if those vanquished, consumed spirits sought to lure fresh victims to succumb to the inner flaws that destroyed them. Their bodiless thoughts whirled in tireless search, seeking, prying, scrabbling to exploit any small chink of uncertainty. The peril of their assault was real, unforgiving. Lirenda's skin rose into prickles of fear. Despite the assurance of Morriel's wards, the danger sang through like the instant before a lightning strike, with her naked selfhood exposed but one breath shy of oblivion.

An inflexible truth, that if the Prime Matriarch failed to subdue the roused Waystone, her frail circle of protections must crumple. If those thin lines of power once faltered or faded, Lirenda would be cast to ruin in the turmoil of upset control.

As never before, the lesson thrust home: to succeed the Prime's power, a candidate must become nothing less than a faultless instrument. No prime applicant would ever achieve dominion of the amethyst without unbreakable strength and no fault left to admit weakness.

Then Morriel made her presence known. Her confidence unassailable, she configured the Waystone's seals of mastery, laid them down in silvered vectors of power, fast and precise as thrown knives. Runes arced into sigils, symmetrical, perfect, to shape raging passions to order. Through the convulsed moil of energies, Lirenda caught the half-glimpsed imprints of past conjuries, the ghost echo of old currents chained through the quartz axis: of storms and disease bent awry or tamed outright; of the very slipstream of time challenged and reversed. She heard, too, the dusky voices of past matriarchs, their words, their deeds, their arguments all melded like the sussurant scrape of dry leaves. Then one last stamp of mastery sheared the whispers away.

The Waystone's sullen stew of resistance tore asunder, then surrendered to limpid clarity.

Lirenda watched, awed, as the limitless vista opened before her at second hand. As often as she had experienced the rushing, exhilarant joy in her mastery of other focus jewels, the Waystone yielded an order of magnitude more. An indescribable passion plunged through her, sensation shaved to an exquisite knifepoint of ecstasy. The fired thrill of self-awareness seized her unaware, left her flushed and craving. She lost herself. Rapture beyond all imagining rolled like sweet thunder down her nerves. As if she stood poised at the pinnacle with all Ath's creation strung on its axle, turning; and her hand, *hers*, to grasp the rein and drive the wheel, to prod the harnessed vector of fate to the dictates of her chosen whim.

Revelation flooded her, a keen exhilaration spiced by addictive longing. *She would own this power herself one day.* At whatever cost, no matter the sacrifice, Lirenda knew she would pay any price to succeed the Koriani Prime. No risk, even death, would swerve her rightful claim to that heritage.

Impatient for that hour, the First Senior envied Morriel's grasp of that seamless course of power. She ached for her chance to let tuned awareness thread through the stone's lattice and frame the runes into sigils of command.

The pattern the Prime chose was a basic scrying. Somewhere upon the world's seas, a brigantine's keel carved westward. A small mote; a dimple pressed into the wavecrests by a hull hand fashioned of planks and sheathed in a bottom of copper. The metal would be subject to personal resonance, stamped bright in imprint of a man's desperation, and his all-consuming hope of escape from the geas that hounded his peace.

Arithon s'Ffalenn sailed west on the summer winds, and Morriel shaped her bidding to comb Athera's broad oceans to tag his current location. For sheer display, the move was impressive. Water was earth's most unbiddable element. Salt of itself balked cast conjury. The call through the Waystone arose in a tumultuous torrent, a whiplash of force before which the wide seas must bow to outright demand.

The search spell released, launched in stamped intent to claim dominance over its target. Yet the connection fell short, maligned by some unseen barrier. Another resonance intervened, then captured its order. Clear sigils were impacted and snarled awry, then diffused away into nothing. The sea appeared lidded by impervious shields, and the scrying failed, its pure force dispersed into aimless puffs of air.

Lirenda cried out, indignant. "So much for the Fellowship of Seven and their claim of unshakable morals! Look! They have broken the code of their own compact, even acted covertly for the sake of protecting a criminal. Did you plan to catch their hand in the act?"

But the Koriani Matriarch kept pensive silence. Beneath her hand, the violet sphere of the Waystone shed chill, its heart a thousand spindled planes of trapped starlight. The noosed perils of its focus stayed poised and still as the glint off an unsheathed axe blade. "The Sorcerers have shown a devious cleverness," she finally said, noncommittal. "That defense ward left no tracks, no afterimage of structural conjury." The resonant signature of Fellowship work in fact had been absent, as though Arithon's presence had been masked by an unseen force, or sea itself had joined in conspiracy to hide him.

That piquant anomaly would keep for later study. Morriel cataloged the nagging incongruity, then moved on, brisk, to the task of granting her First Senior a taste of prime powers expanded through the Great Waystone. She spun the jewel's focus, sent a new probe unreeling over the far lands to the north, where the ice-sheathed crags of Tornir Peaks tore through the spine of the cape, and seas ripped to white spume off the Gulf of Stormwell.

Lirenda shared the majestic swoop as the Prime's channeled powers changed purpose. Delight stunned her. She reveled in a sensation like flight; knew the thrill of rushed passage, as if spirit could soar over jagged summits where no road ran, and Northerly's trappers never ventured. The foothills were cloaked in a straight shag of fir. There, wolf packs hunted by the new silver moon, the fanned effervescence of hunger and slaughter trailing like smoke in their wake. The Waystone's precise focus could pick out the frost-point embroidery of the Fellowship wards which bounded the Sorcerer's Preserve. Through the lens of Morriel's vision, the knitted intricacy of their conjury looked like crocheted water, random patterns twined into an accord beyond grasp of matter and logic. The Sorcerers' works were like no other conjuries, their core of fey mystery fraught with perils and gloved in an unearthly beauty.

Lest those secretive riddles beckon the mind into circling madness, Lirenda marveled instead at the creatures the wards kept imprisoned. Here flew the last deadly packs of winged predators brought to breathing life by the dreams of the bygone dragons. Most murderous of the surviving drake spawn, black Khadrim clustered on ledges of volcanic rock. They warbled unending songs of bloodlust. More of them crouched, armored tails curled over their needle-sharp talons. Warmed by the mud pots, they dreamed, ever restless, drinking in memories of the whistling dissonance as high-altitude air thrummed over thundering, taut wing leather. Here and there, a long, narrow head arched up and breathed flame. Others joined in, until the stony, raked scarps became necklaced with brands like a festival.

Northward, Morriel bent the axis of the Waystone, over peaks mailed in ice, or snagged in batts of drifting cloud. Here, on the rim walls which bounded the Gulf of Stormwell, lay the mountains' living heart, no longer cold, but aflame and bleeding the earth's molten mineral through shattered seams and caldera. The peaks at the North Cape were unstable, a brutalized vista of riven rock. Here, earth and elements raged in endless war. Volcanoes like angry, fuming behemoths hurled hot rock and cinders. Magma spewed scarlet lacework into the boil of gray breakers, ever ripping their voracious, tide-driven channels between the shores of the Trow Islands.

"There," Morriel said, her voice the thin tone of dropped porcelain.

Lirenda sensed the small peak singled out, its flanks carved lambent by lava flows.

"We shall cap that vent in the earth's crust." Morriel spoke without arrogance, without even the prideful overtone a child might show a trapped butterfly.

She brought the focus stone's power to bear, a wheeling spin like forced vertigo. Then, in bursting white lines, she framed the grand seals into sigils. Overwhelmed by their magnificence, Lirenda could not discern whether the Prime traced the figures over the amethyst's surface, or whether she called them up, blazing, from the granite discipline of her mind. Some she recognized, for mastery of rock; dominance of earth; the interlaced patterns for repression and joining and guard. Others seemed disquietingly changed, indecipherable despite a haunting familiarity. The train of the construct shaped an unquiet strangeness that razed her to upsetting chills. Her rational thoughts were flicked on wild tangents to recoil into confusion.

The spell towered, bloomed, achieved finished perfection. Then, like the flight of an arrow from bowstring, the sharp, singing hum of release.

Perception overturned, kicked through an explosive cascade of change. Lirenda screamed with the upset as something spun wrong, and cognizance unraveled with the unbound, wild fury of a thunderclap. All order dissolved, then mastery and rule, leaving dark like the aftermath of carnage. Next, the slipped threads of power hurled into backlash. Chaos clapped down. For one yawning instant, natural law wrenched off course. Every sane tie to reason unhinged, as if torn from the span of creation.

The impact slammed through the mind, then froze there in stopped reverberation. Lawless disorder coiled into itself like craze marks pressed through crushed crystal.

Then the moment cracked free and passed. The earth turned serene. Summer stars burned untouched. Lirenda recovered herself, gasping and dazed, on the tower felted in the mild air of a bay shore night in Thirdmark. Etched in the eye of her mind, she still saw the volcanic basin at Northerly, and the fuming, scarlet lava jetting uncapped through the darkness.

Next she became aware of Morriel's speech, pronouncing maledictions in a quavering, vitriolic whisper.

"Matriarch, are you hurt?" she asked, stressed and shaken, in need of reassurance for herself.

She held on through a racked draw of breath, while the Prime expressed rage in a rising, thin shriek. "Damn them all to the dimmest pit of Sithaer! Fellowship meddlers! Curse their hands and their eyes and the tongues in their mouths. Let them suffer for this!

79

May they die, every one, unmanned and weeping, helpless and unloved and alone!"

Lirenda cowered at the tirade, afraid to move or speak, as the Matriarch spun, her features seamed bone in the starlight. "What's happened? Ath forbid I should have lived to see the day! The Fellowship held our Waystone in custody for five centuries, and oh, we were fools to have believed they never tampered."

"But Sethvir promised me our Waystone was untouched!" Lirenda cried. The order's own tests had assured the Warden's statement was no falsehood.

"Ah, untouched indeed." Morriel's malice changed to bitter admiration. "Sethvir did not lie. He did not disturb our stone. Clever fiend that he is, he never had to. He simply imprinted the Waystone's signature into every cranny of the world through the earth link he gained from the Paravians. And damn his wretched cleverness, he laid no ward on Arithon, nor broke any thread of moral principle. The same trick just upset my scrying."

"I don't understand," Lirenda said.

"You should, given more time and experience." Morriel qualified in that etched, acid tone she used to restore equilibrium. "The key lies in the foundations of Fellowship philosophy, First Senior. The Sorcerers' mastery keeps Paravian precepts. The Seven are bound, and must live by the Law of the Major Balance, itself a stricture of permissions. They believe earth and air, in fact, all solid matter, to be spun from animate spirit. Nothing they do, in craft or in deed, can proceed without an exchange of consent. So they have trammeled us. Our Waystone's signature pattern has been given to all that has form in this world; and by Sethvir's knotted conjury, all physical matter in existence has been empowered *to refuse its channeled force of intervention.*"

Before Lirenda's outrage, Morriel ran on, her rancor fired now by the ancient sting of balked rivalry. "Oh, we're not helpless. Our order can still tune a circle of seniors into focused unity through the stone. We can still curb disease, and even, turn armies. But only to bend influence upon conscious, living beings, and these have wills of their own. Over the earth, against even the lowliest storm, our Waystone has been robbed of power."

The wide-ranging impact undermined at a stroke the triumph of the Waystone's recovery. For the order's major spell crystals were themselves irreplaceable. Brought in when the Koriathain first settled Athera, the stones' offworld origins set them outside the scope of the Paravian-wrought earth link. Only those select conjuries channeled through their matrices could escape Sethvir's observation.

Now, the Waystone's Named signature had been disseminated abroad by the Sorcerer. The unique, patterned aura of its influence lay hampered in ties of recognition. Its forces had been disempowered through rejection by all things over which the Fellowship's compact held sway.

Lirenda regarded her Prime Matriarch, shadowed under her hood of pale silk like a hunting spider noosed in spun gossamer. "What will you do?"

"Whatever I must." Morriel stroked skeletal fingers over the polished, sullen facets of the Waystone. "The Fellowship of Seven have no given right to curtail our Koriani powers. I will go myself and present my demand at Althain Tower. The Sorcerers will heed, or be sorry. I *will* gain back our autonomy."

Three Seasons

In late summer, amid the long train of scholars who bring musty ship's rutters, and the flocked parchments of archived maps, and even, from Erdane, new proof that the Isles of Min Pierens exist in the margin of a faded merchant's lading list, a brawny craftsman bows before Lysaer s'Ilessid, and says in his broad southcoast accent, "Your Grace, I'm named Cattrick, and I've come to apply for the master's position in your new shipyard at Riverton. . . ."

At twilight on the autumn equinox, while the day fades to night and two seasons shift balance on the fulcrum of change, three Fellowship Sorcerers at Althain Tower seal the next layer in the construct which has commanded their unsparing efforts for a year; and clean power spears out in a ruled, white line to pierce the very nadir of the heavens. . . .

On the wide moors of Araethura, while winter's diamond dusting of frosts silver the stems of sere grasses, the child, Fionn Areth, survives his first year, while his mother weeps for the auguries yet to entangle his future, and his father stands taciturn and silent. . . .

III. Sentence

On the morning that Arithon's brigantine rounded up and backed sail off the wind-blasted sands of the far continent, the Fellowship Sorcerer who was Warden of Althain perched in a sun-baked window seat. He could have held that pose for hours, or even days, hunched like a ruffled gray pelican in the comfort of his moth-eaten maroon robe. The lined, ivory knuckles of one hand clutched a sheaf of curled parchment. The other wielded a black swan's quill, fussed sharp as a dandy's rapier point. The pot last used to dip his nib nestled between his braced knees, a tipped fraction shy of a spill. Stray stains and a threadbare shine to his velvets showed Sethvir's small care for vanity. Mere ink could be left to run where it would while his provenance spanned all the world.

Through the gift of the Paravian earth link, Sethvir sensed the distant, salt splash as the *Khetienn*'s anchor plunged to bite into the pearlescent sands of the shallows. Amid myriad sounds, just one patterned resonance of changed air: he heard shouted orders from a half a globe away, to brail tanbark sails to squared yards at the end of an arduous passage. Caught between lines of small, precise script, the Sorcerer furrowed his seamed brow. Then the poignancy of the moment overcame him.

He laid his temple against the old stonework and wept.

If the sea gave the Shadow Master a temporary shelter from the hatred raised among townsmen against him, his cherished hope of finding a haven on Athera's far continent was misled. Sethvir knew as much, aggrieved by the secrets necessity had forced him to keep. Kathtairr, the far land, was familiar to him as the creases grained in his own flesh. Distance offered no obstacle. The grand earth link bequeathed him, moment to moment, its endless, weary vistas of ocher and gray. Sun scorched and blasted by the elements, the continent fanned like a snag of singed cloth cast on the jewel-toned sea. Its rivers were dry, or ran poisoned and alkaline. Its shoreline extended, league upon league, as blank, rippled dunes and swept desert.

Sethvir ached for the tragic truth. To the last sand grain and rock, from the cracked, dusty summits of each nameless mountain to the seared, crumbled fissures of the valleys, the land mass beyond Athera's vast oceans was naught but a lifeless waste.

Even in the early centuries of the Third Age, at the height of their power and ascendancy, the Paravians had shunned the place.

Arithon would find no reprieve in Kathtairr from the bane laid on him by the Mistwraith. If he gained brief escape through the time he spent searching, for each year that passed, Lysaer s'Ilessid would breed more killing sentiment against him. The longer the *Khetienn*'s absence extended, the higher the stakes laid against the Shadow Master's life.

Between Sorcerers, the issue had already been thrashed to exhaustion. In desperate truth, their Fellowship dared not spurn the smallest borrowed margin of time. They would, *and had* wrested from Arithon's blind need that span of uneasy peace. Trapped themselves in a race to stave off disaster, they labored to avert an unmentionable peril, compounded since the hour of the Mistwraith's confinement.

Sethvir straightened, blue-green eyes grown airy as mist. His fingers draped loose across the unfinished last paragraph on his parchment. The quill slipped, forgotten, to drift on a whisper to the floor. Amid his sprawl of opened books, stained tea mugs, and his cluttered, stray oddments of feather and stone scavenged from excursions through the meadows, he looked for all the world like a beak-nosed little grandfather, abandoned to senile daydreams.

In contrary fact, the Sorcerer's trained focus ranged far beyond his tower library. Immersed in the broadscale vision of the earth link, the split train of his awareness encompassed all things, from the mighty pull of Athera's riptides, to the rustle of solitary grass stems. The busy tracks of ants reached his ear, and the singular signatures of sand grains banked in the gullies of the deserts. Sethvir could count at whim the cries of the owl and the albatross, riding the wind's thermal currents.

He sensed the grind of polar ice, north and south, and the thundering shear of each floe calved into the briny arctic seas. The planet itself played its living chord through his consciousness. He knew, like a heartbeat, the molten toss of core magma and the eerie, static pulse of its array of magnetic power lanes. Amid the vast, milling chord of flux and event, two precise notes snagged in dissonance. Sethvir narrowed his sight to frame these, his brows tugged into worry like muddled crochet.

A listening minute later, the Sorcerer moved on. Past the world's motley cloak of spun cloud, he traced the wheeling arc of the moon through deep vacuum, then left its grand dance to encompass the thin, singing tracks carved by stars.

The deeps of the void in between were not lifeless. A massive, near-complete ward construct spread for arc seconds in space. In fan curves, through ruled lines and joined angles that transected time, an intricate chain of seals spindled taut in lace point and sapphire, their phantom imprint a gemstone's planed facets cut intaglio on the dry dark. To the paired entities who labored to close the last gaps in the symmetry, Sethvir sent word, *'Arithon's made landfall on the far continent.'*

"Past time," Kharadmon's brisk comment flung back. Discorporate since mishap overcame him in the course of Second Age violence, the ghost Sorcerer added his usual caustic fillip. "He's Torbrand's true-born descendant, with the same nasty temper when his dignity's rankled, or his principles. When he sails back empty-handed, will you have a ready answer? He's bound to demand why our Fellowship never warned him that Kathtairr's seared lifeless by drakefire."

"Mind well, Kharadmon," a fruity, morose voice admonished. "If you fritter away words restating prehistory, there won't be a living land left for anyone's ship to return to." Luhaine's gloomy nature had scarcely improved since his body had perished in defense of a deposed high king. Once a corpulent scholar who preferred cautious order, in five hundred years, he had yet to savor his free-ranging existence as pure spirit. Nor had his tart rivalry eased into shared commiseration as a shade. "In case you've gone drifty, we've work to complete before the advent of solstice."

"Oh, dance on it," Kharadmon retorted. A ripple of energies shot through by stars, he set to in exuberant relish. "You scold like some humorless grandmother with nothing to do but knit mufflers and roust up windy criticism."

Luhaine chose to ignore him. "Do I surmise we're summoned back to Athera?" His prim query was presented to Sethvir alone, the inflection all plaintive acid. "The timing's a gross inconvenience, as you see." The earth link would show that one last charge of power drawn from the lane tides at winter solstice would see their long labor complete. This first stage protection was urgent, and indispensable, against perils too dire for delay.

'You're needed,' Sethvir insisted. 'The moment can't be helped. Lysaer s'Ilessid just condemned his first clan captives to chained slavery. Ath's adepts have sent their appeal to invoke our duty to the compact. We have no choice but to confront him. In addition, Morriel Prime and her servant are about to camp on my doorstep. I might as well have your company in support when she knocks to air her fresh grievance.'

Luhaine huffed his contempt. "Those witches should be coming to offer their help, and not wasting themselves in frivolous resource to cap volcanic vents whose existence but serves the earth's balance."

"Now see who's nattering," injected Kharadmon. "I'm not for watching you argue the stupidity of inviting Koriathain to mix their meddlesome sigils in our works! If Sethvir wants an interview with Prince Lysaer, I'll just be off to string the energy paths." A mercurial laugh and a swirl of sourceless current marked the Sorcerer's precipitous departure.

"Irresponsible jape," Luhaine grumbled. "Always flitting out." In sour eddies that flowed like rippled oil over a backdrop of stars, he capped a precise flourish to a dangling knit of spell seals. "As if no loose ends remained here that shouldn't be stabilized first." His unseen touch launched a spiraling array of circles and helixes to bridge a crucial expanse of deep vacuum. "Trust Kharadmon to duck like a truant, and meet ugly threats with light raillery. I can't *imagine* why we put up with him."

Luhaine listed each shortfall he saw in his colleague's character, then plowed on to include notable past instances when he had been abandoned to tidy disagreeable details. No answer came back. Only the impersonal, high chime of remote constellations. Already, Sethvir had moved on, his listening presence retuned to Athera, and thence, across the long leagues into Shand to make contact with another Sorcerer.

The discorporate presence of Kharadmon breezed into the royal chambers at Avenor a comfortable interval before noon. His entry raised no notice, passed off, perhaps, as an errant winter draft breathed through the swagged velvet curtains. The room was appointed in rich carpets and gold. Wax candles shone from glass sconces. Against the satin glow of varnished hardwoods, the young valet who served the Prince of the Light fussed to set Lysaer's last diamond stud.

"How right you were, your Grace." Head tipped, the servant stepped back to measure the dazzling effects of his handiwork. "Gold trim was excessive. You shall shine like a star in full sunlight."

Lysaer laughed. "Here, don't feed my vanity." He flicked the last pleats in his cuffs into place, his form all pale elegance, and his features cut marble beneath a molten ore cap of combed hair. "I don't need such show. For the gift of my bullion, the beggars will be suitably awed." Then he smiled at his valet, his unearthly, pure beauty transmuted to intimate warmth.

The boy blushed. He bobbed a clumsy bow, then stammered an apology as his elbows jostled the palace officials who waited, clothed in stiff-faced magnificence. Each one wore a new sunwheel tabard, cut of shining champagne gold–and-white silk.

The realm's chancellor and the Lord High Justiciar forgave the boy's gaffe in cool tolerance. They advanced to attend their prince in full ceremony, paired as if cued to a stage drill. The dense, beaded threadwork on their garments somehow looked soiled beside Lysaer's stainless presence. In his shadow, they swept toward the doorway. There, four silent guards dressed their weapons and joined them, two ahead, two behind. No man looked askance at the unseen arrival which breezed on the heels of the royal train.

A second, more tangible obstruction awaited to waylay the prince. The young boy who served as the royal bannerbearer could scarcely take position while a willowy form traced in sparkling jewels blocked off the arch to the vestibule. She had the prowling smooth stride and rich coloring of a lioness, and for today's prey, she stalked in chill rage.

"Princess, Lady Talith." Lysaer touched the foremost guardsman's shoulder as signal for him to keep station. Hunter's spear to her unsheathed claws, he eased past, on an instant the solicitous husband. He clasped his wife's hand, drew her into the light, and lost his breath a split second, as he always did.

First sight of Talith's beauty unfailingly stunned a man foolish. She had finespun, tawny hair, and features refined to the delicate texture of rubbed ivory. Her dress skimmed over her devastating curves, for this meeting, a calculated, flowing confection of damascened silk and jet buttons, cross-laced at wrist and bodice with silk ribbon.

"My dear, you look magnificent." The words framed an effortless courtesy, since his glance significantly avoided the cascade of yellow citrine which sparkled like poured honey into the tuck of her cleavage. Her smallest move and breath chased teasing reflections over her pearl-studded bodice, until the eye became trapped, then arrowed downward into a girdle fitted tight enough to hitch the air in the throats of Lysaer's waiting attendants. "I'm delighted of course, but won't your need keep? I promise I'll see you directly after I've finished my appearance in the plaza."

Lady Talith narrowed dense, sable lashes over eyes like razor-cut bronze. "The beggars can wait for their alms without suffering." Risen to the challenge, she smiled. Her flawless, fine skin flushed for the joy of a stabbing duel of wits. "Better still, let your chancellor dispense the day's coin in your stead. Dismiss your train. Now. I'll never settle for begging court appointments, or standing in line for an audience."

"I can't dismiss my train. My chancellor is no fit replacement." In grave, caring tenderness, Lysaer clasped her wrist to draw her clear of the doorway. "If privacy matters, we'll save our discussion for an hour when I'm not committed."

"Bedamned to privacy." Talith tested his hold, felt the steel in his fingers, and laughed in a sheared peal of scorn. "Why play at pretense?" She aimed her next barb with all the sugared venom her Etarran background could muster. "*My* pride wasn't stung by three months in Arithon's company." She smiled, digging him with threat and innuendo, even daring his temper, since he had not shared his shameful secret with his courtiers at Avenor. They were never told that the Master of Shadow was in true fact begotten when Lysaer's mother cuckolded her marriage in liaison with his father's most hated enemy.

Gratified by the vengeful jab of his fingers through her sleeve, Talith lifted one porcelain shoulder in a shrug. At her throat, the jewels flashed, enticed, trembled in liquid invitation. "Why not say aloud what every servant in your palace already whispers behind your back? That time enough has passed since my ransom. A year and a half gone, and all your court watching my belly like a pack of starved midwives. What pretense is left? My time in captivity was innocent of dalliance."

Unlike your faithless mother, her swift, weighted pause suggested. Locked eye to eye, his arctic blue to her molten amber, Talith said, "Since you can't claim avoidance for a nonexistent bastard, *what keeps you from sharing my bed?*"

Lysaer stroked a light finger beneath her chin, while a frown of consummate puzzlement came and went between his brows. "My love, you're distraught." By an act of brazen sympathy he behaved as if they stood alone, though the guardsmen behind exchanged discomfited glances. They knew well enough his nights were spent in the royal suite, since their ranks supplied the watch set over the prince's apartments.

"No doubt, you have cause for distress," Lysaer temporized. "I realize how desperately you desire to conceive. But chasing me about in a lather is unlikely to help your fertility."

Talith hissed out a breath at this vicious twist. "How dare you!" Her lashes swept down, a black veil for a murderous flare of hatred. "You'll never be able to bury your lapse with state excuses, or claim I am flawed or infirm. If I'm barren, my ladies-in-waiting all know, it's because your elaborate show of appearance masks the fact that you won't couple with me. Tell me, your Grace, what are you hiding? A mistress? Boy lovers? Revulsion on the chance I fell victim to *incest*?"

"Here, I'll be late. Your troubles must bide for a little bit." As she snapped breath to sink her barb of victory, Lysaer cupped her face, slipped a quick kiss on her lips, then handed her off to his ranking man-at-arms. His low, rapid orders cunningly disarmed her most brilliantly raking response. "See my lady to a healer for a posset to soothe her nerves. Say I'll return to check on her the earliest instant I am free."

She threw him a withering epithet.

In pained sorrow, the prince shut his eyes: as if by flat denial he could pretend for a heartbeat such beauty did not harbor so vile a contempt. Then he roused himself, straightened. Every regal inch of him contained into painful, mannered sympathy, he reassumed his place with his chancellor and Lord Justiciar. Despite Talith's glare like an auger at his back, he expanded the circle of his confidence.

"I'm sorry for the scene." His hushed voice carried backward as his party advanced through the echoing, high vaults of the hallway. "The loss of her brother at Dier Kenton Vale so soon after the months she was kept in duress by the Spinner of Darkness have left Talith strained and unsettled. We must all be patient. Give her care and understanding. I'm certain the moment we manage to conceive our first child, her usual staunch nature will prevail."

The chancellor murmured banal commiseration. Less suave, the guardsmen showed pity, while the red-faced valet who watched from the dressing chamber gave the princess the gawky, bold stare that admired for sheer, brainless loveliness.

Talith swept off with the appointed guardsman, chin raised in smoldering rebellion. Born a pedigree Etarran, she was too well seasoned to the ways of court infighting to augment Lysaer's strategy with protests. If he sought to discredit her as a woman undone by harsh circumstance, he had to know, the new-forged, burgeoning spite in her heart would admit no defeat while she breathed.

"On my life," she called after her royal husband in a tone like dulcet poison, "I'll birth you an heir to make the s'Ilessid name proud, *even as your lady mother did before me!*"

Appalled by the sharp, sudden pallor that blanched his prince's face, the Lord Justiciar of Avenor's state council tipped his gray head in assurance, "Give her time. She'll weather her disappointment over children. Women do." He pursed his lips, prepared to continue his fatherly advice.

But Lysaer raised a hand and touched him silent. "Not here."

The royal train reached the outer postern. Composed and brittle as an artwork in glass, the Prince of the Light mastered the short ceremony while a heavy box of coins changed hands from Avenor's Minister of the Treasury into the care of his chancellor. He stepped with his retinue through the outer doorway into the blast of winter wind. The cold nipped his cheeks back to color. Against the luminous, aquamarine sky, his hair gleamed like the tinseled weave shot through a ripple of Atchaz silk. His poise, now restored, was steel masked in felt as he dealt his justiciar a swift and shaming rebuke. "A year and a half is criminally soon to say whether my lady's unfit to bear an heir. Discretion is called for. Her Grace's distress will fare all the worse if unkind rumors start to circulate."

Beside the bronze finials of the palace gate spread the circular plaza which centered the city of Avenor. This site retained its design since the Paravian ruin underwent Lysaer's restoration. His master masons had found the proportions and placement too pleasing to disrupt. The facades of the formal state buildings had arisen on the rims of Second Age foundations. The ancient worn slates, with their cracked channels of queer inlay, were now paved over in amber-and-white block incised with a sunwheel pattern. The vista with its innate grandeur presented the ideal setting for Lysaer's noon practice of dispensing largesse to the poor.

Since the crushing defeat in Vastmark, the coins struck for this purpose were embossed with the new order's blazon upon one side, and stamped on the other with a sigil of ward against darkness. Dubbed shadow-banes by their recipients, merchants in Tysan took them in trade, then resold them as amulets for more than their value in gold.

No edict was signed to curtail the practice. "Why sap the foundations of the common people's hope?" Prince Lysaer gave instruction to his council. "For as long as the Shadow Master lives at large, their terror is real and justified. Let folk grasp whatever comfort they may. Suffering and losses could harm them soon enough. Folk will fare better for not feeling helpless in their worry."

Speculation became rooted into belief. The name of Arithon Teir's'Ffalenn was anathema, and feared, and the coins, dispensed with the blessing of Lysaer s'Ilessid himself. They could not be other than talismans infused by his blessed gift of light.

Prince Lysaer never walked in the public eye without due presence and ceremony. His daily custom of charity became a dazzling display of royal pageantry, while the poor and the downtrodden elbowed forward to claim the trinkets which held the reputed power to protect them.

This day, the plaza was packed to capacity, despite the bracing wind that snapped the fringed banners on their poles. The out-of-town merchants and the bored rich who thronged to observe from the balconies clutched their caped cloaks and furred hoods. Below, in jostling chaos, the waving, cheering supplicants pressed to catch sight of their savior. More than the city poor and village crofters shouted and surged against the guardsmen's cordon. Petitioners now traveled from far-distant cities to receive Avenor's royal alms. A second row of pikemen ringed the central dais to keep order, their polished buckles and appointments backed by white silk bunting tied up with gilt cord and tassels.

Lysaer stepped through the gateway just before the advent of noon. The wind's icy buffet ruffled his ingot gold hair. His white-clad person seemed etched into air, set off from the commonplace sea of dark woolens like a mote struck into incandescent purity by the silver-ice fall of winter sunlight. The welcoming roar which greeted Prince Lysaer rocked echoes off the high, amber brick of the watch-towers. Engulfed in a mounting crescendo of noise, he ascended the dais stair, his honor guard and high council ministers a parade pace behind him.

The thronging stew of voices grew hushed as Lysaer s'Ilessid took his place. He accepted the bullion coffer from his chancellor, then addressed the adoring crowd. "Hail the Alliance of Light! Through the dedication of all people, moral strength shall prevail against darkness!" He tipped up his face. As though his appeal was presented to heaven, he summoned the powers of his gift. A dazzling shaft speared down from the zenith to lend grand display to his benefi-cence.

Yet this time, the flaring, fired brilliance which answered was not completely his own.

The two officers nearest sensed something amiss: as if the light were too fine, too potent, charged through by an effervescence of force outside the range of mortal senses. They called in consternation, saw their prince jerk up short. His calm shattered before irritation and astonishment as his frosty, white finery spun awry in a flux of uncanny, cold air.

Unseen, unheard, the Sorcerer Kharadmon linked his subversive conjury to the tide of the solstice noon. An actinic blast of heatless illumination exploded over the dais. The ranking royal bodyguards were rocked back and dazzled. They strove to reorient, unsure if they should draw weapons, or what form of enemy might manifest. Through an inrush of winds like a rip in clear air, they heard the crash of the coin chest, fallen from the prince's grasp. Then the cascading treble as the shadow-banes burst free, clanging and scattering across the dais. Plucked off the boards like a captured chess piece, Lysaer s'Ilessid no longer stood among them. The circle of light just made manifest shimmered empty, while his chancellor and bodyguard gaped in terrified astonishment.

For Lysaer, seized fast by a presence that disallowed protest, the upset plucked him bodily and hurled him through the howling eye of chaos. He felt torn in half, upended, spun. Nausea threatened to rip up his guts. He battled to cope in riled anger. Led once before through a spell transfer across longitude, he recognized the forces of outside conjury just before the disembodied voice of Kharadmon informed him, "You are bound at this moment for Althain Tower in answer to summons by the Fellowship."

Then transition ended. The wheeling cascade of disorientation snapped away. Lysaer felt his person restored to firm stone, but not in the plaza at Avenor. The smells in this place were ozone and dust, coiled through an elusive, dark tang of oiled metal. He shielded his eyes, made out a black onyx floor underfoot. The fierce play of light streamed from inlaid strings of ciphers, arrayed in disquieting patterns, concentric circles and interlocked rune lines yet limned silver-white in the fast-fading shimmer of spent energies. He recognized he stood at the apex of the power focus laid out in the keep's lower dungeon. Its seamless walls were pale marble. Gargoyle sconces crouched leering at the major points of the compass. Lysaer's flesh crawled with chills, gift of Luhaine's nearby presence; then that cold intensified as Kharadmon flanked him as invisible escort to prod his stiff step toward the stairwell.

"You won't get away with abducting me," Lysaer ground out in low fury. "Nor can raw power absolve Arithon's bloody crimes, nor the secret of your dirty liaison."

"You're no one's prisoner," Luhaine said, unperturbed. "As for keeping propriety, this meeting you attend shall be bent outside time. Your absence at Avenor will last no more than the wings of an instant." He led up the stair shaft, his spirit reclothed as a courtesy in the image of a corpulent bald man from whose dimpled chin hung a cataract of silver beard. His stooped shoulders were robed in the dusty slate cloth favored by scholars and clerics, and his sandals fussed to a waxed shine.

Behind, manifest as a slim, dapper form cloaked in extravagant green velvet with slashed sleeves and linings of flame orange, Kharadmon showed his foxy smile. "Nor need you waste effort maligning your half brother." He wore a black mustache twisted to raised tips like crossed scimitars. His beard was a spade-point goatee. The rest of his hair fell loose and long to his collarbones, argent combed through jet at the temples. He surveyed Lysaer's pique with eyes a sardonic, pale green. "The only man's fate held at issue today will be yours, scion of s'Ilessid."

Every inch the born prince, Lysaer stayed unruffled by the Sorcerers' cavalier handling. His tread on the worn, concave stair was assured, his bearing never less than a masterpiece of cool statecraft. He filed after Luhaine through the trapdoor to ground level, into the fragrant tang of cedar and the polished, frozen ranks of Paravian statuary. Though past high kings before him had cried aloud for sheer wonder at the antlered, stone majesty of the centaurs that raised hooves and towered above human height, Lysaer would not turn his head. Royally assured, he displayed no catch of breath. Nor did he marvel at the unearthly, stopped splendor of the unicorns, posed in dancing steps, with their spiraled horns struck soft pearl in the muted gleam through the arrow slits.

That veneer of indifference soon became forced. The willful, steel nerve he sustained throughout taxing state councils in this place chafed thin, made brittle as a mask of varnished paper. Lysaer fought the poignant, swift tug at the mind that moved prior visitors to weep. He refused for staunch pride to unbend. The Spinner of Darkness was the Fellowship's minion; moral duty compelled him to stand strong. No matter the price, he dared not let the unworldly grace of a dead past beguile him into weakness. He walked as a man sealed deaf to temptation, while to the right and the left, the joyful, inspired artistry of the smallest ones, the sunchildren, ripped his heartstrings and begged him for laughter.

Ahead rose a staircase of stark, chiseled granite, blackened with centuries of torch soot. Althain Tower had been raised in beleaguered haste to safeguard the records of the Paravian culture. Its library held the chronicles of the First Age, when the ravaging hordes of creatures raised to life by the drakes' dreams had led the world to near ruin. Sealed vaults and storerooms contained old weapons from those times, rare artifacts of Paravian craftwork. Young by comparison, the heirlooms recovered from the plunder of the high king's halls shared shelf space.

The grim stairwell between levels still reflected the primary function as a fortress. Stark, unfinished stone made a wrenching, grim contrast to the grandeur of the commemorative statues. Here, even the most unflinching pride could not evade the imprint of despair. The moan of the drafts and the squeal of a loose shutter bespoke desolation, undying reminder of tragedy and losses endured since the departure of the old races. Lysaer set his chin. He refused to give way to emotion or embarrassment, and that hardened determination to stand down Athera's past was not missed by the Sorcerers who escorted him.

They ushered him across the first landing, past the chamber where the Koriani Waystone had been held secure since the first chaotic hour of the rebellion; they ascended to the next, where Althain's Warden kept his living quarters. On the third level, Sethvir himself awaited, the dusty, threadbare garments he preferred put aside for state formality: a robe of maroon velvet interlaced at sleeves and collar in black cord, and belted with a girdle stitched with river pearls. His beard had been tidied. Silk cord looped his hair at his nape, and his glance of greeting came sharp as a catchlight on fired enamel. "Welcome to Althain Tower, Lysaer s'Ilessid."

The prince's crisp nod offered civilized replacement for the bald-faced accusation, that in his hall at Avenor, hospitality did not include being snatched off by force.

Sethvir met that unspoken fuming with a note of disquieting, pure pity. "Beware how you think in this place."

"I fear no one's censure," Lysaer said, and despite his best care, the pique showed.

"Perhaps not today, but the future's not written." Sethvir unfolded hands like gnarled twine and flung wide a door of iron-strapped oak.

Inside, the tower's rough stone had been paneled over in linen fold patterns of golden maple. A carpet of Cildorn weave graced the floor of a comfortable, warm chamber. The furnishings included a table of waxed ebony, standing lions back-to-back as its pedestal, and chairs

94

upholstered in dark leather with exquisite, chased ivory finials. Beeswax candles burned, both in tall stands and sconces. Rowed beneath the paned, lancet windows, and lent the rich depth of choice dyes, the banners of Athera's five kingdoms hung from bronze tapestry rods. The ambiance held a grandiloquent, trapped weight of history before which Lysaer paused, amazed.

"Behold, the chamber of the high kings. Here, your ancestor, Halduin s'Ilessid, knelt and swore oath to the Fellowship. That blood vow he gave became binding on his progeny, *for the length of his line, and all time*. No light matter." Sethvir's gesture encompassed the cleared space before the table, no invitation, but strict command. "Through the duration of this audience, you will stand."

Lysaer bridled, mocked at once by Kharadmon's mercuric chuckle. "You forget yourself, bantling. Your forefathers were crowned kings on Fellowship authority. Any claim you have to royalty originated here, ruling power granted in accord with Tysan's founding charter."

An added voice gruff in the grain as old bedrock lent that statement full weight. "This is not the world of your birth, to acknowledge right of arms or direct ancestry." Unnoticed until he straightened, another Sorcerer moved from his quiet, leaning stance against the ebon pilaster that flanked the fireplace. "You walk on Athera, in the hall at Althain Tower, where blood inheritance is fully revocable!"

Tall, worn to leathery leanness by centuries of life in harsh weather, Asandir was not clad for travel. The flames' ruddy glow touched and drowned in the velvet of robes the deep indigo of midnight. Sleeves, hem, and collar were sewn in silver braid, matching the glint of his hair. Named Kingmaker in legend for the royalty he had crowned, he looked the part: clean-shaven, with sable brows angled in lines like slashed pen strokes, his cheekbones and nose as rugged as if notched by an axe out of hardwood.

"What brings your complaint?" Lysaer assumed his place in prideful, combative challenge. "I refused Tysan's crown. The sovereignty I shoulder is none of your making, but springs from city law and a writ drawn by Karfael's mayor."

"Is that how you claim your right to set chains on free men, then subject them to branding and lifeterm of forced labor on the galleys?" From the doorway behind, Sethvir sighed. "I think not." He added, "We're all here." Although he moved not a finger, the iron-strapped panel slammed closed.

Lysaer gave a start, but refused to acknowledge the arrivals who filed behind him. He took their measure instead as they assumed their seats at the table. The lead figure was hooded in a full-length

95

white mantle. The face stayed shadowed and genderless despite the sharp brilliance of candles. Lysaer recognized the collar yoke and linked runes in silver and gold which denoted a life initiate of Ath's Brotherhood. He sucked a grim breath. His prior suspicion stood confirmed: the adepts were in sympathy with Arithon s'Ffalenn, and this delegate's presence, an unpleasant, sure proof that their kind had joined ranks with the Fellowship against him.

As dark followed day, a fifth Sorcerer limped after, his caped cloak, short tunic, and leggings woven of somber black wool. A raven rode his shoulder, wings spread over a steel gray thatch of hair. The bird surveyed the prince and the assemblage of Sorcerers, but its mind and its thoughts were not avian. All of its master's shrewd intelligence lay reflected in eyes the hue of ripe chestnuts.

"Traithe," Asandir greeted. A swordsman's swift step carried him from the mantel to draw out a chair. His care for his colleague's infirmity held deferent respect for good reason. Traithe of the Fellowship had been crippled since the terrible day he had raised the wild forces to seal the passage at South Gate against the Mistwraith's incursion. His sacrifice then had cut off the invasion. Though fogbound, the world had survived. If his quizzical smile and listening ear had once eased Lysaer to amity, today, all the laugh lines were stilled. Traithe's visage looked tired, his mouth a taut fold, grim with years and old pain.

Sethvir chose the seat beneath the banner of Tysan, flanked right and left by the mismatched shades of Kharadmon and Luhaine. Between the one, rapacious as a gambler in a card parlor, and the other, staid and somber as a judge, Althain's Warden might seem like a maundering old man, prone to openmouthed dozing. Except the eyes he raised to the prince were no dreamer's, but a surgeon's kept steel, to flay skin from bone on a glance.

Lysaer resisted the coward's urge to plead. Fellowship Sorcerers were not subject to persuasion. Unlike his packs of recalcitrant mayors, they could not be swayed by sincerity. Trappings of ornament or clothing would not impress them. At will, they could strip him down to his naked spirit. To face down all five without trembling in dread required an act of main strength. Lit by the merciless flood of the candles, Lysaer felt sealed outside of time. The tower's very presence distilled his perception into shapes too precise for forgetfulness. Grand causes and ideals were excised and diminished. The strivings of honor and the layered masks of selfhood became turned about, reduced to flat copies in reflection, a purposeless circling like movements of fish behind glass.

Lysaer clasped his hands, steeped to acid resolve. He was the hawk in the falconer's net, and the Fellowship, deadly and powerful conspirators acting in concert with a criminal. The right was not theirs to decry his moral destiny, or to accost him with binding judgment. They could hurl their dire threats, and he could refuse. He had no stake to bargain beyond dignity and life; his sole weapon became his own staunch fiber of principle. Let the Sorcerers break him with brute force and conjury if they could. For the sake of all threatened and innocent people, he would do no less than extend his best effort to stand strong.

Traithe opened in shaded, soft sorrow. "You are aware, our Fellowship acts in accord with the Law of the Major Balance. We bring harm to none, nor does our practice force any man against his given will. The talk in the cities of coercive spells and rituals raised out of bloodshed is no more and no less than the ignorant bluster of fear."

"If choice is still mine, then send me back, now." Lysaer inclined his head, every inch the magnanimous prince. "Or prove yourselves hypocrites, since the conjury which plucked me up out of Tysan was an act done without my consent."

"You will listen." Asandir sat forward, his eyes the washed, pale opal of the tiercel's, and his expression forbidding as granite. "Games of rhetoric will not serve, nor will we bandy obstructive, petty argument. Do you realize, in truth, the place mankind holds in the order of this world? Or do you even care, in your self-righteous cry of public sacrifice?"

Kharadmon flicked one finger. Like the barbed parody of a stage magician's trick, a shadow-bane flashed and arced airborne. Asandir fielded the spinning coin in one fearfully capable hand. At first touch, as if the gold scalded, his mouth flinched into a line.

"Abomination," murmured the adept of Ath's Brotherhood. The soft, fluting voice was female, and young, and the shadowy hood turned a fraction. Unseen eyes bored into the prince and measured his regal stillness. "Ah, no," she said. "A mere hedge witch's sigil to ward against darkness could not turn the might of the Fellowship. But stronger powers lie dormant behind symbols. Beliefs cling to metals. For those reasons, the cumulative resonance of your gold rings unclean."

Asandir held the coin cupped between his palms. Through a span of stilled silence, its cast glow of reflection seemed to light his seamed face from within. He spoke a liquid, clear word. The language he chose was the ancient Paravian, and the inflection shaped sound like struck crystal. Time stopped, suspended. The mystery in that moment

97

held the potential to snap thought, or the latent might to rend mountains. But Asandir's summoning framed only kindness. Lysaer knew an instant of scouring, sore grief, that he was but fashioned of mortal clay. He felt as a child shut in the cold dark, and the wrench all but felled him, that the Name gently spoken was not his.

The shadow-bane melted to that power of compassion. Both sigil and sunwheel flowed molten and smoothed. Asandir was not burned. The disk he laid down and slid back across the table was transformed to a pristine blank. The Sorcerer spread his hands flat and looked up while the prince was still nakedly shaken.

"Tricks and spells," Lysaer gasped. "Would any man argue? At your bidding a stone might be made to wail and weep."

"Even so, the stone weeps for choice, by our code." Asandir's speech stayed dispassionate, uncolored by the fabric of sheer caring he had just summoned to redeem the shadow-bane. "What code shapes your life? The deceptive diffraction of Ath's order you encourage shall afflict miseries to span generations. You style us criminals who break lives and spill blood. Do you not do the same for a feud?"

Lysaer snatched at argument to collect himself. "Why not tell me? Did Arithon s'Ffalenn weigh the full measure of consequence when he tore buildings in Jaelot stone from stone, or placed arms in the hands of Vastmark shepherds?" Flagged confidence returned, became ringing conviction. "What of the five hundred he murdered at the Havens? Or the mountains torn down upon Dier Kenton Vale to crush tens of thousands more beneath the Wheel?"

"Those spirits lived and died in free choice within Ath Creator's ordained order," the adept said in metallic soft sorrow. "Their beliefs and expectations held no more than error. They fought for lies, but not faith. The course you now tread would deny the prime source from whence springs all joy and all life."

Lysaer fielded that sentiment with contempt. "Are they any less dead for their choice or their truth? Arithon, also, can beguile to turn innocents. If I don't oppose him, who will?"

"Beware, false prince," Sethvir interjected, neither wistful nor diffused, but earnest in a concern that terrified for its mildness. "The fears you smooth over in the trappings of moral platitudes will counterbalance nothing. Neither can they build. You will find the just fervor you raise can save no one. In the end, your own followers will dictate your actions. Their will shall rule yours with a needy finality that you will be powerless to gainsay. We can offer no help for you then."

"I was beyond help the moment I fell under Desh-thiere's curse," said Lysaer, succinct. His diamond studs flashed like ripped bits of light as he snatched his small opening for riposte. "That was supposed to be your problem. By what right do you criticize my methods before you have broached your own failure?"

A pause seized the chamber. Sethvir and Asandir stayed wrapped in glass silence; the spirits of Kharadmon and Luhaine looked pressed into the air like stamped felt. The adept made a sound, in sorrow or dismay, and clasped bronzed hands to her lips, while the candles burned on in smokeless, unreal indifference.

A baleful, black cutout given life in a scene without motion, the raven splayed its left wing feathers. Its head swiveled sidewards. One bead eye stayed fixed, a spark of buffed bronze, as it balanced to its master's shift forward.

"There is no pretense here, Lysaer." Traithe's rebuke was rust swathed in velvet. "Desh-thiere's ill works pose the true danger, a peril shared by us all. Subject to a curse to kill Arithon you may be, but that does not rule out choice and action. Mind and will can be yours to command outside of your half brother's presence. Blind hatred can be fought." The raven preened on his shoulder, undisturbed, as he entreated, "You are gifted to seek justice. Don't make that a weapon for righteousness. The misery you seed in your quest to kill Arithon might live on long past your death. Claim your cause as divine, and you found a tradition that will not be lightly shaken."

"You are swift to condemn my role as deceit." Lysaer's fine hair shone a pale, fallow gold beneath the flood of the sconces. When he raised his proud head, all the strain showed, his beautiful face stiff in his forced effort not to weep. "As one human ruler, I may be in error. But in all fair conscience, can I stand aside and let Arithon of Rathain turn his sorceries on an unsuspecting society? What binds *him* to constraint? You who claim wisdom know better than any. A mortal who commands unchecked power becomes ripe for corruption. Jaelot and Alestron have already suffered. Why beg for a large-scale disaster?"

The prince turned his head. Despite a transparent desire for privacy, he pursued his point, dogged, to its finish. "If I sacrifice one value for another, if I choose to create a balance of power, who are you to cry me down? The debt incurred becomes my personal score on the slate of Daelion Fatemaster. I am the Shadow Master's opposite. My place is to check him. Ath have mercy on us both, for the fate brought upon us by the bride-gift of a sorcerer whose ancestor was trained by your Fellowship!"

Lysaer faced forward in blazing, brash courage and hurled his own charge in defense. "If your hand is revealed at the root of our conflict, tell me *why have you not acted?*"

Asandir arose, dark brows drawn down over eyes turned a forbidding, storm gray. "How dare you mistake us for the street beggars of Avenor, to try and wring sympathy by crying lame causes, then playing the puppet martyred for the grand destiny." He leaned on the table, the veins on his hands like vines gnarled into aged oak. "Or do you hope you might finally convince yourself?" His glare flickered over the prince like crossed lightning. "*We have not acted because Deshthiere's curse is inseparably tangled with your life aura.* As Traithe said, our Fellowship does not kill."

"You claim you would let two lives tear civilized society asunder?" Lysaer laughed, his widened eyes locked on the Sorcerers. "Then indeed, I have no hope." Honest rage tore through his gritty resentment, for a second upsetting the ironclad duty dunned into him with royal birthright. "Ath, did you think I *desired* my exile to this world? Or that I asked to become your sacrificial weapon against the Mistwraith?"

"The Fellowship has *never* been a force in Athera to take guiding charge of human destiny!" A creature of movement and action, Asandir thrust up from the table. He stalked to the fire, braced an arm on the mantel, while the flames at his feet snapped and flickered. Their light played a moving mapwork of lines over his hard, shuttered features.

Luhaine retrieved the lapsed dialogue. "Our purpose is rather to stand guard for the land, and to this end, you're being asked some harsh questions. Face yourself!" The entreaty was raised, a knife blade that offered no quarter. "You embark on a dangerous precedent, even beg the ruin of your race! How dare you mask over the miracle that is the prime source! For arrogance, you put yourself on that pedestal in attempt to whitewash a curse-bound directive to end your half brother's life. True justice plays no part. You veil truth for vendetta, for vengeance and base envy, because Arithon will not be seduced by the evil you seek to attach to his name."

Lysaer swayed. His glittering shoulders wavered, almost bent.

The adept swept to her feet, relentless. "Unstop your ears and listen, scion of s'Ilessid. Persist on your present path, and you shall gain your desires." As Lysaer's blue eyes widened, she pressed him, "Oh yes. Your half brother shall walk in the shadow you create. But not before you stand blackened enough to raise despair of a force sufficient to break him. Every mortal enclave on this continent shall fall as victim to your cause. Your memory shall be sealed in the archives by violence, for nothing in creation can stand or flourish in the absence of love. Let us see, in the hour that Arithon's blood stains your hands, whether conviction for your fellowman or overweening pride is your master."

That bleak forecast raised consternation among the Sorcerers. Unmindful of their stir, Lysaer sank to his knees. Tears wet his cheeks. The light snagged and shivered in his diamond studs as he bent his bright head in defeat. "Have mercy," he pleaded. "I admit to my wrong. Lend me your guidance to heal."

Asandir returned to the table and sat, his harsh gaze fixed on his hands. Silence fell, filled by the tormented sobs of the prince, who *perhaps* had been brought to realize the enormity of his acts. No Sorcerer leaped to mete out the last test of surety.

Kharadmon shouldered that burden at the end, his razored, brief style expressing the inflexible Law and just consequence of the Major Balance. "Abjure your call to arms. Publicly renounce your false tie to divine calling. Then you shall have at your side all the help our Fellowship can command."

Lysaer pressed his forehead against the patterned carpet. Hair like combed sunlight fronded the hands he held clenched at his crown. He would not look up. Shamed to abasement, he asked of the Sorcerers, "What do I say to ease the grief of the widows and the mothers whose loved ones were slaughtered in Vastmark?"

"Tell them the truth," Sethvir answered, implacable. "Your mistake should not be permitted to compound, nor be passed to their sons, to die for wrong cause and false sacrifice."

At that, Lysaer regained the will to stand straight. Through shock-darkened eyes, he perused the stilled faces of five Sorcerers, then the shadowy countenance masked by the hood of Ath's adept. In tear-stained magnificence, he looked like one of Ath's avatars, fallen, a sword forged in blood to stand firm against wrongful action. "Ath preserve, you ask me to break my personal, given trust. As I am cursed, so too is my half brother. I can't leave my people defenseless before him. Bind Arithon first. Then take my capitulation on any terms that you ask."

"Ath show you mercy," Sethvir replied. "I am sorry. We now must do more than warn."

A thin, feral smile seized Lysaer's lips. "I thought so!" He loosed a jarring peal of laughter. "Here is the truth. Power begets force, did I not say so? What will you do now, if not call me down by straight violence?"

"You mistake us," snapped Traithe, no longer the listening confidant, but grim as the raven just flown from a field of raw carnage. "Your life in our hands is sacrosanct, and your will, no one's other than your own. But mankind's place in Athera has never been a born right." This was straight fact. The ancestor of every human alive had first come as a refugee begging for sanctuary. "Settlement here was permitted under strict terms by the compact sworn between our Fellowship and the Paravians."

"Did you think kingdom law was written at our whim?" Kharadmon sat forward, his trickster's flamboyance razed away. "The original charters were drawn by our hand, but to the old races' auspices. Their strictures are not mere rules to be overturned for some upstart mayor's convenience."

Not to be outdone, Luhaine plunged on to lecture, "For the acts you have initiated, for setting your seal to chained slavery, and for seeking to supplant Ath's order and the Law of the Major Balance, you have defied the tenets mankind was charged never to violate."

"Now you know." Sethvir tucked folded hands beneath the spilled fleece of his beard. Diminished by sorrow, he appeared to read his next lines from the whorled grain of waxed maple. "Our Fellowship keeps a trust with the Paravians. Each human child birthed here lives and dies on the sufferance of our intercession. We stand surety for mankind, all their works, all their laws. Yes, even for their greed and their strivings that could mar every facet of this world. Understand this. We guard and nurture as we can, but our service is not to our race."

Althain's Warden paused. As if the air to drive spoken words bound him mute, he looked aside, the set to his shoulders gone bird-boned and frail. He seemed an old man without mystery, outworn by relentless attention to detail and a shackling burden of care. "There exists no compromise, no quarter. Any man to defy the compact, who breaks the first order set down by the Paravians, must be cast outside our protection. You will leave Althain Tower. None here would misuse grand conjury to upset the fate you pursue. Nor shall we mourn, or answer your cries when the justice of the old races falls upon you and the followers you seduce into blindness."

"You will not break me by intimidation," Lysaer said. "I stand as the shield for my people."

Sethvir bowed his head.

No second chance followed, no gap for reprieve. The image forms of Kharadmon and Luhaine whisked out like gale-blown candles.

Lysaer felt their presence encircle his form in cold air, while the adept slipped her hood and bared features of frost-brittle clarity. "The ways of the Paravians are not those of men. They are not born of earth, but sprung from the prime source itself." Her upraised finger accused him. "Woe to you, prince. The wrath of Athera's true guardians is no light fate to invoke."

An actinic burst sheared the chamber as a rune seal flamed above Lysaer's head. The cipher blazed yellow-white, then faded to violet. Sensation followed, a sourceless wind of fine energies that hazed through all the five senses. Lysaer experienced no physical discomfort. But the vibration rocked on through his mind. Something inside of him howled wild protest for the irrevocable step being taken. His awareness became pierced by untenable loss. No grief ever savaged the heart to such depths, as if for an instant he had gazed upon paradise, then plunged for all time into darkness. He wept. Ugly, racking sobs closed his throat as something unnamed and brilliant slipped away and consigned him to friendless desolation.

The hurt sieved and tore him, needles through silk, until he felt nothing but numbness.

Then Asandir was beside him. Firm hands took his arm, drew his faltering step away from the King's Chamber and into the black chill of the stairwell. Lysaer reeled as though drunk. Plain air turned his head. The stairs felt absurdly hard beneath his feet, and the shadows pooled under the sconces held menace like teeth, lurking unseen to gnaw flesh.

Lysaer called on his gift to blast out the darkness, but no spark answered. His limbs seemed battened in felt. Again he stumbled. A Sorcerer steadied him. The touch was raw power and limitless strength clothed over in gentleness that plunged a dull ache to the bone.

"You are deceivers," the prince insisted. "Betrayers of your own principle to shield Arithon." His voice seemed a stranger's, and his commitment to honor no more than the soulless whine of spent wind.

Asandir pressed ahead, bundling his charge between the stilled ranks of statuary. Their mystery had gone strangely dull; now, the centaurs, unicorns, and sunchildren seemed nothing more than exquisitely beautiful carvings. Lysaer felt remorse, and then wondered in leveled, pure logic why he should pause for regret. The tricks of the Fellowship were evasively subtle. The guiding hand on his flesh was creased by the bridle rein, *ordinary*, no more than a common old man's. Still the contact was comfort and animal warmth; then even that simple solace was gone as Asandir released him by the trapdoor to the vault.

"Go down." Winter drafts bit deep where the Sorcerer pointed.

Lysaer locked his jaw, sliced again by a glass-edged sorrow. He spoke fast and bitter to fill the void. "The mayors who fear you, did your Fellowship disown them the same way?" Steadier now, he seized the giddy nerve to laugh. "I've read the musty old records of the uprising kept at Erdane. They speak of retribution and vengeance to be claimed for the blood of the murdered high kings. *Yet five hundred years have passed.* Nothing happened." The freezing, dry air braced him back to banked rage.

"The Paravians are gone," Lysaer insisted. "They might never return. Yet you still threaten and raise dread in their name. I say humanity deserves better than empty rules and the coercive threat of your sorceries. I shall spread truth, that your compact has no foothold in present-day governance."

Asandir still said nothing. At the base of the stairwell he stopped, unnervingly inscrutable. His hands hung still at his sides, empty and large knuckled as a quarryman's. Lysaer looked away, unbeguiled by that traitorous semblance of humanity. Before him spread the concave Paravian focus, its patterns strung across in mazed chains of ciphers, white quartz embedded in onyx. Then, touched to life by some spark of bound magecraft, the demon sconces blazed into flame. The Sorcerer's taut face became etched in copper; then that warmth erased to unyielding, struck iron as captured lane force flared the pattern lines active.

"Step forward," said Asandir. "Your people are waiting at Avenor."

Lysaer turned his back. He walked in unvanquished pride to the center point of the focus. "I will see mankind released from your tyranny. Justice will follow war. The land will be given a peace free of shadows, with no help from absent Paravians."

No word came back. Only Asandir's signal to Kharadmon and Luhaine, who poised, unseen, to engage gathered power for the transfer. Then chaos clapped down, and time came unhinged. All links to the senses dissolved through a fireburst of light. Spinning vertigo remained, slashed once by the twined cipher of a sorcerer's mark that spanned the whole axis of creation. Through the deluge of static and the keening explosion of channeled energy, Lysaer came aware of a far-off sibilance of speech . . .

". . . say something fast to avert panic," his captain at arms called out in shrill urgency. "Just name the event as a portent of Ath's favor, and *hurry.* If the mob's left to think our prince was abducted by sorcery, we're going to see mayhem and riot."

No brave line of pikemen could stand their ground if the dais became stormed by panic. Since the play of uncanny, shimmering light seemed the least of two evils, the chancellor had no choice but step into the breech. His orator's shout rose above the crowd's stunned astonishment.

"There will be alms!" Forced to a desperate semblance of calm, he improvised, "As you see, the Prince of the Light obeys higher forces! He goes where he's needed upon instant notice. Are we children to pine for his continuous presence? The shadow-banes are blessed. Let them be disbursed by our own public servants, and leave his Grace free to shoulder the burden of our defense!"

Just as the mob subsided from its milling roar, the light of Lysaer's gift shimmered clean once again. Restored, riled and whole, to his ceremonial dais at Avenor, he was fully exposed to the public eye and the stupefied shock of his officers. The moment was his to recoup what advantage he could.

"I've come back with proof!" he announced, his snap of resolve reborn from quenched terror. "Since Merior, I've known the adepts of Ath's Brotherhood were in league with Master of Shadow. Now they and the Fellowship Sorcerers have joined in conspiracy against me."

Before the stark awe of his ranking retainers, he whirled face about. The crowd in the plaza redoubled their chanting. Cheers pealed and woke to a howl of animal noise. *"Prince of the Light! Prince of the Light!"*

Lysaer drank in the adulation. Spurred to fierce exultation, countersurge for a hatred he had long since ceased to resist, he bared his teeth in a laugh. White clad, gold haired, fired by his gift, he raised his fists in defiance of the Sorcerers who had dared to intimidate and censure him.

"Behold!" he addressed the masses in a ringing, exuberant shout. "You and your children shall be saved from shadow! I am called to serve Athera and oppose the Spinner of Darkness! No cause and no power will stop my pursuit until he lies dead, and the allies to his evil works are thwarted!"

Winter Solstice 5649

Exchange

The explosive surge of spell-turned forces just used to restore Lysaer to Avenor subsided from the focus beneath Althain Tower. Where a prince's mortal senses had lately discerned but rough stone and a mood of pervasive sorrow, for lingering minutes while the lane flux subsided, the guarding wards left laced through the rock stood roused in all of their splendor. A mind attuned to Paravian mysteries could discern their imprint. The fine energies twined into substance like hazed water, everlastingly falling: a lightning-laced lattice of pattern came sheathed in a beauty fit to draw spirit from flesh.

While the fitted block walls of the citadel ceased their sympathetic vibration, the visiting adept of Ath's Brotherhood paused just outside the door to the King's Chamber. Her willowy build and white robes made her form appear cased in brightness against the grimed arch of the stair vault.

Or perhaps the effect arose from the spirit aura thrown off by initiates of her discipline when they chose to walk in dim places. Few in Athera were empowered to keep pace with the mysteries of Ath's Brotherhood.

One such confronted her now, a Sorcerer who, over thousands of years, had been other things in his past.

He leaned on the massive, iron-strapped door in what seemed a deranged fit of woolgathering. His features were glazed in the glow of the candles. Less susceptible than stone to the fluxes of grand conjury, wax-fed flame only danced to the drafts, as winter's cold swirled and snatched at the shutters, and moaned through the chinks in old masonry.

The adept surveyed Althain's Warden with her tuned awareness. Her shapely hands stayed clasped beneath her embroidered cuffs; threadwork of gold and silver which at times glinted back something more than commonplace reflection. The heavier sconces, flaming in iron brackets on the landing, scrawled moving shadow across her Fellowship subject, masked in his disarming vagaries.

Sethvir's eyes alone showed a mind like surgical steel swathed in misleading burlap. Beneath the spiked tufts of white brows, his gaze remained bleak and trackless as ice on the northern flank of a snowdrift.

The adept knew a sudden, deep stab of uneasiness, as if a wet leaf had brushed scraping tracks down her spine. "Never doubt," she urged, her dusky chin lifted under the shelf of her hood. "Your Fellowship chose right and fitting action with regard to Lysaer s'Ilessid."

Sethvir's seamed knuckles tightened on the doorframe. "Right or not, his expulsion was our forced duty."

Evasive words, to mask chains of happenstance that *would come* to shape Athera's future. Ath's adept matched his challenge, unwavering in her regard. Drafts stirred the clogged fleece of the Sorcerer's beard and combed unseen over sinews and flesh he often forgot he possessed, so many years had his consciousness ridden the intricate tides of the earth link. Against flooding warmth and pale paneling, Althain's Warden seemed an emaciated tree, braced and shaped by relentless storms.

The adept laid slim, olive fingers on his sleeve. "Why are you troubled? Should we fear for one man's fate, do you think? The judgment of the Paravians is sourced in Ath's wisdom. They won't err in behalf of your prince."

By their nature, indeed, they could not. Sethvir knew best of any. His sustained, rooted patience *was* the unflinching remorse of a conscience chained still through long years and hard-fought experience. Before such burdensome memories as his, no mere touch in kindness could comfort. Althain's Warden therefore yielded nothing, his face clamped to folds like burled cypress.

The adept firmed her grasp, insistent. "Lysaer shall receive his redemption from wrong."

"*And is his choice wrong?*" Sethvir asked. No kindness could spare him the lacerating vision imposed through the channels of the earth link. Stamped into his awareness, passed on through her contact, the adept shared the keening, hot surge of a crowd whipped on to devotion in the far-distant plaza at Avenor.

"What's left to weigh?" Unperturbed, she let Althain's Warden share the upset Lysaer's will had once imposed upon the sacred grove in her brotherhood's hostel near Shaddorn. "This prince is both willful and flawed."

Outside, a blast of north wind hurled sand like gritted smoke against the tower. As if flesh were scoured by the sting of each grain, Sethvir shook his head. "Lysaer is terrified beyond life to abandon his care for the innocent."

"Never mind they need none of his help!" The adept spilled a silvery, sharp laugh. "Athera's folk can find their salvation very well. They need no misfit savior playing on their fears to shore up a creed reft of spirit." Still probing, she gave Althain's Warden her most bracing pity. "Stay your grief in this hour, you waste anguish on the wrong victim. While Ath's order becomes maligned by false truth, and the masses are fired to worship your Prince of the Light, *rather, Arithon s'Ffalenn becomes the spirit in mortal danger of corruption.*"

"Then you see very well." Sethvir disengaged his arm. "You must know our Fellowship dreads that beyond anything." For an instant, the wells of his eyes seemed rinsed blank, both shield and mirror against her prying concern. "You name just one ugly crux out of many. *Each of my doubts is well-founded.*" He covered her young, woman's fingers with a palm that had worn bloodstains before those of ink, and too much of both for lasting quietude. The strength which led her to the head of the stair was anything but an old man's.

She protested his courtesy as unnecessary.

"As you wish." Sethvir let her go. While the tormented flames in the sconces rinsed his face, Ath's adept read its mapwork of lines and snatched insight: Althain's Warden regretted a hope kept too fiercely.

Swift in riposte, his forthright, sad smile foiled her sympathy. "Your Brotherhood can never serve as priests."

The lady gave way, then, no longer able to match that wise gaze. Shaken, not cowed, she veiled her distress in the screening shadow of her hood. "For all good intent, if we tried, we would seed the very rift in Ath's continuity that Lysaer s'Ilessid shall create through selfish error."

Brotherhood adepts could not intervene in affairs of kingdoms or men. Nor did their high initiates leave their hostels to teach or draw in new acolytes. They dared not set forth to preach, even against Lysaer's threat of false faith, which could raise the sure power to scatter them. Theirs was not, and never could be, a guide to established religion. Seekers came to them to find inspiration; as they chose, they might stay and take the path to life's deeper mystery.

Ath's adepts held to no doctrine and no creed. They kept their way clear, their channel to truth unclouded by the arrogance of moralizing fools, to misinterpret, or by the greedy who corrupted to exploit. The Paravians who had been their example were departed, and with them went the world's pure connection to the miracle of the prime source.

"We cannot let the knowledge we guard fall prey, first to dogma, then to power and politics. If your Fellowship would ask help," the adept admonished, "then search again for the lost. Should the old races return, Lysaer's claim of divinity cannot do other than fail."

"We have sent Arithon," Sethvir said. Nothing more.

Those words should have been arrows, to strike so quick to the heart. "I am humbled," the adept gasped. Tears broke her voice, and trembling reflections sparked over the thread patterns at her collar and cuffs. "Because of your sacrifice, *Ath preserve, yet again*, for the endurance of your Fellowship, the light of our grace may live on."

Sethvir's fingers, reclasped to hers, became reassurance and comfort.

Whatever deep worry he hedged to keep hidden, her standing to pressure him was forfeit.

Serenity undone, the adept quit the landing. Her retreat down the stairwell raised pattering, small echoes, no tribute at all to the sorrows enshrined in the granite walls of this sanctuary. The vast, shifting shadows offered no refuge. Nor did the Warden of Althain's piercing watch ever leave her. His thin, fragile shoulders in their formal maroon robes stayed unbowed, in full command of a desperate history. To one who might hazard the whole scope of that burden, naught was left but to ache. Words were no match for such courage and generosity, that in unequivocating competence assumed Lysaer's dark tangle in her Brotherhood's stead.

Again, the Fellowship chose to brave every fissure of torn continuity that human works brought to the world.

Worst of all, the decision to champion her Brotherhood's seclusion was *not* blind. Sethvir fully recognized the perilous potential posed by s'Illessid folly. He knew too well how events might grow to jeopardize all that his Fellowship had become in their labor on Athera's behalf. Risk and sacrifice, the Sorcerer grasped every possible ramification. No warning could serve; stewardship of the compact might test *yet again* the peace of mind he and his colleagues had earned amidst the strife of two Ages.

They would shoulder this coil, atop the dread quandaries already ceded to their care by the past flight of the Paravians. Tears made an ungrateful gift for such courage; pity fell short as a eulogy.

While the adept sought her peace in the comfort of solitude, Sethvir left his post on the third-floor landing. Circling thoughts left him frayed as a scrap of old rag hammered and wrung by a storm tide. His Fellowship no longer held the Brotherhood's view, that the disappearance of the Paravians posed Athera's greatest setback. That belief had been violently undone a year past, when Kharadmon's foray to the sealed worlds beyond South Gate had unmasked the darker face of Desh-thiere.

Weighed down by the terrifying scope of those facts, Sethvir reentered the King's Chamber.

There, settled into a solitary vigil, Traithe sat unmoving, his fingers with their bands of old scar tissue knotted beneath his cleft chin. His cut gray hair brushed his collar like tarnish as he roused to the clank of the door latch. He tracked his colleague's passage through coffee-dark eyes, while ghost silent, Althain's Warden recrossed the carpet and pinched beeswax candles one by one.

"You did not broach our problem with the wraiths still at large upon Marak," he surmised.

"No." The acrid bite of singed string spindled through the musk of hot wax, and the room's ingrained fragrance of citrus-oiled wood. For each light extinguished, one shadow died also; like overlaid oil stains, those remaining capered in pantomime about Sethvir's feet. "If the Brotherhood won't open their hostels to help thwart Lysaer's proselytizing in Athera, they would scarcely face damnation on the scale we've encountered for lost spirits entrapped on a gate world."

"You don't fault them?" Traithe said, prodded out of the pragmatism he brandished like armor against his own measure of despair.

Sethvir's fleeting smile masked inward distress, *that any Fellowship colleague ever required to beg reassurance*. Years might pass, but the ongoing tragedy of Traithe's impairment never for a day ceased to sting. "The adepts aren't wrong in their stance." No more than the Paravians had been to abandon man's conflict since the hour clean sunlight was vanquished. "I could ask, but not argue. Desh-thiere's works have ever been ours to unravel."

Wings rustled. The raven swaggered the length of the mantel, head tipped askance and one sequin eye fixed on the Sorcerers.

"I hear, little brother," Sethvir murmured, his regard centered still upon Traithe. In the dimmed majesty of the King's Chamber, he waited, the grip of his patience like the earth wisdom contained in old stone.

For a colleague left crippled since the hour of the Mistwraith's forced entry, courage came slowly to define an event too recent and raw to assimilate. "I can't doubt our stern judgment was needed," Traithe broached at length. "But, Ath show us mercy, I need to ask. How much of Lysaer's acts arise from Desh-thiere's accursed instigation, and how much, out of wayward self-will?"

Sethvir moved. The last branch of lit candles spoked his step in wheeling shadows. "Do you wish me to show you the aura?" He stopped again, waited, while the casement panes rattled to the outside barrage of north winds.

"Yes." Traithe shivered, straightened, laid his hands on the table. The fingers would not flex fully straight; the elegant, long bones that onetime were clean as a dancer's lay twisted and ravaged by old burns. His formless apprehension poisoned the pause. *Half the given talent to set shackles on the Mistwraith lay tied through today's condemned prince and his inborn power to shape light.* "I would know what we face for the future."

The issue went beyond the corruption of an ancient royal line. Desh-thiere's threat had increased. The step which cast Lysaer outside of the compact opened yet another pitfall to bring the last plunge to disaster.

Althain's Warden extinguished the last bank of candles. He recrossed the carpet, soft footed, and rested his palms on Traithe's shoulders. His touch in the darkness came feathered and dry as the chance-met brush of a moth's wing. Instantaneous awareness crossed that slight contact and seized his mind like dull pain. He knew as his own the harrowing weariness wrung through the flesh beneath his hands. "Let me carry this," he murmured.

"Take my permission, and gladly at that." Traithe raised a crooked grin, the humor forced through his iron bravado an unvanquished bent for lightheartedness. "You always did like to run things, never mind your crafty knack for making everyone believe that somebody else was in charge."

Sethvir laughed. "I could wish this particular trouble sat elsewhere. Then we could chat over honey and scones, and brew up a nice pot of tea."

He started his work in one seamless second, his bodily senses discarded for the sharp, trained awareness of mage-sight. The chamber around him transformed to that altered plane of perception. Simple objects unveiled themselves in complexity, the weavings of Name and history revealed. The pile of the carpet showed its humble beginning as wool on the backs of jostling sheep; then shadowed in overlay, each dye in its coloring, brewed from plantstuffs and crushed insects and urine; and underlying the weave like the tap of ghost fingers, the thump of the looms dragging warp threads through weft in the hands of chattering craftswomen. The pale shafts of candles bespoke honeyed summer days and the bustling industry of bees. Mere flecks of dust adrift on the air gained the lordly, bright splendor of stars. Metal for latches, and the bronze of wrought ornament whispered of dark beginnings in the earth, then shrilled to the bright heat of smelting.

At will, Sethvir could sound solid matter for its nuance. His mastery could sort through its light-dance to the bundled spin of energy which held the imprint of events long past. The ebony tabletop would still house the echo of the commitment that Halduin s'Ilessid had accepted, in signature and seal and blood oath, when he swore to uphold Tysan's royal charter. The old stone kept vibrations of earlier times, when the flutes of the Athlien Paravians had led the joy of spring larks, and the winds past the casements had thundered to the mating calls of great dragons. Years and change like layers stamped in sediment, through the centuries comprising three Ages, the structure of Althain Tower itself speared its indelible imprint. Its bleak stone crossed time's arc in fired loops. Its guard pattern bridged every facet of existence, then soared beyond, an unvanquished fist of white light: a lofty splendor of desperation and hope, shot through by the terrible defense wards wrought by the centaur mason who, for love of the land, had fitted each mortised joint in the walls, then spilled his own blood to bind the seals into permanency.

Even Sethvir could not encompass Althain's dire beauty without a half breath lost to awe. A disturbed scrape of claws issued from the mantel shelf, cut by a testy croak.

"I won't stay distracted," Sethvir assured the raven. He steadied himself, then narrowed his mage-sense into controlled concentration. Slowly, delicately, he extended his tactile awareness into the aura of his colleague.

Sethvir's whole consciousness embraced that of Traithe. Prepared though he was, a sick rush of vertigo ripped his frame. He broke into a cold sweat; stifled his reflexive recoil though horror chased his skin like the clammy, sharp scrape of wet razors. Intent held him firm as his vision spun and drowned, sucked into the fearful, gapped chaos of a spirit whose vital energies had been sheared into permanent disarray.

The effect was clean symmetry pulled tragically awry, a mistake frozen for posterity as a statue half-smelted in a bronze craftsman's crucible might be quenched in disfigured solidity.

By every lawful tenet of nature, the inviolate whole of Traithe's inner spirit should have gleamed through the damage to his body. A self-aware being transcended mere flesh. On the contrary, the vibrational essence of Name held the changeless template by which a sorcerer's own powers could restore full health and fitness. But outside the scope of Fellowship wisdom, one long past, calamitous encounter with Desh-thiere had snarled Traithe's aura into discord. Unlike Kharadmon and Luhaine before him, he could not shape the crossing to earthplane existence as pure spirit. His awareness had been warped too far out of true, entrapped in its cage of crippled flesh.

Sethvir shared the scope of that damage firsthand. The resonant structure of Traithe's merry essence had been rucked to a madman's tangle. Its bright weave showed odd rifts, as if packs of starved predators had ripped through tinseled lace with claws and ravening teeth.

These, Sethvir must patch with his own resources. His colleague's continuity of function must be stabilized to restore complete access to his talents. Braced for disorientation and mindless, tearing pain, Althain's Warden dissolved his last veil of identity to shore up the wounded spirit that was Traithe.

His mage-sight became shattered. Perception dissolved into crazy-quilt fragments, welted in patternless blind spots. Althain's Warden cried out. Unmanned by the handicap Traithe endured through the ongoing course of each day, Sethvir fought down raw fear. Imagination foundered. In grief, he felt humbled by his colleague's brave struggle to hold fast to humor and sanity.

The heart could but reel before the ultimate cruelty, that such suffering impairment might have no end and no cure. Against sheer despair, Sethvir raised a counterflux of power.

The labor he shouldered was painstaking and delicate. No individualized pattern of his signature precisely matched those gaps riven wholesale through Traithe. The interface was clumsy, a rafted-together construct as unwieldy as trying to join hawsers with thread, or forcing mismatched fragments of porcelain to fuse into a water-tight vessel.

Sethvir closed the last channel. He waited, sustained in pity and patience, while Traithe groped to assimilate, and talents repressed throughout five hundred years flexed from their cramped state of disuse. Lent a fleeting, murky access to the mage-sight once commanded in his own right, the lame Sorcerer made no demands, but waited while Sethvir engaged the next step.

Althain's Warden drew on memory. Without judgment, without prejudice, he shared the reflection of Lysaer's spirit aura on the moment that Fellowship verdict had withdrawn the protection of the compact.

Like some eerie, actinic embroidery spindled against velvet gloom, the recalled vision shimmered into visible light. In curves and angles and blazing, arced spirals, the individual vibrations which comprised Lysaer s'Ilessid lay exposed, the whole of his being excised from the shadow of dense substance for mage-schooled eyes to interpret.

Sethvir held the facsimile static, while Traithe traced the steps of his colleagues' decision in unconditional review. Predictable anomalies were sorted aside: here, the seal of Davien the Betrayer's longevity, and there, in fixed imprint lent through maternal blood ties, the s'Ahelas line's given gift of farsight. Traithe narrowed his study to encompass a transection of angles more jarring, that convoluted mesh of whorls and jags where the Mistwraith's curse to destroy a half brother entangled the true lines of s'Ilessid justice. The instilled royal virtue no longer ran straight, but bent with insidious and chilling persistence into self-blinding misalignment.

Mortal will could scarcely resist such a coil. Set to draw his independent opinion, Traithe could not overlook the surrounding lines carved by princely desire and intent.

Lysaer had been cursed to kill his half brother. The tenets of royal inheritance led him to endorse that violence with a just cause. But nestled inside his ardent need to protect society, an uneasy conscience spun new threads of gnawing uncertainty.

Delusion entered in: a magisterial spark of arrogance fueled by outraged duty. Lysaer clung to the vanity of his privileged royal upbringing. Where the coil of self-perception shaped the ideals of principle, obsession flowered, a hot, hazy spiral that corded through the aura like coils cast off a dropped spool.

Sethvir shared the resonance of dismay through the link, as Traithe resolved his conclusion. Lysaer used his flaws to deafen his ears to harsh truth. A lordly, dark pride that brooked no humility before the misguided masses; a caring, honorable sovereign's undoing, that measure of shame and stark horror. No other descendant of Halduin had lived to lead an innocent people to slaughter. That burdensome guilt crushed thought and will, and gave rise to a desperate denial. Lysaer refused outright to betray his s'Ilessid bloodline. He *would not* beg mercy and assign himself blame for thirty-seven thousand use-less deaths.

A penchant for self-sacrifice fueled that chord of victimized fury and reforged an unswerving purpose. In assurance as cool as a strand of steel filigree, Lysaer chose his next course. For the sake of those who died carrying his banner, he would forbear his born generosity of spirit and embark on a more grandiose campaign. Arithon must become more than a criminal beyond pardon, but the instrument of evil incarnate. For honor, for the sake of past losses and grief, the man who styled himself Prince of the Light would not break down and cry weakness.

And so in that hour the composite of Lysaer's aura showed his tragic, committed dedication. For the enslavement of Tysan's clans-men and the salve of a glorified purpose, this scion of s'Ilessid shaped the course and direction of his fate. Desh-thiere's curse might drive him to fight Arithon. Its pernicious hold might inten-sify and strengthen the brutality of each encounter. But like an addiction to euphoric drugs, its pull could not enslave every facet of self-will; nor had it the power to enforce heart or spirit to give impassioned collaboration with its drive to seed bloodshed and war.

Hate was the province of the Mistwraith's geas, not conceit or vengeance for vanity.

Too aggrieved to stay silent, Sethvir said, *'Had Lysaer's human judg-ment or his gift of true justice stayed uncompromised, he might not have per-sisted in branding his half brother as evil.'*

But outside of conjecture, choices still ended with fact. The damn-ing omission which condemned the s'Ilessid prince was his prideful design not to bend.

'Even so,' Traithe admitted in ringing regret. *'Our oath to uphold the compact leaves us no loophole to give Lysaer a reprieve.'*

Sethvir dismissed the s'Ilessid construct. Prepared to drop contact with his colleague's faulted vision, he shivered, swept across by a vio-lent burst of déjà vu. Trained reflex responded. Practiced from his centuries of tracking the unsorted flux of the earth link, Sethvir tagged the triggering fragment of event. Then he rummaged through memory in pursuit of the happenstance which linked the uncanny association.

The connection became manifest. Breath seized in his chest as the past took him back into the suffocating terror of attack. *Once, for six hours he had been imprisoned in the sheer, slate walls of a warded flask. He had fled there in peril of his life, hunted down by a pack of nine free wraiths.*

115

These had been lured from the dead world of Marak through the Fellowship's effort to learn of Desh-thiere's origins. Threatened by possession, his countermove forced out of cornered desperation, Sethvir had fragmented and scattered his consciousness to deflect the force of the assault. Voracious in malice, the wraiths had closed in. For a nightmarish second, Althain's Warden relived the torment, while malevolent spirits savaged his being like vivisection done with hot knives.

In that darkest hour, while the wraiths had devoured those disparate bits of his spirit, Sethvir had experienced the paralyzing horror of a consciousness wormholed with gaps. Shocked to revelation, he perceived the probable cause of Traithe's plight. In the hour of past crisis, Traithe had engaged grand conjury to unmake the spells which enabled the South Gate as a portal to cut off Desh-thiere's invasion. As battle was joined, the collective mind of the Mistwraith may well have bid for possession.

Traithe had lost memory. Repeated scryings to reconstruct the event had exposed only surface images. But there *had* been a spell unleashed that appeared to recoil in backlash upon its creator. Through logic and theory, Sethvir knew Traithe's act had not been any miscast conjury.

On purpose, a sorcerer beset beyond hope might shear off tainted portions of his being. For the mage-trained, the perils of possession and conquest were too terrible a risk to set loose on the world at large.

Worse, far worse, if such maiming defense had not immolated those truncated fragments. Laced still in shared contact, Sethvir masked dismay. Those severed shreds of Traithe's consciousness might well still exist. *If they had survived the cautery of conflict, they would live in the clutch of the wraiths which devoured them. That lost essence of self could be nowhere else but mewed up under the deranging vibrations of the wards over Rockfell Pit.* The chance was too real, that Traithe's hope of healing lay imprisoned with the Mistwraith's stew of warped spirits.

The Warden of Althain snapped his fine band of rapport. Cast free of Traithe's blinkered awareness, he shivered. The ordinary dark of the King's Chamber enfolded him, its brimstone tang of spent carbon commingling with the faded fragrance of the herbs that kept moths from spoiling the heraldic banners. Sweat drenched him. A bone-deep dread compounded his earlier heartache.

He scarcely dared move, lest Traithe be led to sense something amiss and begin a distressed round of questions.

"Get some rest," Sethvir urged, amazed that his voice should still function. He managed no more. The devastating scope of his findings overcame him, and pity closed his throat like poured lead.

While Traithe relieved the ache of his scars in sleep on a cot in the wardroom, the other four Fellowship Sorcerers in residence gathered in the cushioned nook off the pantry.

The unwelcome impact of Sethvir's discovery had spun into brittle silence.

Asandir's charcoal eyebrows met above his hawk nose. Seated at a deal table grayed with old rings left by flowerpots, he plowed the last crumbs from an oatcake into mazes of meaningless lines. In the window seat opposite, feet tucked up on a tapestry stool leaking horsehair stuffing in tufts, Althain's Warden peered into the dregs of a much chipped earthenware pot. A mug turned for a sunchild's proportions sat clasped between his knobby knees. Sethvir found nothing useful to say. The tracks between soggy clumpings of tea leaves held no remedy to heal Traithe's affliction.

"How often ignorance stings less than knowledge," Asandir said at last.

By then, a wintery aquamarine dusk tinted the room's makeshift casement. Hoarfrost tendriled the bottle-thick rondels, crudely set into leading and mortar to seal the aperture of an arrow loop. Failing light glinted on the diamond inset in some forgotten aristocrat's fancy table knife. The bone handle had yellowed, and a blade lapsed to tarnish wore butter in undignified smears. Nearby, a tin spoon stuck upright in the bubbled glass jar of a farmwife's elderberry jam.

A current of cold out of phase with the season prowled the rim of the table. "What does dung do in a byre but get deeper?" remarked Kharadmon's drifting presence.

To stall his rank flippancy, Luhaine spoke from the niche between the rococo cupboards of the larder. "If Traithe's chance of healing is linked with the quandary of Desh-thiere's damned wraiths, in horrid fact, we're left with a dearth of alternatives."

"Just the sort of crux in a chess game to drive logicians and theorists to fits." Kharadmon crossed the window in a puff of miffed agitation. "We might be advised to set calming wards to safeguard your sanity as precaution."

"How belated," Luhaine retorted. "I'd sooner go mad from your incessant, childish inanities!"

Kharadmon blew back a raspberry. "Leave things to you, we'd hear you pontificate 'til the fish in the sea become fossils."

Long since inured to old spats between shades, Asandir twiddled

117

crumbs, and Sethvir pondered tea leaves, each one immersed in perturbed quiet. None cared to broach the difficult quandary, that Traithe's tragic predicament made the cursed princes' lives all the more indispensable. Their elemental mastery of shadows and light could be needed to sort through the Mistwraith's damned entities. The outlook on that future stayed unremittingly grim, with Arithon half-deranged by the pinch of s'Ffalenn conscience, and named as a hunted criminal; and Lysaer s'Ilessid poised to launch holy war under threat of Paravian judgment.

Traithe's raven fluffed obsidian feathers from the keystone over the doorway, while Luhaine intoned arch opinion. "There could be a benefit to this day's bad work. A reprieve might arise out of darkness, if Lysaer's aberration of prime law would draw the Paravians out of hiding to denounce him."

"No grace remains for discussion in any case." Sethvir raised his nose from the dregs of his tea mug, his mood diffused into vagary. "We've got company. Morriel Prime's just arrived at the gates to demand our immediate audience."

Demand

Winter gloaming cloaked the sedges, and the raked, brown stalks of dry weed heads flattened to the gusts that sheared off the Bittern Desert. At the edge of the dunelands, under sky like translucent enamel, Althain Tower reared up in blunt contour, spidery runners of ivy and splotched lichens clotted to its southern side. Morriel Prime worked age-stiffened joints through the snipped-off fingers of her gloves. Swathed under layers of thick, hooded cloaks, she drew a deep breath of the knifing, cold air, and quashed back a riptide of old rage.

Koriani feud with the Fellowship of Seven had lasted since Third Age Year One.

Behind her, fidgety amid the slurry of mud and rimed ruts which seized the stone flags by the gate arch, her young deaf-mute servant stared with his mouth slacked open. No other but Iyan attended her. Too much power and too many secrets lay housed at Althain Tower. Mortals who asked a Sorcerer's hospitality were wont to reemerge changed, since the impacting force of a Fellowship presence was too heady to encounter without sparking an altered perception. No enchantress dared count herself exempt. Despite the strict code of the initiate's oath, Elaira's faulted faith in the Koriani Order had stemmed from just one illicit talk with Asandir.

Morriel sized up the massive grilled portal, impenetrable before her high arts. That irritation galled her with surprising ferocity. Learned as she was, disciplined in the mysteries and dedicated as fine steel in her convictions, even still, the spelled wards on the gates lay outside her means to command. Seals conformed in dire forces unsettled her attuned senses. The ache of them raised bone-stripping twinges from the longevity bindings laid in live currents through her flesh.

In the moan of winter winds, under a zenith deepened to fathomless cobalt, the thorny coil of past event transferred its harsh sting to the present.

Morriel cupped the wrapped Waystone against her breast, the grip of her left hand white knuckled to secure her cloak against the gusts. Althain's defenses had endured for unnatural centuries, the length of an age before a destitute humanity had embarked on its flight to seek refuge. While spacefaring civilization had torn itself apart in a dog pack scrap over the bones of its fallen greatness, the Fellowship of Seven had maintained an isolate residence on Athera.

Whoever they had been, whatever their unrevealed origin, they chose this place for their work. During the Second Age, they had turned the bloody tides in the Paravian conflict against the ravening packs of drake spawn. Rescued from near extinction, the old races had survived to see peace on their overlooked and uncharted little world.

No such enclave of wise powers had intervened to champion mankind's beleaguered decline.

Amid the suffering and the atrocities of humanity's Armageddon, the Koriani Order had been founded to resist the collapse of higher culture. Their purpose had been to perpetuate mercy, while other specious, greedy factions waged war, and burned a priceless heritage to ashes.

What fragmented knowledge remained to be salvaged hung on the brink of being lost beyond all recovery. Morriel confronted the fast sanctuary at Althain, her mood like fired obsidian. Too many of her predecessors had begged these same Sorcerers for help. Each matriarch had been unconditionally refused. Now, when her own term of office neared its end, the current Prime shouldered the more demeaning errand of petitioning for power that was hers.

The necessity ignited a rage of bitter vintage. She alone guarded access to the imprinted memories of every Prime Matriarch to live before her. To Morriel, sole protector of mankind's banished history, the green earth here was no refuge, but a prison kept warded by tyranny.

At the dawn of the Third Age, when the refugee survivors arrived to beg asylum, the Fellowship of Seven claimed no pretense. They were sworn to guard the land by Paravian law. If mankind would settle, the culture that shaped them must be set aside to keep accord with indigenous tradition. Such were the terms drawn into the compact, for which the Fellowship Sorcerers stood surety.

The Koriani, with their mission of merciful protection, were lent no voice in that council. Tolerance might argue that today's Prime Enchantress should rise above the outworn grievance of the past. Yet the burden bequeathed by her office was too heavy. Time left her weary of the proscribed knowledge she sheltered, records that might only be passed on to the precarious charge of a successor.

Althain Tower's stark dignity only mocked her in that bone-hurting, chill winter twilight, monument that it was against all that time or attrition might erase.

Morriel trembled as the old flare of rage stirred her blood. Truth fed her temper. Behind this locked portal lay power enough to grow past this world's horizon, to restore at one stroke all the shining civilization her predecessors had labored to save; and lost. The accumulated wisdom of those centuries was dispersed, or else confined beyond recovery by the bucolic bounds of a compact sworn by seven Sorcerers in behalf of three vanished races.

The moment was past, to mourn, or waver, or regret. Morriel came to do battle on Fellowship ground, armed with naught else but her righteous indignation and the exhausted rags of her faith.

The clank of a windlass heralded the moment her arrival drew notice. Counterweighted chain reverberated inside the sealed archway as the innermost defenses were winched open. Then firm footfalls echoed through the vaults of the sally port, and the heavy, barred gate cracked open. Asandir's craggy profile jutted through the gap, behind the lowered grate of the portcullis.

"Sethvir bids you welcome to Althain Tower," he called, then challenged in chisel-cut bluntness, "He invites you for tea and specific conversation concerning an arrow let fly three years past by Duke Bransian s'Brydion in Vastmark."

Morriel released a laugh of bloodletting satisfaction, waved Iyan forward, and rasped her reply. "You may tell Sethvir, I accept."

The unveiled presence of the Great Waystone flicked violet lights across the litter of empty plates and the glass sides of the jam crock not yet tidied from the table. The lone member of the Prime's entourage felt comfortably at home. Iyan perched in the window seat with his knees drawn up, contentedly licking traces of elderberry off of the stamped tin spoon. The more elegant butter knife, cleaned the same way, remained in the possessive grasp of the other ham fist hooked to his cross-gartered shin.

Sethvir approved the deaf-mute's simplistic pleasures, his smile all childish innocence. The bearded, sprite's features veiled in the steam which wafted off a fresh tea mug held no guile. As a host he had been faultlessly attentive, and yet, the sparkle to his eyes warned of wayward refusal to address the major talisman Morriel had presented before him.

To her stripped ultimatum to reverse his act of mischief and erase its Named imprint from the earth's eidetic awareness, he sighed with reproachful complaisance. "Done is finished. Who could live up to the conceit you believe I possess?" His irreverent manner expanded to gleeful chagrin. "You embarked on a journey of four hundred leagues *in belief I could sway the will of a planet?* My dear, I am flattered, as well as sorry for the discomfort and inconvenience brought on by your expectations. But no living power in Athera could move the earth to do as you ask."

Morriel hissed in a sharp breath. "You're lying." Nestled in shawls, ensconced in a padded chair like an egg in a silk-lined cup, she shared her glare equally between Althain's Warden and Asandir, who leaned against the doorpost, his bench lately banished to the larder to make room for visitor seating. The afterglow behind the paned arrow slit had fled. Plate rims poised above the pooled shadows cast by a tallow dip spiked on an iron pricket.

Unsinged by the Prime's focused ire, blissfully intent on sloshing the dollop of cinnamon butter just added to flavor his tea, Sethvir shrugged. "What you think doesn't matter. Your crystal has been recognized, and earth will abide by its own nature."

He might have said more, but Luhaine snatched the opening to expound. "Stone and soil, you must know, are susceptible to energy. Like the mind of a mimic, they will copy and retain the patterns of induced vibrations. No made spell under sky could remand that given property." Warmed now to his subject, the invisible spirit ran over the Prime's reedy protest. "And anyway, the conundrum's not linked to a balanced equation. To invoke the attempt to dominate a planet would create an unsolvable backlash. Where could the discharge from such a raised force become grounded? Earth itself would reject the called power to bind it into subservience! Even if this were a mutable truth, how could its awareness of your great crystal's resonance be masked? The memory of land is scribed in the language of epochs. It endures across cataclysm. Ath Creator did not gift its being with forgetfulness."

"Then give me a spell of illusion for blinding concealment," Morriel demanded.

Sethvir looked up from his mug, his eyebrows tipped in patent injury. "Just because you accuse me of deceit doesn't mean I'll change my character to become so." He glanced across at Iyan, who held the spoon in locked jaws, as if he sensed the tensioned undercurrents to words deaf ears could not hear.

Althain's Warden set down his tea. He turned his back, gave the mute servant's arm a kindly pat, then vacated his chair to share the cushion in the window seat.

Balked by his move from polite negotiation, Morriel shifted target and accosted Asandir. "Indeed, the hour has come to discuss that arrow once loosed in Vastmark."

Ghost quiet on his feet, the Sorcerer who arranged the Fellowship's field work moved his tall frame and claimed Sethvir's empty chair. He slid the filled tea mug aside and laced his fingers over crossed forearms. "You provoked an attempt to assassinate Arithon s'Ffalenn by fanning Duke Bransian's urge for blood feud." His riposte matched hers like testing, cold steel. "No light matter."

"For that you hobbled the powers of our Great Waystone, admit it," Morriel accused. Eyes like jet bead bored into the Sorcerer's of impenetrable, mirror-glass gray. "You protect Rathain's prince, peril that he is. A mage-trained master fallen under curse of violence will incite more deaths than that one, on Duke Bransian's arrow. I'll say what I think. Your Fellowship has never regarded the people on this world as more than expendable ciphers."

"We'll set aside the question of whether you're qualified to make any judgment on that." Asandir gave no sign he was perturbed. "The issues are separate, in fact."

"I see." Morriel raked up a disdainful cough. "The nature of an inanimate earth and its resistance to change weighs more than our Waystone's potential to spare cities with children and families from the misfortunes of storm or disaster?" She stabbed a stiff finger from beneath her layered fortress of blankets. "Condemn yourself, Sorcerer, by those answers already given."

The tallow dip flared, streamed by an affronted swirl of draft. But whichever discorporate Sorcerer roused up for rebuttal bowed before Asandir's prior claim to defense. "Lady Morriel, where are your grounds for dispute? Athera's land and natural resource were never placed at humanity's disposal."

"Which point is moot, since your precious Paravians have left their ancestral ground." Morriel jabbed home her point. "Will you endorse bloodshed just to hold your lofty place as guardians of their abandoned heritage? While you mourn for vanished unicorns, our cities slide further into violence. Your Teir's'Ffalenn is too perilous a presence to leave at large in the world. I see you're not blind to the flaws in his nature. If your Fellowship won't act to curb his lethal cleverness, our order must. Lysaer's rule offers selfless governance, a fair concern for the needs of society. The obsessions the Mistwraith has driven him to embrace will fade without fuel if Arithon is removed as his target. I find no justification whatsoever for restraint. How should any one life be worth the thirty thousand left dead at Vastmark?"

"Because we are not speaking for one individual, but of the survival of all life on Athera," Kharadmon snapped with blistering irony.

"That is the root of our quandary," Asandir admitted.

The clipped note to his speech arrested Morriel's tirade. She narrowed seamed eyes and read closer, disturbed by the precedence that Luhaine permitted his rival's remark to stand unchallenged. Through the coarse, ruddy flare of the tallow dip, past the vicious play of static thrown off by the unshielded Waystone, she at last interpreted Asandir's stark patience for the stillness of a desperate uncertainty.

"*What have you done?*" she whispered point-blank. Then in knifing accusation, "How is our world set at risk?"

"The peril is not new, but an ongoing extension of the trouble begun when man first created the aberrated mists of Desh-thiere." Asandir sat forward. "If I may?" He caught up the Waystone in long fingers, impervious, as though it possessed no more hazardous an aura than a chunk of unwarded glass.

The Prime Enchantress bridled. Convinced he had the effrontery to mock her by degrading her grand focus as a scrying stone, she gathered herself to revile him. Yet he did nothing but pass the jewel back across the table.

"Your jewel sets off a disturbing dissonance," he temporized as he ceded its cold weight into her protective grasp. "Better we ease the distraction before the next subject is explored."

Morriel Prime tugged a silk shawl from her knees and veiled the sullen glimmer of the Waystone. She felt disgruntled, manipulated, and pricked by the awareness that Asandir's gently innocuous request urged dismissal of her complaint. She would not be sidetracked from her mission. Nor would she be lulled by the informal nature of Sethvir's bachelor hospitality. Fellowship Sorcerers were ever subtle players. Placed firmly on guard, she must anticipate their ploys, even as they offered diversions that led off on tangents.

"Are the wards on Rockfell Pit gone unstable?" She settled the Waystone in the hollow of her lap and waited in rankling patience.

"Those defenses are secure," Kharadmon assured from his over-head vantage above the door arch. "But Desh-thiere was divided upon its entry to Athera. The greater concentration of its fog was turned away, as we have unsettling proof. The uncontained portion cut off on the gate world of Marak is anything but a dead entity."

Lapped like a mummy in quilts and thick shadows, her reed voice stripped to suspicion, Morriel said carefully, "Dead or not, those wraiths should have no thread of connection to exploit. Unless you've contrived some harebrained scheme to restore the old portal to Athera?"

"Ath forfend, never that!" Sethvir interjected, then submerged once again in his voiceless communion with Iyan. An inimical pause seized the chamber, strung out on the hiss of the tallow dip. Asandir turned his hand palm down on bare wood to thwart a visible urge to strike a fist. "This is properly Kharadmon's story," he said in quick discomfort.

Luhaine withheld all opinion, nor did he interrupt as the nexus of his discorporate rival drifted down to settle amid the used-up spread of light supper.

"The tale plays more like nightmare," the Fellowship's most incor-rigible prankster confessed in chilling sobriety. Over the untidied jet-sam of dishes and a tea mug abandoned brimful, Kharadmon dropped the too casual comment that he had accomplished a crossing between stars.

"I went to Marak with intent to find knowledge to break the Mist-wraith's geas of enmity over the princes. Why look astonished?" He chuckled for the joy of provocation. "Come now, Morriel, were your Koriani spies so inept? Did you actually think we would abandon the half brothers to the affliction of a cursed fate?"

The Prime Enchantress fixed his invisible presence with disdain as inscrutable as a sphinx.

"Well, madam, don't rush to lend us due grace with an apology." A miniature, self-contained wind devil, Kharadmon swept a tempest of crumbs into gyrating circles around the teapot. "I shan't lend false hope. I found no reprieve."

On Marak, where cities had once crisscrossed the continents with glimmering strings of lights, he had encountered a dead waste of freezing winds and ice. No people survived. There, the truncated mists of Desh-thiere brooded still, redoubled in malice, and haunted now by far worse than the original matrix of bound entities that had launched past invasion of Athera.

Kharadmon minced no words. "The fogs still enveloping Marak have inducted the spirits of every slain human victim." His whirling exhibition of crumbs crashed and scattered, released as he swirled on to traverse the casement. "The whole world is a stew of trapped entities, suspended in active consciousness, and driven mad by unrequited hatred."

The tallow dip fluttered and jerked. The Sorcerer's unsettled movement stalked on, to raise the odd shiver from Iyan, who cast a sharp, startled glance past his shoulder.

"Never mind," Sethvir soothed in daft unconcern for the fact the Prime's newest servant was deaf. "Yon shade means no harm."

While Iyan settled and resumed his absorbed, silent dialogue between the silver knife and the jam spoon, a crystalline pause filled the chamber. The moaning winter wind buffeted the tower and sheared all the warmth from the air.

"I was attacked," said Kharadmon at unpleasant length, "beset and pursued almost beyond recourse."

Morriel absorbed this, her lips pinched into a bloodless crease, and the frown lines like pleats on her forehead. For a Fellowship mage to admit to near helplessness shook her to driving unease. This recount was no ploy drummed up as diversion to upset pursuit of her purpose. She measured implications as the grim tale unfolded, of an unexplained silence, then the beacon signal sent off by worried colleagues to guide an errant Sorcerer safely home.

"We believed Kharadmon was disoriented, even lost." Asandir made a small, strangled gesture of frustration, then explained how the sorceries he and Sethvir had raised on summer solstice had been ground-tied through the land's living trees. Last came the harrowing corollary, given in hammered, steady speech. "Until every trunk, seed, and sapling alive completes its allotted span of years, a faint signature trace of that homing spell will linger. We can't dismiss the risk. These loose wraiths upon Marak might find means to track such a resonance. If they should cross the vast deeps between stars, the mists that embody them would sublimate away. Arrived here as free wraiths, they would strike for possession and wreak death and destruction such as this world has never seen."

"But surely they would perish outside their containment of mists," Morriel said.

"These don't," Kharadmon admitted, reluctant. "They haven't. Nine of them pursued on my back trail. Those survived the transition as pure spirit. The measures we invoked to trap and dispel them would never withstand the event of a large-scale attack."

"Which is why you need Arithon alive? How very neat and convenient." Morriel gave her most acid riposte. "If you look to a masterbard's talent to effect a translation of Name and redeem them, that's a desperate, thin straw to grasp at."

"A thin straw's the best hope we have at this time," said Asandir with shattering dignity. "The logic is not hard to follow." Taken individually, the scourging spirits could be bound through Arithon's gifts. His rearing by mages already lent him an advantage of training to resist hostile attack and possession. "We are also in process of constructing defense wards to secure this world from invasion."

"I see," Morriel said. "All this takes precedence over the cities we already have torn into war by the criminal charges leveled against this dubious savior."

Luhaine flared into rebuttal. "Neither one of the princes are expendable. Marak at this time is still choked in mists. Powers of light and shadow might still be used to entrap the wraiths on the planet. Even if the fell entities never try the crossing to Athera, our world is not free of threat. The wraiths in Rockfell Pit are imprisoned, not quiescent. The half brothers' talent over shadow and light will be needed one day to help lay those trapped spirits to rest."

"Then confine the half brother most inclined to cause mayhem if you wish them both to stay living." Morriel sat forward with slitted eyes. "Don't deny you hold the power to do this!"

"The issue of power has no bearing," Sethvir exclaimed in fussy correction from the window seat. At some point, unnoticed, he had lifted the spoon and knife from Iyan's hands. "You speak of two grown men born to free will, and not string puppets. Their lives are not ours to use for expedience."

"Are they not?" Morriel arose, wizened and bent under trains of wool wrappings, but charged to denounce with the stripping, fierce sting of white lye. "What a pitiful excuse! You act when you're moved to, or how else did five royal lines come by their gifts in the first place? Why should your wastrel apprentice have taken the arrow for Arithon's sake back in Vastmark? Oh, you dissemble very well. The curbed powers of our Waystone establish that point beyond doubt."

"Sethvir has curbed nothing," Asandir contradicted. "The earth itself is your arbiter. What spells you impose by way of rank force, the land has been empowered to refuse. That is all."

"And are lives and children worth less than a storm or an earthquake raised by the raw whim of nature? What upstart arrogance!" Morriel startled to a sweet metallic chime as Sethvir tapped the spoon to the knife handle. In no mood for his mooncalf byplay with her servant, she raised her voice over the disturbance. "Release the earth's imprinted memory of our crystal. Our help and its power may be sorely needed, to judge by the botch you have made back on Marak."

That moment, Iyan yelped aloud. He shot to his feet, seized the cutlery from Sethvir, and clashed spoon to knife blade in an energetic clatter of wild noise.

"Daelion Fatemaster wept!" Morriel whirled on Althain's Warden. "What have you done to my servant?"

Asandir burst out laughing. "Let him restore the nerves that afflicted his hearing, apparently."

The Prime Matriarch blanched in shock. "Healed him?" Her dismay filled the room, since the act was no favor. The man's value had been his inability to disseminate her secrets.

Oblivious to all nuance, too elated to perceive a mistress's embarrassing, ungrateful hypocrisy, Iyan whooped for joy, then chortled to experience the music of his own voice.

"You should leave," Luhaine suggested in a solemn bent of humor, "before something else more regrettable happens."

Kharadmon abetted in devilish, barbed irony. "Be nice and smile, or your servant could also acquire speech."

Which effrontery was too much; Morriel Prime lost grip on cold nerves and blazed into rare, scorching temper. "Ath curse you all for frivolous intervention! What you name restraint, I call cowardice! The Koriani Order is older than your Fellowship. Our first Prime Matriarch stood at the right hand of free governance *before* Calum Kincaid sold out his great weapon and became the destroyer of worlds. What are you defending in this land but ignorance? I call you tyrants, rank meddlers with what's left of human dignity. Believe this. I shall not forget. Redress will be found for our damaged Waystone, and your Fellowship shall live to regret your unjust interference."

She grasped Iyan's elbow and pried knife and spoon from his crestfallen hands. "Come. We are leaving." She shed borrowed blankets, scooped the Great Waystone from the cushions of her chair, and demanded to be seen down the stair to the gates.

"Good riddance," Kharadmon announced on the eddy of air as the door slammed in the Prime's departed wake. "The lady has a temper like a snake."

Sethvir disagreed with a tilt of his head. "The years she has endured in the seat of Prime office have driven her just a bit mad. Pity her, instead. She's inherited a charge she can never pass on. Since her last candidate for succession died in the rite of passage, I suspect the complexity of her office has become too much for any new aspirant to bear. No initiate in her order, however well trained, could survive the transfer of power."

"One might have," Luhaine interjected, more than usually thoughtful. "At least, Elaira shows spirit enough to endure."

"And count our good grace for the fact she is cast out of favor!" Sethvir cried in rife exasperation. "The current Prime Matriarch is headache enough, with her penchant to ally herself with Lysaer. A successor tied by love to Arithon s'Ffalenn would yield up a frightening collusion."

Loyalties

In a clandestine meeting, Lysaer addresses the devoted captain of his honor guard, and a well-trusted healer who had tended the maimed through all the horrors of Vastmark: "You are sworn to gravest silence because I must reveal several dangerous truths well before our people have gained faith of a strength to endure them. Arithon s'Ffalenn was begotten by a demon, and his unholy powers have suborned Lady Talith to the point where she'll need to be secretly confined. . . .

Safely returned since his audience on Corith, Earl Jieret, *caithdein* of Rathain, hears in relief the appeal of Caolle, his ex–war captain, who had fostered him since childhood, "My lord, the sword training of young scouts is more properly left in the care of my successor. I beg leave to go to the westshore and await the return of our prince. His Grace might deny the necessity, but a sworn liegeman who bears a strong sword should be there to serve him against the day he makes landfall. . . ."

When spring comes, and rumors fly that Lady Talith will make no appearance for the traditional celebrations, Avenor's royal healer admits in gentle sorrow to the court: that in distraught state for her failure to conceive, the princess has retired into strict seclusion for the sake of her delicate health. . . .

IV. Turnabout

J ust over three years after Lysaer's expulsion from the compact by
the Fellowship of Seven, the brigantine *Khetienn* lay anchored off
the distant shores of the continent half a globe away. An equatorial
sun sliced her shadow in hard outline on the chipped crystal sparkle
of salt water. Few fish swam those jewel-toned shallows. Bird cries
never wove through the air. The only wild voice was the rasp of light
breezes, flapping the single staysail left set to draw ventilation
through the hatches. Throughout the logged course of six voyages,
after arduous problems with restocking stores to provision for
repeated ocean crossings, the brigantine had put into every cove, bay,
and inlet along Kathtairr's blighted coast.

That search of the shoreline, and further expeditions on foot into
the rugged, stony vistas of the interior had turned up nothing living.
Only mineral-poisoned rivers and a limitless expanse of sun-blasted,
wind-raked desolation.

Tanned and taciturn where he leaned on the ship's rail in the stifling heat, Arithon wore only breeches of stained canvas cinched at
the waist with tarred cord. By preference while at sea, he dressed
from dregs of the ship's slop chest, as far from the trappings of royal
heritage as tattered, plain clothing would allow.

His tourmaline eyes raked across the splintered ochre rubble, where
the dun contours of scorched earth stitched the cloudless skyline, and

the knees of the headland met sea in lace petticoat ruffles of spent breakers. An ominous, flat inflection demarked his address to the sweating figure by his side. "How long have you known that Kathtairr offered no refuge?"

The Mad Prophet squeezed his eyes closed against the stabbing glare off the water. "A fair question," he allowed in shrinking misery. "One I don't care to answer." He inhaled the tarred taint of oakum warmed blistering hot in the thought-shattering fall of noon sunlight. More than just heat left him faint. He feared even to expel his discomfited breath, aware to paralysis that if he said nothing, the man at his side would react in spectacular, inventive retaliation.

No use to pretend there had been no intent to lead Arithon in diversion through ignorance.

Dakar regrouped the rags of his nerve. He spoke the truth quietly, anxious to avoid notice from the idle sailhands who sprawled in the shadow by the forecastle. "These shores lay scorched sterile by drakefire long before Ath Creator sent the Paravians as living gift to redress all the sorrows of the world. No centaur, sunchild, or unicorn has ever walked here. Not through any age of known history."

An uneasy interval, cut by an isolated movement; the Master of Shadow turned his head and delivered his most scathing, level glare.

"The Fellowship needed to buy time," Dakar blurted. "They wouldn't say why. Some outside crisis concerning the linked gate worlds has kept them clapped close as clams. The only thing that matters is what you intend to do now."

"What I intend?" Arithon loosed a piercing, soft laugh. "The clans need a refuge. If a sea search was required to seek the Paravians, Daelion Fatemaster's sorrows, Dakar! We need not have wasted *three years*. For a sweep of the oceans, we'll need a whole fleet, and strong captains, and navigators trained to make star sights."

Then came the striking, inevitable pause Dakar dreaded, while thought burned behind half-lidded green eyes. Rathain's prince could connive with appalling invention, until even Sethvir became sorely tested to unriddle the final result.

"You had better hope," said Arithon s'Ffalenn, "that Cattrick has been busy keeping the letter of my design back in Tysan."

The impacting force of that statement took a pregnant second to slam home. "In *Tysan*? Merciful Ath!" Dakar all but shouted. "You're not plotting to lift Lysaer's new deepwater keels from the royal yard at Riverton!"

The lean, expressive mouth flexed amid the sharp-planed s'Ffalenn features. Where a stranger might mistake such expression for amuse-

132

ment, Dakar knew to look deeper. But Arithon swung his inscrutable regard to the sapphire edge of the horizon as he said, "For the sake of my peace, don't share speculation with Feylind."

Night claimed the far continent of Kathtairr like ground quartz sown on dark velvet. Restless airs scoured the vivid, flint scent of dewfall off its vistas of sun-baked rock. The sky spread above the obsidian hills held no kindly embroidery of clouds. The stark, strewn blaze of Athera's constellations scribed the arc of the sea where the *Khetienn* rode at anchor, a stamped silhouette rouged by the glow of her deck lanterns. From his solitary vantage on a shoreside hillock, Dakar could hear the desultory laughter, as sailhands made cracks at each other's expense. The windborne exchange of camaraderie seemed disjointed in time, splashed like fragmented dream against the acid-leached contours of rain-stripped gullies and sere landscape.

Despite distance, and the fast-fallen curtain of darkness, Dakar could pick out the Master of Shadow, propped alone against the stern rail. Whether the Teir's'Ffalenn ached for disappointment, or brooded alone in balked anger, no man dared say. Dakar remained outside his confidence. The festering dispute arisen between them concerning his meddling plots against Tysan's shipworks had abraded those nerves which still remained raw from the ache of a tormented conscience.

For Arithon, Kathtairr's barren shores delivered more than bitter setback. The afternoon's truths had sealed the death of a desperate, cherished set of hopes.

The Mad Prophet rubbed sweaty palms on his thighs and swore at the grit that the land breeze sifted over everything. A decision to put about and sail back to Tysan meant shouldering the risks still left hanging by Earl Jieret's fragment of augury. With Arithon left mage-blind, the unwelcome burden of scrying fell on the spellbinder's shoulders. He had small choice but to sound the future for the source of the execution that Rathain's *caithdein* had foreseen three years in the past.

Dakar felt inadequate. His birthgiven talent for prophecy had always been unpredictable. Despite five centuries of Fellowship training, his unruly, chance-met bouts of vision still blundered roughshod over his efforts to impose reason or mastery. The gift had ever been an affliction to upset the planned course of his life. Even worse, the stresses of backlash inevitably wrecked his digestion and left him sick as a dog.

"Ah, fiends plague!" he groused to his audience of desolate, stern boulders. "It's a born sap who dies of stupidity."

133

A fool's self-preservation should have kept him from opening his mouth to volunteer. Too late, he wished he had capsized *Khetienn*'s dory, and seized the lamebrained excuse to beg off, sopping wet. Most of all, he dreaded to see what his ill-advised search might discover.

Arithon's hot-tempered remark to Earl Jieret still retained its damnable accuracy. Too many factions wished the Shadow Master's death. The question became less the timed moment of his end, but which one of his enemies would snatch first opportunity to slaughter him.

A whistle signaled the change in the ship's watch. Dakar hugged his arms to his barrel chest, while the sere, desert breezes fingered the crimped screws of his sweat-runneled hair. He steadied plucked nerves. In trepidation and solitude, he centered his will, cast his thoughts still, and channeled the untrustworthy powers of his gift. His failure or success would support no observers, far less the discerning eyes of the prince whose confounding integrity had trapped him in friendship and loyalty.

Dakar held no illusions. He was no sorcerer, no grand power to toy with events. Kathtairr's vast emptiness diminished all that he was, left him puny as a dust speck afloat on dark waters as he narrowed his scattered awareness. He resisted the pull of a lifetime's rank cowardice and a sidestepping inclination to indulge in aimless woolgathering. Tonight, for the sake of Arithon's life, he opened the undisciplined aperture of his talent while the sweat of cold dread slid in drops down his temples and moistened his thatched ginger beard. The salt taste on his lips reminded of tears before the blameless, bitter kiss of the seaspray lately splashed by his inept hand at the oar.

Time passed. Dakar held on in obdurate stillness. His gift could be stubborn. Countless times, he had sat with no reward gained but the yowl of a belly pinched to hunger. Yet even as he prayed tonight's scrying would draw blankness, his mind sank into that cavernous silence that seemed etched through a void of black crystal. Forewarned by the first, creeping tingle in his gut that his awareness tipped over the edge, he shook to a drenching chill of apprehension. Then vertigo swooped down and hurled him headlong through an unraveling stream of wild prescience.

He saw pine trees, a bright shoreline where turquoise waters purled into spume, and there, Arithon s'Ffalenn on his knees in white sand, his black sword Alithiel drawn and upraised; and through the bone-hurting chord of grand harmony thrown off by the blade's spelled defenses, a unicorn poised in the rampant, first thrust of a charge aimed to gore him.

Dakar screamed aloud, earthly flesh unable to bear the beauty and the pain, *as the sword Alithiel flashed, then blazed through its star-captured peal of ward resonance. The Riathan Paravian dipped his silver-maned head, a scything horn set to reap*; and vision scattered . . .

Darkness rolled over him, unrelenting and bleak, stabbed through by the rippling, clean harmony of a lyranthe given voice by the hands of a master. Notes plucked out in Arithon's best style fell like sprays of dropped jewels, or sleet tapping brass, while decades slipped by in a drawn-out, mindless slow agony . . .

"No," Dakar whispered. He strove to reach out, hook the free-wheeling thread of his talent and bind it; but change ripped through him regardless . . .

He saw priests clad in vestments with sunwheel emblems, chanting litanies against the vile works of the dark.

"Ath show me mercy, no!" The Mad Prophet struggled, his yanked breath drawn too fast, lungs afire as if he had sprinted flat out with some ravening terror at his heels. "No." He grasped after trained strictures, clawed for the will to wrest back some semblance of control. The vision he wanted was one that Earl Jieret had dreamed . . .

He saw blinding summer sun, and the red, bloodied length of a sword laid across an altar spread in a gold-edged, white cloth.

The image jolted through him, almost slammed his heart still. Screaming now, the Mad Prophet reached anyway, tried to rip past his grief to back-trace the event to its source. But the blood was too fresh, too red, *too real*. In slowed motion, the vermilion drops soaked the white silk, ragged stains scribing an ending too vivid to escape. Dakar shied back, wrung helpless by dread, and the channel of his talent exploded through white sparks to static. His unsteady control crumbled after, like an unfired clay vessel dissolved on a tap to blown dust.

Sunwheel became sun, sinking red to a horizon of weather-stripped hills: Daon Ramon. Before the light palled into featureless night, he beheld a new city embedded in tangled black canes of old briar. Somewhere, somebody sobbed in the throes of a gut-wrenching agony . . .

His own voice, perhaps. Dakar had long since lost wits to tell. String after string of prescience reeled through him, a spate grown too fierce to divert by means of sane thought or strong discipline.

A city, sheeted in fire and burning; a child, dead in the dust.

135

Milled under and weeping, Dakar let go. The dream claimed his measure. His senses rushed on in the plummeting slide into the numb haven of escape. His last thought before unconsciousness drowned him was his desperate craving to get drunk.

Much later, there were stars. Dakar pieced together the awareness that he lay on his back with his eyes open. Returned senses imprinted an excruciating impression of harsh rock jabbed into limp flesh. The pain rushed back then, resolved itself into a skull-splitting headache, to which every nerve in his body responded in a sapping chorus of aches.

Nausea knifed through him. He needed to sit up, but lacked the vitality.

A shadow arrived at the edge of his vision. A touch breathless, the voice of a bard phrased an oath ripe enough to scale fish. Then hands left ice-cold from a plunge in the sea grasped his shoulders and hauled him erect.

That succor given just barely in time; the first, rending spasm failed to catch the Mad Prophet facedown. Grateful not to lie heaving in his own filth, he coughed, spat, shivered, groaned, and finally croaked the name of his rescuer. "Arithon?"

"Lie easy." When that instruction became impossible to carry out, the Master of Shadow held on until the Mad Prophet's stomach stopped churning.

Dakar sagged into the lean, steady arm that settled him back against the lumpy support of a boulder. "I could see nothing certain," he husked out, unwilling to sustain the unspoken query for one second longer than necessary. "Arithon, I'm sorry. You're too strongly fated. The futures involved are too powerful to sort. I have no sure course of counsel to offer. Every fragment called in poured through me as uncontrolled vision."

He rolled his head sidewards to interpret the other man's stillness; no need to repeat what events at the Havens and Vastmark had already proved in spilled blood. Any prescience he tapped in the form of ranging visions was subject to change with the pressures of shifting event.

Seconds passed, filled by the rush of white foam gnawing the bleak, stony shingle. With no word spoken, Arithon settled in the darkness, his shoulders braced to the same rock. No sailhand from the *Khetienn* accompanied him; he had swum from the anchorage rather than roust out the crew to sway out a longboat. The crossing left him drenched as a seal, and shirtless. Kathtairr's hazeless starlight sheened the flex of his fingers as he worked the cork from a wine crock, ferried ashore in one of the mesh nets young Feylind tied to catch shiners.

"Ath bless you," Dakar murmured as the welcome, earthy weight was passed into his hands, then guided through the arc to his mouth. He swallowed, eyes closed in relief. One slug, two, and the sour taste of sickness rinsed away. He savored restored taste, eased and mellowed by the sublime, tart bouquet of a rare vintage red from Orvandir.

A sigh unreeled through a throat skinned raw from mindless screaming. "Bless you again, for generosity. I thought you were saving that bottle for—" Dakar stopped, would have slapped his own forehead for stupidity, had he retained any strength.

The barren rocks of Kathtairr harbored no cause at all for celebration; he had known very well since the day four years past, when the brigantine had first weighed her anchor for Corith.

The prince who sat in iron quiet beside him seemed to have shed his rancor for that. Arithon reached, recaptured the wine, pulled a deep draft in turn. Starlight strung sparks through the phosphorescent runnels on his skin, and streaked premature silver through black hair as he swallowed. He seemed to think better of speech and, instead, restored the crock into Dakar's needful grasp.

The Mad Prophet drank deep to drown a lancing, sharp urge to weep. When he next looked, Arithon s'Ffalenn had clasped both his wrists with exquisite, fine-jointed hands, a habit he kept to mask the disfiguring marks of old scars.

Dakar shivered. The hour had grown late. Kathtairr's harsh terrain had traded the day's heat for the keening, cold winds off the interior. But the gusts which sluiced over his sweat-dampened clothes scarcely touched him, aware as he was of the deeper chill. With his mind still awash in the harrowing images just snatched from the uncertain future, words slipped his grasp before thought. "How can you bear this, year after year? How can you live, self-aware as you are, of the fate that hangs on your choices?"

"I wouldn't," Arithon admitted. His skin pricked into sudden gooseflesh. His thumb traced the thin line healed crosswise overtop of the weals once chafed by iron fetters. The gesture arose from unpleasant recollection of his blood oath, irrevocably given to hold him to life by every means at his command. The terrible vow had been sworn to Asandir just after the destruction of Lysaer's fleet at Minderl Bay.

Sensitive now to the one burning question Dakar had never dared ask, Arithon offered his confidence. "You wonder how the Fellowship Sorcerers won my consent to that binding." A brief pause, while the stars burned in chill unconcern. "I was told the world might not live if I surrendered the struggle in death." Rathain's prince tipped his dark crown to rest against striated rocks that sprouted no kindly lacework of lichen. The steep planes of his face might have been sculpted alabaster, except for the small, tensioned wrinkles which nipped at the corners of his eyes. "I saw that I couldn't trust myself, Dakar. Not once I heard what was left on the gate world of Marak."

"Marak!" The Mad Prophet shot straight to a gurgle of sloshed protest from the wine. "Ath, Marak! A crisis on a link world across South Gate. Of course! What else but the severed body of the Mist-wraith could frighten the Fellowship dizzy? Dharkaron avenge! The Sorcerers bound you for that?"

"You need not upset yourself." Arithon's disarming, peaceful tone but reminded that he owned a masterbard's tongue. Dissembling cleverness was his second nature. Dakar knew too much not to guess at the pain, and beyond that, to forgiveness that was genuine, as the Shadow Master finished, "If the Fellowship Sorcerers sought to divert me to Kathtairr, they will have had urgent reason."

"They've been building wards. I've seen them in dreams when the powers crest on the solstices." Dakar found his palms sweating on cold crockery. He required a single-minded and desperate care not to fumble as he tipped the bottle to his lips. "The bindings they weave are unimaginably vast. As if the Sorcerers strive to stave off the advent of their own defeat."

Arithon replied after a short silence, his fingers knuckled white to his wrists. "We have to find the Paravians, Dakar. For all of our sake, they offer the only sane hope of reprieve."

Those half-glimpsed fragments of augury could bite too viciously, after all. Dakar choked back misery, hating the savage sting that inevitably arose to sour the fruits of his gift. He sucked down wine in one guzzling burst, too racked to set voice to the irony, *that he had indeed seen a unicorn in his vision, and read death for Rathain's prince in the same moment.* Life held no sureties. His talent for prescience was more fickle than a courtesan. One storm in the path of the *Khetienn's* charted course, and that goring on the beach might never come to see daylight.

A gust whipped the chisel-sharp summits of stone. Hazed by the sting of airborne sand, Dakar wiped tearing eyes. He tipped the bottle again, and cursed when it ran empty. The wine had left him stranded far short of the drunken oblivion he wished for.

The torment on his moon-round face must not, after all, have been due to the grit, since Arithon said in that level compassion that always sliced straight to the quick, "Let's get you back. There's more wine on the brigantine, and just as well. If I'm going to get in my cups along with you, it's better done after I've launched and rowed your dory from the strand."

Dakar shut his eyes, beholden beyond utterance. Quick temper and subterfuge aside, the Master of Shadow could be trusted to keep the most damnable letter of his word.

Shepherded back aboard the *Khetienn* and installed under blankets in the stern cabin, the Mad Prophet was plied with shared wine and sympathy until his maudlin mood gave way to exhaustion. By the hour he passed out, Arithon had not forsaken sobriety, though dawn blushed the sky to the east. The last crock stood drained to the lees. Dakar snored in a muddled heap with his cheek pressed flat to the chart desk. Arithon s'Ffalenn tucked the blanket over his slumped shoulder, then returned to the quarterdeck, and shouted crisp orders to roust out the watch. "Stand by to make sail!"

As the sun sliced the rim of the horizon, his seamen turned the capstan to clacking life and raised anchor. Sailhands clambered at speed up tarred ratlines, then lay aloft to slip gaskets.

"Clear away the flying jib! Loose and let fall topsails and main course! Man halyards, sheets, and weather braces! Out spanker! Sheet home!"

Canvas the color of old blood slithered free and cracked taut, and the *Khetienn* gathered way, bound back to old risks on the continent.

Athera's sea winds changed with the advent of autumn, blew in hard, veering gusts, northwesterly, then due north under skies raked in cirrus as the days shortened. Bowled ahead with the wind on her quarter, then abeam, the *Khetienn* logged off the leagues, her exhilarating passage made under cascading sheets of spray. The crew kept light spirits, shearing fast course for known waters. Dakar stayed alone in trepidation. Given his most drunken spree of imagination, he could never have foreseen the uncoiling speed with which planning gave birth to event.

Landfall at Corith occurred after dark, a ghosting, windward approach made on spanker, staysails, and jibs. A coin silver moon threw the archipelago's notched summits into chipped coal relief. Tension gripped the deckhands. Drugged by the scent of bearing land and live earth after month upon month of salt winds and Kathtairr's seared rock, the off-watch crew crowded the foredeck. What

scraps of dialogue wafted astern detailed their eagerness to escape an endless diet of salt pork and beans, and hardtack infested with weevils.

"Don't let me see another ration o' fish soup with the pepper stores gone," groused another, eyes rolled furtively over his shoulder to be sure the cook's ear was turned elsewhere.

Still as a wraith at the quarterdeck rail, Arithon s'Ffalenn held a ship's glass trained on the bulking dark shoreline. His close, raking survey scoured the unfolding jut of the headland, nicked like a tarnished engraving with the unraveling foam of spent breakers.

Dakar, given mage-sight, required no glass to see that the harbor at Corith was not empty.

"Daelion's arse," he swore in a gust of ill feeling. "Damn Lysaer's industry, those are masts! Wear ship! We're pointed straight into an ambush."

Arithon snapped the glass closed on a smile of silken patience.

Too sharply aware of smothered chuckles from the quartermaster, Dakar reinterpreted the Shadow Master's quiet with an unholy surge of disbelief.

"You didn't smell the breeze?" Arithon laughed, the predatory flash of his teeth all the more vivid by moonlight. "I doubt we're in danger of attack from that brig. She doesn't bear a fighting company scrambling to span arbalests. Just a hold crammed with casks shipped in from the orchards of Korias."

"Apples." A mystified frown puckered Dakar's forehead. He shoved back the rumpled screw of hair that the wind flicked back in his eyes. "Why apples?"

A whispered dance of bare footfalls, Feylind arrived aft to claim her place at the Shadow Master's side. His equal for height, and grown into a saucy, long-legged, eighteen, she snatched the closed ship's glass from his hand. The roped braid slid off her shoulder to lick her small breast as she deployed the brass segments. She raked piercing study in turn over the vessel limned dark against needle-worked reflections cast by a low-riding moon.

"Dharkaron's hairy bollocks!" She gave a clear whistle. "The varnish still shines on her figurehead's tits. It's a mermaid, and look!" Fired outrage snapped through. "The ship's carvers at Riverton are a raunchy band of goats. Bedamned if her nipples aren't gilded!"

"Don't lose our heading," gasped Arithon to the quartermaster, who had folded his grizzled face into his elbow to stifle an inopportune smirk of humor.

"Riverton!" Dakar howled in unadulterated fury. "Save us all, you

move fast! If that's Lysaer's vessel, you've had to be conniving at piracy for years! Why am I always the *last* one to hear what's afoot?"

But the Shadow Master was himself left no standing to answer. Unable to follow his own sage advice, he lay curled in snorting mirth against the brightwork of the rail, while Feylind pummeled his shoulder with her fist for the fact he took her offended sex lightly.

He had to shield his head with crossed wrists as she changed tactics and lunged to attack with the ship's glass. "Woman, desist! I'm bludgeoned half-silly and left unfit for command. You'll have to lay the *Khetienn*'s course in yourself. If you ram her on a reef, working in without lanterns, believe it, I'll dock her repairs from your dowry."

"Keep my dowry for gravecloths, I've no wish to marry." Feylind flicked back her braid, the tanned arm with the glass still upraised like a cudgel. "You'd let me strike sail?"

"Under threat of getting my skull cracked, yes." Arithon straightened, disheveled and smiling. "You'll see to ranging the cable and let go the anchor as well. Now be off!"

Feylind yelled for joy, hurled the ship's glass straight for his face, a challenge for even his thoughtless, fast reflex, and spun away to claim the wheel to steer the brigantine in.

"Ath," Dakar made cautious comment from the sidelines. "Take more bribe than gold to find a willing husband for that minx."

"I heard that, you sorry, fat windbag!" shrilled Feylind. Her crisp order to stand by sent the deckhands scrambling to man brails and halyards.

"Don't worry," said Arithon in that thoughtful, grave manner that unfailingly masked seamless subterfuge. "You won't have to guard against finding black hellebore in your beer. The *Khetienn*'s past due for careening, and the moment the sail rig and paint can be hastened through a refit on that brig, Feylind will serve as her navigator to Innish to pay her brother an extended visit."

"You think I should be pleased with the arrangement?" Dakar said. Strong purgatives in his drink seemed a piddling, small nuisance against the chance to roll doxies and breathe citrus perfume in the sun-warmed brothels of Shand.

"What are your prospects?" asked Arithon by way of evasive reply. "Did you really want to stay and play hermit for the winter hunting wild deer on these islands?"

Dakar had two short days to wonder and brood, while the *Khetienn*'s trained crew split forces. They carried out whirlwind arrangements to send their mismatched fleet of two back to sea, and sailed under straightforward orders to raise funds by selling their service in honest charter to merchants. Feylind might swagger and whoop as she claimed her new post, but the Mad Prophet held no illusions.

If the Master of Shadow wished the girl sent away, then danger would dog his next passage. The risk to the ships in his charge might be less, but their pursuit would not stay innocuous.

The course of suspect events started off with an unkindly, rough crossing to the mainland aboard Arithon's tiny pleasure sloop. She made landfall amid the deep coves of Caithwood, under low, leaden clouds and driving rain. A discreet whistled signal drew clansmen to meet her. In silent efficiency, the band of scouts saw her warped into an inlet, and covered in brush and deep cover. An icy drizzle misted the flame red of changed maples. Dakar shivered in the chill, then endured a dank evening in a cave lit by a smoking oil wick, while Arithon's reading of dispatches led to a terse exchange of news.

Swathed like a sausage in his salt-fusty clothing, Dakar bludgeoned through fogged wits to listen.

A grizzled forest captain with an eye patch sat tying new fletching on his hunting arrows. "Can't offer better than deer jerky. Fires are too risky for cooking, with new patrols off the roads out of Quarn."

Arithon's reply came measured, all but inaudible over the trickle of moisture off the evergreen thicket outside. "They've gotten that sharp?"

A grunt gave him answer, while the clansman split a goose quill with his belt knife. "Tracker's a gift from a demon." With the bounties doubled for live capture, muster for headhunters had tripled. "They're crown funded, too. Much better outfitted." A lengthy squint down an arrow shaft, to ascertain the new feather would steer true, then the tart summary, made over the winding of waxed string. "It's an offense against nature, but we've had to set traps for the dogs."

Amid the back-and-forth round of discussion, Dakar fought ebbing attention, jerked out of a doze more than once by grim details of shore patrols and galleymen, and a stockade built to hold slaves inside city walls at Hanshire. His eyes closed at length. Time must have escaped him, because he looked up and saw Arithon had changed out of sailhand's garb.

Reclad in a laced set of riding leathers of sable, and a wool tunic trimmed in dark scarlet, the Shadow Master tipped a sheet of reed paper above the streaming brown fumes off the oil wick. In his hands, what looked like a laborer's tally sheet changed form. Invisibly inked lines first written in lemon juice burned to reveal a message in fugitive script. He read, while the words glowed sienna between the callused, sea tan of his fingers. "Princess Talith confined? *For vapors, due to barrenness, and delicate health?* I don't believe it!"

The clansman gathered his finished arrows, licked a finger, and bundled them with a deerhide thong. "Hearsay. But word from clan sources shows the same. The princess hasn't been seen in public for three years. When Lysaer assembled the train for his journey, our scouts on the west road were sure that no pedigree lady traveled with him."

"Lysaer's left Avenor?" Dakar interjected, snapped erect and belatedly alert.

Arithon threw him an exasperated glance. "You were snoring through that part. But yes." He tapped the report in Mearn s'Brydion's frenetic script, now flattened across his left knee. "Lysaer's taken the road to Etarra to ply his honey tongue in diplomacy. Toss a pinch of salt, sinister, for sheer luck. There's an unguarded henyard left for us foxes once again."

"Scarcely that." All at once too aware of the cold, Dakar hooked up his dropped blanket and snugged the disagreeable scrape of wool under his chin. "I wasn't asleep for that bit about the herb witch who got stoned in Quarn. Or the part about Avenor's troop rolls being tripled in number since Vastmark. Nor would I lay any coin on dim odds, that our spirits stay clear of the Fatemaster's Wheel if you make fires on the snake's home ground."

"Our home ground, too," the clansman retorted. "*Caithdein*, Lord Maenol, has stayed his blood grievance four years preparing for this day."

Arithon broke in, "Then the wait for my timing hasn't chafed?"

"It has, and unbearably." A shrug, then the bald-faced admission, "There were prideful hotheads who railed against your liaison. Only one was given my lord's leave to pursue vengeance. That man had a just cause. He'd just lost his sons in a coffle bound for Lysaer's galleys."

Dakar knew better than to waste futile argument with any party joined to Arithon in conspiracy. He shut his lips and his eyes, while the talk wound down. But sleep left him stranded in weariness. The awful, circling dread of bad prospects harried his mind beyond rest. He kept no illusions in his service to Rathain's prince. Three years of suffering tasteless ship's rations and battering ocean gales now seemed a time of seclusion in paradise. Not least, when the winter ahead promised criminal machinations under the armed nose of Tysan's elite royal garrison.

Morning broke cold and clear as the shell of a robin's egg. Dakar crept from the furling layers of his cloaks like a grub from a collapsed cocoon. His predawn hours of restless tossing had given way to an inadequate, heavy sleep. His mind felt logy and thick. The chirping twitters of foraging sparrows drilled his ears like the stab of tinker's pins to the brain. Frost traced the leaves at the cave mouth. Dakar bemoaned the lack of any fire as he dressed, and wished for cheese instead of hardtack and jerky to appease his growling belly.

He sat for some time, head propped between his hands, before he noticed the voices outside, raised in ongoing contention.

"You should be with your earl," Arithon said, a snap to his tone to scale iron.

Dakar thrashed through the intervening curtain of brush and peered, his nearsighted squint like a mole emerged from its burrow. Amid dazzling shafts of early sunshine, he made out the discreet band of clansmen from Caithwood who guested them. Their scout captain stood near, his eye patch raked low, and the reins of two saddled horses looped in each hand. Beyond their maned necks, past the steaming back of a third horse which drooped its head from hard usage, another man stood dismounted. The newcomer was built broad, an obstinate thrust to his massive, squared shoulders. His head wore its cropped hair like filed steel, bristled to cowlicks at the crown. Born ornery, or else given to brainless bravery, he confronted the slightly made Prince of Rathain, feet planted like a balked mastiff's.

"Caolle?" Dakar called in disbelief.

Neither combatant glanced his way.

"Here I stay, liege," carped the northern-born clansman who had resigned his life's post as Earl Jieret's war captain. "My sword guards your back. Live with that gift or behead me for treason."

Dakar missed Arithon's gloved velvet reply. Whatever the content, the sally made the rugged, older swordsman flush crimson.

"So just damn the day of your birth, while you're at it!" Caolle cracked back. "Since you refused the good grace to die on delivery, Rathain has got a living prince." Immovable oak when charged with his duty, he hurled his next line like a gauntlet. "I serve the kingdom. Since you plan to hang yourself out in Tysan as bait, you'll have me along for the sacrifice."

The Mad Prophet shoved through the thicket in clawing dread. He closed the last steps to an obliterating crackle of dry leaves, too late again to catch Arithon's riposte. Caolle maintained his stance, reduced to contentious, stiff silence. His eyes were red rimmed, as if he had ridden all night through rough country, and a disfiguring, fresh scar crossed his jawline that had not been there in Vastmark.

Those weathered, blunt features that had not changed at all wore a frown like black basalt, and the hand closed upon the sheathed hilt of his sword could have been etched into place.

"You might try a smile of welcome, your Grace," Dakar bored in, well aware how the title would rankle. He pressed brashly on, came between the too-careful expression of blandness that Arithon presented toward his liegeman. "Ice could be turned into sunshine on a wish before you'll talk Caolle home to Strakewood. He's by lengths more stubborn than you are, and besides, this time he happens to be right."

"Say that again to my face, should Jieret's young son lose his father to a slave galley," Arithon ripped back in blank rage. "By my oath as Rathain's crown prince, if that day happens, I'll see you both bleeding and dead for it." All smoldering grace, he spun away, caught the reins of the nearest horse Caithwood's clansmen held ready, then vaulted astride without pause to measure his stirrup length. "For today, keep up if you can."

No more words, and no thanks did he offer his clan hosts, but closed his heels and shouted and startled his mount standing to a canter.

Caolle surged to remount his blown gray.

Dakar grabbed, first the reins, then the wrist of the clansman's right hand. "No. You'll founder a good horse, and for nothing. We'll get you a remount and breakfast, too, if you're hungry."

"Damn breakfast!" Caolle swore.

The Mad Prophet held on, well aware he risked a sword thrust if his grip should give way. Fat, but not gutlessly soft as he had been, he still felt as if he shouldered the part of the numbskull who grasped a bear by the leg at a baiting.

"Curse you, let go!" Caolle dropped his shoulder to battle in earnest, his desperation made vicious by fast-departing hoofbeats as his prince widened his lead through the forest.

The Mad Prophet clung. Despite tendons set on fire by his charge's effort to wrench free, he said, "Don't be a donkey!" Bashed backward, fetched a punch that rattled his brains and left him too jellied to duck the fighter's move set to fell him, he gasped out, "Caolle, have done! I know where Arithon's bound."

Kicked hard behind the knee, Dakar hit cold moss on his back. The jolt robbed his wind. He tasted fresh blood; had ridiculously bitten his tongue for the damnfool belief he could wring reason from the selfsame rock-headed clansman who had raised young Jieret to manhood.

"I'm listening," Caolle prompted, not yet softened, but towering against a sky embroidered with evergreen. He waited in searing impatience, arms folded on his cross-belted chest.

Dakar wheezed, rolled back brown eyes, and let his spinning head thump against a tree root.

"No use," said Caithwood's mustached chief scout where he observed from the sidelines, still holding the horse saddled for the Mad Prophet. "He's down like a clubbed trout." Then, laughing at Caolle's knotted pose of frustration, he stepped in and slapped the victim's cheek with long-suffering familiarity. "Don't worry, prophet. Rathain's henchman can't go 'til we've found him a mount, and none of my scouts are flat stupid. No one in camp's going to waste himself trying to force you to ride without breakfast."

Four days later, in the crowded, grease-pungent taproom of a bargeman's hostel built by the ford over Ilswater, a fat man dressed as a tinker shrugged off the saddle packs slung across his shoulder. He scanned the scattered assortment of patrons seated at trestles and lounging in talk against the upright posts which supported the roof trusses. The light blocked off from the casements in the press was replaced by candle lanterns set behind glass. Their panes had been cleaned of soot, and faces underneath glowed like lit parchment.

The tinker studied them all. His traveler's wise eye marked the dusty boots and badges of the ox drovers; then the barge captains, with their booming, boastful voices and broad hands; and after them, the lean-bodied caravan masters in oiled wool and leather. His survey brushed past the merchant's factors draped in cerecloth capes to protect their brocade clothes as they bargained passage for trade goods by the water route across Korias to Riverton.

The tinker's brown eyes touched, then fixed upon a slim man by the hob who had hair like bleached flax, quick eyes of a heathery gray-green, and whose clothing was embroidered and garnished with river pearls. Two tavernmaids fluttered over him like moths. He gave no appearance of leading them on, but his sweet words and kind manner left them desperate in their wish that he had.

A smile twitched the tinker's tucked lips. He raised a wrist to scratch his snub nose, and behind cover of his sleeve whispered, "That one."

Across the dim room, the ranked trestles and packed benches, and the brimmed felt hats of the bargemen, through the autumn tang of cinnamon and cider, the fair-haired dandy said something which set the girls laughing.

146

"No." A hulking, thick shadow against paneled walls, the tinker's companion raised eyebrows like the grizzled pelt of a badger. Half of his leathery face lay swathed in bandages that seeped pus from a suppurating wound. Black gimlet eyes flicked aside and gleamed back in hot disbelief. Then a dubious mumble emerged from beneath the caked dressing.

"Oh, that's him, make no mistake," the tinker insisted under cover of metallic commotion as a chubby scullion stacked empty tankards on a tray. "He kept fancy clothes aboard the sloop with his lyranthe."

More indeterminate grumbles from beneath the bandages, from which the word "wager" emerged clearly.

The fat tinker cracked a chuckle that turned nearby heads, but notably, not that of the blond man. "So we'll see." He shoved his packs into the arms of his rawboned companion. "Find us a bench in a corner and wait. I'll order beer and pay a visit to the privy. My silver laid on eight to three, the first one who follows me out will be none other than your royal liege."

Riverfront taverns in south Tysan were all similar, built of mud brick and split pine beams and lath. The hearths were always large enough to roast a calf, and the bar tops, a vast slab of fieldstone like a bastion, behind which the barrels were stored and kept guarded by landlords as seasoned as siege captains. On a meat hook behind hung the inevitable cleaver, kept sharp to carve the huge wheels of cheese bought from the dairies in Korias. In rough seasons, the same steel might chop fingers from unlucky pilferers, to mark them for thieving ways. Customs along the river route south of Mogg's fenlands were swift and direct, only generous if a man were honest in his habits, or straightforward about his need in ill fortune.

The tinker was soft-spoken and carefully polite. He jostled no patrons, nor pinched the flame-haired wench who bent to shake out the straw matting by the back entry. He offered her a copper, asked directions to the privy, and stepped out the rear door, whistling.

The path he pursued was well beaten, dusty under the glazed gold sun of late autumn. Leaves burned brown at the edges by frost crackled beneath his slowed step. A breeze blew crisp off the Ilswater, skeined in the scents of wet reeds and black mud, stitched close at hand by the taint of sour leather and urine from the mucky compound of the ox pens. From downriver, a drover called encouragement to his team. A barge rocked at the landing bollards to a whispered creak of chafed lines.

Flecked in the rippled ink shadows of the alders already stripped by the season, the tinker reached the board privy. He heard no one's

147

step on his heels. Just the uncanny sensation of movement at his back, a split second before hard fingers bit into his shoulder and jerked him face about.

The blond man from the hearthside confronted him, his fine, beaded doublet masked under a bargeman's caped wool. "Come," he said in the razor-cut diction of Arithon s'Ffalenn. "We need to take a little walk."

The pair turned right, into the dappled shade of the wood which fronted the river, then veered again, into pine-scented dimness removed from the bustle of the teamsters who plied the towpath.

"That took a great deal of nerve, risking Caolle in there," Arithon opened. "You'll answer to me if harm comes to him."

The fat tinker drew a breath in trepidation better suited to his role as a prophet. "I won't take that blame. You might have accepted his offer in Caithwood."

Arithon stopped cold and clawed back the straw wisp of hair the busy wind flicked at his cheek. "You're risking his life!"

"He's risking his life," Dakar corrected. "I'm flattered if you think my efforts could stop him."

Looking frail boned in his pale-haired disguise, half-swallowed by the bargeman's cloak, Arithon started forward with a visible effort to keep a tight rein on his temper. "We could be quartered in Riverton for months." His bard's instinct for sound seemed to guide his footing. His step fell almost noiseless through the race of loose leaves in the gusts. He went on, "A winding or two of ill-smelling bandage can't hide a clan accent from headhunters!"

"Bandages won't, but a glamour can," Dakar argued. "I can work the small bindings to make the scar on Caolle's jaw seem far worse than it is. He'll wear the semblance of an injury to disfigure speech. In a port town with sailhand's dives, who would bother to look for a spell to bend air? No one will trouble at all. His halting tongue will just seem too garbled for anyone but his friends to understand."

"Ath, Dakar!" Arithon stopped again, one hand pressed to his face. At long last the misery showed through. "He's Earl Jieret's man, and the only foster kin that boy ever had to replace his slaughtered family."

The Mad Prophet spun away, perhaps to lend the pretense of privacy for old grief. Even as the edge returned to Arithon's control, he was unable to meet the appeal in the blank, masking gray of those eyes. Nor was he insensitive enough to try platitudes, or argue that Jieret was now a grown man and father to an heir in his own right. Not when the Earl of the North had been orphaned in one of Arithon's former campaigns.

The loyalties demanded by the ghosts from that past were by far too deep and painful.

"You won't win this one, old friend," Dakar said at last in gruff sympathy. He turned around in the mat of dead pine needles, ducked a low-hanging branch, and forged the way back toward the tavern. "That's Caolle's clan heritage you need purloined ships to try and save. Nor can you shirk all the trappings of your birth or cast off your most sensible liegemen. Some will live and others come to die in the course of your service. That's their picked fate. Yours is to bear it, until the day comes that the Fellowship Sorcerers grant you their lawful leave to abdicate."

That stunned through the force of past sorrows. Arithon s'Ffalenn looked back from his shadow-wrought disguise, his eyes for a second reverted to their native, blazing green. "Then we're stymied." He smiled in that baiting, bright malice he used to divert stinging words. "A match brought to draw, since the end play can't happen unless I sire an heir for Rathain. *You should all leave me.*"

Dakar chose to ignore that. "I presume you'll be going into Riverton as a bard? Well, you've just acquired two servants. You might want to add some gray hair to fill out the part, since as the fair gallant, you'll draw the wrong sort of notice traveling with a doting male retinue."

Design

The Koriani orphanage in Capewell was housed in the refurbished shell of a merchant's palace, a five-storied edifice of extravagant fancy that loomed over the harborside market. Stevedores' calls and the dickering insults of house matrons never troubled its residents. High marble walls enclosed its stables and inner courtyards. Carved with weathered nymphs and the moss-caked cavities of scrolled waves, the scullery entrance fronted a sun-washed courtyard. A row of gnarled pear trees in tubs were all that remained of the formal herb gardens famed far and wide in past centuries. The branches lay stripped now, blackened skeletons shivering in the veering toss of the gusts off Mainmere Bay.

Hatched in their spiderweb shadows, Morriel Prime chafed porcelain stick fingers to encourage her poor circulation.

The days, the years, blended one into another. She wished she could scream for the frustrating labor of discerning one from the next, present from past; the jetsam of old memories become all but indistinguishable from posited future event. If the gardens where she sat this autumn morning had outworn their elegance through change, the routine obligations of the Koriani Order stayed tediously static. Each daybreak came, seamless in sameness as the metallic sheen of pooled mercury.

On Morriel's right, from the close little chamber that once served the merchant as countinghouse, speech droned through the opened window. In muddled accents, a pouch-eyed little cobbler swore the order's oath of obligation in exchange for a sigil of blessing for his craftshop. A fresh-faced girl novice would duly enter his name on the Lists of Service against the day when Koriani need would ask payment in boots or shoes, or some other piece of skilled leatherwork.

The ritual was timeworn as the order's inception. Excepting the small sales of simples and remedies too onerously numerous for record, enchantresses took no coin for the spellcraft they rendered in service. With no wealth to gain, their practicing code of mercy remained difficult for greed to corrupt.

Morriel loosed a shallow, bored sigh. Entrenched tradition blended, not just days or seasons, but caused years themselves to meld together, memories rubbed smooth by repetition until none stood out from another. She endured the monotony. Moment to moment, she carried on with the tenacity of a lichen latched to north-facing rock. This morning's task of selecting new page boys for her personal service had recurred so many times, she had ceased to number or name them.

The children seemed one long stream through time, as similar as pebbles in a brook. Unblinking, her obsidian eyes surveyed the dozen odd choices. They stood in a row with their fair hair combed, and clothing brushed formally straight. In age, they ranged from eight to ten.

Some always cringed from the Prime Matriarch's review. Two stared at their feet. The inevitable coward sniffled and shook, while another near the line's end presented tearful, flushed cheeks in defiant and terrified silence.

Morriel made her selection on a scant second's thought. "That one, and that one." The pair marked apart by her stabbing gesture were close matched in height, and possessed of a china-doll innocence. "Show the others away."

"Your will, matriarch." A matronly enchantress bustled from the archway behind. She comforted those children returned to her charge, then bundled them off to the kitchen with a promise of apple tarts and milk.

The Prime surveyed her latest acquisitions with a vulture's unwinking regard. The near boy watched her back, trapped in awe and macabre fear, as if her withered limbs in their draping purple velvet belonged to a corpse, or some nightmare work of carved calcite. The other child stood frozen with a dripping nose and a chin puckered red in failed effort to dam back his tears.

"You will serve as my page boys until you reach twelve years of age," Morriel informed, not unkindly, but rasped thin as steel set too long to the grindstone. "The work I ask will be light. Do well, and on your day of dismissal, an apprenticeship will be found with a reputable trade which suits your inclinations."

"Yes, matriarch," whispered the boldest of the boys.

The withered twitch of a smile turned a corner of the crone's lips. "How fine, you have manners, boy. Bravery, too. When you are a man abroad in the world, those virtues will be appreciated. My needs here are simpler. Please recall, when I come to address you, I prefer you say nothing at all."

The tearful child whimpered. The forward one shrank in uncertainty from the sting of her mild disapproval. Morriel offered the boys no false reassurance. They would do best to fear her, that the friends and associates they made in maturity should share due respect for her office. Like white-painted iron in the brine-scented winds that keened off the waves of the bay, she also withheld her dismissal. Her eyes fixed ahead like sheared chips of slag, and her hands were unmoving marble.

The rift happened then, without any warning at all.

In one seamless second, she no longer inhabited the chilly autumn courtyard in Capewell. Ten centuries blurred; the friable webs of perception unraveled. The green fields of her village childhood resurged and wrapped her in sun and the fragrant, honeyed heat of summer haze. The boys who rolled tussling and yelling amid the new-sprouted barley were her dark-haired, dark-eyed little brothers. Sprites who clung to her ruffled skirts while she simmered berries into preserves; who brought her their skinned knees and elbows to be nursed; who secreted live beetles inside her jars of dried rose petals.

She loved them like an addiction.

When her talent came on too strong to deny at sixteen, her parents had sent off the young plowman who sued for her handfasting. Deaf to her pleas and her stormy bouts of rage, they sent her dowry to the Koriani Order and pledged her to lifelong service. The boys became the tie that broke her heart. Scene followed scene as she suffered for their loss, huddled under blankets in the echoing, vaulted stone of the dormitory. She wept for her brothers, while merchants' daughters from Cildorn bemoaned their lost gowns and jewels, and sly-faced craftgirls from Narms vied to take illicit lovers before the day they came to swear vows, and seal themselves forever to the celibate ways of an initiate enchantress.

Then the years, passing, and the demands of strict learning claimed all their youthful rebellion. Study of crystals, then endless practice with the sigils of power erased their differences of station. Girls became women, at one with the Koriani Order, and few thoughts remained of the families abandoned in childhood.

The regrets which survived were the strong ones. Even after a thousand years, Morriel Prime would not suffer her pages to resemble the brothers who had grown and gone on to mortal death. No one alive remembered their faces; how they had fared, or where they had breathed their last. If they sired descendants, those too were vanished into forgotten obscurity. The folk who had known them were generations lost; their near kin gone to crumbled dust.

"Prime Matriarch?" A soft voice, then a tentative touch to her shoulder drilled her thought like electrified pain.

Morriel started. Her senses upset, awash in blind static. The moment became nightmare as she fought to reorient. Buffeted by the incongruous, fishy tang of winds blown off of salt water, she knew blank confusion more vast than the infinite dark beyond the veil. Then eyesight returned with a burning, sharp rush. Two robed seniors waited to one side. Their inquiring, smooth faces should have been known to her. Yet her memory would yield up no names; their identities blurred into thousands of others, until rank and personality failed to take on any semblance of importance.

The panic hit then, a slippery, dark wall too sheer for trained calm or reason. Fear yawned before her, that she might never recover her sense of time and place. Morriel shut translucent, webbed eyelids. She willed her breath steady while the trip-hammer pound of her heart threatened to burst through the walls of her chest. Years of forced discipline let her clasp the quartz pendant at her throat. The focusing properties of its matrix should let her grope out the right thread of recent memory.

But that remedy failed her. Sharp, questing thought slid past her guard and mired in the stone's composite layers of stored imprints.

She had outlived her time. The crystal she wielded held a thousand years of memory, too long a span for a reactive mineral to stay in unbroken contact with breathing flesh. Past due for cleansing, any stone's burdened matrix would develop an ornery character.

Its obstructive nature mocked her now, as if to expose her rank weakness. She regained no connection to the facts she required, but fell into the deluge of residual memories left behind by former primes: the disparate, echoed fragments of bygone personalities, strained at random from her use of the Great Waystone.

Morriel choked back a scream, beat down the visceral terror, that her last recollection of her name and identity might be mazed into the stewed thoughts of dead predecessors.

That instant, like a pane of snapped glass, the disorientation cleared away. As if the cogs of her mind had never once slipped, Morriel recognized the swept, white stone of the courtyard at Capewell's orphanage. Against mortised coping and soft, southern marble polished by weathering rains, two small boys stood before her in terrified obedience, shivering in the north wind.

Though they must learn in due time to wait on her needs, today's lesson was unduly harsh; Morriel blinked lightless, jet eyes, chilled herself, and uneasy. If age had eroded her grip on self-command, she had small choice but behave as if no lapse had upset her sound judgment. "Have my new pages taken to the seamstress to be fitted for proper livery."

"Your will, matriarch." The younger initiate shouldered the task, though the bands on her robes marked a rank far above petty errands.

The middle-aged enchantress stayed silent in respect while the courtyard was cleared of small boys.

Morriel refused any moment to compose herself. The dread could take root like moss in dim corners, that a second slip might overwhelm her. Until Lirenda was fully trained to replace her, she must permit no breach of faith in her competence. "You bring news?" she prompted, then gestured her formal leave to speak.

The enchantress gave proper obeisance, and said, "Matriarch, our clairvoyant received word from the lane-watcher stationed in Tideport. She wished you informed that Arithon of Rathain has made his return to the continent."

Morriel's interest took fire. "In Tysan? I thought so!" She wheezed through a gravelly laugh. "Very well! The hour has come to start forcing the Fellowship's hand." A snake's eye glitter of diamond pins loured from under her hood as she delivered imperious instructions. "I'll require a closed audience with your most gifted clairvoyant. She will send my instructions through the lane-watchers. Afterward, summon your two newest initiates and direct them to attend me in the observatory. Once I have admitted them, let no one interrupt or unseal the chamber until I emerge or give leave."

The enchantress in attendance showed surprise. Such obvious steps to undertake a grand conjury would not usually proceed without steps to inform the First Senior of momentous events. "You don't wish a messenger sent on to Lirenda at Valenford?"

"How dare you ever think to question my rule!" Morriel cut back in distemper.

"I bow to your will, matriarch." The initiate took chastened leave, the displeasure of her Prime like the stab of an auger at her back.

The observatory built into the Koriani sisterhouse at Capewell was an edifice evolved through the contrary styles of seven centuries. The

154

dainty, five-sided bronze cupola and the fancifully shuttered casements which overlooked the town's roof peaks were the latecoming
ornaments of folly. Mossy stone walls and the flint sills of old revetments bespoke grimmer beginnings as a watchtower. From its original vantage, merchants had counted inbound ships at the quay. The
stone had been reset with arrow slits later, when townsmen fortified
against vengeance-bent clansmen through the unsettled years of the
uprising. The observatory built on when the keep was roofed over
now served as a chamber consecrated for fine magic.

The inside air had gone musty since the pierced shutters were
darkened with sheets of tarnished silver. Candles of incense-soaked
wax fluttered on the shelves of the sills. The inviting, cushioned
benches that once lined the walls were reframed as cupboards with
bronze hinges. Door fronts and portals had all been replaced with
unpainted oak panels, cut green, dried in fire, then inset with the
knotty, counterlooped copper of a thousand runes of ward. Each latch
had been painstakingly welded, then sealed by tin sigils with guard
spells to deflect any outside prying. The old, timbered floors were
flagged over in black slate, unpolished to accept the scribed traceries
and seals of forced power.

There, an emaciated predator poised over a webwork of ciphers,
Morriel Prime crouched with a sliver of chalk in her hand. If the construct she patterned against the Fellowship's constraints showed a
calculated, terrifying complexity, its driving plot was most simple:
since the Sorcerers placed undue value on Prince Arithon's life, he
was himself made the key to arrange their coercion.

Capture the Master of Shadow as a pawn, and for fear of the threat
lying latent upon Marak, the Seven must bow to Koriani demand.
Better than most, Sethvir must own up to the stakes: Morriel would
seize upon any provocation to see the Teir's'Ffalenn dead. Indeed, the
Prime deeply preferred to end his misspent royal life to forestall the
prophesied threat to her succession.

Between each tormented step of her labor, the withered, old Matriarch cursed the crux that bred such necessity. With spiteful care, she
etched chain after chain of linked ciphers in her wretched, crabbed
script. Here and there, as line crossed line, or a finishing sigil raised
latent energies, a sulfurous light flared from the contact. Shed glare
lined her hooked profile, fleeting as the flit of a sunbeam. The air
became glued into uneasy clarity, until the tapping scrape of her chalk
ripped the quiet like the snap of flint-struck sparks.

Morriel shuffled another step, closed another circle. The rune signs
might skip like torn stitches beneath her palsied, frail touch, yet the

vectored arcs laid to move summoned forces stayed precise, as if scribed by a master mason using a pin compass and cord. At the center of the floor where the sigils converged stood a low tripod. There, looped in a silver cradle and masked in black silk, the amethyst Great Waystone stood waiting, center point for the uncoiling layers of Morriel's enveloping snare.

Regarding its draped globe in stifled apprehension were the two young initiates Morriel had chosen to serve her. Though the shuttered, fireless chamber was chilly, both girls clasped damp hands in the folds of gray robes. Fresh from their novitiate, wholly unmarked by experience, they waited to give what was asked. When their Prime straightened up from her scribery and bid them to place themselves at the north and south poles of her construct, they accepted their role in stilled dread.

"Be seated," Morriel commanded. When she asked them to assume a deep trance, they knew, but dared make no protest. They would not take active part in this spellcasting, but serve as its passive binding. As their Prime required, energy, talent, even life force itself might become siphoned from them. By the strict oath of obedience to their order, their Prime Matriarch could demand any sacrifice against the needs of greater humanity.

"For the mercy of the world," Morriel exhorted them, "do exactly as you are told. I will be threading your personal energies through the Great Waystone. No margin exists for your weakness."

Minutes passed, sluggish under the weight of pent powers. The Prime visited both initiates in turn and collected the summoning crystal each one wore at her neck. She traced each with a sigil, then performed the Prime's invocation to claim and attune their personal powers under her dominion. Time assumed the drugged torpor of dreaming as the circles upon the observatory floor were called active and dedicated to the secret, dark side of the moon. Mystery pulsed through the febrile veil which tied life to its housing of flesh. The paired initiates felt as though a misdrawn breath might shatter the whole firmament of creation into eddies of glittering current.

Then Morriel spoke a word in command. She clapped withered hands, and the spells of prime power claimed the girls, spirit and mind.

All now lay in readiness. The Koriani Matriarch advanced to the tripod. She slipped off its covering cloth, the smoothness of silk a cruel contrast to her ruined flesh. Her skin had grown so translucent with years, at times, she seemed but a spectral shadow, unreal to her own tactile senses.

This moment the allure of death's peace left her hollow. She sorely missed Lirenda's support. If a relapse of blocked memory should claim her now, she had no one to anchor her through the perils which lay ahead. Each time she raised the Waystone's great focus, she shouldered the risk that her will might become overwhelmed. Yet the stakes at play to arrange tonight's plot had never before been so dire. Age had unstrung her sure grasp of self-awareness. Should the crossgrained old jewel finally defeat her, the Koriani Order must continue. Lest this hour's work come to frame her last act, the untried girls who backed this spell's pattern were expendable, as the handpicked successor to prime office was not.

Steeled, heart and will, by fatalistic resolve, Morriel cupped fleshless palms around the faceted amethyst. Its cold pierced in dousing waves to her marrow as she eased into trance. Perhaps for the last time, she locked horns with its spite and grappled to wield its dire focus.

If Fellowship meddling had curbed the stone's reach, its innate strength was untouched. Charged to the familiar, freewheeling exhilaration, restored to the pinnacle of power and command, Morriel bent will to accomplish her desire.

If Sethvir had granted the earth backdoor wisdom to encumber the stone with permissions, the works of man were exempt. She still ruled quarried stone and the milled timbers of buildings, bridges, and diked roadways. The signature energies of individuals left vulnerable through trusting, blind ignorance remained subject to the Waystone's spelled influence. Although the Teir's'Ffalenn's training as a master mage made him elusive prey, his return to the continent had occasioned him to accept other company on the road. The former clan war captain, Caolle, offered as volatile a personality as any tracking enchantress could wish. The signature seals of the spellbinder's glamour which disguised him with scars and slurred speech tagged his presence. Each move he made flared small pulses of static through the world's tracery of magnetic current.

Searched out by the Waystone's piercing focus, Caolle's course blazed like a beacon. Past, present, and future, his movements could be scryed as cleanly as text marked on parchment.

Given such infallible guidance to dog his liege's footsteps, the Prime became the more cautious. The weavings to entrap the Master of Shadow must be wrought with consummate care. Dakar was a Fellowship spellbinder, and guarded. Though Arithon's talents were left blank and blinded since his past misuse of grand conjury, he still held a masterbard's arcane hearing and a trained mage's eye for nuance. The disharmony raised by hostile intent would unsettle his keen sense of empathy.

The interface must therefore be indirect. In velvet-gloved delicacy, Morriel wrought. From the riverside tavern where her quarry last slept, she quested among the dust in the floorboards. Her search yielded three flecks of stubble left from Arithon's grooming. Before the inn's chambermaid arrived to sweep, minute sparks of energy flared in the candleless gloom. The Prime's first tendril of spellcraft embraced those cut snippets of hair, then wound their purloined essence, ephemeral as spun moonlight, into a personal signature to guide the course of her snare.

Next, the Prime Enchantress launched into deep augury. She traced the course of event yet to come, sounding the probabilities of Arithon's close movements as he mounted his foray in Tysan. She narrowed the vast might of the Waystone into tightest, fine focus, and targeted those actions her quarry was likely to take. Then she played the full range of probabilities and allowed for the utmost array of contingencies.

A trap of such delicacy could not follow a schedule. Chance action held too wide a range to predict the precise timing of event. Rather than structure her plot into a single, inflexible binding, the Prime instead tied its course to multiple chains of tagged markers.

This board in a bridge that Arithon might cross on his travels: Morriel set a hair-fine tendril of spellcraft into the wood's grain that would trigger in response to his passage. Here the wax lamps in a tavern's taproom were hazed in small spells of recognition; there, a ferryman's rope on the shores of the Ilswater became twined in ciphers of watch. Next, signposts en route to Riverton were tied into the growing tapestry, then people drawn in as well. *That* official in the royal shipyard who would need to be bribed or misled; a cipher of listening was laced through his jeweled chain of office, keyed to Arithon's voice. Specific cobblestones in certain city streets; the carvings on doorknobs or lintels; then the gate latches of every harborside inn: all became knotted into the weave of an ever so subtle array of spellcraft.

Morriel was patient. She had need to be thorough. One overlooked possibility, and the whole linked network would fail. Her grand construct was shaped, one step to the next, through infinitesimal increments of care. Then each separate facet was masked in a glamour. Dakar's watchful eye must be made to turn elsewhere, through a loosened board set to cause him a stumble; or else the lurking presence of her embroidery of seals must be groomed to mimic the natural resonance of stone, or wood, or wrought metal.

Across the path of Arithon's future, Morriel seeded her small barbs and hooks. To these, in ingenious, connected succession, she attached the seals and small ciphers to drive Arithon into her net. *This* rumor would find its way to the lips of a street beggar; *that* hunch would prompt a certain volatile clansman to raise a round of inquiry and search. When the orchestrated moment arrived for the coup, Arithon s'Ffalenn would be flushed from cover and hazed into desperate flight.

Morriel burned reckless power, affirmed and cross-checked every venue of possibility. Her labors eased options until no choice her quarry might try could win free of her invidious design. She adjusted and fine-tuned; twined tortuous traps in tight spirals.

On *this* hour, when every likely auspice came aligned, an ancient book from the Koriani Order's closed libraries would fall into the hands of a scholar who owed a sworn debt of service. The knowledge and the man would make their way to Lysaer; then war galleys would arm and cast hawsers and sail. The Mistwraith's curse would engage with its victims, and in the heat of its geas-bent obsession, the s'Ffalenn pawn could be spirited away.

A criminal who endangered society would be curbed, and the Fellowship of Seven be served its timely comeuppance.

Only the last, great sigil of ending remained to seal the chain of augured event. Tinged nitrous violet by the glow of the Great Waystone, Morriel grimaced like a skull. Never had she worked so elaborate a conjury upon resources pressed to such limits. While the daylight hours fled into night, then the starry sky paled and birthed the new dawn, she sensed a deep-down, burning discomfort. She had drained reckless power and now suffered sharp warning her strength ran dangerously low.

She pressed on, wrung what she needed to steady herself from the pair of initiates bound to her use through the Waystone. Were the crystal not restored back to unfettered potency, mankind's rightful legacy would stay jeopardized; the Koriani charge to restore civilization to lost grace would remain threatened by Arithon s'Ffalenn. Morriel did not equivocate. She spent ruthless force to shape that last cipher, and set final linkage between the disparate, trip-wire elements arrayed to bring Rathain's prince to defeat.

At the last, the squared circle of sigils dragged at her mind like spilled needles. Exhaustion leached her will, pulled like unseen fingers against her weak housing of flesh. Willful as old iron, the Koriani Prime reached out again to tap the initiates who stood as her anchors.

Something went wrong. The smooth flow of power summoned to her hands ripped through a sharp hesitation. One of the young women rejected the sacrifice, perhaps touched by the sudden, cutting panic of instinctive self-preservation. Betrayed in her need, Morriel felt the balance of raised spells veer awry. She screamed in rebuttal. The forces she grappled seemed shadow and flame, two opposite elements bent toward unbiddable destruction. Lacking her flawless and rigid control, the whole construct could fold into backlash.

Morriel perceived no safe avenue. Poised at the crux, taxed past the limit of her visceral frailties, she grappled harsh fact: without months of recovery, she could never retrace all the steps of this complex conjury. Should this construct tear itself asunder, the jagged vibrations of its collapse would burst even the most rigorous protections. Sethvir would stand warned. The priceless opportunity to suborn the Fellowship would be thrown away for one faithless initiate's weakness.

Fury seared through Morriel Prime. Well aware her demands must claim the life of the loyal enchantress who held firm, even still, she engaged her act for necessity.

Power flared up, too bright, too frenetic. Morriel lashed lawless forces into order, used the channel of the Waystone to reaffirm her cleared will. She joined the last sigil. Her drawn-out, wrenching cry of effort rocked the room. Then the dregs of her strength bled away. Slumped in collapse, her cheek laid to rest on the burning-ice sphere of the amethyst, she gasped out the ritual chant to blinder the jewel's roused focus.

No space to wonder, that these words might shape her last act. Her heart raced and throbbed. Each breath rasped like steel filings in her throat. Vast blackness devoured her senses. While the fires in the heart of the great crystal blazed low and flickered at last to quiescence, the spark of her will bled away.

Morriel Prime closed her eyes. Alongside the risk she might never reawaken, she measured the sum of her efforts.

A momentous labor was done. Time and the unwinding course of events would spring string upon string of chained triggers. Let the scryed snares in her construct play through, and Arithon s'Ffalenn would walk a doomed path into capture. First Senior Lirenda would be called to assume the mantle of prime power. If she held strong, if she proved a fit vessel, the memories of past Primes locked into the Waystone would rise up to channel and guide her.

Morriel rested content with the chance she had snatched back lost hope, and salvaged the legacy her sisterhood preserved for posterity. With the Fellowship brought to heel and the Shadow Master curbed, the Koriani Order could preside over mankind's freed future.

Marvel

For his diplomatic visit to Etarra in the eastern Kingdom of Rathain, Lysaer s'Ilessid and his sumptuous state retinue would avoid the Thaldein passes. Ship's captains seldom dared the North Cape, where tidal rips cut the inlets of a savage, volcanic shoreline. The overland routes through Camris to Miralt Head were preferred by the autumn caravans, as wayfarers and trade goods raced to meet the last of the outbound trade fleets. Before winter churned Stormwell Gulf to a stew of ice floes and spindrift, a raffish breed of northcoast galleymen indulged their sharp rivalries, driving their oarsmen in relentless, fast passage to the ports across Instrell Bay.

Late warmth was wont to linger in the scrub-grown flatlands of Karmak. Each year the alkaline soil of the plain lay ground to fine powder by the ox drays. Leaves and brambles entangled on the verges and wilted under a coating of grit, while air draped like gauze in late-season haze bore a windborne tang of churned dust. The progress of Lysaer's cavalcade raised muffled thunder in the powdery footing. The endless squealing of cart axles, the chink of brass harness, and the sifting grime fouling their trappings drove the prince's guard to clenched teeth. Tempers flared, and armor chafed, and meals came infested with sand.

Six days beyond Erdane, the low ground still stretched the same on all sides. A tireless sun stabbed glare off the rocks, and the horseboys were too parched to whistle.

Here, the mettlesome company chosen to spearhead the prince's

161

retinue rode in a squinting, watchful wedge. They slapped at the flies which lit on their horses and cursed others that escaped to bite flesh.

"We should make Miralt Head by tomorrow noon," ventured the company's captain, a grizzled former headhunter with a craggy profile and tough hands like silk on his reins. The hair on his wrists sprang in tufts through caked grime as he scraped gritted sweat from his chin. "That's if the camp cook can pack up his crockery without hounding his fool scullion for laziness."

"That scullion's my friend, and no layabout," the prince's page boy defended. "And anyway, how can you tell where we are? This blighted plain has no landmarks."

"Used to trap wolves here," the captain replied. "Packs swarm like vermin, come the snows. A man knows where he is, and how far to shelter, or he's like to find his horse hamstrung."

At the page's unsettled review of the landscape, the man-at-arms loosed a gruff chuckle. "Before sun, there's the truth, and may Light strike me down if I'm lying."

"Have a care. His Grace might hear your profanity." The page tipped a weighted glance behind, where Prince Lysaer rode a horse length to the rear of his standard-bearer.

Through the sulfurous silt of puffed dust, the Prince of the Light rode bareheaded, his gleaming, fair hair a diffracted halo in the citrine glare of strong sunlight. Even through dirt, his presence seemed uncanny, a masterwork wrought of alabaster and gilt against the monochrome landscape. The bullion-fringed banner and the stitched silk of its sunwheel seemed brass without luster in comparison.

Voice muffled to awe, the page boy ventured, "Do you believe the realm's seneschal, that his Grace is sent as Ath's servant to drive scourge and shadow from the land?"

The burly captain shrugged mail-clad shoulders. "I couldn't speak the creator's intent, boy. But Prince Lysaer, now, he's real. His powers can be seen and felt." Eyes trained ahead, he finished in respect, "Whether his Grace has divine origins or not, I'll swear by his name as our given defender against evil."

A barely sensed movement flicked a leaf by the verge. To a whickered puff of dust, a whine creased the air.

Stabbed by keen instinct, the guard captain shouted, "Archer!" He reined his horse back, sent it crab-stepping sidewards; screamed for his men to close in. "Move! Shield the prince!"

Scarce time to notice the page boy's mount, shying, and the lad unhorsed in the roadway.

Next a searing, actinic crack whipped the sky. A charge of bolt lightning scalded everything white. Then a slamming report like the hammer of doom thudded echoes across the bare flats. Men were yelling. Their formation erupted to mayhem as they fought the eye-rolling panic of their mounts.

But no casualty had fallen to bowfire. The prince remained astride his blooded cream charger, stopped in the middle of the roadway. Amid a cavalcade churned into panic, he sat with a statue's composure. No mere assassin's ambush held the power to ruffle his uncanny poise. Heaven's own lightning must leap to defend him, and out of a cloudless, clear sky.

The arrow lay banished to a lacework of blue smoke and a fading whiff of dry carbon.

"Angel of Ath!" the guard captain swore.

He stilled his sidling mount between bit and spurs, dimly aware of the men staring dumbstruck beside him; of the page boy's loose horse still plunging against the reins looped through its pasterns. The flat taint of dust and the tang of sweaty leather seemed disjointed and wrong, too earthy a setting for miracles.

Lysaer commanded the tableau like a stage, his lofty magnificence set apart. The moment hurt for pure splendor. For a handful of heart-beats, time's flow seemed erased, the lesser movements of men and beasts jarring.

Then Lysaer s'Ilessid commanded his guard with their half-unsheathed swords to stand down.

The unseated boy moaned and struggled to rise, the fall having injured his shoulder. On Lysaer's gesture, the royal valet scrambled from the baggage train to offer him succor; the loose horse was caught and soothed quiet by a groom.

Still awed beyond speech, the troop's guard captain swallowed in flushed shame, faulting himself for slack vigilance.

Yet the Prince of the Light offered no reprimand as he stirred from that terrible stillness. Swathed in the blinding, stitched glitter of his surcoat, he urged his charger toward the verge. Where the crumbled old tracery of wheel ruts gave way to the tangled brush of the plain, he drew rein. The object of his gaze might have been some beggar's bundle, discarded among the bent weed stalks, except for the hand flung splayed on the earth, blistered with weeping, raw burns.

A barbarian archer, the troop's captain surmised with a horrible twist to his gut. An assassin struck down by what seemed a godlike manifestation of wrath, his bow a charred ruin beside him.

"Bind him up for trial and arraignment," Lysaer s'Ilessid instructed.

When his stunned guard captain failed to react, he added in gentle encouragement, "The wretch is unconscious, not dead. Any henchman of Maenol's who holds murder in his heart can live on to pull an oar for just cause."

Roused from its nerve-edged amazement, the prince's company settled, re-formed, no man quite bold enough to exchange banter with comrades, or speak. The misfortune of the page boy persisted, a knot of disharmony in their midst. Blanched from the pain of a broken collarbone, his forehead and cheek grazed in blood, he stood on shaken feet, supported by the royal valet.

The troop's healer summed up his brisk examination and pronounced him unfit to continue astride on a horse that dragged at the bit, restive despite the groom's efforts to calm it. "The boy can't manage with one hand for the rein, and the break in the bone will fare poorly if he's jostled about in a baggage cart."

"Be still, we won't leave you," Lysaer chided the weeping boy. He then turned with crisp orders to his captain. "Mount the clan prisoner on the gelding and tie it to the back of a cart. Then set the page up behind me. My destrier's gaits are the smoothest."

The valet looked up, aghast, from the boy's dusty limbs and bleeding abrasions. "But your Grace! With all due respect, your surcoat will be spoiled with stains."

"Your Grace, I couldn't," the boy stammered.

Lysaer laughed. His blue eyes held the unshakable, kind censure that melted the hearts of his servants. "Should a man who follows my banner be worth less than a few yards of silk? I think not." The diamond in his ring scribed fire on the air as he extended his hand toward the page boy. "Come, lad. Share my saddle, and save your brave face for some worthier fight against darkness."

Once the captive was mounted and lashed and secured under guard, the cavalcade mustered in disciplined order to resume its northbound march. Surrounded by diffident officers, Lysaer s'Ilessid was pressed with advice not to camp on the open plain.

"Better we ride on through sundown," urged the captain. "Your Grace should rest safely inside city walls, protected by a manned garrison."

Lysaer refused the necessity. "We must not make our entry at Miralt unannounced. Our troops will need to be quartered and fed. As guests of the city, the late hour would pose a discourtesy."

Then that objection was overthrown by the seneschal, who insisted that a cadre of scouts forge ahead to carry word in advance.

"We ride on," the captain said, satisfied. "The mayor's Lord Commander at Arms shall have his due notice of your Grace's imminent arrival."

The royal cavalcade closed the last league to the arched gates of Miralt before midnight. Despite the late hour, they were met by the town's ranking officers in glittering, parade formation. These were accompanied by two dozen armed outriders with rich, matched trappings, agleam under streaming pitch torches.

Their approach was unhurried. Lysaer had time to note the fringed banners, the silver-gilt helms, and bright bardings stitched from costly dyed silk. His forbearing smile reflected his pleasure and dismay. "By the fanfare, dare we guess? Our scouts' tale of a light bolt and a barbarian arrow must have caused an excited reception. Those lancers in front look like they're packing half the city treasury on their backs."

The seneschal, mounted at the prince's right hand, squinted through the flare of the torches. "Don't belittle their pride. That's the mayor's personal guard."

Apparently unwilling to risk offense to an envoy shown the favor of divine intervention, the city of Miralt had turned inside out to arrange a ceremonial entrance.

A taciturn soul who took shocking joy in the occasional gaudy joke, the seneschal observed at bland length, "I imagine they've also planned rounds of slow, pompous speeches."

"Ah." Lysaer's eyebrows rose. "If you're tired, we could duck the long-winded welcome." He inclined his head and addressed the page boy, whose chin bobbed against his left shoulder. "You'd prefer a soft bed and a posset, I suppose?"

When the child returned an appreciative mumble, a curve of lordly amusement bent Lysaer's lips. "Well then, we'll need to outmatch them for pageantry." To his captain, he commanded, "Ready the men. On my signal, I'd have them dress weapons."

"As your Grace wills," assurance came back from the dark.

When the lanterns on the city walls hove into view, Lysaer laid the reins of his weary charger in one hand, raised his right fist, and discharged his gift in a hazed, gold corona over the vanguard of his retinue.

Gemstones and bullion leaped into dazzling clarity. Mail sparkled. Light hazed the sweated coats of the destriers to the gloss of polished satin. A crisp, clear call from the head of the royal column, and the guards in the train raised pennoned lances in salute. The sunwheel standard fluttered in the wash of warmed air, while night became riven to high noon.

Lysaer s'Ilessid in his brilliant white surcoat became the shining center point in their midst. From battlements and gate arch, the rowed ranks of Miralt's garrison watched his advance in gaping awe. Those city ministers and guildsmen called from home by peremptory summons forgot their complaint. The prince's unearthly presence might have seemed an arrogant excess of pageantry, but for the young page riding pillion behind.

As the pair neared the gates, all eyes could see the rich surcoat was not stainless white, but marred with bloodstains and dirt. The boy who besmirched its purity was tear streaked, an ordinary mousy-haired victim of mischance who clung in pain-shocked need for solace. The contrast between the child's needy suffering and the Prince of the Light's remote majesty framed an indelible image of mercy.

The Mayor of Miralt forgot every word of his hastily scribed formal welcome. The herald stationed in the gate keep hid his face, reduced to gawping silence as the prince drew rein in the roadway.

Before any minister could recover the aplomb to smooth over the lapse in state manners, Lysaer raised his voice and blessed the city in flawless formal language. In seamless diplomacy, he begged leave of needless courtesies. His train had suffered an assassin's attack. "No man was wounded, but my page boy suffered a battering fall from his horse."

If ceremony could be excused, a healer was asked, and swift disposition for the men, who were hungry and tired.

Dazzled half-blind, awash in shed glare from the unveiled heat of Lysaer's majesty, the Lord Mayor managed a stammered assurance. His garrison barracks would house Avenor's retinue, and the comforts of his own palace would be placed at the prince's disposal.

Lysaer inclined his head. "Light's blessing on you," he said, the gracious assurance behind such acknowledgment no less than his regal due.

To relief on both sides that the speeches were dropped, Avenor's captain at arms marched his columns through the stone portals into Miralt. Curious onlookers lined the thoroughfare to witness the blessed prince's passage. Shutters cracked open; balconies filled as the sleep of the righteous was shattered by the fiery, fierce light that knifed through the glass in their casements. Folk stumbled blinking from their pillows to gawk. Only when the royal cavalcade reached the city square did Lysaer mute the splendor of his gift. The furor kept on, fueled now by pure force of momentum. As the word spread, the whole city was raised, the streets packed as a midsummer festival.

Hastily clad in his livery and sash, the mayor's house steward issued frenetic instructions. Servants were rousted to light guest rooms and air linen. Grooms were kicked out of their pallets and sent running to accept the reins of blown destriers. Errand boys fetched out merchants to unlock their warehouses and amend shortfalls in wine and provisions. A healer arrived with bearers and litter to attend to the injured page boy.

Somehow amid the upsurge of commotion, the prince's charger was missed. Inquiries flew.

The mayor's flustered master of horse added his vehement insistence. "His Grace never entered my stable yard."

Questions lacked answers. No one seemed to know the royal whereabouts.

"Ath save us!" the mayor's house steward fussed in martyred agitation. "Suppose our exalted savior has taken offense at some fault in my lord's hospitality? Daelion avert such misfortune from our house! He *can't* have sought out a common tavern."

Avenor's Lord Seneschal repeated himself twice, then shouted to make himself heard. "His Grace has gone on to the shrine on High Street to give thanks for today's safe deliverance."

Word passed from mouth to mouth. A suitable retinue was assembled in haste. But the latecoming guardsmen discovered the way mobbed by curiosity seekers who choked the route to the square. The night streets of Miralt were teeming and charged into frenzied excitement. Even the dim byways held unsettled crowds, surging to glimpse the Prince of the Light, haloed in what seemed an exalted radiance as he made his devotion at the crossroads.

The thoroughfares went from tight to impassable. Not even the city guard could maintain their patrols. Balked citizens crammed into the taverns. Inebriated tosspots were displaced into corners as drudges rushed to light candles, and rumor sparked rampant speculation. The anomaly was noticed, that none of Lysaer's weary guardsmen stripped weapons or mail to retire. Half of their hard-bitten number had remained at Ath's shrine, firmly determined to stay through the night on bent knee in thankful prayer. Others whose tastes were more boisterous shed propriety and got themselves garrulously drunk. To throngs of avid listeners, they described miracles and lightning bolts that seared lethal arrows from clear sky.

"He's blessed, our prince," they pronounced in stark reverence. "We've borne witness with our own eyes. The shining powers of divine creation saved his Grace from a deadly attack."

"Where's the wretch who shot off the arrow!" some roisterer called from the sidelines.

That first, inflammatory remark was cut by a shout from a butcher. "There's justice due! Where's this filthy clansman who's in league with the Master of Shadow?"

Noise swelled. Trestles swayed to the surging press of bodies as like-minded celebrants accosted the royal guardsmen over the fate of the prisoner.

"The Prince of the Light is all our defense against darkness," a fist-shaking bystander insisted. "His murder would strand us without help or hope. Should we leave his attacker unpunished?"

More outcries arose. A touch match to tinder, the racket spilled out of the tavern's close confines and erupted into the street. By then, wine and ale lit the mood of the mob to a vengeful, dog-pack frenzy. When an off-duty guard from Miralt's garrison volunteered to force the cell where the infamous assassin was incarcerated, a jostling throng of vigilantes howled their eagerness to help.

The ringleaders seized torches. Less scrupulous citizens pried up cobblestones and hitching rails, or purloined bricks and sharp rocks from the mason's yard. The yelling horde grew. A torrent in spate, folk poured into the deserted market. There, the zealots whipped them into bloodletting passion. They would visit vengeance upon Arithon's henchman, who had dared to accost heaven's grace and deprive them of their protector.

Up and down the side streets, the shuttered, wooden shop fronts echoed to the rush of running feet. A cutler's stall yielded before battering assault. Stolen knives flashed between angry faces, and other fists brandished bludgeons. The mob surged through the commons, across the hollowed stones beside the city well, where women did laundry by day and ragged children begged coppers and filled the moss-crusty horse troughs for wayfarers. Miralt's citizens rioted past the pillared stair to the baths, screaming vicious and frenzied imprecations.

There, progress stalled, jammed from egress where the old harbor storm wall fronted the quays along High Street. From the wharfside mazes, and seamy brothels and sailor's dives, new revelers streamed to make mayhem. The press grew acute as men elbowed and pushed to funnel into the neck of the avenue.

Then the route to the inner citadel became blocked by a mounted figure muffled in a nondescript cloak.

"What passes here?" he cracked. His imperious manner was too refined for a guardsman. Whatever his business, he traveled without escort. He appeared to carry no weapon.

"Make way, man!" yelled an instigator. "We have business afoot."

"I said, what passes here?" The rider wheeled his horse and set its shoulder against the roiling surge of the crowd. A snarl of frustration greeted his stance. More than one hothead screamed epithets. In warning of tension a hairsbreadth from breaking, a brick flew and smashed a merchant's window. Bodies surged and shouting yammered through the costly tinkle of glass.

The rider gave no ground to fury. Target for violence, his destrier jostled by a grinding weight of sheer numbers, he bore in with rein and spur as if clubs and stones held no power to threaten his person. "Halt there, I say!" His timbre of authority now blistered to anger, he cut through the rising clamor. "By my name and the Light, stand fast!"

A shutter clapped open above. Too deaf and blind to sense disaffection, a beldame leaned out of her mansion window and launched into shrill imprecations. "What's become of Ath's peace? You wastrels have worse than the manners of hogs, who shove for the slop in my close stool!" She made ranting promise the contents of that could be hurled on the heads of the rabble.

She ducked back inside to make good her intention, and the sconce from her bedchamber limned the rider below. The thin gleam of flame traced the crest of an unmistakable cream charger.

The front ranks cringed back. They knew whom they faced: Lysaer s'Ilessid, just returned from the shrine, and en route to the mayor's hospitality.

To others behind, the detail was obscured. Due redress for a murdering, traitorous clansman seemed balked by one man, and the threat of a grandame's tossed jakes.

"Just cut down the lamebrain!" shouted a knife-bearing smith.

Others howled in contempt and pummeled their way forward, determined to smash through all foolish opposition. Their fury drowned protest. "Gut the clansman!" came the chanted slogan. "Kill the barbarian traitor! See him burned as a sorcerer's accomplice!"

The outraged old lady raised an arm to shy her chamber pot, then quailed before a roaring wall of noise. Below her, a cataract of humanity shoved and snarled in confinement, slashed here and there by the threatening sheen of bared steel.

The bottleneck of resistance, become focus for mayhem, the solitary rider fought his horse with magnificent skill to stand firm. His effort was futile. Despite ruthless courage, no inspired action could stem that onrushing tide. The prince must be forced to give way, or else trample and maim the front ranks who knew him. In seconds, he would be pulled down in turn, a rag milled under the teeth of a lawless stampede.

Lysaer raised his fist. "This will stop!"

A shattering arc of light clove the darkness overhead. His warhorse reared up and dislodged his plain hood. Like an angel's bright aureole, his crown of fair hair took fire from the glare of his gift. Then the illumination waxed unbearably bright, and banished the night in a wave of actinic brilliance.

The beldame fainted. The rabble recoiled, blinded and screaming. Their outcries were drowned as a thunderous report slammed over the merchants' slate roofs. A howling clap of flash-heated air blistered paint from the woodwork of dormers and shutters. Rioters at the fore howled and shrank. They found no escape from the sting as the skin on their faces and hands became singed by the merciless fall of raw light.

"*No man held in bonds for the sake of royal justice shall be subject to violence or bloodshed!*" Lysaer cried through the well of shocked motion. "Disperse and return to your wives and families, and leave the fate of clan criminals to me."

"Why should he not die?" blustered a wainwright from the shadowed protection of a side street. "He's the Shadow Master's minion! Or why should the lightning have surged from on high to deliver your Grace from his bowshot?"

"He is but a man!" Lysaer rebuked. His gift snapped and blazed. Through that flood of dire brilliance, the diamond white silk and gold trim of his surcoat shot his presence in scintillant outline. "Alone with a bow, do you *really* believe one mortal clansman could bring down the righteous arm of the Light?"

No one arose to dare argue that challenge. The prince on his horse was implacable, cut marble, ablaze in unearthly powers. His fierce gaze searched out one man, then another, and finally encompassed the whole crowd until stones dropped from abashed hands. Purloined knives were cast down in fierce shame.

"No criminal act can be healed by rash action," the Prince of the Light exhorted. "This clansman you would burn was misled by evil. Before execution, he deserves all your pity. My law has sentenced him to chained service at the oar, a miserable fate. He'll know the whip and the indignity of slavery, sore enough suffering for the error of his ways. No one, *no matter how outraged*, will take his life out of hand! Death will deliver him from the galleys soon enough, but only on the hour appointed by powers outside mortal judgment!"

No sound from the mob. Two men near the fore were reduced to stifled weeping. In rustling movement, others sank to their knees in spontaneous plea for forgiveness.

"Go home, now," Lysaer said, his fury reduced to gentle care. The radiance softened and dimmed from his fist, benevolent as mellow spring sunshine. "Take my peace to your hearthstones, and my blessing to your kinfolk. For every man's sake, spare weapons and rage for better causes. If by tomorrow you still burn to fight, my captain at arms will take down the names of new recruits. Should war come again to drive back the Shadow, then every brave heart will be welcome."

For a half second longer, that struck silence held.

Then Prince Lysaer reined his destrier around. Moved to emotion by the fading of his gift, darkened to loss by his departure, a lone voice pealed out his name.

The first cries took root. A man more inspired led into a worshipful chant: "Hail the blessed lord! Hail the Light! Death to the Spinner of Darkness!"

Moments

Ensconced in his diplomatic post at Avenor despite the absence of the prince, Mearn s'Brydion receives a message from a street beggar sent by Arithon s'Ffalenn, and the note requests a clandestine inquiry into the disappearance of Lady Talith, Princess of Tysan. . . .

Far to the east of Miralt Head, where avid recruits line up to swear service against shadow before Lysaer's sunwheel banner, Earl Jieret's scouts intercept messengers calling town mayors in Rathain to Etarra to pledge for the Alliance of Light; and foreboding weighs on him for the inevitable fact that his clans must flee into deep cover. . . .

Against the strapped oak door to the observatory in the Koriani sisterhouse at Capewell, the peeress in charge delivers an ultimatum to her anxious colleagues in the stairwell: "No one opens this door, by Morriel Prime's stated will! If she's died from turned spellcraft, only one holds the right to gainsay that command. Her successor in training has been summoned. Until the hour of First Senior Lirenda's arrival, what lies past this threshold shall bide behind seals, undisturbed. . . .

If tears were hardened stone to carve,
inscribe my cry for life:
Let no man raise his unsheathed sword,
may no man draw his knife,
that this, our sore and grieving land,
waste no more hearts to strife!

verse from the Masterbard's lament
for the widows of Dier Kenton Vale
Third Age 5649

V. Riverton

For three hundred years, the rambling, old tavern had stood below the river fork where Ilswater joined the broad, placid channel which drained off the mudflats of Mogg's Fen. Moss shagged its fired brick walls on the south-facing side. The north wings sliced the brunt of the winds that scoured the leaves from the roof shakes. Its warren of galleries and peaked dormer rooms lay packed, that stormy, cold night. Chimney smoke smudged the deepening gloom, sliced by the needle tracks of rainfall. Bargemen forsook the damp berths on their vessels; drovers left the miseries of open-air camps and thronged in for a copper to spread blankets on the common room floor. Driven indoors as autumn's late chill threatened the first, freezing sleet, soaked wayfarers huddled elbow to elbow over mugs of soup and mulled wine.

They would have squeezed the accommodations past full, even with no bard in residence.

The racket would let no man rest until he lay drunk or exhausted by crude entertainment. The taproom was too packed for darts, and the landlord forbade arm wrestling, since wagers were wont to breed fights. Milling patrons banged the boards and whistled for service from the barmaids.

The hour was just shy of midnight, with long ballads the sole remedy for boredom. The bard on his stool by the settle was kept too relentlessly engaged to retire.

The inn's kindly landlord held one room aside for his use at no charge, for the excessive demand on his talent. The mannerly threw money to keep him sweet. As each song drew to its closing, small coins sliced the gloom to chink on the boards at his feet. If the singer was built a trifle too fine, or his dress seemed a touch over-done, those delicate fingers on silver-wound strings wove sound like a net of enchantment. Through the chiming cascade of gift tokens, the whoops of approval, and a general hubbub of noise, the call of the mousy widow by the casement seemed the lost utterance of a ghost.

"Pray Ath our bard didn't hear that," Dakar said where he lounged, feet braced on a trestle crammed under the jut of the staircase.

"Hear what?" Wedged deep in the gloom with his back to the wall, Caolle elbowed the Mad Prophet's side, then spoke his concern for a tankard left brimful all evening. "You don't drink, man. When that happens, I worry if you're sick."

Despite provocation, Dakar's watchful eyes tracked the woman in her ribbons of mourning. "Trust me, I'm hale and dreadfully sober. The misery's the same, nonetheless." Then, on a break into fierce irritation, "Damn the silly bitch to black Sithaer! He's noticed."

For the coins had ceased falling with the bard's head still raised. All theatrical elegance in his slashed murray silk, he had not launched into some lilting dance tune to quicken the pace since his last air. Instead, he regarded the nondescript woman in stilled and striking intensity.

That indefinable instant, the noise lagged. Rain drummed the slates and the windows, and the widow raised nerve to repeat her request. "Minstrel, play a memorial!" This time, her frail, porcelain treble reached every corner of the room. "Sing us a lament for the brave ones who died against Shadow in Dier Kenton Vale."

"Merciful Ath!" Caolle shoved straight, gruff outrage slurred into mangled syllables by the spell-turned web of the glamour. "He'll refuse her."

"His masterbard's title won't let him." Dakar clamped a quelling hand on Caolle's forearm. "This is sovereign territory to the crown of Tysan! Try and stop him, you'll start a brawl and get us pitched out."

"Sithaer's dark furies!" Caolle yanked free. "Are we girls, to flinch from a douse in cold rain?" Yet he subsided, if only to watch how Arithon would field the unpleasantness.

The bard shifted the lyranthe in his lap. He regarded his hands, fine jointed and stilled, the image of languid elegance. The pose was misleading. To any who knew him, the mind underneath was as unperturbed as drawn steel. While the taproom grew hushed, and storm sluiced the eaves, he spoke in mellifluous courtesy. "Mistress, which of your loved ones was lost?"

"My husband, rest him." The woman cried, bitter, "May the Spinner of Darkness come to suffer Dharkaron's damnation!"

"Lady," said the singer in plangent, fierce pity, "rest assured, he already does."

Then, as if unadorned words caused him pain, he flung back his head, shut his eyes, and struck a chord like a plummeting cry. No chance assemblage of minor notes, this opening, but the pure charge and power of a masterbard's art, that ordered the air and snatched mortal heartstrings and twisted, until all the world became realigned to his measure of gripping, stark sorrow.

A dreadful, ranging chill poured down Dakar's spine. "Caolle," he entreated, in haste to speak before music burned away reason, "tonight, I'll need help. Keep vigil with me at Arithon's bedside, and please Ath, leave your temper behind."

He never heard Caolle's answer. The upwelling surge of an exquisitely made grief enthralled every listening mind. Arithon chose not to play to console. The deaths he had caused at Dier Kenton Vale were too harrowing a loss to soothe over. Instead, he spun melody in soaring lament and seized his hapless audience by the vitals. His notes sheared past thought like hooks in silk thread, unfurling a shimmering net of fine sound. The musician firmed his hold, dragged them under, then drowned them in a surge of emotion like tide.

Fingers partnered to unbridled talent, the bard added song, distilled into lyrics to unhinge the mind and make the most callous soul weep.

> *If tears were hardened stone to carve*
> *a monument to grief,*
> *would we let loss and trouble starve*
> *our spirits for belief?*
> *Our men have gone from home and hearth*
> *and faith has made us weep!*

Arithon played them their mortality in the pressed heat of that dingy riverside taproom; first like keening wind, and then like a blade to cleave through skin and viscera. This was no catharsis to soothe the bereaved. Each line of harmony demanded the question: for memory of those dead at Dier Kenton Vale, Arithon challenged every moral brought to bear, all principle raised as banner and cause for bloody war. He unwound reason, unstrung pride, then snapped the last thread of dignity in regret for the wasting ruin of broken lives. Barmaids and barge captains, beringed merchants and their coteries of servants; all, down to the coarsest, unwashed mule drover wept unabashed, that husbands and sons should ever leave home to kill for reasons of policy.

The music surged on, relentless. No one escaped the leveling shame as those surgical tones unveiled the lie of just trappings. Arithon showed no pity for mourners. He endorsed no heroic act of sacrifice, but stripped away mankind's penchant for self-righteous zeal to its core of arrogant futility.

> *No cause is scribed in fire and star—*
> *then whose truth must we heed?*
> *Why bind the will and blind the heart,*
> *more lives to rend and bleed?*
> *Our men have gone from home and hearth,*
> *and hate has made us weep!*

His last line dissolved in a flood of diminished harmonics. The bard damped his strings. Silence descended with the brutality of a public execution. One second passed, two, with the flames in the lanterns the only movement in the room and the sough of cold rains, the sole sound. People were statues, cast in bowed grief. Breath itself hung suspended.

Then the bard raised his head. His face was bone pale and remote, as if the channels just tapped for his art had undone the ties to expression. His stance as he rose was unsteady. The fingers left gripped to the lyranthe's slim neck seemed nerveless as winter-dry sticks.

Dakar roused first out of song-induced stupor. Before the bard assayed even one infirm step, he broke from his lethargy, squeezed past packed benches, and crossed the cramped space the audience had lent for performance. Coin offerings chinked and scattered to his step. Their dissonance snapped the Masterbard's spell. People stirred out of stupor, then rocked the close room with sighs and frenetic exclamation.

Whatever they tossed to acknowledge this performance, the reward was unlikely to be silver.

Dakar shouted across a mounting swell of noise. "Come on!" His hand closed on Arithon's moist velvets. The shoulder underneath was trembling, no surprise. The musician had played his very spirit into sound and kept no reserve for recovery. For a bard of such stature, the effects could rival the drifting exhaustion imparted by acts of grand conjury.

Arithon swayed.

"Damn you for a fool, don't fold on me now." The Mad Prophet scanned across lanternlit fug; gauged the mismatched cadres of patrons, the resilient ones rising, as yet wrung too limp to react in affront for their shattered equilibrium.

Such backlash would come. The moment their recovery allowed a recap of Arithon's composition, some inquiring hothead would connect that the lyrics suggested a treasonous dissent against Lysaer's vaunted Alliance. Violence might be averted only as long as mass fury was given no target.

"Arithon," Dakar urged, "you've got to leave, *now!*"

Then Caolle arrived, unquestioning and brisk, his broad shoulder set to brace his liege upright and barge them a path to the stairway.

Behind a barred door in the upstairs chamber, a candleflame fluttered in a saucer of puddled wax. The gusts outside laced rain against the shingles, while shifting light stippled the dingy plaster walls and sprawled felted shadow across the floorboards. On the low pallet, stripped to hose and shirt, and warm under clean bedclothes, Arithon s'Ffalenn lay asleep. Black hair fringed the unlaced sleeve and forearm which cradled his face. The fair, slim semblance of the dandy had fled, the small workings of his birth gift erased under force of the spells newly wrought. His awareness lay immersed in dreamless oblivion, but peace had come at high cost.

Worn from his battle to quiet the ferocious bite of s'Ffalenn conscience, Dakar slumped on a footstool, knees drawn up and fingers shoved through the bristle of hair at his temples. For all his care, he felt nagged by failure.

"Those bindings I set may not hold," he warned Caolle. His voice seemed unreal, like scratches on glass, to which rain burst in tireless applause.

Caolle shifted his stance by the doorway, his reflexes set on flinching edge by the laughter which burgeoned downstairs. Each racketing burst from the taproom stewed louder, more shrill, touched to a raw pulse of hysteria. "You're thinking we'd do best to ride out at once?"

"That's not possible just now." Dakar chewed his lip, while the roistering celebrants rattled the floorboards beneath him. "If our horses are made ready and saddled, the precaution is probably sensible."

Caolle made no complaint for the weather, but snatched up his cloak and departed. The bursting swell of noise as he slipped through the door increased Dakar's breeding tension. The crowd's temper built to a vengeful edge, as each housebound riverman sought to rout grief through indulgence. Beer and carousing could not stem their blind urge for catharsis. No genius was needed to forewarn that their mood would grow ugly.

When they turned, the bard who had kindled their emotions must be far beyond reach down the road.

Dakar heaved erect and refastened the bar. The small garret chamber seemed beleaguered by storm and darkness outside, and by the fiery lusts of Sithaer from below. To mask his worry, the Mad Prophet scavenged the crumpled heaps of Arithon's cast-off finery. He folded and smoothed ribboned velvets and fine lace, then repacked the saddlebags, attuned all the while to the prostrate form on the bed.

Left no other diversion, Dakar fretted. His spurious talent for prescience stirred to the targetless hunch that peril stalked at his back. Rather than chafe his nerves into jelly, he delved past the wrapped bulk of Arithon's lyranthe and took up the lethal, cold longsword left propped against the clothes stand. Even sheathed, the blade sang to his mage-sense of uncanny, Paravian origins.

"Bloody death, let me not have to use this," the Mad Prophet whispered. He locked sweaty hands to the stained leather scabbard and hunkered down with the sword laid across his plump knees.

Arithon's sprawl on the inn's saggy mattress never shifted. The uncertain spill from the candle played over his tight-knit frame. Fanned snarls of black hair seemed to drink the faint light, while his slackened fingers curled on the sheet seemed masterfully carved out of alabaster. Such stillness unmasked a frightening vulnerability, a humanity grown too sharply defined in muscle and tendon and bone. Never a large man, Arithon had become alarmingly thin and worn. His wrist might be circled by one finger and thumb, and the cleaved edge of his cheekbone stood demarked in drawn flesh.

Dakar tried to recall the last time he heard the prince laugh. "For mercy, how long can this go on?" he asked an unlistening stillness.

No answer came. Just the unending chap of the rain through the rowdier din from the taproom. Dakar rubbed his eyes. The sword in his lap seemed a wrapped bar of ice, his body like storm-sodden clay. He shifted his shoulders, then ordered his mind in a ruthless effort to stay alert. His gaze drifted anyway. The mingled, fusty scents of wool and hot wax conspired to clog his trained senses.

Then the candle fluttered in spent fuel and went out. Dakar grumbled an oath, loath to rise up and scrounge a fresh light. He never remembered falling asleep. But the transition back into wakefulness came like a drowning douse in warm syrup. The Mad Prophet raised his head. Vaguely alarmed, he fought lassitude and wondered why his mind should seem bogged in a spell weave. He mumbled a cantrip of unbinding by reflex, then chastised himself for absurdity. He could scarcely be misdirected enough to succumb to his own arcane workings.

Yet the counterspell ripped the blank fog from his mind all the same.

"Arithon, damn you!" Fully roused to annoyance, Dakar scrambled upright. His fists flailed limp cloth, the bedclothes his ungrateful royalty had thrashed off. The sword no longer lay near to hand. Dakar dived for it, groped, found its firm length fallen beneath tumbled blankets. He snagged a hangnail, tugged. The hilt remained mired past reach of his burrowing fingers. He shoved erect, frantic, and almost fell flat in collision with a fast-moving body.

"Sithaer's black furies, Arithon!"

His cry raised no answer; too much to hope that the Prince of Rathain possessed anything near waking sanity. Arithon could be bent on who knew what mayhem, seized as he was in the grip of vile dreams, and unable to shake the ties of strong sleep spells wrought over him. Whipped to blind fight, few men alive were as dangerous.

Dakar plowed to his feet. Poor candidate for heroics, he whacked his shin on the stool, howled from frustration, and launched off in blundering pursuit. His toe hooked the table leg. The candle dish fell, splashing the floorboards with crockery. Too flustered to question why his mage-sight seemed trammeled, Dakar dove in a tackling pounce through the murk.

He struck flesh, grabbed. An elbow sledged into his jaw. "Merciful Ath! Arithon, *you're dreaming! Wake up!*"

The mazed creature he grappled spun about, bashed him spine first against the washstand. Basin and tin pitcher clattered askew, dousing his neck in cold water.

"Arithon!" Dakar ripped in a breath that shot branding fire through his chest. "Stop this! Now!" The next hammering blow broke his hold. He dropped, tasted blood from a bitten lip. The jolt as he crashed full length turned his head. Through dizzying pain and a fall of spun shadow, he heard the grind as the door bar slipped free. "Ath, no!"

The latch clanged, gave; the panel swung wide. An influx of chill air from the corridor wafted past Dakar's damp face. He scrambled back upright, agonized to find his recovery came too late to matter.

He rushed anyhow, tripped over the tin basin, and skated through a swath of flung water. Beleaguered, half-stunned, and griped short of wind, he made a futile effort to call warning. This was *Tysan*. Should Arithon step out with no thought for disguise, fate might lead someone to recognize him. If he quenched any lamps in the taproom by means of wrought shadow, mayhem and bloodshed must follow.

No option remained. Dakar resorted to magecraft. He ripped out a rough-drawn spell to warp wood, then barbed its flight in permissions garnered from Arithon for use against extreme need. Currents of raised power coursed through his frame, already shocked into shivering. Dakar let fly his linked ward and construct with intent to trip his agile quarry in the doorway.

Nailed boards groaned and flexed in obliging reply, but not to block Arithon's passage. Instead, Dakar himself caught the assaulting stir of warped forces. He yelped in vexation, too bruised to evade what he only *now* tagged as a mirror-keyed spell of deflection.

Then his own hasty conjury rebounded on its maker and accomplished its end like fell vengeance.

Dakar stubbed his toe on an uneven plank, crashed full length, and skidded. His palms caught a nasty scouring of splinters. The more frightening truth hurt worse than the pain: *beyond any doubt, the Master of Shadow was wielding his talent for magecraft.*

"Curse me with fiends, that shouldn't be possible!" Dakar scrambled upright, vexed to despair.

Always before, the block had remained beyond reach of Arithon's resource, the trained powers of his upbringing shackled in guilt by his imposed royal gift of compassion. Too late now, to avert a disaster past imagining. The Mad Prophet launched in hotfoot pursuit. This was a realm where Lysaer's crown campaign to eradicate sorcery brought victims to the stake without trial. Too real, the chance that Earl Jieret's augury might come due in this backwater settlement.

Breathless, stabbed at each step by the grate of a cracked rib, Dakar reached the opened door. The hallway beyond showed him rows of closed rooms, the end by the stair banked in shadow. Dakar dammed back his rasping breath. Through the masking noise from the revelers, he listened, but detected no scuffle of footsteps. Arithon s'Ffalenn could move like a ghost, even with no gifts to hide him. The darkness he called to mask his escape hung too thick, even to pass the fine, signature energies which underpinned all things of substance. Dakar strained his mage-sight, but recaptured no glimmer of pattern to guide him.

Resigned, he plunged into that blind dark by touch. His best course lay in reaching the stables. Caolle deserved warning. After that, the flimsy hope must suffice, that their combined efforts would be enough to extricate the Shadow Master from whatever brawling havoc arose from his foray through the taproom.

Dakar tracked the wall with a palm stubbed with splinters and minced his hampered way forward. Above the racketing clamor belowstairs, he heard someone bellow: Caolle, returned from saddling their mounts against need, and confounded to find himself under attack as Arithon sought fugitive exit.

"Don't let him get past!" Dakar rushed to stop Rathain's prince from doubling back through the hallway.

Ahead, grunts of effort, then an alarming thump. A body cracked through the oak banister. Caolle snarled an oath. Someone's knuckles smacked flesh. An incongruous reek of pitch smoke spiraled up from the stairwell. Dakar winced through a snort of laughter. Barbarian to his core, the clansman stuck by his cantankerous habit of lifting the coachmen's torches from the stable yard to light his way within doors. Between prince and liegeman, the battle raged on, a no-holds-barred scuffle fought on the steps with fists and fire and fell shadow.

A wooden-sounding thunk bought a surcease from darkness. Dakar blinked to adjust abused eyesight. Against the filtered glare from the taproom, Caolle poised with one massive fist clenched to the haft of his cresset. The flame had extinguished. Sultry coals still flared from the tip, laced in demonic trails of spent smoke. Collapsed in a heap against his braced feet lay Arithon s'Ffalenn, a welted mass of newly raised blisters glistening across his forehead.

"Ath, he went mad!" Still brandishing his bludgeon, Caolle glanced past his shoulder as if he expected another assault from behind.

Dakar made neither excuse nor denial. "Lucky the meatbrains downstairs are flat drunk. We'd best move your liege before some sweaty john wheedles one of the barmaids upstairs." He ignored his own throbbing chorus of aches, knelt over Arithon, and helped Caolle check for lingering injury.

"No broken bones. That's better than he deserves." Caolle for a mercy never stalled over questions. He licked a bloodied knuckle, jammed his spent torch in the stump of the banister, then bent to the task of hefting royalty. "Runt sized or no, his Grace fights like Sithaer's furies." An accusatory glower shot back as he straightened and took note of Dakar's hitched stance. "Kicked you also, I see."

"One rib. Only cracked." Dakar raised a hand to wave off the matter, then gave up the gesture for speech that hurt just as much. "Won't keep me from riding."

Caolle let that pass with a dubious grunt and plowed onward with Arithon across his shoulders like bagged game. "Well, whatever undid him, I'll hear a reason. For this, there'd better be cause fit to stop Dharkaron's almighty justice."

But time was not given, even for Dakar to outline the gist of disaster. On return to the room, Arithon stirred the moment Caolle laid him back on the bed. Since the damaged bindings of the sleep spell were now too perilous an influence to keep, Dakar effected their immediate release.

The Master of Shadow regained full awareness at once, his pupils black and wide in the flare of the candle Caolle brought to measure his reflexes.

"No concussion. You're lucky," Dakar pronounced. Too heartsick to meet the anguished recognition unveiled in those wakened, green eyes, he held out a ripped twist of linen, soaked in the spill from the washbasin.

Arithon took the offering. As wary himself of prying observation, he pressed the compress over his scorched forehead. He asked just one question; heard from Caolle of the torch used at need to take him down. Then he sucked a sharp breath through shut teeth and let the sting to his outraged flesh stall off unpleasant explanation.

Too brusque for tact, Caolle showed him no quarter. "Liege, what evil possessed you?"

"Ath, let him collect himself!" Dakar snapped, detesting the pity that made him speak in defense.

"I can't be spared," Arithon contradicted.

The ground-glass hurt in his voice set even Caolle aback. In wordless embarrassment, the clansman pawed through the fallen blankets to recover the stool. That evasion helped nothing. On the floor lay the Paravian-wrought sword; the bared sweep of black quillons offered stark enough proof of a trust gone desperately amiss.

"You reached for *Alithiel!*" Arithon cried, the name of the blade charged with horror.

The Mad Prophet lost his chance to soften the impact.

"Yes, it's the curse!" Arithon snapped, the admission jerked out like barbed steel from a nerve. "Desh-thiere's touch has warped me, *never for a moment forget this.*" For Caolle, he explained his razor-edged quandary. "The geas which drives me to destroy my half brother grows ever more uncontrollable. That's why Dakar holds my

182

given permission to reach past my deepest defenses. So long as I keep my right mind, the preventative ought to be binding."

A moment passed, rinsed in the buttery glow of the candle. "You're not always sane," Caolle summed up in his usual, hammer-blow bluntness.

Arithon shut his eyes. The rag in the mangling grip of his fist could scarcely mask his expression. Forced to yield his unwilling confidence, he lowered his hand, limp now, the knuckles scuffed red from warped violence. "Yes." A shiver coursed through him. "The curse has invaded by way of my dreams. Apparently, there, it just claimed me." He looked up then, his shaming appeal made the worse by his unflinching dignity. "I'm no fit prince to lead Rathain's clans anymore. Caolle, I beg you, accept my release here and now. Take back your oath of fealty before the worst happens. Before—"

"Before I die by your own hand?" Caolle slammed to his feet. "Never." He spun and paced, his wheeling shadow too large for the cramped room. "Liege, my death is not the worst that could happen. By your oath, sealed in blood before Fellowship Sorcerers, I stand fast. Even if your charge to stay alive was not binding, my heart could not do less. You are the hope for my Lord Jieret's future. The heritage of your bloodline is not revocable, your Grace, any more than my own sworn trust."

"Caolle, could you step out," Dakar pleaded, as much to stop that lacerating contest of wills as to seek word with Arithon in private.

"No. Caolle remains, by command of his prince, if he's too much the fool to disown me." Arithon sat straight, faced them, the spark in his eyes too baleful and steady to wear down. "If he stands endangered through guarding my flank, he'll not take those risks in ignorance."

Aware that statement was pitched to provoke, Dakar joined forces, not just to turn Caolle, but to make Arithon withdraw before ruin overtook them. "This time, your Grace, you tapped into your training. You worked talent and wrought conjury against me."

Arithon went white.

"Not once, but twice." Dakar steeled his nerve and bored in. "My sleep spells were bent back in deflection against me, and not by an outside act of sabotage. When I used force at need to bar your way, all your sworn permissions were revoked."

"You're quite sure?" Arithon looked as if his own knife had slipped and stabbed him through to the heart. "Ath save us all, then the curse has subverted even my royal-born gift of compassion." The forearm half-raised to mask his stark shock dropped nervelessly back in his lap.

"Not when you're conscious," Dakar amended quickly. Aching too much to endure forced bravado, he looked aside, and noticed that Caolle retreated also. As if care for this prince posed too punishing a trust, the gruff clansman busied his large hands to right the crashed washstand and retrieve the dented tin basin.

Dakar strangled pity out of fear and resumed. "Your Grace, we can't argue facts. A masterbard's gift grants you linkage through sound to something akin to your mage-sight. Any performance which recalls the Mistwraith's influence, like tonight's lament for Dier Kenton's fallen, may well open channels for its curse to exploit." While Arithon weighed this, Dakar nailed home his point. "I think you know it's dreadfully unwise to proceed with your mad plots in Tysan."

"I must," Arithon insisted. The entreaty on his features too anguished, too vivid, he bared himself to explain. "We need more ships to seek the Paravians. The clans here require sound vessels and crews to spare them enslavement on the galleys. Lord Maenol's people won't survive the next generation if they are forced to stay landbound. They have no recourse left, since their former *caithdein* gave her life to declare them my allies. Against Lady Maenalle's execution on my conscience, I pledged them my word I would help."

No sensible counsel would move him. A swift, sideward glance showed that Caolle saw as well. Bull stubborn, or maybe cow stupid, Dakar tried again all the same. "You do realize that any encounter with Lysaer could send you over the edge. Not just your sanity, but the whole of this world would be threatened."

"I have to go on." A wry bent of humor flexed Arithon's mouth as the stew downstairs roared to crescendo. Still unapologetic, he delivered his adamant conclusion. "What's left but to run? And if I turn tail, that solves nothing. *You must understand*: this curse just compounds as time passes. Evasion will bring the same downfall. Actions and will are all I have left to stave off my own self-destruction. Worse than Lysaer, despair is my enemy."

"Are you sure?" Dakar pressed. "Do you speak true? Or is your thinking corrupted by the Mistwraith's geas itself?"

"Come ahead and find out," Arithon invited. A testy, backhanded delight lit his face, almost welcome for the change as he shoved to his feet in familiar, acid-bright temper. "I've always liked fighting my demons up front. Since I'm dangerous, asleep, we may as well embrace folly headlong and ride on for Riverton tonight."

Dawn blazed over the deep estuary at Riverton, a veiling of cirrus like cloth-of-gold fringe strewn across dove gray silk. Against that gilt backdrop, the walled inner city spiked a bristle of towers and battle-ments, streamered with pennons and pricked by the rake of ships' masts. Seventeen centuries of commerce had overrun the original citadel. The flats where the barges docked along the river delta spread crammed to bursting with wharves, the arched gateways of coach inns set chockablock with boathouses and ferryman's lighters.

Arithon and Caolle led the horses ashore for stabling with a livery-man. Ten paces behind, suspended over water on the gangplank, Dakar half sensed *something*; a fleeting prickle of spent energy, not unlike the imprint of a dissipated spell. He suffered a swift pang of nausea. Nagged by the oddity, he braced half in dread that his gift of prescience might trigger between steps to the dock.

But his tread on dry boards raised only the expected hollow echo. He frowned, paused anyway, plumbed mage-sense until his head ached. His search yielded nothing. Only the random, silvered dance of energy which patterned grained wood into substance. The air bore only the reek of black river mud, skeined through by the mulch of turned rose beds in the merchants' garden courtyards, and the sea-sonal must of piled leaves.

Dakar rolled his shoulders, irritable and anxious. All week, he had been starting at phantoms, and no wonder. A man with the sense that Ath gave a flea would be anyplace else but in the Shadow Master's company, inside the crown territory of Tysan.

Dakar hastened on before Caolle's impatience could shatter the morning quiet.

If the wide, tranquil lanes by the barge docks met misty daybreak in restraint, by contrast, the harborside reflected a livelihood steeped from the rowdier tastes of men who plied deepwater shipping. There, the sky above the roof peaks teemed with raucous gulls. The puddles in the gutters reeked of flotsam and fish, a furlong removed from the exquisite walled mansions of the riverfront. The division between saltwater commerce and fresh lay demarked by the customs keeper's compound, its seaside encroached on by sagging, tiled roofs and the storm-weathered planks of old warehouses. The market became the hub of activity, with its channeled gutters of herringbone brick spanned by the pilings of squatters' shanties. Behind them, the half-plank tenements loomed three stories above the street-level sprawl of bawdy houses and dilapidated taverns. The mews in between held the seamier sailors' dives, wedged amid tangles of cobblestone alleys scarcely wide enough to pass single file.

Arithon traversed the bayside mazes on foot, his lyranthe slung from his shoulder. His step was unhurried, almost meandering, and everything living made him linger. He dallied to peruse the trinkets spread on open-air tables; conversed with the idlers leaning on lamp-posts, or carters, wolfing hot pastries over their slackened reins. Caolle wore his sword and shadowed his shoulder. Made jumpy by the lazy accents of townsmen and the hated enclosure of city walls, he insisted on keeping his hands free. Which left Dakar to heft his tinker's gear, the saddle packs of spare clothing, and the manful share of complaints.

"Don't pretend you didn't notice that circle of ash in the market square." Disgruntled since he had dismissed the painted redhead whose playful fingers had promised fine dalliance, he groused, "They burned some poor wretch for the practice of unclean sorcery only yesterday."

A pause, filled by the Mad Prophet's puffing as they jagged up a narrow stair and passed a darkened archway through a close. His chorus rang plaintive echoes through a courtyard choked with frost-withered flowerpots. "The merchants should riot. Who will craft fiend banes if everyone with mage-sense cowers in fear of execution?"

Down a rickle of heaved flagstones, the party of three emerged back into daylight, with Caolle's grip white on the sword as Arithon stalled again on his course.

Dakar scarcely avoided crashing into him. Blinking like a mole past the bundles clutched to his chest, he snapped, "If you're going to give silver to every beggar we pass, my back will break before we find an inn."

Arithon broke off a quiet sentence with his latest fascination, a raggedy old salt propped on a crutch. "That's heartless bad manners," he admonished.

Less eloquent, the beggar hawked and spat on the offensive Prophet's boot.

"You toad-humping spawn of a maggot!" screeched Dakar.

The beggar cracked into devilish, deep laughter. "Now didn't you say the same on the day you crammed yourself into that beer cask and we heaved you afloat on Garth's Pond?"

Dakar's eyes widened. The jab of Caolle's elbow into barely healed ribs nipped his cry of recognition just in time. "I'm sorry," he gasped when he could manage civil speech. Through another glare at Arithon, he added, "Our singer here has a soft heart and a head as addled as a duck's egg. We'd all join you in the streets before he'd let a layabout go hungry."

The beggar flashed a tigerish grin, none other than the lame joiner whose past touch at subterfuge had once helped the theft of a princess's ransom. "Ye won't lack for beer and feather mattresses, I'd say. Not in the company of a bard whose playing could charm life into a stone gargoyle. The Laughing Captain, hard by the shipyards, is a tavern to welcome a good singer."

That suggestion passed off in languid disinterest, Arithon pursued, "If Lysaer's royal guardsmen are busy burning talent, what does this city do for fiend bane?"

The beggar scratched his chin. "Well now, the Koriathain fashioned the talismans for the yard. Merchant guilds signed oath of debt for that." An expert lag, while scruffy fingers poked for lice; until Arithon's hand obligingly dipped into his purse. In glad speculation, the joiner delivered. "For the rest, we had a good bell founder."

Arithon's interest lit. "Had?"

"Aye. Man's fair useless to anyone now. Born without perfect pitch, see? Can't rematch the tone since one of his master set's cracked." Nonplussed by Dakar's scowl, the scoundrel joiner palmed coins as though he had begged all his life. "Strolling that way, are you? Yon craftshop's off Chandler's Alley."

Yet if the bell founder's plight concerned Arithon s'Ffalenn, the path he chose to the harborside became everything else but direct. His small party tailed him in and out of three wineshops. Underneath the planked walkways which linked the close tenements, he shared biscuits with the filthy children who lived by picking pockets in the shadows. Dakar battled his shortening temper. Each move seemed to fuel his anxiety. More than once he spun around, certain someone was dogging his heels. He saw only slinking alley cats and rats. His skin stayed nipped into gooseflesh, as if the creatures were golems raised from bones, and set spying by furtive conjury.

Oblivious, Arithon loitered to gossip with a laundry girl, rinsing linens on a gallery, while Caolle dodged wind-scattered droplets of runoff, and Dakar fumed in annoyance. His chastised survey of each chance-met acquaintance revealed no other familiar faces.

The day wore past noon. Arithon jaunted through the sailors' market, loquaciously intrigued with its glass beads and shell trinkets; its whalebone charms against drowning, and its philters and potions mixed against ague and hangover and whore's pox. He chaffed the apothecary and acquired a posy of dried catmint. A second talisman maker sold him assorted tin scraps in a sack.

Jostled by a press of tar-smelling riggers, they withstood the buffeting sea breeze while Arithon purchased a burgundy silk waistcoat trimmed with mother-of-pearl spangles.

Before suffering another zigzagging course through the market, Dakar balked and dropped all the packs on the cobbles. "No more."

Arithon looked at him, eyebrows raised, then unslung the lyranthe from his shoulder. "Hold this," he bade Caolle, then balanced his sack of tin leavings on top of the load.

Right there in the street, amid rumbling drays and carters who swore and reined their racketing teams around him, he donned his ridiculous glad rags.

The maroon-and-gold garment clashed stupendously with moss green hose. Dakar gave way to disgust. "Spare us all, you're a sight to make a corpse walk."

Arithon grinned, an edged flash of teeth. "I agree. After the clothes, who will look at the face?" He asked back his instrument, to Caolle's relief, then waded undaunted through the rows of shawled women packing salt barrels.

Dakar's vociferous frustration cracked echoes off the mews chosen this time for an exit. He sucked in a breath and choked on the miasma of tar and hot wax. His next comment was expelled as a cough. They had entered Chandler's Alley from the north. The craftshop of the benighted bell founder loomed ahead, every casement boarded up, and its signpost demolished to slivers. The cobbles beneath were sugared in smashed glass and the shards of pulverized roof slates.

The Mad Prophet gave the warped door, the bent nails, the litter of bashed casements his expert survey, and chuckled. "Ath. The iyats are having themselves a field day."

Arithon leaned close, cautious in a realm where mage talents lay under interdict. "They're still here? You can see them?"

Dakar nodded. His trained eye picked out the whorled dimples of distressed air which pocked the shop front and the surrounding alley, unmistakable trace of the energy sprites' presence. "The whole place is riddled. Do you guess this is sport, or plain revenge for the fact the warding bells are out of true?"

"Likely both," said Arithon s'Ffalenn in delight, "and for us, a rapturous throw of fortune." He banged on the door, which swung inward on shrieking, bent hinges.

A short step into a lanternless dimness, then a violent stir from the shadows: an angular crane of a man scrunched across a piney spill of sawdust, most likely scattered to cushion the impact of tools the rampaging iyats might throw down. "Are you blind?" he howled in calamitous agitation. "Get you out. We're fiend plagued and closed!"

Dakar cringed, face masked in his hands; Arithon tucked back an exhalation suspiciously like laughter; while the fiends, busy creatures, rocked into a wakened frenzy of assault.

A tin cup chained to a fallen washbasin gyrated in crazed circles in the dark. Something else made of wood, a potstand or a close stool, galloped to life on a circling course to smash ankles. Caolle yelled, stamped down on an offending pair of fire tongs which tried to stab holes in his boots, while a row of tin canisters rocked as if to dump themselves over his head.

"Ath, see what you've done!" the bell founder screeched above burgeoning commotion. "The blighted infestation has started all over again!"

Iyats enjoyed feeding upon human rage. Hand-wringing, dithering hysteria teased them on. Recharged to delight, they obliged, and seized on wild energy to fuel a new round of pranks.

The cup snapped its tether, shot off into space, and clanged into a hamper of metal scrap. The lot toppled with a deranged, belling crash over the workbench with its crucibles and anvil. Filings and scrolls of shaved iron whirred airborne, a threat to eyesight and flesh. Through that scouring storm, and the craftsman's imprecations, a sound to drill through quartz: Arithon whistled a shattering threnody.

Scrap metal dashed to the floor like dropped chaff. The close stool toppled flat and lay with its legs pointed skyward, while from every darkened corner, the artisan's dropped wares belled in resonant, dissonant sympathy.

The rampaging fiends ceased their mischief. Under threat of dissolution from those ranging harmonics, they unraveled their energies from purloined items and fled. Their departure, willy-nilly, raised small flurries of ripped air, the ping of popped nails, and a staccato barrage of cracked boards and burst shutters. Inside a handful of heartbeats, the sawdusty gloom subsided to muffling silence.

"Praise Ath Creator!" The bell founder gaped. His protuberant eyes cast right and left, but saw nothing except blessed stillness. "Here's a bard!" Nary an iyat remained on his premises, and the impact of rescue sank in. "A bard with a true ear for fiend bane." He kicked through his muddle of violated belongings, snatched Arithon's sleeves, then thumped to his knees and gushed out his tearful apologies. "I had no idea. None. Forgive my rude welcome. What amends can I make to beg for a ward on my shop?"

"A fee." Arithon slipped his wrists free of moist fingers, amused and cool, but not unkindly. "You've no cause to plead. I don't have the talent to set lasting protections. But to place the pitch to recast your cracked bell, a sum of ten silvers will suffice."

"Bless you man!" The craftsman scrambled erect and closed on his find with doggish, backslapping eagerness. "That's far less than your talent deserves."

Caolle scuffed sawdust in stiff-lipped distaste, as much for the disrespect shown to his liege as for the frivolous delay. Arithon's humor stayed unruffled. For a private man who disliked being touched, he weathered his patron's unctuous handling with striking equanimity.

Which anomaly at last snapped Dakar to cold thought. He had accompanied Arithon's travels too long not to sense another seamless thread of subterfuge. Nor did his hunch prove misplaced. The reputation the bard earned in that one afternoon won them the most sumptuous, private room in the Laughing Captain Tavern for the rest of the week, free of charge.

Event fell out with natural elegance that, after Arithon's morning of plying gossip from passersby and his fresh notoriety at the bell founder's, a nonstop stream of Riverton's folk should stop to exchange words in the taproom.

Nor did every admirer wear the face of a stranger. Dakar recognized a ropewalker, a handful of caulkers, and two doxies twined through the arms of a suspiciously familiar sailhand. A street child sidled up, brother to one who had served them before as informant through a forced stay in Jaelot. Ath alone knew how the filthy mite had tracked Arithon the width of the continent.

Inevitably also came Cattrick, covert conspirator to the Shadow Master's cause, and paid master of Tysan's royal shipyard.

Dakar caught first sight of him, a bluff, square man whose muscular tread rivaled Caolle's for strength, and whose presence exuded authority. He elbowed his way through the press of galleymen, carousing deckhands, and off-duty royal guards as if he expected due deference, his immense, callused hands broad enough to span the slopping rims of four tankards. The squint to his eye from sighting straight board lengths, or the lines of new keels on their bedlogs, had grown more pronounced through the years since the *Khetienn*'s first launching in Merior. Lank shocks of brown hair still licked his wide shoulders, a new gleam of silver at the temples.

The gruff, ram's horn bellow he used in the sawpits vanquished the taproom's rank noise. "Beer for you, singer, and for your companions. You'll need to get drunk to raise any tune through this racket."

He barged himself a seat on an overcrowded bench. The redolence of pine resin and coal smoke from the boiler sheds laced through the fug, and earned glares from a foppish pair of soap merchants. Cattrick scarcely cared. Braced on his forearms in a loose, sailhand's shirt, he cut an enormous, rough figure alongside the bard, neatly clean in his flashy silk waistcoat and cap of feathered, pale hair. While the tankards brimmed over, his stilled, intense eyes took in Caolle's scars and dismissed them. The weapons concealed by the clansman's caped cloak merited no closer survey. His attention swept over the indolent, small frame of the singer he knew for the Master of Shadow, took note of Dakar's closemouthed expectation beside him, then flickered back. "Demons take all, minstrel. Ye've scarcely the substance to bed a bony-arsed spinster. Are ye man enough, or should I have brought fresh-squeezed cider?"

Arithon grinned. "Man enough to deplore the childish need for contests involving strong drink." That opening salvo cheerfully reversed, he stung back. "Best you stay sober for your launching next month. Or did the street gossips malign you for nothing? They say your last brig sailed hull down over the horizon and vanished. Sunk, no doubt, by her ill-fitted seams, if you rate a man's wits by his bar habits."

"Tongue like a viper, you have. Same as every other skinny warbler who can shrill sour notes to banish iyats." Cattrick downed a vast swallow of beer, his settled bulk like an owl on a branch, his half-lidded gaze still hunting. "Beyond wails for fiend bane, what use is your milk-tongued caterwauling? Lure out my craftsmen to hang moonfaced in their cups, and I'll have smashed fingers in the yard come the morning. Sprung planking too, if the lads get too muddled to sight north and south on a measurement. Mind your step. Go too bold, you'll have enemies vying to spike your feckless head atop the gatekeep."

A smile from the bard, then a challenge. "Let me play this taproom to a standstill, first. If by then you aren't flopped beneath the trestle with the rest, let's find out who's effete over fine brandy in private."

The burly master joiner palmed a belch and gave back a level, hard stare. This game was not new. Arithon chose his associates for excellence; if they came with quirks or unruly character, or balked at being nose led, he must expect to cross wits to extract the service he angled for.

"Well?" needled the bard.

Cattrick slammed the trestle with a fist, the same that had once tortured a man whose interests had thoughtlessly crossed him. He held no regret for that incident; nor would he lose sleep if this latest slick bargainer chose to bury the memory. "You want a contest? Said is done and Dharkaron take the hindmost." The shipwright drained his tankard in cocky salute, shoved erect, and plowed his way back for a refill, while Arithon received an unsettled glower from Caolle.

"I thought you claimed you had Cattrick in hand," the Mad Prophet murmured, voice muffled as he peered into the dregs of the beer the ship's joiner had left him. "Those insults came barbed, or I'm a grandmother goat's arse."

Arithon shot off a sparkling run to retest the pitch of his strings. "It's all jealousy," he agreed, eyes alight with innuendo. "Somebody's welcome was a shade too warm and that clerkish little guardsman behind us returned a bit too pointed an interest."

Before Dakar could weigh evidence to tell if the threat was a glib fabrication to divert him, the bard rollicked into the reeling, first measures of a bawdy dockside ballad. His tempered voice cut the noise like struck bronze, suspending discussion and argument. Nearby drinkers erupted to their feet with yells of delight. Wolfish sailhands stayed their dice games, and merchants, their dickering, while barmaids caught the coppers flung onto their trays and bustled to the tap to fetch tankards. By the time the bard closed the last chorus, the common room rocked to the thrill of discovery. He gave his audience no chance to let down, but flowed seamlessly on to the fast, fired lilt of a hornpipe.

Town ministers started stamping, despite their immaculate velvets. Tar-begrimed deckhands whistled and leaped on the trestles to clog step, then dragged doxies along as the frenzied, wild tempo rocked up one key and took flight. A figure of calm amid heaving pandemonium, Arithon played, head bent and foot briskly tapping. His spirit led the dance, surrendered on demand to the weave of the intricate melody. Precise as stitched gold, each grace note splashed out in ecstatic execution. His was command of a masterbard's style and to any with mage-sight, the air in his presence became charged into glittering brilliance. His listeners could not help but ignite in conflagration, while the trained snap and flex of his fingers wrought joy from wound metal strings and inspiration.

Through stamping applause, the landlord shoved in to extend his pledge of free lodging. "Whatever the house has to offer, it's yours for as long as you're minded to stay."

"A year for one percent from the till, and the coin any well-wishers toss at my feet," Arithon bargained.

"On those terms? Bless you, I'd fund your retirement and welcome!" Unable to contain his disbelief and good fortune, the landlord beckoned to his comeliest serving girl. "Give the minstrel and his two servants any damned thing they might ask."

While her painted, sloe eyes gauged the way the singer filled his clothes and warmed into frank invitation, the landlord moved off, chuckling.

"Any damned thing?" Arithon awarded her lush favors the compliment of his smile and snapped a sprightly run from his strings. "Then keep my friend the tinker in beer. That's work enough for a brigade."

The Mad Prophet's indignant riposte became lost in braw noise as the tap's salty patrons clanked knives on the boards in demand of a repeat performance. Head tipped aslant, Arithon obliged them, song after song, until evening wore away and his listening crowd roared itself to exhaustion. While the standing survivors reeled their way homeward, the landlord gloated over empty casks and filled strongboxes, his smile all but nailed in place.

The bard arose then, stretched, wrapped his lyranthe in no hurry. Caolle knelt unbidden and raked up the abundance of silver tossed down by generous admirers.

"Do you offer the plate scrapings to the street orphans?" Arithon asked.

The landlord bobbed up from the gloom behind the bar, a polishing rag in his hand. "I give the ones willing to scrub pots all the leavings. Do you want to save the small coppers for them? You needn't. That custom's lapsed since my grandsire's time."

Arithon shrugged. "I keep stubborn habits. Just make sure the girl who sweeps up knows how to count in fair portions." The instrument slung from his shoulder, he seemed impatient to depart.

Dakar showed no inclination to move, settled as he was in brosy content with the barmaid cuddled in his lap. "It's grown desperate late," he complained in a beery slur. "Can't you bear to forego the indulgence of sucking down brandy with Cattrick?"

"I daren't," said Arithon. "Caolle can watch my back." His step ghost light before his liegeman's solid tread, he picked a path through prone revelers to attend his match with the master of Riverton's shipyard.

"Dharkaron wept!" The Mad Prophet groaned in low misery as he peeled off the doxie and apologized. "Before you ask, yes. We're surely as moon mad as he."

Desperate not to care how severely he was weaving, he crossed the puddled taproom in Arithon's wake, to yelps and grunts from the inebriated bodies he disturbed on his course for the stairway.

Payment and Bribe

The Laughing Captain's best guest suite still wore its origins as a shoreside madam's boudoir, bed hangings and dagged curtains done in gaudy, flame scarlet, tied back with gold-shot cord. Despite a casement cracked open to catch the sea breeze, an ingrained cloy of patchouli clung to the air and the rugs. The clothes chests were pearl and black lacquer from Vhalzein, new enough that they still smelled of citrus oil. The washstand supported an ewer of gilded enamel flaked with chips at the edges, two rails of embroidered towels, and a pair of pitch-smeared boots just kicked off and crammed with the wads of shed stockings.

Their owner had made himself comfortable on the bed, his back to piled pillows, a cut-crystal decanter propped between the knees of his patched canvas trousers. The brandy inside pooled pale amber in the glow shed by beeswax candles on prickets. Not mellow at all in the haze of soft light, Cattrick tracked Arithon's entrance, slit eyed and primed for contention.

"Ye're a master with that," he opened as the bard tucked his lyranthe away in the wardrobe. "Heard all from here, and it damned well entertained me. Lysaer will be wild when he learns what's afoot."

When and not *if*; the inference bristled like hurled insult.

Arithon folded himself into the least-cushioned chair, the deep pleasure instilled by his music yet with him. "Since Avenor's a scant fifty leagues from this dive, shall we avoid the unpleasantness? If you're too cowed to pour, I want to be brought up-to-date."

194

"Well, here's fine impatience." Cattrick's lip curled in sarcasm. "Four years is damned long to wait for the asking."

When Arithon said nothing, he dug through the pillows and unearthed two enormous glazed tankards. The clink of Falgaire crystal and the trickle of neat spirits did little to soothe a stiff pause.

Cattrick recapped the decanter and poised the filled tankards on his thighs. "Since we've rebuilt and launched a replacement for every galley that burned in Minderl Bay, the crown's been hiring on riggers like ticks. Two-thirds, and the best, are all yours. The caulkers recruited from Havish were no good."

"Too little pay," Arithon supplied. "King Eldir's no fool. He funded his craft guilds to keep the well-trained ones at home."

"Then that's old news." Cattrick shrugged. "Your own crews from Merior have gradually replaced any second-rate labor. Petty infractions did for the rest. The plankers and sawyers all have southshore accents. By Ath, we're so infested with talent a man wonders why none of it's local." He extended an arm in an effortless stretch, passed the most brimming vessel to Arithon, then finished, "Ye ken how I spit on pretty boy hair."

An undignified thump intervened from outside. Dakar clanged the latch and demanded admittance, and Caolle moved fast to let him in. Against a strung stillness, the clansman snapped the door closed, the hands beneath his cloak clasped to the hilts of his weapons.

Too drunken for tact as he sized up the tension, Dakar blundered on, snatched the second tankard from Cattrick's preoccupied hand, and spouted his venomous opinion. "A friend might believe you wanted the thrill of seeing a sorcerer burned alive."

Cattrick's pelt of whiskers parted into a wolfish smile. "I prefer to speak to my associates firsthand." He uncorked the decanter, rolled a long swallow of brandy on his tongue, and switched his regard to frame Arithon. "You're not drinking, either. Does that mean we're too careful to risk any untoward confidence?"

"There isn't an abundance of confidence to share." Arithon sampled his drink, grimaced at the sting to a throat stressed from singing, then tipped his head back in the chair and shut his eyes. He let go a small binding. The shadows he used to disguise his appearance ran off like singed silk in the candlelight. When next he looked up, his eyes were bright green and his hair the sheened black of a raven's wing. His gift had done more than falsify coloring.

Now none in his presence could mistake his frank warning: the exasperation laid bare, or its unwanted corollary, written into the planes of bone pressed against hollowed, pale flesh. If such an unmasking had meant to restore confidence, the mistake escaped salvage as Cattrick leaned forward, eager to test how far he might sway exposed weakness.

Dakar felt a sudden grue ream his spine. Hazed by some thwarted fragment of prescience, or maybe just spurious hunch, he blurted, "Cattrick, are you in Koriani pay?"

"Don't answer that!" Arithon sheared in. "I don't believe it." He did not look settled or sanguine anymore. "Caolle, pass on what we brought from the tinsmith's, if you please."

The clansman slipped the sack from the thong at his belt. Never a man to forbear from sharp action, he hurled it full force toward the bed.

Cattrick fielded the catch without upsetting the brandy. Since its unwieldy bulk required both hands, he nipped off the thong binding and upended the contents in a caroling chime over the red velvet coverlet.

Dakar's eyebrows shot up. The tinsmith had delivered in pristine gold coinage, struck in Havish's fair city of Cheivalt.

Prepared when Cattrick's lips hardened to contempt, Arithon said, "That's no bribe. I thought we agreed. A man of your stature can be paid, but not bought."

Cattrick lost all his angst to disbelief. "No! Don't say we're due wages. The crown of Tysan rewards our work well enough."

"Lysaer's pay is spoils." Enthused beyond weariness, Arithon laughed at the shipwright's flummoxed startlement. "If you can unbend on that fine point, let's drink your nice brandy and celebrate. After all, the miserable galley work's finished. You're laying new keels for my fleet, now."

"Ath!" Cattrick slapped his leg in a stymied explosion of temper. "Fiends plague us all, man, you could've sent some sort of word back after our previous launching! The lads in the yard are the devil to keep quiet, and I take unkindly to guessing. *Did* our new brig shake down in safe passage to Corith?"

"That much and better," Arithon quipped. "The pay for your craftsmen was sent from the sale of the cider she carried as cargo. Now *could* we back off and swill spirits in earnest? You can sell me out to my enemies later if my nasty reputation makes you squeamish. But if we rise tomorrow undamaged by brandy, then all our brash claims to manly pursuit are going to lie forfeit by default."

Dakar woke up to hazed pain, as though moths with steel hammers set to with rivets and fastened the inside of his skull to his brain.

His bladder was full, and his tongue, like furred lead. Well versed with the miseries that came entrenched with cheap beer, he groaned and shoved upright. With his throbbing head plowed facedown into a pillow, he fumbled to grab the first container at hand to catch what his body ejected.

"You look fit to serve time as ship's ballast," said a quiet, etched voice across the room.

A moan escaped the pillow. Dakar unshuttered a bloodshot brown eye and measured his tormentor, who sat tidied and dressed in the flamboyant elegance expected of bards who garnered a taproom patronage. "You shouldn't be capable of speech. By Daelion's fell justice, that brandy would have knocked anyone else down sick as a mule with a belly full of yew."

"You're right." Arithon stood, the slashed velvet sleeves of his doublet tacked with matched studs of black pearls. "I should have been, too, except that I had to render my gorge after Cattrick earned the good grace to fall senseless. He was packed off home in the slop taker's cart for the round sum of two silvers."

"That's thievery." Dakar found the chamber pot. Pillow clenched now to his heaving belly, he sat, torn by two needs and waiting to see which bodily orifice was going to demand service first. "Not to mention a waste of fine brandy." Then, disgusted to be caught just as black as the kettle, he folded in half and gave the selfsame libation to the vengeful god of brewed hops.

Erect once again, and vastly more comfortable, he rinsed his sour mouth and regarded the prince, who thoughtfully seemed to be sorting out yesterday's clothes for him. "We're going someplace?"

Unwontedly serious, Arithon passed over his shirt, then smallclothes and breeches in turn. "Yes. There's something I need you to see."

Outside, the daylight had lost its dawn blush. The wind blew brisk with a warning of rain as the spellbinder trailed in the Masterbard's footsteps through the quay alleys which led west through Riverton. Gulls screamed and called in a pale citrine sky. Dakar made his way with hands clamped to his temples, cursing when his feet tripped him. The fog-dampened cobblestones gleamed like new lead under the deep gloom of the eaves. Even that minimal glare hurt his eyes.

"This excursion had damned well better be necessary," he groused at the crossroads where the wharfside buildings thinned out. The stone road gave way to a rutted, mud track, interspersed by board bridges which stitched an uneven course through the mudflats of the

Ilswater delta. Low ground wore bearded stands of marsh grass, interspersed with the less savory industry drawn by a thriving sea commerce. The air clung with smells. Still sunk in the misery of a tender stomach, Dakar pressed his cloak hem over his nose to cut the reek of the tanneries and the dead animal stink of the stockyards.

"Where in bleak Sithaer are you taking me?" he demanded as Arithon moved ahead like a wraith through a streamer of late-rising fog.

"No place that's civil. I'm sorry." Reappeared in solid outline in his elegant gray silk, Arithon descended a weathered log stair. His high boots wore a fresh coat of wax, no detriment as he picked his way down a meandering path churned boggy with cow slots and muck. The ground oozed brackish water, and marsh wrens flitted off the fluffed heads of the reed stalks.

"Not the barge docks at the estuary." Dakar grimaced as the wet soaked through the scuffed leather shoes he persistently neglected to upkeep. "That's a nasty, rough place to wear pearl-studded clothing. The meat packers there will knock a man flat just on principle, far less to snatch any wealth they think they can clean off of your person."

"We're not dealing with meat packers." Arithon turned sharply left off the path. Ahead, the land undulated, ochre on gray, the tufted sedges and marsh grass skirting the verge of the sinkpools dirtied with crusts of salt rime.

"Damn you!" snapped Dakar, sunk ankle deep in cold water that shot pain like iced nails through his headache. "Since reasonable people don't wear black pearls for a slogging jaunt through the marshes, you might have warned I'd get wet."

Arithon stopped, turned, caught Dakar's moist wrist in hard fingers. "I will warn you now to stay silent. Where we're going, if we're seen, we'll find trouble far worse than a meat packer's mannerless fisticuffs."

The corollary stayed unspoken, that to chance-met observers with too much curiosity, a bard who wore clothing fit for rough country would have business other than minstrelsy. Dakar curbed his complaint. He sloshed at Arithon's heels for a miserable half league, while his headache settled to roost in his forehead, and his beard became snagged with shed seed heads. Ahead, the damp ground arose into a low bluff, combed at the crest with rustling tufts of pale dune grass. The chatter of male voices issued from the far side, cut through by the metallic plink of a smith's hammer. Someone's coarse laughter was met by a shout. As bard and prophet mounted the slope, they heard an intermittent squeal of wood pressed to wood, telltale sign that a barge dragged at fixed bollards in the rip of the tide through the estuary.

"There's a landing here?" Dakar ventured in soft inquiry.

Arithon nodded, then crouched to avoid being caught in stark silhouette against sky. Screened by the thickets of grass, he pressed forward, then beckoned for Dakar to share his vantage point.

The Mad Prophet knelt in his brine-sodden hose. "Smugglers?" he whispered.

"You'll see." Arithon's face stayed attentively trained forward. "Listen." Stilled as a fox, he strained to glean what he could from the windblown rags of conversation.

"Fool dogs didn't scent them," one party blustered. He had rust-spotted chain mail and the stance of a braggart, meaty arms crossed on his chest. "The fiends had masked their back trail using green brush smeared with otter's musk." Through the ongoing throes of involved explanation, someone else cursed the smith for taking a fussy long time with his rivets.

The hammer strokes paused, while a curse was returned, and Dakar parted the grasses. The headland where he and Arithon sheltered overhung an alluvial deposit, piled on the bend in one of the channels which drained the mouth of the Ilswater. The barge dock which hosted the current activity nestled beneath the steep curve of the bluffs. The planking was unweathered and new, but built to outlast winter storms. The bollards were well sunk and braced in roped triplets, with two vessels currently tied. One was a seagoing galley by the chipped strakes and dulled paint which bespoke the hard usage of a trader. The other was a river barge fitted out as a slaver. Half-naked clansmen stood or sat, chained to steel rings in her deck.

Dakar knew a white-hot explosion of rage, then an ache beyond words to express. These were the proud keepers of the old and irreplaceable bloodlines whose sworn bond of service began at the dawn of the Third Age. Now, one man's whim reduced their function to brute labor. By Lysaer's decree of revenge against Maenol, free men were reduced to the lives of kenneled dogs: a priceless heritage thrown to entropy and waste; a wild pride darkened to resentment and despair.

A hand touched Dakar's rigid wrist in restraint: Arithon's, in forbearing compassion. "Those guardsmen can't realize the impacting scope of their action."

Dakar choked down his fury. No excuse salved his nerves; not when he had borne living witness to the past, when the clans had braved their place as the link between mortal men and the burning,

199

dire grace of the Paravians. His gorge rose at the price of an outworn injustice, reduced now to blind hatred and ignorance.

Other cruelties stung for their needlessness. The captives had nothing beyond the crumpled leathers on their backs. Most were torn and marred with old bloodstains, testament to the violence of the hunt that had brought them to capture. They numbered a miserable two dozen, ill clothed and ill fed, their hair wind tangled and their bodies exposed to the chilly caprice of the weather.

Eight guardsmen with the badges of royal authority oversaw the next step of what seemed an entrenched routine. To pass time in boredom, they traded epithets and jokes as the prisoners were off-loaded one at a time from the barge. A small fire flickered on the verge. There, a bandy-legged smith fitted each convict with an iron collar and cuffs. His burly apprentice then closed the steel link which fixed their chains to a bench on the deck of the trader's galley.

"Lookit that gimper. Never guess now, but he's the one who fought like a wildcat." The speaker with the sergeant's badge sliced a thick finger down his cheek. "Left our captain with a scar his wife won't forgive. Man beat the fool wretch half-senseless for that. He only stopped when six headhunters pulled him off. Their kind breathe and piss for their money, I swear. To Sithaer with all else, the bounty was half if the puking clan vermin upped and died."

Sickened now by worse than a hangover, Dakar saw through the marks of old bruises, and recognized just whose wrists were being fitted with permanent fetters. The young man who stood, fighting tremors of pain, was none other than the scout from Caithwood who had provided the spare horse for Caolle.

The sight was one to brand the mind for cruel sorrow: the scout, chin raised, unwilling to show his gruff captors one sign that degradation and suffering touched his spirit. He did not flinch as the hammer blows closed the steel rivets, nor when the soldier grasped his lank braid and hacked the hair short at his nape. His face wore the battering bruises of rough handling. One arm and shoulder showed the livid scabs left from untended wounds. He walked with a stumbling limp as two guards prodded him up the gangplank to the galley. There, his forest-bred nerve almost failed him. The soldiers had to bundle him up to the bench, force him down, and hold him, while the apprentice clubbed his jaw to make way for the tools that would leave him chained like an animal.

Dakar shut his eyes against pity and tears. The chance was too real, that the ships built at Riverton would become the last hope to save Tysan's dwindled clan bloodlines.

"You do see," whispered Arithon. "Maenol's people must be given the fair means to fight back."

Dakar swallowed. He had no argument for stark necessity. Nor could he summon the cold-hearted logic to decry that the dangers posed too grave a risk for a prince already under curse by the Mistwraith. As a vicious, damp gust raked over the bluff and razed first warning of winter in a chill that bit to the bone, he took sharp note of the season. "It's late in the year. Too late for a galley to round Stormwell Cape. The ice will be moving already in Northstrait. That ship can't make passage to Miralt."

"No," Arithon agreed. "There's another incentive as you'll see."

For the galley captain had poked his head out of his snug cabin. His shout carried clearly to the guard on the dock, who wore the sunwheel badge of authority. That one unhooked his thumb from his belt and strode aboard. Amid brief discussion, he pulled something from his tunic. A tied leather pouch changed hands. The galleyman shook the contents. The greed in his smile exposed yellow teeth as he ripped open the strings and counted the coin, the pale flash of gold a bright note under the rubbed velvet of the overcast sky.

"That's a bribe for the harbormaster at Cheivalt," Arithon said. Even through his low tone of voice, the sorrow wrenched through. "They defy King Eldir's edict to move the slaves southward through Havish. Once past Mornos, no mayor in Shand will scruple to disbar slave-bearing galleys from the seaports. These men will be resold in Shandor or Vhalzein. If no one intervenes, they might labor until their death on the southern trade routes."

"We can stop them." Dakar shoved stubby fingers through his hair, thinking furious and fast through his hangover. "Send word ahead that corruption has undermined Havish's edict."

Arithon's answering smile was cold as the north-shadowed side of a glacier. "I trust I'm forgiven the price of wet feet? Without an accurate description of that galley, we could do nothing at all."

Dakar blinked. "Demon," he murmured. "How did you know where to look for this shifty transaction?"

"That guard sergeant drank in our taproom last night," Arithon murmured in reply. "It's a galleyman's dive, you had to have noticed. The fellow made his contact, then got into his cups and bragged of his cleverness to a trollop. Amazing, how men with a chit in their lap think a bard won't take note of plainspoken words while he's playing." The Master of Shadow backed down from the crest then, his eyes grim as fired enamel. "We should go. There are urgent letters to be written and sent, and no more to gain here but heartache."

Liaison

Lysaer's royal galley rowed into the snug port at Narms against the bitter gales which presaged the ending of autumn. Despite wind and rain, the city did him honor by staging a sumptuous celebration. Feeling ran high in the packed state guildhall. Delegates had traveled from the far shore of Rathain to fete the prince's grand entry. The cities of Highscarp, Jaelot, and Werpoint owned a tangible reason to show gratitude, since the crown's generous restitution for every galley destroyed by the Master of Shadow at Minderl Bay. Pensions were allotted for the families left fatherless, and then new ships, replaced out of Tysan's royal treasury; the gifts did not end with fair frames and stout planking. Daily, there arrived the convict clan crews to satisfy losses to labor.

Rathain's grateful guildsmen had underwritten the night's feast. The wine and the toasts flowed freely. The hour was late when the Prince of the Light shook off his ardent admirers. He shed the adoration of the last clinging sycophants and retired at length to his chamber.

The Lord Mayor of Narms had provided his visiting royalty with a large suite of rooms commanding the sweep of the harbor. The furnishings were heavy, varnished black walnut, and the rugs, woven in gold ropes with the deep scarlet dyes for which Narms was famed far and wide. The bedhangings had been scented with dried rose petals. The basin held lavender water. Towels and soap were of the first quality, and a tray of rare vintage wine had been left as a courtesy.

Lysaer paused in the first private moment he had known since the hour his state galley had left Miralt Head. As his body servant latched the door gently behind him, he resisted the frank urge to raise his hands and massage the ache in his temples. His arrival had gone well. The pledges obtained for money and troops to build the resources of his Alliance had poured in, fanned by the bow wake of excitement. Much rode on his ability to fire such sentiment.

This was the first diplomatic visit he had paid to Rathain since the catastrophic loss, when the Master of Shadow had bogged down his great war host on the shores of Minderl Bay. Letters and gifts had kept feelings running high in the Alliance's favor, even after six years. Well cognizant of the snares of intrigue and politics still left to surmount to bring the Spinner of Darkness to destruction, Lysaer stood, feeling leaden. The luxuries placed in the room for his pleasure did not comfort, an oddity that jarred after the privations of a rough and arduous sea crossing.

Then memory smashed through the warm haze of wine. On his last pass through Narms, his best friend and confidant had still been alive. Now Diegan was dead, and Lady Talith estranged. Lysaer had no antidote for the loneliness, except to carry forward the cause of the Light. Arithon's ruin became the last thing in life to have meaning.

Oppressed by the cloy of patchouli on his skin from the smothering admiration of several trade ministers' wives, Lysaer waved off the servant, who moved to close the dagged velvet curtains. "Just crack the latch. I need the fresh air."

Tired, made tense from the drag of his diamond-and-gold collar, Lysaer closed his eyes and surrendered his person to the ubiquitous care of his valet. Stripped, bathed in warm water and clove oil, and reclothed in silk, he settled under blankets loomed by the finest craft-guild in Cildorn.

"Leave the one candle burning," he instructed his servant, though the silent, trained staff who attended him since Vastmark all knew: the one light was never permitted to go out. The prince never slept in darkness lest he suffer the torment of recurrent ill dreams. His servants were discreet. They did not speak of the fear that Lord Diegan had shared like a brother; that the fate the prince shouldered for the greater good of humanity might prove too great a destiny for one man. Lysaer stood apart with his given gift of light. He lived by his promise as defender of the innocent, though the burden to banish threat of sorcery and shadow at times seemed to sear through his blood. Diegan alone had tempered those moments when the mere sight of darkness could fracture his reason and drive him to targetless rage.

Now, Lysaer took no chances. His driving will to see his nemesis dead must not slip his control on the unquiet wings of night's shadow.

The servants had stopped suggesting that he take a mistress. After Talith, no woman born could ease the cruel quandary of his solitude. New staff were warned not to question. Since the friend who had been his right hand died in Vastmark, ever and always, Lysaer s'Ilessid passed the hours before daybreak alone. His honor guard knew to stand fast at his door. They would admit no one short of a messenger bearing word of war or disaster.

Tonight, Lysaer did not sleep. Weary as he was, relaxed to pampered lassitude, an indefinable edge kept him wakeful. The odd feeling plagued him, as though something unseen and unheard lurked in the dimness and watched him. Since the momentous occasion when the shade of a Fellowship Sorcerer had visited with news of his wife's abduction, he did not feel the fool for indulging in paranoid fancy.

For at least the third time, he surveyed the sumptuous appointments of his bedchamber.

The painted door was still closed and latched. His jewels and clothes from the feast had been tidied and folded into the chest by the armoire. The ironbound coffers with his tactical maps and correspondence were locked and stacked in neat order. His servants were efficient. In well-oiled habit, they had arranged the basin and stand with clean towels. The floor gleamed, mopped clean of slopped water, and buffed with a shine of new wax. Beyond the cracked casement, the late-burning torches by the quayside taverns wore cocoons of rising mist. The harbor was peaceful. At the mouth of the inlet, the signalman's bell clanged to guide inbound ships through the channel. A dog barked, and a carriage ground past. Through the distanced chatter of departing celebrants, the rhythmic tramp of a wall sentry carried in on the breeze from the tideflats.

The night seemed tranquil and ordinary in the port city of Narms.

Lysaer combed a last glance through the corner which held the pearl-and-lacquer gleam of the secretary's desk. And this time, he saw that in fact, *the room where he lay was not empty.*

A woman sat on the lion claw stool. Her pose was so still the hands clasped in her lap might have been shaped of smoothed ivory. Her face lay obscured, sunk in the depths of a hood of violet silk. Her sleeves and hemline wore six bands in silver, the sheen of metallic cloth like chrome ribbon snap-frozen into black ice. Only the quartz pendant on its chain at her breast moved in time to her breathing.

"Koriani," gasped Lysaer. Woolen blankets tumbled over his knees as he jackknifed erect in hard startlement. "What are you doing here? *How did you get past my guards?*"

The woman's hood dipped to a fractional tilt of her head. "They knew only as much as I wished them to see." One finger flicked straight in sudden, sharp censure. "No. Don't call. I'm not here as your enemy."

"You were not invited," Lysaer said, his consonants clear as chipped crystal. "Let me be plain. The Alliance of Light is opposed to the tyrannies imposed by the practice of sorcery."

"The glamour which allowed me to slip in with your servants encroached upon no one's free will." The hands were a young woman's, which lifted and removed the dark hood; underneath, a face of baby-smooth skin and a coil of salt-and-pepper hair neatly sculpted with tortoiseshell pins. The eyes were clear brown, and direct, and not youthful at all. She had lips like the pink underside of a conch, turned up in a half smile of irony. "Credit me with some semblance of courtesy. I could have made my presence known while you were engaged in your bath."

If the enchantress sought to unbalance him, the effort fell short. Lysaer turned not a hair, nor blushed, but regarded her with a calm that transcended small vanity. "Under any circumstance, I would have refused your public petition for audience."

The Koriani laughed, a peal of joy like the struck tone of bronze bells. "You fear for your image of morality, I see, far more than for your male pride. Very well. Since I have obtained your close company on my own, you might as well sit and listen. I've came to offer you my order's help to bring down the Master of Shadow."

Lysaer stood up. The quilt slid from the mattress and puddled on the floor, while his hands closed to fists defined in white knuckles and hard tendons. "I am listening," he assured her. "But I warn, be very careful what you say."

He crossed the thick carpet, turned the stuffed chair by the casement, and seated himself on the opposite side of the secretary. An unearthly gleam seemed to burn in his eyes, the pinned highlight touched by the candle as hard as a cut facet in sapphire. His damp hair clung in fronds to his head, tarnished and heavy as spilled varnish.

Through a grave stillness, the enchantress took his measure. Her smile was gone, and her hands cupped the quartz crystal pendant strung on silver chain at her breast. "Our kind make no bargains," she said at chill length. "Nor am I here by any other will but the bidding of Morriel Prime. She would have you know that she shares

205

your conviction. The Master of Shadow poses a threat to the free growth of society. Koriathain will assist your Alliance against that one enemy if you ask. Remember our pledge. Keep your captains at arms vigilant, no matter the season. We have cast auguries on the future. My Matriarch would have me say that your opening to take down Arithon will come far sooner than you think."

The question burned through even Lysaer's state discipline. "When will this happen?"

"You shall have fair warning." The enchantress raised a finger and traced a sigil in burning lines on the air. The glyph flared bright violet, then flashed, shocking sight with its blinding intensity. Lysaer threw his hands up to shield his face. In the second he was dazzled, the light burst and vanished into a soundless clap of heat.

The stool where the enchantress had been seated stood empty in the draft-torn flutter of the candle.

Lysaer shot from his chair. The beautiful carved back smashed into the wall, raising chips and a small puff of plaster. Barefoot, sweating, all over unclean from his bone-deep revulsion for magecraft, he paced over the floor. He searched every corner, banged open the doors to the armoire, even hurled the bedhangings free of their tasseled silk cords. He found nothing. No sign remained of the enchantress who had invaded his chamber. The stuffed cushion on the stool felt ice chill in the breath of the drafts. The street beyond the casement lay shadowed and dim, empty of mongrels or carriages.

Lysaer crossed to the nightstand, uncorked the wine bottle, and sucked down the vintage red from Orvandir in gulps. The dry heat that curled in his belly did nothing to settle the prickle of fear on his skin. He fought for cool reason. The wild heat in his blood was not rational, he knew, but extended back into childhood. The distrust that ripped him began with his mother, a s'Ahelas witch who had married a king, and then undone her vows in betrayal. Her perfidy had created his nemesis, the bastard born Master of Shadow.

Unsettled, Lysaer paced to the window again. The bite of the sea wind bit through his thin silk and set him shuddering in waves of reaction. Too tense to be dreaming, he decided the Koriani presence must be an apparition, brought on by a waking illusion.

Real or not, her words remained with him, a branding gift of live coals well designed to ignite the full flame of his passion. Consumed by the spark of his secret desire, Lysaer stared unseeing into the fog which settled over the dark harbor. He could not rest now. Sleep lay past reach, while the greater good of moral justice did battle with his most staunch private scruple. He sweated and shook, brought to his knees by a need that wrung merit from even this unsavory liaison.

In the self-searching depths of a tormented honesty, he allowed that perhaps his harsh judgment had been premature. Spellcraft could become a tool or a weapon. The outcome depended on whose hands guided the range of its power. The Koriani Order long claimed to champion the cause of humanity. In all fairness, he must grant them their chance to stand by compassionate principle. Now that their arcane support had been offered, he could turn down no prospect of help to bring Arithon s'Ffalenn to destruction.

Dualities

In Narms, after sunrise, when the royal valet undertakes the prince's dressing, he finds his charge in a rare, testy mood; too timid to gainsay the direct order not to speak, he does not mention the oddity that only a personal servant might notice: sometime in the night, a small lock of hair has been snipped from the nape of the royal neck. . . .

A fortnight after Arithon's arrival at Riverton, the master shipwright, Cattrick, sits morose in his quarters, head pressed between his huge hands; diligently he has tried, and failed, to provoke Arithon to distrust, and now time runs out to thwart the betrayal demanded as service for a Koriani oath of debt, sworn years ago to save a young sister stricken with fever in childbed. . . .

Far south and east, oblivious to the greater machinations of her order, the enchantress Elaira smiles upon a black-haired child and promises on the day of his fifth birthday she will saddle her fat gelding and begin his first lesson in horsemanship. . . .

Early Winter 5652

VI. Tangle

Snow silted over the rooftops of Capewell and frost-chilly light poured in with the drafts through the tower's misfitted casement. On the landing beneath, First Senior Lirenda stood shivering in her layers of travel-soaked woolens. Before her loomed the observatory door, laced still with the tracework glimmer of seals kept undisturbed since Morriel Prime's fateful conjury. Raised power had charged the air over time. Even the dust held a singed, acrid tang of charred carbon. An unsettled presence in the gloom of the stairwell, the peeress of the Koriani sisterhouse and her staff of enchantresses hung waiting.

The dignity of privilege bred into her long bones, Lirenda at last gave opinion, her husky, bronze tones sheared into a thousandfold echoes. "The chamber must be unsealed, no matter the risk." She inclined her head toward a spiderworked nexus of sigils. "I sense stayspells in play, ones powerful enough to bend the forward flow of time. That lends cause to hope. Our Prime might still be alive."

The peeress advanced, her soft, oval face dimpled with apprehension. Small need to stress that if the Prime lived, the least upset to a meshed net of wardfields might compound disaster and kill her.

Well aware the woman's silence masked censure, Lirenda faced about, all poured grace in her travel-muddied mantles. "What of the two initiates trapped inside when the spells sealed? Should they also be left entombed alive? Mercy on them, in the absence of our Prime, the burden of their fate becomes mine."

The peeress curtseyed, her deference made awkward by the steep, narrow stair, and the enchantresses close pressed behind her. "First Senior, no one questions your judgment." For more than the lives of three colleagues were at risk; the order's Great Waystone could scarcely be abandoned in the resonance of malingering influence.

A spell had gone wrong within that sealed chamber. Behind seals that blocked scrying, who knew what raised powers might escape conjured channels and run wild. Such deviated forces could not disperse naturally, hemmed in by wardfields of containment that time and attrition would destabilize. Leaked vectors of current might resurge decades later in unpredictable, even lethal flares of backlash. Had Morriel engaged the Waystone's grand matrix to frame the main axis of the construct, a derangement of unbalanced forces could seed anything from cyclones to broadscale cataclysm.

The wise old peeress harbored nothing but dread for her First Senior's designated duty.

Lirenda bent her head and raised her banded hood, but never to hide trepidation. She might wish heart and mind to share the peeress's grief for the fresh risks to Morriel's plight. The icier truth eclipsed sentiment: the challenge ahead did not daunt, but instead, incited the First Senior's strung nerves to a guilt-fed flame of excitement.

On a threshold of perilous responsibility, when the innate flaws of mortality should have shaken self-confidence, Lirenda felt estranged from the shrinking caution of her peers. Authority and rank of themselves did not distance her. No; what marked her apart was her sinful, fierce lust for the chance to acquire supreme power.

Lirenda well knew the deep pitfalls of ambition. Her craving for control could calcify pity, even grow to undermine the Koriani creed of human mercy. Through the long, lonely nights after trials of initiation, she had battled her willful nature. Yet like the addict's secret pleasure, need chafed at restraint. The drive to grasp the reins of command found neither outlet nor surcease; self-contained as the hunting tigress, Lirenda understood herself very well.

She would rule the pack rather than serve.

"I will rest and eat," she informed the peeress and the anxious coterie of enchantresses. "By the advent of noon, I want a containment seal wrought at the head of the stairwell. Set a second one at the lower entrance. Then my work to breach the wards on the observatory will begin."

*   *   *

Reclothed in an overrobe of lavender silk stitched with the silver bands of her rank, Lirenda withdrew from her survey of the stiletto bars of light which demarked the seal construct just raised between the stairwell and the warded threshold of the observatory. The protections laid down by the sisterhouse's senior circle proved flawless, each detail precise in execution. Lirenda had cross-checked each interstice. Should any skewed force slip past her control, the sisterhouse residents and the citizens of Capewell would be safe beyond sound defenses.

"Well-done," she said in perfunctory praise, then opened the box at her side to unveil the quartz point which would channel her will for the conjury.

The senior enchantress inclined her gray head in acceptance, then motioned her twelve colleagues forward to their places. She unmasked a wand crystal to cut and mark the boundary of containment for the conjury about to commence.

No need to review every nuance and precaution; from here, all proceedings would follow an age-old, proscribed set of rituals. Each initiate chosen for the task was experienced with the perils of unstable conjuries. Their nerves or trepidation stayed masked in decorum as they knelt in a rustle of purple skirts to serve the greater good of the Koriani Order. Arrayed in the traditional circle, each one cupped her personal quartz and murmured a cantrip of opening. A slow minute passed, the crystals a mute spark of light between each pair of hands. Then their solitary wills caught and engaged with the energetic matrix of the stones. Each enchantress spun her awareness in trance to channel through the master crystal held poised between the First Senior's palms.

Lirenda engaged the sigils of command to capture each individual thread. Then she framed the binding seals to comb disparate energies into aligned subservience. The familiar, tingling build of drawn force poured down her nerves like a tonic. Her own senses heightened in link with the quartz crystal's burgeoning resonance. The air gained a transcendent clarity, then transformed, a shimmering veil through which the webworked lattice of raised power seemed as ribbons of laced silver light. Lirenda's sole will linked her circle of sister initiates until their collateral talent framed a spearshaft of balanced intent.

Cipher and rune, Lirenda wrought the last seal. Through the moment of consummation, stray thoughts dissolved. Here, at the heart of Koriani ritual, linked with an empowered focus crystal, she found the unalloyed thrill of fulfillment. All the aching, hollow yearning inside her lay banished by absolute control.

211

Her touch, and no other, could order the moment. She *was* the nexus to spin that reservoir of force and break Morriel's wards of privacy over the observatory door.

The sword-edged delicacy of that unbinding took most of the afternoon. Those seniors who assisted emerged from tranced melding exhausted and pale with relief. They grounded their energies, disbanded their circle, then asked formal leave with a dutiful lack of curiosity.

Their First Senior spoke the time-honored release. "Your will is your own."

Outside the slit window, new snow caught the aquamarine tint of the afterglow. Farther off, the eventide chime of the kitchen bell summoned the orphan wards to supper. Lirenda did not crave the teeming warmth of human company. Taxed by her hours of close concentration, she touched tapered fingertips to her shut lids.

The flaring, harsh afterimage of the last, enchained sigils felt branded into her retinas. A tremor shook through her. Dampened skin under smothering layers of silk prickled through an aftershock of chills, as her stressed thoughts skittered across a razor array of dark facts. The Prime Matriarch's workings to safeguard this portal had been unimaginably thorough.

Wrapped in a disapproving silence like armor, the peeress remained stationed in the stairwell. The safety of the sisterhouse at Capewell was her given charge. Far removed from her cozy, first post as a ward matron, and happiest with a toddler on her knee, she shouldered the need to witness what passed, despite her stiff grounds for objection.

Always made to feel unnatural before others endowed with the nurturing, female instincts, Lirenda arose. She closed a chilled hand over the icier brass of the latch. Her untamed thrill of anticipation never showed as she set herself to violate her Prime's most guarded confidence. Aware that such elaborate defenses might stem from a need to thwart observation from the Fellowship, Lirenda loosed the bar. She pushed the portal inward, pressured by passions she had striven all her life to contain.

The door swung wide to a whisper of pressed air. Darkness beyond hung like unmarked slate, sliced through by shining lines of argent. Morriel's spell construct sheared across gloom in breath-stopping, masterful splendor. Circle upon square, each interstice sang in meticulous balance, multiple layers of enchained sigils looped in knots like filigree wire trapped in felt. The weave displayed an unnerving complexity, centrally anchored by a stayspell which fixed its point of origin in the past. Lirenda found herself mazed into wonder. Those entangling radiants resisted translation, nor could dazzled eyesight track every spiral, which channeled the conjury's influence outward to arc through an unformed future.

At a predestined moment, this majestic array of spells would resolve and shape an event of Morriel's design.

"Merciful maker!" Lirenda breathed in awe.

Imagination foundered. The effects of stark beauty and sheer terror stopped her breath. Sparked to hot jealousy and raging despair, she knew beyond question her skills were inadequate to match such a broadscale endeavor. If Morriel Prime had passed the Wheel into death, that one shortfall might brand her successor forever. Lirenda coveted the knowledge not yet in her hands with a passion of savage proportion.

The paradox stymied her raging ambition.

Either she waited to assume the supreme mantle of her order, or she lived all her days galled by the loss of an irreplaceable legacy. A live Prime Matriarch or a shriveled corpse: the cipher which entangled her destiny lurked in fusty darkness, coiled inside of those perilous, dagger-edged spells.

The peeress's tentative inquiry shattered her furious thought. "Did anyone survive?"

Lirenda called back through the entry, "I'm not sure yet." She drew a steadying breath, freighted with smells of dank stone and charred herbs, but no reek of corrupted flesh. An untrustworthy reassurance, since the might of the inaugural stayspell itself would arrest the progression of decay. Nor could she plumb the silence with spells. Wards drawn and laid on the axis of the earth were not permeable. Even cursory review showed the outermost circle demarked a sealed pocket in time.

The purpose which guided the construct stayed hidden. To know Morriel's fate and recover the Great Waystone, her successor must bridge those dire protections, then walk the convoluted maze to its center.

"You may enter the observatory," Lirenda informed the peeress. "I'll need a wise senior to keep vigil."

Three tentative steps masked in rustling cloth; then the stunned gasp as the enchantress arrived and shared sight of the construct's magnificence. "First Senior, for prudence, the safest course would be a ritual cleansing to unmake every line of that patterning."

"I know. Yet we daren't." No flutter ruffled Lirenda's poise as she cupped the spell crystal strung on silver chain at her neck. "The importance of this design must be paramount. How dare we countermand our Prime's signal will? I fear worse, to unravel the least vector of power without knowing the reason for her act of self-sacrifice."

The peeress smoothed back a loose wisp of hair, ill at ease in the face of necessity. "Be cautious, First Senior, for all of our sakes. With the world brought to strife by the works of cursed princes, the Koriani Order cannot afford to lose both Prime and successor."

Lirenda stared back, her eyes impenetrable as flawed amber. "I will not fail. And Morriel might still be recovered alive."

Too aware the ordeal would test every facet of her training, she dispatched her final instructions. "Stay alert. If the energy flow in the sigils turns sour, don't rely on the wards of containment. Collapse the construct immediately, and close the door with a grave seal."

The peeress stepped back, torn into reluctant discomfort. "Your will, First Senior."

But already, Lirenda forged ahead. The chain in her hand stitched cobalt reflections across gloom as she bent her trained mind through the crystal, then dangled its focus as a pendulum over the rimwards of Morriel Prime's outer circle.

Just as a mirror would give back the light, the quartz caught vibrations in resonance. Attuned through its matrix, Lirenda allowed the stone's captured energy to suffuse the waiting, blank eye of her consciousness. Guided by discipline, she allowed Morriel's work to imprint its pattern in her mind.

Guard and defense, the ward showed her emptiness, a fathomless well of negative space to freeze breathing flesh and stop the heart. The crystal spun deosil on its chain. A hint of a smile bowed Lirenda's rose lips. She advanced a half stride widdershins, her quartz poised above the figured ward. Its clear facets flashed like flaked mica, whirling faster, then faster still. Lirenda took another step. The jewel flared brighter, a blue spark gouged out of stygian dark. Still the freezing void gripped its interface, translating through to her mind.

The draw of the circle was steady in deception, its blankness cloaked in a numbing, seductive sense of peace. Lirenda stayed guarded. A Prime Matriarch's protections were to be feared. Any gap in her personal defenses, and the ward's shrouding vacuum would sweep past control and smash her link to conscious memory. An infinite expanse of null energy would draw spirit from flesh, and see her lost utterly and forever.

Lirenda trod the rim of the construct, her palms lightly sweating, the chain between her pinched fingers a vibrating thread whirled by a crystal tuned to madness. Step upon step, she sought the one cipher of opening that *should* be wrought into every formal conjury fashioned under Koriani auspices.

Another pace, another; the spinning quartz raised a faint, waspish hum from the chain. The darkness with its smells of tarnish and dust shrouded the edges of vision. Light-headed with strain, Lirenda forced burning eyes back to focus. She refused the undermining dread, that Morriel's design might have omitted the sigil she required for access.

That moment the chain jerked. Its tethered crystal snapped the links rigid and hung as if nailed to the earth.

Lirenda wrung out a sigh of relief. Her nerve was iron and her left hand precise as she raised power and engaged the prime successor's cipher through the heart of her focus crystal. The quartz flared acid yellow in reply. As that key answered its matching lock, a handspan arc of the ward circle flickered from blue to acidic gold. The access point opened.

Lirenda crossed the abyss. Dread forces held in abeyance through her passage scoured her nerves into tingles. Her skin felt scraped by razor-edged steel and her vision blanched into static. She had no perception, no balance, no will. Only faith assured safe completion of her step. Reason and substance reassembled at last as her foot came back down on solid stone. She was through.

The blinding veils tore away.

Around her, entombed stone and dusty darkness hung with an alkaline scent of chalk. Hemmed by the impeccable vibrations of the wards, Lirenda settled her riled senses. Her course was committed. From the moment she engaged with the spell's inner workings, the sigil which granted her entry would fade. Should Morriel still live, the pattern must be followed through to its end without disturbing the least, subtle vector of laid force. Had Morriel died, Lirenda must survive to contain whatever raging chaos had brought her Prime Matriarch's downfall.

Possessed by a clean, analytical calm, Lirenda surveyed her prospects. Behind her, the defense wards glimmered their fixed, arctic blue. Ahead, scribed in lines like hot fire, the active core of the conjury blazed like a slow fuse, bound to its preset course. The slate slabs underfoot wore a glimmer of chalked sigils, the inaugural runes dimmed to spiderworked tracks where the energy had consumed itself in completion. Among them, Lirenda picked out bronze pans of spent ashes arrayed at each point of the compass. The scents of charred herbs had long since melded into the ambient dust, yet the

215

placement tied the construct through space and distance in ritual alignment with the land.

Lirenda wadded her cloak hem and skirts into the grip of cramped fingers, that no haphazard eddy could smear the febrile chains of dead ciphers. She eased her way along the inner rim of the ward circle until she found the Paravian rune, *An*, which meant prime, or one, or beginning, and without which no work of Koriani spellcraft could be engaged on Athera.

The significating figure interlaced with that rune seemed a knotwork of arcs, configured with maddening intricacy. Lirenda paused there, confounded. This elaborate work of conjury did not frame the foil she expected against interference by Fellowship Sorcerers. Hampered by the unsettled light, the Prime Senior freed her quartz and chain for another arcane sounding. She dangled the crystal above the faint chalk lines, hopeful, yet no residual energy remained for the stone to recapture in resonance. She had no alternative but to refire the sigil, lend it a spark from her own conjured will to trace its original vibration. The quartz as her focus, she bent her will through the matrix. A lifetime of training enabled its virtue to channel her talent into an applicable force.

She stilled curiosity to listening silence, then threaded a tenuous connection. The lines on the floor responded and flared a fleeting, subliminal purple. Their imprinted resonance surged through the quartz link, and touched her ready awareness.

She grasped that the construct framed the individual Name for a man, but no more.

Her sounding of his analog presence stormed through her like tide, an unassailable, blanketing warmth of connection that shattered all pride and restraint. Lirenda could summon no breath for denial; her stunned mind allowed her no grace for retreat. His innate compassion sheared like struck lightning across the quartz interface, to flash-burn her frozen emotions. Unwanted fascination held her in thrall, while integrity unraveled before a force like winged song, an aching, pure expression of melody that pealed through her woman's heart and filled all the hollowness within her.

Lost as she touched what could never be hers within bounds of the Koriani Order, Lirenda cried out. However she cringed and postured, this one man held the potential capacity to know her. His intuitive awareness could strip away pretense and lay bare the self she kept hidden.

Every buried sorrow escaped from containment as water might burst from shocked glass: all of a young girl's mute yearning to refute her mother's withering criticism. Cosseted by wealth and strict expectations, hounded to polished deportment, Lirenda still harbored the sawing, helpless misery left by her childhood feelings of uselessness. Her bleeding retreat from self-expression, then the refuge she carved out of rigid perfectionism had matured to a gnawing ambition. Hurt long denied now became pleasure thwarted, until the mask she wore ripped away. Her present existence became useless motion, a dance step play of meaningless shadows.

Inner barriers crumbled as the male presence tied through Morriel's spell invited her to discard empty posturing and anneal her whole being into change.

Stranger to herself, spun giddy by a siren call to cast off restraint and embrace the freedom of laughter, Lirenda understood that her armor of reserve might dissolve at a touch and bare her vulnerable heart. One man might command such power to change her. She gasped, torn through by a savagery of need beyond the bounds of her past experience. Fear snapped her poise. She gave way to a firestorm of tears, when in callous fact, she had never before let self-pity overwhelm her.

Her violated pride at last sparked true rage, to stab through rank turmoil and redeem her.

Hurled back into still, dusty dark and the comfortless flare of sealed spells, Lirenda knelt in the suffocating velvet of her formal robes of high office. Her quartz pendant and chain hung slack in her hands, as though bone, flesh, and nerve had been scorched. Ath, *Ath preserve*, she knew this man's nature, with his devastating, forthright perception of hidden truths. Never mind he was a living danger to the world, with no thought at all for her dedicated life inside the Koriani Order. His existence was a threat to unstring heart and mind, then whirl her like a moth to its brainless immolation in a lantern flame.

Alone in chill darkness, Lirenda gasped a vengeful curse on his name. For the lynchpin of the construct Morriel had conjured held none else but the imprinted signature for Arithon, Prince of Rathain.

The discovery wounded like double-edged steel, that the Shadow Master's fate lay entangled with Koriani destiny. Lirenda locked her teeth in frustrated resentment. Of course, the Prime Matriarch must suspect her hidden weakness for the ill-starred Teir's'Ffalenn. No other reason explained Morriel's need to tie his movements in dire spells and secrecy.

Lirenda stood. A twisted cry escaped her. Arithon, unholy fires of creation, *Arithon s'Ffalenn* had been the instrument of disaster to trigger the Matriarch's downfall. The irony all but choked her, that he might also became the signal turn of fate to transfer the reins of prime power into her impatient hands. The reason why remained twined with the riddle behind Morriel's grand conjury.

Between the glacial glimmer of the defense ward and the surging, core brilliance of active magecraft, the chalked chains of ciphers which keyed the spell's purpose extended in tangling spirals. Lirenda released the crushed links of silver embedded into her palm. Unable to quell the tremor in her knees, she buffed the clammy fog of perspiration from her crystal. The misfortune of Arithon's Name as significator posed a most thorny complication.

Her annoyance found voice in startling venom. "Merciful Ath, prince, if Morriel's died of this, you'll regret the light of day that saw you born."

Lirenda grasped her quartz and rapped out a cantrip to raise a spark of illumination. Its firefly glow caught the rune *Shayn*, for two, stitched through the seals of a tracking spell. The locus which keyed its activation sprang from a riverside inn along the Ilswater in Tysan. Slaved to that sequence, Lirenda uncovered the Name form for Dakar, then Caolle's as well, hooked and tagged by the spellbinder's glamour to disguise his native clan accent. The reason for the triad presented no mystery. Morriel had wished to trace Arithon's movements. As safeguard against his wily nature, she tied in his henchmen to assure an unbroken connection.

The lines off the third figure held branching complexity. Lirenda recognized the triplicate axis of the seer's rune, then the mazed ciphers for diversion and secrecy, joined to trigger threads for a delicate array of spring traps. The spell became more than a straightforward scrying. Morriel had wrought against the code of the Koriani Order to curtail the freedom of a prince.

Lirenda refused to pass judgment for that transgression of founding principle. Arithon s'Ffalenn was a catalyst of unprecedented and volatile potential. Discomfited herself by unruly attraction, she saw too well how his influence had once spoiled the faith of a promising young initiate. Perhaps in the greater reach of her wisdom, Morriel Prime saw past Elaira's tragic defection to some threat to the sisterhood at large. Or worse: the might of this construct may well have been raised to shield Lirenda herself from temptation. Koriani code held no recourse. Any romantic entanglement would disbar her from prime succession.

"Never that," the First Senior avowed, shamed by demeaning possibility. Hatred scorched through her, that the man could exist with potential to tear the least flaw in her loyalty.

She pressed on to shed her embarrassment. Meticulous strings of sigils fanned into a widening net, until Arithon's movements were not only traced, but stalked outright. As the first chains of circumstance branched right and left to rearrange destiny and entrap, Lirenda felt no surprise. By then, leading evidence established his role as Morriel's earmarked quarry. The progression unfolded with diabolical care, the Prime's plot stitched unerringly through Arithon's machinations at Riverton to suborn Lysaer's royal shipyard.

Lirenda deciphered the unwinding course of events, forced to admire the artistry of invention, as a bard's salty repertoire made the Laughing Captain a haunt for sailhands and shipwrights. Through a season's cagey dealings with Cattrick, while Dakar blunted his worries through drink, Morriel's neat craft passed unnoticed. Spring trap and trigger, Arithon's course became flanked in a narrowing channel, scribed in surreptitious power and plain chalk.

Lirenda paused to stretch a cramp from her hand. The crystal on its chain had warmed from hard use. She nestled it between her palms and chanted clearing cantrips, while her arcane connection to a fragment of happenstance reeled on to display a spectral recast of a dialogue spoken days since. The trace resonance of sound preserved by spent sigils cast whispered echoes through the deadened air of the observatory . . .

'When's the next launching?' murmured a flaxen-haired bard in a voice unmistakably Arithon's, while from a tucked pose in a scarlet-cushioned window seat, the broad-shouldered master of Tysan's royal shipyard weighed his every word with the slit-eyed contention of a lynx.

'Next week,' Cattrick drawled. 'The gilders are still fussing with her brightwork. If the riggers and splicers are left to their gnashing row over topping lifts, the shakedown could stretch a bit longer.' A pause for a smile of provocative, white teeth. 'You know this brig's going to be tougher. The disappearance of the last was blamed on green officers, so this time they've assigned the tried and trusty.'

The bard sheared a needle-bright chord from his lyranthe. Under his hands the music held laughter, belied by the shaded intensity of the gaze stilled and trained upon Cattrick. 'Your craft is the building of excellent ships. My share of the fun is to steal them.'

The spelled record dimmed, faded back into fusty trails of chalk. Lirenda blinked, brought back to herself. She had screened the final, spent frames of the construct. Ahead stretched the fire-strung nets of live power, preset for events yet to come.

The interface with the present spread at her feet, and the next sounding she touched would be volatile. Contact might jar the uncoiling precision of the spell's influence. Arithon s'Ffalenn still possessed trained awareness. Blind instinct could warn him if she raised a disturbance. Now, the least misstep would unbalance the conjury. The smallest disruption of pent power could destroy her if an inadvertent move chanced to unravel the delicate bindings.

Lirenda blotted a forehead rinsed in sweat. Around her, the observatory seemed a sealed tomb; cold dark wrapped its core of inferno. Loop upon loop of slaved power lay spring wound and cocked, awaiting the moment of release. Lirenda strove to read the fine lines inked like magma across the dark. The dazzle whirled her to dizziness, and the Great Waystone remained beyond view. Aware she must risk direct contact through visions, she knew visceral fear. The danger before her was no longer malleable. Should she once lose control inside those nets of voracious power, naught would remain of frail flesh and bone but an immolated silt of white ash.

Carried by her unbending determination, Lirenda stilled her awareness. Blank as cooled glass, she stamped down her traitorous, cringing unease, raised her jewel on its chain, and doused its bared facets in the surging, live current of the spell. As the upending rush of seer's vision claimed her, she braced herself to receive . . .

The taproom was jammed to an airless, close heat of packed bodies and uproarious noise. By nightfall, drawn in from the frost and the leaden chill of coastal winter, every yard craftsman and beached sailhand in Riverton crammed into the Laughing Captain. Celebration ruled the hour. That day had seen a successful royal launching. The new brig rode at anchor behind the seawall, sparkling with lanterns hooked to her yards as the riggers tied in her last running lines. The crew selected to man her for shakedown attended the madhouse festivity. They sat apart, under orders to moderate their drink. Despite the close eye of an iron-willed captain, they howled with laughter and accepted the beer mugs passed across by congratulatory friends.

Only the bard at the settle had elbow room. With the same stilled deception of a storm's sunlit eye, he stirred the jammed room to a feverish, wild energy through a reeling succession of dance tunes. The crowd responded, and stamped, and roared with fine spirits, dry tinder raked for the spark.

Dakar's clumsy, inebriated trip came perfectly timed to fetch against a bald sailor. The pair of them toppled in a tangling heap, and a trestle crashed over to a flying gush of spilled beer. A bystander's screeched insult provoked a swung fist. From behind their captain's cordon, several of the brig's crew laughed and shouted in scathing amusement. As though uncoiled from a spell, an agile little caulker whose dinner had been upset snatched a pitcher from a barmaid's laden tray. He hurled its foamy contents to silence the ridicule and doused their small pocket of decorum. Through yells of blind outrage, the bard's measures changed key, then leaped a surreptitious beat faster. His disingenuous skill burned the very air to abandon, while tempers frayed red, and brawlers set to and sowed mayhem across the packed taproom . . .

"Dharkaron *curse* the man's effrontery!" Lirenda swore as scried vision dissolved and freed thought.

Lysaer's handpicked sailhands had been fearlessly targeted, and a fool's guess could forecast outcome. To sideline the men of unswerving crown loyalty assigned to choice berths on the brig, the bonesetters in Riverton would be given a busy night's work. Arithon would claim his diabolical triumph as the scheduled shakedown raised sail with an alternate crew.

Burning to uncover how Morriel's construct might serve the s'Ffalenn prince his comeuppance, Lirenda mapped a parallel strand in the weave. She found a fresh spring trap interlinked to a marvel of scried forecast, and already engaged by the Riverton launching. The construct arced across distance and time, and conjoined with another, inset with the trefoil seal of a sworn obligation. Some minor Name who bore oath of debt to the Koriani Order received his call to deliver due service.

In the stale dark of the observatory, under roof beams nicked scarlet by the agitated light thrown off by arcane powers, the First Senior set her will once again and pitched her crystal to imprint its moment of due consequence . . .

Amid the gaudy appointments of an Etarran hall of state, a lanky scholar with soft hands arose from his self-conscious bow. Clad in wine velvet, his bristled, white hair tamed by a cross-laced silk ribbon, he raised his chin to squint at the imposing, blond figure on the dais. Fingers damp, and heart pounding, he offered up the aged vellum he had asked private audience to deliver.

"Milord Prince of the Light, my translation is done. By Koriani request, the fruits of rare knowledge are to be freely given to your cause. What you hold in your hands is an early–Third Age treatise on the lost arts of ocean navigation."

A deep, rolling thrill pricked Lirenda to gooseflesh. Morriel, in collaboration with Lysaer, against Arithon; the piquancy of that manipulative use of politics raised a sharp gasp of astonishment. Seldom before had a Koriani Prime used power to move sovereign players as pawns. Lirenda traced the spell's ranging reach toward the future. Curiosity fed now on the drive of ambition, she *saw* the sealed dispatch from Cattrick which would soon prompt Prince Lysaer to assemble a picked following and leave Etarra in whirlwind secrecy and haste. Cause to consequence, the mighty construct converged, with Arithon flushed into desperate flight. Once he took to the sea, the grand plan would close on him, its culminating force dovetailed into an ingenious, orchestrated opportunity. The last stroke would fall amid the stormy, broad swells of Mainmere Bay. Lirenda reached *Alt*, the rune of closure, and the construct's cycle showed the end game to crown its set purpose.

Morriel's clandestine trap would strip Arithon defenseless, then bind his mettlesome fate into impotence through Koriani captivity.

On her knees before the last sigil, Lirenda pressed narrow palms to her lips to stifle vindictive laughter. Humiliation lanced through the rags of her mirth, that Morriel should judge her too fragile a vessel to bear knowledge of Arithon's defeat. If the Matriarch died of such overweening arrogance, fate's backhanded justice was worthy of Dharkaron Avenger.

Lirenda regarded the inner circle of traced, dusty ash and singed herbs. The arced patterns of ending and ward were precise. She sobered to fact, that the old Prime had left no loose ends. Past the dribbled stubs of dead candles, beyond the ceremonial braziers burned cold on their stands, the amethyst Waystone gleamed in sullen quiescence. No vestige of strayed power smoldered unchecked to draw backlash. Lirenda would require no ritual rune of passage to cross this last ward of protection.

These vital defenses, set to shield the spell's creator from the scalding blast of fused energies, had been breached long since. The break had been instant. No vestige of guarding virtue had survived long enough to bleed away through attrition.

Lirenda raised her skirt hems in shaking fingers, irrationally reluctant to disturb the fine lines whose sigils had failed to protect. She encountered the reason for the lapse soon enough. A girl scarcely sworn to initiate service lay sprawled across the perimeter, hands outflung on the charred slate floor. She breathed in a queerly arrested rhythm, her hollowed, pale features stamped in frozen panic by the passage of arcane forces.

Deep rage shattered Lirenda's dispassion.

Morriel Prime had not fallen to a flux of miscast energies. She had been betrayed. The failed nerve of this inadequate chit had undone the entire circle. Recognition followed, that the Matriarch had anticipated, even planned for disaster. Seven chains of stayspells wrought over the observatory kept the construct in fugue through that unbinding moment of crisis. Awe remained, that Morriel had called up the strength and sheer will to force her spell to consummation. In mortal pain, perhaps dying, she had impelled her grand construct to live on.

Lirenda straightened up and moved on, leveled to realize she owned no such depths, nor any grand bent for self-sacrifice. Beneath the scintillant eye of the Waystone, she confronted the last tragic figures. They lay in their layers of crumpled robes, youth and age like two dolls dropped through a fracture in time. The first throat she probed for a life sign lay cold; the steadfast initiate who had held to her vows had perished, her life's spirit drained out of ruthless necessity, that the Prime might survive long enough to stabilize the conjury.

One bundle remained, cast down like dry sticks in a shroud of fine velvets. Lirenda sucked in a steadying breath. Lit by the gleam of the Waystone's chill presence, she knelt down and braced herself to touch.

The wrist she raised felt insubstantial as bleached parchment wrapped over substanceless bone. But a pulse still threaded the blue network of veins. Though cool, the flesh was not corpse chill.

Against all adversity, Morriel Prime still survived. Unconscious, weakened, perhaps strayed beyond recall, indomitable will kept her breathing.

Lirenda bent her head, while heated tears welled through her eyelids. There and then, amid the musky, flat ash of spilled offerings and the alkaline tang of scraped chalk, she weighed an unthinkable choice: to collapse the grand construct and draw Morriel clear, or to let the spell burn on undisturbed to completion, and hope the Prime's tenuous reserves could hang on until the last sigil reached its planned closure.

Arithon's freedom weighed against Morriel's life; Lirenda snagged her lip between teeth like small pearls, shredded in the cruel crux between desire and ambition. Prime power in hand, and the chance to seize her autonomy; or a sheltered subservience with demeaning awareness that one man, still at large, held the means to unstring her whole character.

Lirenda arose. A laugh ripped from her patrician throat, shrill with leashed-back self-loathing. She was prideful and flawed, too desperately consumed by desire to rule. Temptation had set its steel claws in her vitals, and she was too threatened to tear free.

Alone in the dark, without voice beyond conscience, Lirenda turned her back on the fallen Prime. She shouldered the task of retracing her steps without jostling the spell's course of alignment. She held no regrets. At heart, she was exactly what her mother had claimed: a spirit born lacking the female kindness Ath granted to natural womanhood. The man who might have unchained her closed spirit held too potent a power to ruin her. Once she was confirmed as Koriani Prime Matriarch, her authority would be unassailable. No one alive need ever know of the emptiness masked at her core.

Midwinter 5653

Tidings

The port of Innish had been known as the jewel of the southcoast for as long as oared ships ranged the seas. During the hard winters, when the Stormwell Gulf capes seized with ice, warehouse space at the dockside rented out at a premium. Every shed and stable loft near the waterfront became pressed into use by the insatiable demands of commerce.

In years when the seasonal snows also sealed the northern passes, the inland attics with sound roofs lay crammed with the silks spun in Atchaz, then packed through the desert by caravan. Crated oranges from Southshire towered in stacks under awnings, awaiting sea trade to the eastern ports along Eltair Bay, or the western cities of Havish. The streets teemed. Sailhands on leave lounged under the shade of the damson trees. Merchants with their trains, breathless errand boys, and half-naked stevedores shouldering bales breasted the chaotic commotion. Busy men cursed the languidly idle who obstructed their frenetic course. The side alleys and the louvered windows of the wineshops rang with the brass bells of the prostitutes. In gilt-dusted lashes, heavy scents, and soft paint, the paid women of Innish could lure a man into dalliance and drown him in pleasure for hours.

Just crossing the wharf district for a day's business could tax an honest man to short temper. The sights themselves were temptation, the stucco colonnades with their tiled roofs and pierced finials a puzzle of artful complexity. The allure of Innish could waylay the senses in the whirl of its milling crowds, its exotic scents, or its outright, seamy misfortune, dealt out by the riffraff who skulked and preyed off the wealth that changed hands in the streets.

Feylind's brother, Fiark, had as much as he could handle as a journeyman trade factor. Left wan from the hours spent working over his master's accounts by lamplight, sweating under his beautifully tailored broadcloth in the lush southland heat, he had no patience to spare, even for thrashing through arguments with the twin sister just called back in port.

The years spent on shipboard with Arithon's crews had not blunted her feckless temperament. Her decorum was still nonexistent. No woman he knew but a dockside hussy would pick her fights amid the racketing press of the wharf at noontide, where shouted conversation could scarcely be heard, and rumors flew mouth to mouth at the least possible whiff of a scandal.

"Why can't you give us a cargo bound for Ostermere," Feylind shrilled. Clad in the man's dress she wore at her post as navigator on board the brig *Evenstar*, she spun sideways to avoid a servant bearing a crate of white doves. "Don't tell me the ladies of Eldir's capital have given up buying fine silk! Not when the King's Grace just issued a public proclamation of his handfasting!"

"What would you know of court women and their refined ways, gallivanting in slops on a ship's deck?" Fiark sniped back.

Feylind eyed him askance, unable to accustom herself to his adult dignity, nor the golden hair trimmed neat at his collar, and his genteel, quality clothing. No trace remained of the barefoot boy as he paused by the bollards and hailed a lighterman to ferry him out to a brig at a remote anchorage.

"You can't duck me so easily," Feylind retorted, her pale braid flying loose strands in the breeze, and her full-sleeved man's shirt and pearl-sewn scarlet waistcoat enough to turn heads for sheer gaudiness.

When her brother merely shrugged, she shot out a toe and expertly fended the inbound lighter away from the dock. The oarsman cursed her. She fielded his insults with a phrase by lengths more inventive, then crossed her arms and glowered down her freckled nose at her twin. Except for appearances, nothing was changed between them. Either they connived hand in glove at appalling acts of mischief, or they fought each other like stoats.

Feylind tapped her foot. Fiark would know she would heave him into the bay in his finery before she let him ignore her.

He glared back in anger for only a moment. Then the smile she loved best turned the corners of his lips, and merriment sparkled in his wide cobalt eyes. "You want to gain news of him?" That pronoun, between them, required no naming; they had spent half their lives in Prince Arithon's shadow, underfoot, or attached out of bold fascination to the strings of his far-flung machinations. "Well, you don't need to finagle a passage to Corith to hear."

Feylind's eyes of identical color lit into shrewd recognition. "That ship you're in such a hurry to meet?"

She laughed, spun about, and flicked something bright in a careless arc over the turquoise water which roiled in mishmashed chop against the seawall. The offering clanged into the cockpit of the lighter: a coin from Perdith, minted in heavy red gold.

The craft's slighted oarsman yelped in mid-oath. He recovered the bribe, then stood, face upturned, and bowed his unctuous appeasement. "Where would the lady like to go?"

"Such a way you have with men," Fiark teased, then stung her pride back by extending his hand like a gallant to assist her off of the dock.

"Do that again, and you'll swim for it," Feylind said. Limber as a monkey, she stepped off the wharf, trod down on the gunwale, then startled the lighterman all over again by claiming his unoccupied bench. She unshipped his spare pair of looms, threaded their leathers through the rowlocks, and scarce paused for Fiark to board at the stern before she dug the blades into a ferocious stroke.

"Now I'm in a hurry," she confessed as the lighter shot forward. Two other craft in the way veered aside, the owner of one snapping oaths. Feylind ignored him, intent upon Fiark. "Tell the man where we're pointing this tub."

When her brother took his time to indicate direction, Feylind jabbed down one oar like a rudder and shot the lighter craft sideways. Head twisted, she sized up the motley collection of boats, small and large, riding over their slice-cut reflections in the shelter of Innish harbor. Her grasp of detail quickly winnowed the clutter of merchant brigs: the slipshod ones with their sails tied in gaskets, and others run by more rigorous captains, rolling neat at their moorings with yardarms varnished and stripped. She assessed crosshatched rigging, the swept decks with baled cargoes, then unerring, spotted the one vessel set apart.

"Hah!" she whooped, triumphant. "Belay Fiark's word, I already see." She backwatered, hauled, and jacked the lighter onto her self-determined new heading. "We're bound for the brig with the shameless bronze tits on her figurehead."

"The *Cariadwin*," Fiark admitted to the muddled-up oarsman, who sat with his looms raised and dripping. "She's the new-looking brig on the far southwest mooring, and if anyone's shameless while still fully clothed, it's my sister. Please accept my regret for her manners."

"Shameless, is it?" Feylind jabbed in her right blade and sent a rocketing arc of water dousing over her brother's neat head. "Take worse than a wetting to cool down your insolence, but that will do for a start."

"Wench!" Fiark laughed. "For each salt stain and watermark, I'll see you chained to the washtub at home. Our stepfather won't spare you from drudgery either. He swore he'd help if I held you down. We've all got ripped hose and holed stockings for darning. High time you sat for us, mending."

"You conspired against me?" Feylind accused.

"Well yes." Fiark flipped back the dripping bangs plastered to his raised eyebrows. "Don't look so wounded. Your mother and I share the general opinion that you could stand more practice at needlework. You ought to cultivate some womanly graces for the day you weary of seafaring."

This time, he was wise and fast enough to duck as the water grazed over his head. "No chance at all," countered Feylind, carving into the pull of the next stroke. "If that means getting soft and thick bearing babes, I'd sooner swim with the sharks." Her expert handling shot the narrow lighter into the choppy crosscurrents alongside the *Cariadwin*'s side strakes.

Not to be outdone, Fiark dug into his scrip and pressed another coin in the palm of the flummoxed lighterman. "Come back at sundown. Our appointment should finish then." Despite his town clothes and his love of staid commerce, he proved then and there he could still beat his sister up the battens of a deepwater trader.

The *Cariadwin*'s captain sauntered on deck to meet them. He was a thick man, swarthy and wrinkled, with one eye crimped to a permanent squint from judging the set of his canvas. Wind and sun, and the tireless barrage of the elements had gnarled his joints, and his unlaced shirt ruffled against a chest broad enough to muscle a siege ram. He tucked away the rigging knife just used to clear a jammed block, his sharp glance touching Feylind and swinging at once back to Fiark. "Your sister, yes?" His thick, frosted eyebrows tipped upward with inquiry. "She have a strong stomach? There's business we'll have to conduct in the hold that's no pretty sight for a woman."

"Nor for a man, either," Feylind retorted, stance braced against the mild swing as the brig turned to the wind on her beam. "I promise not to puke first."

The captain threw back his head and roared with bass laughter. "By Dharkaron's vengeance!" He dealt Fiark's twin a slap between the shoulder blades that might have staggered her forward, had she not reflexively shifted her footing. "Why couldn't I have found a lass like you before I had a wife and eight weans, not to mention six lusty mistresses?"

"Because lasses like me have no use for weans, and even less for a husband." Feylind grinned back, her teeth like fine ivory, and her hair a gold rope in the sunlight. "Keep your eyes and your insinuations out of my shirtfront, and get on with what Fiark came for."

Not chastened at all, still very much taken with the female curves underneath the breeches and waistcoat, the captain waved a lanky arm toward the opened hatch amidships. "Step into my lair, then, shewolf." He sidestepped to the ladder and led the way down. More of his peppery invective boomed up from the cavernous opening. "First or last, if you puke, lady, you'll be the one handed the bucket and rag to swab up the mess on my deck."

Fiark elbowed his sister aside before she could effect a reply. "A man might think you had bollocks in those breeks, the way you carry on." He ducked Feylind's punch through a hasty descent, then laughed at her scowl, framed in cloud fleece above him as she swung onto the ladder. "Step on my fingers, minx, you'll be sorry."

Feylind's retort came more thoughtful than barbed. "Trust me, it isn't your fingers I'm itching to flatten."

They descended into the brig's lower deck, enveloped by gloom and the fusty miasma of damp arisen from the bilges. The hull was new, the fug of lamp oil and mildew not yet entrenched through the tarry bite of the oakum worked into her seams. Feylind knew ships, in particular ones fashioned by Cattrick's exacting craftsmen. Attuned to the hull like a sounding board, she analyzed the chafe of the lines and the slap of wavelets transmitted through the thick timbers; in her critical judgment, she determined the captain was competent. No fittings banged, and no halyards thrummed loose to tap and spin kinks at the masthead. The small talk of three hands at work mending sail drifted down from the forecastle. In the aft cabin, a nasal-voiced purser conducted an inventory of stores with the cook, standard enough practice for a ship between legs of a sea passage.

A blue-water trader just cleared into port followed a preset routine. The lower hold beneath would be cleared and swept, ropes and nets tidied in smart readiness for onloading new cargo. Aboard *Cariadwin* the main hatch was not open in welcome, but shut fast in the velvety gloom. No lit lamp burned in the ring overhead. Rather than roust

229

out his sailhands for laggards, the captain crouched and whispered a password.

The countersign returned was a sequence of taps. Then, from the inside, the hatched grating cracked. A brown eye peered upward. Against total darkness, the bared gleam of a knife scribed a thin line of silver.

"It's himself," assured a low voice in clan accents. A stirred exhalation came from below, as listeners released pent-back tension.

"You carry convicts freed from Lysaer's galleys?" Feylind whispered in excitement.

"Aye." The captain muscled the heavy grating aside. "They've got the news out of Tysan and Havish your brother's been sweating to hear." To the clansmen below, whose lives would be instantly forfeit if the authorities at Innish caught wind of their presence, the brig's master assured, "You're kept safe enough. Fiark's loyalty's true, and I've three hands with good eyes sitting guard on the forecastle. They'll shout if anyone boards us."

The face moved, then the knife in token of cautious trust granted. "For me," the man said, emphatic, "I'd slit my own veins and leave my blood to the sea before I'd risk freedom again."

Warm air swirled up from the close, musty darkness, made stifling by the lack of ventilation. Someone below unshuttered a candle. The weak illumination showed the upper-deck planking had been tacked over with canvas to seal off any chance gleam of light. The men who inhabited this miserable den numbered an odd forty, faces upturned in keen wariness toward the visitors brought by the captain.

For all their cramped confines, they were reasonably clean. The few knives shared among them kept them shaven and groomed. Torsos roped in muscle from hard labor at the oar were decently clothed, some in the mended rags of forest-tanned leathers, and others in shirts gleaned by sailhands from Innish's used clothing stalls and motley from the ship's slop chest. No face looked healthy. Most were sorrowfully thin. The wrists and ankles rinsed by the flickering light were disfigured and angry where steel and salt water had chafed into permanent scars.

Feylind felt sorrow before sickness, then a ripping fresh anger as she reached the base of the ladder and a younger scout brushed by her to replace the hatch. A chance flare of the candle touched the raised, ugly mark left by some mayor's harsh practice of branding men sentenced as convicts.

Fiark sucked a shocked breath, then said without preamble, "What

230

are your needs? You'll have anything in my power that doesn't jeopardize my patron or require an outright act of theft."

The clan spokesman pushed forward, squinting through hanks of salt-and-pepper hair not yet regrown long enough to braid. He limped badly, his right ankle fused from a poorly set break. Still, he had not lost the grace of his manners. "Fiark?" He extended a forearm for the traditional clasp of amity. "My loyalty belongs to the Earl of Taerlin. In his place, hear my gratitude for your strength of heart."

"Speak," Fiark urged. He need not stress that each hour *Cariadwin* lingered in a port ruled by townsmen, the risk to her fugitives increased.

The clansman bowed his head, for a moment overcome. "Provisions, first off. Fresh meat and fruit. Bad diet has left many of us sickened."

"Clothing," Feylind added. "I'll supply funds."

But the freed man touched her wrist in restraint. "Bless you, but no. We won't be beholden for what our cousins in Selkwood are able enough to supply." To Fiark, he summed up, "For that, you need only sign us a legitimate cargo bound upcoast to Elssine or Telzen."

"Have to be luxuries," the captain chipped in from his laconic, square stance by the ladder. "Our lading list out of Cheivalt says our main hold's chock full of wool bales and barley bound for the brewers upcoast."

"Fine brandy in bottles and some Sanpashir gemstones, will that do?" Fiark measured the clan spokesman afresh, a warning hard glint in his eyes. "Should they be underwritten?"

Someone else's barbed dialect jibed from out of the darkness, "What, you don't truly want to stay honest?"

Before light words caused umbrage, the captain reassured, "The cargo you consign will be safe, with one small delay. We've an unscheduled stop on the coast of Alland to take on what our lists say we shipped out of Cheivalt."

"That's Erlien's territory," Feylind broke in. Her quick mind leaped ahead, taking stock. The barley would have been grown in Orvandir, and the wool shorn from Radmoore sheep. The *Cariadwin*'s pending illegitimate cargo would be nothing else but the spoils from a caravan raided en route to Sanshevas or Southshire.

In typical fashion, her brother's thought flanked her. "Are the High Earl's scout raiders in conspiracy with Arithon?"

"Not precisely," the *Cariadwin*'s captain corrected. "Don't have to take sides to hate chains and slavery. The High Earl's river inlets in Selkwood make an ideal place to load contraband. I used to shift cargoes from there before Arithon hired me. And anyway, these days, a number of brash younger scouts want to ship out to Corith as volunteers for sea training."

"Volunteer pirates, more like," Fiark said, no stranger to the marauding ways of Erlien's chieftains. The factors at Innish knew well enough: the best silk from Atchaz always moved overland rather than risk the river route into Telzen. "You'll want a return cargo?"

"Not just then." In soft words and darkness, the plans were laid out. The brig's share of gold from Erlien's plunder would fund new rigging and canvas from the Southshire shipyards. "Those supplies and provisions are critically needed at the Shadow Master's outpost at Corith. Cattrick's crews have been busy," the clan spokesman said. "Maenol was told to expect three more brigs for refitting early in the spring."

"Why can't the *Evenstar* bear these men to Alland?" Feylind broke in, still angling for her chance to escape another decorous run down the southcoast.

Fiark shook his pale head. "The *Evenstar*'s bills of lading are clean. Need one ship honest and yours was elected. If you didn't know, all her profits are going to buy weapons to outfit the ships purloined out of Riverton. With luck, by high summer, the clans will have their fleet of sail to play havoc on Alliance shipping."

"Slave-bearing galleys won't pass with impunity," a hard voice affirmed from the darkness. "Once our people have the armed ships to strike back, we can make rags of Lysaer's new edict by putting the screws to his trade."

Feylind was not mollified. "Looks to me like you've already started with that." She turned upon Fiark, tenacious, to nail home her point. "If the *Evenstar*'s clean, I don't see any reason why I can't run cargo to Capewell. The outpost at Corith's a short leg away. Supplies and dispatches could be left on a regular schedule without any undue risk."

"No." The clan spokesman caught Feylind's shoulder and gave her a fatherly shake. "You care for Prince Arithon?" At her stubborn nod, he bore in. "Then see sense! Stay where he's placed you, or see him hurt if you fall to grief!"

Pearls flashed in the shadows as Feylind stiffened to argue.

The clansman cut her off, merciless. "Then look at these men and the cruelties they've suffered! You have no idea just how tense things have grown, and not just in Tysan. Havish's king is caught in contention as well."

They heard the news then, of how the forty men in the *Cariadwin*'s hold had come to be freed by the seal of King Eldir's justice.

"Three galleymen and the fat harbormaster at Cheivalt were just arraigned for treason." Seated once more, elbows braced on his knees and his hands jammed through the uneven hair at his temples, the clan spokesman qualified. "Those were put to trial for an exchange of bribes to refute Havish's crown edict. They'll die, and not nicely. Lysaer's bailiffs have been rebuffed twice, denied any right of extradition."

Amid the dense quiet lying on all sides, Fiark accepted the tied packets of correspondence from Arithon's westshore contacts. Sweating and sobered, he knelt by the candle to read. As always, the broad range of sources astonished him. From sheets soaked in the incense from the intrigue of court brothels, to others, encasing filched documents with official ribbons and cracked seals, the damning, grim picture unfolded, with warnings phrased in stark language. Feylind shared the written pages alongside her brother, cursing as he turned yellowed leaves too slowly, or the flame fluttered low, making thin, ciphered script too difficult to peruse.

In letters sent by prostitutes, officials, and tavernkeeps, the political brangles unfolded, of relations gone from displeased to contentious at every level of government. The coastal mayors resented King Eldir's sharp justice. Inbound trade from Tysan would suffer without galleys, cut off altogether while the winter's rough weather closed the north passage to oared transport. Tension waxed to distrust at the border, as Alliance officials were forced to discover their Prince of the Light's bold policies received no margin of tolerance in Havish.

The royal counselors at Ostermere might accept that their king would never back down.

"It's the rock-brained coastal mayors who refuse to hear sense," the clansman explained at agitated length. "They're howling protest. Most won't understand that charter law can't be changed or repealed. The crown's execution of a few arraigned traitors isn't going to deter them. Bribes will just double. Nobody's fooled. Enough gold will tempt any man to dishonesty, and the headhunters in Tysan are bringing in captives with no heed at all for the season."

Feylind perceived the stakes well enough. Until the ice broke in Stormwell, galleymen had no open route except southward through King Eldir's territory. Oared ships demanded more fresh water and provisions; their vulnerable low freeboard required close access to safe harbors, since storm swells could cause them to founder. Only a blue-water hull with full sail could achieve the passage from Capewell round West Shand in one leg.

Fiark tapped the last document against his shut teeth. "I see back-lash and dangerous pressure coming to bear on Cattrick's shipworks at Riverton," he said softly.

"Man, we know that!" The clansman sheathed the knife he had used to scratch maps of Alliance troop movements and shoved to his feet in bursting, sore agitation. "Maenol himself's said Prince Arithon should leave. Though how we could help to spirit him cross-country is a right sticky point at the moment. Can't even protect our own *families* in the forests, Alliance patrols are so fierce."

No need to voice the full scope of the problem. With guild profits affected, more than ever, the Alliance would covet the new vessels targeted by the Shadow Master's delicate plotting.

"One thing's sure," the clansman insisted, his fists clenched in sorrowful emphasis. "Those ships are the last and only hope to save my Lord Maenol's people."

Under mounting persecution from the Alliance, the last bloodlines in Tysan faced an increasing threat of extermination. Their loss would open the gates to disaster, since the territory the clans spilled their blood to keep wild would become razed by the axes of townsmen.

"The cry is raised to seize land for development," the clan spokesman finished in a grief sharpened to desperation. "We are the grass roots of the Fellowship's compact. Kill us off, and all ties to law end." No proven line of descent would remain to keep faith with humanity's petition for sanctuary. "Ath help us all, if the Paravians return, and the Ath-forsaken mayors have the power in hand to cast off the Fellowship's sanctions."

Midwinter 5653

Succession

The Fellowship Sorcerer crossed the barrens of Rathain in the teeth of a howling storm. The gale which blasted the swept landscape of Daon Ramon razed over the rounded, low hills in an assault of horizontal sleet. Stone and dry gullies lay marbled in ice. The wind screamed and flayed, lent the cruel edge of a billion dashed shards of quartz. In weather that vicious, posted sentries were useless, even at the narrow mouth of the draw which sheltered the small clan encampment. The first Earl Jieret's scouts knew of Asandir's arrival was the presence of a steaming dark horse in their midst.

The young swordsman who wore his braid tied with fox tails gasped and reached in shot panic to draw steel.

His wrist was caught and yanked brutally short by the clamping hand of his elder. "No. That's a friend." To the muffled figure on his blowing mount, the veteran called, "Kingmaker?"

A nod answered. The cowled Sorcerer dismounted, cloak snapping in the whiteout scream of a gust.

"Take his horse, boy." The older scout turned the younger one loose with a companionable clap on the shoulder. "Don't be shy. If there's Fellowship business, and not just a traveler's need to ask shelter, our guest will ask for your High Earl."

Asandir surrendered his wet reins. His reassurance fell like a struck mote of sunlight against the gray storm that kept the land mantled in winter. "Is Jieret in camp?"

The older scout nodded. "I'll fetch him. You'll find his wife Feithan in the lodge tent, the one with the stag antlers hung on the javelin rack by the door flap."

"I'll find my way." Asandir peeled a glove, used the back of his wrist to scrape the ice from his eyebrows. His level gray eyes then measured the scout, who was shivering, his buckskins soaked through to the skin. He said in tacit handling of stiff pride, "When you find Jieret, give him my word. There are no headhunters out reiving within eighty leagues of this site. No need to stand guard until this weather has lifted. I left wards on my back trail and a spell of confusion to spin any tracking hounds widdershins. The seals won't release for three days. If dogs or armed townsmen try to push through, they'll just make themselves dizzy running themselves into circles."

"Ath bless you for that!" The scout's reddened features broke into a pleased smile, masked as he shouldered head down through the gale.

Asandir tucked his bare hand back under his mantle, then footed his way over iced rock and the rimed crusts of dead grass to the cluster of wind-beaten lodge tents.

The antlers on the rack proved still fresh from the hunt, and the small, dark-haired woman who unfurled the door flap was wet to the wrists from a fatty emulsion of boiled deer brains.

When she saw who awaited outside her threshold, her thin, gamine features blushed scarlet. "Come on in. The place reeks." Her shrug framed apology as she let the flap fall, enclosing her visitor in a steamy fog of white woodsmoke and the odorous stench from the pot where two scraped hides were set curing. "Couldn't be helped. If I waited for sunshine, the boys wouldn't have the leggings they need to cover their new growth of ankle."

She stepped back to her labor, one skin draped and dripping over a rope stretched taut between the two lodgepoles. "Let me just wring this out, and I'll see to your needs. No doubt you're famished. Hang your cloak, if you want, by the fire."

With competent, chapped hands, she flipped the ends of the hide into a neat loop, tucked in the edges, then inserted a stick through the center and twisted. The raw leather gave up its burden of moisture, pattering runnels into the beaten earth floor.

Asandir watched her in light, alert silence. The unassuming movements as he cracked the cased ice off his shoulders and peeled off his layers of soaked wool were deceptive, even ordinary. Yet Feithan's blush remained high in tacit awareness that everything about her was being measured, from the sable coil of hair fallen loose at her neck, to the skinning knife on its thong that had thinned from too many years of sharpening. She felt like that steel: worn with use, but still strong, still keen, still able to cope with the hardships that seemed to increase with each year as Alliance patrols pinched and harried clan movements.

"The scouts have gone for Jieret," Asandir said. Unasked, he had bent. He caught up her forked stick and fished the next hide from the pot, his upturned smile flashed through his austerity like quicksilver. "I'm already wet, yes?" He slung the saturated buckskin over the rope and lent his arm to the heavy work of wringing.

"You shouldn't," Feithan chided. "You'll stink just like me." Then she whooped like a girl as she realized just what he was doing with his hands.

Magelight flared soft indigo over the wet hide, then brightened, changed, slid down the spectrum to bloom into clear, fiery scarlet. The leather steamed and unfurled, dry and warm from his spell seal, finished inside the span of one heartbeat for its final curing in smoke.

"I won't have to stretch this?" Feithan asked, dumbfounded.

The Sorcerer shook his head, running his testing touch down the velvety surface. "Nor smoke it, either, unless you wish to darken the color." Luminosity trailed where his fingertips passed. The thick air seemed to shimmer through an unheard song, as though a resonance of his blessing did honor to the dead buck. "The hide wouldn't have dried before nightfall, and this storm could be better spent sewing. Do you wish me to treat the next one as well?"

"I thank you, yes." Flushed now with pleasure, Feithan stepped back and let him lift the moist pelt still draped on the rope. "Though, Ath, I could have used a few of your tricks on the morning I tackled the scraping. The camp boys were to help, but my truant of a husband spirited them off to go hunting."

She untied the taut cord, then knelt to collapse the frames used earlier for stretching and drying. Immersed in false brusqueness, she tried not to care how desperately her fingers were shaking. But her uneasy questions loomed too large to ignore, and the forceful quiet of Asandir's presence was too palpably real at her back. She would mask her sharp worry in chatter before she dared to ask why a Fellowship Sorcerer should visit her hearth in the comfortless misery of deep winter.

Stilled as old oak, his silvered hair lying lank on broad shoulders, the Sorcerer spoke as if he heard her thought anyway. "I'm here to Name the next heir to Jieret's title."

Feithan closed her eyes. The rank smell of deer brains all at once seemed to unstring her senses. Fighting a tight chest, then wheeling faintness, she crouched half-unmoored, as if the dependable solidity of the earth must give way to a yawning void. She hung on, her lips clamped shut against desperate fear, and her arms clutched into an awkward embrace around a disjointed bundle of ash sticks.

While the moment hung, she forced her stunned thoughts to sort out what the Sorcerer had told her.

Jieret's life was not endangered. An heir for his title as steward of Rathain was only chosen by the Fellowship when the s'Ffalenn royal line became threatened.

No confirmed ill news, then; not an immediate disaster to her family, but too likely a larger one pending for the realm. In mechanical habit, she continued to tidy the collapsed slats of the hide frame. Then she drew on raw courage and a forced, hammered steadiness. "Which son should I call?"

A hand touched her shoulder, light as a moth's wing, and uncannily warm for a traveler just spared from the battering siege of harsh weather. "Neither son, lady."

Asandir had reached her side in one long, soundless step. Another move saw the wood lifted out of her hands. His understated strength raised her upright and gripped her in bedrock support. "Dismiss every fear for your husband as well. He stays here in Rathain, under my binding command if need be. This appointment of succession is but a formality and, life willing, should stay so for many years to come."

Steadied enough to stop shivering, Feithan tipped up her angular face. She surveyed the Sorcerer, who topped her by a head, his patience like glacial scarred granite. Then the wonder broke through and wakened a flutter in her veins. "You want *Kei?*"

Asandir's smile was quietly luminous, subtle and fleeting as the spill of a moonbeam in the sultry flare of spent coals. "She will be Kei no longer. And yes. Be proud. Your daughter shall become the next Teiren's'Valerient, steward to the royalty of Rathain."

"She's with the neighbor," Feithan explained, straightened now with relief. "The smoke from the tanning sometimes bothers the newborns. Let me just rinse my hands and fetch her back."

The Fellowship ceremony for Naming the *caithdein's* heir took place in hurried solemnity. There was no feast, no celebration, no joyous gathering of far-flung clans the tradition usually warranted. Only Jieret and his wife attended the ritual when Asandir in his travel-stained leathers accepted the infant from Feithan's arms.

On that day scarcely one month old, she was tucked in a sheepskin laced at the front with plain thongs. Her gems were the glints of melted sleet caught in silk of the fleeces. Her wide eyes were blue, still uncolored from birth, but tracking the Sorcerer's finger as he traced a glyph in white light over the dome of her forehead. "You who were Kei shall be Jeynsa Teiren's'Valerient henceforward."

Translation from the old Paravian meant successor to power. For a moment, the Sorcerer's presence seemed raised to a level that transcended mortality. His hair, his large hands, the very life in his veins seemed to sing with a subliminal silvery aura. The babe in his grasp seemed both flesh and light, surrounded and infused by the majestic force of a power too fierce to be captured by reason. Feithan raised cramped knuckles to dash away tears. Jieret stood silent, perhaps in remembrance of his own hour of oath taking, years past in Strakewood when his parents stood living beside him.

Slashing winds and the singing whine of the sleet ruled the moment as Asandir's arcane rune sank and touched. Its intricate angles blazed bright as a meteor, and then dimmed, softly melded against the smooth warmth of the girl child's skin. "Jeynsa, little spirit, be strong. Prove worthy of the destiny you will come to carry forward from the time-honored lineage of your ancestors."

Then the choosing was done. The Sorcerer raised the bundled child. Smiling and dazzled, she was returned to the care of her mother. More than Name had changed. Jeynsa's future was sealed. A sign like a gossamer tracing in starlight gleamed under the rim of her hood.

"My mark will bear witness, she is Fellowship chosen." Diminished once again to a weathered old traveler, sturdy, but worn from long service, the Sorcerer gave last instructions. "The sign will fade in one cycle of the moon. Raise the girl to bear the proud title of *caithdein*, with all of the powers and charges therein. She will swear formal service to her prince in the fullness of time."

Earl Jieret touched his daughter's soft cheek. Still wrapped in the crumpled furs he had worn in the thorn brakes, his wolf-pelt hat dripping ice melt through his braid, he raised his bearded chin and regarded the Sorcerer who stood unmoving before him. In all of Athera, he was one of the few who stood tall enough, and bred of a stern enough fiber to endure a prolonged, level stare. "You're not staying?"

Asandir's silence became palpably heavy. For a second, he seemed a phantom figure, pressed out of velvet against the dimmed hides of the lodge tent. "I can't," he admitted at unpleasant length. "The Koriani witches have been much too busy for anyone's peace of mind." The regret in his words held the masked strain of dangers unfit to be shared.

Yet Jieret was no man to settle for platitudes, far less from a Fellowship Sorcerer. "If the enchantresses pose any danger to my prince, best tell me." His courage was agony and his heart, hammered steel, as he refused to back down under pressure. "I know from Dakar that Morriel Prime once laid a plot to assassinate him."

Asandir did not try to evade brutal truth; neither would he answer directly. "Your liege has Caolle at his side. Bide here. There's nothing more you can do for your crown prince or your realm in the west, except suffer the most ugly of deaths."

When Jieret drew breath out of protest, the Sorcerer spun away, snatched his cloak from the stool by the fireside, and flung it, still wet, over the squared frame of his shoulders. "No, Jieret. You cannot come with me. I am bound now for the focus circle at Caith-al-Caen, and from there, with all speed, on a mission more urgent than this one."

Hands clutched to a child whose life was now promised to the service of people and realm, Feithan sucked back a small gasp for the hurt unexpressed behind Jieret's wooden dignity.

Asandir fastened his cloak. In the close, reeking air, still befouled with smoke and the lingering, grease stink of tanning, he shook out his damp gloves. Deliberate in each precise movement he made, and with no spell expended for comfort, he slipped the chill leather over his capable hands. Then he looked up. His eyes were rinsed slate, utterly blank and unreadable. "Jieret, we are not stewards of any man's life, no matter how precious his bloodline. What can be done, will be. Sethvir has cast auguries. His assurance was this: the enchantress who works healing in the moorlands of Araethura has not been recalled by her Prime Matriarch. Whatever the Warden at Althain perceived, he said, keep you here in Rathain. Until the Koriani initiate named Elaira is pressed back into active service by her order, your prince should fare well enough under Dakar's wards and protection."

Jieret bent his head. Better than most, he understood the strict limits the Law of the Major Balance set over Fellowship actions. The fists at his sides locked in helpless, white tension. Unwittingly recast in the image of his father, his anguish screamed through every restrained joint of his bearing. "You will tell me, at once, if there's *anything* I can do?"

Asandir reached out his gloved hands and grasped the *caithdein* of Rathain by both forearms. "Trust us that much. For now, for your people, there will be small reprieve. Lysaer's convocation at Etarra is going to lose impetus. All the armed resource the guilds raised for the Alliance to scour the forests of Rathain will soon be diverted elsewhere. Pack up your camp when the storm breaks. For this year at least, you can summer in Halwythwood with no more than the usual precautions."

There was no more to say. Too proud to plead, too stubborn to ask where Lysaer's crack officers at Etarra would march troops, if not into Rathain's hidden glens to hunt clansmen, Jieret watched in numbed frustration as the Sorcerer touched Feithan and murmured his formal farewell. Then he slipped back into the chaos of the storm, drawn away by more desperate crisis.

Turnings

In the fullness of night, amid pelting sleet, Lysaer s'Ilessid and his closest retainers mount in urgent secrecy; given covert knowledge of the Shadow Master's piracy at Riverton, they ride from Etarra's postern gate and swing west on the Mathorn Road, their intent to seek passage by sea out of Narms and effect swift return to Avenor. . . .

Late night, under broken clouds and the stabbing-bright glints of hard starlight, Earl Jieret walks the wind-beaten crests of Daon Ramon and curses his Sight for the snatched, fickle dream, which has shown him no sign of his liege's predicament; but only a circle of Koriani Seniors, gathered whispering around a white crystal, while a Fellowship ward of protection is smashed wholesale, and the cries of winged predators whistle enraged off a backdrop of snow-covered mountains. . . .

Dakar the Mad Prophet suffers fitful, ill dreams until a flash of prescient talent rips him awake with an entangled warning of danger laced in dark images of fire and smoke, and hot blood on a battered main gauche; through the course of another violent row, he entreats Arithon s'Ffalenn to leave Riverton, with no more success than before. . . .

VII. Hunters

Since Arithon made his covert request for an inquiry into the fate of Princess Talith, Mearn s'Brydion grew back his lovelock. A thorough and leisurely round of seductions of ladies-in-waiting and chambermaids would yield him sure word whether Lysaer's public declaration of retirement covered a madwoman's seclusion, or incarceration of an unwilling prisoner. When pillow talk bought Mearn no more than the court knew, and uproarious drinking with the palace garrison drew owlish blank looks and speculation, his prowling search slipped past locked doors. By night, he perused the private ledgers kept by Avenor's tight-faced Minister of the Treasury.

Even there, outright facts stayed elusive. One odd, recurrent entry for high-council security allotted gold to six guardsmen without recorded names. Another, in Lord Eilish's fussy capitals, awarded a stipend for the princess's retreat that was suspiciously meager to support a full staff and the comforts for a cosseted royal wife.

Mearn's lips quirked in jaundiced thought where he crouched, lightly clad in bitter air, his chosen vantage now the wind-raked slates atop the ornate, spired roof of the council hall.

Yesterday's snowfall had cleared off to a brilliance of winter constellations. Beneath, emptied streets traced a gleam of tarnished silver, frozen to ruts sliced by cart wheels. The respectable taverns had closed for the night, their banked kitchen fires trailing thin smoke from the chimneys. The upper-story window frames lay paned in dimmed glass, pocked by the odd candleflame where a restless eccentric clung to sleepless activity. Mearn's furtive presence passed unseen. Left a cold trail by the happier pursuits of loose-living females and beer, he snugged coiled rope across his trim shoulders, then chalked resin on the soles of his thinnest kid slippers.

By the dark of the moon, he set out to test the one lead pried loose by dint of his maternal grandmother's advice.

'Townborn will always dissemble and cheat,' he recalled her admonishing through a youthful attempt to talk his way through a scrape. *'That's what nature breeds out of landowning avarice.'* White haired, diminutive, as flawlessly neat as a porcelain lily, she peered up at him, her chuckle all vinegar delight as she jabbed home her point with the blackthorn stick she brandished in old age like a weapon. *'Ath above, boy! You keep all your brains in your cock? To know a statesman's true heart, you must first track his wealth. Only his gold never lies.'*

By coin's sterling testament, the keep which fronted Avenor's state palace held the realm's most fugitive secret. At least, Mearn had learned after tailing the self-important senior clerk who paid wages, the anonymous six guardsmen played watchdog to the locked and barred tower attached to the building's south wing. The structure was hexagonal, built of the fired fawn brick used to expedite the restoration of Tysan's capital. From Mearn's stance by the pillars which braced a dome vaulting, the keep's north facade cut a ruled silhouette through the smoke silver stipple of stars. No pennon flew from its blunt, leaded roof. The banded masonry beneath the upper battlement held no carved follies or gargoyles. Only the simple sunwheel emblem graced the dressed-granite lintels of the entry below, a cavernous portal of strapped oaken doors, studded in steel and square bosses. This, Mearn discovered, stayed barred to all but a handpicked cadre of the realm's highest officers.

Avenor's new fashion of zealous idealism made bribes too chancy to contemplate. Hands tucked in the crook of his elbows for warmth, Mearn suppressed a dry snort. Never mind his recent, scapegrace reputation, earned in the boudoirs and wineshops; as the ducal ambassador for his clanborn brother, Lysaer's officials clung to their prejudice against his credibility.

Townborn rancor ran deep as the root of the Fellowship's compact. A man who preferred his grudges blood fresh, Mearn doused pricked temper to taciturn silence time and again, while the courtiers spun to their hatreds like weathercocks. He observed, his knife hand locked into stillness, when tempers flared up during councils of state.

Always some merchant who lost goods to Maenol's forest raiders would yammer the old accusations. Then every pigheaded guild minister in sight would ignore five centuries of history: s'Brydion of Alestron had *never* preyed upon caravans. Mearn met each outburst and pigeon-brained insult with cynical, ingrained suspicion. Since even his most innocently posed inquiries were likely to worsen his questionable clan standing, he chose to sidestep the quagmires of intrigue. The bare-handed adventure of scaling the tower held much more to his taste.

A gust hissed over the cornices and snapped the royal pennons on their lanyards. No comfort-loving sentry would stand his watch exposed to such lacerating cold. Mearn snatched his chance to cross the roof peak unseen. By touch, he avoided the patches of glaze ice; his soft soles made no sound against slates raked bare by the elements. Below him, the snow-covered gables of Avenor wore the night like a mantle spun from frost opal and woodsmoke.

To the west, his view commanded the black sweep of the sea, flecked by carnelian watchbeacons. Eastward, over the square walls and past the crowned turrets of the gatekeeps, a ragged mound tore a scar in the flank of the hill. There the Paravian stones cast down by Lysaer's builders lay jumbled as lichened bones, silted in rubble where the crumbled Second Age towers had been razed off the foundations to make way for his grander design. The dells the ancient ruin once defended fanned inland, pocketed in winter-silent drifts. Forest had encroached on the older boundary where mankind's tilled acreage ended, and the inviolate expanse of Paravian provenance once began. Horned centaur guardians no longer trod under the massive oaks crowning the hillcrests. No sunchildren danced in the vales, with their tangling skeins of shallow streams. The glens where Tysan's dead high kings had met to hold council with Athera's lost races lay grown over with holly and briar, forgotten except by the deer and the hare, the mice and the night-hunting owl.

Clansmen might stubbornly adhere to past ways, but inside town walls, the land's former heritage was scorned. A carriage clattered over the cobbles, bearing some late-going gallant to the sea-quarter wineshops where friends met to vent youthful spirits. A cur yapped down by the exciseman's sheds. The commotion set off an answering chorus from the stables next to the barracks, where Lysaer's coursers were kenneled alongside the lean hounds bred by headhunters to worry the fugitive clansmen.

Among them, deep toned, Mearn's own couple of deerhounds gave tongue. For their heart, he loosed breathless laughter. While his dearies kept up the commotion and diverted the bored wits of the sentries, he tucked up against the beaded cornice where the tower joined with the roof.

Kiln-fired masonry offered no purchase to climbers, an advantage for defense. To offset its prime weakness, that brick inclined to shatter under stoneshot launched from siege catapults, the vulnerable angles had been laid and faced with blocks of field-hewn granite. Scarcely as inviting as a stairway, Mearn thought as he sighted aloft to weigh his prospects. The mortar at least was unlikely to crumble. No standing structure in Tysan's restored capital had stood for more than a decade. Though exposed to the elements, the roof line of the council hall masked the first stage of the ascent. The blast of the wind would press him into the wall, and drive the keep's anonymous, paid guards to huddle on the leeward side.

Since Mearn looked on caution as a mealymouthed word for gutless procrastination, he tightened the laced wrists of his sleeves and stripped off his gloves. Hands hooked to chill stone, he wedged his toe in the crack of the first course of granite and forsook his safe stance on the roof. Either Princess Talith was locked away in seclusion above, or he could send honest word back to Arithon s'Ffalenn that she was nowhere inside of Avenor.

Shouts from the kennels at last quelled the deerhounds. Mearn's raised vantage over the wall walks chiseled even the small sounds into unnerving clarity. Above the hiss of his breath through locked teeth, he picked out the warbling flute of distressed pigeons, wakened by a thief in the falconer's dovecote.

Clamped to exposed rock, shivering from an unrelenting exertion that scarcely left room for thought, he could do little else but cling and hope the desperate wretch would wring the birds' necks with dispatch. Never mind the s'Brydion posture of alliance, now placed in irrefutable jeopardy. Mearn set his jaw and groped another determined handhold, then forced burning thighs to straighten. The breast of his jerkin scraped another foot up sheer granite. For pure, demented folly, he resisted the breathless urge to laugh. His brothers would gripe themselves prostrate should he become caught by some guard rousted up for a servant's inept pilfering.

If risk of ignominy was not bad enough, an unexpected light flared scarcely ten yards above. Mearn flinched like a cat. Reflex alone saved his balance. A fleeting glance upward showed a gleam of new flame behind a row of slit windows.

Someone had entered the keep's third-floor chamber.

Mearn gasped out a virulent oath, wishing pustules and pox on palace officials taken with urges to burn candles in towers past **mid**-night. No afterthought, he added his prayer that the crazed individual disregard any notion to admire the stars or the view. The niches where the sills pierced the wall offered the only secure ledge for him to pause. His predicament was not mutable. Not through an unbroken ascent, with the next set of casements a distance of forty feet higher up. Fatigue already ran searing tremors through his limbs. His own labored breath turned his head. He must snatch that stop to rest, or succumb to exhaustion and fall.

Wind hissed across masonry and thrummed the thick frames of the casements. Mearn shut his eyes against a blurred sting of tears from the cold. On a grimace of effort, he unlatched his numbed fingers from a handhold, fumbled, then hooked the rough edge of the sill.

The light flickered. A thickset body shadowed the glass, and a complaining voice Mearn recognized as Quinold, Lord High Chancellor, drifted to the casement overhead. "Beastly drafts at this season."

Behind diamond mullions, a scant span apart from the knuckles which suspended the climber from a lethal plunge to the roof slates, Lord Quinold's pudgy hands seized the tasseled cord to draw the curtains. Brass hoops slid on the rod and a heavy fall of velvet doused the candlelight down to a slit.

Mearn hissed with relief. Shaking and runneled in icy sweat, he shifted his weight, hitched himself up the last, saving foot to the level stone of the window ledge. The knifing winds which had been his ally now sheared through his clothing. His skin had worn through at the fingertips. A forthright inspection revealed flesh underneath gone too numb to feel the abrasion. Mearn's heart raced with the unpleasant awareness that nothing more than thin rondels of glass and the untrustworthy mask of a curtain guarded his niche from discovery.

Let him be caught inside Lysaer's guarded precinct, and no tribunal would trifle with charges of treason. Town law was explicit. Execution of clansmen brought public dismemberment without benefit of a hearing, followed by death from a sword blade run through the heart.

Mearn wrapped his forearms around his tucked knees, as much to contain his outright contempt as to foil the ripping north wind. His diplomacy at Avenor could scarcely bend five centuries of ingrained disrespect. The ways of city governance confounded and astonished him, that these twit-brained townborn with their manned walls and libraries, their obsessive filing of ledgers and written record, could so arrogantly disown the founding facts of their heritage.

The fugitive forest clans their conceit named barbarian kept no inscribed histories. Persecution by headhunters denied them safe haven to live in shelter and comfort, yet they preserved memory of the purpose behind their unmixed bloodlines and ancestry. Mearn's restless penchant to challenge authority made him rage, that unbridled greed could ever have raised this bloodletting rift between factions.

As if to bear out his cynical view, the Lord High Chancellor stumped past the gap in the curtains, his diction precise as he resumed brassy carping. "Ath, there's no wine. Some dimwit neglected to restock the cupboard. Damn those breeding pests of barbarians, you know how I hate climbing stairs for these meetings."

A gravelly voice Mearn did not recognize answered too low to overhear. Pricked to curiosity, well practiced from a boyhood spent eavesdropping on his short-tempered older brothers, he set his ear to the glass.

". . . scarcely a matter of clan raiding this time," the bass speaker finished in stiff censure.

A chair scraped. Lord Chancellor Quinold sat down, his next line filtered through a barrage of squeaks wrung from rush caning and wood. "No wonder you're thin, Vorrice. You fret like a nesting pack rat. To judge by your maundering, one might mistakenly think the Fellowship Sorcerers were omnipotent. Or are you worried the Paravians might return in their full and fatal glory overnight? Really, we'd all fare better if you could relax your obsession with burning convicted talent. The perils posed by the Shadow Master are far more immediate, since his overt collaboration with Maenol's clansmen."

"But the old races aren't dead," the one named Vorrice lashed back. His grainy voice stabbed with conviction. "If they were, the accursed taint of practicing magecraft would be banished from the world altogether. Obstructions by meddling sorcerers would be ended, besides. Until that day comes, public cleansings become my bound duty."

Outside on the sill, a chill gripped Mearn that bit deeper than any assault of mere wind. He had watched Lysaer's interdict against sorcery seed spurious arrests across Tysan. On the street, not a whisper of rumor had emerged to suggest a fanatic invested with high office to enforce a campaign of persecution.

A knock sounded at the door to the inside chamber. "That must be Tellisec and the other guild ministers," the Lord High Chancellor surmised, then huffed through the bother of raising his bulk to admit them.

From below, a ruddy flicker in the stairwell arrow slits warned of another imminent arrival. Mearn hunkered down against icy granite, amazed to have stumbled upon a clandestine conference between Lysaer's trusted inner circle. He listened to their exchanged greetings, and by names and accents identified the realm's Lord Justiciar, Avenor's High Gate Keeper, and Lord Mayor Skannt of the head-hunters' league. Tysan's ranking seneschal was away with Lysaer in the east, but his appointed seat was not empty.

Another man with soft, fruity vowels assumed the authority to officiate. "Where's Gace?" that one snapped. "He's late. Does anyone know why?"

Gace was Prince Lysaer's household steward, a closemouthed, stringy wisp of a creature who tended to slink. Mearn misliked the man's habit of lurking in dim corners, unblinking and watchful as a rat.

"If Gace is delayed, he'll have sound reason," Vorrice made grating objection. "We need his goodwill. As the Prince of the Light's closest servant, it might be politic to trust him."

A whining blast of wind obscured the reply. Mearn braved the brunt, given no other choice. Meeting or conspiracy, he needed to tell which, then make clean his escape. Cold and inactivity were now deadly adversaries. Prolonged exposure on a north-facing ledge would soon impair his reflexes. He dared not linger beyond the point where he became too chilled to climb.

"Our man has arrived," announced the fatuous spokesman. Inside the chamber, the door from the stairwell opened to a decisive click. Pressed to the casement, his breath fanning frost rime across rippled glass, Mearn snagged the newcomer's name from the brisk exchange of introductions. A frown nicked his brow. What breeding mischief would lead a rich trade minister to leave his plush comforts in Erdane to convene with Avenor's cabal of power? Mearn gave the quandary ferocious thought. He had never met Guild Master Koshlin, but clan rumor from Camris linked the title to a bullish, short man with sly eyes and a penchant for endowments in gold to further the head-hunters' leagues.

While chairs bumped inside, and the cozy assembly settled itself down to deal, Mearn chafed stiff fingers, riled to slit-eyed concern.

"Your welcome is accepted here only because of your overtures to support Prince Lysaer's alliance against evil," the man in authority addressed, his peach-syrup inflection at chilling odds with a blunt-ness that ran contrary to the ingrained town penchant for stylized manners and ceremony.

"By all means, let us speak plainly." Lord Koshlin's ruffled suavity trailed through a considering pause. "Your prince shall have gold in support from a faction in Camris I have been asked not to name. The moneys will come with no strings attached. If your self-styled savior can bring more than folk at Miralt Head to hail him as an avatar, no one of us will denounce him."

That raised a bristling rustle, as someone of size roused himself to take umbrage.

Ever smooth in diplomacy, the High Chancellor intervened. "Let us not quibble over unfounded truths, Vorrice. We few are privileged. Elsewhere, the awareness of Lysaer's blessed heritage has not been made common knowledge."

"Divine will shall triumph, but the time must be right," a supporter chimed in to placate Erdane's minister. "His Grace has promised each man must find faith and belief for himself. Until he wins due acclaim, our prince poses as mortal."

Lord Koshlin pressed on, impatient. "Why waste any breath on theology at all? Let your prince inspire the whole world to bow to his moral righteousness. Every conversion he makes serves our need, in turn. We are dedicated men bound to break the constraint of the Fellowship's compact. Our followers in Camris already have instructions. They'll serve your Alliance of Light in coin and information, and even raw resource. By whatever means, they want sorcery suppressed and the old clan lineages eradicated. The s'Ilessid claim to immortal birth is not germane. We view his criminal charges against the Shadow Master's allies as a powerful political convenience."

While Mearn battled the rise of his gorge, Vorrice raised abrasive opinion. "Your hatred of Maenol's barbarians runs deep. Do we also surmise you fear the restoration of the Paravians?"

"Don't mistake, we fear nothing." Koshlin paused through what felt at second hand like a lingering, oily smile. "Let me suggest, any force in Athera who stands for the old ways poses a dangerous impediment. We wish the Second Age mysteries forgotten."

On the sill, tucked and bitter, Mearn squelched seething fury, while Koshlin's bland monologue expounded upon the self-blinded creed of the townborn.

"Those bygone beliefs stunt the interests of trade. Why should a hidebound adherence to past ritual disallow more seaports and better roads?" A fist thumped on wood, to a flickering splash of leaked flame light through slitted curtains. "Since the Paravians abandoned the continent, mankind should claim rightful use of the land." Koshlin cleared his throat. "The faction I speak for will back Lysaer's cause. In secret, we've labored to abolish the compact since the overthrow of the last high kings. Those of our heirs who incline toward religion will scarcely care which name they invoke when they mouth their prayers to a deity. Once humanity is free to reap this world's wealth, society will flourish. You wish the Prince of Rathain brought down and his supporters suppressed to save the peace. We wish to escape the Fellowship's tyranny. Our ends lie along the same course, won't you see?"

"You want the slinking barbarians dead," Lord Mayor Skannt observed in his drawling, perpetual contempt. "For that end, I'll take in any man's gold. But first, I'd hear your conditions."

The proposal branched into particulars and questions, while Mearn shivered and fretted on the ledge. The moment had arrived to press on, or jeopardize all of his success. Against the murmured backdrop of debate, then the Lord High Justiciar's scathing accusation to the realm's chancellor for fence-sitting, the clansman eased his tucked stance. A second he lingered, heart torn into conflict by blood loyalties.

"Damn all your shortsighted bickering!" Vorrice burst through in surging vehemence. Mearn started tense. Inside, a chair rasped back from the table. He flattened against stone as crisp footsteps carried across the chamber. An angry hand snapped the curtains aside and bared the centermost casement. Time froze. Cramped against the adjacent lintel, Mearn stopped breathing, pinned down a fatal handspan away from the executioner's suffused profile.

"Barbarians or sorcerers, their twisted nature is the same." Vorrice jabbed passionate fingers toward the gathering behind him. "The sooner they're exterminated, the better."

Escape was not possible. Mearn clamped his quivering sinews into rigid stillness. If he moved, if capricious luck left him now, he would be caught as a spy. All Vorrice need do was glance sidewards.

Unblinking, Mearn memorized the man's jowled features. If by Ath's grace he came through unscathed, he determined to know this new enemy.

Vorrice's pale eyes fixed unseeing upon the frost-sharp sweep of the rooftops. He worked fleshy lips, pinched to tight discontent at the corners. His stance seethed with nerve-fired agitation, the stalker's impression intensified by a thin nose, and eyebrows napped like wet burlap. He wore his hair cropped. The thoughtless clench of his fist to fringed velvet contrasted a manic neatness. White robes and gold band of office hung stainless and straight, glittering with the golden sunwheel device.

"We should take the Lord Master's offer, believe this." His adamant diction flecked spittle as he gestured his conviction. "Let his coin help rout out the canker of sorcery. What should we fear? Prince Lysaer will shine as our maker intends. Let the faithless beware. The light of his presence shall banish corruption wherever man's works embrace evil."

"Vorrice," admonished the unseen authority, his fulsome voice glacial with command, "this is not an inquisition. No sensible gift will be spurned by this gathering. Not if the coin and the services offered are being presented in good faith."

Vorrice made no reply, but snapped shut the curtains to a sliding clash of yanked rings.

Veiled in safe darkness, Mearn loosed his pent breath. Moisture plumed from his lips, whirled away by another keening gust. The cold at his back seared down to the bone, while rage hazed his mood to fierce recklessness. He seized a short moment to steady his mind, then quit the ledge, athletic and sure as he groped the next handhold higher up. His mind stayed unsettled, each circling thought struck from a mold of hot fear. Erdane's guild ministers had not forgotten their history since the uprising which dethroned the past high kings. *They knew the clan bloodlines were an irreplaceable legacy.* To judge by Koshlin's least sinister insinuations, they understood the connection between the oldest and first ruling families, and the guarded liaison once maintained between mankind and lost races.

For few spirits were born with the tenacity to withstand the living presence of the Paravians. Mearn knew as much from the chronicles preserved in Alestron's archives. Those moldered histories read with the fierce ring of legend. Mortals who survived the experience of contact quite often went mad, driven distraught by their limited human perceptions. The fortunate who were stricken found solace with Ath's Brotherhood. Most others simply wasted away, reft witless by a thirst for a splendor too majestic to sustain reason. Daily cares, kin, the very necessities of survival fell into eclipse before Paravian presence, which reflected unsullied the grandiloquent grace of the power which sourced Ath's creation.

For this, the Fellowship in their wisdom had sworn and sealed the great compact. Their act of intervention took charge before the grief of more limited human awareness could tear the fabric of society asunder.

Men like Koshlin still fueled the misunderstanding which gave rise to the slaughter of the high kings. Sunk in dangerous resentment, nursed by ignorance and hate, they mistook the clans' past rule for repression, when in fact charter law compelled bygone sovereigns to a guiding burden of defense.

S'Brydion clan record said Melhalla's twelfth high king had set seal to Alestron's original city charter. Like many another chosen family, the new overlords made their residence in an abandoned fortress. The old races had forsaken walled keeps after the binding of the drake spawn whose marauding had ended in defeat in the middle of the Second Age. Every duke since then swore himself to life service, and the peril as acting intermediary between his demesne and the consecrated wilds inhabited by the free Paravians. They held vested authority, but only in trust. Forests were never to be cut down for fields, nor were fences and roadways ever built, except by grant of permission. Mankind had settled Athera on sufferance. Their works and their governance had been cautiously allowed, that the great mysteries maintained by Paravian wardship should remain in perpetual harmony.

Rule was not based upon power or privilege, but on the fraught perils of sacrifice. The pitfalls were documented. Lords and crowned high kings most often died young, heart torn between dedicated care for their own, and the terrible, exultant conflict of spirit as they treated with beings who formed the living bridge across the veil.

Mearn hugged his shivering body to the granite, groped a toe into the next crack, and shoved upward. The whispered scrape of his shirt over stone, and the moan of the wind through the gulf of starry darkness left him too much space to brood. A natural gambler, he measured the odds and concluded that fate dealt the clans a bad throw. His brother the duke had initially backed Arithon for matters of family honor. But as politics and greed built on the grand impetus of Lysaer's cry for armed justice, that chosen loyalty could well become an act of desperate survival.

Five centuries past, a misguided war cast off crown justice. Dissenters had seized the protection of the towns to wrest Athera's unexploited wilds from the sway of the Fellowship's compact. Now Lysaer's bright new Alliance of Light lent a glove for the hands of those factions who still sought to raise mankind into dominance. The sinister purpose which first launched the headhunters' leagues regained its original impetus: to exterminate the link preserved in clan bloodlines and end the resurgence of Paravian mysteries.

Mearn reached the next windowsill winded, his knuckles and fingertips raw from the granite. The chamber inside was curtained and dark, its purpose impossible to fathom. If a living princess was held captive above, sleeping guards or attendants might be quartered here. Mearn shut his eyes, listening. Small sounds drifted up from the street in diminished, wind-snatched fragments: a slap of hurried footsteps, then the head falconer's surly phrasing in complaint of a dishonest scullion. Between oaths and blasphemies maligning the oaf's character, the reference to stolen pigeons surfaced in recurrent disgust.

"Daelion Fatemaster's almighty debts!" harangued the falconer. "If your duty as Avenor's royal steward won't see the miscreant punished, who in creation's going to act? Should the Captain of Avenor's Royal Guard be yanked in to box the ears of a feckless boy? Well, kiss my dead granny's arse, if that's what you think! Bedamned if I'll show my face at his door to say why he has to roust out."

Mearn twitched narrow lips, his soft snort of laughter damped by his sleeve as the brangle destroyed the night quiet. Echoes bounced, multiplied, through the tower entry. The theft in the dovecote seemed the cause of Gace Steward's delay, a setback to nettle his weasely temperament into a snarling row. The falconer refused to give back any ground. Delighted to seize on the chance-met diversion, Mearn s'Brydion nipped from his niche and embarked on the grueling last ascent of the upper battlements.

The watchtower's turret had a crenellated guard walk, inset with drains to gutter rainwater. These offered the climber a precarious left handhold while he unslung his grapple and line. He timed his throw between gusts, lest the wind spoil his aim. The carrying, metallic chink as the hooks slid and caught prickled his nape into gooseflesh. He could not shake the unnerving conviction that an archer took aim between his shoulder blades. Imagination harried him on through the moments he was forced to trust his weight to the rope. Eyes shut, sweat branding the acrid taste of salt on his lips, he swung out over air and scaled the line hand over hand.

Gusts battered at his progress, fetched him against stone in repeated, bruising impacts that tore through his shirt and skinned a shoulder. Then he reached the crenellation. He dragged himself up and through, and crouched head down, sheltered at last from the buffeting cold.

Had guards been stationed there on the wall walk, he should have died, betrayed by teeth that chattered from fraught nerves and chill. Yet no man-at-arms came to skewer him. Gray stone and pale brick wore nothing beyond ice, except where the reaching scour of the elements swept the battlement clean. Mearn thrived on escapades. He shrugged his scuffed clothing back to rights, licked a scraped knuckle, and raked his lovelock free of his collar.

The tower's turret chamber had windows secured with oak-plank shutters strapped in iron. No light shone through the gaps at the edges. With his ear pressed to the wood, Mearn sensed no activity. A questing touch confirmed a barred fastening, likely fitted with a lock and hasp from inside. The hinges were mounted prison fashion, onto the outer wall. Mearn unlaced the thong ties from his collar points, ripped off his shirt cuff to muffle stray noise, then looped the heads of the pins with the leather and worried until they slipped free.

Left the play in the hasp, and one side unanchored, the shutter gave just enough to allow him an opening to push through.

Mearn deferred his first move. While the gusts slapped and pried through the rip in his shirt, he peered into the stillness, poised as the predator who tested the lair of unknown and dangerous prey. Faint warmth touched his skin, dense with the charcoal smoke of banked embers and a lighter fragrance of lavender. He detected no movement, could see little beyond the bronze-bossed handles of what might be a lady's clothes chest. Bulked corners of other furnishings lay limned in the starlight admitted by the breached shutter.

Mearn raised his thigh, tautened his grip, and hoisted soundlessly onto the broad sill. A feathered brush of his jerkin across studded wood, a whisper of calfskin on stone, and he was through, flattened to the curve of the inside wall.

He waited.

Nothing; just the breathy draw of coals in an unseen grate, and the fret of the wind outside. His wide, straining eyes discerned the frame of a curtained box bed, the harder gleam of a porcelain ewer on a stand, and the pale linen oblong of a towel. The chamber was appointed for basic comfort, but not in the grace of high luxury. An Etarran-bred princess accustomed to society and the gregarious convolutions of city intrigue would be like to go mad from sheer boredom.

That moment, from nowhere, fierce fingers grasped his lovelock.

Mearn whirled. His sudden, lithe reflex ripped off the hold. His wrist bone jarred metal. The shuttering cover of a hand lamp chinked back. Caught in the flaring, sudden haze of light, the woman he seized with a wrestler's strength was all molten gold hair and pearl skin. She was fire, gilt-and-white porcelain, and a vision to stun a male witless. Widened bronze eyes flashed up to meet his, black lashed and deep, with pupils to drown him in primordial night.

The sound that impacted his closed throat wrenched his larynx. Mearn lost all grip on his senses. Swept head to foot by a physical awareness to freeze thought and unstring his reason, the swift, building pressure of desire in his loins ran him through like the shock of a sword thrust.

"Ath!" he gasped in a wrenched whisper. "Save us all, lady. You are like the Avenger's own spear, too sharp to touch without bleeding." Cramped fingers could be forced to unlock; dumb flesh, be compelled to step back.

Her Grace, Princess Talith touched cool fingers to his lips. "Be wary. A handmaid sleeps in the chamber beneath, and her loyalty is not to me."

Mearn shuddered and broke her restraint as though burned. He had heard all the rumors, even glimpsed Lysaer's wife at state functions before her incarceration. At safe remove behind a retinue and attendants, she had been a sight to turn heads. Nothing alive could prepare any man for the impact of her at close quarters. Mearn discovered himself helpless to tear his gaze from her face. The delicate, ivory line of her shoulder entrapped him, and the sheer fall of the nightrobe whose folds by turns offered and obscured a form of breathtaking loveliness.

Words came like bruised increments of noise, struck by a faltering tongue. "You're a prisoner, then?" Mearn forced a next sentence. "The party who sent me believed so."

A brute turn of will let him recall the danger posed by the lamp; he snatched back the presence to lean through the casement and close the skewed board of the shutter. Faced away, wit and speech gained a measure of reprieve. "Word at court insists you've gone into retreat. Stress and overwrought nerves, Gace Steward says. The upset is attributed to barrenness."

"Lies," Talith said on a barb of stung spirit. "My bed has been barren." Bitterness made her laugh, but in venomous, smothered quiet. "No husband, no seed, hence, no child. It is Lysaer who fails to get us an heir." She dimmed the small lamp and restored it to a soot-streaked niche in the wall. "For hatred of his half brother, the prince thinks to put me aside."

"The abduction by Arithon caused this?" Mearn straightened and set his back against stone, acute in his private discomfort. The lady's tower quarters were too cramped to pace. If he stirred one step in any direction, his retreat would not bring him more than an arm's length from her. "But why? Eight hundred thousand coin weight in gold brought you home with your virtue intact."

Talith flung back a ripple of bright hair and regarded him. The contempt that fired her topaz eyes seemed to roil the very marrow in his bones. "You say. Yet what proof can I show for my loyalty?"

Mearn swore. A stride carried him to the box bed, impelled by a pity too fierce to keep still. "Prince Lysaer's a fool. I can't change that." He locked hands to the spare rope coiled across his shoulders, flamed to ridiculous, boyish embarrassment for his sweaty state of dishevelment. Torn shirt, ripped fingers, and wind-tangled hair, he felt rough as an unsanded plank. "But I can offer means to escape."

"To what?" Talith answered. This time, she spun away in swift violence.

Not in time; Mearn saw the lucent, gold rims of her eyes dim to a sudden flood of tears. He ached to take her into his arms, to circle her glass-and-gold-leaf fragility inside a bastion of comfort. Pride stopped him, then the first, warning prick of intuition. "You still love your husband."

Her rancor a core of iron in silk, the princess rebutted, "Should my heart lie with duty, in Avenor?"

But the statement struck cold to a gambler's ear. Hatred could breed twisted passions, Mearn knew. He watched. The lady opened a drawer and fished out a striker and candles. Her hand stayed too steady as she lit the fresh wicks. Tears might still glitter through her ebony lashes, and vulnerability sharpen an allure like thin crystal, and yet, she had been born a pedigree Etarran. A clansman forgot at his peril: her breed fed on intrigue and betrayal since infancy.

Three years of solitary contemplation in this tower might foment a thousand deadly hopes of revenge. If Lady Talith of Avenor wished no escape, she would angle to gain something else.

"I need to conceive a child," she announced without prelude.

"*What?*" Mearn exclaimed.

"You risked much to find me. I trust you like women?" She gave no more warning, but closed in and cornered him, one exquisite, warm shoulder exposed by an artful slip of her night rail. The curve of her breast underneath was too perfect to endure without touching. Mearn felt the bang of raw physical sensation hammer the center of his chest. Her soft scent filled his mind. Rife chaos struck through his labored, trapped logic. "You want," he began in emasculated anger.

She tipped back her head, cupped his jaw in fine hands, and did not smile at the violent flush to his skin. "Don't be a hypocrite. However much you posture and prickle, you want me in bed well enough."

"That has little to do with good sense," Mearn gasped. His breath failed him. His next utterance came out strangled. "A child—"

Reason fled, words dissolved to a groan as she stretched up and laid her softened lips against the sped pulse in his neck. His arms closed around her through no sane volition. Touched off by explosive, violent need, he pressed her slim heat against him. The fingers still torn and stinging from his climb locked in her cascade of bright hair.

Her seduction was no longer passionless or steady as she slipped her hands through his collar. Prolonged years of loneliness ripped away pretense. "You are very fine," she murmured beneath his chin. "Brave also. Sire us a prince to make the realm proud."

"Ath, this is madness!" Mearn twisted free. "My get would be half-bred." He caught her wrists, his birth accent snapping. "Lady, you have *no idea* what you're asking."

"Oh?" Talith laughed, deep and low in her throat. If his strength was too harsh, she did not pull away. Chin lifted, her taut, aroused nipple a hairsbreadth from his tormented flesh, she let her pose become her sweet challenge, well assured he could not resist.

Mearn cursed.

Talith returned a slow smile. "Can a princess be faulted for taking a lover if she is cast off in neglect? Let the court in Avenor hear I'm not barren, the disgrace will become my fresh victory. My child of course won't be Lysaer's. For that, his much vaunted manhood will be laughingstock."

"Things aren't that simple," Mearn wrenched out. She was too close, too desirable. Her appeal for just vindication was too potent to let him think. Nor had he the means to let her down with any proper kindness or subtlety. "I can't. Lady, your spirit is great, and your beauty unmatched. I could lie with you for sheer pleasure. But I can never, ever presume the right to make a new life between us."

She broke then, her tears a bright, rolling spill over her flawless cheekbones. "Ath's mercy, help me! Won't you see how I need this? A shamed wife could gain freedom, some measure of autonomy. Yes, the worst could befall. Lysaer may cast me off. At least I could return to my cousins in Etarra."

"I can't," Mearn said, helpless before her unhappiness. "It's a matter of honoring my family bloodline."

Her features stayed blank, confounding Mearn's pity. Etarra was a city founded too late to have any record of the uprising. Unlike the persistent guild minister from Erdane, Talith would not know of the facts behind clanborn descent.

Mearn shut his eyes, anguished. He dared not explain; not after the clandestine overture just presented to Lysaer's high counselors. Clan numbers in Rathain were dangerously dwindled from the impact of the Mistwraith's curse. The damaging truth in Etarran hands, that the old family bloodlines were not replaceable, might hasten their final destruction.

"Lady," he said through bleak anguish, "let me help you escape.

Once free, you can flee to Etarra if you like, or even conceive your bastard at will on any other man that you choose."

She did not answer.

Mearn sensed the stir, then the chill kiss of draft on his skin as she widened the distance between them. As he looked, and interpreted her proud determination, he felt as if his powers of cognition had suffered a dousing in ice water. "Lady," he said, more dangerous now, "what do you know? There's something to this you're not telling me."

Talith smiled. Her neat, narrow fingers adjusted her night rail and reclothed her inviting nakedness. "Tell all and give nothing? How like a man who has bloodline, but apparently no measure of heated blood in him. Why am I not surprised? I should be asking, instead, who has sent you."

Mearn grinned. "You sound like my grandmother Dawr. Sharp as vinegar and sand when her males won't do as she pleases. I have no intention of saying which party takes active interest in your predicament. Shall I end our sweet impasse and go?"

That shook her. "We are bargaining, bloodless man." The glass edge of solitude had eroded her strength. Both fear and contempt rang true as she spoke. "Did you plan to climb down as you came? Then I'll have your rope and grapple to reel in once you set down on the council-hall roof. Deliver my note to my lover of choice and let *him* scale the wall for my favor."

Mearn inclined his head. "I'll bear your note. The rope I would leave you in any case, to escape or invite whom you will. The person who sent me shall hear of your plight without any need for persuasion."

He shrugged off the hemp coils, nettled by more than fresh scrapes and the stinging of his grazed fingertips. His refusal of her sex lodged an ache of unassuaged need in his gut. Still, he felt her gaze track him, fierce as the heat thrown off magma.

"If you're dedicated as you seem to the cause of Lysaer's Alliance, this won't matter," Talith said in sudden, terse resolve. "But if you speak to other clansmen, or have sympathy for ones in Tysan at risk of enslavement, I offer this much. The Koriathain are in league with Prince Lysaer against Arithon. Their kind have sent word: my lord husband has left Etarra. He returns to Avenor with all speed, in secret, for he knows the Master of Shadow has suborned the shakedown crews at his shipyard."

Mearn blinked. Set upon dangerous ground since no suspicion of doubt must touch on s'Brydion loyalty, he tossed off an insouciant grin. "You lay claim to a knowledge of state secrets, *from here*?"

Talith met him with the thinnest of smiles, spiked in thorns and malice. "You didn't know?" She stepped sideward, flicked back a felt curtain, and seated herself in the box bed. "Beneath lies my jailer and handmaid, who also is mistress to Lysaer's appointed High Priest of the Light, Cerebeld. I married a man who now claims to be god sent."

She paused. Mearn said nothing, preferring to listen, while his thoughts spun on tangents of frightful speculation.

The focused intensity of his stillness must have reached her. "Oh yes, you suspect the very truth," Talith affirmed. "The meetings in this tower seek to seed a religion. Cerebeld and his mad-dog fanatic, Vorrice, have been consecrated to carry out a divine mission. Lysaer makes long-range plans to unleash a holy war against the Master of Shadow."

Touched by the fluttering play of the candle, Talith gave a small, resigned shrug. "The s'Ffalenn prince might be a pirate, might ply his sorcery and connive against innocents, but he does not spin fair lies to justify his killing. Remember that, if you stay to fight him." Her hands had laced themselves taut in her lap, white knuckled in response to sharp memory. "Arithon's criminal and clever, but he's truthful. If I can smear Lysaer's reputation just enough to tear down this false claim to godhood, the world might come to bleed a little less."

Again she looked up. This time, her striking beauty held no subterfuge, but an appeal stamped in hard desperation. "I might win back a husband who is human if his gifted power to win a following is besmirched."

"You love him, not his cause," Mearn confirmed. He could rely upon that to protect the s'Brydion good name. "If you plan to keep my rope and grapple after I've lowered myself down, what will you do about hinge pins?"

Talith looked blank for a second, then chuckled low in her throat. "Pick the lock on the hasp, what else? The Etarran daughter who failed at that skill was judged unfit to be married." She arose, too wise to offer him meaningless thanks, and too worldly to press further claim on his personal loyalty. "If you'll wait, I'll pen my appeal for a bastard."

Mearn laughed, enchanted by her spirit. "Dear princess, if you are cast off and left lovelorn with cousins, allow me to visit and pay court. If you liked, I'd spirit you out of Etarra and invite you to tea with my grandmother. The result would certainly repel boredom."

"With vinegar and sand?" Talith rose in wry grace, tore a leaf from a book on her nightstand, then dipped water from the ewer and ground makeshift ink from a handful of ashes in the grate. "I'm not sanguine."

A thin quill drawn from the stuffing in her mattress, cut and split with Mearn's knife, made a pen.

"You've brought me precious hope," she admitted as she scribed her perilous invitation to lure a lover. "If you fall getting out of here and break your silly head, I'll entreat your grandmother's shade to come haunt you."

"No need," Mearn quipped. He shed his coil of rope. Volatile in movement as sparked flame, he took her folded missive and tucked it away in his belt, then kissed the warm fingers of her hand. "Dame Dawr has already sworn to do as much anyway, if she doesn't find a way to live forever." He blew out the candle. Removed to the window, he tipped back the shutter to an unwelcome blast of night wind. "Fate's blessing on you, princess. May you win back your joy outside the walls of this tower."

Much later, returned to the security of his bedchamber, he penned his own messages for Maenol's clansmen to bear warning to his duke, and also the Master of Shadow. As he inked his dire findings in close-spaced, ciphered script, Mearn s'Brydion could not set aside his last sight of Avenor's royal lady, erect in a silvery outline of starlight, the silent tears falling and falling off the breathtaking, proud slant of her cheekbones.

Early Spring 5653

First Upset

No sound destroyed Lord Maenol s'Gannley's sleep faster than the inbound drumming of hooves.

Shot to alarm in the misted, predawn gloom, too nerve wound to snatch for his boots, the man who bore title as Tysan's *caithdein* rolled headlong from the cloak which also served him as blanket. While crossing barren scrublands and open territory, he slept clothed in jerkin and breeches. His main gauche and daggers stayed sheathed at his belt. Damp earth and tender spring grass chilled bare feet as he snatched up his longsword, ready on the instant to fight, hide or flee to keep his small company living.

"Don't trouble," he murmured to the scout come to wake him. "Guard yourself as you can."

Edging the salt flats, en route to their next seacoast rendezvous to embark with three more of Arithon's purloined ships, none of his party slept disarmed.

The rest of his band stirred amid fog-choked hummocks, as hair-trigger wary as he. Their discipline became their young chieftain's sole pride. No chink of weapons and nary a torch marked their movements. Their presence blended like chaff upon burlap with the rise of the inland dunes and their low crests, fringed with wind-harried sedges. Stained dark with walnut, their exposed hands and faces melted into the rank stands of cattails and brush. Yet here, even the most covert care could not ensure their survival. Fourteen leagues south of Hanshire, their picked destination a hidden tidal estuary, their foray offered choice bait to headhunters ranging in search of scalp trophies, or worse, the double bounty routinely paid by the crown to muscle the galleymen's oars.

Breezes still spiked with the late season's chill wisped the loose strands from Maenol's clan braid. Every sense trained alert, he breathed in the lushness of green-budding willow, and the brackish fish taint of the bogs. The threat was still closing. Around him, the shrilling pipe of spring peepers fell silent before the oncoming hammer of hoofbeats.

"Just one light-boned horse," relayed Jyce, whose barrel-stout frame was small help in an ambush, but whose hearing made up for his clumsiness. "Not a destrier."

Maenol stayed wrapped in habitual silence, too spare with words to confer. Armed patrols seldom swept this landscape by night, unless they were dealt provocation; and over these reed-choked, stream-tangled lowlands, a war-bred charger would mire too deeply to canter.

"Nobody moves out of cover," Maenol said in a terse whisper. "We might face a traveler strayed from the road. With luck, he'll pass by without finding us."

Yet the rider came on, relentless. The swish of bent willows and the splash of muddy shallows marked an arrow-straight course through the bogs. On Maenol's signal, men prepared to ease steel in a soundless draw from their scabbards.

Then a low, trilling whistle signaled warning to the sentries. No chance-met arrival, the horseman reined in his foam-flecked mare. He dismounted, sweat drenched himself and half-winded, and shoved through the last stand of reeds under escort by one of Maenol's own watch scouts. "Tysan's *caithdein*, is he here?"

Any courier who knew to search these wilds for that name could bear only calamitous news.

"More slave raids," Maenol surmised. He stepped forward, gut tight and braced, his bloodless grip jammed on his sword.

The sardonic male voice which hailed from misty darkness belonged to no Korias clansman. "No. Not this time." The rider resumed with hoarse urgency, the peppery snap of his eastshore accent now clear enough to be recognized. "A trap's to be sprung on Arithon at Riverton."

Maenol advanced another step, piqued by an unwelcome hunch. "Mearn? Mearn s'Brydion? Merciful Ath! You have no business risking yourself here, even for such word as this."

"No time for passed messages. These tidings can't wait." Mearn's chin jerked up in a spasm of startlement as a second scout slipped from the brush at his elbow to take his reins and attend his blown horse. Prince Lysaer's increased bounties to slavers had pitched the forestborn clans to a wariness even sworn friends found unnerving.

Lord Maenol gave no apology, but pinned his close scrutiny on the mare. Relief eased some of the bite from his manner as he marked a rented hack with nondescript markings, and tack without blazoned trappings. The clan envoy from Alestron had been canny enough to seize every desperate precaution. Marshy soil would hold a shod horse's track for days. Skannt's headhunters might pick up his back trail. If they chose to pursue, the animal must be cut loose for expedience, or else bled to death lest her noise draw the hounds to full cry.

In the s'Brydion style of rapid-fire summary, Mearn broke the news that had brought him. "Lysaer's returned." He caught the *caithdein's* wrist in a grasp like wound wire and drew him aside to speak privately. "You can't imagine worse. His Grace has reached Avenor even as we speak."

A woman scout on the sidelines overheard. "That's not possible!"

Others echoed her incredulity. To the north, the mouth of Instrell Bay and every northern harbor remained locked in the grip of green ice; the mountain route through Camris was sealed shut with drifts. The severity and strength of a lingering winter left the West Road trade routes impassable.

"Tornir Peaks are deadly, razed by avalanche at this season, and our scouts from the Thaldeins say the Orlan pass will stay blocked thirty days past the equinox," Jyce protested.

"Yes. That's the lynchpin of Lysaer's strategy." Mearn plunged ahead, straitly grim. "I presumed the very same, a near-fatal mistake. Lysaer's forged a liaison with the Koriani witches. They parted the floes with spellcraft to row a galley into Mincress, then breached the Fellowship's wards to bring him southwest through Teal's gap."

"You claim he's crossed Tornir Peaks through the Sorcerer's Preserve?" the woman cried into stricken silence. "That's insanity!" No mortal company could survive that terrain. Every savage pack of fire-breathing Khadrim held confined by the Sorcerers would descend, and tear an armed supply train to pieces.

"The Prince of the Light's in Avenor," Mearn insisted. "He had arcane guidance, and could have arrived no other way."

The outspoken scout swore. Her young chieftain met the disastrous news like unflinching oak, hands firm on the hilts of his weapons. Over the rattle of breeze through stiff sedges, through the muffling, salt-heavy mist, he said only, "Give us more detail, if you will."

His *caithdein*'s composure and straight stance revealed nothing. Unable to measure his courage in darkness, Mearn matched his tone, talking fast. "The prince arrived in close secrecy. The town's not been informed. The outrider's servant I bribed for the gossip said his Grace planned a conference with the inner cabal of his council. He will board a waiting galley and put to sea by this dawn's tide, then slip ashore again at Hanshire. You can expect him to take the direct route by road and rejoin his specialized assault troop."

Before Maenol's steadiness, Mearn ticked off a trip-hammer listing of hard facts. The company came on special levy from Rathain, a division of Etarran field guard, handpicked, and deadly at infighting. These had already marched south under orders to cordon the roads and the ferries, and cut off all routes out of Riverton.

"Seven days," Tysan's *caithdein* extrapolated. "You say that's all we have to break through with a message, and let friends spirit Arithon out."

"You've got less," Mearn rebutted. "The elite company bypassed Avenor. They took remounts with them and parted from Lysaer's guard past the Melor River bridge. They've gone straight across country. I traveled at speed through the night out of hope the high spate off the peaks may mire their passage by Mogg's Fen."

Maenol seized the gist. The torrent fed by the snowmelt might open a frightfully narrow margin for clansmen who knew the high ground to engage and delay the advance of the enemy company.

"You'll need to move like Sithaer's winged demons. Damned *well* I wish I didn't need to be here," Mearn added, vehement. Yet he could not shirk inescapable facts. More lay at risk than his s'Brydion family honor. The next shipyard launching was due a week hence. Bold plans under way aimed for clan crews to abscond with not one, but three stolen vessels. The temptation to expose Arithon's interests for reward would be great for a man without a blood stake on the outcome.

"Anyone notices where you've gone, and why, you could be put to the sword," Maenol said, then instantly shouldered the risk of that debt. "You have my free welcome to take sanctuary among my clans."

Mearn snorted a disdainful laugh through the graying, salt-burdened air. "Don't mind *my* back. I left town in fine order. My chambers are barred, with word out I'm drunk to incapacity. For added assurance, three whores fill my bed. The house servant's keeping them occupied, blissful man. That much gold in their hands, I'll just have to hope the trulls won't exhaust him too soon, nor care whose prick stands to greet them."

"Come or go as you please, then. Make free with our stores if you're hungry, but hurry. You'll know we can brook no delay." Too rushed for more than that bare thread of courtesy, Maenol stepped aside to mete out instructions to his war captain. "No help for it, we're going to get bloodied. Send runners in relays. We raise call to arms. Also, word must be won through to Riverton to warn Arithon. Spend lives as you must. We'll see no free children if those dogs of Etarrans pin down Rathain's prince in their cordon."

As he caught wind of Mearn's clipped request to grain and refresh his tired horse, Lord Maenol spun back. "Where are you bound before morning?"

The youngest s'Brydion sibling bared his teeth in acidic self-mockery. "South, wherever else? I have Lysaer's note of safe conduct. Should your efforts fail in the fenlands, this fresh Etarran company has no clue that I'm prostrate, easing a thick head with doxies. If they won't be weaned from bullheaded prejudice, I'll just indulge them and uphold my ill-bred reputation."

"For harebrained acts and wild barbarism? I see." Maenol regarded him, thoughtful, his mustache quirked at an angle that almost smoothed the furrows from his brow. "As Duke Bransian's envoy and Avenor's pledged ally, you'll seed uncivil chaos in the chain of Lysaer's field command?" Before Mearn could muster a mettlesome retort, he burst into deep-throated laughter. "Go softly. You'll call down your brother's ducal vengeance on my head if you pass beneath the Wheel on this foray."

Mearn eyed him askance. A lethal spark of fury smoldered through his lean frame as he ended discussion with a shrug. "Better worry more whether Arithon's killed."

While the Alliance of Light gathered strength through past feuds and political incentives, both men held no illusion: the Master of Shadow became their last hope to stave off decimation of clan bloodlines.

Downfall

On the same misted daybreak that saw Maenol's scouts race east to attempt their desperate stand by Mogg's Fen, the first gold blush of light rinsed the high battlements of the tower where Princess Talith of Avenor was sequestered.

As always she opened her eyes to deep gloom. The strapped shutters leaked only pinpricks of light. Airless and chill, the flinty dankness of the brick enclosed the fusty odors of soot and beeswax, the lavender sprigs in her clothes chest too refined to drive the must of mildew from her blankets. Talith lay still, never so agonized by her plight that she gave way to helpless resignation. Where once she had commanded chattering maids to serve up scalding tea and the choice snippets of the night's gossip, now she had only her ears to record the ongoing events outside. Born and bred a pedigree Etarran, she would lie dead before she renounced her belief she could wrest back her place in court politics.

On calm mornings such as this, at the tide's turn, the exchanges of oaths between the stevedores and crown customs men winnowed up from the harborside. By the number of epithets relating to oxen, she deduced that a carter backed his dray down to the dockside. Talith heard the exchange of bawdy jokes, then laughter, which faded once the inspection was complete. An excise officer duly stamped the bill of lading; then a grinding, hollow thunder tore the quiet, as the dockworkers off-loaded the wainload of barrels. Left to conjecture, Talith wondered if the casks held water for a ship's stores, or whether another cargo from the brewer's rolled down the quay to burden the hold of a trade galley.

A ruled sliver of sunshine struck through a crack, the only snippet of natural light to brighten her chamber all day. The slow hours of her isolation racked her like torture and stretched highbred nerves to drawn glass. As if to compound that sawing misery, the bastard growing in her belly, contrived by liaison with a worshipful palace page, made her feel drawn and queasy. Talith cherished the still interval after each dawn, and the cozy warmth of the box bed. All too soon the chambermaid who served as her warden would burst in with wash water and firewood. Made arrogant by her position of propriety, the woman always grumbled in monotone while her fussy, brusque hands girded the princess into chilly clothes to endure another day of grinding emptiness.

Talith became afraid if she retorted in frustration, the screams she had smothered through four terrible years would escape all restraint, and leave her mewling with madness. If she could not hear the trills of skylarks at the meadows' edge, the spring brought her swifts and cliff swallows, nesting under the eaves on the battlement. Through their sprightly chirps, she heard the wind freshen and snap the banners streaming from their poles on the vaulted dome of the council hall. The bustle from the docks became erased by the gusts, replaced by the clop of hooves on the paving as a tight, fast-moving cavalcade cut through the daily grind of farm wagons crossing to market.

An officer called. His querulous order was answered by the deferent footfalls of a servant. The ponderous, leaved panels to the lower vestibule were unbarred to the uneasy bristle of activity which spoke of an arriving delegation.

Once, Talith would have arisen to pace the floor in a froth of balked curiosity. Prolonged incarceration had not sapped her spirit. Female wisdom and cold rage let her stop beating caged wings long since. She had learned in her desperate patience to rechannel the cutting edge of her mind to more subtle venues of subterfuge.

She shrugged off the empty comfort of her blankets, now impatient for the maid's prompt arrival. The woman had a haughty temper, when provoked. She was ambitious and vain, covetous of her position as a high priest's clandestine mistress. Rich all her life, and born to position, Talith knew by her huntress's instinct which jabs would rankle the most. The maid was a gold-digging, servant-class whore, and her nettled retorts to a princess's needling could sometimes spring knowledge of outside events.

Yet the mincing, slippered step and piqued puffs of exhalation she expected came replaced by the grating tread of boots, embedded against the rumble of masculine voices.

Talith exploded to her feet. She snatched a quilted robe from a chairback, and whirled, heart pounding, to confront the charcoal shadow which demarked the barred arch of the doorway.

The approaching steps ground inexorably upward. An explosion of pure rage made her blood race like magma, for this invasion came with no polite notice and no dignity; then that ire seized to ice, as the steps outside halted and isolated her maid's obsequious soprano from the stairwell.

". . . missed her courses, my brave lord. The linens for such stayed unstained these two months, though on my word, no man entered her bedchamber. Each night, I slept across the threshold to the upper staircase. Below me, always, were the guards sworn to serve the divine Light. They answer to no man but your exalted self, and to his high eminence, Cerebeld."

A man murmured something placating. Then the steps paused. The bar clashed and the panel swung inward.

Barefoot in her nightshift and the dangling toggles of a robe just barely donned, Princess Talith received no warning beyond a dazzling scintillance of diamonds. Then a damascened glint of pale hair shone by the rags of new flame in the sconce. A lightning clap to unsuspecting rock, her senses imprinted the form of the man who entered her chamber.

Least likely of visitors, her s'Ilessid husband strode in unannounced, prematurely returned from his state delegation to Etarra.

Four years had changed him, Talith saw, eyes narrowed to the influx of light, and her arrested breathing resumed to sped rhythm from the recoil kick of shocked nerves. His stainless white dress, simple jewels, and lethal charm had been welded into new purpose. He had always had majesty. Now, presence lay on him like gold thread in velvet, or fine silk wrapped over tempered wire. His eyes of water-rinsed sapphire upon her showed no shadow of strain. On the contrary, as if passionate love had never aroused his desire, his mannered tranquillity held a luminous focus that seemed to command the dead air to forced rarity.

Despite her contempt, Talith felt the force of him ripple her flesh to a stabbing prickle of awe.

She could not sustain the keen edge of her anger. Every bastion of her cynical, Etarran pride wavered. Nor could she tear her gaze from his features. Almost, she lost to the moonstruck fool's impulse which urged her to rush into his arms. If Lysaer saw her weakness, he had not come to gloat. His face stayed expressionless, its lordly, fair symmetry remote in perfection as a spirit carved from light and air.

Talith could have wept then for unjust debasement, that his mere reappearance held the power to sear her shunned heart like a brand.

She wrestled to shore up her fractured composure. A wrung moment passed while she recouped resilience, then noticed the other three officials who mounted the landing behind him.

Raw fury then stained her cheeks heated pink, that her unjust state of incarceration should be made the public butt of a formal audience. She realized in cringing embarrassment that her hands fumbled to fasten the front of her robe, but failed in their task through her racking torment of raw need.

However much she had cause to resent Lysaer, her love was the stronger, a force as unruly as the surge of the tide. Left weak at the knees, she had nothing else left but her verbal wits and a hamstrung drive to vent outrage.

"How like a man and a craven, to arrive with a bootlicking dog pack to heel," Talith said. "Or have you come in overdressed force to collect my soiled linen for the laundry girl? The gallants in Etarra would think it the rage, to see royalty wait on a servant."

Lysaer seemed not to hear. Lordly and unruffled as masterworked crystal, he assayed neither riposte nor civil greeting, but addressed her instead with the incisive clarity she had seen him use once on an officer who had deserted. "We'll have no display of false modesty, woman. Your robe must come off. Strip your night rail as well. I'm informed you are bearing. Shall we see?"

His train of officials pattered in from the stairwell, no doubt summoned to stand legal witness. The sallow-faced leader with the stalking tread swept her with obsidian hard eyes, his voluminous cloak of ermine and gold fretted with chains and wired pearls. The sunwheel emblazoned his cowled robe of office, and one fist, squared blunt as a mason's maul, clutched a scepter encrusted with citrines. Behind him minced the stooped person of the High Seneschal, the sills of his cheekbones windburned to old leather by days of inclement travel. Beyond middle age, and stymied by events outside the ossified mores of state politics, he gave the cracked stone in the floor his discomfited contemplation. Vorrice came last, as the Light's new-made instrument to seek out and destroy petty sorcery. He gave her a leering, suspicious inspection, preened as a fighting cock hung with steel spurs for a match with inferior rivals.

Talith felt their collective awareness, avid as crows lined up in an abattoir waiting to gorge on a carcass.

Her tone was syrup as she let fly her unwounded contempt. "Whose shame shall we celebrate? Yours, gutless prince, for the pathetic excuse of my barrenness?"

Lysaer never blinked. "You heard my command. I need not repeat myself." A crook of his finger brought the traitorous handmaid scurrying to assist her disrobing.

Talith raised her chin, too proud to give way to a physical struggle, or invite them to lay hands on in force. Nor would she assist the ignominy herself. Doll stiff, she maintained every breathtaking inch of her bearing, while the maid tugged and circled, divesting each layer of her garments.

The kiss of chill air was too sharp to hide. Shivering as the cloth slithered down and bared her defenseless shoulders, Talith relied upon words for her knives. "If there's truth to this claim, dare you brand yourself cuckold?"

The handmaid recoiled in prim righteousness, ready to repeat her avowal that no man had passed through her guard; yet the princess, her disdain fixed like acid upon Lysaer, gave that unctuous objection no chance. "Why not ring the bells in praise of another miracle? Ath's all-powerful avatar shouldn't balk at a child conceived by sublime intervention. Let your bitch of a watchdog swear by her truth. Give the realm an heir begotten by miracle, and blessed by the glory of the Light. Another lie is scarcely more preposterous than the last. What a stirring opportunity to fan the ardor of your campaign, and win more adulation from the masses."

Lysaer gave back his pitying patience. "I am truth's minion. My born calling can't be sullied by the rags of false gallantry, even to protect your infidelity." His eyes on her stayed an implacable, blued steel. "Nor would I exploit an honest servant's gullibility. The Master of Shadow is at Riverton, and sorcerer enough that he once gained covert entry to the most rigorously guarded keep on the continent." No one could forget the furor over that, since Duke Bransian's citadel had been widely considered impregnable. Lysaer closed his point. "If you chose to be my enemy's lover, this tower would pose his demonic skills small impediment."

"Had Arithon wished, he'd have done his work earlier, without the inconvenience of skulking." Talith held herself erect, ablaze with the unalloyed arrogance of pedigree, while the plain, dull cloth of her night rail slipped down and puddled around her cold ankles.

"Bring the torch," the priest Cerebeld snapped to the handmaid. The High Seneschal flushed red to his wattles, pecking her with swift, sidelong glances as he opened cupboards and chests, and fingered the contents to mask his driving discomfort.

Princess Talith endured, desperate and unflinching, her fine skin fretted to gooseflesh. While the one man she loved with her whole heart in marriage showed her nakedness no trace of natural humanity, others who were enemies leered in unconstrained male amazement. The exquisite torment of her beauty became her last weapon against tears, as Lysaer's state witnesses sweated in their clothes and ached in stifled frustration. Their lust left them slack jawed as they cataloged her attributes like an ornament unveiled for private auction. The subtle details lay beyond her to hide: the giveaway pallor of morning nausea; the ripe fullness of breast, and the first, softened curve of hip and belly. Nor could she mask the smooth, dewy skin that seemed lit like the satin reflection on a pearl.

"Let the light be brought closer," Vorrice urged, sand on granite, while the thick, hurried breathing of the High Seneschal sawed through suspended silence.

The ordeal seemed a puppet's play, distanced by the sudden clangor as the bell tower tolled the hour. Outside in the freedom of sea-bright, clear air, gulls still cried and swooped. The snatched, wind-torn cry of a ship's officer called for his galley to cast off her lines.

Talith felt every current of disturbed air on her skin. The minutes dragged by, until the frame of the ordinary must splinter away under tension. Her bravado became a meaningless shield before an unbearable, annihilating shame. *Please Ath; let her waken to safe, lonely darkness and the after-sweat of a nightmare.*

Yet the ponderous, honeyed vowels of Lysaer's new High Priest crushed hope into damning testimony. "My Lord Prince of the Light, I corroborate the handmaid's suspicion. The woman is certainly bearing."

The High Seneschal coughed in queer, strangled haste, then blurted, "I concur."

"By the Light of Divine Presence, I would see her burn for infidelity with a sorcerer," Vorrice intoned, then licked his moist lips, his pouched eyes shining with eagerness.

Lysaer looked aside, magisterial in rebuke. "No such cruel sentence shall occur without proof, nor shall the law act without a proper hearing and tribunal."

Talith broke into a violent shiver. "My lord prince, I must speak."

Lysaer gave her plea no reaction, but removed his steady gaze from his officer. The torch flame hazed his pale figure in light as he pronounced in gentle sadness to the handmaid, "Our business is finished. You may help the accused with her robing."

That frightening, unnatural distance warned Talith that her last option left was escape. She still had Mearn's rope and grapple secreted between the boards of her box bed. That private option braced up her pride as Lysaer stepped toward the doorway. He chided his officers that Ath's tide would not wait. Vorrice and Cerebeld came to heel like two dogs dragged stiff legged off a fresh kill. The seneschal followed, still cringing. Lysaer's muted words of disposition arose, wreathed in hollow echoes from the stairwell, as if the wife he had once cherished was deaf and mute, and a stranger.

"Keep the woman in good health until the child's birth. If it is dark, Vorrice, have it ritually killed as the accursed offspring of darkness. If the infant is of any other coloring, consider it mortal, and blameless. Let my seneschal send word to Etarra in appeal to its maternal relatives. If they show offense at the babe's bastard blood, then consign it to a Koriani orphanage. The realm's justice cannot be sidelined for sentiment. The adulteress must stand trial for treason against the Crown of Tysan, under pain of death by the sword."

Consequences

Under smoking veils of spindrift hurled aloft by swift oars, an unmarked galley speeds westward; and below her sluiced decks, the state splendor of his jewels set aside in private pain, Lysaer s'Ilessid weeps the desperate tears he could not shed for Talith in the tower, and the love forced to ruin by the wiles of an enemy anneals his heart to dread vengeance. . . .

Midst the bubbling mud pots and rank steam of Teal's Gap, lit by a misted new moon, Asandir of the Fellowship paces the unstable ground, unwinding Koriani spells of concealment like clockchain, and sounding each link in the boundary wards for weak points which might unravel to free bloodthirsty packs of Khadrim; and he knows, as he works, that his stopgap seals will hold scarcely more than a decade. . . .

Near dawn in Avenor, crouched in the rags of the sea mist, an archer under the High Priest's secret orders discharges his crossbow to dispatch a thorny state problem and deliver the divine prince from a base and damaging embarrassment; his bold shot shears through rope, and the adulteress suborned from the faith of the Light falls with a cry to her death. . . .

Early Spring 5653

VIII. Spring Trap

The morning began innocuously enough. The Mad Prophet set out to get drunk and the written verses, commissioned by a merchant for his love-struck young bride, lent the first opportunity to absent himself. Arithon asked for a servant to complete the delivery. Flushed since their horrendous argument at dawn, still unnerved from the sting of the Masterbard's refusal to abandon his wiles at Riverton, Dakar volunteered for the errand.

"I need the excuse to get out," he snapped in bruised candor as he snatched up the ribboned parchment. Only the anonymity of another tavern would let him drown his sorrows in peace. Stay, and he risked the inebriated folly of marching upstairs to battle the same cause all over again.

On the subject of increased risks at the shipyard, Arithon stayed deaf to reason. To break off as resident bard at the Laughing Captain within days of another launching would risk his connection with the men now set in precarious position to spirit the new ships from the harbor.

In due course, the infatuated merchant received the promised scroll, his jewels subdued like sunken treasure in the depths of his pillared foyer. His expansive contentment left three Shandian sovereigns in the hands of the bard's scowling courier.

The Mad Prophet blinked. Dimpled into a smile of moist-eyed

275

gratitude, he asked leave to depart through the merchant's back courtyard. He plowed through the daily mayhem of commerce: baled goods and sweating men loading wains, and made for the seaside quarter.

Dakar wasted no time. Racked by distress as devouring as guilt, set after by worry throughout the Shadow Master's string of reckless successes, he reeled from the taproom of the Oyster ten minutes after it opened. He knew better than to stay. The proprietor's two heavies took a dim view of patrons who lolled in seamy stupor on the floor. Cheerful from the foresight which spared him their attentions, Dakar clutched a crock of Orvandir's best red in each fist. The contents of a third one sloshed in his belly, and the day seemed suddenly very fine.

Languorous, honey sunlight poured over the checked boards of the quay. A man in search of quiet could find a sheltered niche if he poked between the hogsheads of salt pork stacked for bulk sale to the pursers. The spring season also offered up rotting heaps of fishnets, discarded as salvage for ragmen.

Dakar felt no shame for his lapse into debauchery. If Arithon s'Ffalenn could ignore every sensible warning, then the fool who elected to stay at his shoulder must squelch a sane conscience by whatever means lay at hand.

Yet in the cramped alley between the quayside brothels, the best of laid plans went astray.

A chubby, tousled potter linked Dakar's arm, soon joined by a journeyman cobbler who was lanky as a pole, and snared in the teeth of misfortune.

"Man, it's my temper gets my fat in the fire, every time," he lamented, while the potter peered up, arms folded like a judge, and Dakar marked time, scuffing a stripped bone in the gutter. The tale unfolded, a swan song of dismissal from a master's craftshop for pinking a fussy customer with an awl. "What a piss-mongering shrew, never pleased with anything. I went to chalk her size, and let me tell you! The bitch threatened not to pay if the outline looked undainty. Kicked like a mule each time your finger grazed her ankle."

The cobbler rolled his eyes. "As if any man with the itch would tup a cow like *her* for relief. Likely that's what keeps her broody. I shouldn't've jabbed her. But a patten in the groin's a fighting provocation. Damn me! For such a piddling wee trickle o' blood, she scarcely had to squeal like a hog dragged by the haunches to slaughter."

"Never mind," the potter soothed. "Women get themselves born to cause trouble." He added a suggestive nudge to Dakar, who obliged and surrendered the crock.

Two shopgirls and a passing sailor's bawd fell in with the consolation party under the plank walks of a tenement. Pinches were exchanged amid trilling giggles. The cobbler shrugged off his disaffection. Enlivened by the surge of merry spirits, the bawd drew the cork on the last crock of wine, the name of her jack-tar forgotten.

By then, Dakar had insinuated a hand under one doxie's blouse. The other, who was blond, kissed him silly until his means to escape into a numb stupor had been squandered. He tried to take his leave, but his chance-met acquaintances towed him along, disregarding every protest as they rollicked their way past the shops on Weaver's Alley.

Nobody was either upright or sober. To missteps and shrieks of uproarious glee, they ricocheted off signposts and buildings. The doxie donned a wig of yarns cut from the warp ends of a loom, then embarked on a simpering impersonation of the crown exciseman's second wife. Hurting with laughter and winded as well, after dodging some spiteful matron's barrage of flowerpots, Dakar folded in half to catch his wind. When the placement of a lamppost stopped his list toward the pavement, he seized the moment to take stock.

A hooked sprig of gentian trailed from his ear. Crumbled earth and shards of terra-cotta sifted down his collar from his hair. He suffered the twinges of a bounding headache, and wine fumes made it difficult to think. Instead of drinking himself painlessly senseless, he found himself perspiring and itchy as a dog in the untidy wool of his jerkin.

His uncoordinated squirms to shed the hot garment dislodged his last sovereigns. The pair rolled in chiming duet down the gutter.

Shopgirls and whore butted heads as they pounced. Since the cobbler waxed morose, they rescued Dakar from the jammed wads of his clothing and chivvied him down a back alley to purchase more spirits.

"We need a rum seller," slurred the potter. "Since the day those blighted ships sailed and vanished from the harbor, every dive in the quarter's turned lousy with off-duty guardsmen."

Dakar agreed. As principal henchman to the pirate responsible, he held no enthusiasm for hobnobbing next to crown soldiers. Distressed by untimely reminder of his angst, he latched onto the first available crock and sucked rotgut spirits until his middle felt tight as a blowfish.

Afternoon passed in a dizzy whirl of noise, the indistinct moments overlapped on themselves like a salvager's haul of glass and flotsam. Dakar stayed transfixed while the cobbler fell prostrate. Cart traffic jammed. Burly teamsters shook their fists in an argument over which should step down and drag the lout clear of the thoroughfare. The Mad Prophet bet a penny on the outcome, then wandered in circles, confused. A swarthy cooper insisted the combatants were knocked senseless, while the potter swore by the toes on his feet that the town guard had dragged off both parties. Dakar blinked like a turtle. Sunk in cogitation to recall which cheating craftsman still owed him a winning portion, he tired of walking, and wound up parked on his hams in a bakery.

The potter seemed content, crunching down the stale shortbread stars left over after the solstice. When his gestures grew vehement, he fell off his stool. The baker tried to right him and got his eye blacked. Tossed back on the street, Dakar had to stop and grope for the coins to buy another jack of whiskey. His doxie had vanished. He refused to go farther without a replacement, and there she stood, scaling cod over a bucket by a cookstall. The potter settled down, obliging, while Dakar kissed his newest find, his gaze gone dewy from her overwhelming perfume of fish oil.

The shops closed. Dusk loomed like smoky pearl through the drifting snags of river mist, while Dakar swore and wept, half-prostrate across the butt of an unopened keg. Four apprentices from the blacksmith's helped him free the jammed bung. The singing after that became damaging, with Dakar by then doubled over in the gutter, caught in between a whistling bout of hiccups and the necessity of rendering his gorge.

Night fell, and the crabbed old torchman lit the lamps. Stumbling past the flare of his wind-jerked brand, Dakar reeled and collided through streets grown inexplicably crowded. He felt no premonition, no compelling sense of urgency. His tipsy curiosity led him to surmise that some disturbance had arisen in the market square. Rather than fight the press, he tacked that direction. The throng soon jostled him away from his companions. If they had gone because his wallet was empty, the fine point scarcely mattered. Mazed by the muddle which foreran a damning hangover, Dakar pawed the sleeve of a maidservant to ask why the festival should happen five days late. "Can't anybody see? The moon nearest to spring equinox passed her full phase last week."

Her words about captives and barbarians at the gates seemed a ridiculous fiction.

Dakar called her a liar, swore back as he was sworn at, then reverted to unctuous, smiling beneficence as her burly pack of brothers grasped his collar. Their fists shot him reeling through a mailed cordon of armed men, and he escaped getting skewered because he fell.

He flung out his arms to break his headlong sprawl and plunged to the wrists in a warm, clotted mass of bloodied straw. The spill was fresh. Dakar recoiled, slammed witless with revulsion. He yelled and scrambled upright to denounce the royal guardsmen for staging their unruly public spectacle in a slaughter yard.

Yet words never came. Speech foundered, as if nervous reflex reacted a heartbeat ahead of trained mage-sight. Jarred from his drunken stupor as water might slam into rock, Dakar pulled up short, crumpled over by mangling nausea. The pale, phosphor haze twined through the night air was not steam winnowed up by the chill, but the imprint of spirit light shocked free of live flesh at the moment of violent death.

The aura dispersed by this recent act of bloodshed resolved no animal's dumb agony. Dakar retched with horror, caught in reverberated pain pitched too fine to be other than human.

The spasm sapped all his volition to move. Dakar hugged his griped middle and wished the rest of his awareness would stop functioning. Then perhaps he could deny that what arose above his head was a scaffold for a public execution. He dared not look up lest he find himself damned. *Ath preserve, while he drank, Arithon had been left undefended.* Lord Jieret had delivered them a warning and a prophecy. Regret came, too late, and the sorry, wretched fear: *that the blood on his wrists could be royal.*

"Come on, you! Move along! You're in the way." The guardsmen had outworn their patience.

When they prodded with pike poles and gained no response, they hauled the barging miscreant to his feet without care for his mewling denial. Garbage thrown by the screaming mob splattered against the boards and someone's poor aim raised a bold round of raillery from a prisoner. The accent sounded too clipped to be townborn. Since no city officer or tribunal seemed in evidence to restore the crowd to civil order, logic at last wakened reason. The condemned men had to be clanborn. Dakar's chastened glance showed one already dead, with two more bound up for disembowelment.

He lurched against restraint and rounded on the guardsmen. "Ath, you can't do this!" He shot a drunken kick at the nearest man-at-arms, impelled by white rage and urgency. The law's murdering, thirsty sword must not reap another irreplaceable bloodline. "Your prince has commandeered these captives as galley slaves!"

A mailed fist smashed back and silenced him. "Not this lot. Now be off."

Dakar was ejected by two brutes with maces, who rammed him into the surging onlookers, then closed ranks to re-form their cordon.

279

"Gutless sheep!" Dakar yelled through a stinging, split lip. "Whose order commands this?"

"Be still, you fool!" A woman snatched his elbow to restore his good sense. "These skulking clan curs tried to slip through our gates. For that, their lives were called forfeit."

But Dakar shook off her well-meant restraint. "Do I look like an idiot? No clansman would visit a walled city unless he was crazed with a death wish!" Yet even as he spoke, he discerned the contradiction: messengers from Lord Maenol might attempt such a course if they carried a warning for Arithon.

Belligerent with rum, Dakar rammed the soldiers, screaming to demand a stay of mercy.

Too late; across the pale span of boards overhead, amid the streamed sparks from crude torches, the sword fell and rammed home. Blood sprayed from a man's opened chest. Painted in gory, flittering light, his death spasms splashed Dakar in a hot, obscene rain. "No! Save us all! Stop lest you call down disaster!"

The executioner heeded no outcry amid that raucous sea of noise. Raised above a crowd that howled for a spectacle, he angled his stroke to claim his last victim.

"Let the man live!" Dakar ducked a pike staff. Citizens hemmed him in too closely on all sides. No spell of illusion his power might fashion could sway them in time to matter. Left no better course, he jammed his shoulder in someone's ribs and tried a fumbling charge to fling himself onto the scaffold.

The bite of armored hands ripped him back. He fought and clawed, flayed the skin off his knuckles in attempt to land punches on chain mail. The one soldier he felled clamped a hold on his ankle. Another's blunt weapon clouted the back of his neck.

Vision imploded to a blast of white sparks. Dakar swayed as his knees gave. The torches upended. The studs of a guard's armored bracer rasped his cheek. Then howling darkness arose and engulfed him; not from the blow. Nor yet from the hammering kicks which tumbled his body on the paving.

"Spare me, no," Dakar gasped. But no round of pummeling could avert his cascading slide into precognizant trance. The noise of the crowd dimmed inexorably into distance as consciousness frayed into the welling, black tide of his spurious talent for prophecy.

He beheld the low, serried flats near the marshland of Mogg's Fen. Bare tufts of brush snagged through a floss of pale mist and moonlight. Amid mounded hummocks and the quartz sheen of streamlets, men skirmished.

The light-footed, furtive ones wore the undyed leathers of clansmen. Their opponents sloshed ahead in a body, encumbered by shields and byrnies. The glint of their helms bobbed like bubbles in lead as they hacked at cattails and sunken logs in attempt to rout out lurking foes. Southward, they pressed, to the beat and clang of metal. Harried officers kept them moving, while arrows hissed in, and ambushes and traps minced at their flanks and impeded their forward progress . . .

The vision spun away like a scene in dropped crystal.

In its place, Dakar viewed the high frame of the scaffold. As if he were drifting unseen as a spirit, he saw Riverton's executioner flick the gore from his wide, fullered blade. Bloody handed, the man shed his hood. His stubbled, lantern jaw pebbled the light like red sandstone as he ran his gloved fingers over his sword to test for nicks in the edge. Behind his set profile, the three condemned clansmen sagged naked and broken in death. The posts which held them spread-eagled stood as pillars against the stars, flicked into coppery, shifting relief by the streaming billow of the torches. Slack fingers still wore the glazed sweat of suffering. Unclotted blood seeped, glistening, from the corpses' hacked chests. Dakar failed to banish the horrific vista before his seer's gift veered sighted dream into nightmare:

The gaped-open maw of dead jaws clicked shut. Glazed eyes swiveled in slackened, dead faces and fixed in reproach upon him. Then dead tongues stirred in dead mouths. 'We failed in our task. Our life's charge becomes yours. Warn the Teir's'Ffalenn! Forsake plans in Riverton and see him away before sunrise. Lysaer s'Illessid marches from Hanshire to close a Koriani trap . . .'

The whispered chorus of the slain leached into a future scourged through by light like a cleaver: *a storm-torn night ripped apart, and the air recoiled to a fell slam of thunder. Ripped out of darkness, a mercury ocean frothed and boiled into steam. Like dropped spills touched to flame, a thousand riven fragments of cordage and wood rained down upon the flecked foam. The wrecked shreds of ships and the frayed wisps of charred sails hissed through the roiling vapors . . .*

Dakar screamed for the agony of a world gone mad, and then knew nothing more.

The stink of rat urine and musty, rotted straw told Dakar where he was before he opened his eyes. His scapegrace past had dumped him, manacled or caged, in city dungeons times beyond counting. The drip of condensation down nitrous walls seemed common to stone cells everywhere. Nor was he stranger to the twinge of stiffened bruises, or the dull, throbbing aches brought on from an unconscious night lying supine on dank floors.

A headache of exceptional virulence made him feel as if demons with steel hammers played carillons on the bones of his temples. Through excruciating pain and the soured taste of vomit, Dakar clutched his crown to keep his skull from flying to pulverized bits between his fingers. His brain felt like jelly mashed through a sieve. The evils of strong drink were never so punishing. By contrast, vile sickness and palsy never failed to afflict him after an episode of pre-science.

Against the grandiloquent maceration of his hangover, a racket of echoes spiraled down a stairwell: ". . . disorderly conduct, attacking royal guardsmen, not to mention disrupting the peace at a public function." The speaker added in nasal superiority, "There's certain to be a stiff fine."

Dakar plugged pudgy fingers in his ears, too late to evade the dismal conclusion. "Those who can't pay get hard labor on the hulks towed out for dredging the harbor."

The talker scraped to a stop outside the barred cell gated shut with riveted-steel strapping. "He's in here. You did say the man you want's the fat loony?"

Dakar cracked an eyelid and winced through a spearing dazzle of torchlight. "Is it night, or next morning?" he rasped. He could not recall why he felt nagged by a shadowy sense of urgency.

No one gave him answer. Outside the cell, hatched in squares by forged bars, Caolle flourished the slate he carried to overcome the glamour which slurred his clanborn accent. His tough, swordsman's hands scrawled sincere imitation of a yokel's straggling script, then thrust the message under the turnkey's beaky nose.

"You say he was drunk?" the jailer huffed. "That's no excuse. You'll find the offense with the minor charges listed after disorderly conduct. The fat wretch is your friend? Then toss a penny in the tide to give dame fortune her due. If the raving idiot hadn't been sotted witless, our guards would've seen him spitted beside that pack of condemned barbarians. Best take him in hand. He won't have a long life, showing pity for that breed of felons."

Caolle scratched out a new sentence, then flipped his slate like a tray and cast a chiming spill of coins over the letters which spelled, 'fine, paid in full.' Then he tipped his laden tablet toward the turnkey.

Gravity obliged; the gold pieces slid. The jailer watched what amounted to a generous year's salary tumble toward the stinking, runneled floor. Decision became reflex. His spidery fingers swooped to capture the bribe. "This is irregular," he grumbled, in no haste to unhook the keys from his belt. "The city's grand magistrate ought to be called to preside over due process."

Caolle proved impervious to argument. He snatched the loose key ring, tongued the iron in the lock, and clashed open the hasp and grilled portal. Dakar cringed from the clangor of iron. His evasion saved nothing. His rescuer caught his wrist and hauled him headlong from his noisome nest in the straw.

"Damn you, for bingeing," Caolle muttered as he towed his redeemed miscreant toward the narrow turnpike stair.

Dakar moaned. "Let me stay. The risers are too steep."

When he tried to collapse, Caolle shook him. "Sober up, fool! You're needed." Steel shackles in putty, his hold never loosened as the Mad Prophet stumbled and tripped. "Arithon's taken with some sort of fever."

"If you have to shout," Dakar groused, "at least wait until we're outside."

"I'm not shouting." Caolle slammed shoulder first through the upper-landing portal, and chivvied his charge through the magistrate's chamber, a cavernous space of scarred wooden benches and the fetor of old sweat and dried ink. The Mad Prophet shivered as they passed the justiciar's dais, then the prisoner's dock with its rows of forged rings for manacles.

Torches still burned by the entry. Gagged by a billow of oily smoke, Dakar missed his stride. His fragmented vision resurged and gave birth to a hollow spasm of alarm. He bludgeoned dulled senses to gauge the turn of the stars. Only two hours left before dawn.

Caolle was still energetically speaking, his words unintelligible gibberish to the sentries standing bored watch by the portal. "We have trouble afoot. Those clansmen who died were Lord Maenol's own cousins. They would scarcely have wasted their lives in a town without the most dire reason."

Dakar lagged again as full memory returned like a battering onslaught of cavalry.

"Don't mind the guards," Caolle snapped in abrasive impatience. "I bribed them on my way in."

The Mad Prophet gave up his effort to shield his tender eyes from the sconces. Tugged stumbling into the sea-damp night, and a mist like dew-sodden velvet, he grumbled in plaintive injury, "You needn't tear off my arm. I know the message those couriers carried."

"What?" Caolle plowed to a tumultuous halt. "Ath, man, you spoke to them?"

"No." Necessity and pain made Dakar succinct. "Their execution wakened my prescience. And Arithon's not ill." He broke off, wrung by a pestilent shiver.

Caolle suffered the delay in steaming, clamped patience. Around them, the clogged air clung like silt. Lights from the wharves shot ruddy spears through the tenements, and seepage off the overhanging eaves splashed echoes through the darkened alley. Dakar ground on between dry heaves. "We're in deadly trouble. If I'm right, your liege has been touched by the madness of Desh-thiere's curse."

Never slow to grasp threat, Caolle began running. "Then someone's told the s'Ilessid prince we've compromised the shipyard?"

"Worse," Dakar panted. Even crimped like a bolster, he made every effort to match the increase in pace. "Lysaer's marching on Riverton with a fighting company at his heels. They would've arrived yesterday, but clansmen from Korias slowed them down. Lord Maenol's messengers died to bring warning. We have maybe two hours left to force Arithon away before a royal cordon seals the gates."

"Much easier said than accomplished." Caolle added a string of pungent epithets. Too real, that Earl Jieret's dreamed vision might happen on Riverton's fresh-bloodied scaffold.

The Laughing Captain's upper story lay dark, the candles set burning to guide patrons to their rooms long since drowned in sooty wax. The door to Arithon's chamber was closed. No light leaked under the sill.

Dakar stalked down the corridor, his flesh napped with chills as he touched Caolle's sleeve. They had agreed he should disrupt the bard's privacy first.

A board squeaked underfoot. The hallway with its ingrained tang of lye soap and floor wax, and the stale fust of overused bedding raised too clear a memory of another tavern hallway, and the Shadow Master hurled outside reason.

No lingering pinch of guilt plagued his royal Grace this time, but the proximity of Lysaer himself. Dakar rolled back his sleeve cuffs. Perspiration snaked down his neck. If he misjudged and the fatal balance tripped, disaster would follow beyond any power to contain.

The unlocked door latch gave at a touch, the plink of the bar like a cry against silence. Unnerved by apprehension, Dakar eased open the panel.

Darkness met him, thick as warmed felt and stamped with indistinct shapes. The mullioned casement latticed diamonds across a rectangle of indigo sky. The feeble, ruddy gleam of coals in the grate brushed the textured bedhangings, and scattered sequin reflections over the yarns of gold tassels. Steeped in the mingled fragrance of citrus oil and beeswax which toned the wood of the Masterbard's lyranthe, Dakar searched the gloom.

His mage-trained acuity found nothing amiss. The silk shirt and pearl velvet breeches Arithon had worn the day before were draped over a chairback, creased by an ornate clasped belt. The bard's full-length cloak hung in order from its peg. His wrapped instrument rested on the clothes chest. The accustomed coils of refined wire lay on the marquetry table by the casement, nicked to scarlet glints where the light caught; nearby, the spare winding pegs and pearl-handled knife the Masterbard used to trim lyranthe strings. Everything kept its accustomed place, except for the item that counted.

The Paravian-made sword was not on its hook by the armoire.

Dakar shrank to a stab of alarm. Innocuous stillness became sinister as he moved on and surveyed the bed. The hangings were tied back: recessed in the shadow of the dagged velvet curtains, the blanketed outline of a sleeper. Dakar shut burning eyes in relief, then advanced in quick stealth to take down his quarry unaware.

Movement sighed from the shadow behind, a friction of leather against cloth. Dakar caught his misjudgment a split second before a chill pinpoint pricked at his nape.

He swore in venomous consternation. The uncanny attunement of his mage-sense informed that the irreplaceable blade he required now threatened to skewer his neck. Lost, his one chance to deflect Deshthiere's geas; *the sword's enspelled virtue would only deploy if the defender held to a just cause*. In Arithon's hands, the malignment of the curse would keep its defense spells dormant.

"If you plan to wreck the peace, make your stroke count," Dakar accosted. "You were awake."

"In fact, I never slept," said Arithon s'Ffalenn in his most abrasive ill temper. "Whatever else did you expect?"

"Not words of brotherhood and courtesy." Dakar chattered on in the spurious hope he could mask Caolle's presence in the hallway. "Your promise to Lord Maenol has become a bad risk. If you know Lysaer's coming, we'll agree, you can't stay here, no matter how ugly the fate of chained clansmen."

"But I can," Arithon contradicted. "I've a launching in two days, and plans I've no wish to abandon."

If the voice held its usual pared sting of mockery, speech offered an untrustworthy gauge of a masterbard's state of mind. Dakar cursed the sword, which forestalled his need to turn around. Even in darkness, his trained senses must discern more than Arithon wished to reveal. The inimical bite of the blade turned informant as a fine-grained tremor ran through its steel.

"Arithon, hear me. You're not yourself." Through the pound of his heart, hammer to anvil against the wound pain of his headache, Dakar forced himself to keep talking. "If you stay, you'll be letting Desh-thiere's curse overset your mind and integrity."

The sword moved, as if Arithon noticed the price of its bearing pressure. "And what if I planned this to be the last bloodbath?"

Dakar gathered up the rags of his courage and spun face about in the darkness. "If you had," he said, tremulous in terror and entreaty, "then as I was born, I'd not stand here." He pitched all his resource to unmask the man facing him, and desperately wished he had not.

The sword blade divided the air in between, an obsidian line against a less palpable darkness. Arithon no longer wore his delicate pale-haired disguise. Alert and reverted to his natural coloring, he had also cast off fancy clothes. "Since I didn't cut you down as you came through my door, you may accept my invitation to leave."

"You know I can't do that." Dakar licked dry lips. His headache redoubled, the throb of forced blood at his temples a trip-hammer misery of pain.

Arithon said nothing. Reclad in fitted riding leathers, his form seemed sheared out of black watered silk. He did not look deranged or demonic. Excised by the curse from the encumbrance of loyalties, he looked ready to scythe down any obstacle in his path.

"I won't move aside," Dakar said in ultimatum. "To get past, you'll just have to kill me."

A tensioned thread of suspension snapped. Mage-tuned intuition sensed the event as a frisson of vibration shot through the weave of Ath's creation. Only then, too late, the Mad Prophet realized what his tactless handling had cost. *Until this instant, Arithon had been aware, and still fighting the pull of curse-driven directive.*

"Stand me down at your peril," came his silken invitation from the dark.

The infinitesimal shift in tone speared chills down Dakar's spine. Opened to mage-sight, he witnessed the change as the last sane controls burned away.

Now wholly ruled by the Mistwraith's design, the Shadow Master showed the fixated viciousness of a cat as it tracked a lamed kill. "I'm sure the whole Fellowship would applaud your good sense for dying to stop the inevitable."

"Mercy on us all," Dakar whispered, unable to outface the ferocity in those unprincipled green eyes.

This was what Earl Jieret stood down at Minderl Bay; and another time as well, on the banks of Tal Quorin, when as an orphaned child, the boy had thrown himself between Arithon s'Ffalenn and the abyss of geas-bent destruction. The Mad Prophet was made of no such stern stuff, to stand firm as a friend's private self came undone. Nor did he own even that child's advantage: the direct, binding tie of a blood oath sworn in amity, while Arithon still commanded his mage talent.

"Could I remake my choice, I'd be far from this place." Yet even Dakar's cruelest honesty had lost any power to wound.

"Drunk, surely," Arithon mocked. "Or else buried to your short hairs in some willing woman's flesh. *You'd have been better off.*"

However one might ache to hear regret in that tone, none existed.

Then, "You've interfered enough," the Master of Shadow said. Without further warning, he attacked.

Dakar escaped the first sword thrust because his knees gave way as he ducked. He had poor success with the well of bleak shadow which clapped down and masked his trained sight. He resorted to magecraft, begged help from the air, then drew on its reserves to fashion a banespell to stop Arithon. The exchange of raw force settled chill through the room as warmth fed the draw of his need.

Before Dakar framed the seal to balance the conjury, the energies ripped from his grasp. The next breath he drew sheared his chest like white frost. *Just as before, the effect of the curse let Arithon wrest his own powers against him.* He gasped, coughed, wrung his lungs empty before killing cold stopped his heart.

Dakar's warding cantrip emerged as a whisper. "Avert!"

Defense and counterspell locked and unfurled. Barely in time; through a ratcheting, starved breath, Dakar heard a low, trilling whistle. He felt the ward bend, like stress applied to a green stick clenched in his fingers. The sound built and focused, and the symmetry of the spell suddenly let go and twisted. Whatever fell package of magecraft rained down, the shock lanced Dakar's nerves like spilled needles. He rechanneled the worst. Backlash smote the floorboards. Wood squealed and burst into smoking cracks under the kick of wild energies.

Half-paralyzed by pain, Dakar resisted. "Arithon, don't!"

But pleas could not save him. At his peril, he dared apply no more talent. Arithon's refined ear picked up the vibrations of sorcery.

Though the powers were not of the Shadow Master's making, he had knowledge enough, and a fearsome command lent through his trained gift for music. *He would simply keep on retuning the pitch to augment and reverse summoned forces.*

Edged steel sliced the darkness. Dakar blundered clear. The sword snatched a rip in the doubled-up cloth of his shirtsleeve. He rolled to evade the next cut. Each desperate move, each flurried thought but entrenched the bite of the spell turned hostile against him. His flesh felt stitched with white-heated wire. Each effort to think cost him agony. He denied his need to enspell a release. Any arcane defense would only be hurled back in hostility against him.

If he could not fight back, he still held Arithon's given power to bind. Dakar rushed through a string of entangling cantrips, then laced these through with the true power of Name, enforced by ritual permissions. The stayspell deployed and sealed. If the mangling pain seemed to let go a fraction, or the blind of wrought shadows relented, the sword hissed down in a cut to his head like the howling descent of pure vengeance.

Dakar flung open the door to the armoire to break the force of the blow. Lacquer-worked ebony jounced to the scream of turned steel. Chipped abalone pelted his knuckles. He rammed the slivered door hard into his attacker and deflected the following thrust. Something hard bashed his shoulder: the pommel of the sword. His arm went numb, and he crashed into a chair. Through a rain of split rungs and a mire of bard's clothing, he snatched what defenses he could. Rolled fabric muffled his bludgeoned forearm. The chair seat made a temporary shield.

The sword Alithiel whined off wood and snicked a hungry tear through the silk. Dakar gained a scratch instead of an amputation, but the sting rocked his mental equilibrium.

"Saved," he wheezed, while the blade zinged and clanged, "by the shirt off your back." As the barrage whittled slivers out of the chair seat, shrill fear and the limpet throb of his hangover impelled him to inane hysteria. "You know you've gone mad. Arithon."

No word came back. Only the clang as a murderous riposte gouged another scallop from the wood. Splinters rained down on the spellbinder's cheek. Flat on his back like an upset turtle, Dakar cringed as stout oak gave way in his hands. A whimper escaped through locked teeth.

One heartbeat; two; the lunge he expected would come to impale him never fell. Dakar heaved in a raxed breath. He recouped the presence to map a defense ward and cast another snare across the doorway.

He felt Arithon sense the surge of channeled energies. Braced, he absorbed the counterpull as the strength of his binding by permission was grappled, and then sorely tested. Now aware he was bound, Arithon eschewed all attempt to match sorcery. He smashed the glass casement instead.

"No, you don't." Dakar clambered clear of the mangled chair, then shed on the fly the entangling veils of silk shirt. The belt he retained, and swung like a sling, which Arithon's blade intercepted.

Silver clasps sheared off and clanged into the wall to a pattering fall of chipped plaster.

"Stop now!" Dakar snapped. "Don't you realize how closely you just came to shattering the lyranthe Halliron Masterbard passed on as your legacy?"

Arithon used the emerald pommel of his weapon to sweep broken glass off the sill. "That's a touching concern, but irrelevant. My half brother isn't going to lie down and die from the glorious rapture of music." He set his hand on the frame, but Dakar had anticipated. White sparks ripped out. The branch snare of the spell set to seal off the doorway stung Rathain's prince into recoil. "Curse you for meddling!"

"That was your own permission just blistered your skin!" the Mad Prophet cried in correction. "Don't try your birth gift of shadow. You'll find yourself curbed there, as well." He seized the washbasin and pitcher from the stand, dumped out their contents, and sought for a point of aim by the casement. "Why not simplify things and hold still?"

The solution required no genius. He need only batter an armed and demented adversary into a state of unconsciousness. The sulky thought followed, that long before, Caolle should have seized the advantage bought out of his desperate diversions. As Arithon's liegeman, the man must try *something* to bring his sworn charge back in hand.

"You're not speaking," the Mad Prophet accused. "From you, silence never bodes well."

He shied the pitcher, waited for the smash as sword steel fended off porcelain, then winged the basin on a corrected trajectory. That vessel also became deflected by weaponry. Arithon must have seized his sly chance to fetch out his quilloned dagger.

Dakar met the changed odds with a vexed string of oaths, and finished in plaintive injury. "Two blades make for butchery. You know when I'm drunk I don't even carry a penknife!"

No answer; armed now with both sword and main gauche, Arithon bid to wrest back his mastery of shadow.

His geas-bent will slashed against sealed restraints and deflected onto the spellbinder. No surprise to Dakar, that the attack brought a fragmenting explosion of agony. Arithon's talent encompassed the command of elemental darkness. He required no effort to raise simple shadows. If a ward of permission denied his access, he need do no more than apply testing pressure to wear down the inhibiting stayspell.

Dakar held firm, teeth locked in misery through a pain that plucked him at random. He suffered the bearing, innovative feints as Arithon quested to find weakness. The scalpel-swift slice of each forthright attack hazed him dumb with torment. Wrenched and pulled as though milled in a spate, he hung on, though his senses shut down at each onslaught. Leaching numbness beset his extremities. Next, his balance succumbed to mangling weakness. He toppled. Only the intervening bulk of the armoire saved his doomed effort to stay upright.

He clung, victim tied to ruthless antagonist through the grant of permission which founded the first rune of stasis. The spell which curbed Arithon from use of his mastery keyed into Dakar's fast-failing strength. No recourse lay open to retaliate. A call for assistance from air or from matter would invite a flank strike from the bard's use of dissonant sound.

"Ath, where is Caolle?" gasped Dakar, as his sight dissolved in a howling rain of white static.

His chest felt cumbered in molten lead. Each nerve end felt dipped in raw acid. The fight had been futile, outmatched from the start, with him pitched alone against an opponent beyond his depth and resilience. Dakar had no genius reserves of bright talent. Only a fool's suicidal tenacity to bear up and sustain under pressure.

"Arithon. Listen." Pain racked the plea to a whisper. "I can't let you go. A sword and a dagger can't stay Lysaer's army. *Fight for your sanity, damn you!*"

No answer from the creature claimed as Desh-thiere's instrument.

Dakar crumpled. A horrid, sucking pull swallowed his mind as the force of resistance drained him. This was a contest drawn outside of mercy; wise limits were long since abandoned. The only way left to stave off disaster was to borrow off his own life force.

Weeping, Dakar tapped that last well of resource, though he knew the end was upon him. Arithon stayed in thrall to the Mistwraith's dark violence. Already he advanced on his victim. Paralyzed by throttling agony and dizziness, Dakar scarcely tracked his murderous, light tread. The dormant spells in the Paravian weapon gave

mage-sense fair warning of his peril. Air brushed his skin with preternatural clarity as the blade poised to cleave hapless flesh.

Then the Masterbard's voice, cold as no man ever heard. "Be a
dead fool, then, for interference."

The whetted, steel length of Alithiel descended. Dakar shut his
eyes. Limp as a hare stunned and stretched for the knife, he kept
obdurate hold on his bindings.

"In Earl Jieret's name, leave that spellbinder be!" Metal clanged in
a screeching collision and arrested the sword in midfall.

Dakar flinched. Whimpering beneath a trip-hammer exchange of
fierce swordplay, he realized a burly figure with a torch had rushed in
to claim his defense.

"Merciful Ath!" The prince's gruff liegeman had not abandoned
him after all. "Caolle."

"I went for my mail shirt," the clansman flung back by way of testy
apology. Harried across the carpet by Arithon's attack, he beat off a
rain of furious ripostes with blunt and deliberate competence. The
years he had served as Earl Jieret's war captain matched Arithon's
fierce brilliance through experience. The pair had sparred often.
Caolle knew his opponent's fast style and quirky, unpardonable
tricks. But this was no straightforward match in the open. The mad
drive of Desh-thiere's geas set him at extreme disadvantage. The
caithdein's sworn man, he dared take no life. His slighter antagonist
obeyed no such scruple, but sidestepped and angled to kill. Nor did
Caolle have better weapon than his accustomed hand-and-a-half
longsword.

In cramped quarters, the blade's greater reach spoiled accuracy.
Close and tight as he parried, the tip clanged off furnishings or
stabbed and hung in the curtains. The torch in his left hand spat
hellish sparks as he turned the wooden haft to deflect the swift fury of
Arithon's dagger hand. Cinders showered the carpet. A sickening
reek of singed wool laced the room.

Caolle flicked his wrist to haze off the flame which streamered and
singed his leather bracer. Through the clangorous dance of thrust and
parry, he resumed his belabored dialogue. "Nor would I fight a possessed demon again without light. You just keep tight hold on those
fiend-plaguing shadows." A feint, a disengage; Caolle's sword battered against the smoky sheen of Alithiel, then screamed through a
sliding bind. "If I'm blinded in darkness, we're dead men."

A pillow struck the floor, slashed to leaking feathers, close followed by a crash as the pricket was raked from the nightstand. Caolle
slipped as the candle rolled under his boot. "Dakar," he entreated

through beleaguered balance, "if you aren't injured, please Ath, *I need you to move.*"

Dakar scuttled clear as the fight clattered past him. He coughed sour fumes, swiped sweat from his lashes. "You're oathsworn to Jieret!" he accosted the Teir's'Ffalenn. "Dare you murder the very man who raised your *caithdein* from boyhood?"

"Never mind parley, his Grace won't hear you!" Caolle grunted. A scorching scream tore the air as sheer force of strength cleared his blade from entrapment on Arithon's crossed sword and dagger. The torch absorbed another lunge. Sparks flurried and peppered spilled fragments of glass with pinpoint stars of reflection. "As you love life, prophet, move your fat arse and do something to back up my light."

Roused to the danger, Dakar winnowed up eddies of loose down in a hands and knees scrabble across the chamber.

Backdrop to his effort, a half-snarled curse as a fighter snagged in the bedhangings. Velvet tore. A hacked tassel sliced into the gloom. Dakar wrenched open a drawer, tossed out papers and pens, but found nothing of use to strike a spark. A toe gouged his calf; Caolle's, in retreat. Again the duelists clashed in attack over the crown of his head. The puddle by the washstand slickened the footing. Caolle slipped, ejaculated a stringent oath as his guard suffered an unlucky break.

Arithon's weapon licked in like black lighting; rang into an improvised defense. Blood flew. Caolle sustained a nick above his bracer. The whirl of his torch barely foiled the following left dagger thrust, while the jerking, snatched flame chased glints across quillon and guard.

Both men felt fatigue. The fight lagged a split second. Dakar, looking up, caught a glimpse of green eyes. The prince who was born to s'Ffalenn compassion, whose music could raise tears from stone hearts for generosity, appeared to be vanquished beyond recall. Soulless, inhuman, the creature who advanced to take down his own liegeman seemed unreal as a fetch wrought into the form of a dreadfully familiar body.

Lips peeled back in murdering ferocity, the Master of Shadow lunged again.

Dakar flung back from that killing bash of steel and cowered behind the clothes chest. "You'll have to disarm him!" If means still existed to salvage Arithon's mind, the Paravian defenses held dormant in Alithiel offered the last avenue for hope.

The washstand crashed over. Back and forth, the duel raged, while Caolle's fast-pressed weapon gouged slivers from furnishings, or stabbed jagged furrows in plaster. The belling crash of swordplay roused sleepers from their beds. Someone's raised voice shouted from the outer hallway, while weapon clashed to weapon, a tireless roulade of raw fury stitched through the descant jingle of Caolle's mail shirt.

Dakar cursed a head still melon thick from drinking. The din drilled his ears and scattered his labored train of thought. Caolle's cause could not be helped. That quicksilver exchange of thrust and blocking parry confounded his blurred eyesight. His effort to rise was undone by the palsied, nauseated weakness brought on by over-played talent.

Caolle fared no better. Veteran though he was, his strength was not speed, but methodical, polished execution. Rucked carpet and the hazards of upset furnishings presented countless pitfalls to defeat the reach and sweep of his weapon. Again and again he was forced to defer to the darting strikes of Arithon's dagger.

The Mad Prophet snagged the wrapped bundle of the lyranthe, shoved her clear of the fray as clansman and prince sprang apart. Heaving rasping gulps from exertion, the pair faced off, the stolid, iron-haired veteran like a battered stone buttress, and the Shadow Master opposite, light boned and slim, and possessed of a weasel's poured grace. Blades raised, eye to eye, they stood locked through a measuring pause.

Caolle surveyed his liege, a study that flickered over carriage and mien, and ended infallibly with the hands; a habit begun in contempt and adversity, done now as an unthinking sacrifice in behalf of a prince he had learned to respect. Then its heartbreaking counterpart: the echo of the grave, listening intentness Arithon served those who had won his most difficult trust. All his empathetic gifts of perception stood reversed by the curse. He subjected Caolle to a combing search for the first fatal weakness to exploit.

Against razor tension, some concerned citizen knocked at the door and inquired for the safety of the bard. The latch rattled, foiled by the bar Caolle had dropped as he entered.

Suspension shattered into movement. The renewed, wailing onslaught of metal beat at metal in relentless intent to draw blood. Arithon's dagger scored once, then twice, as Caolle's sword scythed through the bedhangings. Swagged cloth slowed his counterstroke. Again the striking main gauche sought his flank.

The clansman parried, squarely in form, but the torch cracked at last under punishment. The lit end sheared away. Shadows wheeled through its arc as the spluttering stub bounced under the clawed feet of the tipped washstand. Streamered flames lit the towels. The Mad Prophet chose not to stop the conflagration. He owed Caolle better than uncertain light. Since the Laughing Captain's landlord required strong incentive to enforce his house rule against brawling, Dakar hooked the unlit end of the cloth and hurled its burning length across the tossed sheets on the bed.

Fire blossomed. Close walls banked the heat and flung back a hellish glare of light. Smoke billowed, licked through by the flicker of steel. The combatants met and parted in circling concentration. While the racket in the corridor changed pitch to alarm, Caolle ran out of options. Another bind; his wrists flexed in practiced response. Tempered steel shrieked and parted, leaving him pinned to the crackling blaze of the mattress.

Dakar perceived the last choice as it happened. "No! Caolle, don't! Let the smoke haze him dizzy. We can take down your liege as he falters."

But the clansman saw well enough how the stakes lay. He accepted the one fleeting opening and lunged. His sure stroke rammed home through Alithiel's cross guard. Faultless in timing, steadfast in sacrifice, he recovered his stance, set both hands in leverage, and twisted.

His right side, exposed, took the thrust of the dagger he lacked any weapon to parry. His grunt as cold steel bit under his mail shirt entangled with a dissonant outcry of metal: his blade still engaged with Alithiel's cross guard. Falling, his warrior's reflex at last broke the Shadow Master's grip.

The Paravian-made sword arced free.

At that instant, Dakar spoke her Name to engage the bright powers instilled by the centaur who forged her.

Light ripped the air, hard followed by sound, a struck chord to raise the wild elements to exultation. Wrought in a terrible, undying harmony, the note reshaped perception, until earthly existence seemed a shabby reflection to be suffered against loss that carried no tangible name. No one in range of that resonant, clear power proved exempt from its force. Time suspended. Thought and memory and awareness lost meaning. The shattering peal of Ath's primal mystery shocked the tie between spirit and flesh.

Arithon screamed. "Caolle!" His voice pierced through the sword's diminished vibrations in a transfixing agony of restored wits. "Ath's mercy on me, Caolle!" He fell to his knees. Undone, distraught, he laid horrified hands on the bleeding wound in his stricken liegeman's side. "Dharkaron strike me, it's death I have dealt for your service."

His remorse rent through the whispered harmonics of the sword's fast-fading vibration. Flame light laid bare his terror and his tears as he labored in feverish need to stop the ebb of life beneath his fingers. "Dakar, in the clothes chest. There are shirts to staunch the wound. Hurry! Shove my sword in the fire. The blade will be needed for cautery."

Dakar pushed erect, crossed the chamber, but not to fetch rags or follow orders. He recovered the dropped sword. For tragic and sorrowful necessity, he reversed the grip and struck Arithon a blow on the back of the neck with the pommel.

The Shadow Master dropped in a slackened heap of limbs across the shoulder of his dying liegeman.

"Well done," Caolle gasped. "Now, heave him up and haul him out of here." He paused, rendered silent by a shuddering spasm, then labored through another ragged sentence. "Take his lyranthe. He'll be grieved if he finds we let her burn."

"Caolle," Dakar said. He coughed on rising smoke.

"No! Leave me! You must!" The clansman snatched Dakar's arm in a frightful, harsh fist. "Don't spurn my sworn duty. If Rathain's prince is lost, I have just thrown away all I was ever born to serve."

Dakar scrubbed sweat from his eyes and trembled with anguished denial. "Ath, if I do this, what about Arithon? You know the force of his grief could turn inward and cripple him."

"See it doesn't." Caolle gasped, seized again by a quivering paroxysm. Eyes shut, jaw clamped, he forced will to prevail against the extremity of agony. "If this is my fate," he resumed, "inform my Lord Jieret that my last service was to fight the Mistwraith at my prince's side." Through a horrible, wrenching lag, he wrestled to draw breath and finish.

"Tell my liege . . ." As though he sensed refusal in the harrowed quiet of the Mad Prophet's attention, he grew frantic. *"Tell him!"* He had to speak over the yammering noise as alarmed citizens pounded at the door. "Say to Prince Arithon, when the Fellowship Sorcerers crown a s'Ffalenn descendant as Rathain's high king at Ithamon, on that hour, he will not have failed me."

The bar on the door burst to a flying rain of plaster. Flames fed on draft and leaped high and licked in a roar across the ceiling.

"Go!" Caolle begged. "You must, can't you see?"

Shouts hailed from the doorway and thrown water flailed through the murk. Coughing back tears, Dakar bent, found the sword, rammed its scabbardless length through his belt.

"Daelion keep you, I won't let your liege die." The ripped shirt sufficed to cover the exposed s'Ffalenn features. The Mad Prophet remembered the lyranthe, then caught Arithon's slack wrists and dragged him like deadweight through the smoldering litter of smashed furnishings.

Hands from the corridor reached to assist him. Someone astute hung the lyranthe strap which had fallen askew off of his shoulder.

Dakar snatched breath for thanks and responded to the landlord's hysterical inquiry.

"A thief," he improvised as someone's servant stepped in to help shoulder his wrapped royal burden. "Broke in and knifed the bard's servant. Smashed out the window to make his escape." Before anyone thought to question the lie, he entreated, "My master's man still lies in there, wounded. I beg of you, do what you can for him."

Two bystanders arrived to help fight the fire bent at once to soak cloth and mask their faces. Dakar never knew if they managed a rescue. Slave to the demands of desperate necessity, he stumbled on toward the stairs and started down in a dumb fog of misery. To the volunteer bearing Arithon behind, he snapped, "I'll need to borrow a cart from the stable. At once! The bard can't be left on the street, unconscious, and someone needs must fetch a healer."

A stableboy passed off his two slopping buckets and sprinted ahead to commandeer horses and harness. Dakar leaned on the newel, half-blinded by tears. The excuse of the cinders masked his undignified sorrow as he played arcane seals through the smoke. He ensured what he could: the fire would not spread. Through the bedlam raised by the bucket brigade, his furtive acts of conjury were certain to pass unremarked.

No one would notice his furtive escape, or recall Arithon's precipitous departure.

Feint

Dawn mists loured over the estuary at Riverton, stained as dirtied fleece where the gate lanterns leaked sulfur light through the gloom. The company of mud-splashed guards sent to seal the city's north postern established their post in smart expectation of the Prince of the Light's formal entry. The captain entrusted to seal every egress out of Riverton was a stocky, scarred veteran, flushed in the face and run to vile temper from a cross-country march beset by unimaginable difficulties.

The last men under orders reached their designated checkpoints at the docks, wharves, and gates through his incandescent drive to mow past upset plans and diversions.

The most recent and diabolically irritating of these still remained, a thorn in his side in the shape of a lean, impertinent clansman. The fellow knew field war. His laconic, whip-stinging criticism held an accuracy that shamed the men scarlet and generally fragmented morale. Flights of high temper seeded shouting between rankled officers and flustered subordinates. Bright eyed, avid, the clansman picked fights. With them since midnight, and onerously underfoot through the exhausting, last leagues of forced marching, he clung to their company like a pill on knit wool until most of the officers would have been pleased to ram unsheathed steel through his gizzard.

None did. The s'Brydion claim to alliance against shadow was unfortunately backed by a safe-conduct bearing Lysaer's own signature.

"Horsemen, inbound," called the watch from the tower.

The mists hoarded sound like an arras of dank felt. Strained minutes passed before the oncoming thud of hoofbeats reached the commanding captain on the battlement above the main gate.

His rank, furrowed frown raised more volunteer comment from the old blood duke's pesky brother. "Look lively, my friend. Your luck hasn't changed."

"What?" The disgruntled Etarran swung his cast-iron glare from the road to the impudent speaker beside him.

Mearn s'Brydion showed him the insolent grin he saved for his killing hands at cards. "We aren't getting the reinforcement you expected."

"You say!" The troop captain peered through the fog, beetled brows sequined with moisture.

"Torches," said Mearn, his accent succinct.

Comprehension dawned as the cressets streamed in, socketed in the upraised fists of the outriders. The vaunted and glorious Prince Lysaer s'Ilessid would not light the column with pitch pine.

"A pity for me you're too griped to bet," Mearn baited. "I could've claimed a delightful small stake, since you'd never have imagined the women."

The captain managed not to rout dignity and retort, since the maddening assessment was true.

Emerged like blurred tapestry through the silver-gilt tarnish of dawn, the disciplined cavalcade which reined under the archway served escort for three cowled Koriani seniors.

"Black Sithaer and Dharkaron's bloody vengeance!" swore the captain. "What are *their kind* doing here? And where in creation is Prince Lysaer?"

"A very sharp question." Mearn s'Brydion's irksome, bright smile gave way to intent speculation.

As the captain stamped jingling toward the stair through the keep, the barbarian followed, cheerfully assured of his blood-given right to shadow Etarran authority.

At ground level, the air hung like vaporous cotton, masking the bleached hue of daybreak. Horses stamped like animated shadows to the pealing, treble chink of harness. The officer in command of the inbound party proved a stranger wearing guard's colors from Hanshire. The name he gave back when challenged was Sulfin Evend, pitched in a snapping, aristocratic arrogance.

The mist cased the loom of the gatehouse, blurring texture from stone, and spangling the lichens in dew. Etarran men-at-arms held their stance in the turrets, defined by the bog reek of mud on their leggings, and by pebbled gray helms, pocked where the dents of late combat snagged glints from the moving torches.

While Mearn held his interested stance by the postern, the Etarran commander called puzzled inquiry. "Where's his Grace of the Light?"

No one answered. The captain from Hanshire vaulted from his high saddle, cloak flung back like a mantled hawk. He turned his lean profile away and held bridles as the trio of women dismounted. Two bore purple mantles with scarlet-sewn borders, plain warning their errand today was not for humanitarian charity. The third wore the gray robes and white hood of a healer.

The one with the triple-tiered bands of a seer's rank bent and consulted a scrying crystal. The Etarran commander hissed through his teeth, ill at ease in the presence of spellcraft. More familiar with the ways of Koriani practice, the Hanshiremen played at their bridle reins to distract their mounts as the faint, tingling current of uncanny forces unreeled through the battening mists.

Two men-at-arms made signs against evil as the cowled seer finally straightened. She pronounced in a young woman's voice, "I've confirmed. The Master of Shadow left Riverton before Lysaer's cordon closed down the east gate."

"Dharkaron avert!" the Etarran commander exploded. "That's not possible. My men were in place before anyone here could gain word of the force sent to take him."

"Peace on you," said the second witch, the one wearing eighth rank, which set her seniority high enough to intimidate. "All is in order."

Preoccupied by something she held in her hand, she murmured a staccato run of syllables that sounded like arcane ritual. The lines finished with *Alt*, name for the Paravian rune of ending. When she turned to stow her fetish in her saddlebag, the officer glimpsed what looked like a doll, fashioned from strips of white velvet and pearls, and twisted with strands of fair hair.

A shudder of distaste made his protest too shrill. "I can't believe this! You *expected* the Spinner of Darkness to go free?"

The enchantress faced him. Her collected voice and superior bearing matched a refined oval face, silk black hair, and eyes the turned gold of aged varnish. "The trap to take the Master of Shadow is proceeding exactly as planned."

The Hanshire officer who commanded her escort seemed to share her high-handed disdain. "Send a man to summon the Lord Mayor."

The Etarran ignored him. "Where's the Prince of the Light? I still hold his orders to seal off these gates."

"Be still!" snapped the enchantress, imperious. "Our snare to entrap the Spinner of Darkness was never meant to close here. Lysaer of Tysan is scarcely so reckless! Blameless lives are at risk if there's bloodshed. Your liege is a just prince, and merciful. He would never corner an unprincipled sorcerer in the midst of an innocent populace."

"I don't trust what you say." The Etarran stayed planted, arms folded over his breastplate, while his men in the gate towers clasped dampened hands to their weapons in chill fear of provoking fell sorceries. "Show me you carry Prince Lysaer's authority."

The Koriani senior regarded him, tranquil. As if a man's history lay etched in a face, she said, "You may address me by the formal title of First Senior. I admire your staunchness, but don't be a fool. In this, we work for the same cause." Her eye for detail sought the root of his obstinacy and as swiftly divined the reason. "We know you for a veteran who survived the fight at Tal Quorin."

When her uncanny statement redoubled his unease, her cut-coral lips framed a smile. "Fear nothing. No one expected to take the Shadow Master unaware. We have him hazed into open flight, and the moment shall come when he's vulnerable. Do you hear? The s'Ffalenn outpost is offshore, in the Isles of Min Pierens. Prince Lysaer has already sailed west with his war fleet to intercept him. The Master of Shadow will fall to an ambush at Corith. Now send for Riverton's mayor. We require his council's sealed writ to proceed."

While the Etarran capitulated and called for a runner, a dry-voiced observer remarked from the postern. "You intended the Master of Shadow to slip through?"

"But of course." Lirenda disdained to glance at the speaker. She guessed his name already. The Prime's initial scrying had shown her his presence. He had an indispensable role yet to play to ensure the trap against Arithon. Through the bustle as horses were led off for stabling, and the bristling talk to establish a hierarchy between the Etarrans and the guardsmen from Hanshire, Lirenda's reply filtered back. "The cordon here is set by design to take down all of Arithon's accomplices."

Her curious exchange with the s'Brydion envoy became supplanted as the scryer touched her elbow. "The liegeman from Rathain you asked me to track has been moved from the inn where the fire struck." She finished in soft urgency, "He's been sheltered in the cook's quarters on Haymaker's Lane. We haven't much longer. He's dying."

First Senior Lirenda murmured a terse reply, then amended her instructions to the guardsmen. "When Riverton's Lord Mayor answers my summons, inform him to gather his magistrates and have them await my arrival at the shipyard."

The three Koriani commandeered a guide from the local garrison. Through imperious autocracy and the well-oiled use of their power to intimidate, they swept smoothly on to their business inside the city gates. The main body of their escort from Hanshire remained at large, without assigned quarters and food. Beset by their flood of unscheduled demands, the Etarran commander took harried notice that fortune still granted small favors. The temperamental clansman with the waspish tongue had finally removed himself elsewhere.

Lirenda's small entourage sought the burned shell of the Laughing Captain Tavern. By now, the fire had played itself out. Smoke smudged and coiled through a rickle of fallen beams and the last sullen pockets of shimmering embers the bucket brigades labored to extinguish. Persistent questioning led them at last to the bedside of Arithon's stricken liegeman.

Caolle sprawled like felled dough on a ticked straw mattress in the kitchen annex left standing untouched by misfortune. The scullion sent for candles never came back, no doubt out of fear his petty thefts in the buttery might be disclosed by some trick of divination. The room that held the pallet remained dimmed in shadow, the squalid miasma of old grease and turned onions congealed in the heavy, close gloom. At the First Senior's bidding, the Koriani healer knelt to perform her examination.

"Burns and blood loss," she concluded. "He's in shock still from cautery." She laid down the rawboned, sinewy wrist she had clasped to take Caolle's pulse. Her thin face turned toward the stray quill of light which fell through a knot in the shutter. "In an hour, perhaps two, his spirit will cross over, however he fights the Wheel's passage."

In fact, his obstinate flesh would stay breathing until sundown, one of a laddered array of small details embedded in Morriel's grand scrying. Lirenda stirred, a form out of place against plaster whose grimed coats of whitewash were streaked where condensation had rinsed through the tallow soot. Her long, sculpted fingers flicked ash from her mantle, and her face showed supreme unconcern. Through the ongoing grind of the salvager's wagons across the cobbled yard without, and brief outbursts of oaths as men soused the timbers that stubbornly sprouted new flame from the ashes, her voice was enamel and silk. "Could you save him?"

The healer's hands hesitated, paused, returned to trace over the stained linen bindings swathed around Caolle's flank. Her cape-cut gray sleeves stirred the scents of goose fat and seared tissue, and roused a sullen chink from the chain mail no one had dared to remove for fear they might restart the bleeding.

Lirenda smoothed down her disarranged mantle. Her eyes antique gold and her face like milk cameo, she watched while the healer touched her crystal and traced through an array of testing runes and seals.

A drawn moment passed before the enchantress dared a prognosis. "His wound was taken in the name of his liege. There lies our opening. A binding tapped into his past oath of fealty might command enough power of obligation to stay him. But he's dangerously weak. A forced regeneration of the blood must come first. If we stabilize his condition, his body could recover. Wards and sigils can be used from there to arrest the infection and fever."

The Koriani First Senior folded her arms, her fine, sculptured nails sheathed under her cuffs. Her banded silk hems caught on the board floor as she crossed and surveyed the man on the pallet. The glamours set by Dakar to mask clan identity had dispensed in the spellbinder's absence. Caolle's strong hands rested slack on the coverlet, scabbed on three knuckles from the trials of an impatient character. The cantankerous clefts of hard living and grief were brought now to unwilling release. Lastly she studied the indomitable broad chest, where the heart beat unvanquished through the draw of each stertorous breath.

Lirenda shut her eyes. Her fingers, masked in silk, dug the flesh of her forearms as a white force of rage arrowed through her. An unswerving devotion to Arithon s'Ffalenn had wrested this clansman from life.

She could not stop the hurtful comparison to herself. The felled liegeman lay oblivious in extremity and mocked her, that she might become just as haplessly subservient to the drawing force of the same master. Unlike Caolle, she lived in resentful rebellion, a latent pawn with potential to be claimed as a vulnerable, unwilling sacrifice. Just once, she desired to reverse her own punishment, to humble Rathain's prince and make him suffer the impacting cost of the loyalty he won and then spent without thought.

Moved to a vicious, inspired stab of impulse, Lirenda seized her initiative. "Do all you can," she charged the healer at her feet. "If the clansman survives, I would take him captive to sail with us on the chance he may yet prove useful."

The woman bent her head and took up her quartz crystal. "Your will shall be done, First Senior."

By the order's own tenets, no subservient enchantress could question her decision. Lirenda shared nothing in confidence. She took satisfaction in her autonomy, that the crowning fillip to Morriel's grand design would bear a twist of her own devising. The defeat of her nemesis would bring sweet revenge by the deferral of one clansman's death. Caolle would make a devastating addition to the shipyard's score of hostages when Koriani power at last cornered Arithon at sea.

Early Spring 5653

Quarry

Two hours past daybreak, the mist broke and rolled, torn as snagged knit, over the fields which rimmed the shore of the estuary southbound from Riverton. The trade road to Middlecross at the mouth of the bay snaked through rutted mud, bounded by timber fences to keep cattle, and hedgerows of thorn, budded with clockvine and bittersweet. The terrain was flat. Trees grouped in huddles, salt burned and stunted on the ocean side by gales, and raked like a drunkard's grope to leeward. The blue pan of the sky held the swirling black flocks of swallows returning to nest in the hay byres, swooped and chivvied by gusts off the Westland Sea. Just past spring equinox, their winter-sharp edge could still flay through a drover's cloak of oiled wool.

Before the uprising threw down the old rule, the mild, boggy summers grew the bull grass shoulder high. Here, the secretive hare had grazed, her black-edged, velvet ears attuned to the speech of the breezes. Midges and dragonflies danced in the sun which streamed like gold oil, and daylilies had bloomed like outbursts of wildfire. Now, across the wide vista where young dragons once stretched drying wingleather and flew, wattle-and-thatch farmsteads clumped like brown mushrooms, surrounded by goose pens and pigsties. The rustling, graceful stands of bull grass had gone. Reseeded pastures were grazed to shorn stubble, or chopped into hummocks by the milch cows who plodded their mindless daily rut from farmyard to gate.

The stiff winds of equinox did not rustle and whisper off the sea, but burned over the razed ground with flattening force. The squat drover of the oxcart narrowed his squint eye and muffled reddened hands in the rug thrown over his knees. His beasts nodded onward in their yokes, their vast, splayed hooves chinking through glaze ice where low sun had yet to thaw the puddles. The wain racketed behind them, a rattletrap conveyance of squealing, pegged boards and spoked wheels which sucked and dragged through black muck and runoff to a labored creak of worn axles.

Hunched over the lines, the drover looked as if he suffered the pangs of a pestilent headache. He did not look up as the armed riders streamed past, to shouted orders and a military snap of royal banners. Nor did he curse the mud spattered up by their hooves, or protest as they waved whips or weapons and demanded he roll his cart to the verge to make way. Had he carried apples, they might have stopped him on demand for provender. Since the wain's unsavory, manure-stained bed held nothing but musty sacking and an empty goose basket chalked with guano, no guard seemed minded to search. A straightforward cipher which prodded the senses to revulsion was all any competent spellbinder needed to be left to resume his interrupted way south.

As the sixth such patrol galloped jingling by, the drover cast a soured eye across his load of potato sacks. "You have no idea just how lucky you are." He received no reply. Only the grinding chirp of the axles and spring birdsong, blithe, from the hedgerows.

The rider who passed an hour later came alone on a lathered chestnut. The saddlecloth bore the guard's emblem from Hanshire, but the man wore nondescript leathers beneath the braid of his captain's cloak. Nor was the blade hung by rings from his baldric the issue of any town cavalry. The acerbic scrutiny he gave wain and drover could have scraped verdigris off a bronze tack.

Then a grin like a whip disarranged his thin lips. "Ath, it's yourself. I *thought* the stink was by lengths too extravagant. Where's that shadow-bending little bastard you nursemaid? I bear him a pressing message."

By the sniping humor and an accent like shot darts, Dakar recognized the s'Brydion scion who had been the first man in twelve decades to fleece him at both cards and dice. "I've disowned him."

But Mearn had not missed the sidelong glower directed at the ruckled sacking.

"He's there?" The s'Brydion blasphemed through six sentences of admiring incredulity.

Drawn pale by the drummed-out dregs of a drink hangover and the diminishing spasms of palsy, Dakar shrugged. "I'm not at all certain I'm going to survive the invective when he wakes up."

The clan envoy's gaze lingered, riveting sharp, while his forced stab at levity floundered into brooding, and his eyes stayed trained ahead, circled and darkly haunted.

"Bad, was it?" The chestnut shook the bit to a spatter of white foam, while Mearn played her sideways to keep her abreast of the creeping oxcart. "You won't like what I have to tell you any better." Never one to hold off delivery of ill news, he plowed on. "You're caught in the teeth of a Koriani conspiracy, did you know? They flushed you from Riverton in full expectation of netting your Teir's'Ffalenn in an ambush off the Isles of Min Pierens. Lysaer's been at sea for six days with trained navigators. His fleet's destination is Corith."

Dakar swiveled sideways in dumbstruck shock. "At *sea?* Lysaer s'Ilessid? Ath, he can't be! Arithon was driven to break his disguise by full onslaught of Desh-thiere's curse. Only Lysaer's immediate proximity could provoke such a fit of murdering insanity!"

Mearn shook his head, the thick stubble on his jaw graining the hollow of his cheek. "Spells and trickery." He suddenly sounded every inch as tired as he looked. "Yon curse was triggered by Koriani intent. I saw the accursed tangle of hair and silk scraps they used to shape Lysaer's proxy."

Horror whitened Dakar's rumpled features, and the cloudless spring sun sparked small, silver glints on the hair roots at his temples, changed from ginger to white overnight. "You're saying the witches *brought on the whole incident by means of a conjured fetch?*"

"Why else would their First Senior be carrying a wee doll made of tied rags and blond hair?" Since the ramifications were too grievous to grapple, that Arithon could be hazed hither and yon by a bundled spell created by a Koriani whim, Mearn traced the flight of a marsh falcon who snapped from its high, lazy spirals to stoop. "His Grace can't flee to Corith. He'll find Lysaer waiting with a war fleet well primed to carve his s'Ffalenn liver into stew meat."

Dakar glowered down the roadway, which unreeled straight ahead, between the capped horns of the oxen. "I won't ask what you risked to deliver the warning."

Mearn laughed. "There's not enough gold in Ath's whole creation to pay the whores to preserve my randy reputation."

"What?" The starting ghost of a dimple dented the cheek above Dakar's rumpled beard. "Past experience should have taught me. The s'Brydion line runs to madmen who are born addicted to danger."

Mearn's grin widened, then became the triangular smile his brothers had learned to regard with extreme trepidation. "You never saw me," he said. "For the past seven days, I've been in bed at Avenor jousting the lights out of three willing doxies."

"I see." Dakar rolled a walleyed glance of apprehension toward the muddle of lumps in the sacking. "Forgive me when I tell you I wish that had been the plain truth."

"Oh man," Mearn agreed, turned sharply restive as the horse which stamped and curvetted underneath him. He glanced over his shoulder, and the Mad Prophet heard too: through the weave of the gusts, the oncoming hooves of yet another patrol sent to scour the roads out of Riverton.

"You should go," he advised Mearn. To be seen under questioning by a man with Hanshire trappings would draw perilous attention to them both.

"As you suggest." Mearn's humor changed to a wicked slice of malice as he gave rein to his head-shaking mount. "I leave you the road, and wish you joy on the moment when yon testy mountebank wakens. Upset his temper, he's got a tongue can raze scales off the innocent fish."

The ox wain rolled on into the afternoon, while the blue sky clotted with high-flying clouds, and the sun dimmed and vanished into haze. Dakar ate cheese with the gritty, hard bread provided by the farmwife whose goodman had sold him the wagon. He absorbed himself licking sticky crumbs from his fingers. The lines threaded unattended through the fist on his knee when a sneeze and a shudder beneath the potato sacks reminded of his fugitive passenger.

Dakar tossed off the last crust for the birds and halted the oxen. He considered, then decided against releasing his mild spell cipher.

The next moment, the burlap stirred and parted. An angular face shaded in beard stubble emerged, capped by moldered stems of oat straw stuck through untidy black hair. Eyes of a burning and terrible emerald blinked and regarded the wind-flattened briars in the hedgerow, ragged border to a ladderworked mesh of fallow fields, then absorbed the rutted groove of the roadway. The intelligence behind stayed mercifully baffled and blank.

"Potatoes," the bard murmured, puzzled. His glance turned to Dakar, inquiring, and his light touch explored a clotted scab on one cheekbone. "No doubt a just punishment for tupping the farmer's eager daughter, except that I can't recall the chit's face."

A pause; hands that in daylight showed the scuffs and congested bruises of a ruinous combat received an absorbed inspection. Reassured at last that all his joints flexed, Arithon raked clinging chaff from his collar and lapsed back to a dusty puff of rot from the sacking. "Dakar," he said, muffled, "the guano is a stroke of pure brilliance, I admit. But may we dispense with the manure and the offal? If I suffer my fair deserts from a hangover, I could manage rather well without the stink."

Then, from a shattering and sudden break in thought, a ripped intake of breath: Arithon s'Ffalenn came fully and finally awake. His next words reviled in distilled venom. "Should I curse you or thank you for my deliverance? Or better, give you the whip hand to send me straight on to damnation and Dharkaron's black vengeance?"

His unspoken anguish hung on the pause, 'For Caolle, there exists no redress.'

Dakar clamped helpless fists to the lines and slapped the worn leather over the backs of the oxen. "You swore oath at Athir," he reminded through the squealing protest of stressed wood as the wain sucked free of the mud and rolled onward.

"Oh Ath, that I hadn't, or better that I could have renounced life and breath on the day of my birth." Arithon sat upright, his face pressed behind his opened, marked hands and his shoulders braced against trembling.

"Your survival had to come first," Dakar insisted, unmanned himself, and too much the coward to watch. Nor could he quite mask the flick of an honest revulsion as he made tactless effort to ease an impossible grief. "All hope isn't lost. Arithon, your stroke didn't kill him, not at once, I swear this. Caolle still breathed when I left him."

"Ath, no!" the Shadow Master cried, shot straight and sawn through by redoubled remorse. "He is clanborn, and hurt, and what have I done but left him helpless among enemies? His own people would have served him a mercy stroke!"

The cry drowned echoless in the winds of the flats. While a wedge of flying geese sliced the gray sky, and the oxen nosed brainlessly forward, Dakar found nothing to say. Nor could he ease the unbearable distress of the prince who refused even tears in his locked and horrified silence.

Fragile as a silk moth's spun filament, the blood oath alone stayed the force and fury of Arithon's natural reaction. Moment to moment, while the warm life in his veins seemed a cruel violation, and the beat of his heart framed insult to his integrity, he sat in bound quiet. Eyes wide, hands slack, he dared not even flinch to be served the unconditional gift of the land's beauty. Not now, Dakar sensed with a wounding, sure pity: not when all sound and all movement revolted the nerves, and a mind lay torn and trapped in the grasp of transfixing grief.

The sough of the breeze in the budding briars, and the mournful cries of the hawk and the marsh wren filled all the world with oblivious industry, while the wain rolled and bore the Master of Shadow into the cheerless dusk.

They made camp in a hollow with a stream, under the leafed-out crowns of a willow grove. The trees were ancient. Their dry-rotted trunks offered nest hollows for owls, whose plangent hoots and gliding, swift flight made the oxen whuff and back against their tethers. Low clouds shed a steady, fine drizzle that sluiced a varnishing glaze of damp over man and beast, and made the fireless night a bitter misery.

Dakar served out the last of the farmwife's provisions, a heel of rye bread and strips of jerked beef cured hard as glass through the length of winter's storage. The spellbinder chewed without appetite. In oathbound responsibility, he noted Arithon's attempt to do the same.

But exhaustion and stress exacted their toll. Two unobtrusive trips into the brush came and went before the Mad Prophet noticed anything amiss. Every scrap of sustenance the Shadow Master dutifully forced down was rejected with wretched persistence.

Dakar could have wept and sworn both at once for the cost of the blood bond imposed by the Fellowship at Athir. Since straight pain was suddenly preferable to the ongoing cruelty of silence, he scrounged out the flask of sour wine he had hoarded and shoved it toward Arithon's chilled hands.

"Drink. You need it. And talk, for Ath's sake. If you can make such a dogged effort to eat despite the fact you're too sickened, you can try just as hard to make plans."

Arithon looked at him. Wrists hugging one on another about his drawn-up knees, and his fingers like clamped bone under the soggy, grimed cuffs of his sleeves, he said nothing. Neither did he accept the offered solace of the wine.

"Well, you can't risk sailing to Corith!" Dakar exploded. "You know if you try to face Lysaer again, you'll become slave to Deshthiere's curse."

The ruinous fact could not be evaded. The awful limit *must* be faced. Intent had not served; free permissions had proved woefully inadequate; the working of the geas strengthened with each contact. Dakar gnawed a torn thumbnail, demoralized and mute. As well as he, the Shadow Master knew: *if not for the saving intervention of the sword, he would have lost his mind into irreversible insanity at Riverton.*

Dakar dragged in a breath that felt heavy as liquid glass. "You don't know the worst yet. Koriathain are involved." Pained for the necessity which made him twist the knife, he repeated what Mearn s'Brydion had seen, the terrible proof that the flight out of town had been launched by means of a golem wrought of spells. "To assist Lysaer's cause, they deliberately triggered the bane of the Mistwraith's geas."

That unbearable news carried vicious implication, *that Lysaer s'Ilessid had been leagues at sea, and no threat.* Plans for the launching and abduction of three ships were upset for naught. Lastingly worse, Caolle had fought and fallen to Arithon's sword for no true threat at all, but only manipulative illusion.

In comfortless grief, set isolate by the needling fall of fine rain, Dakar could not bear to strike light and measure the scope of Arithon's anguish. He feared worst of all to broach what no empty offer of solace might disguise, that every associate and accomplice brought in for the launching remained still in Riverton, unwarned and defenseless against whatever machinations the Koriani First Senior might devise.

Dakar chewed his lip in agonized suspension. He waited through a pause grown dense as lead crystal, while soft rain wet his cheeks and trickled from the untidy bristle of his beard. No night birds called. Just the whispered tap of droplets, and subliminal rustles as willow fronds bowed to their burden of damp. The weather promised no surcease; clouds would sheet in from the north until dawn. Nor did a mere spellbinder know of a palliative to ease wounded pride, or shore up the wreckage of a man's priceless care and integrity.

Human balm did not exist to relieve an inhuman quandary. No friend could mask the impact of inborn s'Ahelas farsight, that would turn the birth gift of a ruthless insight ahead to map the course of a poisoned future. Helplessness remained, of a dimension to grind thought down into despair for a balance inevitably foredoomed.

A masterbard whose compassionate heart had been torn out thrice over in the cause of meaningless destruction could not have limitless strength.

The rain and the dark embraced Arithon's stilled form. The wine flask lay untouched by his feet, while the drizzle pattered and seeped and leaded the tender shoots of new greenery.

Against every interfering impulse, despite the oblivious, brash decadence that prompted his fleshly excesses, Dakar kept his palms jammed over his lips. He would not speak. Even through the tormenting, perilous awareness that the blood oath sworn to the Fellowship Sorcerers allowed but one terrible course.

If Arithon kept faith and held his gift of Shadow in reserve against the greater threat of the Mistwraith, he would be forced to spare his own life through the ruin of uncounted others. No reason could ease that abnegation of free will. The wait seemed to span the arc of oblivion, while time wound into a brutal, shared tension to shred the most steadfast patience.

"I dare not attempt to save the men or the outpost at Corith," Arithon announced at drawn length. With Koriani led into conspiracy with Lysaer, he saw well enough. No place remained inside the five kingdoms where he could depend on safe refuge. "Nor can I recover the launched ships for the clans. No course is left but to recover *Talliarthe* and sail south and east to regroup."

Dakar set his chin in his hands. He could make no answer, overwhelmed as he was by the sweet rush of astonishment and gratitude. Nor could he repress his outright awe for the character of Rathain's prince. He knew no one else capable, no spirit with the outright, mulish fight to reach past such branding ignominy and guilt, *and for nothing* if not another compounding act of self-betrayal. The torment of Caolle's tragedy did not end here, but extended to embrace losses unbearably larger.

As if no friend wept for the grievous depth of character that carved up such tenacious resilience, Arithon laid out his decision with the icy dispassion a surgeon must find, when forced to amputation with no time to spare for anesthesia. "There's a fishing village south of Torwent in Havish remote enough to lend short-term sanctuary. From there, I'll send word to Fiark at Innish. He can release the *Khetienn* from her current merchant charter. The *Evenstar*'s not to be compromised, for Feylind's sake. Her runs can enable safe drop points for stores to extend our blue-water passages."

His admission came in agonized quiet, that no shred of his hopes could be salvaged. That because of his presence, Lysaer's deadly, trained force from Etarra was drawn into Tysan, where clansmen fought now for survival. The men, the ships, the months of meticulous and dangerous work to redeem threatened bloodlines: all designs fallen short on the brink of completion, then abandoned in one cruel stroke.

The last line in summary, dredged up in pain for a world future bought at a damning price in shed blood. "We must sail offshore, alone, and quarter the seas until the Paravians are found."

No mention was made of the third brig, *Cariadwin*, sailing under a clan crew to Corith, where she must inevitably fall to Lysaer s'Ilessid as a sacrifice. Nor did Arithon belabor past choices, or wallow in self-castigation for what might have been saved, had his bid to free Maenol's clans from enslavement been pursued in less brilliant aggression. But Dakar knew him too well; having seen the s'Ffalenn prince through the atrocity at the Havens, having offered the shoulder that steadied him after the horrors unleashed at Dier Kenton Vale, the dispassionate, stark outlines of tonight's recast strategy spun him no false reassurance.

He could do no more than stifle his sorrow for what went unsaid in the dark and the rain. The change he had most feared to witness had come. Never through even the ugliest setback had he heard Arithon's voice turn flattened and dull in defeat.

At the time which spanned the midpoint of night, that suspended hour equidistant from sundown and dawn, the Mad Prophet gave up his failed effort to rest in the clammy shelter of his cloak. He stole to his feet and listened. Arithon lay still, huddled limbs furled in oiled wool and his breathing soft and regular. He was not asleep. The rain had freshened, and the pattering stream of moisture from the willows' arched canopy conjoined into trickles of runoff. Rising wet drove the mice to their burrows. The owls had ceased silent flight.

In trust that his absence would be taken for a routine call to relieve himself, the Mad Prophet crept from the campsite. He followed the throaty voice of guttered water and crossed a ditch with a streamlet. The eddies flowed clogged and tan with drained clay, too muddied to serve his intent. A few paces on, he found a wide puddle cast to the sullen gleam of pooled mercury under the haze of the storm scud.

The water proved clear enough for scrying.

Dakar knelt. He raked away sodden leaves and a sandy detritus of gravel. Into the softened mud on the verges, he traced out the radiants invoking the cardinal points of direction. Then he settled himself, cleared his fraught mind, and immersed himself into mage-trance. Between the night's whispered rainfall and the fluting shrieks of spring peepers, he sought the voice and the essence of water. He asked and exchanged a permission. Raindrops still fell fine as pins, pocking the puddle with their fleeting circular imprints. A soft word, a rune, and the surface sheeted still. Palms sweated now with the concentration of refined talent, Dakar invoked a star's Name, the one which rode the meridian on this particular hour, at the nadir of night's span of darkness.

Lastly, he ripped off a thread from his sleeve, rusted brown with dried blood spattered from Caolle's wound. This he soaked clean in the puddle. He restrained his fretted nerves as he waited, while the essence dissolved and released its magnetic aura.

A minute came and went, sevenscore heartbeats set to the impact of a numbered fall of raindrops. The rune traced over the puddle's surface flared like weak phosphor and drifted. Dakar gathered his inner faculties, ordered will into balance, and murmured, "*tiendar*," the Paravian call to invoke the linking tie between spirit and bodily flesh.

Had Caolle died, no such connection would remain and the conjury just set would fade away unrequited.

But as Rathain's prince had so desperately feared, the liegeman from Deshir yet clung to life. In the shadowy depths of the puddle an image formed, a scrying forged through the delicate energies of one star's ascendancy, and a clansman's fierce will to survive.

Candlelight in a cramped chamber, where a youthful woman in gray-and-white robes labored over a brazier and pot, brewing a steaming herb tisane. She paused as she stirred to attune small magics through the crystal on the chain at her neck, and to chalk sigils on the stiff squares of paper which held her medicinal plants and dried rootstock.

Just past the edge of that circle of light, eyes like bored gimlets of obsidian, Caolle watched her, his colorless, blunt features sweating in the extremity of his pain. He still wore the mail shirt, though the links and the gambeson beneath had been dragged up his torso to bare his wounded side for the Koriani healer's ministrations.

As if his fixed gaze were abrasive, the enchantress glanced aside from her work. "No," she informed with acerbic exasperation. Though he had not spoken, she answered his direct thought. "The mail can't come off without tearing your wound. Your life's to be spared by command of our First Senior, and I won't risk restarting the bleeding."

Caolle's life given over to Koriani design; Dakar spared no second to mourn this sure confirmation of disaster. Nor did he delay to size up the anguish the news would inflict upon Arithon's already shattered peace of mind. A scant interval remained before his conjured connection to the star's power waned and passed. A rune, another cipher, swiftly composed to exploit the connection with First Senior Lirenda, who had intervened outside of mortal consent to stay the natural course of death. Dakar's construct widened to summon another image in the puddle.

More candles burned in the loft above the clerk's shed. Here the royal shipyard's hired master stored his drafting pens and his tools. The closely kept plans drawn up for his three-masted brigs lay unrolled on broad trestles, weighted at the corners with gray, rounded rocks from the river bottom. Though the hour was past midnight, Cattrick's personal domain was not private. The benches by the wall where he issued his daily instructions to his laborers were still occupied. Clad in their dark robes of judgment, Riverton's tribunal and justiciar sat in formal session, while a secretary scribbled out transcript.

Before them, a wretched southcoast rope splicer knelt in sweaty, shivering fear from the aftermath of an interrogation made under the burning compulsion of arcanely wrought sets of truth seals. His shock held him passive while the shipyard's blacksmith hammered the rivets to close the steel shackles on his wrists.

"That's the last of them," pronounced the aristocratic woman with a disdain to slice through the clangor. Her expression was abstract porcelain, and her gown, a sweeping purple robe with red borders. "Lock him away with the rest until the launched hulls are made seaworthy."

The smith finished his task and shouldered his satchel of hammers and tongs. Blinking and stiff from the long hours spent hearing testimony, Riverton's officials arose. Uneasy, without talk, they shook the creases from their clothes and made their pompous way through the door to the outside stair.

Lastly went the guards with their workaday armor and drawn swords, to remand the chained prisoner into custody.

The Koriani First Senior remained, composed as fine ivory in the unsettled spill of the flame light. The focusing jewel she had used to wrest open the privacy of men's minds lay tucked between her clasped hands, each curled, slender finger arranged into line like the fluting on a blush-colored shell.

She was not alone. A broad-shouldered man stepped out of the gloom and skirted the laden trestles. If the eyes set amid his measuring squint stayed nervelessly direct, his step held a stalker's sharp caution.

"What now?" challenged Cattrick. He extended his work-hardened, sinewy wrists in a gesture of mock supplication. "Have you no shackles for me? Or am I to stay free in reward for my peerless service?"

Lirenda returned an imperious flick of her nails. "Busy man. Never presume to take freedom for granted. Be grateful. Your place remains here."

As Cattrick's brows frowned in distrustful surprise, she deigned to proffer explanation. "The gossip must eventually reach Arithon. When he learns you were the one who effected his betrayal, your worth will be sadly diminished as a hostage." Her enameled gold eyes shimmered with contempt as she swept her gaze head to foot, and dismissed him. "You're Lysaer's man, now, and if you have sense, will remain so."

High overhead, behind banked layers of cloud, the star crossed the zenith, its span of ascendancy past. The scrying linked through its energies flicked out. Left staring at raindrops stamping faint rings over and over in a puddle, Dakar gripped his knees through an unpleasant shudder. Beset by the aftershock of sorrow and distaste, he engaged the familiar, ritual steps to release the used frame of his construct. Three handclaps and a breath disbursed the life tie to Caolle. A scribed rune of passage unwound the spiraled energies bound by permission to water. A green stick blessed and borrowed from a bush made a sweep to erase the directional markers. Once the leftover traces of his craft were disbursed under blessing, Dakar stretched his sore shoulders. He gathered himself, but stopped short on the point of arising.

Some intuited warning of disturbance made him glance over his shoulder.

A whiff of rain-wet leather and a shadowy presence: Arithon s'Ffalenn stood like a wraith at his back.

"Dharkaron's bleak vengeance!" the Mad Prophet swore, then shut stinging eyes. A high surge of relief combed through him for the fact the prince's mage-sight lay blinded. His Grace may have borne witness to every step of arcane ritual, but the train of summoned images would for a mercy lie beyond the reach of his five mortal senses.

As if private thought had been shouted aloud, Arithon contradicted in searing irony. "Trust me, I heard the whole coil all too well."

No apology sufficed to fling back in rejoinder. Nor was space given for Dakar to venture even a token attempt. While he ached for a pity beyond words to express, the Master of Shadow spun on his heel and strode off.

Recoils

Infuriated that their quarry escaped them at Riverton, the Etarran officers hold an argumentative council to salve the pride of their chafing troops by sending them reiving after the forest clansmen who might lend the fugitive Shadow Master shelter; while they deliberate, the Hanshireman, Sulfin Evend, requisitions forty men on fast horses and leaves the gates under Koriani orders to pursue Arithon's trail with sharp fervor. . . .

Upcoast, at Avenor, the crown council of Tysan releases formal public announcement of Princess Talith's fatal plunge from a high tower battlement; and the verdict delivered to the shocked and mourning court names her death as a suicide brought on by despair and a tragic inability to conceive her fair husband an heir. . . .

On the third day, the Koriani healer reports to First Senior Lirenda concerning her charge's condition. "Caolle will be well enough to move, and can sail with the hostages if he's given a secure berth. His wrists cannot be set into irons, as you hoped. It's a paltry enough setback, but the gashes on his forearms for some reason seem to have festered. . . ."

IX. Setback

Night lidded the sky over Korias Flats like a bowl of thick cobalt glass. Yesterday's bleak weather had blown away south, chivvied out by a cutting north breeze that moaned over the barren lowland terrain with its swept slabs of calcine granite. Stands of witch hazel and thorn, and the storm-trimmed fronds of bent willows rustled and tossed in the gullies, twigs dusted in the faint light of a waning crescent. North of the river course, where ancient glaciers had plowed up a shoal of dry ground, the land fell away in a gradual slope that eventually cradled the steaming, dank pools of Mogg's Fen. That way, alone, fared a lean rider nursing a trail-blown horse.

The traveler knew his purposeful way in the wilds. He tracked steadily north, the polestar lending him guidance. His mount went shod, but no chance grate of steel rang upon unclothed granite. Sparing of the animal's last strength, he moved where he could up the throat of the gullies, and avoided the scoured brush on the rims.

Despite his most diligent care and sly knowledge to foil observation, his stumbling, spent gelding could not pass entirely without noise. Mearn s'Brydion reined back in nettled annoyance as four men with drawn steel stepped out of the thicket in his path.

Their challenge was alert and crisply professional. The nasal ring to their speech identified them as the elite muster Prince Lysaer had marched from Etarra.

Against fitful shadow and the mottled ink patterns of bare thorn and hazel, Mearn made them out, clad in mail dimmed with soot to damp the chance gleam of the moonlight. Each one was outfitted with horn, bow, and steel, unafraid to meet trouble with force. Their carriage reflected a centered, light balance, decidedly more lethal than their garrison-trained countrymen who wore the sunwheel blazon at Riverton.

Caught without knowledge of the password they demanded, Mearn refused answer until their advance had brought them inside one stride of him. The hand under his mantle rested taut on his knife. He kept his spurs ready to wheel his spent mount into immediate, hard flight, for no saving grace could lift the hair-trigger potential for disaster. These were townbred veterans with hard-core disaffections. Here in the free wilds, where clan accent alone could provoke a bloodletting misunderstanding, Mearn had no wish to claim the protection of Prince Lysaer's Alliance with his family. A s'Brydion presence abroad with credentials, but no escort, would raise all the wrong sort of questions.

"Who passes?" the sentry repeated. "Say your name and your purpose!"

Mearn let his dragging exhaustion sap the lilt of clan origins from his tone. "Courier, northbound."

Then more crawling chills flicked the length of his spine. The whispered rustle of branches from behind gave warning as more men closed at his back. His straits were now unequivocal. He rode alone, with no lawful witness within miles to gainsay the right actions of men who held him surrounded with drawn steel.

The next query carried a cold snap of suspicion. "What brings you here? Your path takes you far from the public road."

Mearn kept his birth dialect blurred, and his hands light and taut on his weapon. "Alliance business." To his right, where the gulch held pooled water, the chorus of spring peepers had silenced. These men would have concealed archers placed there, backing them up against mishap.

Ready to wheel his horse's startled weight and ram the two swordsmen behind him, Mearn measured his odds. If the bowmen had poor eyesight and miserable aim, he might narrowly manage to beat an escape through the brush. Very likely he would be wounded. Any lead he might gain could last only as long as some headhunter thought to set dogs on him. Without knowing the size of the camp these men guarded, dissembling stayed his best option. Mearn assayed an impatient, townborn inflection. "I have northbound dispatches. Very urgent."

The Etarran officer was steady enough not to kill out of hand. Scarcely a day's march away from the river, he must know an overt barbarian presence was unlikely in the middle of wide-open country. Mearn waited, unbreathing, to see whether sweet luck or mischance was going to present his next opening.

The duty officer called for a torch. "Let's have a look."

Flint and steel were produced with no fumbling. One of the sentries had rags soaked in pitch already prepared and waiting. As the flame burst and flowered, carnelian light played over Mearn's leather-clad knee, then the sable and scarlet colors of the officer's cloak he had purloined from the gatehouse that morning. Behind the folds of his mud-spattered hem, his gelding still wore the matching saddlecloth with its Hanshire blazon, that he had forgotten he carried.

The Etarrans fixed on the city mayor's device, and troubled to look no farther.

"Dharkaron's bollocks!" somebody carped from the sidelines. "Not another of you louses! Gave up my bed to your kind last night. The peacock disdained to fold up his blankets, far less say thanks in gratitude. Treated everyone he met like the get of a bootlicking scullion."

"Be still, you!" Defined in the light by the braid on his surcoat, the authority proved a man of middle years, rangy and fit and intolerant of nonsense. To Mearn, he made swift disposition. "All right, sir. You need not prove out the unpleasant reputation your countrymen left with my troops. You pass. Then you speak to the captain on watch. If your needs can be met, he'll look after the arrangements."

Mearn masked a thrill of delighted inspiration behind faintly sneering reserve. Weary, hungry, and hagridden by the urgency to move on, nonetheless, the gambler in him refused to ignore the dubious gifts dame fortune cast in his lap. He tipped a superior nod to the sergeant. Then he gathered his reins, risen to an arrogance no less withering than the Hanshire aristocrat who preceded him.

"Fiends plague!" a plaintive voice announced in oversight. "He'll need tonight's password if he isn't to find himself skewered on the swords of the inner watch."

Mearn pulled the gelding up short, his expression sure prelude to a burst of reviling temper.

The sergeant grumbled his unembarrassed apology and shared the prearranged signal. Mearn inclined his head, touched firm heels to his horse, and passed by, girded to wring what advantage he could, starting with a hot meal.

Behind him, the disaffected patrol indulged their dismal opinion of Hanshiremen. "Not a trustworthy lot, never have been. Hate royalty like plague. The fish-eaters consort with witches and soothsayers, as well as abet Koriani. You knew their Lord Mayor's high council is said to dabble in black magic?"

"Stow the loose chatter!" snapped the sergeant.

His chastened men broke up to resume their lapsed posts, while Mearn moved on out of earshot. In apparent routine, he let his exhausted mount pick its own way through the rim-lit gulches and low brush. The farther he progressed, the more fresh unease chafed at his overtaxed nerves. Again, he surveyed the plain. The shaved moon textured a panorama like etched lead. He detected no sign of a camp. Only a storm-raked wrack of bent trees that marked the dry confluence of a watershed. The hollow he crossed was scarcely a notable landmark in the lowland face of the Flats. He heard no human sound. Just the rustle of a fox, and the endless sough of the wind through the budding twigs of bare branches. Whatever business an armed camp had here, these Etarrans knew enough to use even this barren terrain to advantage.

Mearn slowed the gelding, sobered by an ingrained campaign wisdom to revise his original estimate. Given two lines of sentries, and no discernible activity, cold instinct lifted his hackles. An armed presence that maintained such secrecy would not be inept, or unleashed for any other Alliance agenda than the harrying of Tysan's free clansmen.

Made aware like a douse into ice water that his danger was far greater than he realized, Mearn combed the shadows more closely. He saw nothing still. His palms sprang a cold sweat and his warning instinct changed from mild to rousingly urgent. A covert retreat now carried more than chance risk in this country, where a mouse could not cross these stands of dry brush without telltale rustles of sound.

Mearn weighed a dangerously cruel set of choices. Best odds of survival were to bleed the horse dead, then try and creep back past the alert ring of sentries he had just hoodwinked to protect his identity. If he slipped through unseen, he would then be on foot, easy prey for the tracking dogs dispatched to run him to earth. Hot pursuit would inevitably close at his heels. A horse carcass would draw notice, perhaps even before the watch reported his presence at the next routine change of the guard.

He could trade his anonymity for short-term escape, or he could play for high odds and act out his guise as a bullying blue-blooded Hanshireman.

Had the stakes been less grim, Mearn could have laughed for the damnfool straits of his predicament. By that hour, he had been moving at speed through rough country for the better part of five days. His rest had been snatched between showers in the thorn brakes; his last meal, a chunk of sour cheese bought from a farmwife out feeding her geese. His judgment was failing, each separate thought strained as though drawn through a pall of black silk. Had he not been about to nod off in the saddle, he might have bypassed the first pack of sentries altogether.

Mearn stroked the neck of his flagging mount. To reward the poor gelding for trusting service with the furtive thrust of a knife seemed the ungrateful act of a coward.

An insatiable gambler, Mearn let the rash heat in his blood call his fate. Since trained soldiers were likely to dog his path anyway, he might as well snatch the bold opportunity to gain provisions and a fresh horse.

"Oats and a rubdown for you then, old man," he whispered in wisecrack resolve. His bluff would carry more thrill for wild stakes, never mind the maniacal temptation to gripe the Etarrans in the most evil manner he could. He pressed the gelding's scrambling, tired gait, swearing as noisily as any Hanshire townsman whose urgent orders sent him across an inhospitable wilderness.

The inner ring of sentries came at him like sharks in their haste to issue their challenge. Through snapping sticks as the horse fought bad footing, Mearn gave the password in the sloppy, soft vowels that centuries of affected fashion had evolved into citybred speech.

"State your business," the guard demanded, unsatisfied.

"Courier," barked Mearn. "You can't see with the two eyes Ath put in your face?" He added a phrase in the west coastal dialect that would raise a ripe flush on a galleyman.

"From Hanshire?" The flustered guard jerked up his chin, then snapped for a henchman to unshutter the light.

Slit eyed in the blinding flare of a lantern, Mearn gave his obstreperous opinion. "Fiends plague! You Etarrans always check on the obvious with the plodding stupidity of fed ticks."

Three guards slapped swift hands to their weapons, insulted. No fool, the young officer waved the arrival on quickly. He could do little else without risking a brawl unlikely to stop short of bloodshed.

Mearn smiled like a fox and rode past.

A bowshot ahead, he encountered the camp, a row of dark tents hunkered into a hollow carved out of the stony debris of a floodplain. The site lay well masked, set into the willows that knitted the low ground in the flats. The shelters were invisible unless an observer all but stumbled into their midst. Mearn saw no loose ends, no telltale gleams of chance firelight. The fitful, hard gusts did not slap at slack canvas, nor did stray talk ride the breeze.

This field troop displayed deadly, meticulous care. In sheer size alone, their presence bespoke a planned devastation, the work of trained reivers moving fast into enemy territory. Mearn disliked the unpleasant bent of his hunches, that Lord Maenol's clan scouts were going to receive a grim retaliation for upsetting the late march into Riverton. Nor did informed hindsight applaud the decision to beard the wolf pack in its chosen lair. This strike force was seasoned by the wiles of headhunters, and likely as fast to take scalps without question if they caught wind of an infiltrator inside their camp.

Though contentious escapades were Mearn's personal specialty, the banner which flew above the command tent made him wonder if even his brazen wit could pull off a challenge this grand. For the field captain in charge here had served the s'Brydion family as a mercenary until the campaign at Vastmark had brought an abrupt change of patron. The duke's brothers were far more than passing acquaintances, and Mearn's false claim of identity as a Hanshire courier would be seen as a killing offense.

A stick snapped on his back trail. Mearn spun, saw the two-legged shadow that stalked him, and snarled a silent obscenity. His presence had apparently stirred enough doubt that a guardsman had been sent to tail him. Most likely the creature was instructed to make sure he reported straightaway to the acting officer of the watch.

Hazed to a spurt of riled temper for this latest unlucky setback, Mearn drew a deep breath, then turned to engage every twist of cunning wickedness he could raise to secure his stake in survival.

"If you're going to follow," he drawled in contempt, "might just as well do so up front, where you won't take the point of my knife in mistaken belief you had thieving eyes on my purse."

The stick-cracking rustles hitched through a pause, then resumed as a stocky, perturbed soldier elbowed his way through the prickles of a hazel copse. Despite his large build, he moved well. His balance reflected a swordsman's neat tread, and though self-controlled, his temperament was by no means phlegmatic enough to withstand the barrage of Mearn's baiting. If he dared not strike back at a Hanshire courier, he would settle for shedding an unwanted responsibility as fast as humanly possible. "Head groom's still awake. He'll care for your horse."

"*I'll* care for my horse," Mearn shot back in distemper. He dismounted and loosened his saddle girth, running on in snide language under his breath about the ineptness of rattle-pated grooms. For sheer, stinging mischief, he added an insolent phrase in dialect he picked up by the Riverton gates, when the officer whose mantle he filched had swept in.

"Fatemaster's bollocks!" The stout guardsmen peered past the sloped neck of the gelding. "Is every living one of you also related to the priggish family of the mayor?"

Mearn smiled, sly in malice as a weasel. "Thick witted, are you, to take so long to notice the connection."

The pair crossed inside the camp perimeter, the alleged Hanshire courier all peevish-sharp nerves, and the heavyset soldier tagging his heels in contrasting, subservient awkwardness.

No torches burned, even damped behind canvas. Those men who had not turned in for the night hunkered down in small groups, conversation held to low whispers. They blended into the pitch shapes of the shadow, faces and hands stained with walnut dye to mask the pallor of bare flesh. Their shelters were sturdy and weatherproof, showing the odd scuffs and mends of hard use, and a layout taken from a headhunters' practice, with tents placed in rows of predictable width to allow ease of movement in darkness. Mearn lightened his tread, made cautious by the lethal stamp of competence reflected in every salient detail.

This camp was laid out for instantaneous action, from swift relocation to surprise attack. Men called to arms from the deepest of sleep could move, fight, and organize without tripping over tent pegs and ropes. No clutter lay about, no stray gear or strings of washed clothing. At a table with camp seats placed near the center, three wakeful officers clustered in conference, a tight-shuttered lantern between them. Yet no gleam of flame gave their presence away in the faint, mottled fall of the moonlight.

Led into their presence, Mearn used the snagged hair of the gelding's mane to obscure direct view of his face. His posture stayed straight, every inch of him arrogant. At length the camp watch captain broke off discussion and issued a testy inquiry. "Don't stand there dumbfounded! If you have any purpose here, state it."

Since the uppity Hanshireman deigned not to speak, his disgruntled escort was forced to step up and explain. "Here's a courier, bound north bearing urgent dispatches."

A drawn pause; the watch captain waited, braced on mailed elbows. His expectation made the silence unbearable. Red-faced, the sentry resumed his report, unable to refute the implied chain of command. "Yes, he needs food. Care and grain for his horse."

Mearn forced his breath steady as the lamp was raised up, and a cautious, brief finger of light flickered over his cloak and the Hanshire blazon on his saddlecloth.

Blunt as the mace he wore at his belt, the watch captain pressed his gruff inquiry. "You know him?"

"Sithaer no! Thank the power of Light for that blessing." The soldier glared with pure rancor at Mearn, who gave back a smile full of teeth.

Across the table, one of the subordinate officers clapped a hand to his beard to mask humor. The duty captain noticed, and snapped, "Swellhead or not, he can't stay in camp unescorted."

The guard braced his posture in bitten-off protest. "Respectfully, sir, I'm posted on the inner perimeter until midnight. Since this dandified errand boy requires a servant, will you hear my advice? Assign him somebody's unseasoned page. Preferably one with an insolent tongue that's deserving a stiff round of punishment."

"Just make sure he knows how to clean a man's boots," Mearn remarked from the sidelines.

The watch captain lost his breath to astonishment, then struggled not to laugh at the stilted discomfort of the soldier caught in the breach. "I understand your position," he said, straight-faced. "By all means, we don't pander to mincing state guests." He nodded dismissal to his disaffected veteran. "Return to your post with my compliments."

Relieved at vindication, the heavyset guard grinned in parting. "Be sure the daisy attends his own horse. He's already told me our grooms aren't fit to pluck the arse end of a goose."

Left with the watch captain and two inimical senior officers, all of them thankfully strangers, Mearn held his ground, wary. His airs and affectations in fact bought no immunity. This strike force was not warmly disposed toward strangers, nor did it welcome unannounced couriers who impinged with a claim of hospitality.

"You will leave all your weapons with us," the watch captain instructed, stretching the hard muscles of his forearm. Moonlight snagged on the links of his mail as he leaned his massive weight over the table. "No one here knows you. We don't leave men armed who aren't vouched for."

Mearn said nothing, but yanked loose his sword belt. He knotted the ends of the leather around the scabbard and, in masterful presumption, pitched his offering toward the seated officers; as if all his life, any man near him would naturally scramble to vie for the favor of his service. To judge by the fast reflexes of the brute who received the catch, his best chance was to stay on the offensive and discourage too close a scrutiny.

Before the captain could phrase a demand for his dagger, Mearn blistered back in disdain, "Since I'm not an assassin, will you insist that I eat with my hands?"

Any competent killer would use a noiseless garrote before steel; a fine point the watch captain was shamed to concede since the dagger remained in Mearn's custody.

The first throw fell to s'Brydion wiles, that freewheeling complaint proved a grating embarrassment in this bastion of prideful authority. No more argument ensued as a page boy was rousted and assigned the mean task of dogging Mearn's presence in camp. The steaming horse and its troublesome rider were dispatched straightaway to the picket lines, to long-suffering sighs of relief.

Granted limited autonomy and a precarious state of safe-conduct, Mearn adopted the sneer he liked best to intimidate crews on the decks of his brother's war galleys. Cardplay had taught him the elegant fine points of intimidation without the crude bluster of exertion. In one withering glance, he sized up his escort, a swaggering, lanky boy of sixteen who tripped over his own feet at each step.

Since braggarts typically feared contradiction, Mearn spun on his heel. He tugged his mount in the wrong direction, his blunder a certainty since the wind in his face carried no tang of manure.

The boy plucked at his sleeve, then flung back as Mearn bristled.

"Don't touch me, whelp." In sterling offense, Mearn faced forward and continued on his way. The page followed. Three dozen strides passed before the boy raised the nerve to correct the displaced orientation.

By then, the s'Brydion envoy had finished his count of the tents, and by swift extrapolation, set a crude limit on the strength of Alliance numbers. This force kept no camp followers. Servants and support troops were pared to a minimum, and an overheard scrap of conversation had informed that even the healer bore arms. More than one shelter's ridgepole displayed trophy scalps, clan braids knotted together like rope, or wound in the blood-crusted thongs the living man's wife would have tied in before battle.

Enraged and grieving, Mearn came at last to the picket lines. This division was light horse, the animals all prime, kept glossy with grain and condition. By contrast, the hack he tied up and rubbed down was thin and straight shouldered, an eyesore of a livery horse outclassed by its neighbors.

The page boy fatuously pointed this out.

Mearn ignored him. By clan belief, all things alive were made equal, no animal given more worth than another, and no man's life valued above either. Moved to cross-grained annoyance for the boy's townbred ignorance, he fixed his whole attention on tending the tired gelding's legs.

Just like the chained dog spurned by the free one, the snubbed page inflated his boasting to compensate.

Mearn did not comment. Thin features cast to indifferent disdain, he listened and absorbed each stray fact the boy spouted. By the time the gelding was cooled, fed, and groomed clean of sweat, he had cataloged a major array of tactics used in past raids against Red-beard's clans in Rathain. When the page boy wound down, he ventured laconic opinion that as yet, he remained unimpressed.

Done with the picket lines, his saddle and the Hanshire horse cloth slung over his shoulder, he pursued his quest for a meal. At the cook's tent, a well-placed disparagement sent the boy inside to fetch bread and jerked meat. Mearn waited, sharp-eyed and observant on the sidelines, overhearing stray phrases and talk from the men who came and went about unnamed business.

". . . give the forest-slinking lizards their comeuppance," a pikeman said, chuckling.

Through a lull in the breeze, a companion enlarged on the story, his gestures expansive and vehement. ". . . for what they did in the bogs. Let them suffer Dharkaron's fell vengeance for all eternity . . . nothing else but a tenday of sharpening weapons. Have blades in our band could split hairs with a cat's breath behind them . . . "

Low talk from another quarter cut in between gusts of wind. "Man, they'll be swept up like leavings. No chance. . . . other troops moving in through the mountains. . . . them surrounded, and clan scalps enough to make felt to restuff our Lord Mayor's upholstery."

Riled as a cat doused in rainfall, Mearn capped the blaze of his temper. Bit by bit, patient, he assembled each garnered fact. Under Alliance orders to sweep northward, these crack Etarran troops held a crown disposition to hunt down free clansmen in Tysan. Stung pride would be vindicated. Having suffered and bled through laid ambush in the wetlands, these men were rested and hot to take down the barbarian vermin who had abetted the Shadow Master's clean escape. Nor were their officers anything less than prepared for the tricks cornered clansmen could mete out.

Mearn had quartered the camp. As s'Brydion knew war, he recognized excellence. After five seasons spent plowing the forests of Rathain for Jieret Red-beard's unscrupulous breed of scout, they were hardened veterans, lethally practiced at keeping a near to invisible presence.

He ate what the page brought, suborning racked nerves to assuage his body's demand for replenishment. Emerged from a seamless tempest of thought, he laid down the wild card hand he had cut from the cloth of desperate courage and chance.

"I'm tired," he announced without preamble. Lest the flustered page seek a superior officer to ask for bedding and shelter, Mearn caught the boy's wrist with insistent fingers. "I won't sleep under canvas. Too smelly. Fetch me a blanket. I'll choose my own place set out of the wind, where I won't scratch from picking up head lice."

Once the blanket was found, he crossed the camp again, the saddle and cloth still carried across his left shoulder. He took painstaking minutes to cut and skin a green willow branch. With that oddment in hand, he acquired a seemingly limitless enthusiasm for exploring the brush between tents. He poked under bushes. His vexing, erratic course wound in circles around a structure of tight-lashed canvas, then stalled into another confounding silence.

The page grew rebellious. "That's the supply and the armory," he volunteered in exasperation.

"I do have a nose, whelp." Not to be hurried, Mearn extended his search and turned over each leaf on the ground. "One can't be too careful. Tracking dogs might have pissed here."

"They're kept caged in wicker," the page disallowed.

Since Mearn had detected neither barking nor whines, he made chill conclusion that this company practiced the headhunters' cruelty of cutting the dogs' vocal cords to make them run silent.

Scarcely able to mask his shudder of distaste, he unloaded his saddle, folded his lean frame in the blanket, and lay down full length on bare earth. "Good night."

"*What?*" The befuddled page glowered.

"I said, good night." As a final eccentric foible of privacy, Mearn arranged the crusted saddlecloth with its bold Hanshire blazon over his exposed head and face.

The page stood at a loss with his mouth open. As Mearn's breathing steadied, then slowed to soft snoring, the boy paced, kicking stones in bilious frustration. His orders to watch this high-handed courier included no avenue for relief. Nor was an officer nearby to consult or say where his irregular duty left off. The boy stood; he deliberated; he went foot to foot in sore doubt. Finally, resigned, he sat down in the brush to keep boring vigil. The prospect of watching a prig sleep through the night underneath the ripe felt of a saddle-cloth seemed a stupendous waste. Where a man might lodge a complaint among peers, a boy could do little but sulk and endure the injustice.

Hours crawled. The watch changed. The last wakeful men retired to their tents. The courier from Hanshire did nothing but lie in unmoving, oblivious quiet, while the page leaned his back on a sapling. Tired, he dozed once or twice. The final time he opened his eyes, the brush over his head rang with the chirps of spring sparrows. Dawn had broken. Through a pearl haze of fog, men stirred, seeking breakfast or the latrine ditch. The page stretched, rubbed his eyes, and through the complaint of stiff muscles, ascertained his charge had not strayed. The courier's boots and spurs still poked from the blanket. Naught else had changed; the red-and-black saddlecloth remained creased like a tent over his insufferable, swelled head.

The page endured privation in eye-watering discomfort, then finally gave in to bodily need and relieved himself in the brush. The Hanshireman slumbered on, oblivious. The sun rose, melting the streamers of mist and unveiling a day like a chisel-cut diamond. The camp was fully aroused before an irritable petty officer sent by the watch came inquiring to see why the courier had failed to make an appearance.

"He's asleep, still." Grouchy and feeling unjustly martyred, the page boy tossed a pebble just shy of the blanket. "Probably lies in silk sheets until noon in that decadent city he comes from. You kick him awake. He has thankless manners."

The petty officer stroked his clipped beard. He eyed the man-shaped muddle of horsecloth, saddle, and blanket with visible trepidation. Then, touched to a sudden, chill plunge of intuition, he stepped forward and stamped his booted foot with full strength onto the courier's midriff.

Sticks snapped. The blanket collapsed, sagged in folds that revealed the form underneath to be nothing else but an artful arrangement of twigs and dry grass.

"Murdering *fiend*!" the officer gasped. "The confounded dog was a spy!" He elbowed aside the gaping page and raced headlong to raise the alarm.

The Etarran camp erupted like a nest of kicked wasps, but not to a wild stir of noise. Men reacted in a chilling, oiled flow of discipline, tearing down tents and searching through every nook and cranny of packed baggage. Twenty minutes after the stunning discovery, the officer of the day watch stood in straightlaced formality and delivered the raw news to his captain.

"The man's not in camp, though his horse, his sword, his saddle and cloth are still here. The outlook is no good. He slit the tent canvas with a dagger and crawled into the armory. All the tactical maps are taken from the locked chest. He snatched an excellent sword, then caused enough mischief to make us all choke in embarrassment."

"Sabotage?"

The officer swallowed. "Yes sir." He shifted huge shoulders under his mail, braced his nerve, and recited the list. "All the steel broadheads were cut from their shafts, and the fletching stripped off the arrows. Sword blades were unwound at the tang and separated from their hilts. At the horse lines, we found all the bridles cut apart. We'd fix them with string, but no one in camp can find a damned bit for his horse, or a girth that has any buckles."

"Embarrassment, you say?" The captain stabbed his eating knife upright in the crust of his scarcely touched bread loaf. "I call it mayhem." His eyes narrowed with thought and a chilling, leashed temper, he snapped his strong fingers, causing the page who knelt by his elbow to jump. "Go. Fetch my parchment and seal."

Then he leveled his blue eyes at the duty officer, and said, "You're not finished?"

The man caught under scrutiny fidgeted, the sweat rolling from under his steel helm. "No, sir. The kennelman claims the meat for the dogs was tainted. At least, since he fed them, every last one's fallen sick."

The account suffered a break as the page boy returned, bearing the troop commander's lap desk and the tied leather bundle which protected the state seal with its sunwheel blazon of authority.

"Keep talking, man." Resigned to the setback that spoiled his breakfast, the captain unburdened the page boy. His hard fingers flipped open the lap desk. "If our scouring of the clans is no longer a surprise, the other troops have to be warned. You can talk while I write." He accepted the wrapped packet containing the sunseal, then paused, his frosty brows snagged in a frown.

"Something wrong, sir?" The duty officer blotted his moist face.

The troop commander showed his teeth, an animal response to murderous fury as he snatched up his knife and slashed the thong ties. The rolled leather fell away and revealed an old knotted root left in place of the sunwheel seal to attest crown authority. "Why, that slithering get of a snake! For this, I'll see his entrails torn out by dogs and his scalp taken under my dagger!"

The page boy launched into panicky excuses. "The lock wasn't loose on your coffer, sir. No papers were missing." Then the damning worst, from the lips of foolhardy innocence. "Whoever stole the seal from your things had to know just where to look."

"Be silent." The captain fingered his steel, his temper leashed through hardened experience, and his slate-colored eyes fixed back on the man whose report was unfinished, and whose perspiring features showed inordinate lack of surprise. "There's *more?*"

"Yes, sir." The forbearing sigh this time seemed to rise from the harried man's boot soles. "The groom on the picket lines was given a requisition order, sealed and signed in what looks to be precise forgery."

"What did that groom give, say quickly." No idiot, the troop captain thrust to his feet. "The facts are by far more important than the blame."

The reporting officer braced himself. "Six horses, half of them saddled and bridled, and the last three apparently on lead reins. We've examined the tracks. The creatures were roped in pairs. The dawn patrol saw someone they believed to be ours, leaving with remounts in tow. He carried packeted orders under your wax seal, and we can't fault them, the sunwheel blazon was genuine. A short distance from our outer line, the trail scouts say the horses slowed down. Then their tracks diverge to all points of the compass."

"You tried dogs?" said the captain, not truly expecting the obvious had not been covered.

"First thing, sir." The watch officer rubbed his moist hands on his surcoat. "The two bitches well enough to stand up lost the scent next to the picket lines. That's where the groom said the rogue mounted. We can follow that horse, but that's wasted motion." This spy had proven inventively clever. He had likely climbed from one saddle to another before he sent the loose horses packing.

"All right," said the captain, all ironbound purpose. "I want action. Now. Each one of those horses will be tracked and brought in, I don't care if their trail leads through Sithaer itself. Every man will be questioned. If anyone saw this traitor's face clearly, I want his detailed description. Next, we assume he's barbarian blood. Why else steal the tactical maps, if not to send word to the enemy? We're marching north anyway. Last night's little blunder just lit the fires under our order of march a bit hotter. At the end, we'll face men who are warned and desperate. By the Light, if there's justice, our line sentries are going to stand front and center when we close with the murdering fugitives."

A searing, short pause, as the captain recalled the humiliation that he had no seal for his orders. Nor could he verify his dispatch to Avenor to send formal complaint of the infamy.

"Damn the motherless, slinking little weasel!" he exploded in livid heat that promised a reckoning in bloodshed. "When we net his close kin, I will personally sew their damned scalps as a fringe on my saddlecloth."

By noon, sweating in the humid spring warmth that chafed blisters under gambesons and made chain mail weigh like poured lead, the men ran down the last horses. Not one bore a rider. The spy's tracks were not found, though the hound couple which survived the morning's bout of poisoning whuffed and milled in baffled circles. They sprawled on their sides, muddied and panting, while their irritable handlers persisted. The next hour entailed the miserable, wet labor of leaping across hummocks and scouring the verges of the waist-deep, dank pools in the fenland. Sedges and cattails waved in the wind. Half-budded maples trailed lichened branches and tough roots into the peat black waters of the sinkholes. Hard effort flushed nothing but otters and the flap of displaced crows. Nothing moved but the high-flying hawk, while clouds gathered and plumed like combed silver overhead and threatened more rain before nightfall.

In due course, the search was called off. The guileful courier had left no trace of his passage, and his clanblood relations would inevitably receive the premature warning of trouble.

The setback raised grumbles, but no loss of morale. These were seasoned fighters who had marched against clansmen before. They knew to expect balking tricks and sly tactics that time and again deferred victory. This campaign might go hard, but the ending was assured. Without ships, the barbarian enclaves in south Tysan were doomed, soon to be reaped by the vengeful steel of Lysaer's Alliance of Light.

In the late afternoon, the gathering storm rode the west winds raking in off the ocean. The rain drizzled, then gushed, then hammered down in white sheets. The barrage chased the dark pools in the marshes to stippled pewter, and glazed the bent limbs of the maples. Mearn s'Brydion waded shin deep to keep dogs off his scent, his wet leathers clinging like glue at each stride, and his fingers locked to the straps of three rolled leather map cases. The brass-capped ends bashed his thigh when he stumbled, his ankles caught back by the sawing tangles of sedges. Only the relentless chill kept him wakeful.

His thoughts came in fragments, their meaning unmoored by the expanding spirals of exhaustion.

He slogged his way past another islet of hummocks. The sucking pull of the mud continually mired and slowed him. Yet he dared not traverse the high ground, not with an Alliance armed force at his back, enraged by his suborning trickery. Some of the dogs might survive the pulped water hemlock he had used to taint their dried meat. Etarran field troops were not fools in the wilds, and no lack of bridles and girths would swerve them from their orders to march north.

Breathless, shivering, gnawed to the bone by the ache of spent muscles, Mearn perched his hip on a deadfall. Rain pocked the water in rings at his shins. Premature dusk banked deep shadows beneath the stained boles of the trees. The low, misting clouds showed no sign of lifting. Rain blew and swirled and trickled from his eyebrows, and rinsed streams through the garlands of watercress plastered over his thighs. Failing light was going to upset his bearings. Mearn tipped back his head and fought off a flattening rush of disheartenment. He had only the lichens for orientation. On the south sides of trees, the salt winds from Mainmere burned off their splotched growth; and the shag moss did not grow north-facing.

Mearn shut stinging eyes, every nerve end and instinct alive to his danger. Range too far east, he would find only distrustful fenlanders in their lowly wattle-and-mud huts. Pass too far west, and he would encounter high ground, fair game for a second armed troop the maps showed would be beating a line inland from Hanshire. South lay the Etarrans he had riled like jabbed hornets, and north, and if luck saved him, he might find the armed bands of Lord Maenol's scouts who had foiled the Alliance's cordon of Riverton.

Geese called in the reeds. Daylight was fast waning. The gloom seemed cast in lead silver between the plummeting curtains of rainfall. Mearn shoved off through the vast, empty maze of stilled bogland, no longer able to mind his own noise as he snapped through the sticks of the thickets. He tripped again, slamming his shoulder on the knob of a willow bough. "Forgive," he gasped, breathless, by timeworn clan custom acknowledging the mistake of his own clumsiness. The nurturing trees might overlook his offense, but the needs of his body could not be deferred for much longer.

The willow grove thinned. Hedged by gathering darkness, the ground snaked away into tarnished, dull pools inked with the knees of dead tree roots. A lightning-struck oak thrust a blackened shell skyward, the stripped husks of burned saplings angled like spears through the rioting tangle of briar. The past fire had scorched off the moss and the lichen. A few sloshing steps brought the water waist deep. Mearn paused, half-immersed. He wiped streaming wet from his eyes, while the wind slapped and battered at his hair and his clothing. He hitched the map cases up to his shoulder to protect their waxed hide from immersion.

Rain blurred the landmarks. The sere, muddy banks held no sign of an otter's den, or any other small animal burrow to hint which direction lay south. Only the unreliable, buffeting west winds lent their unkindly semblance of guidance.

These fens were not safe to traverse after dark, with mud sinks that could swallow a man's foot in one step and suck down his bones beyond finding.

Mearn slogged ahead, splashed into a hole, then managed a clawing recovery back to raised ground. He would have to double back. The effort would certainly turn him around. Trail instinct did not apply in this land, with its puzzle-cut maze of tangled, brown hummocks, and meandering pools inscribed by hammering rainfall.

Immersed in deep thickets, clawed raw by green thorns, he lost his bearings again. Faced by a deeper stand of water than before, he now shivered uncontrollably. The relentless chill stole his body's reserves. He knew his survival hinged upon finding immediate shelter and food. Sleep now was his enemy. To yield to his craving for overdue rest would see him a skeleton picked clean by predators. The urgent warning he carried would become lost, and the maps, which detailed the Alliance sweep through south Tysan for the purpose of eradicating clan bloodlines.

Mearn thrashed into another grove of maples, hampered by closing darkness. A gray heron startled into flight from her fishing. He recoiled from the noise. Twigs clawed at his burden. He caught back the loosened bundle before the straps gave, and clasped the rolled leather to his chest. Breath sucked through his locked teeth. He no longer knew if the whine in his ears was the shrilling of spring peepers, or yet another warning of overtaxed senses about to let go and fail him. He kept moving regardless, unwilling to give way to the beckoning void that offered him painless unconsciousness.

Through the sheet-lead expanse of another shallows, Mearn lost north again. He groped for a tree, a stripped stump, any firm object that might still harbor a telltale colony of shag moss. His touch met cold mud. Reeds slapped his face. Cattail down snagged in his nostrils and smeared yellow fuzz on his eyelids. He coughed into darkness that seemed too thick to breathe, and shoved on against a battering tempest of cold wind. The rain sluiced and hissed and rinsed through wet leaves. He knew he must stop, find some sort of shelter, and wait out the night or the storm. Vertigo threatened to unstring his balance. Already he could have become turned around and be moving back into the armed camp of the enemy.

Time slipped. He became aware that he sat underneath the dripping crown of a marsh maple. Gusts roared through the branches, and clattered the loosened, dead runners of vines. Far past feeling cold, he crimped his hands on the straps that secured the purloined map cases. Fear and worry were numbed, his cognizance flattened to insipid and dangerous lassitude. The rain drove down, relentless, and scattered thin trickles off the wicked ends of his hair. Only the otters fared well in this weather. Mearn heard the splash as they dove from the banks, hunting small crayfish, or cavorting for sport in the darkness.

Or perhaps their noise masked the doings of men. He could no longer tell. The vise grip of exhaustion left his skull feeling packed with wet cotton. Overcome by inertia, he attempted more than one brutal measure to regain his feet and keep moving.

Nothing changed. His last strength was long spent. Mearn sat, huddled with his forehead bowed on his knees, and his smeared wrists tucked at his ankles. Weariness sapped his last spark of vitality, but not stubborn will. He still held the map cases clenched to his breast. Asleep or unconscious, he did not respond as the splashing disturbance approached him. Nor did he stir in the flare as someone unshuttered a wick lantern. The breath of the storm winnowed the reek of hot fat, then the must of wet clothes, sewn from the skins of small animals. A skiff made of bark glided through the shallows. From a perch in the bow, a wizened little grandmother raised a horn lantern, while two younger male relatives pointed and whispered in the singsong dialect of the fenlands.

The poleman paused. Shoved by contrary wind, his boat drifted.

On the greening bank, the spearpointed sedges bent and flattened, streaked like ruby glass with reflections. The juddering light picked out the arrivals, with their stitched leather caps tied with talismans fashioned from feathers, and strung acorns, and little stars woven of flax straw.

"It's a man sitting there. Has no boots on, that's odd," the grandmother observed in a mollified, half-toothless warble.

Rain slanted through the purl of the mist. "Could be dead," mused the squat uncle, who rinsed the offal from the last kill from his hands. He jabbed a thumb rubbed shiny from endless hours spent twisting fish twine. "Has a sword, see? Could be dangerous."

"Isn't moving," the third party ventured.

The skiff jostled closer. The thwart gouged the peat bank.

"Still breathing," said the trapper, kneeling down. "Just barely." He stabbed his bloody knife into the reed basket shining with the scales of gutted fish, while his companions reached out tentative hands and lightly fingered the stranger gone lost in the bogs.

"Clanborn, and in trouble," the grandmother determined.

Another chimed in soft counterpoint, "Shelter then."

In silent efficiency, the two men arose from the skiff and stepped onto the marshy bank. Shadows wheeled, stitched with carnelian where plummeting raindrops sliced through the flickering lamplight. They bent, grasped Mearn's arms at the elbow and shoulder, then startled back with hissed breaths as their find stirred and lifted his head.

He had gray eyes, the pupils wide and black with shock. The two fen folk poised, stilled as scared rabbits, while the rain sang and splashed unabated. The man squinted through the downpour. His vision seemed reluctant to focus, as if the skiff and its occupants were a nightmare come visiting, or a madman's distortion of Dharkaron Avenger's Black Chariot, filled with wizened little people with bloodied knives and insistent plucking fingers.

Then he spoke, the ingrained courtesy of his ancestors set in the antique speech of his breeding. "Please. I beg help. If you know, if you can spare a runner to seek, let these cases I carry reach Lord Maenol s'Gannley or his kinsmen with all possible speed."

The grandmother clicked her tongue through shut teeth. "Whist, bring him in. Or this one that he seeks will receive his cold bones for naught but last rites and a burial."

Early Spring 5653

Appeals

At Althain Tower, the mood changed from downcast to grim in the darkened, chill hours before dawn. Sethvir sat, chin on fist, at the massive stone table in the library chamber, half-swallowed by the gloom which gathered under the star-patterned beams of the ceiling. As his mind ranged through yet another chain of auguries, his forehead stayed pinched into creases. The last such cast sequence had already fretted the white ends of his beard into finger-caught tangles. The dark, polished table before him was swept clear of books. By his elbow, a filled mug of tea had gone cold. The casement windows at his back were latched shut, the tight fastenings kept under tireless siege by a barrage of sharp winds that, farther south, coalesced as a rainstorm.

The one dribbled candle alight in the stand fluttered anyway, tormented by the gyrating presence of a visiting discorporate colleague. "Just say what you see," Kharadmon urged at length, his pique the snarl of a mewed-up predator, and his worry unsubtle as the flaying edge of a storm front. "I'm well aware the news out of Tysan bodes no good. Can the details make things any worse?"

Sethvir shut his eyes. Unmoving, he answered, "Dakar's warning framed an accurate judgment. Arithon eats, but his body rejects sustenance afterward. He speaks, he perseveres. He stubbornly enacts all the movements of living. But the fire, the passion, his sense of self-worth and entitlement have all been strangled by grief. Like the Paravians, who waste away in the absence of hope, our Teir's'Ffalenn tries

336

to endure against the grain of his born nature. He keeps the very letter of his oath to survive."

Through a plangent, fierce pause, Kharadmon spun in suspension. "Say on. I can already guess."

"Oh, the gist isn't new." Sethvir stabbed distraught hands through the hair at his temples, the farseeing span of his vision all bitterness. Morriel Prime had foreseen this crux years ago, that Arithon's inheritance from two royal bloodlines created an incompatible legacy. "The gifts of s'Ahelas foresight cross-linked with s'Ffalenn compassion poisons all that he does, all that he thinks. Now he's forced to betray the loyalties he holds sacrosanct, he has no defense against guilt and despondency."

While his colleague's roving angst churned a crock of quill pens into rustling agitation, Althain's Warden summed up. "In the absence of grace, entropy triumphs. The flesh loses its natural drive to renew itself."

"Then you fear our Teir's'Ffalenn will succumb into wasting disease, over time." Kharadmon's presence sheared over the bookshelves, raising dust like fine smoke from the rows of old, musty covers. Pages flipped madly on another opened tome propped on a lion-carved lectern. "Well give him some news." The self-contained tempest paused on its course, reversed direction, and whirled the quill pens on the opposite spin like small weathercocks. "Find him some word of encouragement."

The Warden of Althain simply looked up, his gaze the blank blue of a robin's egg.

Kharadmon stopped, a poured well of cold that exuded biting frustration. "There are moments your mind's just like knotted string, too vexingly layered to unravel."

Sethvir stirred, unfolded crimped fingers, and with a fingernail showing a black rim of ink, traced a circle on the obsidian tabletop. "You won't like what you see."

"Well, that's nothing fresh," Kharadmon breezed on. "These times are rank chaos. Though Luhaine is a pessimist, and his theories are galling, I have to agree that entropy's been winning since Desh-thiere came calling through South Gate."

"Peace, here." Althain's Warden traced a glyph in blue light on the air.

Then he laid light palms on the table and pronounced a phrase in the slow, rolling consonants that awakened the Name for the primal awareness of *this* stone which held his attention. A permission was exchanged in language and pitch beyond range of ordinary hearing.

Sethvir traced another glyph inside the closed figure, and awaited an inward alignment.

A connection closed like a spark in his mind. He framed his intent and sank his awareness into the dance of meshed energies which bound the obsidian into solidity. His grasp of grand conjury accomplished what no other arcane order on the continent could achieve on the wings of pure thought: he invoked shift in resonance, and raised the vibrational frequency of dense matter.

Within his drawn circle, the stone's matrix dissolved, transmuted to a state of pure light.

Rinsed in a flare of actinic brilliance, Althain's Warden reached out again. He said, hand poised, the spiked snow of his eyebrows trained toward Kharadmon's breezy fidgeting, "The fish, at least, led the proper fishermen to the catch. I give you the brightest thread in the tapestry."

"Well, we can't all be scatterbrained and capture such nuance by dreaming." But this once, Kharadmon's baiting humor fell short.

Althain's Warden did not smile as he touched the field of unformed matter with his forefinger and imprinted the reenactment of a scene drawn in through his tie to the earth link . . .

Rain splashed and guttered through the reeds in Mogg's Fen, where a soaked party of marsh trappers poled their skiff northward through night's inky maze of shoals and mudbanks and flat water. Wrapped in furs and greased hide, a shuddering clansman lolled half-unconscious, raging curses against an Alliance invasion in feverish fits of delirium . . .

"Mearn s'Brydion? Taken north? But you know his warning will come far too late." Kharadmon wheeled over the shadowy aumbries, sarcastically unimpressed, since Lysaer's gathered forces were already present and closing upon Maenol's clansmen. "What's one coal raked from the flames of a building conflagration? Merciful Ath! If that's a success, you'd better show me the failures. Or Luhaine will claim I've traded my bollocks for outright, shrinking faintheartedness."

Sethvir bowed his head. "Wiser, perhaps, to discount pride and praise the one gift as a blessing." But he honored Kharadmon's bidding and set the small linkage between transmuted stone and his powers of earth-linked perception. The scenes he translated through the ring of his scrying were indeed unrelenting bad news.

Lysaer's war galleys swept down on the Isles of Min Pierens and overran Arithon's small outpost at Corith. The site had no defenses. The ramshackle sheds, the tools, the small sail loft which refitted the stolen hulls from River-ton were razed and burned inside the first hour of landing. The laborers had been trapped, killed as they resisted, or run down and captured as they fled through the brush by headhunters and trained packs of tracking dogs. The handful of survivors now languished in chains with the wounded, shortly to see the Alliance destroy their last outside hope of a rescue.

Into the harbor, unsuspecting, ran the Cariadwin *with her crew of freed galley slaves and her hold filled with clan scouts just signed on as untrained volunteers. These expected to man three forthcoming new ships, and were yet unaware of the setbacks inflicted by Koriani intervention. None of them knew of the launching just gone bad at Riverton; neither they nor their cap-tain realized as they sailed that an Alliance trap lay in waiting.*

Sethvir spoke a word, and time bowed to his bidding. The colors in the scrying on the tabletop bled into the ghostly gray prescience that unveiled the unformed future. The sequence firmed into sharp-ening focus, as the few tracks of possibility in play merged into a remorseless junction. Kharadmon saw that the coming sea fight at Corith would end in a vicious defeat. Against an outfitted war fleet, caught in confined waters, the *Cariadwin's* fierce defense was fore-doomed.

"*Alt*," Sethvir murmured, the Paravian rune that marked closing. The silver-point tones of unborn event bled away, replaced by another vision, this one a view of the Alliance shipworks at Riverton, grained in a mist of falling rain.

"What you see next occurred just this afternoon," Althain's War-den added in subdued explanation; and Kharadmon shared all the sorrowful details of Caolle's survival, now entangled with the last thread in the Koriani design that devolved from the arraigned yard workers and sail crews kept hostage to force Arithon's capitulation. Sethvir's scrying perused the firelit chamber where Lirenda, First Senior, signed the requisite papers of extradition in the smug com-pany of Riverton's mayor. With a crystal wineglass poised in one hand, and an expression serene as milk porcelain, she delivered her order for the prisoners to sail on the dawn tide three days hence.

"I don't like her eyes," Kharadmon observed tartly. "Vindictive as nightshade to stop a man's heart in his sleep."

"She looks that way when she's hiding something." Althain's War-den considered the sorry prisoners held in chains in the cramped cell that once had confined Dakar. "The three new brigs will be diverted from crown orders by her Prime's will to form a blockade. If our Teir's'Ffalenn crosses through Korias without mishap, he could certainly fall to Morriel's conspiracy as he sails his small sloop out of Mainmere."

A wind like black ice, Kharadmon's course riffled a stack of loose parchments weighted down by a chunk of iron meteorite. "You sent me summons. What do you ask? *What else have you seen that you are so loath to tell me?*"

Still reluctant to answer, Sethvir raised one finger. His soft word sang release over his suspended conjury, and the bindings inside his drawn circle let go. The sustaining, fine energies carried from the Prime Source spiraled downward. Spell-fired light sank to a pale halo, then vanished. Residual heat fanned and stirred the pale ends of the Sorcerer's hair and beard, while spent forces dispersed, sighing away to stilled silence.

Between Sethvir's elbows, the stone table reverted to form, seamless black as before, the sole remnant of change the upright candle, now snuffed to a febrile ember. Out of chill darkness, a stir of worn cloth as Althain's Warden stood up. "I can't say what tomorrow will bring. There are too many free-will choices involved to guess whether Arithon s'Ffalenn can achieve his escape into freedom. Yet one fact can't be argued: at large or held captive in Koriani hands, he cannot long sustain a despair of self-damning proportion."

Sethvir's library suffered another tempestuous dusting as Kharadmon seized on the gist. Neither one of the half brothers had escaped the deranging sorrows linked to the bloodshed at Tal Quorin, Minderl Bay, and Vastmark. But where Lysaer s'Ilessid became driven to self-sacrifice for morality, ennobling his losses through a public campaign of justification, Arithon s'Ffalenn more quietly bled in compassion until his solitary resilience ran dry. No need to belabor the painful necessity, that the one threatened life held the lynchpin of the Black Rose Prophecy's resolution. All hopes for the Fellowship's restoration back to seven still hinged upon a crowned prince for Rathain.

"You want a mitigator," Kharadmon burst out, his mercuric impatience the springboard to seize on the direction of Sethvir's thinking. "Someone to reforge the bond of his trust with *himself*? Who's to ask? Daelion Fatemaster wept! We're talking of Kamridian s'Ffalenn's direct descendant, and nothing we tried in *that* hour of trial turned his mind to seek self-redemption."

"I know." Sethvir reclaimed his tea mug and sipped its cold contents as he shared consternation and the grievous past memory of a valiant s'Ffalenn high king, driven to his doom in the Maze of Davien, where the Betrayer's insidious coils of truth spells faced a man with his own mirror image. Arithon's ancestor had died, torn apart by the pangs of guilt-driven conscience. The thread which had seen him undone at the last was his line's royal gift of compassion.

"We lost King Kamri despite every conscious protection, and he had no damning entanglement with the effects of s'Ahelas farsight." A spark jumped and grounded into the stone floor as Kharadmon vented his testiness.

"I thought you claimed Luhaine was the pessimist." As if the dregs of his tea showed him nightmares, Althain's Warden secreted the mug amid the snarl of old twine he scrounged when he needed a bookmark. He knew by Kharadmon's complete lack of argument that he could not mask the bare truth. Out of today's breeding quagmire of circumstance, the same tragedy that had ended King Kamridian's life could be repeated with Arithon. Sethvir pondered bad odds, while outside, the wind slapped and whistled against his sealed shutters, and within, Kharadmon expended his angst in small fits that raised havoc among his belongings.

As if the innate peace of the darkness had fled, Sethvir touched the wick of the candle alight. The feeble spear of new flame creased shadows over the timeworn hollows of his face. Worry pinched his lips like cracked leather, and lent his clasped hands the transient fragility of flesh that was fallibly mortal. "I know of only two individuals with the power to lay claim to Arithon's heart."

Kharadmon froze into ominous stillness. "The enchantress Elaira and Earl Jieret s'Valerient."

Sethvir nodded, brooding over the relentless perils implied by his posited remedy. "The lady could heal Rathain's prince the fastest. Her influence would be reliable and sure, but she must first step forward in free will and transcend the limitations the Koriani Order has imposed between her and the man she would love."

"I can't take that risk!" Kharadmon protested, all trace of the prankster razed off by uncoiling horror. "What if she martyrs herself as a sacrifice? She might well break her vows and accept self-destruction!" The quill pens flurried airborne and circled, caught up in the shade's consternation. "By the Avenger's black Spear and Chariot, Traithe already questioned her once. Luhaine also. Both met the same obstacle." Elaira had seen no truth beyond Morriel's binding; nor did she perceive her own power to ask help to claim back her right to free spirit.

Althain's Warden could not argue the razor-edged chances involved with breaching Elaira's self-imposed solitude. Shoulders bowed, arms tucked to his chest, he crossed to the sill of the casement. While the storm raged with unrelenting raw violence against

Althain's spelled stone and latched glass, he did not share his caged pain, that often his wardenship weighed on his heart like lead shackles. The mighty protections of a dead centaur stonemason could offer no comfort, nor provide any haven against the pending potential for disaster Desh-thiere's curse stewed up in south Tysan.

Nor was Kharadmon left blinded to nuance, that a discorporate spirit could accomplish the errand to Araethura with neater dispatch. His capitulation came barbed with the sardonic fire he used when he masked hurtful sentiment. "If Luhaine went once, I'll bear that role now. At least the woman won't have to put up with his windbag style of lecturing."

Sethvir's lips twitched with the barest thin irony. "Elaira stalled him point-blank with her woman's sensibility, in fact. Take warning from that. Her superiors never did break her streetwise impudence. Airs and authority of any kind still raise her blistering contempt."

Outside, the gusts ripped and savaged the runners of ivy latched into blunt stone. By lengths more obdurate, Sethvir laced chilled fingers under his beard, his elbows propped on the sill. His statement blurred into the dream of the earth link as he summed up his final appeal. "If you fail in Araethura, and Earl Jieret is called, his people in Rathain will be left in the hands of an infant successor. He will ask our help for safe passage. Even so, his journey will take several months. We could lose the short margin of time that is left to spare Arithon's equanimity. Go swiftly."

By the time the echo of the words died to silence, Althain Tower held no outside company. Sethvir was left to his own disturbed thoughts and the aimless whirl of the dust motes unmoored by Kharadmon's soundless departure.

In distant Araethura, where the herbalist's small cottage snugged into the sweep in the moors, the spring downpour drummed in balked thunder against thatch netted down with twine and stout stones. Deep night wrapped the land. In velvet-grained darkness, the incessant winds rattled shutters and door, and moaned litanies under the eaves. After six years, the complaints of harsh storms were familiar enough that Elaira did not stir in her sleep.

When Kharadmon's presence poured under the gap in her doorsill, the enchantress lay curled beneath tumbled blankets, wrists tucked to her breast. The spell crystal defensively cupped into one fist held her guard, the signature field spun off its facets like smoke hazed to a glow of spun phosphor. That shifting, uncertain luminosity picked out details a discorporate mage could perceive with no shift in vibration.

Sethvir of Althain had said for years that this woman's hands held the threads of Arithon s'Ffalenn's future happiness. Since the fate of Athera also rode the same course, Kharadmon gave the sleeper his most exacting survey. The thin, elfin profile pillowed in waves of her deep auburn hair was serene. Her closed lips had softened from the habitual wry tilt of impertinence. Open to plain view was her heedless sensitivity, the vulnerable heart she would defend with attacking dry wit when aware.

Brushed by a finger of inquiry from behind, Kharadmon stilled. A pinpoint of cold amid the rough play of drafts, he revolved in place, amazed as the touch came again. Apparently the woman had placed small defenses on her cottage. His embarrassment stemmed from the astounding oddity that her contrary wardspells had picked out his presence before he had noticed their existence.

He swept her surroundings. The tiny cottage reflected a character too large to contain it, from the fleece-lined boots flung off helter-skelter, to the clothes lopsidedly hooked on the tine of a deer antler. Her pleasures were simple. Elaira had planted jonquil bulbs in a crock. Two quilted pillows stuffed with lavender and dried catmint seemed the gift of a moorland matron. She kept a vase filled with fallen owl and crow feathers. Three slate bits with holed centers strung on a thong hung over a black bowl lined with marble for water scrying.

The crammed trestle table where she mixed her herbals showed no trace of the frivolous dreamer. The brazier, the worn pestles and cups, the stone knife, and earthenware jars of the healer's trade lay jumbled together with scarcely a bare space between them. More herbs dried in bundles dangled from the rafters. Last autumn's rootstock was wrapped in willow baskets, carefully labeled, and preserved with sigils against rot. The runes and seals radiated a faint golden glow and the razor-edged haloes of energies that landscaped a spirit's perception. Shoved by another questing emanation of inquiry, Kharadmon sent back a pure touch of compassion, and back-traced the carrier ray to its source.

Beside the wand crystal used to potentize the fine energy properties of herbs, four rounded chunks of river granite rested in alignment with the cardinal points of direction. Their awareness was raised, and glowing faint blue with the intent the enchantress had set upon them to serve her as guardian protection.

Kharadmon found their awakened perception most piquant, since practice of earth magics ran against strict form. The peculiarity spoke volumes, that a small wisdom kept by field witches and country grandmothers should find credence here, in the dwelling of an initiate

343

Koriani. Since he was a friend, and brazenly uninvited, he held to strict manners. Each of the stones received his polite greeting in turn, phrased from the pure tones borrowed from the grand chord that sowed form in the void when sound first conceived Ath's creation.

"The language is lyric, but scarcely an offshoot of anyone's local dialect," observed the woman whose cottage he had invaded. Aroused, propped on one elbow with eyes like gray smoke fixed on the blank air by her worktable, the enchantress challenged her visitor unabashed. "Nor do herders address plain stones from thin air. If your presence is honest, please show me courtesy and reveal yourself."

Kharadmon did her bidding, and proffered the image of a tall, dapper personage furled in a flamboyant green cloak. He had seal-dark hair swathed white at the temples, a sharp, spade-point beard, and eyes the flat jade of a cat's. He swept into a bow, his hands clasped like a courtier's. "No sweet language of mine could have coerced your guardian stones to betray you. The one to the east has the temperament of a crone."

"That's why I placed her opposite the door. She won't bend for flattery or nonsense." Elaira sat up, mantled in blankets and a magnificent, arrowed fall of bronze hair. "You're Fellowship of Seven?"

For all her bravado, the import behind that query revealed a quick tremor of distress. Kharadmon straightened, still the posturing gallant. "Sweet lady, I'm the fourth to be granted the privilege of meeting with you face-to-face."

A shiver seemed to run through the woman's thin frame, though she masked the unease behind movement and tucked the rough wool up under her chin. "Should I thank Sethvir? Or doesn't he usually dispatch shades to pay unannounced social calls while his victims are disadvantaged and in bed?"

Touched to delight by her quick, stabbing humor, Kharadmon raised his peaked eyebrows. "For you, like the cat born with all of its claws, there exists no inequity, lady." His image lit with the wicked, bright smile he used to deflect Luhaine's baiting. "I see where your stones acquired their ripe tongues."

"Were they kind, they would have barred you from entry." Now the tremor caught hold, let the Sorcerer read into the deep, ragged pain behind her effort of seamless composure. "If you've come to speak of Arithon s'Ffalenn, be warned. My Prime Matriarch is his implacable enemy, and I but a tool to her hand."

Kharadmon flowed into pacing, carelessly letting one shin pass through an oak stool that lay in his path. "You are never a tool, lady, except by allowance or consent." His glance darted questingly side-wards.

The enchantress had gloved both her hands in the blanket and pressed the cloth to her mouth, as if the gesture framed a bastion against her own thoughtless and desperate speech. There were tears, bright as jewels, brimming her eyelids. Yet the pride in her silence was stark iron. "I was a six-year-old fool in trouble with Morvain's authorities," she admitted. Her voice held its timbre through sheer stubborn strength. "Nor are four crotchety old stones from a river bottom quite proof against the might of the Skyron aquamarine. Since my vows are not revocable, why are you here?"

"Why indeed?" Kharadmon pressed, and waited, poised utterly still.

But the woman did not ask for his help to unravel the conundrum he posed her. Raised self-reliant, too resourceful to seek pity, she lowered her fingers and laced them, sure and still, on the tent of her drawn-up knees. "Say what you came here to tell me, since you've already stolen my peace."

Kharadmon spun into vexed agitation, the breeze of his passage gone bitingly blunt as the frost that sang through his consonants. "Your prince has just learned that Koriani spellcraft can raise Lysaer's essence as a fetch. In fact, your Prime Senior laid a trap to ensnare him. Her minions used that cheating, uncivil trick of spellcraft at Riverton, to sad and disastrous effect. Earl Jieret's past war captain fell to his sworn liege's steel."

Elaira drew in a shaken breath, stilled as white marble in the darkness. "Ath's mercy, Caolle? Arithon's sword took down *Caolle?* Then what you have is a man torn by grief and entrapped in a web of despair. Is *that* why you came here? For advice to contain the Prince of Rathain's bitter conscience?"

Kharadmon stilled again, wholly noncommittal, but the volume of his silence became mistaken for consent.

Eyes shut, her hair like wound bronze tanged with rubbed glints where the ends curled, Elaira said slowly, "As I love him, I can tell you the truth. Give him his release from your blood oath sworn at Athir."

At Kharadmon's specious startlement, she stared back, nerveless as coal-fired steel. "Oh, I knew of his oath on the hour it happened. You had to have seen. Since the healing spells we engaged in tandem at Merior, an empathic link still remains open between us."

"You could use that to spare him the pitfalls, as you choose," Kharadmon ventured in angling argument to coax fresh review of her logic.

But Elaira shook her head. "I won't be his crutch. He needs none of my weakness. Nor will he thrive on any feminine instinct that gives him the child's role through mothering a grown man's mature pain. I urge you instead, return his free will. Give back his choice to own life or death. As things stand now, the very fact his hand is forced will only add coals to his anguish." The flex in her modulation snapped for a second, and revealed all the tenderness beneath. "Ath, I know him, none better. He has strengths and depths even he doesn't yet acknowledge. I believe with all my heart he will endure and survive even a grievous remorse such as this."

Kharadmon pressed her. "You could risk his life on that premise?"

Elaira stared back at him, level. "I'd let *him* risk his life. There was no evil done. He did not succumb to the Mistwraith by choice. Nor would he endorse a forced act of insanity by turning the craven and destroying the royal heritage Caolle sacrificed himself to preserve."

"He has lost everything," Kharadmon pointed out.

Elaira swallowed, fighting down the passionate need to give way, to lean on the Sorcerer's power and presence and find ease for her own stricken heartache. "His Grace of Rathain has already lost everything twice before this. What has changed since the banks of Tal Quorin?"

"Brave lady," Kharadmon conceded, forced to yield at last before the unflinching moral fiber of her love, and her relentless display of raw courage. "I see we have also underrated your strengths. Be very sure, I shall argue against any one of us making the same mistake ever again." His image snuffed out, leaving a turning, chill vortex of air that even the drafts treated deferentially. "With your stones' permission, I will leave you a ward, that your Seniors not know I have been here."

Then he was gone, in the space of a breath sped on northward, where, between Daon Ramon Barrens and the deep glens of Halwythwood his charge was to extend his appeal to Earl Jieret, *caithdein* of Rathain.

Behind him, he left the hollow drum of the rain and the cry of the winds on the lonely, dark moors of Araethura. Huddled in blankets, shot through with sorrows, Elaira released the hot flood of tears she would not shed in his presence. Her vows to her order left her no grace and no quarter. A child and a prophecy yet hung in the balance. Worse than death, she dreaded her inevitable fate, that on the day she next met with Arithon s'Ffalenn, in all likelihood she would be forced by her Prime to arrange for his final betrayal.

Legacy

The rain still smoked down over the marshlands of Mogg's Fen, ruffling the pools to a sheen like dark pearl, and greening the spears of the sedges. Through the passage of day and into the next night, the singsong language of running water seemed to leach endless tracks through Mearn's dreams. Undone in delirium, he raged aloud for Dharkaron Avenger to give him a place in Sithaer where, if he suffered, his nerves might be spared from the trials of incessant moisture.

Hands touched him, pressed him back and down into a maddening mire of clinging, smothering dampness. Mearn shouted. His protest emerged muffled against the rag somebody forced to his mouth.

A voice that splintered into a roar like flood tide implored him to be silent. Since he could not swear his outrage, or make his will known, he struggled, inflamed by the red rage of fever. Nobody succored him. A woman came instead, her hair strung with feathers. Red cheeked, dark eyed, and wrinkled as a harridan, she dealt his wet cheek a ringing, hard slap, then shoved a sticky wad of medicinal herbs into his mouth. Then more hands clamped his jaw while foul juices numbed his tongue, and the world spat white sparks and turned black.

Later, he rubbed open sleep-crusted eyes. Detached from all rage by debilitating weakness, he blinked. The sky had rearranged from weeping gray clouds to an opaque roof of pressed mud and sticks. He swallowed, and discovered his throat scraped nearly raw and a tongue furred in what felt like the wrack from a bird's nest.

Off to his right, somebody groaned. Mearn shut swollen lids, aching and limp, and too spent to unravel the straits that had left him flattened and disoriented with illness. His sinuses felt wadded with red-hot rags. Someone he could not recall had peeled his leathers from his body. A throw of sewn rabbit skins covered his nakedness. If the tanning was poor, his clogged head mercifully blocked his sense of smell. He lay, too inert to fight his discomfort, though the silky fur clung to his sweat-runneled neck, and gave rise to pestilent itches.

Reason eventually assembled the awareness that he sprawled on dank clay, enclosed by the dim mud-daub walls of a fenlander's hovel. The dwelling had no windows, just one door of rough planks set into an uneven frame of peeled logs. A rushlight burned in a niche lined with slate. The groans of human misery he had heard in his sleep were not any figment of dreaming. Arranged like bundles of inert cloth around him, he made out the shadowy forms of faces and limbs strapped in splints and stained bandages.

Mearn wrinkled his nose in distaste. He had seen enough field hospitals to recognize the close and fetid quarters where men thrashed in the throes of wound fever.

"Ath, how did I get here?" he croaked out in cankerous irritation. He struggled to sit up. Assaulted by immediate, wheeling faintness, he swore, then started halfway out of his skin as somebody gripped his left shoulder.

"Lie easy. You're safe." The deep voice of assurance was male, and sure in the grain as burled oak. "The fenlanders brought you among friends."

Mearn swiveled his head, his neck still mired in the garroting cling of damp fur. "Maenol? Lord s'Gannley of Camris?" Horrible, chilling fear ran him through. He might already be too late, with the casualties around him brought down by the very Alliance cordon he had tried and failed to thwart by his timely warning. "How long have I been ill?"

"A day and a night." The hold on him released, and the backlit shadow at his side revealed itself as the square, solid presence of the *caithdein* of Tysan. Sympathetically aware of Mearn's burning question, he answered in the same measured steadiness, "The men here were hurt several days ago. Their tactics delayed the Alliance's first march on Riverton."

Not too late; sapped by relief, Mearn clawed the offending fur from his throat and rubbed his lids to clear his clogged vision. Even dim rushlight showed him too much. The young man who held chieftain-ship of Tysan's clans looked more worn, more drawn, his dependable nature fretted into a hagridden mask of desperation since their meet-ing on the tideflats by Hanshire. Strips of white-and-black hide laced into his clan braid signified mourning for the blood cousins who had died to take warning to the Master of Shadow in Riverton. Raw endurance remained, of a stripe to rival a mountain for tenacity.

"My sorrows are yours, for the lives of your kinfolk," Mearn began. "I see you have word of their fate already."

The sturdy line of the shoulders under Maenol's mud-spattered leathers stayed unbowed. He said gravely, "You informed me your-self, though not in the mannered condolence you wished."

As Mearn stiffened, horrified, the Lord of Camris held him down. "No offense. Quite the contrary. In delirium, your rude opinion of Riverton's mayor and council delivered a more satisfying consola-tion." Nor was this *caithdein*'s settled patience in any way forced as he waited for an invalid to compose scattered thoughts and rejoin the tumbling mainstream of life.

Mearn drew in a breath like dipped fire. "Sky and earth! How much was I raving? The maps—"

"They are here. Your message of the Alliance invasion has reached us." Maenol's pale eyes, intense as his mother's, saw deeper than most through a difficulty. In response to an agonized, unspoken ques-tion, he said with sparse clarity, "When the fenlanders brought you in, you carried three map cases with seven sets of tactical instructions. If that's your concern, we have already acted."

Mearn sank back amid the drowning clasp of the furs. A hard chill speared through him. He had to struggle to keep his teeth from chat-tering. "Too late," he ground out. "I stumbled into that Alliance encampment by chance. By the time I lifted those plans, Lysaer's cor-don was already in place and closing."

The wind whipped against the gapped planks in the door. Traced in flickering rushlight, Maenol leaned forward, his rawboned hands clasped to his drawn-up knees. "Not all is lost. We've set lines in defense, and no few traps to slow the Alliance advance. Hounds can't trail in these fenlands. Many of the women and young ones may yet find escape through the mountains." Born of harsh times and a cruel practicality, he faced the unflinching truth with an unyielding equa-nimity. "We still have our hidden refuge in the Thaldein passes. That will just have to serve to safeguard those bloodlines that survive through another generation."

Mearn swallowed, silenced by the overwhelming weight of sorrows

Maenol tacitly faced without speech: that the high mountain defiles might foil the Alliance campaign for a short time. The *caithdein* knew, none better, that long-term safety for his people could not be assured without the ships just torn beyond reach by the Koriani conspiracy at Riverton.

"You stay to fight," Mearn managed at last. "Why?"

In the dimness, the hiss of the rushlight became the thread upon which existence loomed its firm fabric. A wounded man groaned. The wind outside bespoke more rain pending, and time stood as the comfortless enemy. Maenol regarded his interlaced fingers. His features were too grim for his twenty-five years, and the conviction that shaped the steel of his character lent his answer the grit of scaled carbon. "As Tysan's *caithdein* how could I leave? We are kingless. The land's charter, therefore, becomes mine to uphold, in line with my ancestors before me. I will not see living acreage carved up into boundaries, or trees and streams and hillsides exchanged as spiritless deeds of writ that ignorant men believe can be bought and sold without penalty. Earth's life and town greed share no common ground, and I have no stomach for compromise."

"Brother," Mearn said. He fought a hand free of encumbering furs and touched Maenol's wrist in the sympathy of their common heritage. In Third Age Year One, clanblood had been consecrated to uphold the Paravian law of unity which kept the earth's mystery intact. The world's bounty and heritage were the binding fiber to hold Ath's design, and no man's to unwind for the divisive reasons of domination and profit.

"We are not yet defeated." Maenol shifted, straightened, the dignity knit into the blood and the bone of him like the dauntless, stilled majesty the rooted oak must show the honed axe blade. "While there is one patch of forest in Tysan still free, I stay to resist the wrong thinking that threatens the peace of the Fellowship's compact."

"My heart would stand with you," Mearn s'Brydion said fiercely.

"Save us, you cannot!" Maenol's objection turned forceful. "Lysaer's Alliance has no respect for limitations. The day must never come, that your duke in Alestron should face the same forces of destruction our cursed prince has unleashed in Rathain and Tysan." Too large a spirit for the cramped gloom of the hovel, Maenol exhorted in sorrow, "Our people are scattered. Every man and woman who carries a bow has a vengeance arrow with the name of Lysaer s'Ilessid engraved on the point. There is no joy in this impasse. I implore you, do nothing. The very suspicion you had betrayed Lysaer's interests would break a most fragile balance. That would serve nothing, but call down sure ruin on your fugitive clans in Mel-halla."

"A sword in the hand would feel better, nonetheless." Mearn's frame sagged into his rough pallet of rushes, but his eyes held the banked fires of resentment. "The truth gives no ease. Not when the wind is likely to blow the Alliance's troubles our way anyhow." Hating the fact he must deliver ill news while lying flat on his back, he gave terse explanation why those engraved arrows were unlikely to find the man they were fashioned to bring down. "Koriani duplicity ran far deeper than we knew."

Diminished by the *caithdein*'s sudden, prepared stillness, Mearn faltered. The chills as his fever broke racked him in waves, and the difficult words he must now assemble weighed like piled rock on his chest. "Lysaer sailed for Corith, not Riverton," he forced out at length. Pinned now under Maenol's unnerving attention, he related how Koriani design had enspelled a fetch of Lysaer s'Ilessid to awaken the Mistwraith's geas and drive Arithon s'Ffalenn into madness. "The spells did exactly as the witches had planned, and set him to purpose-less flight."

The pause as Tysan's *caithdein* measured the root cause for the ruin of his people, contained a stunned force of sorrow to etch the moment into wretched clarity. The next breath Maenol drew could have made the air bleed, or the rain to change into salt tears in midfall.

When the first shock let go, and speech could be managed, the *caithdein* of Tysan had but one word. "Why?"

Mearn shook his head, without answer. "Who knows the mind of Morriel Prime? Her works always have run contrary to Fellowship concerns."

One of the wounded stirred from thick sleep. Maenol arose. All stripped grace and silent economy of movement, he crossed the hovel, dipped water from a leather pail, then borrowed the fen-woman's long-handled horn cup and made rounds. For the power of responsibility he carried, he wore neither ornament nor jewel, nor any token of finery to set him apart from his scouts. His brown, weathered hands offered drink to the wounded without care for rank. He gave encouragement as he could to those whose voices were fret-ful. With the natural dignity of a man who had never been pampered by servants, he rearranged soiled bedding for others who had slipped beyond conscious awareness.

On the cot, helpless and weak in the sweat of his broken fever, Mearn s'Brydion watched the care the *caithdein* held for his doomed people. He knew, then, whose hands had tended him through his

351

own illness. The rage rose up, blistering hot with the bite of an unendurable grief. He had read every one of those maps before Maenol, had seen how improbable lay the margin for hope. Truth and plain tactics held no ambiguities. Of the clansmen who had embarked to delay Lysaer's Alliance from containing Arithon s'Ffalenn in Riverton, few would escape to reach safety. The routes into the mountains from Caithwood would be sealed by armed troops within days. That would leave only the coastline, already set for blockade at Mainmere by the selfsame ships that, by Arithon's intervention, could have opened the way for clan freedom.

In the squalid, dense gloom of a fenlander's hovel, the sturdy *caithdein* in his ordinary leathers seemed unmarked by the immanent finger of fate. Divested of his weapons, except for a hunting knife, he paused on one knee to laugh at a woman's rough joke. He flipped back his braid of ash-colored hair, abandoned to a moment of boyish embarrassment as an older woman half-hidden in shadow called something back in rejoinder.

"My grandmother should be alive to hear that," Maenol said. Fingers still busy, he replaced a slipped bandage in frowning concentration. Then, as if disaster were not present and closing to put an end to the spirited joys of small byplay, he moved on, in meticulous care attending the needs of his wounded.

Mearn shut his eyes, too agonized to watch. Though his family was not fugitive, he knew forestborn customs too well not to shrink. In these wilds, the clan codes of survival imposed since the uprising held no space for pity or compromise. Any scout here who was unfit to walk would not be permitted to fall into the hands of the enemy. With Alliance troops marching in force on Mogg's Fen, those wounded would ask for a mercy stroke rather than burden their hale companions.

Under the faltering flare of the rushlight, whether man or woman, each face showed determined calm in the face of such shattering uncertainty. It was the outsider among them who battled the urge to stem fate and scream outrage for the injustice imposed by a prince turned false to his bloodline.

When Maenol had finished, he returned to Mearn's side, bearing the sewn-leather bucket and horn dipper. The citrine gleam of the rushlight traced the stubble on his cheek, and the gaps torn in the fringe on his deerskin where thongs had been cut off at need to mend, or tie bandages or tourniquets. Lives and blood would be given as generously to defend the needs of the land.

Mearn labored to regather the lost thread of his composure. Before accepting the same care from the hands of the man who was Tysan's reigning *caithdein*, he demanded in rankling honesty, "My Lord of Camris, why are you still here?"

The unaccustomed use of his formal title touched the younger man to stiff wariness. He crouched. The water dipper all but snapped as his hand clenched, and his face showed a startled and sudden vulnerability that exposed the youth in his twenty-five years. Carefully, slowly, he set down the water. Clan habit did not waste the gifts of the earth, nor take life's bounty for granted. He settled on his heels, strong wrists draped on his knees, while the carnelian glow of the rushlight mapped the small scabs ripped by briars, and the deeper scars left by war on his knuckles. In the same grave steadiness that flinched from no hardship, he answered, "I had to ask a boon of you, in behalf of my clans."

Thirst forgotten, Mearn refused the wringing weakness in his limbs and elbowed himself half-erect. Inadequately braced against the wadded mat of the rushes, he shook back the stuck ends of his hair and matched the other man's courage headlong. "Whatever you need will be given. My word on s'Brydion clan honor."

Maenol looked away, perhaps overcome. "I accept that word from you. Ath bless your willing heart." He paused, then added through a harsh burr of regret, "Sleep now. We'll speak of this later."

He arose, clasped his benefactor's shoulder in salute. Moved by uncharacteristic reticence, he averted his direct glance, and Mearn, in suspicion that the *caithdein* was weeping, did not press, but left the man to his dignified privacy.

The fever had left him light-headed in any case. Drained from his effort to keep focused composure, he gave in to the sapping demand of his flesh and lay back. Despite his fierce worry and his musty, uncomfortable nest of damp fur, sleep came like an ambush and dropped a black cloth over his thought and his senses.

When Mearn s'Brydion reawakened, the rain had cleared into a chill, gusty night. The rushlight burned now by the cracked open doorway, where a fenwoman bent, stirring fish stew in a cauldron. She was typical of her breed, built rawboned and short. Hair of an indeterminate color was bundled beneath a string cap. Feathers swung from hoops in her earlobes, and her layered skirts were sewn with dark threads into queer, whorled patterns and luck signs. Three purses made from the shells of marsh turtles dangled from a cincture at her waist, and two raggedy children sucked their fingers and peered from the well of deep shadow behind her. A third infant waved from the carry sack she wore strapped to her back.

If her household was typical, her fenlander husband would be faring out in his skiff, trapping and fishing for the family.

Mazed in the lassitude left by his illness, Mearn took too long to notice the hovel was emptied of wounded. The furs where the clan scouts had languished were rolled in neat bundles, lashed with fiber twine twisted from wild flax. Maenol s'Gannley was gone, replaced by a toothless elder smoking a root pipe. Beside Mearn's shoulder sat the last of the clansmen, a boy of twelve years. He had blond hair tied into a neat braid, and hands too large for his still-growing frame. Sword and knife rode in sheaths at his waist. His belt was his only ornament, sewn with simple designs of wooden beads and otter fur. He waited, stiff backed and composed in the tight, sober silence that came over the young in times of crisis.

Touched by foreboding, Mearn fisted the hand hidden under the covering furs. "My word as given," he said at careful length. "Just what have I bound into promise?"

The boy started. His dark eyes went wide, the pupils dense black as he realized his charge was awake. He said nothing, but instead drew two letters out of his jerkin and passed them across to Mearn's keeping. Then he rose. He seemed all knobby joints, rail thin for his growth. Despite tender age, he knew how to move to accommodate the adult weapons he carried. His voice had just started the change to a man's bass timbre, yet the cracking child's treble which intruded as he addressed the fenwife put no crimp at all on his dignity.

"Mistress," he requested, then thanked her generosity in fair dialect as she surrendered the use of her rushlight.

The flame jerked and fluttered as the boy brought the wick. Mearn ran his thumb over the wafer of wax, impressed with the ancient seal employed by Tysan's *caithdein* for personal use through the centuries of fugitive exile. The choice of devise confirmed a most risky necessity, unrelieved by the fact the first missive set down upon formal parchment was inscribed to his Grace, Eldir, High King of Havish. The second note bore Mearn's own name in a script astonishingly erudite. He had never seen Maenol's written hand. By wary habit, the forestborn clans wrote no messages for fear such might fall into the hands of town enemies.

That Lord Maenol had seen fit to wield pen and ink bespoke desperation and appalling finality. Mearn gripped the note, reluctant as stone. For an agonized instant, he wished himself far from this site in the marshes, that he not be the one left to carry whatever burden the sealed parchment was bound to contain.

Then, as if stung into branding impatience, he ripped the seal open. Wax bits arced through the gloom like flung gravel. Tagged by the flickering, uncertain flame light, eyes stinging with humility, Mearn read.

The first line requested his assistance to deliver an appeal to King Eldir. Tysan's *caithdein* would beg sanctuary in Havish for the refugee survivors who managed to win free of Alliance persecution against clanblood. The cost in pride, in pain, in the sheer magnitude of that understated defeat raised a knot of remorse in Mearn's chest. Scarcely seven years since the massive downfall at Vastmark, Prince Lysaer had succeeded in unseating a clan presence whose roots went back five thousand years. Words were inadequate to express grief and heartache, that without the trials of the Mistwraith's curse, these same clansmen should have sworn the same man their loyalty.

Now naught could be done but watch entropy march through the breach. The bottomless demands of trade and crown treasury held small care for the great mysteries. No means existed to soften the blow, that Arithon's loss of three brigs at Riverton might impact all future generations. A clan abdication of Tysan's free territory would leave townsmen free rein for desecration. Unwilling to admit such a weight of despair, Mearn stamped back bleak thoughts.

The boy watched his face, restrained into choked stillness that bespoke an unkindly awareness of consequences. The hovel's thick warmth and the fenwoman's welcome lent him no ease.

Mearn tucked the missive for King Eldir away, then fought for the presence to peruse the second request.

There, even Lord Maenol's steady hand faltered, the letters formed into jerked lines of reluctance as they charged s'Brydion by word of honor to admit the boy named Ianfar s'Gannley into Mearn's personal household as a page.

'*The boy is my uncle's son,*' Maenol's words stated, torn by small gaps as though more than once the ink had dried on the quill nib. '*As of this moment, he stands as my heir. He will inherit should I pass the Wheel without leaving progeny. My scouts just brought word the Alliance forces are closing the east passes. I see no better way to ensure the boy's safe deliverance from Tysan's sovereign territory. I charge you, by your family Name, keep him safe. If my war captain in Camris survives me, the raising of Ianfar must fall to him. Should that one perish, seek fosterage with any forestborn family you see fit. Be sure he learns what he must to rule after me.*'

Mearn closed his fingers, crumpling the parchment with a burst of animal savagery. Too grim to weep, he used all his anger to resmooth the crushed leaf, which he then rearranged into razor-sharp folds and tipped into the spill of the rushlight. Smoke billowed black. The acrid reek of burned hide rode the air, and the fenwife shot upright, exclaiming.

One look at Mearn's face shocked her silent. Through the dirty orange flame that crawled up the charred missive, the brother of Duke Bransian s'Brydion met the paralyzed gaze of young Ianfar s'Gannley. "I accept both charges laid on me by your chieftain. Will you formally agree to my guardianship?"

The boy tucked his hands under his arms, too brave to show he was shivering. He knew well enough his consent entailed the unspeakable possibility that his clans might be driven to yield up their sovereign charge in Tysan. Almost, his heart seemed to fail him. The underlit shadow thrown by his lashes made his eyes seem too large and too bright.

Then the stark, gritty fiber of his people shone through. "I bow to the will of my *caithdein* and the demands of necessity." His dignity far more in that moment than many men managed in a lifetime, he bowed. "In gratitude, s'Gannley gives thanks for the generosity of s'Brydion."

"This is not charity, boy," Mearn denounced, gruff. He tossed the last flaring embers to the floor, which was earth, and damp enough not to lend fuel to the sparks. "Under my roof, you'll have standing as a brother. Be sure, if my family has any resource to give, you won't end your days in foreign exile."

Had the child been younger, even by two years, a grown man could have extended his arm and gathered that awkward, stiff form into an embrace for comfort. But hardship had imposed too early a maturity. The boy stepped woodenly forward and offered his wrist for the clasp to seal a pact between adults.

Mearn blinked. He hoped the scalding blur to his sight was solely due to his fever. With his jaw clenched hard against any words that might unmask the pity that tore him, he pretended the wrists he accepted were not cold, or drawn taut with fear and uncertainty.

"Don't you mind, boy," he said in dry humor. "We're in poor state together. If I'm not mistaken, our first act must be to beg help from these fenlanders to thread a safe path through the mires. Then we might need to pilfer a post horse to make our way back to Avenor. We'll need to go swiftly." One corner of his mouth crawled up in fierce irony as he remembered the gold and the compromised straits of his house servant, still embroiled in the ruse concerning several sly doxies. Their extended service to cover his absence by now must have seeded a staggering collection of wild rumors. "If I'm going to look peaked, it's all in good form. A man who's been worn to his bones by three women over the course of a fortnight would be nothing else except prostrate. Do you bet?"

A tentative nod. The boy's fingers stopped trembling a fraction.

"That's good," Mearn assured, and lightened his touch. "We'll get along fine. I'll stand you five silvers for the bone buttons on your boot cuff that when my brother the duke learns about my randy reputation, he'll send sealed word by fast courier. He'll say that my dallying is shameful, and for clan's sake, the time's come to marry."

By then, Lord Maenol's bitter note of appeal lay in immolated bits on the floor. The fenwife bustled over, indignant, and poured water over the ashes.

"I could have used that to drink, pretty mistress," Mearn said in reflexive protest. He released his steadying hold on the boy, grabbed the empty bucket, and tucked it into Ianfar's stilted grasp. "Go, man," he urged. "Refill this for the lady, and take as long as you like."

The release came no moment too soon. Run to the end of his flagging strength, Ianfar bolted outdoors to unburden his anguish in private.

Left to the breathless scolding of his benefactress, Mearn shut his eyes against branding pain and the flame of a burgeoning headache. When the fenwife understood he was not going to argue, he managed a beautifully worded apology that sapped the very last of his reserves. Before the maw of oblivion claimed him, he made a vow with the unyielding endurance of black iron. Once back in Avenor, when Ianfar was delivered into absolute safety, he would seek out the name of the man who had betrayed Arithon's faith and precipitated the premature flight out of Riverton. For Lord Maenol's losses, and for the clans' forced abdication of their age-long stewardship of a kingdom, that one would suffer the harsh edge of s'Brydion justice until Dharkaron Avenger himself interceded to ask human mercy.

Three Moments

In a tavern along the road south of Middlecross, a middle-aged minstrel clad in scarlet sits down and tunes his lyranthe for his night's round of performance; and his accustomed audience of tradesmen and farmhands is swelled by a half company of crown soldiers under command of another man, whose nondescript mantle covers the sunwheel blazon of authority, and who hears through each ballad with mounting suspicion and a frown of incensed disapproval. . . .

A fortnight following Arithon's clean escape out of Riverton, his imprisoned accomplices are boarded into the holds of the three brigs newly commissioned; while the appointed royal captains call orders to make sail, Cattrick stands at the trestle in his loft, a sharpened shim of graphite clenched in his fist, and his heart lit with rage fit to murder. . . .

On the same day, Mearn s'Brydion returns to Avenor, Ianfar s'Gannley alongside him; and the first gossip he hears as he hands off his blown livery horse is the word of Princess Talith's fatal plunge from a high tower battlement, named by the shocked and mourning court as a suicide caused by despair. . . .

X. Pursuit

The three brigs newly commissioned under Lysaer's sunwheel banner raised anchor to a windward tide. Before the rip grew too stiff to ride for advantage, the pert little fleet raised stainless, fresh sails and began its mincing, piloted run down the estuary to ply open waters to Corith.

Confined in the narrow gloom of the mate's cabin, and crammed head and feet in a hammock ill suited to the frame and muscle of a man given lifetime service as a war captain, Caolle listened to the tense strings of orders which maneuvered the flag vessel, *Lance of Justice*, through her intricate, bending course down the narrows. Since his complaint that the fumes of fresh varnish turned his head, the door to his quarters was latched back and open. His ankles by then were already chained to forestall him trying escape. By the free air through the quarterdeck hatch grating, and the brackish miasma of the salt bogs, he mapped the layered headlands of a shoreline he could not see.

Moment to moment, Caolle rode his taxed senses. However his wound ached, he asked for no posset. Too easily, the reins of clear consciousness might slip his grasp and spin him back into circling delirium. The Koriani healer meant him well, but her remedies gave him sleep that brought nightmares, and no peace of mind when he woke.

359

Like a crippled, old dog, he felt he had outlived his usefulness. The enchantresses' meddling fed his unease, tick tight as they were with Lysaer s'Ilessid's Alliance. Dread fanned that anxiety, that his part in his liege lord's flight out of Riverton might become their best tool to clinch Prince Arithon's downfall.

Now the brig was under way, ostensibly to reinforce the s'Ilessid assault on the outpost at the Isles of Min Pierens.

Caolle was not resigned. Discomfited by the roll of rough passage as her crew worked ship in the tideway, he traded straight pain for awareness. The hammock swung and creaked from its rings as the vessel slipped astream of the ebb. Canvas cracked overhead, square sails caught aback, and steering cables hissed as the quartermaster spun the helm hard alee to swing her stern down the channel. Terse orders volleyed through the rocking lag of the stay, as drift bore the vessel past the sandy tongue of a spit. Then the shivering bang from aloft as her yards braced full to the wind; new foam dashed off the rudder. The brig regained way and sailed close-hauled down the neck of the Riverton Narrows.

Caolle's hammock rocked to the heel of the deck. He clamped his teeth and stifled the oaths that would draw unwanted attention. The straits of his captivity were worse than demeaning. The least cramp in his limbs could not be eased without begging outside help. His weakness was not deemed a reliable jailer: the festered wounds on his forearms were poulticed, dressed wrist to elbow in bandages which also served as restraint. Immobility left him more time than he could use without fretting.

Abovedecks, the leadsman called off the mark. The captain barked for a two-point change in course.

"Smarten up on those braces!" howled the mate to some laggards. "Are ye blue-water hands, or a pack o' coast-hugging galleymen?"

The lookout sang out and the lead line confirmed shoaling water. Other crewmen stationed at the port cathead let go the ring painter. The cockbilled anchor splashed to windward to a rattling fall of cable. While the bow was stayed through the tug of an eddy, Caolle pitched his forest-sharp senses to take fullest stock of his surroundings.

By now, he judged the ship's company included twenty-five combat-trained guardsmen. Half of these sprawled idle, polishing mail, or shooting dice for small coin in the galley. Their less seaworthy fellows shared the rail on the main deck, unmercifully rousted hither and yon by rushed seamen as the brig wore again, and the lee side changed port to starboard. Two dozen more sailhands berthed forward as crew, each one vouchsafed by merchant references or a paper with a justiciar's seal to affirm lawful background from a city of lifelong residence.

Others on board, Caolle recalled from the Laughing Captain's taproom. These included the brig's handpicked officers, a captain, two mates, a grizzled and temperamental quartermaster, and the serving-class appointments of cook, purser, and cabin steward. At large also was a street brat, caught stowing away, and pressed into crown service as ship's boy. His vociferous, guttersnipe insolence came and went through the companionway as he fetched and carried for the Koriani First Senior.

Since spells and scryings wrought through quartz-crystal resonance could not be made to span open salt water, Lirenda and the healer, brought along to tend Caolle, made passage on the same vessel. They shared the captain's quarters in the stern cabin, while the displaced officers occupied the chart room a scant breadth of a bulkhead away.

More orders sang out, and the brig hauled her wind; the changed quarter of the breeze wafted the smell of fish stew from the galley, mingled with soldier's oaths and the cook's nasal carping. By the bite of his temper and a doleful emphasis on assignment of unfair duties, Caolle learned that seventy-two of Arithon's accomplices, exposed by Koriani conjury languished, chained, in the brig's hold as well. By default, the two vessels trailing the flagship must bear the Etarran fighting companies imported to defeat the Shadow Master at Corith.

A war captain's instinct died hard, to know the strength and position of his enemies.

Caolle closed his eyes. From habit, he reconstructed the mate's cabin in detail from memory. On his right hand, a hanging locker leaked a tanner's tang of new oilskins; then a stand and basin, rowed with latched hooks holding buckets of drawn seawater and a mesh bag with lye soap for washing. To his left lay the mate's berth, and a small niche for an officer's sea chest, with a brass lantern mounted in gimbals overhead, swinging unlit to the toss of the hull. Caolle gave no ground to discomfort. He quizzed his recall until he knew he could find his way without mishap, even in total darkness. Then he catnapped as he could, restive with distrust and the incessant throb of bound wounds.

For a while, the rush and slap of rip currents in the estuary kept time to his uneasy dreams. He drowsed and woke and drowsed again. When sunset faded into silver-gray dusk, the vessel cleared the last shoals at the mouth of the inlet. The commotion as she raised topsails, then the change to the long, swinging roll of fresh sea swells sharpened Caolle back to full consciousness.

Flaring light jinked through a seam in the bulkhead as the cabin steward kindled the lantern in the chart room adjacent. A discussion in progress resumed on the heels of his departure. Through the staid clump of the captain's seaboots, a woman's soprano raised a snag which burgeoned into rife argument. The captain's bitten authority clashed into female rejoinder.

"We will not lay our course for the Isles of Min Pierens," Lirenda contradicted, chill as new ice on a freshet. "That was sheer presumption on your part since, in fact, our quarry will not sail there either."

The first mate's gruff bass backed his captain's disagreement, whelmed into thundering canvas as crewmen aloft shook out the reefs in the mainsail.

Then Koriani reply, in dictatorial steel. "No. By no means. Not only has the future been scried for full surety, but we have deliberately allowed Arithon s'Ffalenn to hear warning of Prince Lysaer's plans." In clipped, sulky venom, the First Senior qualified. "The Shadow Master knows an Alliance blockade will close over him if he sails to Corith. We've foreseen his reaction. He'll flee south for Torwent. Sealed forecast has already shown us the cove where he'll reclaim his sloop and embark. His point of vulnerability lies in the estuary at the head of Mainmere Bay. If our spellcraft restrains his shadows, your three ships plying the mouth of the inlet can pin him down as he bolts for open water."

"That's a coast run," cracked the captain, tired and brittle from the long, fussy hours of seamanship required to run the Riverton Narrows. "You'd have been better off to charter a galleyman who hauls cargo through Tideport and Mainmere."

"You're afraid?" Lirenda's derisive accusation chilled Caolle to ugly foreboding. "I'm surprised. Three ships with armed companies against a pleasure sloop crewed by one man and a bumbling, fat drunk would seem an auspicious engagement."

The captain's slow-strided pacing stopped short. "Do you take me for a fool? You speak of the shadow-bending sorcerer who caused the trade fleet to burn at Minderl Bay."

"Against whom you've the backing of the Koriani Prime Matriarch. Gainsay her will, and you also betray the Alliance of Light for refusing your help to corner the Spinner of Darkness." Lirenda cut off debate with aristocratic dismissal. "Do fetch out your charts, captain. Our course is a foregone conclusion. The trap which my order has set will be sprung, the fate of your enemy is already destined and sealed through multiple wards of grand augury."

Distressed to alarm in the salt-muggy confines of the mate's cabin, Caolle heard the captain expend his last argument. "I don't like your odds, witch. This felon commands the very fabric of darkness. No mortal fighting company can close on a prize they can't see. Nor can my quartermaster steer clear of the reefs if he's reft blind on lee shores in an inlet!"

"You worry for nothing." Lirenda arose to a breezy rustle of silk. The crack in the wall flickered as she crossed through the light to leave by means of the companionway. "The Master of Shadow will come readily to heel once he learns of our cargo of hostages."

"Are you mad?" The captain of the brig banged frustrated fists on his chart table. "The man's a fell sorcerer and a thrice-confirmed killer! Do you actually believe he'd give himself up to spare a mere coffle of lackeys?"

The latch clicked and held as Lirenda paused at the threshold. Her conclusion came freighted with menace to seize the hottest man's blood. "Then, captain, you must lay us a course for the Lanshire coast on the strength of my Koriani Order's requirement."

Lashed prone in his hammock, Caolle measured the stakes and weighed his own judgment concerning Prince Arithon's chances. He held no false hope. Set against the entrenched s'Ffalenn gift of compassion, the undermining sense of guilt engendered by just one accursed sword thrust seeded the opening for disaster.

Caolle understood he was not made as the realm's sworn *caithdein*, to test and grapple the fires of s'Ffalenn royal conscience. Nor could he swerve from implications that nagged like a poisonous aftertaste. He could not stand down, not for his life's sake: not after overhearing the harsh, focused hunger which charged the First Enchantress's tone at each mention of Prince Arithon's name.

Forty years with the burden of command left Caolle a sharp judge of character. Whatever Morriel's successor believed, her reasons for seeking the Shadow Master's ruin were entrenched and intensely personal enough to raise the hair at his nape. In defiance of despair, and the straits of mortal pain, Caolle gritted his teeth. He linked his fists through hemp netting and began in stark need to chafe the linen bound over his poultices.

Midnight brought the change in the watch, with the flagship leading her sister vessels on a dogleg course which would bear straight offshore for a clandestine passage, then bend on a rhumb line to make landfall through Mainmere Narrows. The fleet of three ran before following winds when the Koriani healer closed off the mate's cabin and laid down her satchel of remedies at Caolle's side. Each night and noon, she came to renew the regenerative spells on his wound, that strict schedule kept since the First Senior had remanded his care to her charge.

The lantern lit by the ship's boy at sundown had burned low, its weakened flicker made worse by the strong pitch of the swells kicked up by the equinox shift in the wind. The brig tossed stem to stern in long, rolling corkscrews, doused under back-fallen arcs of carved spray. New varnish sweated to the influx of sea damp. Snatched in crawling shadows and sliding spears of wan light, the convalescent stirred in his hammock. A groan escaped his clenched teeth.

Moved to pity for the wearing discomfort caused by the rigors of sea passage, the enchantress sighed and deferred her intent to trim the neglected wick. The sigils she required to reverse fatal wounding carried an unkindly resonance. Enspelled tissues closed at the price of nagging pain, and the clansman was stubborn as grit. He rejected those possets she mixed to bring ease through the gift of oblivious sleep.

Yet tonight, even his stiff pride seemed forced to bow before the demands of his suffering. "Something's not right," Caolle ground through a gasp. "The dressing's turned sodden."

"Easy. We'll see." The enchantress touched his brow, found him clammy with chill. Her frown deepened. She thrust a palm under the blanket. Caolle's shoulder and chest were also running fresh sweat. "You're fevered," she soothed in that bedside gentleness she used to disguise deep concern.

For the ciphers and seals still actively binding spirit to flesh were far from safe or beneficent. If Caolle's wound had gone septic, the same conjuries which regenerated torn tissue would outrace their proper intent. Sigils as a rule were unselective, a vectored spell of forced impetus. A starting suppuration would engage their figured energies, then turn on itself and run rampant. All risks came redoubled. Misread the first signs, and Arithon's liegeman could die in an hour, consumed from within by infection.

Now grateful for the dimness which masked peripheral distractions, the Koriani healer hooked out the silver chain which hung her spell crystal from her neck. She dangled the jewel above Caolle's flank, then shut her eyes and smoothed her awareness into trance. The peace of her craft settled over her mind and distanced the ship's clamor of stray noise. The squeal of the rudder cables dimmed into the mirth of the hands who idled on the afterdeck to share a lewd joke with the quartermaster. Channeled to heightened sensitivity through the attuned matrix of her quartz, the enchantress sounded each of the sigils intermeshed with the clan liegeman's life energies. Naught seemed amiss. The layered streams of vitality interlaced through his aura showed no ominous stain of dull gray. She listened, diligent, and rechecked her findings. The first sign of dissonance could be subtle in warning of fresh inflammation.

The explosive attack took her without warning. A hand grabbed her hair and yanked her headlong toward the hammock. Trance dulled her reaction. The sharp break from mage-sight hurled her dizzy, and the shock never let her assemble her balance to strike back.

Too late, she regretted her reckless compassion, to treat a man's pain before thinking to test the intent he might hold in his mind. Something hard clubbed her neck. She toppled with scarcely a cry. Panic coalesced into split-second instinct. She framed a sigil of air to alert her First Senior. Then power of defense slipped her grasp altogether as ruthless fingers snagged her spell crystal. The quartz tore from her hold. She felt the chain snap as her senses upended in spinning descent through bleak darkness.

Jerked out of sound sleep by an air-fired sigil of distress, First Senior Lirenda shoved erect on her berth in the stern cabin. The detested inconvenience of seafaring extracted rough payment for haste; her head thumped into the deck beams. "Motherless hell!" She thrashed free of damp blankets, her hatred of ships unabated as she rammed an elbow on the timbers which crowded the edge of her mattress.

"Dharkaron avenge!" She stood up and staggered as a bucketing roll nosed the brig down the face of a swell. No friend to water, the more so since her gifts of power were founded in firesign, she clawed back tumbled hair in annoyance.

Whatever mismanaged turn of disaster had upset the healer, ill temper would lend her no asset. Lirenda soothed her rattled nerves back to cool equilibrium. Gooseflesh raked her bare skin. She groped through the darkness to find the hook which hung her violet over-robe, then listened as she wrapped the silk over her shoulders. She sensed no overt disturbance.

Canvas and timber worked to the drive of fair winds. No deckhands shouted. Since naught seemed amiss with the crew, she chose not to summon the watch officer. The draw of filled sails and the surge of rucked foam rushing under the counter would defeat her best effort to keep her inquiry unobtrusive.

The captain's outspoken show of dissent still rankled the subordinate seamen. All on board knew the brig's easterly course had been charted under duress, and the enchantress was a fool who would give the ship's officers fresh grounds to challenge Koriani authority. Whatever had arisen to upset her colleague, the First Senior would have facts before she abandoned discretion.

Lirenda cupped her white crystal on its chain. Clad in the ankle-length fall of her robe, her porcelain shoulders doused under drizzled-ink snarls of hair, she strode on bare feet from her cabin.

The signature trail of the sigil led her past the chart room. The plank door was shut; she engaged her quartz focus to augment her senses, but no waking activity stirred in the darkness behind. The brig's captain slept, or else walked the deck, fine-tuning his vessel through shakedown.

Beyond the stepped bulk of the mizzenmast, the entry to the mate's quarters cracked open. The streamed phosphor track of the sigil originated within. Lirenda stole closer. She extended her awareness in tacit, light contact with her crystal, prepared at need to raise conjury.

The brig slogged through a trough and rose at the bow. Newly forged hinges swung free to her roll, and the panel gaped further open. The sultry glow of a failing wick etched the interior of the cabin, with the bulk of Caolle's hammock a dim silhouette overtop. Lirenda heard a woman's groan. Quickened to alarm, she made out a female form, held pinned and struggling beneath the rucked folds of a healer's mantle.

"What ails you, wench?" teased Arithon's liegeman in muffled, derisive clan accents. "Only boys mind a virgin. Keep still and enjoy the fine sort of fun you've been missing."

A hissed breath of rage escaped Lirenda's clenched teeth. "How *dare* you!" She closed the last steps, shouldered into the small cabin, and unfurled a barbed spell to stun the male occupant of the hammock into unconscious paralysis.

"First Senior, my lady," murmured Caolle in obliging regret, *from behind*, as the door panel crashed shut at her heels.

Before she could whirl, something hard struck her nape. Lirenda lost wind to curse her mistake as she measured her length on the decking.

She roused to the chill splash of water on her face. Restored awareness brought her the sawing throb of a headache. Her hands, her ankles, and her mouth were bound with strips of bandage filched from the healer's satchel. She was still in the mate's cabin, the velvety gloom thick with the scents of copal varnish and new planking. The ship's heel pressed her backwards. Someone had propped her shoulders like a doll's against the shut door to the companionway.

Runnels of water seeped down her brow and combed through the strands of her lashes. She blinked to clear her bleared vision.

"Now, don't ye look fit to murder," Caolle mused in soft threat. Not a half pace away, he sat braced on the sea chest with his back to the hanging locker. His feet were still fettered. The heavy iron chains had been inventively muffled with a slit length of sleeve off an oilskin.

He had unhooked the gimbaled lantern during the interval while his victim recovered full consciousness. The wick was now trimmed. A clear, bright flame stabbed mirrored reflections in the depths of inimical, dark eyes. "Foolish, to think I'd sully myself with a witch who kept me living as bait to bring down my liege. Not to mind," he ran on, as Lirenda jerked stiff. "She's there, in the hammock, triced up neatly as you are. How obliging of her to struggle and moan just as you made your appearance."

Caolle paused, flexed his shut jaw, and shook through a visible tremor. "Oh, I know I might die for my troubles," he admitted when the spasm of pain let him speak. "That's why we'll rush things along. Take my point straightaway, I'm a man who makes promises rather than blustering threats."

He raised his left hand. Something bright skittered and flashed to the bucketing toss of the hull: a quartz crystal on a sparkling length of fine chain.

"This belongs to your colleague," Caolle said. "But you're damned right to worry. Your own isn't still linked around your pretty neck."

Eyes pinned wide, pupils expanded and black in a stark and impotent hatred, Lirenda matched his stare like a baited tigress. Her dignity was rags. Whatever the cost to her rankled pride, she dared wait no longer to summon the help of a crewman. Bereft of her voice, she raised her bound ankles to hammer her heels on the deck.

Her captor had already foreseen that resistance and muffled her feet with nothing less than the folds of her mantle of office. That moment, the lingering chill of the draft gained a horrid and leveling significance. The gag stopped her shriek. Stripped naked as well as bound wrist and ankle, Lirenda paled to an explosion of rage all the more deadly for being mute.

"I didn't like being fingered by ladies I don't know, either," Caolle agreed in unswerving complaisance.

The length of his forearm was laced in fresh blood. His struggle to strip off both poultice and dressing had torn open his wounds, a just and fitting penalty for the unwise demands made upon half-healed flesh. Lirenda savored the petty satisfaction that the pain undid his dexterity. He made a rough job of tilting the lamp. Several minutes fled by while he fumbled to lift the latch which fastened the pane.

Yet he was not unnerved. Every ruthless art of Koriani observation failed to strip his cragged profile for other significant weakness. Bodily discomfort did nothing at all to blunt his tactician's mind. Caolle watched her conclude this, unfooled. He was too seasoned a campaigner to entertain false belief that an enemy held captive was no threat. In stony dispassion, he raised the strung jewel above the opened cover of the lamp. The healer's dedicated quartz jounced and spun on its tether as his unsteady grasp teased it back and forth through the flame.

Given liberty for speech, Lirenda could have explained that the wards on the stone would offset the ravages of fire. She displayed no uneasiness, that the attuned focus of her colleague's born talents should become this deadly man's plaything.

"She's a bonny enough flower." Caolle inclined his head toward the healer, his features filed iron, each suffering hollow bruised in dull shadow where crinkled flesh masked the bone. Never had he looked more the part of the hardened killer.

The healer who had obeyed direct orders to spare him watched back in glazed fear, her shining loops of blond hair netted through the rope mesh of the hammock. Each roll of the hull rocked her trussed form to and fro like a sausage.

"Would you say that her youth's an illusion?" Caolle mused. "There's a fact or two whispered in the lore of our clans concerning the ways of your kind." He lifted the gemstone, heated now, the unquiet shimmer of its facets thinly tarnished under a layering of soot. "Do you know, I've a perverse curiosity to find out how ancient your colleague really is."

Russet light wheeled as he shifted the lamp. The bent of his cruelty struck through at last as First Senior Lirenda realized he held an iron bucket braced between his tucked knees.

Her cry pealed into a defeating wad of cloth.

"Yes, the water was dipped from the sea," Caolle said in affirmation of her ghastliest nightmare. "Salt water and an iron bucket, I believe, were the talismans listed for the ritual to ground and clear a spelled crystal."

'But not elemental fire, never that,' Lirenda raged in gagged anguish.

Caolle's jet eyes held her pinned like a shark's as he opened his fingers. The chain with its irreplaceable pendant slipped free.

Hot quartz struck cold water. A sharp hiss, a shot geyser of steam, as the crystal shocked out of resonance and shattered. The fragments sliced in terrible, thin clangs against the metal confines of the bucket. Trapped helpless in mage-sight, Lirenda beheld a cloudy burst of static. Then an actinic flare of silver bloomed above the rim as wrought sigils let go, and a lifetime's figured energies bled off and vanished into air.

On the hammock, death visited with wrenching finality as the stabilized seals to retard aging gave way. The healer's slim body bucked once. An inhuman screech shrilled through the linen wound in layers across her mouth. Muscle, nerve, and bone, her body convulsed, shivering the hammock on its rings. Her bound limbs thrashed. Joints cracked and cartilage popped to the lash of unnatural stresses. Spasmed hands jabbed and fought their restraints, then seemed between heartbeats to shrivel. Tendons contracted. Splayed knuckles bent. Bone clenched to bone, leaving not fingers, but claws, cranked tight into rigor like the leg-folded husks of dead spiders.

Then the fit which contorted the woman's wasted sinews let go. The remains sagged limp and the covering cloak slid away.

"Daelion Fatemaster's mercy," Caolle gasped, despite himself stunned into pallor. Throughout his rough life, he had killed countless times, but never so hideously as this.

For the hammock now cradled the shriveled corpse of a hag which could have languished three centuries in the grave. Leached cobwebs of hair trailed off the wax skull, swaying to the roll of the ship.

Caolle recovered himself first. Having grappled the horrors of death all his days, he averted his eyes, more concerned with the living enchantress held captive at his feet.

Lirenda gave him back a sheet-gold glare of pure murder.

For of course, he possessed a second purloined crystal to spin in cold threat above the lantern flame. Despite features pinched by sleeplessness and suffering pain, his glacial deliberation left Lirenda in no doubt that her peril was real. This was the clan war captain who had helped Arithon s'Ffalenn engineer the atrocities at Tal Quorin and the Havens, and after these, the most unconscionable of all, the thirty thousand casualties which had bloodied the field in one hour at Dier Kenton Vale. He owned no unmoored nerve to revolt. The First Senior watched, wholly defenseless, as Caolle hooked up the braided chain which fastened her personal crystal. He rebalanced the lamp, played the stone through the flame, his ultimatum served up in a silence like dammed acid.

No threat, but a promise: he could repeat his lethal act if he chose, and strangle his conscience pangs afterward.

"I'm glad that you grasp the true reach of the stakes," he observed as he measured her stillness. "Now listen up sharp, because here's how we're going to play this."

Lirenda heard him through, racked by humiliation. The shame bled her sick, that she had ever dared to take personal liberties with Morriel Prime's intricate plan. When she stayed Caolle's death, she should have recalled he was a scarred veteran, clanbred to serve s'Ffalenn royalty. Liegeman to the bone, he would see her killed, and care not a whit if he lost his own life in the balance. The pitfall of her pride lent him his foothold for victory.

He survived by her weakness, and refused her even the face-saving mercy of asking her word of agreement. Pragmatic as earth, he rifled the dead healer's satchel, then used her stone knife to slice through the ties which bound his live victim's ankles. While Lirenda's fire-hot quartz swung suspended over the maw of the bucket, he skidded the blade across the wood deck for her to fumble and clasp. Through seemingly endless, awkward minutes, she wrestled to manipulate tied wrists and brace the haft between her bare knees. She was left to saw her bonds free on her own, and to cut away the sour knots of the gag.

Caolle's gaze never wavered despite the pounding the ship's motion dealt the reopened wounds in his flesh. He knew his limits, and had sounded hers: he expected she dared raise no outcry.

"I don't envy the death my order will mete out for your acts of coercion and murder." Scuffed dusky red with the marks of his handling, Lirenda arose with a glacial sangfroid and a fury beyond all forgiveness.

Caolle's brows met in a frown of contempt. "I'll shrug off their sting, you bloodsucking spider. Nothing else matters but that my prince should escape from your unclean web." He flicked the chain. Her crystal shivered a bare fraction above the rim of the bucket; close enough to make her heart shrink and skip, he well knew. The quartz would not escape sure destruction if she tried the least hostile move with the knife.

"So, die with me, bitch," the clansman invited. "Lacking your guidance, I very much doubt an untried fleet of three can take on Prince Arithon and survive."

His frank male regard became statement enough he was content to rest on that judgment. Lirenda snatched the folded silk from under her feet. She reclothed herself in graceless, clipped jerks, then spun on her heel to depart.

"Ah, no," Caolle snapped. "That knife stays with me. And remember, the oil in this lamp won't outlast a quarter of an hour."

That was the paltry allotment of time he gave to complete his demands. "You'll shut yourself into your cabin after that." The quartz flashed and spun its unequivocal, dire warning. "One step wrong, raise one whisper of alarm, and your doom at my hand is a certainty."

Lirenda quashed back her overwhelming blind rage. She had no recourse. Perform as he asked, and Caolle might keep his word and set her ashore to go free. Guarantees were all forfeit. His perilous ploy must be launched and forced through before his promise could be put to the test. Nor was Lirenda's own risk of exposure assured a felicitous outcome. She could shrink a man's bollocks out of fear for her rank, but sham could not survive direct challenge. Deprived of her quartz link to empower her drawn sigils, she had no sure means to conceal the betrayal this fell bargain would level against the brig's unsuspecting crew. With her crystal under the threat of annihilation, she could fashion no spells. Even the petty illusions devised by the least tutored hedge witch lay outside the reach of her talent.

The predicament galled her to singular bitterness. Brought under coercion, and alone on the sea, she could blame no one else for her downfall. By her own headstrong miscalculation, the end play to Morriel Prime's grand conjury might fall to an inexcusable reversal.

The latch to the mate's cabin clicked shut after the First Senior Lirenda's departure. Caolle slumped back against the bulkhead of the hanging locker, his large frame shaking head to foot from the pain in response to unwise exertion. He dared not acknowledge the grisly remains in the hammock. His nerves would revolt. The bucket would become an immediate catch basin for the rejected contents of his stomach. The minutes crept past, while he sweated. Ath knew, he set small store by prayer. Nor would he yield to his hypocrite fears, and beg the creator's indulgence.

The plan set afoot rode now on the strength of First Senior Lirenda's stung pride. For Arithon s'Ffalenn, *everything* hinged upon her counting ambition above her own life as a bargaining chip.

Caolle braved another shuddering wave of discomfort. Well seasoned to danger, plagued by agonized doubts, he flicked the small chip of quartz crystal through the lantern flame like a talisman. While the light sparked in demonic patterns from the facets, he reviewed all the small things which could spin awry. One single upset would create a cascade, calling down risks like rowed dominoes.

The witch could stop him, and die. Or she could pitch her wits against his word of honor, and hope for a mistake to spin the odds back in her favor. Few men aboard ship would gainsay the will of the Koriani First Senior. Not without reason. Her orders would not raise immediate questions; nor would anyone think to deny her a visit to the convicts in the hold.

The brig pitched through a trough. Caolle locked back the groan which threatened to rip free as the jostling speared fresh torment through his flank. His vigil over the crystal and chain must not flag, though his vision blurred, and reeling spells of dizziness leached at his will to stay conscious. On deck, he thought he heard the watch call the hour. No shouting started, nor did he pick up any other small sign of anything gone amiss.

The sails creaked to the bearing pressure of the winds, and the foam slammed and lisped through the rudder.

Caolle clung to the reassurance of each sound. He endured the grim seconds one after the next in tight-breathing, bulldog tenacity. Inside a few minutes the lamp would burn dry. By then, the last of Arithon's collaborators must be set free from their chains. Either their little hired captain, a foul-tongued West Shandian, would arrive bringing confirmation, along with the keys for the leg irons and also the brig's forward arms locker; or Dharkaron damn the consequences, Lirenda's quartz focus would be dropped in salt water to shatter.

No loophole existed, outside total failure. Whatever the outcome, Caolle understood the harsh stakes. He might buy his prince one last chance for reprieve. In the unlikely event he survived abused wounds, and won this wild gamble against fate, for himself, the days he had left must be numbered. For his cold-blooded murder of the healer, if not for balking Lirenda, he was now a man marked apart for Koriani vengeance.

Second Upset

Night advanced. In the open waters of Mainmere Bay, the turn of spring stars crossed through the zenith to the complaint of raw winds, chasing their freight of fretted wavecrests. The sea heaved black and molten, web silver beneath cloudless skies. Across a tableau like spilled indigo, the three Alliance brigs sailed in convoy. In the main crosstrees of the second vessel in line, the lookout hailed the watch on the quarterdeck.

"Trouble's here. *Lance o' Justice* looks to be listing to starboard."

Minutes later, the fitful flash of a signal lantern confirmed that the flagship was taking on water. The mate himself climbed the ratlines to the crow's nest to translate the lines of blinked code.

"Deck there!" he called. "She plans to heave to! We're asked to round up alongside and take on most of her cargo of prisoners."

The surly first mate snapped closed the ship's glass, considering, while the air plucked moist fingers at his cloak, and the dark rim of the horizon swung like a plate. By the time he completed his descent from the rigging and conferred on deck with his captain, their ship's compliance was settled. The exchange made plausible sense. Many of the criminals packed onboard the *Lance* were craftsmen trained as skilled shipwrights.

"Can't be a blighted loose timber in her hull their sort can't be press-ganged to fix." To those crewmen who were wont to dodge sail drill to eavesdrop, he snapped, "It's the other wretches who are dead-weight we'll pick up. Sailhands set in chains for conspiracy with the

Master o' Shadow. Their carcasses litter the decking in the hold. Dharkaron's black arse, that's all got to be pulled to see which faulty seam the *Lance* has sprung in her bilges."

Return signals were sent, then sails and course altered to draw the two vessels side by side. The swell was running too high to grapple. Boats were swayed out to a melee of shouted orders and uncertain flickering lanternlight.

Then, through moonless dark, the longboats rowed back, trailed by others put off by the *Lance*. Each craft breasted and slogged down the waves, made unwieldy by their protesting burden of prisoners. The first boats reached the brig, to redoubled confusion, since convicts in irons could not climb the side battens. One by one, they had to be hoisted aboard like landlubbers in a bosun's chair. The clumsy maneuver raised a running, obscene commentary from those among them who were seamen. The most ribald and ruthlessly damning remarks were volunteered by a swarthy West Shandian captain who proved vitriolically loyal to Prince Arithon.

The brig's snappish mate peered down his nose at the turmoil fanned over heaving, jet waters. "Pitiful waste, that leg irons do naught to crimp shut the yap on that wretch."

For no mark proved exempt: the prisoner possessed a deadly sharp eye for slack seamanship, and a tongue to scale rust from black iron. Worse yet, his railing came poisoned with wit to crack the most dour man's ribs. The oarsmen who ferried him across in the longboat lost their timed stroke, unraveled into helpless laughter. They arrived, doubled over their banked oars, shut eyes leaking tears, while wind and drift fetched them headlong against their mother ship's side strakes.

The sea rose and dipped; varnished gunwales raked new planking to a roaring scrape of gouged wood.

Screams from the outraged officer topside collided with the Shandian's peal of ridicule. "Ath, you blind ninnies! It's a wonder you all managed to get yourselves born, if you'll row for a coxswain who rams a brig broadside with his eyes open."

The victimized oarsman shot from the stern seat to defend his maligned competence. In calamitous mistiming, the shove which fended the longboat off the ship rocked into the rising lift of a swell. The coxswain windmilled his arms and sat down with a smacking splash in the ocean.

"Dharkaron's arse, lookit you!" cried the Shandian in amazement. To rounds of explosive chuckles from the other boat's crews, and against jeers from the gallery of idle hands just arrived to crowd the brig's rail, he ranted, "I'd have to give my one-legged grand auntie the better odds to stay upright! Not only can Lysaer's brave seamen not *row*! By Ath, cold sober, they can't even keep their bungling butts dry in a longboat! If this is the measure of an Alliance royal ship, then for mercy strike my chains. I swear, I'll drown sooner if I'm forced to ply my fortune under the same breed o' captain."

"Silence that upstart!" the brig's master called down from the quarterdeck.

His command passed unheard. An oar splashed to a murderous yell from the swimmer.

"Toss the poor wretch a rope!" cried an onlooker.

"Better not," quipped the Shandian. "He'll just get it looped round his neck."

His bent of hilarity turned from harmless to obstructive as derisive suggestions flurried down from those sailors on deck who were still safe and dry, to the oarsmen who manned the indecorous longboat. Each remark proffered a more outrageous solution to fish their soaked coxswain from the water.

"Why bother?" The Shandian laughed in withering disgust. "Sharks don't care beans if they eat stupid meat."

"I said, shut that wretch up!" Flushed with ill temper from being ignored, the brig's captain stormed from the quarterdeck.

He plied elbows like rams and laid a path through the pack of shirkers amidships. Forced to stumble over clusters of chained prisoners, he shoved aside the last gawkers. But his new vantage at the rail gained him small satisfaction. Below him, wild splashes and a steady round of oaths issued from beyond a rocking circle of lamplight. To his left, some inveterate pest was taking odds down for wagers, as though anyone on shipboard could reliably sort out the roistering mayhem ongoing under cover of darkness. Scribbled reflections thrown off murky swells defeated the most determined attempt to sort out the salient details. Nor could a captain enforce his chain of command without correct names to assign to the faces of the miscreants.

Left no sure target for reprimand, he locked horns at last with his mate. "Are we running a shambles?"

"Well, ding me dead!" whooped the Shandian in renewed delight. "We're getting the old man himself, come to teach us lowlifes the obvious."

The captain lost his temper. "You oarsmen! Let that oaf in the water shift for himself. I want every Sithaer-forsaken one of these prisoners clapped in the hold straightaway! We make sail in an hour.

By then, the last boat will be stowed in smart form. If I hear any laggard's still bumbling at the oar, he'll be cast off as flotsam for the sharks!"

"Oh, smart thinking," cried the Shandian in whetted, bright sarcasm. "Leave the shirkers adrift. *I* wouldn't want to strike topsail yards, either, underneath of some louts who can't hoist their flea-bitten bones up a side batten."

"Gag that prisoner, or kill him," snapped the captain to the mate, who still chuckled at his shoulder. "Whatever it takes, bring our men back in line. I don't care if you have to break heads, just show me a diligent crew!"

Far from cowing the sailhands back to order, his enraged threat of violence only seeded a frenetic, new snarl of confusion. Sailhands jostled and yelled oaths from behind. They pressed their captain's stance, apparently possessed by a brainless urge to start brawling. More shouting erupted from the oared boats port *and starboard*. Then both lanterns were doused in unison. Darkness clapped down, an oddity which meant the brig's deck lamps had also extinguished. Screams ripped through the laughter before anyone realized: the boats alongside were not friendly.

The prisoners themselves were escaped from their chains and bearing arms in a battering attack.

"Ath preserve, we're being boarded!" The brig's captain shouldered past his first mate and fell flat, still yelling. Other men went down with him, raining blood from slit throats. More onlookers skidded and crashed from missteps in warm puddles as the enemy's murdering steel chewed through their disorganized resistance.

"Daelion save us all, it's the Shadow Master's treachery!"

For the crews who brought in the longboats from the *Lance* were not the same ones who had manned the oars at the launching.

In belated distress, the brig's captain screamed for his quartermaster to ring the alarm. "Sound warning to the third vessel! Let them hear that we're under assault! The *Lance*, save her, must be already fallen to the enemy."

"Can't, sir!" His officer's explanation filtered back, harried, through the percussion of steel striking steel, and live flesh and bone in maiming thuds. "Some whoreson has cut down the ship's bell!"

"Sithaer, this can't happen." The captain locked his teeth, fought his way upright, and ducked a bloody sword. He plowed through the chaos and grabbed his first mate by the scruff. "Get below! Now! Roust out that useless Etarran fighting company! We need them to kill as they're paid for."

But the bad news returned, that the royal men-at-arms were not sleeping or deaf, but confined. Some fiend had battened the hatches.

"They'll come out disarmed, or be poisoned with smoke," said a stranger with soot-blackened features who must have crept aboard through the thrashing display put on by the posturing coxswain. "Since we don't rightly care if the poor bastards suffocate, you might want to declare them our captives."

"You won't get away with this." The captain stiffened to the prod of a sword at his spine, then flinched, as beside him, his arguing mate was cut down by a stroke that gutted him to the navel.

Then, the insufferable last straw, the Shandian captain swarmed up the strakes and leaped the rail in swaggering insolence. "Strike your colors and surrender this vessel." His grin came and went, all uncivil, sharp teeth. "Or die valiant while we run up the leopard of Rathain. It's all one to me. This brig's already befouled to her scuppers. We're going to have to find pails and swab up your mate's liver, anyway. Refuse, and you'll just make that unsavory task the more grisly."

Reckoning

The meeting took place just past dawn in the *Lance*'s overcrowded chart room, the aftermath of hard action reshaped to crisp order by the Master of Shadow's freed henchmen. Fate and Caolle's courageous ingenuity had bought them a stunning reprieve. Theirs now to decide, the new course of action for the Alliance's two suborned vessels. In addition, they held the Koriani First Senior and fifty smoke-sickened men from the Etarran fighting company, kept alive for use as hostages. The latter had been imprisoned in the hold where, lately, their ebullient captors had escaped the selfsame misfortune.

The vessel still listed, albeit suspiciously. No hands could be heard manning pumps. The defeated captain rowed across from the other prize cursed in hindsight, now aware the flagship's ballast must have been shifted to lend her the appearance of leaks and sprung planking. On deck, in the pale flood of daybreak, he had deciphered the sequence of signal flags being strung up on a halyard. In due time, the third brig still sailing in legitimate crown loyalty would receive placid word that the *Lance of Justice* intended to retire to Tideport. Her course change made plausible sense; once in sheltered waters, the convict shipwrights she carried could ostensibly mend her stressed timbers.

The two other brigs, in tandem, would sail east for Mainmere Narrows to effect the blockade intended to trap Arithon s'Ffalenn. No break in procedure hinted of problems. With appearances maintained, the assumption followed suit that the flag captain's sealed orders had been transferred to a sister ship with sound seams. The third vessel would have no reason to suspect her command ship was now manned by armed enemies. Undisturbed, still serene, she remained unaware of the past night's nefarious piracy.

Tired to the bone, his breeches and shirt splashed with dried blood from his murdered first mate, the brig's deposed captain currently languished in the same chains lately struck off his Shandian counterpart. The ignominy left him indisposed at sea for the first time since he was a ship's boy set free of his tearful mother's apron strings. His shame was not eased by the damning sharp seamanship displayed by a band of rank criminals.

Behind the chart desk, bound in plain rope, sat his fellow officer in misfortune. The dispossessed captain of the flag vessel, *Lance*, appeared disheartened and pale, unmarked by signs of rough handling. His clothing was still uncreased and clean, and his face showed no worse than the wear of taut nerves and lost sleep.

Packed around the chart table, in swift, whiplash dialogue, the escaped shipwrights and crewmen, and another man who proved to be a clanborn scout, exchanged viewpoints. The course and direction their strong words debated had nothing to do with Tideport as a first port of call.

"Dharkaron avenge!" the brig's captain whispered in bleak fury. These devils can't just spin us around and start gutting trade galleys for spoils!"

The iron-haired flag captain turned a face with sad eyes, his shrug strained by the pull of his bonds. "You think our last brig can fight past surprise and prevail?" His mouth flexed in resignation as he looked at his boots, worn at the toes from his distinguished record of crown service. "No. You'll hear, if you listen. They've planned the last move. Our sister vessel will be attacked after sundown. She'll surrender or burn, her fate to rely on the fight put up by her seamen."

The beaten man's tone shocked for its flat certainty.

"Why did you give in?" asked the captain, painfully aware that he addressed a colleague he had once respected as his senior commander. "When you suffered attack, you sent us no signal. What made you betray the Alliance?"

"They suborned the Koriani First Senior, Ath knows how. She called me below, and I walked straight into an ambush. Is it so hard?" The fleet captain coughed, eyes averted, while he shifted his shoulders to accommodate the splash of the wavecrests retreating beneath the stern counter. Concerning the proud ship he had relinquished to the marauding use of the enemy, he had disgracefully little to relate. "That fiend of a West Shandian gave me a choice. Leave this vessel intact to Lord Maenol's barbarians and endure a five-day run into Caithwood, or else stay in chains and be bound over as hostage to the Master of Shadow. Better, I think, to survive as a traitor, than to risk death and Sithaer knows what sort of evil at the hand of that servant of Darkness."

But the brig captain dared not say what he thought, that after the royal edict condemning clan prisoners to lifelong misery as galley slaves, he very much doubted Lord Maenol's scouts would let any townsman walk free.

Much later, the conference in the chart room broke up. The brig drove east on her bearing, and the Alliance prisoners settled under tight guard, when a man tapped quietly at the door to the stern cabin. He awaited no answer, but slipped into the stillness within.

The one who kept vigil by the berth where Caolle lay arose, gave a nod, and departed. The newcomer settled down in his place, and without asking, volunteered all the news.

"Everything's been decided just as you wished, and no argument. The brig's to be rechristened just *Lance*. She'll sail as Arithon first planned at her launching, and take on a crew of Earl Maenol's clansmen. We can't speak for them, here. They'll have to determine which course to take, whether to pick up the Shadow Master's orders at Innish, or to sail west to Corith and bid against Lysaer for any of ours who may still be alive."

Caolle lay with his eyes closed, his breaths fast and shallow and his skin like limp parchment with suffering. "The plan's sound enough," he whispered at long length. If the men chose the fight in the Isles, they would have the brig and the Koriani First Senior as bargaining chips, as well as a sea captain and the Etarran company to play for an exchange of hostages. "The First Senior's jewel is well away?"

The man he could not see paused a moment to smile. "Aye, so. She let fly with unlovely language when she heard. If the brig's crew wins through, they'll do as you asked, and send her spelled quartz on to Prince Arithon with your compliments."

For certain, Caolle knew, he himself would not live to see through the events he had used his last wits to enact. Still as he lay, he could feel the warm life seep from his limbs. This, his last campaign, was fought against an enemy no steel could conquer. Spellcraft had no remedy that his straightforward war strategy understood. In slow and insidious progression, his extremities were invaded by a crawling, unnatural numbness he could only presume was the backlash set loose when he had shattered the healer's quartz crystal. No recourse remained as the Koriani seals which kept his body alive undid themselves through attrition.

In time, he asked if it were nightfall, the cabin seemed so cold and dark. The roll of high seas dissolved into the spiraling spin of blank vertigo. He could not feel his blankets. The breath in his lungs felt insubstantial and light, not like true air, but some vaporous drug which wafted his mind into dizziness.

"It's afternoon," the man said, never far from his side. His accent had the syrupy vowels of the southcoast, and his hands, a shipwright's thick callus. "The curtains aren't drawn. You can't see the sunlight through the stern window?"

A pause came, through which the clansman said nothing, and upon which cold truth paid attendance like a vulture.

Then, in a tact striking for its compassionate acceptance, warm fingers closed over Caolle's shoulder. That firmness he could feel distinctly, and the craftsman's straightforward kindness as he spoke. "Never mind. Day or night, should it matter? Say whatever you want to Prince Arithon and your kin. One of us will see your thoughts reach him."

Across a span of gluey distance, Caolle regrouped scattered wits. He had no words, then or now, to express what he felt in his heart. Gruff to the bone, no dabbler in niceties, he could not shed his flint-edged habit of honesty. Nor could he let go of life in false peace. He gave in, content to let his ornery nature have his last breath. For his final, most lacerating care and his need to release a friend's burdened conscience, he assembled his thoughts as sparely as arrows to be shot in hard arcs toward the future.

"Let my people and my prince hear that I died in the assault to toss out the Koriani witches. No less than plain truth." Caolle denied clutching fingers of pain just enough to wrench out a gritty, disparaging grin. "Tell the Teir's'Ffalenn, too . . . every word I said to Dakar at Riverton is still binding. But add one thing more. . . . I've survived many worse than the pinprick he gave me. His Grace has a puny sword arm, and may Dharkaron Avenger damn him for a weakling if he doesn't choose another liegeman to stand at his shoulder in my place."

Turning Points

In the Isles of Min Pierens, where Corith's ruined fortress notches a sunset sky, Prince Lysaer s'Ilessid reviews disposition of his troops, his war galleys, and the captured brig, *Cariadwin*, awaiting with keen anticipation for the hour when Arithon s'Ffalenn will be led by the Koriani witches to sail into his preset ambush. . . .

In the mountain wilds of Taerlin, Maenol s'Gannley and his dwindled band of scouts meet the swords of Alliance forces, and while clan blood flows yet again to allow the threatened families to flee behind them, the *caithdein* whistles the retreat, too aware that no more time can be bought for his people; either King Eldir will grant his petition for sanctuary, or all will be lost on the wooded shores of Mainmere. . . .

Stopped to water horses on the Middlecross road, the Hanshire captain, Sulfin Evend, straightens up from discussion with a dairymaid, and his sudden flush reveals his elation as he calls his armed troop to attention: "We're onto him, now. The Shadow Master and his fat henchman passed yesterday, apparently driving an oxcart. There's a company of sunwheel soldiers with Lysaer's Crown Examiner ahead of us. If we move fast without springing the alarm, we could catch our quarry by nightfall. . . ."

XI. Fire and Sword

Rumpled, hungry, all but giddy with fatigue, the Mad Prophet reined his rackety oxcart alongside the wayside tavern's stone wall. After a seven night of sleeping in thorn brakes, he smelled little better than his draft animals. The beasts stood with lowered heads, tails switching to dislodge the black, biting flies which descended upon the Korias flats from the moment the sun thawed the soil.

"Ath, are you certain you're up to this?" He filched a glance sidewards, not trusting appearances as the Masterbard stepped down, his lyranthe slung from a strap at his shoulder, and the silence like poured lead between them.

The lacerating despondency settled since Riverton this morning seemed tightly leashed. Arithon had washed and shaved at a streamside. His torn shirtsleeves were mended in meticulous stitches; the tailored cuffs cleaned, old bloodstains bleached away by the lye soap begged from a dairymaid. His dark leathers had been brushed until the singed patches were scarcely noticeable. Gaunt from eight cold, wet days of foraged meals, the Master of Shadow looked more the part of a courier or light swordsman than a bard on itinerant sojourn; until he turned his head.

Then the light touched his face and revealed what he was: a self-haunted fugitive with exhaustion etched down to each fitted angle of bone.

"You're unwise to try music in public so soon," Dakar berated, concerned for the exposure an honest performance must demand.

"We have to eat. We haven't got a coin between the two of us, and I'm up to this because it's safer than risking my fingers trying to skin coneys with a main gauche." The gathered, black brows let go of their frown and tipped up in acidic inquiry. "Unless you prefer snaring songbirds? I thought not."

"Sithaer's dark furies," Dakar swore. "Why do I stay with you?"

"For maudlin entertainment, no doubt." But against every precedent, Arithon s'Ffalenn was first to turn aside.

One charged moment led into another, an abrasive progression unbroken since the hour Caolle had fallen. Beyond the wall, a woman soothed a crying child, and a stableboy's rush broom scraped rhythmically through the lazy spring warmth.

Standoff, while the Mad Prophet held his mutinous seat on the buckboard. Then the Shadow Master's lips curled in sarcasm like a razor cut, at odds with his careful speech. "We haven't seen a patrol in two days. Stop looking over your shoulder and fretting, or I'll have to mix goose grease and wintergreen to treat you for cricks in the neck."

Dakar felt too heartsick to return the slight. "You aren't up to this," he insisted.

Arithon hitched up his lyranthe with hands that betrayed all his stress in fine tremors. "All right, I'm not up to this. That's why we agreed. You're staying to mind the wagon." His departing stride held that tigerish poise which warned when his temper was rankled.

Dakar watched the sunlight fall like white ice over his trim shoulders and back, the sleek ends of black hair feathered into the drawstring ruffles of his collar. In the nerve-racking boldness which trademarked his style, Arithon refused a disguise. People, he insisted, were least observant of things left out in plain sight. He passed the inn's gate, and the broom of the stablehand stilled to his clear call of inquiry.

Abandoned in the company of cud-chewing oxen, Dakar crossed his arms to muffle his yowling stomach. Unease scraped his nerves, though the road stretched empty north and south. The ruts carved up by recent thaw lay hemmed in puddles, tinted lapis and moonstone under a sky sliced by diving black swifts. Brisk trade moved by sea on the southcoast of Tysan until spring dried the mud and the grass offered fodder for caravans. Midmorning was too late for the farmgirls bearing spring eggs to the Middlecross markets, and too early for the afternoon relays of post couriers to clatter in asking for remounts.

An early breeze riffled the blossoming apple trees. The droning industry of bees cut the air, and the thin bleats of lambs, grazing at large with their dams on the flats.

Dakar sulked. His natural penchant for long naps in bright sunlight seemed permanently displaced. He had small taste for idle lurking in a rattletrap cart that made him a creeping target for sunwheel guardsmen and headhunters' arrows.

Nor did he like stringy game eaten cold in the brush, a practice now likely to continue. From inside the wall, Arithon's mild speech raised a howl of vehement distress.

"Another bard? Here? Spare us all, send him packing!" A heavy door slammed. Then a hail of agitated footsteps slapped across the cobbled yard, and a voice of indignant propriety cut off Arithon's next question. "I'm sorry. You mustn't stay, times aren't safe. An herb witch got herself stoned last week. She only sold a girl a love simple, but that was enough to raise trouble. Tysan's Crown Examiner came with a half company of sunwheel soldiers who could ride back any moment and clap you in irons for singing the wrong sort of ballad."

"Fiends eat my liver and lights!" The Mad Prophet snapped up straight, shot off the buckboard, and raced to the heads of the oxen. "Back! Hup!" He grabbed at their headstalls, snatched green-slobbered bits, and gave an almighty jerk. "You splay-footed whoresons, *move now!* Or by Ath, I'll singe your hairy rumps to blisters! We'll have roast tongue for supper. While I think of it, we'll hack the rest piecemeal and string out your entrails for fly bait."

The oxen rolled reproachful brown eyes. They shook their capped horns, bawled through whiskered nostrils, and begrudged him a lumbering half step. The shaft groaned, jackknifed, and the wain squealed to a chorus of gapped boards and stressed pegs. While the Mad Prophet yowled epithets, all four misfitted wheels rocked askew on warped axles and jammed.

Dakar clenched his teeth in forbearance. "For mercy," he pleaded into four tureen ears. "For Daelion's sake, *save* your miserable hides!" The fact he could hear no oncoming hoofbeats offered him small reassurance; a dozen crown mercenaries could be taking their ease unseen in the innkeeper's taproom. Still hauling rein leather, he sized up the merits of hazing the beasts with his drover's cape.

Then another cool hand slipped over his hot ones. Arithon's voice said, "Desist. We're not followed."

"I should believe you?" Dakar cranked his head around like a turtle who suffered a pinched tail. A bay, muscled shoulder filled his whole view.

The Master of Shadow pried the spellbinder's fingers off the lines and replaced them with a supple length of bridle rein. "Leave the cart. We're going astride."

"What?" Dakar gawped at the post horse attached to his fist. "Have you taken leave of your senses?"

A fine-boned, race-bred mare snorted behind the bay, ears rammed flat, as a barefoot horseboy hauled in her girth with indecorous haste. The horse nipped in protest, caught short by an elbow as Arithon looped his lyranthe to her saddlebow. Dakar's urgent questions were ignored. Back turned, the Shadow Master scrounged underneath the cart's filthy cargo of sacking, then straightened, buckling on his baldric with its sheathed burden of sword and dagger.

From the innyard, the fussy infant wailed on through commotion, while some unseen servant shouted to a scullion, "Hurry up and fetch that satchel from the loft!"

"Damn you! What's afoot?" Dakar shoved between stamping horseflesh, his cloak wadded up in the crook of his elbow, and his feet in grave threat of maceration. "No innkeeper in his right mind trades prize post mounts for two bone-skinny oxen and a wain overdue to be hacked up for kindling."

Arithon flipped the mare's reins over her high neck and mounted. "There's a free singer in trouble." His fingers, flying, adjusted the hang of a stirrup. "Time's short. You'll hear as we ride."

Dakar stuck his toes in to argue, while the horseboy disappeared. A potbellied graybeard scurried from the yard, burly arms clutched round a saddlebag. Slung across his shoulder was a fleece-wrapped bundle that looked to contain a second lyranthe.

"Here." The man wheezed to a stop and unloaded his burden into Dakar's already taxed charge. "The singer naturally couldn't take his belongings. Left here in irons, poor wretch." A coin sack teetered onto the top of the load, forcing Dakar to bobble sidewards to avert a spill.

"There's his silver, as well," the innkeeper explained. "Mine's an honest house. Won't take advantage of a man caught aback by misfortune."

"*What misfortune?*" Dakar ejected through the horse-reeking leather of the saddlebags.

"You didn't hear?" The landlord scrubbed moist hands on his apron. "Sunwheel soldiers and a weasel-faced examiner arrested the minstrel I had quartered here. Condemned him to burn. They said that the singing of legends threatens innocents. I tell you, what's happened to good sense? Unkempt louts drew cold steel in my taproom and bedamned to any grace of hospitality. Never mind it's my inn will suffer the blame and the satires."

"This has nothing to do with us," Dakar insisted. He juggled his load, and ineffectively tried to return the unwieldy collection. The lyranthe slipped and banged his knee with a ringing, hollow clunk, and a harness buckle snagged in his mustache. "Will you listen?" he cried in breaking, fresh temper. "My companion and I are not interested."

But the landlord only shouted to roust up some laggard from the tavern. "Wenj! Jump on it! They need those provisions now, not next week!"

The prospect of victuals deflated Dakar's protests. He stood, breathing hard, while the innkeeper narrowed incensed, dark eyes, saying, "Dharkaron's Spear strike the unsavory brutes! My reputation's in ruins. Better I ask for the Fate Wheel's turning than see a free singer take harm during his stay in my tavern. There's curse and misfortune in the breach of a bard's right to shelter."

"You'll have no such bad luck," Arithon assured, then beckoned for haste as the horseboy trotted out with a third mount, this one a fancy iron gray gelding with snowflake dapples, and a bridle which trilled, sewn with bells and flamboyant red tassels.

"The singer's own palfrey," the landlord explained through Dakar's flabbergasted glare of mutiny. "Bless you both! If you can spare that poor wretch from the fire, the horses are yours with my compliments. That's the best I can do. Grain-fed mounts aren't easy to come by, not since the season's been harsh. But you'll need the advantage to outrun the sunwheel guardsmen."

"Guardsmen?" The sidling horse trod on Dakar's toe. Before he fell over in an avalanche of goods, the horseboy stepped in, hooked the lyranthe and packed saddlebags from his wobbling grasp, and secured them onto the palfrey.

"Rip off the bells," said Arithon, succinct. "We don't need the noise to betray us."

"If you think we can save anybody, you're mistaken," Dakar snapped.

"Oh dear." The innkeeper wilted. While the horseboy paused, the plink of bronze bells choked in dispirited fists, he implored, "Who else is left?"

Dakar shot a venomous glower at Arithon. Green eyes watched him back, implacable as glints in sheared emerald, with all the fresh sorrows of Riverton like a spiked canker beneath.

The Shadow Master insisted, "I gave my promise."

No plea, but a warning; Dakar shut his teeth in balked temper. As the inn's kindly matron fluttered out with a bulging pannier of provender, he shrugged; and discovered the coin sack still grasped in the hand underneath his rucked cloak. That saving fact raised his smile like gilt on bad tin. "Well then. We'll give your bard's rescue our diligent best."

Dakar crammed the silver down the neck of his shirt before the innkeeper recovered his aplomb. The venture perhaps made plausible sense. Gifts of coin and horses were no sort of boon for two fugitives to spurn for the overnice scruple of honesty. While the innkeeper gushed his effusive relief, and Arithon took directions to the hamlet, the Mad Prophet busied himself checking the bay's girth to make sure his fat bulk could stay mounted.

"The burning was to happen between the flour mill and the glassworks," the inn matron finished, while the horseboy tossed over the palfrey's neck rope, and Arithon set heels to the mare.

Caught flat-footed, Dakar forgot to shut his mouth. Departing hooves churned up a gobbet of mud, which vengefully clipped him in the teeth. Hornet mad, he spat grit, clambered astride, and gave chase, while stirrups too long to suit his short legs clanged and battered his dangling ankles.

A league down the road, stretched flat at a gallop, he shouted through a stinging lash of mane. "You can't mean to try this. The risks are enough to serve up our guts raw on the sword of Lysaer's executioner! Even if we bolt now, someone will remember our foolish exchange at the tavern. Since you chose such rash lengths to be quit of those oxen, we'd be wise to turn off of the thoroughfare."

"I spoke in good faith," Arithon flung back, breathless, while the horses careened neck and neck through a turn. "Didn't you recognize the silver bosses on the gray palfrey's saddle?"

Dakar's rank epithet allowed he had not.

Arithon steadied his mare's stride and urged greater speed, rankled to acid impatience. "The free singer they're to execute is Felirin the Scarlet." As his mount stretched her nose and thundered ahead, his voice eddied back through the turbulence. "You'll remember Felirin once helped save my life."

"Red tassels, oh Ath, of course!" The Mad Prophet regained recollection; as well as loud clothes, the free singer affected complete indiscretion before bone-headed, townborn intolerance. "Felirin always did know just the right ballad to set headhunters brawling with fists." Dakar tried and failed to match his companion's sinuous agility astride. His seat smacked the saddle, his mount jibbed and pecked; left trailing by three lengths, he hollered admonition, "You know you're turning one minstrel's misfortune into a lunatic's play for disaster."

But Arithon by then had forced too wide a lead to bother to frame a reply.

The Mad Prophet scrubbed sweat from his neck and sagged against the gapped boards of the glassmaker's shed. "Ath, I'm too old and fat for this."

His breathing ran ragged. His heart sped too fast. The muffled thunder in his ears came as much from the beat of his own rushed blood, as from the rumble of the mill's vanes, turning. The two frame buildings notched the mild rise, and beyond them, the tide-driven thrash of sea breakers, ripping a white, sandy headland. The hollow between held a spindly row of cottages, a cobbler's shop, and a blacksmith's: the hamlet they had lathered good horses to reach before the free singer's burning.

A glance at the gathering packed onto the commons showed that the plight of the minstrel was hopeless.

"You don't have an obligation," he exhorted to Arithon, crouched motionless behind the glassmonger's rickle of supplies. "What you face is a clear invitation to suicide, and if you try, I'll have no choice but to invoke the blood oath you swore under Fellowship sanction at Athir."

"Who would answer? The Sorcerers are all gone to Havish for King Eldir's wedding." Arithon did not turn his head, but shifted his vantage between the piled quartz sand, the green piggins of iron oxides, and the sacks imported from the fens of West Shand where saltwort was burned into soda ash.

"Why can't you hear reason for once in your born life?" Dakar clapped his cheeks in frustration. "Now would be a nice time to start listening."

Sweat trickled down his spine, steamed through his clothes by the kilns, which beat rippled air through the gapped boards. While the miller's dogs yapped, and a woman's railing punched through the sonorous bass of crown authority, the sun scudded under a burl of cloud. Catcalls from the bystanders maligned the prisoner on his pile of oiled faggots, no encouragement. With at least ten guardsmen attached to the official now citing the formal charges, Dakar read bad odds. The crown soldiers were from Lysaer's elite division, their sunwheel cloaks white as strewn snowdrifts amid the drab motley of the countryfolk.

Arithon regarded the tableau with the unswerving attention that boded the worst sort of consequence. "Felirin is condemned for singing the ballad of Tal Quorin, as written by Halliron sen Al'duin," he said. "Ath knows where he learned the rendition. He must have spent time with the clans."

"Daelion's bollocks!" Dakar shivered, hands latched in his cloak to shut out the plucking breeze off the sea. "Small wonder they'll burn him."

"They won't." Arithon ducked, doubled back, and slid down beside Dakar. "Since I can't turn that crowd with steel in plain sight, I'll need to borrow your mantle."

The Mad Prophet rammed upright, swearing. "Man, that's a death wish! You dare not be seen here!" Certainly not after an unexpurgated ballad which maligned the s'Ilessid prince as a butcher made blind by self-righteous morality and arrogance.

"Your cloak," Arithon repeated. "Dakar, *stop arguing!*"

The Shadow Master spun in fraught urgency as the door banged at the front of the glass house. A boy hurried out with a torch from the kiln fires, streaming a tang of dark smoke.

Still Dakar hesitated. "I can't sanction such risk."

"Then I must." The Shadow Master snatched up the drover's oiled wool, ripped the cloth through unwilling fingers until his companion stood stripped to his jerkin.

"Felirin delivered no less than the truth! A free singer's rights should hold his life sacrosanct, and *I am Halliron's successor!* If I don't stand forth and protest this injustice, can't you see? Any minstrel in Tysan could burn for composing an ordinary satire!"

In Arithon's hands, the vast, caped cloak flared and settled over taut shoulders. "I need you to frame up two runes of mastery for elemental fire. Draw them here, in my palms."

He pressed a twig of charcoal scavenged from the glassmaker's midden into the spellbinder's nerveless grasp. "Damn you, think! Dakar, I can't douse live flame with bare shadow. Not when my mage talent's blinded."

A surging cry from the onlookers marked the moment the sun-wheel guard captain bent and set torch to the faggots.

The Crown Examiner hailed over their noise, "May Daelion Fatemaster find you repentant as you pass his Wheel in judgment!"

"Dharkaron, Ath's angel, avenge me instead!" the condemned musician hurled back. Disheveled, not young, his face scraped and bruised, he let outrage fuel his dignity. His voice sliced through the burgeoning crackle of flame and carved the first lines of a bard's curse.

Dakar pressed stubby fingers to his face. He could not look, lest he weep. While the singer's defiance clipped short in a rasping cough, speech failed him. His throat closed, too parched to shape words to garner the ritual permissions.

Arithon's prompt spurred on laggard memory. If his talent was silenced, he still had trained knowledge. The graven discipline of a masterbard's diction bridged a channel for clear concentration, even through the first stifled whimpers from the victim chained on the pyre. Then his slim, urgent hand, thrust through Dakar's damp one, firm enough to steady them both as the branching runes to blight fire were inscribed in crumbling ash.

"Touch anything, even your weapons, and the marks are going to smear," Dakar cautioned.

Arithon tossed off a nod, tucked cupped hands out of sight in the folds of the cloak.

Irrevocably committed, he emerged from the cover of the glass-works, strides limned by the diamond-shard heaps of white cullet. He advanced past the rain-channeled mounds of pure sand, straight as Dharkaron Avenger's ebon spear in the furling layers of his leathers. When his head tipped that familiar listening angle askance, a friend could do naught but feel the heart tear for the moment's brazen, doomed courage.

"Daelion Fatemaster wept!" the Mad Prophet ground out. "For merciful sense, turn back."

For one hagridden moment, dogged by the leaping surge of the flames, Arithon raked and measured the backs of the crowd ranged against him. They were fifty against one: the curs circling the fringes in whining excitement; the knots of weeping women; and the glassmonger's burly craftsmen, bare arms and furrowed foreheads ruddied by the heat. They still wore hide aprons smeared with ash and the singe prints of cinders, while the rods and tongs of their trade hung cool between idle fists. Beyond them, drawn in from the plow, farmsteaders watched with their droves of barefoot children, the clappers to scare the wild birds from the seed grain clenched silent in slender fingers; next the hands from the mill, blanched head to toe with musty flour; then the grandames and old men, stoic as aged oak with the soldiers between them, impassive in their white-and-gold cloaks and prideful, expressionless faces.

All eyes tracked the fire, braiding hot tongues of carnelian through the snagged heap of faggots. In horror, in macabre, slack curiosity, the manifest presence of death held them riveted. The free singer writhed now for their sick fascination. His suffering became a spectacle, supple hands rammed taut in steel bonds, all the gifted splendor of his voice broken hoarse as the inevitable, blistering pain cracked through its fallible timbre.

Arithon's survey touched last on the crown's high official, his brilliance sullied by the risen smoke of his sacrifice, and his righteousness backed by the helmed ranks of his retinue.

Lord Examiner Vorrice sat enthroned on a plank propped across the clouded bricks that were pigs of raw glass, stacked ready for export to town craftshops. He wore the sunwheel of vested authority with an unswerving dedication, his jowls shaven, and his fleshy mouth tucked like pleats basted into raw silk. His view was untrammeled as the slight, dark-haired Masterbard broke his stance and stepped forward, voice raised and soaring in song.

The verses and melody in sere a cappella were the same ones performed long ago for Halliron's widow at Innish.

Dakar heard the words, mute. He sensed the true notes spin their harmonic magic. This was the appeal that Arithon's dead master had written for his art, a plea for mercy and a cry for understanding from a family abandoned through the demands imposed by his talent. In an expression of distilled pain, Halliron had claimed freedom to pledge his life to the immortal tradition of music.

Flattened against the glass shed, Dakar felt the first lines stab through him, whetted to a lance of bright power. Stripped of accompaniment, Arithon's voice became a honed weapon. The spare, severe handling of each flowing lyric came tempered to unassailable force. Another step, a second verse; song unstrung every tie of resistance and stormed the floodgates of emotion.

Arithon crossed the beaten earth of the commons. Through the riptide of release as his powers reached resonance, his directive held true: to captivate, then to bind, through a suspension of irresistible beauty. On his makeshift dais, the Lord High Examiner's pouched chin jerked in startlement. Below him, heads turned, those hatless and wind tangled and bald, and others in gold-blazoned helms. Then the bard who demanded in naked, clean song reached their midst.

He *would* be recognized. The yelping cur silenced. Humanity paused, pierced through by a masterbard's construct of absolute, unalloyed sorrow.

A figure alone, Arithon parted them. His nerve stayed as iron. Above the evil crack of caught flame, his melody unreeled, simple and fine as poured water.

The sea breeze now wafted a sickening stink of singed flesh.

Sheltered, still safe, Dakar laced his hands over the clench in his gut. "Ath, merciful Ath."

Nearest to the pyre, Arithon s'Ffalenn must endure through the reek of the fumes. His concentration must not waver. Pitch and syntax must cleave to perfection, even through the ugly, shuddering moan as the victim's gray head thrashed to the first nip of agony.

The bard's step trod its measure, nerveless, detached. His voice did not quaver. Each sustained note razored out in true pitch, harmony and word interlaced to create one matchless tapestry. Power as wide as new morning forced the horror at bay; drew each of the onlookers singly and turned them. Pitted against time, and the fire's cruel lead, Arithon s'Ffalenn weaned the watchers away from their morbid fascination. He thralled them to his art with spellbinding clarity. Each step, each staid beat, he *must* be aware: once Felirin gave way to a full-throated scream, his effort would be shattered wholesale.

The enchantment he fashioned was founded on nothing beyond a fugitive brilliance of sound.

Second to second, he fused his art's focus. His will, his voice, his irrefutable bearing netted guards and bystanders, and held them in rooted attention. Dakar watched them, terrified, aware of the flaw in the odds; his heart skipped for cold knowledge that *one* whelming dissonance would splash those superb ties of empathy to ruins.

All eyes tracked the bard, now, except for one rheumy, bent grandmother.

"Damn her, she's deaf," Dakar whispered through the unbidden, salt taste of tears. Sweat dripped through his beard. His lungs felt strapped in lead. The thud of each heartbeat slammed hammer to anvil against the locked bone of his sternum.

Arithon threw back his head. Face tipped to sky, he hurled all he was into the song's final verse.

The talent he commanded ran through him like light, and snatched the stilled air into feeling.

Nothing moved but the flames. Dakar, himself paralyzed, felt mage-sense cry warning. Such winding power as this could not be indefinitely sustained. The tension had climbed to the threshold of peril, with each listener poised like blown bubbles of glass that the first jarring tap must collapse.

Then, at last, elbowed by the wizened grandfather at her side, the recalcitrant old woman turned her head.

"Now!" Dakar whispered. "Arithon, you have them, *act now!*"

Immersed mind and heart in the throes of his art, his audience netted like fish, the bard freed his hands from the cloak. Dakar croaked the ritual word of release; and the sketched charcoal runes to bind fire laid into Arithon's palms raised their element to primal awareness.

393

The bard responded, still singing. Through that offered gateway to conjury, his gift of spun shadow descended, sharp as the snap of flung wool.

While all eyes were averted, an unnatural darkness clapped down and smothered the flames on the pyre.

Felirin broke into choking, hysterical sobs.

Throughout, the descending beat of sung melody never once missed precise rhythm. Each note rang true, each word stitched its place to hold the disparate bystanders enthralled. In timing to raise the fine hairs at the neck, Arithon s'Ffalenn reached the dais. He stopped. He hurled down his falling, last line like a gauntlet; and fell silent at the feet of the crown's Lord Examiner.

In the absence of art, the unchanged voice of nature ground as a shock on the ears.

Past the ramshackle eaves of the craft sheds, surf slammed and hissed over unyielding sand. The racketing creak of the mill's turning vanes, and the shrill calls of gulls grated on dream-wakened nerves. Against that structureless absence of melody, Felirin's whimpers struck like a whiplash of shame.

Through the riveted focus cauterized by his art, Arithon s'Ffalenn addressed the robed man on the dais. "What is a song, or a word but a thought given wing? A man should not burn for expression of ideas. The sentence passed here offers frightening precedents. Or has forthright speech become one and the same thing, to be tried as a deed that caused harm? Do we allow you to end a man's life in a fire because you disagree with his music?"

"That's rank impertinence!" Vorrice leaned forward, one hand raised to summon his guardsmen, and the knuckles of the other splayed over the pristine lap of his robe. "This was a crown trial, held under seal of the realm's lawful regent." His tight, narrowed eyes refused the appeal, and his brows clumped above his wedged nostrils. "I see no grounds for any commoner to intervene with the works of Prince Lysaer's justice."

Arithon stood his ground, arms lightly crossed beneath the caped shoulders of the drover's cloak. "I'm Athera's titled Masterbard, affirming the law of the land and a free singer's right, as you see." Chiseled, imperious, yet in the crowd's sympathy through the spelled meshes tied by his song, he cracked a command to the guards. "You there! Unshackle the minstrel you have wronged. He's no felon, but the victim of injustice."

The ploy almost worked. Two soldiers broke ranks in reflexive obedience.

Vorrice surged to his feet. "Hold hard! Are we half-witted dupes to jump for the first softhearted meddler who speaks?" To Arithon, he shouted, "You presume far too much!" The snap of his rage reordered his guardsmen, and a murmur arose, as one, then another of the bystanders awakened to the fact that the flames in the pyre had extinguished.

"There's sorcery here, sure as the mother who bore me," someone cried.

Farmhands and craftsmen made signs against evil, while matrons snatched their children and hustled them to safety inside the craft sheds and cottages.

Dakar ripped out an oath, while fear stirred a palpable current through the gathering. The unarmed onlookers crowded a step back, while first one, then another guard's sword sang from their sheaths. They advanced, bristling; not to unlock shackles, but to hem Arithon s'Ffalenn inside a nervous circle of steel.

"You mistake what you see," Vorrice said, his confidence oiled by the shielding ranks of his guardsmen. He smoothed a wrinkle from his robe and explained in condescending forbearance, "Felirin does not burn as a singer. He stands duly sentenced as the minion of the Master of Shadow. As such, every man must agree, he poses grave danger to all of us. No masterbard's privilege can excuse those who side with the Spinner of Darkness. Such license would lead us to ruin. My given office, by the seal of this realm, is to rout out hidden servants of evil. You could be one of them. Tell me your name."

"Tell me yours, instead, puppet!" A brazen contempt sharpened Arithon's voice, clear over the crowd's stirring murmurs behind him. "Or do you not wear another man's gloves, and parrot another man's lies to give yourself airs and importance? Show these people here you can think for yourself. Or take my promise, you'll have a satire the five kingdoms won't readily forget!"

"Remove him!" snapped Vorrice. "He has upset proceedings."

The guardsmen pressed in, hampered. They were many ranged against one, without proper space to wield arms. Dakar watched them close in, racked by agonized helplessness. Like the stag menaced by the jaws of a wolf pack, their quarry must know: the least step in retreat would trigger aggression against him.

Arithon's feet shifted stance beneath the cloak as he answered in searing, soft mockery. "A contest of force cannot make your cause right. You're a misled zealot, or else hopelessly stupid."

Vorrice bristled. "Should I care what you think?" Gold braid flashed at his cuff as he snapped knobby fingers at his guard captain.

"Clap him in irons! He'll share the minstrel's pyre. Let him die in anonymity. The mother who named him won't even weep when the sea wind has scattered his ashes."

"But his mother didn't name him," a gruff, broken voice cut in.

"No," Dakar groaned.

Forgotten at the stake, sick and bewildered from inhaled smoke and the blistering pain of burned legs, the condemned minstrel cleared his throat and spoke out. "You don't know whom you address?"

Felirin raised his smudged face and laughed in dazed triumph for the fact he still breathed, singed and degraded, but graced with an unlooked-for protector. "You face the Master of Shadow himself, called Arithon by his maternal grandfather. And burn him? Just try! With my own eyes, in Tornir Peaks, I once saw his birth gift quench the fires spat from the jaws of a Khadrim."

Arithon's shout pealed through the crowd's shocked astonishment. "Fool!" he cried to Vorrice. As though he were not cornered, nor help-lessly outmatched, he surged ahead, seized the towering mistake of Felirin's loose tongue as a tactic of raw desperation. *Did you think you could threaten a sorcerer's minion with a mere ten guardsmen to defend you?*

He hurled off the cloak. The scream of black steel drawn from his sheath came entwined with a soundless descent of pure darkness.

Then that seamless, unnatural night burst in turn, smashed asunder by unbridled light.

The guardsman singled out as Arithon's first target reeled back as the runes in the longsword, Alithiel, flared into white mage-fire in just cause of Felirin's defense. The Paravian blade in a masterbard's hand could not but welcome a free singer's right to disseminate truth, clothed in the fine art of music.

Its cry of bright power sheared the air into recoil.

Undone by terror before blows could be struck, the sunwheel soldier fled. Behind the glass house, Dakar dropped prone as the untamed chord which had first Named the winter stars knifed through the ramshackle hamlet.

Seared blind by fierce light, struck deaf by a peon of resounding celebration, every man ranged against Arithon s'Ffalenn lost his will to attack. Thought faltered and stopped. Grand harmony grown too refined to endure held them rooted, until mortal spirit longed to escape the bounds of its own living flesh. Onlookers unmanned by sheer splendor broke down and wept for a rapture too mighty for reason to encompass, and for a beauty too sharp for the clay of earth-bound senses.

The enchantment built to a shattering crescendo. Reduced to shrill screams, Vorrice cowered on the dais. His less fortunate guards lost wits to flee as the land itself woke in reply. The ground shook to that spiraling resonance of celebration. Dust flew as the wild winds sprang aloft, to spin the arch of the sky into ecstasy. Caught in the breech, man's works became winnowed like so much chaff set to the flail.

The glass pigs whined into crystalline cracks. First one, then another of them sheared through and collapsed to a sleeting slide of white fragments. The crown's Lord Examiner toppled from skewed planks and landed, raked bloody and weeping. None heard his distress. Any whose feelings had maligned Felirin became trapped in the well of raised force from the sword.

Deadwood burst new leaves. Forged metal heated in sympathetic vibration, until swords and armor racked apart into smashed links and tinseled shards. Within heartbeats, the prostrate, stupefied guard stood stripped to the shreds of their gambesons.

At the apex of power, charged head to foot by a wave of unbridled joy, Arithon s'Ffalenn cried aloud. Athera's titled Masterbard, sound was his element. Ceded a cresting tide of roused earthforce, he required no mage-sight to apply the fine dictates of his training.

Dakar thrust to his feet, prepared for the outcome. The Teir's'Ffalenn had accomplished much the same feat before, when an accident of song had unleashed the grand mysteries during a summer solstice in Jaelot.

Arithon raised his schooled voice. Merged with the harmonies fired by the sword, he sang the exacting resonance to wake steel. The bolts snapped in Felirin's fetters. Chain and shackles clanged free. Limned in the glare of the Paravian guard spell, Arithon kicked aside smoking bundles of faggots. Cinders whirled, sullen, in his wake as he reached the dazed singer and shouldered the man's failing weight.

"Run!" he implored.

In his hand, the sword passed through its crescendo. The sheeting flare off the runes bled from white to silver, then sank, sparkling into subliminal haze. While Arithon spun shadow to confuse their escape, Dakar reached his side, hands outthrust to stave off Felirin's collapse.

He said, urgent, "You don't have to walk far, we have horses."

Together, he and Arithon hauled the singer away from the charred bundles of faggots. Drunken flight carried them through the dazed guardsmen. They wove past the stacked saltwort, and ducked under the eaves of the craft shed, to explosions of fragmenting glassware as the sword's diminished vibration unleashed fresh destruction inside.

To Arithon, in horrified admiration, Dakar gasped, "Ath preserve! If you planned this, you know you've just handed Lysaer's Alliance all the fighting cause they need to raise the whole countryside against you."

Running as though traced in a frozen strobe of lightning, Arithon stung back in dry irony, "That's presupposing we manage to survive the next hour. Once that examiner and his guard find their wits, they'll be at our heels like fell vengeance."

Parchment and Seal

Nine years into crowned rule, King Eldir of Havish still bore the weight of royal office like the encumbrance of effete finery draped on the shoulders of a laborer. His blunt nose, square face, and bluff manner were misleading. More than his high council and his guild ministers had been fooled into believing they could intrigue as they pleased, masked in deferent manners and false honesty. When the shrewdest of them all, the Lord Mayor of Westcliff, took a hard fall in his effort to thwart the disbanding of the headhunters' leagues, the king was barely eighteen, still fresh from his Fellowship coronation, and nicked with scabs from inept first acquaintance with a razor.

By the hour of his Grace's twenty-first birthday, those titled officials left standing knew not to regard the Westcliff affray as a slip of poor luck or chance accident. By main strength and hard wits, his Grace of Havish had routed the most entrenched town policies from their bloodletting feud against clansmen.

At the age of twenty-six, the realm remained in firm hand, with the Second Age site at Telmandir crawling with stonemasons working to lift tumbled walls out of ruin. If Eldir still donned his state jewels with reluctant, stiff-shouldered forbearance, only those outside ambassadors who were deaf to advice misread his farmbred appearance. Even in private conference with a Sorcerer, his peat brown eyes stayed disarmingly direct. His hands, square and blunt, rested at ease. Beneath them, the inked script of state parchments unfurled across the battered deal planks which served as his council-hall table.

"Choose your stance firmly," said Sethvir of Althain, perched opposite. His woodsprite's face peered out in concern from a wren's nest of tangled white hair. Shadowed by the gloom under soot-darkened ceiling vaults, he seemed a bundle of discarded maroon velvet, crossed legs tucked up like a child's in the ostentatious gilt chair Eldir kept at hand to mollify disputing merchants. His inquisitive fingers traced the earthenware mug nestled askew in his lap as he added, "I pity the need that makes this step necessary, and I warn, what peace you buy will be temporary."

Without visible emotion, the king snapped his fingers to his secretary, then accepted the waiting, dipped quill. He jagged the bold loops of his signature as if the act by itself framed defiance. In truth, no footing for compromise existed. The ban on slave labor was a point of charter law, held in faith by the Fellowship Sorcerers' sworn compact with the Paravians.

"Since I don't plan to abdicate, pity has no place." Eldir's dark regard rested back on Sethvir. "I won't have my edict against slavery defied. Nor will I see my harbormasters tempted with bribes that beguile them to treason, or bend them to the whim of Tysan's botched politics for the sake of a shipping guild's profits." The king's eyebrows knitted in distasteful memory of the death sentence just enacted against three high-ranking offenders. "My relations with Prince Lysaer are already strained over principle. Well then, my port magistrates need waste no more trials collaring the scoundrels who meddle in the breech."

If Prince Lysaer's guilds pursued trade with the cities of Havish, they would ply the king's coast in galleys rowed by free crews.

The pen was passed back. The efficient, mousy secretary had wax already heated, Havish's great seal and scarlet ribbons prepared from long habit as the royal fingers snapped again.

Eldir impressed the realm's blazon, the formality of his words at odds with his gesture as he skated the parchment across the worn trestle to Sethvir. "As King of Havish, sanction is asked with my sealed intent. This day I request Fellowship assistance to enforce the realm's charter, bound to me by oath from my line's founding ancestor, Bwin Evoc s'Lornmein."

"By your leave." The Sorcerer traced an apparently negligent finger over the wafer of warmed wax. His gaze stayed fixed on the other hand, aimlessly rolling his mug to and fro, while his drifty regard seemed absorbed by the shifting, whorled patterns sluiced through the grounds by the dregs.

King Eldir knew better. Moment to moment, immersed in the

world's multiplicity of events, Sethvir tracked the life threads of men, and sparrows, and flies. On that one second's effortless thought, his consciousness unriddled a chain of disturbance that whipped the southcoast of Korias to a burst of unseasonal activity.

His far-flung awareness sensed three riders in flight, two of them unwell; and a storm brewing; and the shouts of post riders dispatched at speed to raise Alliance guardsmen from Middlecross. In the immediate quiet of the king's patient presence, magecraft bloomed under the Sorcerer's touch. A star of etched light flared over the fresh wax. Deft, precise, Sethvir traced a circle of glyphs. Spells stitched the air like the indelible glitter of foil ribbon. When he lifted his hand, the cipher remained, a fiery imprint cast across the royal blazon to seal promise of a Fellowship binding.

"Post fair warning," he murmured, while untold miles to the north, a gray palfrey stumbled and her rider whimpered in pain. Speech maintained his divided train of thought. "In thirty days' time, Traithe will travel your coastline to raise an enchained spell of proximity. When his work stands complete, any galley to raise sight of Havish's shores will have no fettered oarsmen, on peril of Fellowship intervention. Every man set in manacles or kept under duress will have his steel struck by cold sorcery. Slave convicts go free, with their captains and crews to be held at the mercy of crown justice."

"And the ships?" the King asked. "They'll remain tagged with banespells?"

Sethvir shifted, his half-lidded gaze rinsed the lucent turquoise of a sky-caught imprint in a rain puddle. His distracted reply whispered echoes across the lofty expanse of the hall. "Impound them. Or set them afire as you please, though they'll float without hindrance for a paid crew."

Outdoors, the sun emerged from a cloud. Barred light streamed through the west bank of lancet windows, hazed with airborne dust. The sliced edge of the mote crossed the Sorcerer's bent knee. Against the lit flare of wine-colored velvet, his hand clamped into a fist.

"Trouble?" asked King Eldir.

"Not yet." Seconds passed, while the secretary fidgeted and Sethvir's pixie features retreated into the semblance of doddering blankness.

A dutiful page boy poised by the doors rushed a step to rescue the tea mug, in danger of upset amid the folds of the Warden's robe.

The king's quelling gesture deflected the kindness. "Let be, lad."

A minute trickled by, elusive as the fall of sand grains sieved through an hourglass. Then Sethvir blinked, stirred, and linked

401

crooked knuckles through the rumpled fall of his cuffs. He flashed a conspirator's wink to the page and rescued the canted mug himself. "A trip to the kitchen would not be amiss. Could you bring back a fresh pot of tea?"

His pert smile saw the boy off on his errand, yet the glance he bestowed back on King Eldir stayed as lapsed into distance as a fog-bank. "Merciful maker," he grumbled. "If I'm overtaxed by any one thing, it's intransigent princes who run amok without the saving bad grace of planting even one bastard on a tavern wench. When you marry next week, grant our Fellowship a boon. Breed up a clutch of royal heirs."

A cough as rich as aged oak escaped Eldir's sturdy palm. "Dare I guess?" Only one other childless scion in Athera was the last of his family line. "Is Arithon being difficult again?"

Sethvir raised miffed eyebrows. "That sort of indulgence would be blessed relief where the Teir's'Ffalenn is concerned, well you know as much."

King Eldir curled his knuckles against his lips to nip his impolitic laughter. One disruptive visit to his court had been enough; Rathain's prince had countered Tysan's public campaign of eradication through a volatile mix of unlawful conniving and a devilish bent for playing unconscionable stakes. No matter that Havish stayed neutral through the feud sown by Desh-thiere's curse. All spring, the dockside at Ostermere had seethed with bold talk concerning the rigged ships disappeared from their Riverton launchings. If rumor held truth, the marauding crews included disaffected clansmen from Tysan.

Since no mind might fathom the full scope of Arithon's design, the King of Havish asked outright, "What's Rathain's prince done this time?"

Sethvir blinked. "Raised a hue and cry that has every crown-commissioned guard in south Korias lathering good horses to kill him." He scowled into space, while the reflexive span of his consciousness mapped the speed and direction of more than one far-distant set of hoofbeats. Then his branching thoughts riffled like cards through a player's deck, testing the probable offshoots of consequence.

Amid myriad moments of unformed possibility, one stood forth, a diamond-clear crossroads of movement and intent pared to the fixed edge of destiny: *in three days' time, guardsmen under a Hanshire captain named Sulfin Evend would close upon the three fugitives. The spells of illusion and misdirection the Mad Prophet spun to evade them would fail, because in the past, their commander had studied with the boy wards of the Koriathain. He understood very clearly how spellcraft could upset the hierar-*

chy of political power. The grown man had sworn his sword to the Alliance to confront the source of that fear.

The King of Havish said something.

Althain's Warden replied, his mind still enmeshed with the whirl-wind array of unborn happenstance: *when Dakar the Mad Prophet would come to scribe a distress rune in blood upon the surface of a stone. Under the light of a chilly, gray dawn, he would dry the figure in flame, then cast the construct into a streamlet. At the hour his appeal for help reached the Fellowship, time would be too short to act.*

Sethvir shifted the arc of his thoughts. A fraction of an instant let him catalog what resource he might call to hand. Though his powers as a Fellowship Sorcerer were overwhelmingly sufficient to effect complete rescue then and there, he would not, *must* not, do other than allow the threatened parties to act to save themselves. The reprieve he had won from a past outside of Athera's historical record still haunted; still seared his waking awareness. A stock of experience too bitter to endure had stamped its mark of immutable truth.

By the Law of the Major Balance, his Fellowship could not use direct force to intervene without unseating the course of the world's destiny.

The audience with King Eldir suffered a small lapse as the grievous pain of past losses weighed on the Sorcerer's heart. He was not complacent. Once, before drake-dream had snatched the Fellowship of Seven to Athera, he and his colleagues had enacted their will for a cause. They had paid for their meddling with appalling consequences. He could not but ache before the chill wisdom that for Desh-thiere's curse, his Fellowship must resist the temptation to relive the same choices again.

By the compact's clear terms, their powers were sworn to preserve the Paravian mysteries; mankind might accept steering counsel and assistance on request, but the ultimate course of humanity's survival must be shaped through self-will and free choice.

"Your tea has arrived," King Eldir prompted.

Sethvir looked up, found a smile for the page, then exhumed his mug from the folds of his robe and set it upright on the table. Worn as he was, and tested by conscience, his gnarled grip held no palsy. Through the interval while a royal servant refreshed his cup, the Sorcerer unreeled his considered response in the form of three direct appeals.

A call arrowed out to touch Asandir, just ridden the breadth of Tysan to test the new patterns of prejudice fanned by Lysaer's campaign to repress mage talent.

A second tracer flagged down Kharadmon, on watch amid the grand ward against a cold backdrop of stars; and tied in a request to the brewing spring storm in Athera's arctic latitudes.

A third touch raised the awareness of a patriarch tree, wind beaten and twice seared by lightning, and exchanged a pact of permission.

One last vectored inquiry mapped cause and effect, and gauged their impact on the future. Sethvir foresaw no trend of enlightened understanding arise out of Arithon's brash rescue of Felirin. The summer would bring on more trials, more burnings, more sunwheel recruits led to enlist by unsettled fears and strained politics. The spiraling trend of Prince Lysaer's maligned belief would gain heated impetus, fresh spark to the trend which drew men to embrace the cause of the Alliance of Light.

Misunderstanding of a sword's gifted powers served only to ignite a new wave of fear. The price of Fellowship assistance as always touched off wider ramifications.

Sethvir sought prosaic comfort from his mug of scalding tea. When he raised his tormented gaze to Eldir, he offered his sorrowful forecast, "Very soon you will be pressured to take sides on the issue of practicing sorcery. The mage talented will come seeking refuge within your borders before the advent of summer solstice."

"There's no decision to be made," Eldir said, his strong hands reaching to gather up the spelled parchment. "Tysan's burnings are unjust. The condemned are not criminals." For the scion of a line renowned for mild pragmatism, he finished in vehement force. "My crown is a mockery if Havish can't provide them with sanctuary. We've already spoken for the refugees who flee Tysan's persecution of the clanborn."

Sethvir touched his crabbed fingertips against his closed eyelids. Shadowed by the finials of the massive gilt chair, he could have been mistaken for an arthritic grandfather, mantled in velvets too voluminous for their framework of brittle, aged bones. His voice was subdued as he tendered the only bright truth he could offer. "Your Grace, because of your mercy, more than one irreplaceable clan bloodline will be saved. That could be the one act to salvage the balance on the hour when the Paravians choose to return."

The spin of the Fatemaster's Wheel meantime would scarcely stop for a platitude. The Sorcerer diffused his attention back into fragmented awareness; *while far off to the north, amid the hummocked landscape of Mainmere's ruined keeps, Asandir drew rein, wheeled his stallion, and sent it thundering back down the road he had just traversed through Caithwood. Elsewhere, a storm gained intensity; a battered tree consented to*

*the hour of its death; and the Hanshire captain named Sulfin Evend clattered
into a Middlecross posthouse, shouting for provisions and remounts with a
zeal the laziest horseboy must attend.*

Beyond these small happenings, hazed into momentous event with
the passage of years; snicked warp through weft with the turn of seasons, and the fall of changed leaves, and the byplay of iyats, Sethvir
saw sunwheel priests raise vast armies, to carpet the summer landscape. Rank upon rank crossed the Lanshire border to bring Lysaer's
cause by fire and by sword into the Kingdom of Havish.

Unwilling to dwell upon the sorrows Desh-thiere's curse might
inflict on the future, he immersed himself in particulars. "Please
extend to your bride my Fellowship's profound regret," he said. "Due
to an unforeseen difficulty, Asandir will be late for your wedding."

"No matter." King Eldir arose, staid as plain granite against the
stitched silk of a tapestry. He thrust the rolled parchment under his
arm and returned his rare, even smile. "We won't see hurt feelings.
Every city mayor and guild minister your colleague shamed into
compliance for my coronation will more likely be silly with relief.
They've complained in the past that Asandir's scrutiny just makes
them sweat rings through their expensive brocades."

But Sethvir sensed how the lightness was forced. He and Havish's
king matched an agonized glance of understanding.

Then Althain's Warden clasped the royal wrist. "Trust your heart,
your Grace. Your decisions today have been fitting and right."

No longer did the Sorcerer seem aged, or careworn unto fragility.
His myopic air of fuddled inattention could not mask what he was: a
spirit annealed to unassailable strength through a past few others
would survive. He owned the endurance to brave trials yet to come,
and King Eldir s'Lornmein was too wise to stay blind to consequence:
the impact of the day's event would not happen in his reign, but must
fall like a blow upon the shoulders of his unborn descendants.

Spring 5653

Impasse

Days later, shivering in the predawn chill of the Korias flats, Dakar the Mad Prophet licked blood from a nicked thumb and cast his stone construct into the shallow current of a streamlet. He ached from the soles of his mud-spattered boots to the uncombed crown of his head. His vision held the treacherous shimmer brought on by overstrained hours of mage-sight. He linked pudgy hands and stretched a kink from his back, then swore aloud for the misery that the landscape offered dim prospects for a trio of fugitives. Driven off the coast road, a rider could find himself mazed amid farmsteads, with their yapping dogs and screaming geese, and where treacherous stands of pasture fencing could yield up angry bulls or lethal delays spent backtracking from unexpected cul-de-sacs. The low roll of the fields carried sound far too clearly, and extended visibility for miles. Those expanses too thin for tillage or grazing formed a vast, washed floodplain of poor, stony sand, patched over with scrub too sparse to mask fleeing hoofprints.

Huddled amid a witch-hazel thicket wadded with morning fog, the horses nosed the ground for straggling shoots of sawgrass, ears limp and coats matted into dry whorls of sweat. Felirin could do little to tend them. Salt leached into the raw burns on his hands, though every plain shirt in his saddlebag had been torn up at need to make dressings. Arithon had packed the worst blisters and weals with burdock sprouts beaten in egg whites before he himself had succumbed to his backlash. The inevitable penalty he must pay for channeling unrefined earth powers with his mage talent blinded left him drained near to incapacity.

Prone amid the stripped saddles with his head cradled on his locked arms, he made small complaint, though the tight-lipped expression he wore when he moved told Dakar how deeply he suffered. Nor had the sorrows inflicted at Riverton been lifted by his keeping good faith with his charged duty as Masterbard. Like snags in deep current, that unseen despondency leeched him, ebbing his reserves without letup. He needed henbane tea and a bed warmed with stones to ease the spasms which racked him. But sunwheel guardsmen searched door-to-door. Farmwives would sell him to his enemies out of fear before they would offer him shelter.

Faint gold rinsed the clogged, misty air. The fog was starting to thin. Dakar clutched his ribs to suppress a chill, aware that the thicket provided inadequate shelter. The mists would lift in less than an hour, leaving horses and riders a sitting target for the oncoming Alliance patrol.

The mare chose that moment to fling up her head and whinny a deafening inquiry. Dakar swore. "Just let the whole world know we're here, you worthless bundle of dog meat." He dealt a pebble by the streamside a temperamental kick.

The stone arced aloft, but the predictable crack of its impact never happened.

Wary, Dakar glanced up.

Five paces ahead, an inked phantom against mist, a black horse and cloaked rider confronted him, their approach uncannily silent. Even the clang of shod hooves on rinsed rocks failed to raise telltale clatters. The horse halted, meeting Dakar's sharp start with pricked ears, but no trace of a shy. A ghost eye gleamed like frosted glass through the veils of dawn mist. Under a dark mantle, the rider stirred. A hand unfurled from a gray-banded sleeve, and let the abused pebble drop to the streambed with a murmured phrase of apology.

"You!" Dakar cried. "Did you have to scare a hunted man out of his living skin?"

The Sorcerer Asandir inclined his head in reproof, his regard on the spellbinder's thumb. "You did send a summons."

Dakar glanced down, caught aback, then closed shaking fingers over his still bleeding cut. "We need help," he admitted. "I've scried warning. The patrol I can't shake will close in by noon. If Sethvir doesn't already know, Earl Jieret's had Sight of a public execution, the condemned man being Prince Arithon."

Asandir sat the black stud, patient, but without speech.

The Mad Prophet flushed slowly crimson. "I ask for Arithon's survival," he defended.

The Sorcerer touched the black's neck, soothing it from stamping off the midges which swarmed at its mud-spattered fetlocks. "Arithon suffers backlash, yes? As well he should expect from his prior experience, when he raised the Paravian mysteries at Jaelot."

"You won't see him?" Dakar demanded.

"He has not asked." The Sorcerer touched his horse again, and as if language had passed between master and beast, the stud backed a half step and wheeled to go. While Dakar stood, helpless, his bleeding hand clenched to a frustrated fist, the hooded head turned. Silver eyes met his, and one bristled brow tipped up. "How you've changed," Asandir commented. "I should have expected at least an impertinent question demanding to know where I'm bound."

One moment; two; the birdsong rang loud through the thicket, and the horse stamped. Asandir gave him rein, and nearly too late, Dakar caught the drift of abstruse insinuation.

"Wait!" He surged forward, hopeful, while the stud snorted his annoyance at being checked back to a halt. "Where are you bound?"

Asandir glanced over his shoulder, his mien like graven flint. "There's a Paravian grimward northeast, did you know? I will be testing its guarding boundary for soundness, and since Luhaine is busy, no one will check on my back trail. A foolhardy traveler might stray inside. Should that happen, the perils are unforgiving."

Well aware he was cued, and blanched to hollow nerves by the implied suggestion, Dakar recited, "Kill no beast, break no branch or leaf from a living tree, set no fire and remove no twig or pebble."

"Just so." Asandir's smile seemed lit as a shaft of breaking sunlight touched his mouth underneath his deep hood. "A horse should be muzzled to stop him from browsing. Let Arithon rest, he'll recover. And bring Felirin with you to Shand. If the friends you have there won't take him in, Halliron's daughter surely will. She's been lonely and morose since her mother's death, and the city could use a new storyteller."

Dakar drew a weak breath to proffer his thanks, but an influx of fog surged between. When the air cleared, both horse and Sorcerer were gone with no sound to mark their departure.

"Did you have a successful scrying?" husked a voice at the Mad Prophet's shoulder.

The spellbinder gave yet another bounding start. "Dharkaron's black vengeance!" he hissed to Felirin, crept up on poulticed feet.

"Does everyone in creation have to sneak in here and scare me out of my skin?"

"I'm sorry." The singer padded to a halt, his soiled cloak tucked around his shoulders like a blanket. He had always possessed elegance, with a handsome, straight nose and cleft chin. Stress made his prominent bones appear gaunt, and the hair that once spilled in waterfall waves to his shoulders now clung to his skull, frizzled and singed like matted wool in the damp. "I thought I heard you say something. Wouldn't you rather somebody checked to make sure you weren't lost in a fit of prescient trance?"

The spellbinder focused his discomfort toward his boots, as if the hard, stony soil underfoot might sprout untrustworthy sinkholes. "I've had guidance from the Fellowship, after a fashion."

"And they said?" Felirin probed.

"Daelion's bollocks!" The outburst set a meadowlark to flight, but did nothing to lift the Mad Prophet's rumpled scowl as he stomped off to untie the horses. "We're to lose our pursuit by crossing through a grimward."

Felirin blanched. Hazel eyes still inflamed from the pyre showed bloodshot rings of disbelief. "You do know it's said that those sites guard the sleep of the great drakes. Perhaps the very ones whose true dreams led this world to the brink of destruction before the dawn of the First Age." He slipped a wrapped hand from the layers of his cloak to discourage a sprig of briar that latched its green thorns in a tassel. "Are those legends true, as the sun was?"

"I never asked," Dakar admitted, his moon face furrowed in distress. "Althain's Warden himself never said. Asandir refused to discuss the grimwards, except to relate they were ceded to Fellowship trust when the old races fled from the continent. Ath knows what those circles confine. I could wish we'd never find out."

Another rolling billow of sea fog shredded itself under sunlight. By the time the horses were saddled, the land would be laid nearly bare.

"I hope you like Shand," Dakar finished, the spur of haste driving him breathless. "Because if we escape from the sunwheel guardsmen, there's a very good chance you'll end up there."

Chain of Event

On the Korias flats at the hour of noon, a headhunter tracker soothes his cringing hounds and refuses to cross the shimmering light which frames the boundary of the Paravian grimward; despite all advice to the contrary, the brash captain from Hanshire swears through his teeth, calls his forty select men, and overrides their quavering dread to continue pursuit of the Master of Shadow. . . .

Three days later, a gale off Stormwell Gulf brings rain and winds that raze trees like a scythe, and one of those fallen is a patriarch oak which sweeps a sunwheel courier from his saddle; he recovers from a sharp blow to the head, forgetful of the tidings which dispatched him to Avenor: that of the riders who followed Sulfin Evend into the Paravian grimward, nary a one has returned. . . .

In the observatory at the Koriani sisterhouse at Capewell, the last spiraling glimmer of power fades from the grand conjury made to trap Arithon s'Ffalenn; and like old, dried paper, the ancient Prime stirs from her coma and opens sealed eyes to the galling discovery that her quarry has slipped through her net without scathe. . . .

XII. Grimward

Inside the shimmering, mercurial barrier which bounded the Paravian grimward, the natural progression of time dissolved. As spellbinder, Dakar noticed the alarming development when his subliminal connection to sun, moon, and stars became cut off like snipped thread. Footsore, exhausted, and snappish from hunger, he shut his eyes and milked his recalcitrant memory. He retained a shamefully sparse store of facts for his years spent in Asandir's tutelage. What fragments he gleaned could be counted on three fingers, jumbled as trivia between detailed reminiscence of his past trysts and wistful hours spent wenching.

By contrast, each one of his two-silver harlots stood out with a jewel's exotic clarity. The quirk moved him to teeth-grinding worry, that the fragment of lore that might key their survival would stay obscured by the decadent pursuits of his past.

"Well how was a drunk to know what his life might come to depend on?" Dakar snapped to Felirin's sensible inquiry.

Distempered and soaked in cowardly sweat, the Mad Prophet drummed his heels against his horse and drove its balky steps through the ward's shifting bands of coiled energy. The bard and the Shadow Master rode behind him like shadows, the former reduced to a petrified silence, and the latter, too undone to care where his mare's herd instincts might lead him.

The Mad Prophet wished in jangled irritation that Arithon's wits were not scattered. This once, the other man's unmerciful perception would have posed an indisputable advantage. For his own part, the spellbinder found such exactitude wearing. Escape into thoughts of a lush woman's favors seemed resounding good sense beside the outright insanity of braving the perils now at hand.

Dakar yanked a wrinkle from the knee of his trousers before he chafed a new saddle sore. He needed no scholar's insight; nothing about a Paravian grimward would seem canny to human awareness. The location of all seventeen known phenomena might be charted at Althain Tower, but whole years at a stretch, a man might pass those marked sites and encounter no trace of their presence. Through his five centuries as a Fellowship apprentice, Dakar could not remember one time when the Sorcerers did not attend to the grimwards alone.

The protections which turned the inadvertent traveler from a disastrous step through their boundaries were laid down with ruthless potency. When the seals required adjustment or rebalancing, the task was always shouldered by Asandir or Sethvir. Their discorporate colleagues Kharadmon and Luhaine might sometimes assist from the sidelines by misdirecting strayed game or even the occasional two-legged trespasser, but Dakar retained the distinct impression that such places held consummate danger for any spirit left unshielded by mortal flesh.

At any cost, a man must not come to die here. Not unless he wished to be struck from the Fatemaster's Wheel for all time. Of all the trials suffered in Prince Arithon's service, this one trod the surest course to folly.

Dakar tugged a snarl of hair from his mouth, his rude stock of oaths an inadequate quaver as three muzzled mounts bore his small party of fugitives irrevocably into the unknown.

Ten paces ahead, his unsettled senses ripped back into clarity. As if an eyeblink had remade the landscape, the vista ahead showed seared trees and sterile dust, charged in a flat tang of ozone. Currents of wild energy flicked over riled nerves. The Mad Prophet found his teeth set on edge, and his vitals clawed with unease. The interlaced spells which defended this border threw off a debilitating resonance. Leaves shriveled as they unfolded from the bud, and trees became stunted, shedding skeletons. The blight on the land fed Dakar's disquiet; he knew of the Fellowship's aversion to cause harm to anything growing.

Yet in this place, that dearly held tenet had been broken with stark and appalling violence. As if this circle of spelled seals confined something unworldly that would not respond to the kindlier magics wrought out of natural forces.

The air wore the musk of seared earth and dry rot. What sky glimmered through the clawed fists of bare branches loured under blank haze, unblessed by the face of sun or moon.

Dakar attributed the eerie, flat murk to the proximity field of the wardspells. He glanced behind. Felirin found courage in lilting gentle nonsense to his horse. Arithon had shaken out of his stupor enough to gaze about. His features might seem as blank as chipped chalk. Yet the man who held his intimate trust could unmask that expression and discern the agonized frustration of a master driven sight-blind to mage talent.

"Keep close," Dakar warned. Exhausted as he was, and unfit to ride point, the others were plainly in worse state. Felirin's wrapped hands fretted and fumbled to maintain a grip on his reins. If hazard threatened, Arithon could scarcely stay erect in his saddle. Which perhaps was as well; Dakar had a nasty stab of intuition that the black sword, Alithiel, should not be drawn in this place.

Its uncanny, bright power framed too stark a contrast to the shadowy forces he sensed, laced into queer, subliminal eddies by the blameless stir of their passage.

That disturbed awareness was torn short as his mount balked with a jarring snort. Dakar curbed its rank fear. He peered ahead, wary, then gasped in outright awe.

The sere ground gave way to an expanse of polished granite. Ancient, quarried stone was veined in tangled strata of obsidian and milk quartz, and incised with grand arcs and figures scribed across with Paravian runes of glowing silver.

"You're wise to be jumpy," Dakar cajoled his timid gelding. "But I'm the best chance you have to stay breathing. Throw me off, you'll end up as fly meat."

He dug in his heels, to no avail, until Felirin's more willing gray thought to pass him. The bay's competitive nature reasserted with a bounding start forward. Dakar swore and snatched mane as his horse clattered onto the massive, smoothed block, the mare at its heels, her breath sucked in fast, nervous snorts. The unease of the animals was justified. The array underfoot was centaur work, each dressed stone fitted seamlessly into the next with matchless and uncanny precision. The charged coils of power in the joined ciphers made living skin burn and tingle in waves, and threatened a ranging headache.

Dakar could take no measure of their strength. The magic knit here reached beyond mortal senses, mighty as time, as stately as the steadfast turn of the earth, and wrought on a scale to strike terror through his armor of knowledge. Through a shrill, singing dizziness, the spellbinder counted the eight seals for banishment. His horse skittered over the directional, six-sided figures for safeguard, matched to the cardinal points, and vectored above and below. These stood laced through by ward after ward of containment. He identified *an'alt*, the configured symbol for infinity, stamped over and over in ribboned light. Other runes he did not recognize at all, but the force in them struck like blades of ice through the thick leather boots in his stirrups.

"I don't think I've ever seen the rune for safe-crossing aligned with so many ciphers to annul power," observed Arithon, ridden up on his sweat-draggled mare.

Dakar swiveled in surprise. "You can read these?"

"Only some of them. My grandfather's library at Rauven was limited." Arithon frowned through a fallen thatch of hair, more than weariness making him haunted. "The resonant harmonics I can hear through my bard's gift are dissonances, all. Not what I'd call reassuring."

Then, with no warning, the paved expanse ended. The horses crabstepped off a razed edge in the stone and into a rustling growth of forest. *One heartbeat before, no trees had been anywhere in evidence.* To the rear, the rune ring had vanished away into shadowed, random avenues of oaks. The spellbinder took that for an ominous sign. The guarding sigils at the portal had sealed the way closed behind them. No return course was possible by the path they had entered. If another safe exit to known territory existed, they must endure whatever perils lay ahead and unriddle the grimward's dire mysteries.

"Ath, where is this place?" Felirin gasped. "No timber of this size grows on the Korias Flats."

"Well we aren't there anymore," Dakar ripped back, testy as he bludgeoned his upended senses to gain the full use of his mage-sight.

Yet a discipline which should have responded like reflex escaped his effort entirely. Trained access seemed blocked. He could trace out none of the underlying patterns to this forest's vibrant energies. The too-sharp barrage of his unrefined vision rattled him down to the pit of his vitals. Sight framed an impossible discrepancy. The foliage of these giants grew out of phase with the season, cinnabar and gilt with the fireburst palette of autumn. The maples, the beeches, and the crowned, ancient oaks soared aloft in vaulting splendor.

No such stand of primal forest should exist inside the fifty leagues separating the grimward's location from the old tracts the clans held in Caithwood.

Dakar withstood his craven impulse to rein in by tugging his beard with brisk worry. "We'll need to make time. There's no guarantee we're not still being pursued, if those guardsmen were fools enough to follow us."

But the terrain itself thwarted haste. No paths cut these wilds. While the party of riders ducked vines and low branches, their mounts picked their way in uneven steps over ground laced with roots like snagged rope, and through hollows where stones were deceptively quilted in moss deep and lush as a king's robe. Felirin marveled in monologue under his breath, as though he sought to commit such strangeness to verse. Arithon curled on his mare's crest, fists crushed to his forehead in pent-back, dazed misery, leaving Dakar to tax his bewildered wits and effectively function as guide.

He soon discovered the impossibility of keeping straight bearings through a grimward. The place was possessed by bewitching strangeness. A man might choose an opening between two pillared oaks, only to find his steps redirected him ten paces further to the left, and on through a different byway altogether. What passed for sunlight shone a pale, lambent gold, with ruled shafts slanting through glades of stippled shade. Maintaining a constant sense of direction should have posed his trail-wise party no difficulty, except the unnerving tricks of the landscape mazed and bemused the awareness.

While Dakar puzzled to unravel the anomaly, Felirin broke off his ongoing composition. "Whatever sort of magery's afflicted our senses, we seem to be traveling in a circle."

"Spiral," Arithon corrected, half-muffled through folded fingers. His speech seemed almost drunkenly slurred, the inflection lapsed back to the antique dialect of the splinter world of his birth. "Don't you hear? A harmonic resonance patterns this existence that guides the placement of each footstep."

"What?" Dakar swiveled to stare, startled enough to ignore the branch which slapped his exposed side. The surprise seemed unfair, that Arithon had observed more than anyone else while apparently lapsed into a stupor. A tug on the rein stopped his gelding, while the Shadow Master's mount followed suit by dumb instinct.

Felirin halted his gray, his plain, honest face charged to wonderment. "Masterbard," he murmured, "in truth, Halliron's teaching unveiled your true destiny. My life has been spent in devotion to music, and yet, my ear can't detect this nuance you speak of."

Sunk as the Shadow Master was in discomfort, his precise sense of language never left him. Caught back in reflective speculation by one word, Dakar twisted aside to pursue inquiry. "Existence?"

Like a child in creased clothes jogged out of a dream, Arithon straightened. He blinked unfocused green eyes. His hands ran hot sweat where he changed grip to the saddle out of shameless need to stay upright. "Don't say you hadn't noticed the landscape is unstable."

"Damn you!" Dakar resisted a hysterical laugh. Through the trees to the right, he had just glimpsed a broad, grassy plain. Beyond lay a skyline edged in mountains whose shattered white peaks belonged to no range in Athera. "Why not use your boot and kick me awake? I'd be eternally grateful."

But this time, the victim was too spent to counter that lame attack of sarcasm. His painstaking effort to order plain thought became a trial to witness. Felirin politely averted his gaze, while Arithon sought to translate impressions with comprehensible clarity. "I might add that the earth where your horse treads is anything but solid ground."

"Well, try the next riddle with an answer at the end." The Mad Prophet looped his reins in the crook of one elbow and massaged his pounding temples. His balked effort to plumb the phenomena by mage-sight had left him high strung and dizzy. "If I didn't know better, I'd swear my talent's gone blind and dead as your own."

An hour spent immersed in furious thought had left the spellbinder no whit the wiser. Here, the sparkling energy ties which laced the very substance of creation did not follow any pattern laid down by natural forces. The aberration chewed him hollow with dread, that the trees, the moss, the very sun on lit leaves remained dense and elusive to mage-sense. Petrified to plumb the extent of his helplessness, Dakar shrugged. "If I could accept the impossible, I'd say nothing in this place has an aura."

Eyes shut, Arithon snapped off a nod. "You're surprised? This reality isn't alive by any founding law of Ath's creation."

Dakar bridled to hear his foreboding confirmed. "However can you know?"

Too stressed for impatience, Arithon said, "I still have my bard's ear. The vibration of this existence is not myriad, but seems to be loomed from one thread." He labored to qualify. "The song of its being does not change register, not for a tree, or a rock, or an insect. Since the shadows as well won't answer my gift, I have to presume they're illusions. The logical end point is scarcely reassuring. We must be traversing a path through a dream."

A chill splashed over Dakar's moist skin. "Save us all, don't say that. If that's true, somewhere there must be a great drake, still alive and sleeping."

But Arithon had retreated back into dazed silence. The bay mare bore his suffering weight, hunched and half-senseless in the saddle, leaving Dakar floundering and alone with his terror.

The warning strictures remonstrated by Asandir posed a fearful array of hidden pitfalls. Their small party dared not disturb any aspect of symmetry in this unworldly place. To take even apparent life, or to strip so much as one green branch would cause a strand of continuity to shift resonance. A balance would change, demanding harsh forfeit, and no power of mercy might spare the offender from the fate of that unknown consequence. Whatever fell power enacted this sphere of illusion must not be aroused to the presence of trespassers.

"As you love life, walk softly," Dakar entreated, aware the least act could distress the loomed pattern of integral consciousness surrounding them.

Their footsteps were now guided by a force of unknown magnitude, and retreat of any kind was impossible.

Felirin alone retained the brash whimsy to flirt with poetic phrasing. "Will we or nil we, we're drawn toward the center. I wonder what we're going to find?"

"Something Asandir never spoke of, even on his good days." Fed up with the minstrel's feckless temperament, Dakar let fly out of pique. "Take great care you don't snap any twigs."

For whatever unearthly pocket this grimward carved out, they had no choice but to grapple its uncanny mystery headlong.

The first time the apparent season changed, Felirin cried out in shock.

Dakar gawped and inhaled the frizzled ends of his mustache. His perception had not lied. The leafed autumn wood had transformed at one step to the cobalt gloaming of winter twilight. Low, rolling hills lapped away to a snow-clad horizon. Treeless, the crests wore mantling drifts like honed cleavers. The wind snarled and gusted. The breath Dakar drew to indulge in rank curses sieved cold like spilled mercury through his lungs.

The forest was gone as if expunged from existence, and the new vista offered no shelter. Too exhausted to bolt, the horses shivered and stamped, their labored exhalations trailing white plumes against the deepening purple of dusk. The stars blazed overhead like chips in black ice. No moon arose to diminish their splendor, nor did the constellations form any pattern familiar to Athera.

Arithon volunteered his sparse comment through a pause to share the brandy the innkeeper's wife had tucked into the provisions in the saddlebags. "I know this sky. The stars were never so bright, but on Dascen Elur, ships' masters navigated by these same constellations." He passed the flask on to Felirin, and added, "I wonder if our thoughts could be bending the dream?"

"Then you recognize this plain?" Dakar swiped off the ice crystals lodged in his brows, too dispirited to show disappointment as the Master of Shadow shook his head.

"This landscape doesn't match my memory of Dascen Elur. At least, no landmass encountered by my father's ships seemed this wretchedly desolate." Arithon's voice seemed leached of all feeling as he qualified. "Even on those barren archipelagoes where families mined salt from the silted lagoons, scrub thorn grew on the high ground."

Worried afresh by the lifeless flatness to the Masterbard's expression, Dakar attempted to hold his gaze and measure the depths of his internal despair. But Arithon refused even that slight contact, his mouth a taut line of strained nerves.

The small party pressed on when the brandy was finished. Felirin rode with his eyes shut, lips working, perhaps in a verse from some ancient ballad, or in prayer to Ath. Huddled in his singed cloak with both hands swathed and poulticed, and his pert scarlet tassels shredded to threads from unkindly fire and hard usage, he seemed a tatterdemalion beggar left witwandering in the night.

Dakar pondered their changed surroundings, not a bit reassured that the sky overhead seemed to match Arithon's recollection. He had never thought to ask Althain's Warden whether dragons had flown past the Worldsend Gates. That fine point might come to matter dearly in the future. If in fact the great drakes had not cached the memory of these far-off stars as a backdrop for their present-day dreams, then trouble would shadow the chances of their mortal survival.

The danger could not be discounted or ignored, that this disjointed frame of existence might prey upon human thoughts, then manifest their dark contents. If such linkage occurred, then Arithon's shattered equilibrium could couple with Felirin's penchant for foolhardy fancy and brew up an unconscionable risk. The chance was too frightening, that the impassioned knots of subconscious pain might weave themselves into the loom of the uncanny forces that clothed this alternate reality. If so, the unimaginable guilt held in check by a blood oath could unleash, all unwitting, a murderous, tormented revenge as a subjective nightmare of horrors.

Shaken stark silent, Dakar sketched a sign to avert the ill thought, that the grimward's effects might come to magnify Arithon's despair. The best-willed intent to repress a death wish might twist free of constraint and remanifest in this place as a parallel act of self-punishment.

Through the pound of his heart, Dakar leaned across and spoke directly to Arithon. "Use your mage training. Wrap your mind into silence, and don't for a second drop your guard."

The Master of Shadow opened tortured green eyes. "Ath save us all, I've already done so." He cast a weighted glance toward Felirin's turned back.

For of course, the free minstrel owned no such schooled discipline to lock down the unrestrained play of the mind.

Dakar chewed his lip. He knew illicit lore, had knowledge of sigils to force the will and bend a man's acts through the use of sheared lines of power. Such craft broke the Law of the Major Balance. Eddies of recoiling damage could backlash on both the victim and wielder. Yet here in this place, such a safeguard might mean the difference between life and death.

Left cold to the bone by the bent of his thoughts, even granted the impetus of a terrible expediency, Dakar startled to the sudden restraint of a hand on his wrist.

"Don't, Dakar," said Arithon s'Ffalenn. His shackling grasp did not loosen. "I thought the same once on the banks of Tal Quorin. Believe me, no stakes are worth such a cost. I've lost direct access to my mage talent as a penalty, and would give any price in my power to reverse that decision."

Dakar swallowed, undone by the leveling force of an honesty he could not match. Nor could he restate the horrid, cold fact, that the harmonious continuity of Athera yet hung on the thread of Prince Arithon's life. "If need warrants, even you cannot stop me," he said finally.

The hold on him released in an unspeakable surrender. That act, and the numbing silence that followed ran against every tenet of fight in Arithon's character. An ominous sign, with no joy in the victory, that Dakar held such sway over a friend whose innate strength had always outmatched him. "I'll hold my decision," he temporized, to no avail.

The Teir's'Ffalenn had retreated past reach behind the stone mask of his training.

Very quickly after that, all concerns became moot before the raw cruelty of the elements. Gusts bit through every inadequate layer of clothing. Horses could not withstand such punishing cold without rations of grain and fodder. Half-shed into their sleek summer hair, they were already suffering. Nor did the queer, bending track through the gloaming permit a retreat by retracing their steps into autumn. Concerned that Arithon and Felirin were left in more fragile condition than he, Dakar insisted that the pair ride double on the gray and share the warmth of the drover's cloak between them.

The small party plowed on, horses laboring chest high through sifted pockets of snow. Stuffed like a sausage in two of Felirin's court-style tunics, Dakar blinked melted snow from his lashes and startled to the clang of shod hooves on rock. The frigid air left his lungs in a gasp as the stars and bleak snowfields all vanished.

The three riders moved now under a sky streaked with dawn, across sands grooved and black as raked basalt. The air held the forge-tang of desert and a flint-dry cloy of fine dust. No birds flew. The arid vista seemed lifeless as Kathtairr, except for the massive, clawed tracks of a predator which scored the ribbed flank of a dune.

"Seardluin," Dakar whispered through a throat parched to paper by a devastating stab of fresh fear. In Athera, Fellowship intervention may have battled the monstrous killers to extinction; yet in the sheltered existence of drake-dream, the creatures would prowl still, their marauding thirst for blood raised to a scale of unimaginable viciousness. "If even one catches wind of our horses, we're finished."

Felirin pushed back the limp folds of the drover's hood. "Arithon's unconscious," he said softly.

The Mad Prophet vented an explosion of oaths. No telling, now, whether the defenses ingrained in the Shadow Master's mage training might contain the subconscious poison past memories and grief might engender.

Between blowing on numbed hands and fighting to slip the stiffened straps of the buckles on his saddlebags, the Mad Prophet flung back stopgap instructions. "Felirin, pack up that cloak. You may need your hands free. And we'll have to shift Arithon back onto the mare."

The spellbinder scrounged out two stout pairs of horse hobbles. Focused and made desperate by full awareness that he must safeguard the body that housed the self-haunted powers of s'Ffalenn conscience, despite the latent potential for disaster that same mind might seed to envelop them all, Dakar tossed the restraints to Felirin. "Tie your Masterbard astride. Don't think of pity. Strap him down tight, or he's lost if we have to gallop."

"The horses are spent. We ought to be leading them." Felirin fumbled with poulticed hands to assist as Dakar directed. Together, they fastened the stiff leather cuffs around Arithon's wrists and ankles, and bound his slack form to his horse's girth and breast strap.

That grim preventative was scarcely completed when Dakar looked up. "Dharkaron wept!" A massive, dark shadow slunk sinuously into the hollow where they took shelter. He snatched the bard's wrist. "Don't move or breathe."

Felirin glanced back, aghast. The next moment the three horses shied sidewards and tore at the reins trying to bolt.

Dakar held on, half-weeping, though both of his hands were skinned raw. Standing or running, they had no chance at all once the monsters that approached charged to hunt.

There were four of them, coats like rippling sable, and horned heads burnished to polished gold under the harsh desert sunlight. The powerful, maned shoulders stood high as an ox. The forefeet bore fearsome talons. The muzzles extended into jaws with scaled plates, and fangs that were cruelly poisonous. The eyes were pale as poured oil, and slitted like a snake's. Dakar was aware through the hammer of his pulse that nothing alive looked more lethal. While at large on Athera, Seardluin had outrun the gazelles of Sanpashir, which took bounding flight like racing shadows over parched grass and flint sands.

Never had the spellbinder known such blank fright as that moment, when the creatures on the dune paused to snuffle the wind, ears pricked to strain out the footfalls of prey. Those wide-set, mean yellow eyes swung and fixed, and seemed to stare *right through him*.

Then the lead creature howled in a key to bristle the hair and tear a hole through a man's slackened bowels. Slumped on the mare's crest, Arithon groaned.

Dakar reached out, pitiless, and muffled the cry with his palm.

Then, as if tuned to one thought, the Seardluin moved on, lithe, deadly, and uninterested. They passed not three yards from the horses, who quivered and dripped sweat in rank fear.

Felirin shrank, shaking, against the damp heat of his gelding. "Ath's blessed mercy, I don't think they knew us."

Weak kneed with shock, Dakar resisted the urge to collapse where he stood. "We must not be visible to them in this spectrum of dream. If we were, I assure you, we'd be torn limb from limb."

Felirin offered no argument. Once the horses had settled enough to walk calmly, he remounted and pressed on, trailing the mare which bore Arithon. From behind, the wind carried a drawn-out howl, then the sounds of a snarling fight. Screams that sounded human sliced the baked air, then the drumroll report of hapless horses set to flight, sheared through by a chilling clang of steel.

"Hold fast!" Dakar tightened his grip on Arithon's reins, and twisted to see over his shoulder.

Five horsemen burst over the ridge at his back, mounts stretched to a lathered gallop. Down a grade unsuited to headlong flight, they slid and skated. Sand caved and gave way beneath panicked hooves. Against the fierce, copper glare off the dunes, Dakar made out the Hanshire town blazon sewn on their saddlecloths and surcoats.

"Felirin!" he cried, tensed to stab heels to his own mount and run. *Even here, the Alliance pursuit had overtaken them.*

Yet even before reflex could spur startled flight, the last guardsman cleared the crest, shouting like a madman and driving his horse with the unsheathed flat of his sword. A grue like the precursor to prophetic sight caused Dakar to hold back raw instinct. He reined in. While the guardsmen plunged closer, and the sand scarp ripped loose like unraveled knit beneath their destriers' pounding sprint, he spun a fast cantrip to mask his horse's copycat impulse to bolt.

The stayspell locked down barely in time. Arithon's mount hit the rein in a spinning plunge, shredding new skin from Dakar's fingers; then hot on the heels of the Hanshire guardsmen came the predators which hazed them.

Seardluin burst over the skyline, four streaks of muscle and bared talon that came on like shot oil to overtake. Plowed sand and ripped footing caused them no missed stride. Nor was time given for prey to react or defend.

The lead creature sprang with sinuous speed. It overtook the trailing rider, closed a stride and a half lead in one bound, its thick, plated tail streamed behind. One snap of armored jaws decapitated the horse. The animal pinwheeled, fountaining blood. Its rider catapulted ahead. He crashed in a rolling spray of sand, but never came to rest before the predator pinned him. One goring swipe of its horn left him a disemboweled carcass.

The survivors pounded on through another mired stride before the Seardluin charged among them. Their horses' berserk panic scattered them right and left, chaff before the oncoming stroke of Sithaer's scythe. The king male snatched a mare by one hind leg. Half her haunch tore away in one razor-clean swipe. His Seardluin mate cleared the steed's scissoring struggle in a powerful leap. She landed ahead of the next horse, tucked and rolled, then extended a taloned forepaw as a hook. The horse was jerked out of its run like a gaffed fish. It crashed, splayed and gutted. The downed guardsman died as fast, bludgeoned silent by a swipe of the Seardluin's armored tail. Blood pattered a fine rain on parched earth, the spray masked by the whistling shriek of another gelding, collapsed with a severed windpipe. The final horse thrashed in a heap of maimed limbs, its rider crushed in the tangle.

Dakar never knew how the last came to die. The butchery ended too quickly. Nothing alive remained standing to kill. Seardluin stalked narrow eyed through the razed carnage, their frenzy of bloodlust unsated. They slashed and snapped at the slain underfoot, while the rent limbs of horses and men shuddered through the tormented spasms of flesh torn untimely from life.

The furnace-dry breeze wafted the reek of ripped bowels and the stench of violent death. Dakar's bay gelding and Arithon's mare sidled in demented fear. The gray trembled, with Felirin doubled over the pommel of his saddle in the throes of a gut-rending nausea.

The spell cantrip on the horses was fading. The Mad Prophet yanked the mare's bit before flight instinct could revert into stampeding terror, then curbed his own milling horse by forcing its panic into frustrated circles. While Arithon's mount jibbed and jolted against the lead rein, he shook off stunned shock and strove through a virulent attack of the shakes to sort out what mage-sight now showed him.

"Those men, those horses had no auras," he forced out in a strained whisper. "If they were alive when they entered this grimward, they became *changed* into something unnatural."

As though the recent deaths had not signified, no shocked discharge of animal magnetism hazed the air with blank light; and yet, the Seardluin had tracked every hapless victim that they slaughtered on sight.

Felirin straightened, wrung pale as a specter. "What are you saying?" He wiped his mouth with the back of a wrapped hand, and insisted with gritty disbelief, "Those were guardsmen from Hanshire. *I knew them.*"

Behind, on the dune, amid the strewn gore of carnage, the predators crouched down to gorge. Snarls carried downwind, punched through the snap of cracked bone. The horrors worried their kills as they ate, tearing and ripping through meat and entrails with greedy, savage abandon.

Dakar's stomach turned. "I don't care if those men were your milk brothers from childhood, we'd better get out of here, *now!*"

The slightest release of his hold on the rein, and the horses he gripped plunged ahead. Dakar resisted their snorting, brash lunges.

He could do nothing more than cling to blind faith that their party would not be attacked. Headlong flight could not outstrip a Seardluin's charge. If he gave way to nerves and let the horses gallop on, the loose sand would tire them beyond any chance of recovery.

Felirin eased his jigging gray up beside Dakar's flank. "Why don't those drake-spawned furies see our presence?"

Dakar swallowed hard, yet the rank taste of bile stayed with him. "I can but guess. In some way, we haven't crossed fully into their realm of existence. We traverse a dream. Our lives are not part of it, but only passing through."

"Those guards," Felirin started, then coughed back a heaving spasm. Wretched beyond speech, he shook his head.

"I can't know for certain." The mare plunged ahead, yanked short yet again by Dakar's iron hold on the reins. Swearing, he lost another patch of raw skin before he resumed his snagged thought. "Those men must have interfered with the dream in some way. Dragons are unruly and powerful beings, a law unto themselves. Their conscious minds could seed life. Why not the reverse? If a man in careless ignorance killed game in the wood, or lit a small fire for comfort, then a thread of continuity would be torn by his act. A kinetic balance would become inadvertently upset. In forfeit, the drake might well bleed off the offender's life aura, and knit the repossessed magnetic energies into the dream's fabric to restore the gap."

"Ath's mercy on them," Felirin murmured, his sad, lined eyes fixed ahead. "If you speak the truth, they are lost for all eternity, and yet, their fear and their suffering was no less for the fact that their spirits were unstrung before death."

Dakar had no word of comfort to assuage the minstrel's sorrowful insight. Nor did he dare broach the evil possibility that Arithon's unguarded mind may have seeded that vortex of killing violence. He nursed his tired mount over loose, sliding sand, or the brittle salt of cracked hardpan. Though the site of the slaughter might lie behind, the ugly memory persisted, too vivid and sharp to unburden. A man led in circles by worry and privation could not help but imagine what fates might befall the rest of the company from Hanshire, drawn here in determined and foolhardy duty, and left to the perils of their ignorance.

Other packs of Seardluin prowled the desert. More than one clawed spoor stitched across the spiraling track carved out by the horses' labored passage. By the wayside, the hacked and gutted corpse of a young dragon lay broken. Splayed wing leather shriveled, half-silted under blown sand, and the ripped coils of entrails were strewn like sun-blackened rope in clots of rank, congealed blood. Here, most oddly, Dakar sensed the hazed energies of torn life force; as though the continuum of Fate's Wheel still contained the unmoored wraith of this creature's whole being at the moment an untimely death claimed it. The enigma gave rise to a headache, out of phase with the throb of his skinned palms. Dakar endured. He refused to acknowledge the chorus of complaint from an overweight body kept in the saddle too long. Nor would he hear the fool's urge to dismount and ease the discomfort of racked joints.

To guess by the pug marks pressed into stained sand, the Seardluin which had stalked the slain drake weighed as much as a draft horse.

Then that kill, too, fell behind. As the riders' blown mounts breasted another crest in the dunes, the desert with its perils melted away, replaced by what seemed like a southland orchard gone wild. Glossy leaves rustled, stirred by kind winds to a ruffled embroidery of orange blossom.

Another chill puckered the hair at Dakar's nape. No natural trees should bear ripened fruit and spring flowers in the same season. Almost, it seemed as if the grove was presented in temptation, inviting tired travelers to forget the firm strictures by which they might walk this existence unscathed.

"Don't pick any fruit," the Mad Prophet cautioned. He wondered in stark honesty whether Arithon's deranged guilt could be party to this latest invention; or whether Felirin's loose fancy offered the deadly peril of a sleepy, spring grove whose climate encouraged tired travelers to linger.

Those creeping suspicions entwined with another current, elusive and powerful, but *there* as a sparkle of unseen energy that invaded the periphery of vision. Dakar knew spellcraft. Step upon step, his suspicion gained impetus, that *something* or some power tempered each new train of event, and dammed back the cascade of disaster. Yet each time he tested to fathom the source, the currents he searched for slipped past him.

Felirin brushed a shower of shed petals from his hair, too pained and dispirited to indulge his ebullient imagination. His gray was stumbling tired, and fretful in its efforts to evade its rope muzzle and snatch at the knee-high grass under the fruit trees. Out of pity, the bard dismounted to walk.

For the bay mare, they could offer no such relief. Arithon remained fallen into a stupor. The drawn angles of his face were mercifully eclipsed by the shadow of the drover's cloak, and his hands dangled slack from the restraints which secured him to the saddlebow. He would not arouse, despite Dakar's efforts. Even a spell-turned invocation to his Name failed to raise any flicker of awareness. If the last s'Ffalenn prince was lost in the dreaming quagmire of his conscience, the combined debilitation of backlash and despair would find no healing in this place. Nor could aught be done to reverse his deep malady, but keep on and hope for the relief of escape.

"We can't journey on indefinitely without water," Felirin husked at long length.

Dakar drew rein, sucked clean of the will to laugh for the irony. "We aren't likely to find water here. If we did, it would be too risky to drink."

"What makes you sure?" No matter how desperate his state of privation, the bard's curiosity knew no bounds.

"Great dragons hated a drenching worse than a cat does, or so Sethvir once explained." Dakar stamped back the ripe fear that threatened an explosion of temper. His nerves were drawn wire. He heaved his fat bulk from the saddle and almost collapsed in a heap from the spike of sharp pain which shot through his cramped knees and hips. In mulish rebellion against abused dignity, he pursued his thought to the end. "Rainstorms were said to send the great drakes into rampaging fits of irritation. That's just as well. We dare not interact with anything we didn't bring with us. Heed well. The penalty could be to share the same fate as those foolish guardsmen from Hanshire."

The minstrel breathed in the incongruous, sweet tang of the orange trees, morose. "For a creature that gloried in live flame, wet weather would naturally pose a problem." The tightening scabs on his burns made him seem a slouched and arthritic old man. "How long do you suppose we can survive in this place?"

The Mad Prophet had no answer that did not offer outright discouragement.

Overhead, the sky burned a lingering gold, lucent as marigold enamel. The grove melted away like a lifted curtain into a wind-beaten vista of steppelands. Dakar set his back to the task of driving on balky horses without help from the switch he needed, but dared not braid, out of plucked stems of tough grass. He could not fathom how far they had traveled, nor yet, how much longer they could venture without falling victim to lethal mishap.

Seemingly out of nowhere, the deep, booming note of a centaur's horn call shook the ground, answered like echo by the clarion reply of a mature male dragon. Felirin stopped short with a gasped cry of wonder.

Dakar stared also, amazed and gaping. High over the beaten-brass furrows of the plain, a mated pair of dragons cavorted, sleek as shot quarrels as they closed leathered wings and swooped from the zenith to the horizon. Sun-caught scales flashed fire like tipped gold, and tails streamed and snapped like armored ribbon. No legend, no awed description, even from Sethvir's keen memory, could do justice to the searing, unworldly grace of the great drakes at their prime strength. Before their vast size, the Khadrim were as toys, and the wyverns of Vastmark no more than petty and quarrelsome vermin.

The drakes spiraled upward and dwindled to gilt flecks, lost at last in the molten brass dome of clear sky.

Dakar expelled a gusty sigh, brought back to awareness that he had suspended his breathing.

Felirin shed his awe in an uncharacteristic bent of practicality. "Before we see more inhospitable country, do you suppose we'd be wise to rest?"

"Better to push on," the Mad Prophet disagreed. "Whatever is spinning this dream we experience, it's being tempered by some outside influence." He resisted another tug at the reins as the mare tried again to snatch grass. "I can't imagine the immensity of power needed to stabilize this existence enough to allow for our presence, but there won't be a second chance should we outstay the limit set on our welcome."

In stark proof of concern, the ground changed again. Plains and grass flowed away, replaced by volcanic rock and a blackened, clogged sky. The air churned with smoke like stirred sludge, and the footing rippled with heat haze. Jagged stacks of porous rock notched the scarp, scoured to red veins where magma had leached glowing sores through the crust.

The horses tossed their heads, sidling, tails high and nostrils distended. Their hooves clanged on rock, a rugged array of slabbed basalt ledges, seamed with the angry flows of lava and bubbling, sulfurous mud pots.

"If this is a drake's dream," the Mad Prophet ventured, "what we now cross would be their preferred habitat." He broke off, forced to cough from the acidic bite of swirled ash. "Sethvir told me once the dragons used to roll in molten rock the way birds splash their feathers in a rain puddle. Burned the dross off new scales as a snake would shed an old skin."

Had the horses not been dull with exhaustion, main force could not have coerced them to abide such a crossing. The ground was hot enough to blister through boot leather, and singe nasal membranes at each breath. Scoured eyes streamed hot tears. The porous, sharp edges of solidified lava slit skin at a glancing touch.

Suffering still from smoke-damaged lungs, Felirin hacked and spluttered. Then Arithon's mare gashed her fetlock in a stumble. Though she moved lame, Dakar feared to stop. The ground was unstable. Too much could go wrong if they tarried to shift the prince's slack form to another mount.

"If we linger, we'll sicken," he rasped through a raw larynx. "The fumes here are poison."

No choice remained but push on, each stumbling stride accomplished in unalloyed misery. Through the plodding, grim labor, Dakar could not tell if the spiral they walked seemed smaller and tighter, or whether the effect was the offshoot of headache and dizziness. Feathered drifts of ash caved in to hide tracks. Canyons of etched lava confounded each effort to sight lines for orientation. He could scarcely manage the task of tugging his horse and Arithon's forward. All hope was lost if the spiral's last coils departed from a safe track.

At weary length, the lava flows faded to smoking pits of used ash. The stone smoothed, bleached to a powdery, fine dust as clinging as pulverized porcelain. Smoke and fumes leached away to a turbid, blank haze, and the heat ebbed to dry, cruel cold.

No moss grew; no trees. What passed for sky seemed a drumhead of cloud, stretched the flat, dull pallor of scraped chalk. Against that unmarked, monochrome backdrop, a skeleton loomed like spired iron. The ribs spanned through air in vast, gabled arches. Long, scything horns on the knobs of each vertebra spiked upright, a gigantic array of pronged tusks. The bones gleamed a glossy, unearthly pearl white, with stripped cartilage lucent as quartz.

"Dragon," breathed Felirin. He blinked, rubbed soot from gummed eyelids. The splayed, flint black curves of three talons pierced the ground, of a size to paralyze reason. A destrier could have walked underneath without hindrance. Speechless, stunned, the minstrel stared, riveted. "Ath, the terrible size of her!"

Dakar as well felt his flesh bathed in chills. As a child, he had seen living Paravians, whom none could encounter without change. This behemoth wreckage was long dead, and yet, it commanded a presence which rankled his nerves into shivers. No feat of mortal imagination could capture the monumental grandeur of what *was* scribed in these glyphs of naked bone.

Braced in arched rows, such ribs could have served as the vaults of a palace; and had, Dakar recalled through a vague flick of memory.

Melhalla's last high kings had convened court and served judgment under just such a buttressed hall. The domed, copper roofs had been shingled in drake scales, a legend even before the great uprising, when the ruling seat at Tirans had been gutted by fire and cast down into ruins.

The tail, with its delicate, vaned rudder and needle-thin spines rested curled in an exquisite, neat grace that bespoke the coiled threat of a predator. Despite such vast size, no creature from any past era in Athera could react with the speed of a dragon.

"Sethvir once confided the great drakes were agile enough to brave the crosswinds in a thundercloud." Dakar shook his head, bemused to amazement. Credibility balked at the scale of such feats. These shining remains had tasted the ice crystals combed into white cirrus, when once, clothed in glittering gold scales and wild malice, the live dragon had knifed through the riptide currents of high altitude.

The skull they encountered loomed the size of a hay byre. Its black, shadowed eye sockets did not seem empty. Even in death, their uncanny survey guarded the shadowy realms past the Wheel. They appeared alert still, broodingly hooded in massive, spiked horn, and overlapped plates of etched bone.

Felirin ventured a timorous query. "Is it so, that the relics of dragons carry a bane?"

"Who knows?" Dakar stamped back his shivering dread. The inescapable fact remained that their steps were being guided ever nearer to the colossal skeleton. "There's truth to the saying that where centaurs fell, the stones of the earth weep in sorrow. Dragon bones are much older and by lengths more eldritch. I've heard the skulls of the unhatched younglings have ties to dark magecraft, but that could be taletelling, for all I know of the details."

They rounded the serrated spurs of a forelimb. Ahead, like sheared porcelain, the long, scything fangs propped open the gates of horned jaws. Rows of incisors gnashed through the blanketing dust, razor tipped as the prongs on a whipsaw.

Nor were the three exhausted fugitives the first to arrive at the site.

Light shattered the clogged air like hurled blades, fanned through the points of knobbed bone. A figure in dark robes astride a black horse shouted in pealing urgency. He bridged the small gap where the dragon's forked tongue had once flickered, his outstretched hands streaming power like beacons. The flux of raised forces stormed across mortal senses like the roar of impending cataclysm.

Felirin froze in his tracks, undone by dread. "Ath Creator keep us safe."

"Not Ath at all. That's Asandir." Dakar shot out an arm and hauled the bard forward. The unwholesome fumes seared his throat as he croaked, "We can't linger."

No Fellowship Sorcerer ever burned reckless power without cause. By the singing charge that lashed his awareness, Dakar understood the danger loomed too vast to grapple. Only once before had he seen Asandir unleash his full strength, and that on the hour the Mistwraith had attacked Lysaer and Arithon at Ithamon.

Then as now, the power streamed outward in crackling rays, no brute stab of force, but the unbridled might of fine energies called down by a spirit schooled into peerless unity with every facet of Ath's creation. The result ranged harmonics like a hammer blow to bronze, showering light in waves of continuous vibration.

"Come on," Dakar gasped. "We're in deadly peril." The unshielded might of a Fellowship Sorcerer could derange mortal thoughts, even leave a man witless and paralyzed.

The spellbinder fell back upon ingrained reflex and impelled his stunned limbs to keep moving. However he cowered and shrank from close contact, he feared worse to cross the outright command of a Sorcerer raised to the flash-point pinnacle wrought from bridled chaos and immaculate intent. Dakar prodded the horses' stumbling strides to narrow the last distance between.

Felirin hung back, stupefied, until an appeal from Asandir yoked the gray with a word that could have moved rooted granite. The horse led the minstrel, bonded in light, and a mystery outside plodding reason.

They crossed inside the proximity of the Fellowship conjury.

"Well-done, but hurry," Asandir exhorted. "The currents of this dream state aren't kindly or biddable." His voice cut through actinic bursts of refined power as if speech had been honed by something beyond sound. "I won't be able to temper the forces here to keep you alive for much longer."

Dakar forced the question. "Then this isn't Arithon's creation of despair?"

"Never that," Asandir flung back, strained. "Move him on. Hurry. He's unconscious because his own trained defenses are killing him."

But the order itself proved most difficult to carry out. The potency of the Sorcerer's wards of themselves seemed to hamper free movement. Dakar felt as though each of his steps was dragged through shimmering mercury. The powerfield scoured his mage-sight until vision dissolved behind a deluge of silver-tipped sleet. His tired mind could not compensate.

He was vaguely aware of passing the gateway between the dragon's front teeth. Two horses followed, their breath hot on his neck, and through that sensation, the ghost-feather touch of Asandir's guiding hand on his shoulder.

"Keep going, as you love life!" The Sorcerer's raw strength steadied him over the pothole of bone that yawned between the vast jaw-bones. "Don't worry about shielding. I'll see that Felirin comes to no harm."

"The dragon," Dakar asked. "Do you fear she'll awaken?"

Asandir faced him, his surprise etched in glare, and his eyes the flecked gray of rinsed granite. "Ath, no. She's been dead for two ages. You don't see? This grimward contains the left dreams of her haunt."

"A *ghost's* imprint?" Dakar stared, his skin ashen. "Dharkaron's own tears! You're saying a live one would dream the more powerfully?"

"Enough to reweave the known fabric of creation." Asandir's brisk push sent him onward, under the ribbed vaults of the gullet. "Go now. To leave, you must enter the inner chamber of the skull. The passage won't be smooth or comfortable, but rest on my word. You'll emerge unmarked in due time."

The Mad Prophet tightened his sweaty grip on the lead reins. The horses trailed at his heels without protest, thralled to submission by spells. "You're not coming yourself?"

Asandir shook his head. "Forty Alliance guardsmen crossed into the grimward's sealed circle. Twenty eight have perished for their folly. If they killed game, or broke off so much as a leaf in this place, my powers could not stay their spirits from entanglement. More will be lost ere they reach my protection. For the sake of any who may live to win through, I have obligation to stay. Once I lift my influence, the dream will revert back to entropic chaos. Only another great drake could survive, and then solely because it could remake the torn structure of its being."

The Sorcerer's last words splashed a patter of echoes through a thousandfold crannies of chambered bone. "Dakar, caution your prince." The admonishment filtered through the ringing reverberations of hooves striking the slagged plates of the fire vents at each side of the dragon's throat. "Any guardsman who emerges alive from this grimward will remember his fear and cry vengeance. Be wary. Blame will fall on the Master of Shadow for all of Hanshire's slain company."

"Tell *my* prince," Dakar grumbled. He resisted the craven urge to shut his eyes and ignore the forbidding cavern which yawned ahead of his quaking steps. "Since when did I *ever* swear fealty to a madman wanted dead by half the townsmen on the continent?"

Any future concern seemed a pittance before the crossing still left to surmount. From behind, a flurried prayer as Felirin braved the dark on the tails of the glassy-eyed horses. Dakar crept into the fusty darkness. His boot soles slipped and minced across a surface like watered marble, while the unseen, vaulted cranium flung back echoes of each wheezing breath. In blind trust, the Mad Prophet hoped Arithon stayed on the mare as the lightless cavern engulfed him. Sound just beyond the high range of his hearing seemed to ripple like ribbon across his ears. Then his vision shimmered, punched through by sparks and sequins of chipped obsidian. A rash of fine prickles stabbed over his skin, and vertigo twisted his senses.

Then a magic wrapped in energies he had never known bathed all of his nerve ends in fire. Every last tie to creation unraveled. Sucked into the well of primal oblivion, Dakar realized in panic that this crossing was nothing like a guided spell transfer from a familiar Paravian focus circle. As his mind spiraled down toward the heart of null darkness, he cried out in sheer panic. He did not know how to untangle this pattern. Nor had he the clues to the necessary knowledge cached amid his muddled memories of prostitutes. No one had taught him the guidepost to relocate the haven of Athera's known territory.

Recall

Just before solstice, the nights in Caithwood held a soft, breathing warmth, the air thick as milk in the pearlescent moonlight which streamed through the dense crowns of old oak trees. These ancient groves had never tasted the axe blade. Nor had black soil known the bite of the plow, or the turned iron rim of the cart wheel. The pale, whorled bark of ancient copper beeches wore mottles like coin silver where the strung-floss motes speared the darkness. Rolling combers off Mainmere Bay lisped through, sea and earth joined in dialogue by the whisper of the leaves that stirred to the tireless breezes. The mockingbird's song and the whistles of nightjars spilled liquid notes through the stillness, much as they had in Paravian times when centaur guardians had reigned, and the sunchild dancers had called down the mysteries that moved, incarnate, with the wild grace of the unicorns.

In Third Age 5653, no Athlien flutes rang through Caithwood's glades to celebrate the joy of the season; nor did centaur horn calls reverberate under the eaves of the oaks. Yet in their absence, the low, sandy shoreline which faced Havish and the sands at Torwent did not pass unpatrolled. In furtive, tight bands, Lord Maenol's scouts kept watch for oncoming Alliance ships.

A month past, the contents of Mearn s'Brydion's warning had reached them, word of the coming blockade brought in by runner from Mogg's Fen. The Caithwood clans knew of the Koriani conspiracy at Riverton which had set Arithon s'Ffalenn to blind flight. They received the worst news with grim determination, that three finished vessels had sailed from their launching, packed with Etarran men-at-arms and sealed orders to cut off Mainmere Narrows until nothing alive could slip through. At all costs, the handful of scouts understood they must hold the coastline open, that the families set to flight from the north could stay free to seek promised sanctuary in Havish.

Never mind their strength was insufficient for the task, their numbers pared thin by bloodshed and necessity. Lord Maenol's appeal asked no quarter, allowed space for no preference or pity.

Despite closing threat, no one thought of desertion. The Caithwood scouts kept their posts, their forest held sacrosanct by a hard-bitten few, sworn to lay down life and safety for their *caithdein*.

Not even the lean fisherman's dory run in by dark escaped their exhaustive vigilance.

"Two occupants," whispered the woman who had just sprinted in from the lookout at the mouth of the Narrows. "One passive, and the other manning the oars. Neither looks armed. We saw no glint of weapons, but then, sure's storm, they haven't come here to go cod fishing."

The stern elder who captained the outpost made his immediate decision. "Watch then. They don't leave the shingle unchallenged." A hand signal sent two reserve scouts off on foray, with the elder himself at the fore.

By the raked dunes at the shoreline, the three clansmen crouched wary in rustling stands of sea grass, while the dory knifed in to make landfall. Its sharp prow and muffled oars formed a cut black phantom against lucent lace sheets that billowed and surged where the froth of spent breakers receded. As the curl of the surf shot the craft through the shallows, the old scout made comment. "Torwent fisherman. See the woven string bracelets? He's also damned good with the boat."

The man dragged his broad looms, and in dauntless competence, let his keel gently ground into sand.

The other figure in the stern seat clambered out, the brimmed hat he wore obscuring his face from clear view. While the inbound combers fountained over his shins, he leaned down and recovered a satchel he had tucked safely under the stern seat. An older man, he seemed an enigma, his simple, dark clothing too plain to identify a regional origin. Though his burden was not heavy, an odd hitch to his movements bespoke stiffened scars or old injuries. The hands that clasped the dory's thwart and redirected it seaward were gnarled and bent, if still competent.

His spoken farewell did not carry. The oarsman nodded in

clipped respect, then dug in his looms to hurry his return passage before the riptide raced through the Narrows. The one he had covertly delivered to Caithwood waded shoreward, his limp grown pronounced as the wet sand mired his ankles. Once on dry ground, he paused, the flat spill of the moonlight licking the hanks of white, shoulder-length hair. He tipped his face skyward. Beneath the brimmed hat, his features were cragged and intent, as if he expected an omen.

Out of the night, a raven flapped down and settled upon his raised wrist.

He lilted a greeting. The bird answered back, then sidestepped to perch on his shoulder.

"Here's a friend." The scout captain stood in the shoulder-high dune grass, his distrust melted into glad greeting. "Traithe?"

The Fellowship Sorcerer turned his clean-shaven chin and smiled. "My blessing, yes. You're Maenol's captain?"

"For Caithwood, I am." The elder strode forward, then beckoned for the other hidden scouts to reveal themselves. While the velvet thick breeze stirred the fronds on the seed heads, and the raven on Traithe's shoulder stretched a coal wing to preen, the older captain presented the courtesy of the clans to visiting members of the Fellowship. "How may we serve the land?"

Traithe hooked the strap of his satchel, and stroked the bird's breast with his knuckle. "My tidings aren't joyous. I need you to tell me where I might find Earl Jieret s'Valerient, who serves Prince Arithon as *caithdein* of Rathain."

"Please Ath, not a death!" The female scout fanned off trailing mosquitoes and strode forward. "Or do you bring warning of the Alliance attack we've expected for over a fortnight?"

The Sorcerer reached out at once and touched her tense wrist, laced into its bowman's leather bracer. "Not a death. But I can't keep that promise without your help and swift action. Is the Earl with your band?"

"He's four hours north of here, quartered in a hidden glen." The scout captain extended a hand to assist with the satchel, then deferred as Traithe chose to retain the burden himself. Since a Sorcerer's ways were no man's to question, the captain moved on without embarrassment. "Shore's not altogether safe with Alliance galleys plying the bay on patrol. We'll send a runner."

But Traithe shook his head as he fell into stride. "Spare your man." The play of the breeze riffled his platinum hair, while the hat's looming brim threw a shadow like ink over his urgent expression. "If you know the way to this glen that you speak of, describe the terrain. My raven can lead me."

"The path is straightforward." The captain's pinched gaze swung away from his uneasy survey of the offshore horizon. "Best we finish the details out of sight from this beachhead. If your bird can fly under guidance, the camp where Jieret's quartered keeps horses."

Traithe's gratitude showed as a gleam of white teeth in jet shadow. "My raven can summon him, then. If Earl Jieret can manage to be here before daybreak, the land will be served very well."

"You bring news of the Alliance?" pressed the other scout. Lanky, and just come to early manhood, he kept a swaggering fist on his sword hilt. More than the others, he seemed drawn by the stress of the pending Alliance invasion.

"Nothing so simple." Traithe no longer smiled, the bracketed lines at the corners of his mouth grooved deep with the wear of hard travel. "In a desperate move to cut off pursuit, Prince Arithon crossed through a grimward."

"Ath preserve!" the woman scout whispered.

Before her aghast fear, the Sorcerer used what logic he had to feed hope. "Rathain's prince was well trained by a master at magecraft. He survived the dangerous passage well enough, but his conscience is troubled. He required more than self-discipline to keep his despair in check. Now those defenses have driven him far beyond waking consciousness. He will stay lost between dimensional realities unless Jieret s'Valerient can reach past the veil and find him."

Surrounded by worried clan faces, and a quiet that bred desperation, the Sorcerer flexed his shoulders in a tight shrug. The raven croaked in complaint, its wings unfolded for balance. "We have no choice. The ties of the blood pact sworn between the *caithdein* and his prince must be enacted to recall the Teir's'Ffalenn across time and space." In gentle reminder, Traithe hastened his step toward the sheltering dark of the forest. "Timing is crucial. The opening spells to bridge the connection must be enacted at dawn."

He did not speak of the dire hurdles to be crossed, nor mention the unconscionable intensity of Arithon's grief, or the mind-stripping, ingrained misery which might come to thwart his best effort. The prospect of failure was too real, too immediate. Arithon's downfall might lie at hand despite all his help, and Earl Jieret's willing duty to be called to shoulder the sacrifice. A Sorcerer left crippled by past conflict with the Mistwraith could do naught but listen, as his bird did the same, head cocked to one side, while the Caithwood captain gave terse description of the location and landmarks of the camp where Earl Jieret took shelter.

"Go brother," Traithe murmured. A testy croak answered. The raven flapped silken wings and launched on its errand. Its flight clove the falling, gossamer moonbeams like a silent, obsidian cleaver, then arrowed up through a gap in the foliage.

The Sorcerer stared after his bird's vanished form, hands knotted over the strap of his satchel. The bird bridged what access he could wring from maimed talent, and until it returned, he was both mortal and blinded. Too aware the comfort of polite hospitality fell short, the scouts pressed close and took charge. "You must be tired. Let us know if you're hungry." In soft words and brisk movement, they shared every amenity they could offer under the eaves of the forest.

Their outpost was temporary, a narrow, hidden glen tucked behind the bulrushes of a tidal marsh. Maples and oaks leaned over a brook whose banks were entangled in brambles. The scouts not on watch dozed on piles of bracken, cut fresh to drive off biting insects. They lit no cookfire. Swords were kept within immediate reach, and no one packed belongings beyond skinning knives and a hunting bow. Through the lush season, they foraged fish and game, and smoked food for the trail when hunting would slow their swift progress.

At ease with the untamed fabric of night, Traithe's form melted into the tangled darkness under the leafed crown of old forest. His tacit awareness tracked the flutter of moths and the rustles of mice in the undergrowth, while someone's shy boy offered him dried meat and berries, and a chilly dipper of springwater. Weary though he was, he chose not to sleep.

Patient for the return of his raven, he spoke his thanks in a resonant baritone, one knee drawn up and clasped to his chest. If sheer calm could command the elements, his poise could have arrested the fugitive trickle of water over rocks in the streamlet. His ever-present worry lay perfectly masked, while each minute fretted past, and a hunting owl flew, and a late-singing mockingbird caroled a solo through the last hours of darkness.

His vigil did not pass without camaraderie. While the wind stroked through the boughs overhead, and summer stars marked and measured their courses, three wakeful scouts exchanged jibes and desultory small talk. "Not to worry," assured one, caught napping between topics. "Quiet's thick enough to suffocate. An inbound horseman is going to draw notice like a drum squad."

The scarred veteran who wound bowstrings from a coil of dried gut resumed listing the particulars of the Alliance campaign that savaged the wilds of south Tysan. "No good news, from upstream. We've a precious narrow margin, and no hope at all if our seaward horizon doesn't stay empty. It's plain once the ships come, we haven't a prayer."

The battle-scarred woman raked her whetstone in a vehement pass across the weapon bridged across her bare knees. "Sunwheel troops are riddled through the vales above Mainmere. Person can't walk to the riverside to piss without being set after by dogs."

Another scout wearing an otter-claw necklace filled in laconic detail. "They've swept the forests as far south as Cainford. Nobody escapes their patrols, it's that tight. We have families trapped in the mountains who've had to hole up past the snow line. They can scarcely brave the open plain to cross Camris. Armed companies can move in too fast off the trade road, and time's now our bitterest enemy."

Traithe worked his scarred knuckles to keep the joints supple, unable to deny the assessment. Scarcity of game, or bad weather in autumn would eventually drive the trapped clan fugitives out of hiding. Already, the Alliance net spread over the lowlands to snare them.

"They could survive well enough in the heights," another scout picked up. "But no one can win past to send them provisions. We've bloodied ourselves trying. Too many armed companies with sunwheel banners are camped tight as ticks in the foothills. Gold from the trade guilds keeps them supplied, and their dogs have been cut to run silent."

"And Lord Maenol?" Traithe asked, carefully neutral lest his deep apprehension burden the troubled scouts further.

The one blacking his features with charcoal in readiness for patrol tossed his used stick into the streamlet, his frustration a whisper of leathers in darkness. "Our *caithdein's* trapped down in the marshes. Fenlanders shelter him as best they can, but he's been on the run since the springtime."

A jagged gap held the dammed-back questions no one dared ask concerning the overdue Alliance ships. For well past a fortnight, the watch on the shoreline had expected armed forces to seal a blockade over the Narrows. The Alliance's crowning strategy would cut off the last avenue of escape for the clan families driven south, who might claim safe sanctuary under King Eldir in Havish.

Traithe stared at the scarred knuckles laced like braid over the sound knee tucked to his chest. He could give no encouragement. News from the Warden of Althain always ran through his raven, and the latest sending had held only the images of two brigs in convoy at sea. He had not picked up any visible landmark to guess their proximity to Caithwood.

"I'm sorry. I bear you no news, ill or good." The Sorcerer chafed, pulled a raw breath, then admitted, "If Earl Jieret can pull Prince Arithon through, the spellbinder Dakar will be with him. Our combined efforts can bridge a clear contact to the Warden at Althain Tower. Sethvir will have the answers you need."

The earth link would show where the danger lay, and give accurate account of the *Cariadwin*'s fated landfall at Corith.

Despite the gravity of clan woes in Tysan, one sharp-eyed young strategist picked up the unspoken thread. "You imply Rathain's prince may not be successfully recovered?"

"There is that grim chance." Traithe looked up, his coffee eyes bleak with an honesty that admitted no shame for his weakness. "The Fellowship Sorcerers are beleaguered with troubles. At this time, I was the only one able to come here. Ath grant us the grace that Jieret's courage and my services will be enough to bring Prince Arithon through."

After that, there was indeed little to say, and nothing to do but wait out the night in defined, silent tension.

Ink against darkness, a shape rode the air in the stilled, murky hour before dawn. The scout captain started, hand closed on his sword until a touch from the Sorcerer calmed him. "Peace. No harm's come."

The raven fluttered down and settled with a boisterous croak on its master's black-clad shoulder. The rider it had summoned cantered in a moment later and dismounted at the head of the glen. Unasked, the younger scout rose to take the reins and care for the horse. The arrival himself made almost no sound as he strode into the encampment. Jieret s'Valerient was clad in laced deer hide with fringes that accentuated his firm breadth of shoulder. He smelled of bruised greenery and overheated horse, underlain with the tang of oil from the well-kept weapons at his waist. Adverse to language where actions would serve, he raked a glance over the seated forms of the scouts, then fixed on the Fellowship Sorcerer.

No hesitation marked his greeting as he sank before Traithe on bent knee.

His clan braid had been freshly bound, a reflection of his quiet pride and sure bearing, though his straight posture gave clear enough indication that he sensed the gravity of this meeting. "What do you ask for the realm?"

"*Caithdein*, Steward of Rathain," Traithe intoned. He arose in formality, while around him, Caithwood's scouts backed off to grant a respectful privacy. "I ask by your oath to your kingdom, that you risk life and limb for your prince."

Jieret's reply was clipped iron. "By my ancestor's promise to the Fellowship, my consent lies in your hands already."

Traithe shifted his weight, unable to find surcease from the pull of old scars. More than bodily pain plagued him as he reached and caught Jieret's wrists and raised the younger man before him.

The clan chieftain loomed a handspan taller. His leonine head bent to the Sorcerer's regard, Jieret said, "You're distressed. Why? Do you fear that I carry the weal of the realm as an unwanted burden?"

"You should fear." The Sorcerer released his clasp in trepidation. "What you face could become far more than a burden. I invoke free consent because the need you must answer lies outside the world you understand. I come to beg your willing heart to let your spirit ride the winds." A pause, while the impact of that statement sank in. "If your prince is to be safely recalled to Athera, that's the last way left to draw him."

Jieret shivered despite his most firm resolve. "Where did you send him?" he demanded, the first dangerous edge to a trust already granted without question.

Traithe did not rebuke, nor distress his set loyalties, but met challenge with a sincerity that could have breached the interlocked matrix of diamond. "To escape certain death at the hands of the Alliance, Asandir allowed your crown prince to pass through a grimward."

Jieret flinched. Force of will held him steady for a running string of heartbeats. Then his hands clamped, and he tipped back his face. "How my father would weep." Eyes shut in agony, he swore until he ran out of breath.

"That's scarcely the evil fate you imagine." Traithe drew him aside where the whisper of foliage could settle and ease his cranked tension. "Your prince sealed off his mind, that his poisonous guilt for Caolle's death would not ruin him. There's the problem, you see. Arithon's trained barriers are unimaginably strong. He's locked his mind behind a protective unconsciousness few things alive could break through. That kept him safe from the grimward's dire influence. Only now, he has sealed his awareness too deep. Even Sethvir cannot cross his defenses to reach him."

Jieret reached out and braced against the rough bole of an oak. His profile shone pale in the waning moonlight, and his stance stayed wide set, as if earth itself threatened his balance. "Ath guard my prince." He managed to stay the biting unease from his final reply to the Sorcerer. "My consent is yours, freely. Now, what do you need?"

"Your trust, first of all." Traithe's unbroken calm remained steadying despite the discomfort to his lamed leg. "I will give you every advantage I can, believe it. Prepare yourself. Such a passage is best started in the gray hour of twilight."

Saddened for the strain behind Jieret's set face, he added, "You won't like the method. I'm sorry. My powers are not whole, and because of that damage, we're going to have to use blood magic."

"I gave my agreement," Earl Jieret said, stiff. "There are no conditions. By whatever means, to bring back my liege, I serve the need of Rathain."

"Bless your straight courage." Traithe's break into gratitude could have masked tears as he bent and shouldered his satchel. "We haven't much time left before dawn. If you can bear this, we'll have to start now."

The wind rustled through the dense crowns of the trees, and coiled through brush fringed and heavy with the foil and pearl droplets of summer dew. Enriched by greenery and bearing soil, the dark spanned the forest like uncut velvet, still scribed by ruled rays of moonlight. Yet the sky seemed more indigo than sable, and the mockingbird's solo had silenced. All Caithwood seemed poised at the cusp, while the world's axis turned toward the ending of night.

"I'm ready." Jieret flanked the Sorcerer, his rangy stride shortened in deference to the other's halting gait.

Traithe moved upstream. A short walk led into the grotto the scouts used to draw their fresh water. An underground spring welled in streamlets from a crack in the rocks. Trickles of runoff channeled through moss and boulders to form a shallow pool that spilled into the dagged foam of the creek. There, the current lay divided in the dry months of summer by a washed islet of rounded stones. Traithe splashed through the ankle-deep channel and laid his satchel among the lush cap of moss strewn with the fragrance of shed pine needles. The site owned an innate tranquillity, alive with the melodious splash where the split watercourse rejoined, to gutter and leap down a winding channel that widened and eventually rippled into the pewter stands of the tidal marsh.

"Sit," the Sorcerer instructed, his voice like worn silk and his grandfatherly understanding pitched to transcend ragged nerves. "I have some brief preparations to make."

A pause, while he murmured a phrase to his bird. The raven croaked. Every bit the miffed gentleman, it shuffled sulky wing feathers, then sidled down its master's arm and hopped off. One effortless glide saw it settled upon the bough of a nearby maple. Traithe spoke what sounded like a Paravian epithet in reply to its avian impertinence, then resumed his dropped thread of human dialogue. "My lord Jieret, whatever happens, you may rest assured you will never experience any pain."

The raven cocked its head, avid as a critic, while the Sorcerer knelt. He nursed his scarred hands with relentless patience and undid the knots on his satchel, then removed a thin quartz crystal. In sequence, he took out a stone knife, five clay bowls, and a clean beeswax candle. Last came a leather-wrapped bundle that contained folded packets of dried herbs. He placed each item on the moss before his knees with its Name and a ritual blessing.

Then he looked up at Jieret, whose apprehension all but sang aloud like a strand of overcranked wire. "If you have tight clothing, loosen the laces. The ground here is soft. Choose a place where you can lie down and be comfortable."

Jieret scraped his wrist bracer across the bristled red beard on his jaw, then busied himself stripping off his sword and the bone-handled throwing knives that he had claimed from his father's dead body. "Will I sleep?"

Traithe stood once again, a clay bowl in hand. His reply floated back as a disembodied whisper as he trod careful steps to the spring. "Your body will. Not your mind."

He spoke over the water in the cadence of Paravian, then dipped the bowl and placed the filled vessel on a nearby stone. Jieret watched, heart pounding, as the black-clad Sorcerer crumbled an aromatic herb into another readied bowl. This one had painted animals on the side that seemed to shift and move in the darkness. Traithe closed his eyes. His features were seamed like the ancient, white birch, mapped by rough usage, yet wholly tranquil as he asked a formal permission. Jieret recognized the Paravian phrase for the living fire, then started as a spark jumped between Traithe's spread hands. The herbs in the bowl sprang into pale flame. Smoke arose, a twining silver braid that turned in the air as if alive. It sifted a veiling haze through the breeze as Traithe stood erect and offered to each cardinal point of the compass, then harkened to the elemental powers of the four directions. Last, he took up the thin crystal. More words of invocation, the symmetry of each syllable fluid as liquid light. Jieret could not tell whether the play of the smoke or the language eased his nerves into harmony. He sat, relaxed and half-mesmerized, while a soft glow arose from the palm of Traithe's hand and kindled the crystal into an adamantine blaze of raised force.

The Sorcerer used that summoned power to scribe a clean circle around the small islet of stones. Where the quartz wand passed, a thin sound keened, striking a blade of pure energy that parted a rip through the air.

"Not to fear," Traithe assured as if from great distance. "These are but simple protections to bind and contain the regenerative forces we'll raise here."

Yet somehow Jieret sensed the import was more weighty, as if the spelled circle cut ties through time and space and engaged powers beyond mortal understanding. The raven launched into flight. Dense as pressed ink against the substanceless night, it shuttled in patterns overhead. The rings of its passage dizzied the mind. Jieret blinked, disbelieving, as his eye seemed to track an uncanny energy combed into alignment by the bird's feathers. Each quill seemed attached to a streamer of light. Rather than lose himself forever in bewitching mystery, he settled for the ordinary task of unbuckling his belt.

Around him and past the water's purled edge, Traithe moved about his work, his lamed tread uncannily silent. He placed what seemed an empty bowl to the east, then the fire bowl to the south, water to west, and one he had filled with plain dark earth to the north. Each pause involved a singing invocation that ignited another strand of unseen current, and wove its flow to the joined circle.

Jieret clamped back the unease that surged through his gut. As if violence could somehow reground his turned senses, he yanked the leather tie on his braid, then plowed stiffened fingers through the hair at his temples, dragging the plait loose at his nape. Another glance, darted sidewards; "You're making my hair stand on end."

Straight on his feet with his eyes closed, Traithe appeared halfway removed from the world, his cragged features remote as chased marble; and yet, when he answered, his human warmth was never more real and immediate. "Not to worry. There is no power raised here that is not a part of Ath's order." At the center of the circle, he took up the final bowl and shook out the last packet of herbs. This plant loosed a fragrance biting as snow, and a pungency that stripped all five senses to preternatural wakefulness.

"Tienelle," Traithe explained. He tipped back his hat to unstick damp hair at his temples. "What you commonly know as seersweed. The properties of the flower break down the barriers between space and time, and release the mind to an unclouded view of the continuum. For your safety, the full potency will be weakened. You'll receive just enough smoke to loosen the ties to your body, that your spirit can be freed to search."

Jieret said nothing, his throat dried to sand that left him unable to swallow.

Traithe's glance held a grave and reassuring kindness as he noticed the earl's knotted fists. "You don't have to go through with this. We can stop now."

Jieret jerked up his chin, just shy of offense. "Keep on. I am blood bonded with my prince. This is my job and no other's."

"But a straight battle with steel would be simpler," Traithe admitted in bald understanding. "Be steady. I stand with you, never forget that."

He called fire and lit the herb. The smoke whirled and twined, spun silk against a darkness ingrained with the faint paling imprint of daybreak. Jieret drew a fast breath, apprehension tightening his chest despite every verbal resolve. He had but one moment for shattering fear. Then the herb's fragrance burned through the floor of his lungs, seized his heartstrings, and hurled him into a spiraling vertigo that whirled him headlong from the earth.

Dimly he realized Traithe was still speaking. Hands touched his skin, a nagging distraction that badgered him to lie down. Wrung through and disoriented, he fretted at the contact. His mind rampaged through turmoil, then found its release like a beast sprung out of a trap. His awareness burst open. The shrill song of stars threaded the gaps between leaves, and the wind sighed through his being. Its rustling passage through summer green branches framed a language he could almost understand.

Traithe loomed above him, his dark clothes the same shimmering, iridescent obsidian as the plumage of his raven. He towered, a figure of primordial mystery punched through the spun cloth of twilight. He raised the stone knife, its blade of white chert trailing filaments of blue light.

Jieret blinked, while the earth turned, the majesty of her dance a vibration that thrummed through his bones. The stars paled, then burst into pearlescent sparks that burned through the backdrop of daybreak. Then the clouds ignited also, their drifting serenity shot into fire-opal patterns. Nesting thrushes sang out a chord that knitted the air into ecstasy. Jieret felt warm fingers clasp his right hand, then bear down, pinning his forearm. The textures of cold dew and mossy stones screamed detail like etched light down the trackways of over-stimulated flesh.

He heard Traithe's voice, a whisper of sound strung on a filament that corded the arc of eternity. "By your blood bond to Prince Arithon s'Ffalenn, by the ties that lie beyond life and limb, you will seek. *Let two become one.*"

Then the knife traced the scar of a much older cut, taken before a past battle that left the banks of Tal Quorin soaked with the reaped fruits of hatred. The stone edge of the blade that was *now* scored and bit. Its savage, hot sting raised a sleeting, bright numbness. Freed blood scalded hot over the *caithdein*'s bared skin. The knife's edge smoked light. Through half-opened eyes and a mind deranged by the herb smoke, Jieret watched the uncanny, cold fires off the sharpened chert meet and join with the haze that misted from the flow of his opened vein.

"Ride the winds with my blessing, Jieret s'Valerient!" Traithe scribed a sign that melded the trifold forces of stone knife, flesh, and life. The twined powers blazed, then towered, transformed into resonance fierce enough to blind vision and scatter the last vestige of reason.

A wind out of vacuum rushed through Jieret's mind. He cried aloud, his voice a splash of raw noise amid the howling expanse of the infinite. Then his last tie to human awareness hurled up and out though the crown of his head. He whirled on the vast chord of sound and light that wove the span of Ath's universe, insignificant and frail as a leaf unmoored by the chill gales of autumn.

The sun rose, spilling dappled gold spangles over the spring, and cascading sequined reflections off the small stream. But inside the scribed circle, where Traithe sat on vigil, the gray half-light of dawn hung and lingered. Time froze in place there, poised on the filament of Earl Jieret's courage and the Sorcerer's cast force of intent. A small stone pipe by Traithe's knee held the spent ashes of more tienelle leaves, the last ember gone cold with the morning. Submerged in deep trance, poised as a bridge across the veil of the mysteries, he cupped his scarred hands over the brow of the prostrate Earl of the North. The stone knife was cleaned, the cut wrist neatly bandaged. Jieret's hawk features were a stilled casting in wax, his fox hair a cry of bright color against a pillow of emerald moss.

Nothing moved in that tableau. The raven kept watch, its eyes amber beads that scarcely shifted or blinked though the days came and went in their natural rhythm outside of the spell-circle laid through the crystal.

Then, as if summoned by some unseen cue, the bird launched into flight and disappeared. Traithe's tranced awareness sensed its departure, as under the distant guidance of Althain's Warden, it departed the plane of dense matter and crossed into the spirit worlds, strung like infinite cast shadows between the poles of primal energy and firmament.

Though Traithe's eyes remained closed, he stared beyond the brink of time's prison and into the limitless unknown. He held guard in that place marking space for the gateway, while a finespun trail of magnetic light traced the path of Earl Jieret's journey. Behind the *caithdein*'s lead, a shot arrow of feather and bone, a bird who was more than mere life and flesh flew on a mission of recovery. There existed no recourse. Either the blood tie would call Earl Jieret to Prince Arithon, and afford a firm contact to draw from, or all three would be lost, bird, man, and prince; and the prophet and bard along with them.

"Fly brother," Traithe urged in spun dream to his raven. "Follow, and bridge the connection to bring them all back."

There were no guarantees. Earl Jieret's awareness might ride the winds seeking for an untold span of time. If, in that interval, the Alliance attack swept through Caithwood, or if even one man disturbed the precise spells of suspension Traithe had laid down, the *caithdein* of Rathain would be torn back into the linear patterns of time and entropy. Should that misfortune happen, his comatose flesh would again become subject to the cruel passage of days. Severed from consciousness, Jieret's tie to breathing life would fade and weaken. Attrition would claim his body and organs, until his vital signs failed and Fate's Wheel turned, bringing final oblivion and death.

Discovery

Summer sun streamed through the wide windows of the Koriani sisterhouse at Capewell, laden with the tang of green herbs from the gardens, and the brisk tonic of salt winds off the sea. The fish markets teemed under pale, golden light. Elderly women exchanged gossip at the well, their pails and jugs clumped on the cobbles, while through the lingering heat of afternoon, the craftsmen's wives gathered on the colonnaded balconies and sewed sequined masks for the harvest festival. In the shade of the walled courtyard, the orphan boys shouted at their games, free through the indolent days while the crops slowly ripened, and the crofters required no labor. If the waterfront inns catered to men-at-arms wearing sunwheel surcoats, or if the roads wore the passage of couriers and patrols in hanging clouds of fine dust, Tysan's crown treasury honored its debts for their lodging. In the lazy month while the barley ripened, the season left time for indulging the gifts of earth's bounty.

The Koriani Prime Matriarch harbored no such soft sentiment through her tedious days of convalescence. Imprisoned by her debilitating weakness, and fed on the brew of yet another bitter defeat, she lay swathed in thin coverlets. Her eggshell flesh showed each blue track of vein. Bones pressed against skin seamed and worn to translucency, the joints like knobbed pearl beneath. Through the weeks since the spell construct's release had roused her from coma, her glistening black eyes lent the sole spark of life to her visage.

She refused idle company. The least small disturbance barraged her strained nerves. Sound and light taxed her senses past endurance, as if the trial of living exhausted repetitive discipline. The bedchamber appointed for her recovery was always kept dim for that reason. Thick curtains were drawn over the paned windows to close out the noise and the frenetic stimulation brought in on strayed currents of breeze. The dammed-in heat of the summer afternoons burdened the stilled air, dense as a wool blanket, and choked with the scents of the medicinal teas to cosset her wasted flesh. The gnawing needs of her intellect were more difficult to appease.

Each day, by the sweltering light of a beeswax candle, a senior-rank seeress in dove gray silk sat in strict attendance with a scrying crystal tucked on her knees.

"Matriarch," she responded, as she had countless times to the same scantly whispered request, "I search, but find no sign or presence of Arithon s'Ffalenn. The crystal shows me naught yet again but the cold fog of the veil."

A dry breath stirred the bundled form in the bedding. "He's too clever by far. That's the bane of his mother's lineage." Morriel forced out another thready whisper, rough as scabbed rust in the gloom. "He is not on Athera, then." Her hands lay half-curled, crabbed as the feet of a petrified songbird, each hideous detail exaggerated in shadow spun by the crawling spearpoint of flame. "Proceed."

"Your will, matriarch." The seeress bent to her travail, the bound knot of her hair bone ivory in the gloom, and her collar stuck to her moist neck. The drill she enacted would follow repetitive routine, her efforts divided between three futile searches, none of which changed from one day to the next. Already, the resident Senior Circle at this sisterhouse whispered in corners that the Prime had lapsed into her dotage. The rumors were kept guarded, with no successor at hand to receive an appeal for review. The peeress stayed loyal, and as an outsider, the seeress chose not to speculate. Bound by her vows to unquestioned obedience, she blotted the steamed moisture off her palms, then rebalanced her mind and gazed once more into the vast depths of the crystal.

This time, her intent was cast to draw in the location of First Senior Lirenda.

Ever since her awakening amid the spent ash of her construct, the Koriani Prime had been consumed by frustration. Her mind would not rest. Not until she knew what had destroyed her laid plan to capture Arithon s'Ffalenn.

Always before this, the crystal scrying had shown darkness, a barrier of blank, impenetrable density that the most gifted talent could not pierce. Resigned to another failure, the seeress tuned her effort with all the skilled force her experience could command. Her will became the refined filament, drawn like steel thread through the aperture of the mysteries.

This time the wall yielded as if no impedance had existed. The seeress gasped. Her mind reeled into vertigo as her gift met and tapped into a scene of turbulence and light. She centered and grounded, by instinct steadying the contact. Sound immersed her, a welter of voices all shouting at once. Jubilation reigned, amid a rushed tumult of tumbling impressions. Somewhere on a beachhead, a small knot of clan scouts were pounding each other's backs and whooping in ecstatic celebration.

The kaleidoscopic chaos of this scrying resisted even the best-trained discipline. The seeress shifted her seeing crystal and probed for the reason. The scenes jerked and spun, spliced one to the next, tethered by what looked like a sparkling strand of silver chain. Darkness and blinding sunlight interfaced at random as the viewpoint swirled and jounced through a packed mass of bodies clad in the plain fringe of forest clansmen. A voice filtered through, distinct above others. "Ath, be careful! That trinket's no booty to send to your sweetheart, but the spell crystal of a Koriani witch, and bound for another hand than yours."

The seeress's horrified gasp ripped the sanctity of Morriel's bed-chamber.

"What has happened?" came the Prime's drilling treble.

"I'm not sure yet." The seeress clasped her stone, desperate not to break ugly news until she could verify her first impression. "Let me make better sense of the images." Sweat stuck her skirts to her thighs as she engaged a sigil to force order through whirling turbulence. Imagery continued to assault her trained senses. The smelting heat in the bedchamber dulled her touch as she grappled to find a thread to seize continuity.

"What do you see?" Morriel asked, querulous. Her hand twitched on the coverlet. "Has mishap befallen my First Senior?"

Eyes closed, hands cupped light as a butterfly's shut wings around the warmed sphere of quartz, the seeress at last captured one angle of contact. She framed another sigil of control and froze the vision in place, then engaged the trained logic of observation to assess the stilled scene by its content. "I see a beach where clansmen weep, run, and shout in celebration. They are hunters or scouts, to judge by the carved-bone talismans laced into the cuffs of their boots. One is a chieftain, the son of a duchess by the four stranded knots in his braid.

In the cove, at anchor, ride two blue-water brigs. They're not under command of Lysaer's Alliance of Light. The banner flying at their masthead is no sunwheel, but a crude rendition in dark colors." She paused, tipped the crystal, but failed to extract any further helpful detail.

On the high bed, Morriel hissed in displeasure. "So. My plan failed at sea. *What went wrong?* I had allowed for every possible setback and contingency." She ranted on, relentless, her words the grate of dead leaves dragged over unyielding granite. "What of my First Senior? She should have sailed with those ships. Is she held captive among enemies?"

The seeress swallowed, her dampened palms clouding a fog on the crystal's slick surface. "Matriarch, no." In distress and uncertainty, she blotted the moisture on her sleeve and exerted her powers of analysis. "I keyed my scrying to Lirenda, as you asked. It would seem that I did not find her directly. Instead, I appear to have captured the resonant signature of her personal quartz pendant." A pause, while she braced to conclude the unthinkable. "What I read is not the First Senior herself, but the crystal that has come to be separated from her presence."

The closed quiet of the chamber acquired the tension of the drawn bow, or the measured arc of the spear as it rushed to transfix flinching tissue. On the bed, the silk coverlet stirred to snatched movement as the Prime's fingers closed into fists. "Who has caused this desecration?" She never asked whether Lirenda still lived; that fact was made obvious. A long-distance scrying could not have connected in the first place if the imprinted crystal had lost its energetic tie to the woman.

Gilt touched with sweat as she leaned to trim the wick of the candle, the seeress resisted the folly of platitudes. Well aware Morriel's ire would find small surcease, she bent again to peruse her crystal. Past the flames' renewed glow, the sealed darkness soaked her in thick, scented silence. No sound intruded. Remote with trance, the seeress suspended cluttered thoughts and quested through the deep focus of her quartz sphere. Now aware her linked imagery arose through an unfiltered contact with the matrix of another mineral, she aligned her intent to compensate for the random sequence of imagery.

Somewhere inside the stone's spiraling lattice, caught in frozen light, she should find an imprint of the desecrating thief who had dared to strip a First Senior of her focus jewel. The stored memory would be encoded as a sequence of vibration from which her linked stone could reassemble a sequential string of events. Through the powers of sigils designed to draw truth from falsehood, she might sift through the traces and unveil the purpose of the stone's present-day mishandling.

Long minutes passed, pressed in the musty atmosphere of sun-heated felt. Morriel's breath rasped in and out, stirring through the stale musk of age. The astringency of brewed herbs hung over a room that resonated with the hollow stillness of a sealed drum. Silence reigned, fraught with the Prime's brooding fury. The candle burned, a smokeless, bright finger in its graceful bronze stand, the floor tiles and the tapestries glinting rich colors only inside of its inadequate light. The spun gold of its touch edged a corner of silk counterpane, and mapped each infinitesimal crease surrounding Morriel's black eyes. Nothing else moved. The Prime's features seemed a cast-porcelain impression, assembled from a caricature of knotted old rags pinned on a framework of skull. Her fingernails gleamed dulled ivory, the skin shriveled beyond any inclination to give or take simple pleasures.

Only power remained, a dragon's balefire caged in sapped flesh by the thorns of bound duty and a dauntless, implacable dedication. Though each passing second bespoke final failure, and the allure of oblivion and death, the Prime's obsidian pupils stayed focused and sharp, sparked by a dangerous impatience.

If that last, held bastion of will should give way, the Matriarch would pass from her office unsucceeded. None other than she could measure the scope of such loss, or comprehend the risk of backlash into cataclysm as prime power ranged free with no prepared vessel at hand to contain the accumulated burden of stored consciousness. Too aware of the fragility holding the balance, the seeress responded, her words like scratched glass against her Prime's nettled expectation. "The crystal was parted from our First Senior by a liegeman of Prince Arithon's. He bore the name Caolle."

"*What?*" Morriel's screech of astonishment shocked the dense quiet, and the quilts jumped to the lash of her fist. "That man should have perished in Riverton of blood loss brought on by a sword thrust!" Hurled into rage beyond reach of aged strength, the Prime Matriarch ranted on in a whisper. "*What has my First Senior done?*"

"Your pardon, matriarch. I do not know." The seeress cringed, shaken out of contact with her talents. "I cannot see her. The crystal will not show her presence, no matter where on the continent I search."

Morriel blinked, her eyes two jet rivets. "That's because she is masked by salt water." One forearm twitched, as if under the skin, the nerves leaped to jolts of pure fire. Next to the duller agony of stiff joints, the torment of pure gall burned the hotter. The Koriani Prime had spent painstaking centuries grooming a successor, only to suffer this balking defeat at the hands of a dying clan swordsman. "More to the point, where is Lirenda's spell crystal now? Who guards the imprinted key to her life, and for what unprincipled purpose?"

Another strung interval, while the seeress bent her head and sought answers across time and distance. Behind tight-latched mullions, the curtains did not stir to the crack of the late-afternoon sea breeze. Morriel lay, her shut lids like blued eggshells. In one of the windows, a trapped fly buzzed and battered for freedom. Its wings striking glass made her nerves flare and sear in sparks of pain from the sound.

In the end, submersed in a suffocating tension, the seeress's answer came clear as flung acid with the impacting force of ill news.

"The crystal resides in the hands of Lord Maenol's barbarians. They have instructions to give it into Prince Arithon's keeping. There can be no chance of its rescue, even by the invasion of Caithwood by the Alliance troops. The clan scouts are jubilant with the fresh news that the ships out of Riverton's royal yard were retaken. Due to Caolle's intervention, and our First Senior's coercion, every one of the Shadow Master's condemned henchmen escaped from captivity while at sea."

Morriel's eyes flickered open, her weighted quiet an obsidian knife that could have scored lines in new iron. "There has been a betrayal," she announced at raw length. Her clawed forefinger crooked on the counterpane. "Come here," she directed. "I would know where our First Senior hides now. I can find out by means of your talents, but only if your link to her spell quartz is given over to my disposal."

The seeress swallowed. Sweat trickled at her throat. Though she knew her free will was demanded in sacrifice, her vows left no recourse to refuse. Her talents were at the command of her order to spend for the greater good of humanity.

"You will come to no harm," Morriel assured, brisk, and beckoned again for close contact.

The seeress arose; not young herself, her knees stiffened in complaint from the hour spent seated on bare flooring. She offered the crystal between her cupped hands in surrender to the will of her Prime Matriarch.

Morriel extended a skeletal finger. Her palsied touch traced a dark sigil over the quartz sphere. If her body was wasted, her powers were immense. A force rocked the sealed room like the shock of a thunderclap. The seeress quailed outright, chilled by recognition that she witnessed none other than the cipher of prime dominion, imprinted upon each initiate who swore oath. The one mighty cipher set a brand like a shackle, and granted the Koriani Matriarch her authorized ascendancy over all aspects of free will.

The sigil sieved into the clear quartz like a stain, a shadow wrought from the stuff of deep nightmare that spilled and frayed and darkened the crystal's bright depths. There, the force hovered, pulsing with currents that shocked through live flesh and negated the most passionate coil of desire. Lightless and cold, it realigned the core matrix of the quartz, then spilled over and laid claim to the seeress's awareness.

She flinched in recoil. The crystal's transmission released a shearing sting of heat against her cradling palms. Engulfed by vertigo, she was unable to move as Morriel Prime pronounced the guttural words to key mastery. The sigil fired and took form. Its barbed force claimed thought and mind, then erased the last imprint of individuality. The resonance of subjugation shattered the frail web of the seeress's consciousness. Will, self, and senses sucked away into vacuum, first dashed to powder, then whirled into void by a tide of cyclonic intervention.

Oblivion remained.

Seconds passed, or eternity; time lost all meaning as the spiraling force of the crystal's transmission ranged across distance.

Then, like smashed ice re-formed through smelting heat and dire cold, new sensation reassembled. The seeress no longer beheld the sun-drenched beachhead by Mainmere, noisy with exuberant clansmen. The eyes she gazed out of were not her own, but those of First Senior Lirenda . . .

Under a sky silted in low-hanging stringers of cloud, the harbor at Corith lay untenanted except for the churned phalanxes of whitecaps as the brig *Lance* threaded her inbound course through the chain of flanking islets. She dropped anchor against a stiff wind. The rock basin which gleamed fired russet in sunlight, under dampness wore the blotched tang of rusted iron. Slate waters rolled, and the air smelled of wet rock, and the faint trace of ozone which warned of an oncoming gale.

By the aft rail, the Alliance captain deposed by Caolle's bold strategy stared shoreward. His locked hands stayed braced on new varnish, while over and over, the unraveling spume of the breakers sheeted the jagged crescent strand. The testy temperament once raised in defiance of Koriani sailing orders had deflated to fretful humility since the loss of his flagship command.

His pride was ashes. Anxious to please lest the First Senior's testimony reveal the sad fact of his damning lack of fight before surrender, he volunteered his opinion concerning the vacant anchorage. "The Alliance fleet from Hanshire included oared galleys. Weather's set up to blow, as you see. If Prince Lysaer's ships are still here, they'll be tucked up tight in deep shelter. Captains who'll row on blue water know weather, or they don't survive. They'd have winched up on land, high and dry on log skids. Else they're crammed into some cove behind a barrier reef, where Sithaer's own demons couldn't raise enough swell to kick up a rank sea into combers."

Another gust thrummed through the stays. First Senior Lirenda clamped manicured fingers over her billowing silk. A wayward strand of dark hair escaped anyway, to stream and snap a refrain to her fierce irritation. Her lighter mantle buffeted against the captain's oiled cloak, while the silence magnified her indifference toward particulars. Whether or not the Prince of the Light would agree to trade off hostages with a pirate crew loyal to the Shadow Master, the stakes to her personal dilemma stayed unchanged. Moment to moment, she lived in blank dread, besieged by the knowledge her bonded crystal was withheld on the mainland, guarded by enemy hands.

The Min Pierens archipelago, with its forbidding, scarred cliffs and wind-mangled stands of crabbed cedar, wore its mantle of storm cloud in savage reflection of her mood. Yet where nature could stir the unrestrained elements into primordial fury, she must guard her vulnerability behind a mannered facade of restraint. She could do *nothing* but suffer her impotent rage for talents removed beyond access. Beneath anger and poisonous humiliation, she wrestled the insidious fear, that mishap could unstring every thread of her ambition and ruin her beyond salvage.

She had scarcely spoken through the weeks since the *Lance* had made covert landfall in Havish. There the prize crew loyal to Arithon had boarded a mannerless cohort of fortune-seeking mercenaries. At sea, the men had no enemy but boredom. They wrestled and grew crapulous and picked fights. Rather than suffer their attacks of lewd humor, Lirenda stayed out of sight. The fortnight's offshore passage to the Isles had been spent locked in the privacy of her cabin. She came on deck for the landfall well aware she must keep up the semblance of appearances. Clothed in the eighth-rank robes of a Koriani First Senior and the empty trappings of power, she despised her reduction to female uncertainty, disposition of her fate given into the hands of these rough-cut, fallible men.

The lookout hailed down from the crosstrees. "Longboat sighted! Bearing in on our starboard quarter, and flying the sunwheel blazon!"

Lirenda throttled the urge to cross the deck and gawk alongside the sailhands. Nor would she acknowledge the vanquished captain's self-blinded lift of optimism. The rippling gilt snap of Prince Lysaer's banner against the crocheted heave of the wavecrests promised her no deliverance. Reprieve from captivity would not remove her from jeopardy. Not when a thousand ways existed to erase the attuned bindings which linked her lost quartz to the spells that extended her vitality. If few rituals offered the horrific severance that Caolle had arranged for the healer, some were deadly innocent enough to occur through ignorant mishap.

A moment's inept handling might plunge the stone into the sea. Saltwater cleansing would follow, a gentle dissolution of the wards that would span the course of several days. The first symptom might bloom with a nagging, dull headache. Weakness would follow. Then a fumbling loss of reflex, which would progress into fits of sick trembling and convulsions, until she died at last of paralysis, as her internal organs failed and ruptured, torn apart by the unleashed backlash of stayed time.

The slap of raw winds made her feel her mortality, and the unblemished hand held clenched to the rail only mocked her: she could wake any morning and find herself trapped in the witless, shriveled body of a hag.

Jostled movement beside her upset her dark thoughts. Lysaer's displaced captain had turned aside to make inquiry, while on deck behind, a clipped shout in clan accents called for the deckhands to sway out a boat.

"Koriathain, my lady?" The deposed captain faced back and addressed her. "Signals have been relayed through an officer from Lysaer's royal galley." Uncertainty checked him. His palm left a broad, misty print on new varnish as he shifted to scrape at the beard stubble he now owned no blade to raze off. "The clan brigands agreed I should plead for an exchange of prisoners with the Prince of the Light."

"Those plans have changed?" Lirenda gave him her haughty attention. "State what you wish."

The man cleared his throat, his diffidence laughable. Deprived of her crystal, Lirenda owned no powers to cow him beyond glacial manners and deportment. If keen observation could still let her fathom the gist of his disorganized thinking, no schooled methodology could restore her lost key to access the complex sigils of spellcraft. "State your wish," she repeated. To hide her distaste for his jettisoned male pride, she fixed her tigerish gaze on the tumbled and desolate shoreline.

The man's knot of dread and embarrassment loosened. "An officer from the Alliance flagship has insisted, by word of his Grace, that you be the one sent to speak for the hostages."

Which warped twist of fate held a piquant justice; Lirenda could have howled for the irony. Had her towering rejection of intimacy not forced her need to defeat Arithon s'Ffalenn, Morriel Prime's design to ensnare him would have succeeded without setback. No fool's round of bargaining over prisoners and slave oarsmen would need undertaking at all.

Caolle would have passed the Wheel back in Riverton, with Lirenda spared from her present coil of entanglement.

The First Senior made certain as she sealed an empty promise that her voice masked her sorry self-derision. "If human lives can be redeemed from the Shadow Master's henchmen, the vows of my order require me to act to the absolute limit of my resources."

Individual awareness reawakened. The seeress snapped back into herself, disentwined at a stroke from Lirenda's close thoughts, and the leveling sting of shared shame. Jerked back into the heat of a Capewell afternoon, she raised her damp head. Her heart raced too fast. The lingering horror reeled through her from the secondhand taste of the First Senior's appalling disgrace. The seeress blinked, then shuddered in revulsion, unable to bear the closed, cloying dimness of the Prime Matriarch's bedchamber.

The quartz burned, the etheric web of its matrix torn by the masterful force of the sigil Morriel Prime had rammed through its transmission. Pillowed in stained lace, the Matriarch lay motionless. Her features were an expressionless skull, swathed in crimped skin, only animated by the devouring intensity of jet eyes. Her glance in that hour could have pierced flesh and bone to plunder thought straight from the mind. Of all harbingers of disaster, this day's scrying had delivered the penultimate stroke of ill news.

No setback could strike with such profound impact: the continuance of Koriani power had hung on Lirenda, First Senior.

Terrified to breathe lest any slight motion rip the dread stillness and ignite Morriel's leashed wrath, the seeress froze in suspension. Alive to the unseen currents of danger, she hesitated to ask back her scrying sphere from the Prime Matriarch's clasped fists.

Then the decision was spared her. Morriel unlocked her grasp on the quartz, though nothing else moved under the tucked layers of the counterpane. The pleats at her brow seemed starched into place. Her bitterness poisoned the stifling shadows that speared where the candle's flame faltered. Her seamed lips held the limpid pallor of killed fish as she waved the seeress back from her bedside. "You may sit."

"Your will." The enchantress sank down, unsure whether she dared ask permission to cease further efforts at scrying. She knew of no precedents. If a betrayal had ever happened this high in the ranks during the order's long history, none of her colleagues remembered. Lirenda's defection left her stunned to incapacity, with the Prime's disappointment an unvoiced anguish all the more deadly for being suppressed through an invalid's weakness.

Nor had the seeress ever witnessed an augury cast across open salt water. She had always believed such a practice lay past the reach of the most advanced Koriani arts. The chill truth struck home, that the Matriarch's seat required more preparation and knowledge than a senior enchantress imagined. Given the harsh fact, the enormity became crushing, that the one groomed successor had failed to maintain her integrity.

"Well you should fear," said Morriel Prime. "There is only one glyph that can span the salt ocean. That is the sigil of mastery which I hold over each and every one of you, impressed on your oath of initiation. Spells spun through its vortex will track an enchantress, beyond every defense and safeguard. No place in this world lies exempt. There is no hiding. One who breaks faith cannot escape forfeit, no matter how far her flight takes her. Even death grants no surcease. Such spells have been used at need to call halt on the spirit in its final passage across the Wheel."

The seeress knotted wet hands, shaking now, and unable to discern whether her Prime's words were a warning, or a threat laid against the damaging evidence of Lirenda's disobedience.

Nor did Morriel waste hoarded strength to volunteer clarification. "Leave me. Your duty is finished. You will tell nobody what you have witnessed concerning our order's First Senior." If setback and defeat at last undermined the tenacity of the Prime's will, she yielded no sign. Her faint, husking voice still delivered her authority in snapping short consonants and clipped vowels. "The matter must bide until Lirenda returns. I will choose the day and the hour when she stands before me to receive my formal charge against her conduct."

Reprieves

Inside the circle of the Paravian grimward, Asandir defers his exhaustion and looses another net of spells to hold the dream of the ghost drake stable; while inside the bewildering coil of its spiral, yet another sunwheel soldier meets oblivion in spilled blood, leaving but three survivors of the original forty who followed the Hanshire captain, Sulfin Evend, in pursuit of the Master of Shadow. . . .

In the null gray mists between the veil of the mysteries, Jieret s'Valerient's naked spirit rides the winds, called ahead by the draw of a blood bond with his prince; and on the faint trail of his passage flies Traithe's raven, bearing the tracking presence of Sethvir, who waits and watches at Althain Tower in the poised hope of effecting a rescue. . . .

Steaming mists rise off the pools of Mogg's Fen, where Lord Maenol crouches with a blooded band of scouts; and they move to crash the lines of yet another Alliance patrol, as yet uninformed that the campaign to break his clan foothold in Tysan has been defanged in the south: that two brigs from Riverton have made landfall at Mainmere, but flying the leopard blazon of Rathain. . . .

Summer 5653

XIII. Reversals

Lirenda's meeting with Prince Lysaer was not to take place in the warmed comfort of a state galley's cabin, but ashore, on the open cliff top. The same shattered ring of First Age foundations had sheltered the Shadow Master's sailhands before his unfruitful voyage to Kathtairr. No trace remained now of that habitancy. Six years of winter storms had scoured off the ashes of the cooking fires. The bones of fish and hunted game tossed onto their midden were long since cleared off by scavengers. Even the sail canvas Dakar had used to roof the shell of the sole standing watchkeep had rotted, the frayed threads picked away by industrious kittiwakes to line their nests in the rocks.

Set ashore by her escort of officers, First Senior Lirenda had been left to manage the ascent by herself. On that hour, the low-flying storm scud wore the gloom of a premature dusk. The gusts which lashed and moaned through bent cedars, in these heights shrilled across barren stone. Lirenda's light mantle flailed and snapped at the hem. Each blast assaulted her layers of silk robes, as if the elements conspired to strip her naked. Her pinned coils of jet hair succumbed as well, first torn from confinement, then flogged into tangles like whipped ink against the flushed pink of her cheeks. The dark, congested clouds overhead streamed like frothed smoke in a vat, chased by intermittent thunder.

Raised in cosseted wealth, accustomed ever since to the mannered regime of Koriani sisterhouses, Lirenda held no love for wild heights. She minced over stones too rough for kid soles, and battled to keep the proud, erect grace of her carriage. Stressed to primal nerves by the oncoming gale, she chewed her lip, while the discharge of far off lightning glazed mercury over the upthrust tangs of sharp rock. She could imagine no motive for Prince Lysaer to insist on holding an audience in the midst of a ruined fortress.

Logic spurred on her intuitive unease. *The setting was all wrong.* Based on the observations drawn from years of Koriani lane watch, the indulgence of demeaning gestures matched nothing of Lysaer's ruling style.

Denied her reflexive access to power, Lirenda felt her nerves the more keenly as she swept the barren summit in search of a sheltering pavilion. No such royal trapping met her eye. Just the wind-fluted rims of tumbled-down walls in the poured tones of rust, lead, and ink. Stone here had been witness to violent death, and under bruised cloud, the sorrows of antiquity seemed to cry out for the voice of a bard to waken their brooding memory. When the fortress at Corith had stood in defense, the site had been burned desolate by drakefire. Abandoned to wreckage, even the tenacious island cedars could not pry a stunted foothold to take seed. Too late, Lirenda considered the pitfalls. The Prince of the Light had ever been wont to wrest full advantage from the lofty affectations of court ceremony. His character did not incline toward brooding. Never before this had he been a man to choose a glowering, windswept terrain to conduct his crown business of state.

She saw him at last, against every precedent unattended where he stood against a backdrop of gale-ravaged sky. His elegant silk doublet leaped out like the sheen of found pearl amid the stripped blocks of a rampart's foundations.

A gust screamed. Lirenda wrestled the billowing tug of her mantle, then snagged its purple folds in a death grip to keep it from flagging like a sail. If she wished to turn back, the moment was forfeit. Prince Lysaer turned his head and caught sight of her.

No option remained but to close the last yards over treacherous, uneven footing.

Lirenda's fluttery uneasiness could not be dismissed in brash pretense. Koriani life was communal. Those rare occasions she had spent in male company afforded untrustworthy insight. No man within her living memory had owned the presence of this prince, daunting and polished to flawless grace as he inclined his head and acknowledged her arrival. He offered his hand to steady her last step, his grasp firm and warm around her cool fingers, and his hair like snagged gold against the jeweled edge of his collar.

"Come," he greeted in unsmiling courtesy. "I invited you here to share the spectacular view."

Three steps down a defile, one sharp turn to the right; the abrupt cessation of the wind all but rocked Lirenda off-balance. Lysaer's sure strength caught her back from a stumble. He steered her downward into the niche where the ancient foundation arched over a gully in the cliffside. They halted in that isolate pocket of hushed air, while the gusts shrieked on unabated up above, and balked eddies careened through the defile, shearing through spindly stands of racked trees and harrying their branches like weed stalks. Far beneath, the strand met the sea in stepped ledges, a jumbled bulwark of silt gravel and boulders where the raging surf hurled itself ragged.

The gale was still building. Already the bay wore the loomed stripes of spindrift, where wind sluiced the tops from the wavecrests.

On the pending edge of twilight, the beaten stretch of shoreline tugged the heart with its pristine splendor. Time could be felt here, the mighty deeds of bygone ages compressed against the present like a telescoped view through a jewel facet. Lirenda gripped her thin silks, diminished by awe, and eroded by the demeaning recognition that her life span mattered to the earth not at all. She gave way to a contradictory relief, that she did not wear her crystal in this place. Had her quartz been in hand, its channels would be quickened. The past might have burst forth and shaken her with the vast, deep tones of the horns that centaurs once used to call dragons.

"You may sit," Lysaer said, breaking through her inadvertent absence of mind. In seamless, reserved grace, he handed her onto a fallen slab of coping.

She would not cast off pride. Rather than decry her spell-blinded straits, she bent her cool gaze to wring the uttermost from her Koriani arts of observation. "In my sisterhouse, it would be I granting you that permission."

Lysaer smiled, his candor a weapon's cleared edge. "This site adheres to its own grand sovereignty, except for the Shadow Master's meddling."

"We need not stand upon dignity for that." Lirenda gathered the spilled folds of her mantle and made space for him on the stone.

He chose to stay standing. She scrutinized his poise, unblinking and still as a snake that sized up choice prey. Lysaer met her regard without qualm, a feat few men dared to sustain beyond the brute span of a moment. The bedrock calm that lent this prince majesty was in fact the intent of a spirit schooled into a seamless, listening patience. Whatever she did or said in his presence would be heard without personal prejudice. No judgment would be passed until their exchange had been weighed in its entirety.

That striking attentiveness, paired with the grave impact of male beauty, lent the man his stunning charisma. Lirenda searched his clean features for the fine, marring evidence of selfishness, and found no line in the flesh out of harmony with its framework of bone. He was all substance and firm moral courage. His skin wore its youth like an oak tree's new leaves, and yet, he was not young. Lirenda tried to imagine him as a boy with scraped knees and tousled hair; and failed utterly.

Even here, where the elements lent no man contrived artifice, Lysaer's natural bearing bespoke inborn royalty stamped all the way to the marrow.

Made aware through her own armor of deportment that she and this prince shared more similarities than differences, Lirenda gave rein to her impulse. "If you could have chosen the course of your life, would you be here today?"

Lysaer did not lift his regard from her, nor did the scoured, limpid blue of his eyes once deviate from directness. "I was born a king's heir. I know nothing else."

But his hands gave the lie, unrelaxed against the foil thread of his hose. Lirenda sensed a glass edge to his poise, as though he had made his first stance on the cliff top in challenge, daring the gale to rise up and smash his works into oblivion.

Lirenda said, "This seems an odd site for a king's heir to hold audience. What made you come here?"

"I needed solitude in which I could be myself." His answer yielded no shred of shared trust as he settled his shoulder to the rocks. "However, even here we are not alone. Our ties of responsibility still bind us. Can you see them?"

The seed pearls on his sleeve pocked the gloom as he pointed toward the carnelian gleam where the *Lance*'s stern lantern bobbed amid saw-toothed wavecrests.

Lirenda maintained her tight survey of his face. "Do you speak of the hostages who are offered in exchange for the clan slaves kept chained on your galleys? You could bend to demand. Or do you believe the Teir's'Ffalenn's allies drive too high-handed a bargain?"

"A prince must give way to no man. His guide must be the principled tenets demanded by justice and mercy." Yet new lines crimped the corners of Lysaer's eyes. A fractional tautness to his jaw exposed his fleeting, raw edge of discomfort.

Some recent event still caused him an intense and personal anguish. A thrill piqued Lirenda's interest, that Koriani arts might allow her a glimpse of his most private core.

"The common subjects of the realm must receive the same law as others born to wealth and position," Lysaer qualified. "My will is not at issue, lady enchantress, now or at any time. Today, I must pass sentence on men who failed in their orders. Tomorrow, for the weal of the realm, I may have to sign an execution for treason against the woman I took to wife."

There lay the hidden vulnerability, a raw nerve betrayed in the trembling flash of his jewels. In Princess Talith lay the source of the agony Lysaer lacked human outlet to express. "You loved her," Lirenda accused, aware through his front of equanimity that the confidence she probed for was unlikely to be shared with anyone.

The temper of his voice came back like sheared metal. "The Shadow Master knew. He sought to use her to ruin me."

Lirenda studied Lysaer's shuttered features, the pain embedded so deeply that not even tears might flow; a wounding as bloodless as the blued tang of steel broken off inside vulnerable flesh. If this was how love could mangle free choice, she was all the more determined to keep her own spirit unencumbered. "Why did you bring me here?"

"Did you not guess?" Rings and gold braid sparked to a faint play of lightning. "This is a trial, your hearing, for my impartial royal judgment, since the *Lance* has not delivered the Master of Shadow in chains. Your order's part was to drive my enemy to flight out of Riverton. I want to know how he chanced to gain warning of my trap set and waiting here at Corith."

Lirenda all but shot to her feet in stunned shock. Barely in time, her reflexive poise slapped back the impulse and saved her. She pulled in a chain of deep breaths.

Lysaer watched, his eyes on her impartial as sky-printed water.

Relief surged over her like a shot pail of ice as she recouped bludgeoned wits and reminded herself he was not yet aligned in decision against her. The Prince waited, prepared to hear her explanation, the only ruffled part of him now the gilt hair left snarled by the wind.

"You must understand," he pressed, gentle as though he mistook her silence for reluctance to name a guilty party. "No inquest could be made in the presence of the men-at-arms who serve with my fleet. Each has lost brothers and loved ones in the war against the true dark. For the fact that Arithon s'Ffalenn slipped the net, they would respond like a dog pack. Unveil a conspirator, and they'll cry for fresh blood until a death has righted the balance."

Some sly fact stayed unsaid. Lirenda caught the shrewd set to his stillness, alongside the unpleasant insight that more than royal judgment would be passed in this unwitnessed hearing. Like his half brother, Lysaer s'Ilessid bore the royal gifts of s'Ahelas on the distaff side of his pedigree. However he pronounced sentence for the misplay at Riverton, his indictment would bear a calculated stake in the future. While the night deepened, and the storm broke in turbulent force against the headlands, she realized that Koriani observers too often neglected to allow for the mother's inherited farsight.

"The wise man knows the master always outlives his hounds," Lirenda threw back in provocation.

"Only one opportunity has been lost to take down the Spinner of Darkness," Lysaer s'Ilessid allowed. "We agree, that's no cause to indulge in the hysteria of disappointment."

Against five centuries' longevity, the event lost its impact. The Prince of the Light would not trifle with recriminations. He would instead reshape this setback in deliberate calculation to steer later events to his purpose. Lirenda's suspicion bloomed into swift anger. Morriel Prime would be mortified to learn any Koriani Senior had strayed inside the reach of such usage.

"Is this royal prerogative?" Lirenda provoked. "Are we not to brand your conspirator in public?"

Lysaer withheld response; and the fear shot cold through her, since she had no way to fathom how much he knew, or how much he relied upon guesswork, concerning the reverses brought on by her meddler's choice to prolong Caolle's survival.

Across gale-torn waters and thickening gloom, the firefly dance of the ship's lantern mocked her. She found herself mortal and exposed in this crux as the *Lance*'s miserable, deposed captain. The gutted pride of her First Senior's rank made her loath to cross moral wits with the man hailed as Prince of the Light.

This moment's freight of uncertainty became as grueling a punishment as the loss of her link to prime power. Against masterful statecraft, Lirenda had no true shield, but only bare wits and a scathing self-contempt.

At length, without censure, Lysaer gave his answer. "There can be no conspiracy. The orders you follow are not yours, but your Prime's."

The multiple snares of innuendo bit deep. "Must you insist on attaching blame?" Cornered behind her last shred of confidence,

Lirenda fell back upon pretense. "If so, you have no guilty party, but only a poor choice of scapegoats. No man broke your faith. For reasons of mercy, my order spared a liegeman of Arithon's. Caolle's wounding was mortal. At the end of his strength, no one foresaw he might become the weapon to turn in the hand and wrest the Shadow Master's capture off course."

"Caolle, who once served as war captain to Steiven s'Valerient, and later, to the heir, Jieret Red-beard? My lowliest Etarran foot soldier would have weighed that man's character with better prudence." Dangerous now as struck flame, Lysaer faced the sea. A sudden, sheeting flare of lightning scoured his profile to the ennoblized stamp on a coinface. "Such a man could never be harmless until he lay dead." He waited again in sly pressure, prepared to let silence condemn her.

Lirenda would not stoop to volunteering the Koriani role behind the question he posed by implication.

Lysaer raised his eyebrows in acidic irony. "Weren't you planning to importune me about hostages? Or does the *Lance* not sail under a barbarian crew, with my sworn company of Etarrans held locked in her hold as their captives?"

"Is that an issue?" For surely he had noticed: the inbound storm stripped the night's secrets. For minutes on end, Lirenda had marked the ongoing flurry of activity around the hull of the anchored *Lance*. Another bolt of lightning rinsed the ocean dull pewter. From the cliff top, wrapped in the scent of gathering rain, one could make out the busy flotilla of oared boats bearing fugitives off the moored ship. As she watched, the leading party made a sheltered landing in a cove notched into an offshore islet.

"Of course," Lysaer said, "we came for the view, since the script is too obvious. My men-at-arms and original sailhands are still imprisoned on board the flagship. Since they'd not be left free, the crew in the boats are undoubtedly Arithon's, leaving. They work for a pirate. What would they expect except shiftless treachery, no matter whose word should be asked as surety for their safety? Dogs forced to skulk know well when to cringe. As my father learned in Amroth, to his everlasting sorrow, there is no dealing with s'Ffalenn hirelings through any honorable exchange."

Lirenda uncrimped her hands from balled silk, displeased to find herself sweating. "Why make them a display for my benefit, then?"

Lysaer gave her his complacent survey, as if he might memorize the precise pattern of loose hair trailed across her domed forehead, or set a mold to the secretive slant of her eyelids. "For my own men, naturally, there can be no choice. And I asked you here to bear witness."

Full night had fallen. Beyond the white crash of breakers on the headland, the dark between forks of lightning became a wind-textured veil of black air, pinpricked in distance by the solitary flame of the abandoned flagship's stern lamp. Lysaer in his doublet of milk satin and worked pearl seemed no ordinary man, but an avatar sent down to earth in a form wrought of silvery light. Lirenda saw him turn from her, his expression resolved into a stern serenity she found terrifying for its perfect absence of uncertainty. Then he raised his right arm.

She foresaw his intent a heartbeat too late.

"Mercy on them, you can't!" Her cry entangled with a tortured shriek as his raised gift of light slammed land and sky into recoil.

Thunder fit to crack rock shook the ruins. This was no discharge brewed by natural forces and clean storm, but the retort of lethal fury unleashed as an act of vengeful judgment. Heat sheared in backlash. The fresh-whetted tang of ozone rode the air as the bolt arced down to meet the sea and its defenseless target: the fragile, wood-chip frailty of the ship which swung unsuspecting at her anchorage.

Deafened, dazed half-blind, Lirenda reeled backward against crumbled stone. She saw the point of impact as a blooming, orange star. Timbers and furled canvas and cordage ignited, and with them, Tysan's entrapped subjects exploded amid a horrific maelstrom of fire and debris.

Then all light extinguished. The pealing echoes of spent force quaked the hills and slapped the ground, while the gusts dispersed clotted streamers of flame. Wreckage and cinders settled and snuffed out amid a scrim of storm-racked waves.

The next snap of ordinary lightning unveiled no more than shredded drifts of smoke.

Lirenda clawed back upright. She smoothed the disarranged folds of her mantle, raked back fallen hair, and through flash-burned vision, saw the Prince of the Light turned back once again to face her.

His posture was straight as Daelion's justice, and his eyes, the unrelenting, fierce blue of zenith sky.

"For mercy," he said, his gaze locked to hers. "Behold the true cost of your intervention in my plan. Every death upon that vessel must lie on your own conscience, lady."

When Lirenda tried speech, he cut her off with brute sovereignty. "Far more is at issue than the Shadow Master's destruction. You will advise your Prime that mankind deserves a future unencumbered by the meddling intervention of factions who manipulate our society with magecraft."

Lirenda felt steel rise up with her gorge. "Why you arrogant butcher!" Sickened, appalled, she regrouped her shocked nerves. "Is this pique, for balked plans? Some berserk fit of hatred?" Summary justice was a high king's right, and he, granted less than legal sanction as crown prince. "What have you done here, but show in cold blood you can self-righteously murder the innocent?"

"Yes, but *were* they innocent?" Lysaer's formal civility clashed at odds with the heat of her roused female outrage. "You alone would know, First Senior." He took her hand, drew her to the cliff path with such vehemence she nipped her tongue. "Take warning, enchantress, lest your kind cross my wishes again."

Lirenda resisted his urge to call an end to the audience, even as the force of his close presence tested the depth of her ire. The rocks themselves conspired against planted feet. She stumbled, caught the hem of her mantle beneath her heel. Silk tore like the whisper of screams the wronged dead had been granted no time to utter.

"You have no authority over Koriani affairs," Lirenda snapped.

"You believe so," Lysaer corrected, and then qualified with that magisterial arrogance that brought the most obstinate guild ministers to their knees. "One captain, a ship's crew, and a company of men-at-arms failed in completing my orders. Whether they did so through negligence, or if they were coerced by the power of your Koriani sisterhood *does not matter*. Their fate at my hand became a foregone conclusion on the instant they permitted the *Lance* to change course for a landfall in Havish."

Another step out of shelter, and the gale winds would tear away words. Lysaer let her pause to lend his conclusion due emphasis. "I can afford no loyal officer to fear others before me. Such a weakness could only open the sworn honesty of innocents to risk. Let your Koriani Order learn well from your mistake. The men in my Alliance will not be allowed to become the ready tools of outside powers. *I will not have them suborned!*"

He let her go. The sudden release staggered her backward and bruised her heel against an unkind angle of rock. Men's lives had been sacrificed, and an insolent ship's boy, not for their own acts made in guilt or innocence, *but for hers*, as example to an absent Prime Matriarch.

Lirenda pushed straight, shook the chaff of winter-burned moss from her robes, while the rising gale screamed, and lightning jagged like sullen cracks shot through crystal against the blackened horizon. Her eyes caught the glow, lit balefire in reflection, as she dismissed Lysaer's face and fair person. "No prince, but a manslayer. Tysan's clans were well advised by their *caithdein* not to entrust you with kingship."

His effrontery showed flawless and deferent manners as he clasped her hand to escort her away. "I'm gratified to see my point taken so courteously to heart."

Lirenda stiffened. She would not ask what measure of justice would befall the Shadow Master's men, gone to ground as maroons with no shelter beyond the overturned keels of four longboats.

Lysaer widened the breach by telling her in detail. "Traitors and pirates are condemned through fair trial under the written annals of the realm's law. My governance of men who are not my sworn liege-men is a matter of public record. No harm will befall the fugitives from the *Lance* until they've been captured and arraigned by due process."

Lirenda drew breath to warn him: the renegade crew from the brig yet included the cleverest of Riverton's turncoat shipwrights. Pure instinct stayed her. She observed the prince with her arts until the false complacency sprang stark to the eye and belied his impartial statement. The line of Lysaer's mouth was too knowing, too hard. His quiet was not born of calm, but an act to smooth over a keen, introverted calculation.

Lirenda's trained perceptions pierced that facade and exposed the underlying face of the truth: that for the linked network of Prince Arithon's supporters, the end would come later, upon the hour of Lysaer's choosing. Whatever rebellion their actions fomented would first be used to leverage further impetus toward Alliance consolidation of power, and then to extend the quest to wreak the Shadow Master's downfall into a force of dominion to command every kingdom on the continent.

"You think I don't mourn for the waste of good lives," Lysaer said. "I've watched as you base your calculations upon the careful begetting of a power base. But your thinking is flawed. You reason without pity. Otherwise you must see, I act for this cause *because there is no one else capable*."

Lirenda stopped cold on the path as the impacting power of Lysaer's sincerity rocked her. Game pieces and conflict acquired new meaning. Now she could not evade the overwhelming recognition of the pain he had managed to hide behind the artful trappings of state dignity.

"The Fellowship of Seven refused the burden," Lysaer admitted as her gaze returned to reassess every majestic angle of his face. The barest note of leaked bitterness strained through as he dismissed her from private audience. "Today, to my sorrow, I have found your Koriathain cannot be trusted to act with me for the common good."

The gale pounded over the Isles of Min Pierens in bands of rampaging winds and white rain squalls. In the cliff caves where the main body of Lysaer's fighting companies and ships' officers took refuge, the gusts took voice and fluted in diminished minor tones where the eddies snagged across rock. The caverns had been carved by water and winds, before the mazed array of branching tunnels had been bored by the hot breath of dragons.

Attrition still reigned. Like the fortress above, time crumbled the stoutest stone bastions. Flooding and springs had crystallized limestone into a petrified silt that smoothed over the scored marks of drakes' claws.

Amid echoed bickering, men vied over the best alcoves to hunker down with their bedding. The convoluted ceiling allowed but one fire, and that was reserved for their prince.

First Senior Lirenda kept to herself. Given a dry cranny, a meal of smoked fish and ship's rations, and the blankets an officer shared out of courtesy, she observed the royal men-at-arms as they diced or bandied lewd jokes and smart talk; in grumbling, closed groups, they polished the rust the sea air raised on their weapons and mail. One boisterous party chalked out a circle, stripped their shirts, and arranged bouts of wrestling. The enchantress in their midst was ignored. Whether at Lysaer's order, or through the inherent dread most townborn felt toward spellcraft, every man in the company gave the Koriani First Senior wide berth.

Like any other who had sworn life service to the sisterhood, Lirenda was inured to overt signs of distrust. Long experience let her disregard the unsettled glances, the furtive signs to ward spellcraft cast her way when men believed her attention lay elsewhere.

Not all of the posturing sprang out of ignorance. Lysaer's ranking officers kept their scrupulous distance as well. The Koriani First Senior was excluded from their council concerning the sprung news that the Spinner of Darkness had slipped through their net. Nor did any man in her hearing mention the summary execution of those comrades just burned alive in the hold of the *Lance*.

Whether Lysaer s'Ilessid had given them notice of his justice, or whether they would be left to believe the vessel had been sunk by a stroke of natural lightning, Lirenda was not privileged to know. Reduced to the rankling role of an eavesdropper, she strained to catch what fragmented conversation she could as a rain-sodden courier came in with word from the fleet snugged down in safe anchorage.

". . . galleys are hove up in the coves on the lee side of Caincyr Isle, as planned." The young man peeled off his dripping oilskin. His rough-cut features and perfect teeth gleamed with avid good spirits, touched to copper relief by the fire. "The convict oarsmen and the other Corith prisoners are held in chains ashore, under close guard by the ships' crews."

Lysaer's reply lost itself in a dissonant screeling of steel as two zealous Etarrans put their shoulders into sharpening halberds. Lirenda caught no more than the clipped inflection of the royal query, implying some detail failed to satisfy. She gathered the gist concerned the prize *Cariadwin*, surrendered to the Alliance, but having no loyal crew of her own.

"The brig's keel drew too much water," the courier explained, shoulders squared and voice risen in loyalty to the royal fleet's commanding admiral. "Daelion preserve! My Lord said to tell you her blue-water captain has a temperament like a spring nettle. As he was the Shadow Master's minion, he won't cooperate, and our galleymen get twitchy under sail in strange waters. Would your Grace risk men's lives? The shoals in those inlets shift with each tide. The rutter we're using with a gale at our backs is six centuries old, and written in archaic language!"

A pause, while someone with seagoing experience injected a quelling comment; then laughter, cut by Lysaer's stark inquiry, "Well, if the *Cariadwin*'s not in the coves with the galleys, where in the Light did your officers decide to snug her down?"

"At anchor, your Grace. She's secured in the narrows of the cut."

Silence, of yawning and disastrous proportion; the spirited factions by the wrestlers stilled. Men honing weapons were asked to desist. Even the rowdiest dicers held their next throws, heads turned to follow the rising altercation.

"What's wrong?" asked the courier, made the isolate center of attention by the revealing firelight. "The brig is unmanned, for common sense. Storm could snap her cables any time and set her down on the rocks. No crew could save her. She'd break up in minutes. Riptide's too fierce the way the swell's running to allow a stranded company to launch off boats if she wrecked."

Across the weather-stained vaults of the cave, over the heads of men-at-arms and Alliance officers, Lirenda saw Lysaer glance her way. His eyes were hard blue, and scarcely amused: the cliff-top vantage of his audience with her, and the summary act of his judgment had not yet been shared with his people. None of them knew that men loyal to Arithon had been left at large in the storm. Since the longboats which accomplished furtive escape could not have been seen from the shoreline, she alone shared the clandestine awareness that Arithon's crew from the *Lance* had more than likely survived.

Those men could not be traced now. The ferocity of the gale would have covered their tracks, even if a boat could venture the crossing to the islet where they had sought refuge.

"Your fleet admiral said risk no lives for the prize," the courier answered in earnest response to the sudden outburst of questions. "If a watch crew stayed aboard, what good could that do? They'd be left to fate's mercy. The brig can scarcely beat her way out. Wind's like a funnel at the eastern inlet. To the west lie the Snags, submerged reefs and rocks fit to mill a hull's timbers to wreckage."

Lirenda arose. Having breached Lysaer's trust, she felt moved to offer a gesture to salvage what she could of her order's damaged integrity. She gathered her damp mantle and stepped through the grouped men, while hands snatched their strewn dice up out of her path, or made signs against spellcraft at her back. She paid the inimical gestures no mind. The smells of moist cloth and oiled steel and humanity oppressed her as the mass of the company quieted. All eyes fixed her way. Her wet kid shoes made less sound than a wraith as she traversed the sweating limestone floor to reach the fireside enclave with the prince.

"Loan me one of your diamonds," she said.

Lysaer asked no question, but drew his knife and cut a stud from his doublet. His hands retained their enviable poise as he placed the gem into her keeping.

Lirenda knelt before the fire. She pushed back the lush, sable fall of her hair. The beat of close flame dewed a sheen on her forehead as she turned the small jewel between her fingers. She rotated the chased setting and measured the illumination which played through the starred planes of its facets, until an arrow of frozen light threw its focused reflection across the centerline of her palm. The stone's imprint was not dedicated to her; she could exert no will through its matrix. But given the sensitivity of her inborn talent, and guided by knowledge of runelore, she might link the stone's resonance into Lysaer's need to know, and shape a rudimentary scrying.

The enchantress closed out the furtive rustles as the curious gathered at her back. Her mind brooked no distraction. She unreeled her awareness deep into the stone's core until she captured the still point at its heart. Then she raised her distanced vision across the fire's emission of rippling smoke and hot sparks. She narrowed her eyesight upon the planes of Prince Lysaer's face, that no nuance of expression should escape her.

"Stare through the flames and gaze deep into the matrix of the diamond," she instructed. "Hold to your wish. Let your thoughts not stray from your purpose. While you own your desire to its fullest extent, I'll scribe an amplifying rune-field. If your will stays steadfast and fortune favors, the answer you seek will become manifest in the fire."

As Prince Lysaer concentrated, Lirenda stretched and extended her awareness. The distraction of the fighting company dissolved as relaxation stilled her outer senses. Preternaturally conscious of the grounding quiet rooted throughout the cavern, she embraced the weighty tonnage of the earth, then expanded her consciousness beyond. The gale outside touched her nerves as a tantrum of wind and element. She felt the white waves which drummed through Corith's headland, and the vibration of thunder through bedrock. This place, which had been the past lair of great drakes, made her effort feel sadly diminished. She fought the sudden, overwhelming futility, that her order's works seemed little more than the industry of ants, which died to raise cities from sand grains.

Through the muffling calm of her inner alignment, she heard Lysaer's word of dismissal. Changed air brushed her skin. She sensed the dispersal of men from the fireside, and wondered what secret the Prince of the Light wished to keep from his ranking officers. Then her last thought dissolved into full trance. Held in suspension between prince and diamond, she raised her hand and scribed the opening cipher for the first ordained rune of power . . .

The bright scrim of the flames gave way to combed sheets of rain, and another live fire, quenched in a darkness measured between the static bursts of new lightning. The scrying lent vision where the storm reigned supreme, and the waters of a rock-bounded estuary lay thrashed to boiling lead by the brunt of the whipping winds. The snubbed hull of a brig loomed in faint silhouette through the veiling rags of spindrift. The Cariadwin *had been secured by competent seamen, her spars and topmasts struck for foul weather, with spring lines made fast and a double length of cable payed out for added security. Storm made a mockery of even the most stringent precautions. The brig tossed and slammed like a maddened beast. The sheltering influence from the islet to windward afforded her scanty protection. Behind the roll of her counter, the peril of a lee shore: a spit of raw boulders sieved through by ribbons of green water and spume. Jagged reefs gnashed the froth in the shallows, seething up geysers of spray.*

Despite the fury of wind and wave, the brig's decks held men, struggling against the murderous elements to hoist her topsail yards to her caps. In determined struggle, sails were bent on, with spunyard stops, and gaskets cast off, to ready her canvas for setting on instantaneous notice. The spell-caught vantage sharpened into focus and revealed their desperation: the slipped hand or foot as gusts raked the ratlines; the cried orders lost or not heard at all as rain and waves drummed white torrents on her decks. And yet, even blind, even deafened by the gale's thundering tumult, the men worked in concert. They cajoled the ship like a reluctant maiden. First fore-sails and main yard were hauled aback; then the silvered stroke of an axe blade chopped her anchor line at the hawse.

The wind claimed her then for its own.

A bone in the teeth of a maelstrom, the Cariadwin *spun, slewed abeam as her foresail was cut free. She heeled under her flogging yards of canvas. Then more sails bloomed from mizzen and spanker gaff. To the peal of someone's exuberant whoop, she backed, stern to. Another unheard, frantic order sent crewmen scurrying to haul the braces. The helm was reversed. Stressed sails slammed full, laid for a starboard tack.*

"Saved!" cried her distant, gamecock captain in a paean of exultation. Through a brash feat of daring in defiance of all odds, the brig recovered in Prince Arithon's name skirted the foaming fangs of the reef and ran the open channel, to be lost into howling dark.

"Show me the cove where my galleys are snugged down," Lysaer broke in with hard urgency. But cold logic scarcely required a scrying to confirm the extent of the enemy's resourceful sabotage. The *Lance*'s crew had included forty war-hardened clansmen set free by King Eldir's justice. They had predictably matched a choice opportunity with thorough tactics. Nor had they shown any mercy in vengeance for the kinsmen they found enslaved with the royal fleet. In shadowy images, the bad news emerged: of hulls left holed and unfit for pas-sage, and a score of dead sentries, dropped at their posts with slashed throats. All that remained of the two hundred clan convicts Lysaer's justice had chained for the oar were the sheared-off ends of their fet-ters.

"A victory for your nemesis," Lirenda observed. Her laughter welled up for the lofty irony, that Lysaer's self-righteous public scru-ples had led to his own comeuppance.

"For today, one might think so." The prince's response was too calm, too knowing, and his gesture, a courtier's indifference as he extended his hand to recover his borrowed diamond. "The sweetest gains fall from the jaws of defeat. What seasoned galleyman could

473

possibly believe that brig could sail clear in the teeth of a gale, except through an act of dark sorcery?"

He let that sink in, while a crook of one finger brought a page out of nowhere to secure the loose stud in his baggage. The boy blushed under his blinding smile, then retired out of earshot as the exhilarating impact of Lysaer's attention fastened back on the enchantress. "Our departure from Min Pierens will be delayed for some weeks. Since no message can be sent until my damaged galleys are made seaworthy, my council ashore will be tied. If Maenol's rescued clansmen strike to plunder before then, affairs back in Tysan will be primed and set for a righteous retaliation. My deferred reappearance will repay every setback. I'll find public fervor whipped to a fever pitch the instant we make landfall on the mainland."

Lirenda stared, while the stopped air in her chest compressed into stunned disbelief. "Ath's mercy, you could not have intended this!"

"I will prevail, for the good of this land and the innocent people who rely on my protection." Across the dwindling rags of the fire, Lysaer s'Ilessid resumed in a flawless and chilling sincerity. "None would have been more surprised than I to see this small venture succeed. After the slaughter at Dier Kenton Vale, what fool could presume the Shadow Master's capture could occur without hardship and sacrifice? My inner council at Avenor is scarcely naive. Each man was selected to outlast small defeats. Between the warning your Prime dispatched to Etarra and today's predictable setback, I have gained my sure proof to expose wider truth. Mankind's endangerment does not spring from the Spinner of Darkness alone. The pitfalls of spellcraft pose an equal threat to society."

Lirenda's appalled comprehension came magnified by the telltale rustle of her mantle.

Lysaer granted her unease a statesman's smile, laced with dangerous irony: reversal of his high-handed strategy *was in fact no setback at all*. His dedicated quest to bring the Shadow Master's downfall had been expanded to eradicate the practice of great and lesser sorcery; for that cause, he would let conflict widen and foment. In due course, his call to arms could extend his control across the entire continent.

"You begin to understand," Lysaer said, satisfied. "Davien the Betrayer's fountain in the Red Desert has expanded the game board across the next five centuries. Time enough to usher in sweeping change. As the guilds suffer predation from s'Ffalenn ships and renegade crews, I'll gain for Avenor and my Alliance the omnipotent support to raise standing armies across the continent. My crowning strike must be withheld until I have won the sworn loyalty of every city in

Athera. Then I shall bring down the s'Ffalenn bastard, and with him, the Fellowship of Seven, and *any other factions in the land who obstruct the growth of human destiny.*"

Lysaer arose, the majesty he carried like an extension of his flesh made no less by a setting of uncivilized rock. "Now my warning to your Prime is explicitly clear." His pearls and his diamonds snagged baleful lights from the coals as he stopped, and faced her, and gave his dismissive conclusion. "Be sure she hears the extent of my disappointment for her false principles."

While the embittered calculation of Lysaer's long-range purpose swept her damp skin into chills, Lirenda felt his eyes on her, fierce and wholly dedicated. She now had the measure of him; could sense the trapped depths. His pose of self-honesty shielded some deep and unconsoled anguish. "What will you tell your men of the sacrifice you will demand of them?"

The smoldering spark of his righteous rage struck through his quick laugh like a barb. "Should I not use the same lie you thought to foist upon me for your order's covert conspiracy? Are we not alike, lady? Both capable of committing errors of mercy for men whose criminal acts lie outside the constraints of human decency."

But they were not alike, First Senior Lirenda sensed in hard-core certainty; *not yet.* She had ordered Caolle's survival out of hatred, with precise intent to ruin the man whose character might ensnare her through unbidden emotion of the heart; for no living being would she endure the blind agony Prince Lysaer s'Ilessid suffered in secret for the love he had rejected in Princess Talith. Nor did she seek the accession of prime power for the purpose of public crusade.

Lirenda seized on the opening she had gleaned to inflict the last stinging word. "On the day you command your princess's death, your royal Grace, I invite you to present the same question again." Then she gathered the spoiled folds of her mantle and removed herself from the grace of Lysaer's presence.

Crossing

The darkness burst into shards and smashed rainbows. Dakar recaptured the distinct impression he was screaming, while a painless distress tore him limb from limb and flayed all the meat off his bones. Through one wrenching moment, he passed the shuttered eye of time.

Then perception reassembled with a jolt that slammed like an axe at the base of his skull.

The veil ripped away to a redolence of midsummer greenery. Through somebody's cry of hysterical terror came the shout of a stupefied clan sentry. "Avert and protect!"

Dumped headlong upon a rich fragrance of loam with a hot blanket of sun on his back, Dakar found no breath to respond. Whether he came to die for his failure, he had no choice but to let his unruly stomach take charge.

Doubled over with dry heaves and thoroughly miserable, he almost wished a clan spear in the back to resolve his shattering upset. Half-unmoored by the disorientation that racked him, he gasped in recovery. The air seemed too rich and thick; *too real*. Delivered from the irrational side of the veil, his return to the solid terrain of Athera came as an assault upon body and mind. Befogged faculties fumbled the sharp-edged barrage of sensation. His wits were reluctant to function. He did not want the obligation of reassembling the pieces of problems more comfortably left abandoned.

Already in dread of the consequences, he sat back on his haunches, blinking. Birdsong laced the treetops. A dragonfly lit on his forearm, unfazed by the stink of singed wool and the holes where volcanic cinders had burned through the weave of his jerkin. Dimly he realized that he wore the wrong clothes for the season. The steady, rich warmth of high summer laced sweat through his cold chills, while the rattled clan sentry slammed out of the brush and repeated his challenge again.

Eyes shut, Dakar rediscovered the function of language. "Where in the name of Sithaer's furies are we?"

Clipped accents changed from belligerent surprise to indignant complaint. "Ath! Is that Dakar? You're in Caithwood, as if dropped through the sky by a lightning bolt. If you planned to whisk Rathain's prince out of Riverton by means of magecraft and thunderclaps, did you need to keep him stashed for *three months?* Earl Jieret half killed himself in a cross-country run through Havish. Then the Sorcerer Traithe came, and both of *them* vanished also. The comings and goings have been fair hard on the nerves, these past weeks." The scout paused as he took in the sorry condition of the bay gelding, then accused, "We've worn out a dozen couriers trying to find all the folks who've gone missing, in particular since the crew of the *Lance* left us some liegeman's ashes to be given the grace of last rites."

"The *Lance*? Brought *Caolle's* ashes?" Dakar raised his head and cracked open bloodshot eyes to find three muzzled horses with cinders in their manes regarding him in mournful reproach. "Then he didn't die in Koriani hands at Riverton?"

"Aye, well, she did, and damn well, he didn't." The scout was a young man with frizzled brown hair, and foxy, irrepressible good humor. He peered over the hindquarters of Felirin's gray. His plain leathers were soaked through, though the sky showed no rain in evidence.

"You're wet," Dakar blurted.

"Aye, well." The scout swiped runoff from the fringes of his buckskins. "I fell arse first into the stream when your ruckus erupted from nowhere." He blushed, still disgusted enough to try and excuse his bruised dignity. "Who wouldn't? An arrival like yours was damnwell nothing canny. The game will be scattered for miles."

To Dakar's stiff and forbearing patience, he laughed. "You're behind on events?"

The Mad Prophet scrubbed at his face with his knuckles as if a smith had forged spikes through his temples. "Last memory I have, it was springtime."

The scout squeezed his wet braid, wrung out his cuffs, and plunged in with loquacious relish. "Lysaer's new flagship made landfall here, but flying Rathain's royal leopard. Came in last month with word that Caolle had killed a Koriani witch before he found grace and passed the Wheel. There's a feat by a clansman worth a masterbard's eulogy!"

Dakar planted his palms into grass in determined effort to ground out his giddy rise of dizziness.

The scout rattled on in excited adulation. "What a fighter, was Caolle! His pyre was laid out with full honors. The raid plans he left when he gave his last wishes won two other vessels for Prince Arithon. Then the *Lance* took on mercenaries and set sail for Corith. They say she burned there, but not before her crew had freed every clansman that Lysaer's royal fleet held in chains. Under cover of a gale, they stole back the *Cariadwin* and left Avenor's force stranded with holed galleys. Near two hundred clansmen sailed home to their families, and we've had to feed a whole pack of refugee shipwrights. They have nothing to do, but they say they won't leave until they find out if the Master of Shadow will return with plans to employ them. Where is Rathain's prince, anyhow?"

"I'm sorry," Dakar said. "We've missed all the news." Then feeling overcame him. He ducked his head between his knees, caught between bursting laughter and tears, and a rush of overpowering relief. *Caolle had not died by Arithon's hand after all. Nor had the men at the outpost at Corith been abandoned wholesale to the Alliance. The joy seemed unreal, that the Riverton ships were reclaimed to fight the oppression of Maenol's clans.* Life and breath suddenly became unimaginably precious. A friend could dare to hope for the reprieve those snatched victories might bring to the Teir's'Ffalenn.

Hunched and dripping and loquaciously oblivious, the young clansman circled the nose of the gray and poked an inquisitive finger into what seemed a wadded lump of charred rags draped over the animal's neck. The bundle shifted to expose the marble features of Felirin the Scarlet.

"What trouble did you bring us? You know this one's out cold?" Reverted on a breath to forest-bred wariness, the scout took fast stock of the second form tied to the back of the mare. "Is the other one brought for last passage rites, also?"

"You'd better hope not!" Dakar snapped, recovered enough to scramble erect. "That's his Grace of Rathain, and if he's not tended, I'll let your *caithdein* apologize to Earl Jieret for your mannerless lapse of hospitality."

The scout raised his eyebrows, prepared to repeat his glib testimony that Earl Jieret had disappeared, leaving no tracks.

His words were lost to sound as a stupendous thunderclap rocked sky and earth into recoil. The horses startled. Dakar was thrown to his knees with the lead reins clutched in blistered hands. He yelled warning to the scout, who moved just in time to catch Felirin's unconscious tumble from the saddle.

"Ath's very grace!" The scout staggered under the minstrel's slack weight, caught in a misstep as his sword scabbard swung and hooked the back of his knees. "Why'd you *do* that?"

"I didn't." Dakar barely managed to calm the stressed horses before their deranged instincts shredded the last patch of whole skin on his fingers. "You can lay the singer down in the grass before you trip and fall flat."

The scout looked offended. "Is he sick?"

"I don't think so. He probably fainted." The Mad Prophet had no chance to see whether Arithon suffered the same problem.

The next second, a bursting flash of light erupted from behind the trees. Dakar howled as the horses shied all over again. A deafening report shivered the ground, but this time he managed to tag the signature phrase of the spellcraft. "That's a Fellowship ward circle coming down!" he cried, before the scout lost his last wits and bolted. "Hold steady."

A confused, milling moment, while Dakar tugged the bridle of the mare and shouldered the bay gelding from trampling his toes into stew meat. "Steady." His assurance lacked confidence. Whatever protective binding the Sorcerer had raised was being released in blind haste. The pungency of ozone raked through the sweet scent of the meadow and a razing spin of energies puckered his mage-sense as a slipstream in time intercepted with the present, and shook like a wind through the leaves.

The horses milled in terror, despite every effort to stay them.

Then the problem was lifted from Dakar's stripped hands as a black raven swooped down. White light trailed from its wingtips, combing disturbed energies back into alignment under the remote guidance from Sethvir's earth-sense. The horses snorted and settled, while the wild gusts slackened, reduced to small eddies that winnowed and spiraled through the grass heads.

"Traithe?" Dakar said. Pelted by grasshoppers and the odd butterfly released from the dissipated vortex, he surveyed the wood. Presently, a familiar figure in dark clothing and a broad-brimmed black hat emerged, limping from the shadow.

At the Sorcerer's shoulder strode another, his large hands clenched to an unbelted bundle of weapons, among them a matched set of bone-handled throwing knives. Dakar took in the tall frame and wolfish stride with a leap of glad recognition. "Earl Jieret s'Valerient!"

The *caithdein* of Rathain looked like a man just shaken from sleep. His clan braid was undone. The mane of red hair fanned over his strong shoulders was caught with odd tangles and small twigs. A bandage covered his right wrist. His windburned, cragged face and hawk nose wore a blank frown, and he failed to acknowledge Dakar's greeting.

Traithe touched his wrist, directing his bemused attention to the cluster of horses in the glen. "Look there. You've succeeded."

Jieret turned his head. As if drawn by a magnet, his eyes fixed and locked on the figure of his prince, still tied over the neck of the exhausted mare. His disoriented bearing transformed on a cry of alarm. "My liege!"

He cast down his weapons, uncaring, and sprinted, too centered to respond to Dakar's reassurance that Arithon s'Ffalenn still breathed.

"He won't for much longer if you don't lend your help," Traithe said, arrived in uncanny quiet to clasp the spellbinder's elbow. "We need a fire. At once. Can you see to it?"

Dakar knew enough not to delay for questions. He surrendered the reins of the horses to Traithe, who turned his scarred fingers to unbuckling girths and bridles. He heaved off the bay's saddle and addressed the stupefied scout, "Explanations can wait. If you have provisions, stew and a blanket would be helpful."

"I have only jerky." Aroused to the crisis, the clansman snapped to and stepped in to assist stripping tack. "There's a buried cache in the glen with a cooking pot, but no meal. We always forage at this season."

"Then go hunting, please, once these horses are turned loose. As I know Sethvir, you'll find a deer waiting if you allow my raven to lead you."

Traithe accepted a headstall from the scout's hand, then slapped the bay's rump with the gentle admonishment, "Go roll, brave heart. Eat grass and find water and rest."

Once assured the animals would be competently handled, Traithe strode through the grass and knelt by Felirin's prone form. He ran swift hands over the minstrel's body, while the raven flew circles over his hat, a slice of cut nightfall set intaglio into the hazed summer brilliance of sunlight.

"How bad is he?" Dakar asked, returned strewn with leaves and an armload of dead oak branches clutched to his chest. His plump hands left sweated prints as he shifted his hold to contain the unruly, loose wood.

"Nervous exhaustion." Traithe moved tacit fingers above Felirin's scorched tunic, touching unseen points in the air. A spark jumped from his fingers each time he paused. The raised power diffused into a bloom of faint light, which misted downward into the free singer's aura, then sank and absorbed through the cloth into flesh.

"Sound sleep will set him right." Traithe's ministrations moved down the right arm. There, he held still, with the singer's limp wrist clasped left-handed, as his right trailed over the grimed rags that covered the burns. "His hands are another matter," he concluded sadly. "The fire left damage."

"He already knows he's lost his fingertips." Dakar thumped the wood at his feet, too nettled to wrestle the earth's gravity. "He's said he can turn his bard's talent to storytelling. Asandir suggested he'd find a warm welcome at Innish."

Neither spellbinder nor Sorcerer belabored the tragedy, that if Traithe's faculties were still whole, or if this crisis had been met by any other member of the Fellowship, Felirin's disfigurement might be ameliorated.

After all that had happened, the frustration flared too hot to contain. Dakar bent and began snapping dead sticks into kindling, determined to offer what sympathy he might. "Truth lies with the fact we stand here together. Don't count the small losses. Without your assistance, none of us would have wakened to see air and sunlight, nor walked on Athera's soil again."

A shadow flicked over Traithe, cast by Jieret Red-beard, who approached with the slack form of Arithon s'Ffalenn cradled like a child in his arms. "He's cold as death and scarcely breathing."

"I don't wonder." Traithe's lined face tipped up, drawn with concern. "Lay him down in the sun and get him stripped to his skin. We'll need his clothes. Also every cloak you can find in the saddle packs."

The Mad Prophet stood, stricken. His glance flickered quickly past Arithon's slack face, then flinched from the pale, lifeless hands that dangled, grooved on the backs from the prints of the hobbles, which for expedience had secured him to his horse. The normally scintillant aura of the Masterbard seemed dimmed and gray to his mage-sense.

Alarmed by the rapid ebb of a life that could not at any cost be replaced, Traithe turned brusque. "Dakar! If you're planning to grow roots with that bundle of wood, the fire's more important. We'll also need a pit dug in the open."

The rumpled, fat spellbinder wasted no argument. "You'll use hot rocks?"

Traithe's smile came out like the sun, rekindling the lost lines of humor that ran in starbursts from the corners of his eyes. "Yes. Choose willing ones so they don't shatter. There's a creek bed ten paces inside the trees. And find six straight saplings that are willing to make sacrifice."

Dakar moved off, intent, to reaccess the rusty tenets of his training. Caithwood was sealed under Paravian law, which demanded strict form and fine harmony with the earth, no live wood taken without proper blessing and a clear gift of permission. "Fiends plague," he muttered, still fighting a thick head. "We haven't come back just to lose Rathain's prince for want of a sweet-tempered tree!"

"Just use plain language and say whose life's at stake," Traithe suggested. "Without Arithon s'Ffalenn, the Alliance will triumph. Clan bloodlines will die, and every green thing in this forest is well aware no centaur guardians will return if Desh-thiere survives and claims final conquest."

The clan scout dragged the cleaned carcass of a buck into the glen an hour later. As he broke through trees, the pleased whistle carried over from his successful hunt died into openmouthed silence.

Miracles had happened in his absence. At the center of the clearing, on a bent framework of willow poles, Dakar finished tying the drover's cloak and the gaudy layers of the free singer's court doublets into a shaded enclosure. Traithe stooped by the entrance, bearing a long-handled stick. The fork at the end cradled a stone from the riverbed, baked red by fire, and crackling to the caress of the breeze which kissed its glowing surface.

The scout gawped. "Ath! That's not possible!" He was no born fool: mere flame took at least the length of a day to raise a river stone to extreme temperatures.

A reedy voice answered his doubt from the grass. "A fine piece of spellcraft, yes?"

The scout leaped back startled. The dropped carcass of the buck slumped into a heap, its glazed eyes fanned with stirred dust. "Fiends plague!" He backstepped before he spotted the minstrel, seated upright, and busy fussing the tangles from his hanks of singed hair.

"Dharkaron's own spear! Last I saw, you were prostrate." The scout vented relief, that he had not entirely taken leave of his senses. "Man, you fair lifted me out of my skin."

Slouched in his motley rags of smudged clothing, Felirin sighed with forbearance. "I'm sorry." His bandaged hands returned an expressive, wry gesture. "The day seems made for surprises."

Bent over to reclaim the buck's tined antler, the scout shot a suspicious glance toward the fire pit, where the Sorcerer plied his stick and scooped out another glowing rock. "How did he do that?"

"What, heat the stones?" Felirin unhooked his tarnished pearl studs, and flapped his stained shirt open at the collar. His manner stayed amused as Traithe shoveled the stone into the darkened shelter of the willow frame. "He called sunlight down through his crystal." The minstrel's gaunt features showed delight at the memory. "The event will become my first epic story, how a blinding light shot out of blue sky, a bolt of tamed golden lightning."

Visibly miffed to have lost his listener's attention to a gutted, dead deer, Felirin peered disdainfully down his long nose at the sticky blood painting crushed grass stems. "I suppose you want help. That was the last rock Traithe just shifted. Though I'm not fond of fire, I could help roast your game if you like."

"Soon as you have the skin off, I'll need to haul water," Traithe said.

Felirin and the scout both started in unison, spun, and discovered the Sorcerer standing quiet behind them. "Time," he said gently, as if the one word could explain his uncanny comings and goings. "We have none to spare." He knelt, his drawn knife in hand. The blade was plain steel, unmarked by runes, or any ritual sign of power, and yet, its metal glowed blue as he spoke a Paravian blessing over the wound where the scout's arrow had pierced the buck's heart. A fine mist of energy spun away at his words, then disbursed into the black soil of the earth. Peace remained, and a sense of core balance restored as Traithe turned his deft blade to the work of skinning and butchering.

To the clan scout's reddened embarrassment, the Sorcerer had the green hide worked free within minutes. His fleeting, mild wink acknowledged the marvel that such haste had not torn holes through the pelt, or left even one hacked edge. "No tricks or spells," Traithe admitted. "My knife is old and knows this work very well." He arose with a mild wince at the twinge in his bad knee, and rolled the raw skin hair side in. "Dakar will cut you a spit for the meat. Then pray to Ath that Earl Jieret and I can deliver a live prince to share venison with you at sundown."

Inside the willow frame, masked under patched layers of tied clothing, Jieret s'Valerient kept vigil with the head of his liege in his lap. The changes he saw would have torn out his heart, had worry not done so beforehand. Arithon s'Ffalenn lay full length on the earth.

The glow of rocks in the pit mapped his frame in dense, ruby warmth, the gleam of old scars written over gaunt flesh, and the angry ones fresh from his battle with Caolle. Despite the radiant heat, his cheek felt ice-cold. Each pulse through slim wrists seemed a vestige without force. As though life stayed by rote, his lungs scarcely carried the function of breathing from one moment into the next.

Jieret clenched his swordsman's fist in black hair, tied between rage and regret. "Live, damn you," he exhorted. "Caolle died content in the belief you survived him."

The hard-edged triangle of daylight at the entry dimmed one last time as Traithe entered with the deerskin sloshing with creek water. "Close us in, please."

Outside, Dakar battened down the heavy wool cloak, then sealed the last gap with one of Felirin's belled shirts.

Limned in the vermilion glow from the stones, Traithe poured the water into the pit. Steam shrieked and exploded, whirling the air into a scalding, opaque curtain. Jieret shut his eyes, dizzied, and momentarily confused by what seemed like voices, embedded between the meshed cry of four elements, wedded amid the primordial darkness and circling his frame in a chiaroscuro dance of wild energy.

"Don't mind if they speak." Rendered formless in shadow, Traithe knelt and sprinkled a handful of crushed herbs, which showered bright sparks and infused fragrant smoke through the darkness. "They are spirits born of fire, earth, water, and air, and they arise to help call your prince back to himself."

Jieret began a deep breath, then stopped short as the scalding steam burned into his nose and scoured the back of his throat. He realized by the fact that his forearm was cramping that his fingers had fastened a death grip in Arithon's hair. "You're saying the earth knows how important he is?"

Traithe sat, the hide with its reservoir of drawn water cradled between his tucked feet. He had removed his boots. By the pulsing, carnelian glow of the stones, the sole of the right one showed a puckered mass of scarred tissue, drawn like the mark of an old burn. "Athera knows all of our names," he admitted, thoughtful and pleased for the rarity of indulging in philosophical discussion. "No one person's ranked ahead of another. In Prince Arithon's case, the elements plead aloud for the sake of the service he may yet be asked to perform."

"Service!" Irritable as sweat trickled and stung through a brush burn acquired from his hurried, rough ride, Jieret gave vent to deep bitterness. "It was unstinting service that exposed my liege to unreasonable peril in the first place. The needs of this land are what kill him by slow inches. He would not be undone by a poisoned conscience had he not been asked to face troubles a sorcerer would be hard-pressed to handle!"

"He is mage-trained," Traithe reminded.

But Earl Jieret was not mollified. Though he faced no enemy, he felt unreasonably impelled to birth his wedged hurt into the concealing darkness. "A hundred stout liegemen would not be enough to manage the burden he carries!"

"You're right, of course." Still mild, the Sorcerer splashed a cupped handful of water into the pit. Again, the steam swirled, dark-patterned tarnish on shadow. Beyond that blank veil, his words came disembodied. "Duty won't be what calls Arithon back."

"What else does he have?" Once started, Jieret found his restraint had slipped reason. The moist heat made him careless, and the slack weight of his prince made pity a dull blade that sheared off every civilized platitude. "Or will you release him to follow his preference for music?"

Traithe responded to the first question only, his cragged face and pale hair wreathed in sweet smoke from the herbs. "He has his friend, who is living and with him. That matters far more than anything."

"Your logic is flawed." Shaking and savage, Jieret failed to note that the lean, hollowed cheekbone pillowed on his thigh showed the faintest, thin flush of rose. "What can his friends do other than die for him?"

"They can live for him," Traithe said, acerbic at last. "Do you think Caolle would change his fated end if he could?"

"Ath, no!" Earl Jieret's surprise burst through as a breath of free air. "He died as he lived, for love of his prince. I've heard the details. He could have stopped fighting and chosen a less painful passage. As I knew him since infancy, I'd swear this for truth: however much he claimed that his duty came first, in fact, he gave out of personal loyalties."

Traithe's correction came gentle. "And are you so different?"

The scald of the steam choked Jieret's instinctive denial. He snorted, coughed, then let grief tear asunder to release as a leveling of soft laughter. "No," he admitted. "My days would lack savor without the deep caring to give the bad moments their meaning. This prince holds my true heart." Eyes shut while Traithe sprinkled the rocks yet again, and the heat rolled in waves to strip the last pall from restraint, Jieret lapsed into reminiscence. "I think that's been so since my boyhood, on the night when I trailed his Grace into the forest. He'd just sworn his royal oath as crown prince, and was savage with misery for it. Did you know that I eavesdropped on his tienelle scrying? He never lost patience. Nor would he admit that my prank cost him agony, though he had to have seen. I was just a fool boy come with mean intent to belittle him."

"As well you should have," a rusted voice interjected. Scarcely audible through the coiling hiss of the steam, and by far less fluid than the wraith language used by the elements, the limping speech stumbled on. "Certainly then, I was a prince seeking to escape the burden of my people's hopes. In hard fact, nothing's changed."

"Arithon?" Jieret jolted straight, his hungry eyes struggling to pierce veiling murk. When vision fell short, he resorted to touch. Battened about in whorled darkness and moisture, the cold flesh of his prince was now heated, and streaming thick sweat. Yet the hand Jieret fumbled and grasped was still limp.

Then a flare from the stones as the steam eddied; Jieret saw the green eyes were opened, and wide, reawakened to a pain-filled awareness that violated privacy to witness.

Elation wrenched through him, then brought sharp remorse for straight guilt. His joy of recognition could not be denied, even in the face of such suffering. Helpless, Jieret could not even look away. "My liege, I have no words at all."

"Words are not necessary." Sweat or tears threaded down the hollows at Arithon's temples. The slicked whorls of black hair were dripping. "Your love calls too strongly, and mine, it would seem, is destined always to answer."

A break like cut glass in the suffocating womb of close shadow. "Don't apologize. I'm the one who owes restitution. That was an ugly reward I gave Caolle."

Jieret yanked breath to protest, caught short just in time by Traithe's quelling gesture and silent, mouthed words, "No! Let him rant!"

"You should know, he died true to himself." Arithon's flesh spasmed through a violent shiver. His grainy, scraped voice bore no semblance of the grace gifted to him through bardic tradition as he labored through his distressed confession. "His courage and his loyalty were of priceless coinage. I could live my whole life without fault from this moment, and still fall short of repayment. Nothing is left for you, Jieret. My hands are more empty than a beggar's. I have nothing to give back but the bankrupt husk of my sorrow."

"Your hands are not empty," Jieret forced out past the rock-hard wedge in his throat. "They hold a masterbard's talents, and more, the living promise of crowned sovereignty for a whole people. If you never sit on the throne at Ithamon, you can still keep that trust through your progeny."

Which words pierced twofold, for the fact of a burden unwanted, and for the ruin Desh-thiere's curse had ripped through an oathsworn integrity. Arithon shook with the force of those sorrows, then turned his face, helpless as his agonized shame unmanned him.

Jieret's hands held steady and strong, unwilling to relinquish a tormented spirit to the throes of a solitary grief. Without prompting, this time, he found the wisdom to let the torrent unleash. "You're not alone, ever, despite your belief we would do better outside your company. The Mistwraith's hold is a wound we all carry. Some of us bleed for it. Others give their lives. Those who survive receive the priceless gift of your sacrifice, and the ones closest keep faith and friendship as we may."

But no words could succor the pain that escaped in riven bursts. Arithon's stripped body curled under the force of an anguish his dwindled strength could not deny. Jieret's arms gripped him, circling his wretchedness with unconditional compassion. "Brother, we are one. My sword does the killing, no less than yours. I can offer forgiveness for trials no man could pass without scathe. You and Rathain's people are one mind and one heart. Never see yourself as separate, no matter how far the curse madness drives you. If you bear the insanity, let us be the unity that draws you back and receives you. Won't you see there's no blame? Caolle's content. He knew, as I do, that *ours is the easier portion to bear!*"

"You could die for those words," Arithon gasped. His splayed hands pressed into the sides of his face, as if physical pressure could somehow contain his coil of untenable torment.

Jieret stroked back coal hair, fingers callused from handling weapons infused with near reverent gentleness. "We all pass the Wheel. When I do, I'll know peace, no matter the cause. Believe this, my sons and my daughters will be there to steady your next steps in my place."

"For what price?" snapped Arithon, the wounded edge of his sarcasm striking in savage rebuttal. "Your shackles are wearing! For Dharkaron's punishment, how many times must I sing a lament over Steiven s'Valerient's grave cairn?"

Earl Jieret fought back, planted granite rejecting the thrust of fine steel. "For as long as it takes to defeat Desh-thiere and seat a crowned king at Ithamon."

"Is that so?" Arithon resorted to premeditated viciousness. "Then how many times must Lady Dania's descendants suffer rapine and slaughter under the swords of sunwheel fanatics?"

Jieret flinched. That dart pierced and struck as no other could, the family he had lost to the horrors of Tal Quorin still coiled in memory and the black nightmares that ravaged the peace from his sleep.

Yet Caolle had trained him.

He clung, dogged, his mind pitched to grasp for advantage. From the shocked reverberation of his own pain, he could gain the measure of Arithon's: a thousandfold worse, to have used such a personal weapon to strike with intent to wound. And there lay the vulnerability and the weakness at once. This was not attack, but defense of a vile and desperate proportion.

"You have a vicious tongue when you're bleeding," Jieret managed. His voice shook. He steadied it, determined, and smashed past the barrier of empathy that could have, *would have* stopped him short, if his care had existed only for an ironbound duty to a kingdom. "Makes it harder than plague to bind up your wounds. Even so, Steiven loved you."

"He's bones in cold earth, as you will be," Arithon slashed back. Had he one bodily resource to break Jieret's hold, he would have risen and fled elsewhere. Trapped helpless, he could only use words for his weapons, and no shield to spare his naked awareness from the lacerating impacts of remembrance. Left unsaid, all the unassuaged hurt of his severance from mage-sight, a brilliance of talent choked off in blood on the banks of Tal Quorin; there existed no weal for its absence.

The Earl of the North was not swayed by pity. "Dania loved you equally well. She would call you impertinent, and say to you now that because of your sacrifice, her bloodline survives. Her four daughters still live unspoiled in my memory. If by Ath's grace you defeat Desh-thiere in my lifetime, then every one of my family will stand with me in spirit on the hour a Teir's'Ffalenn accepts his coronation."

"*Let me be dead, first!*" Arithon gasped. "What rightful prince ever murders his feal liegemen?"

The despair, the deep canker of shame stabbed by guilt, at last was laid bare between them. Across misted darkness, Traithe leaned sharply forward. "The moment has come. Jieret, speak now!"

Rathain's *caithdein* set his jaw. Hardened against heartbreak, he bent and dealt his prince a hard, vengeful shake. In stark force, he said, "Listen to me! Stop crying martyr! Caolle chose not to die of your sword thrust. He got up on his feet and marched back to war wearing bandages! Nor were the ships lost, or the craftsmen and crews arrested in Riverton. Arithon, he triumphed, despite every obstacle. By his choice and devotion, he gave back your design with only a few torn stitches. *Cariadwin* was even recovered from Corith, and full half of the men from the outpost."

"This is a dream," Arithon whispered, the spirit leached from his words, and the fight in him flattened to a whisper.

"No." Jieret held him, his unvanquished courage enough to cause pain, and his grasp unrelenting with the promise of the bittersweet dichotomy of life. "Everything's real! If you run now, prince, you'll never see the fruits you spent yourself penniless to reap."

Steam billowed. Traithe splashed more water on the rocks, which showed scabrous gray patches from cooling. The stifling darkness spun time into fluidity, while the herb-scented heat rose in waves and eroded all barriers between mind and emotion. Jieret waited. Each breath in his chest flamed new agony. The stillness in the body held clasped in his arms became harrowing, and despair crushed out hope like the immovable wall of a glacier. He understood too well: this was the crux point, the fragility of moment when victory or defeat hung in the balance, awaiting the flick of fate's finger.

Ever the swordsman, taught to fight for as long as his hand held one weapon, Jieret Red-beard launched his last, stabbing thrust. "Caolle left you a legacy in the form of a Koriani witch's spelled quartz."

At Traithe's start of astonishment, the clan chieftain laughed, broken free like snapped wire from the unmerciful, cranked pressure of strain. "Yes, it's true."

Another racked moment; then Arithon's frame began to shake, first in small jerks, and then in running tremors that caused Jieret a spurt of stark panic. He shoved to his knees, dragging Arithon half-upright. His lungs filled to howl for a loss he had no fiber left in him to withstand.

But Traithe touched him still.

The s'Ffalenn prince was laughing in jagged, hysterical spasms. "A spell crystal?" Arithon ground on through a shrieked, wheezing breath. "Morriel must be spitting like a goosed cat. Whose is it?"

"I'll tell you," Jieret promised, stunned stupid by relief. Somehow he found the aplomb to sort language. "But not until you have eaten and rested. You're so worn right now, the irony would kill you, which was not what Caolle intended."

Lapsed back into quiet by weakness that skirted the brink of collapse, Arithon turned his head into Jieret's strong shoulder. "Caolle was a rabid fox, and you are more devious than that fiend of a father who sired you. I will do as you ask, just to share in the joke. Now you have my word, can we please let in some fresh air?"

But Traithe had already anticipated. Dakar pulled the muffling cloth free from outside, and light streamed in on an inrush of cool breeze that started Jieret shivering. While hands reached to assist, he turned his glad strength to pull Arithon out into daylight. Before they could bundle his spent limbs in the drover's cloak, his prince drifted into a faint.

"Don't worry," Traithe said, his face all wry delight as he peeled the soaked hair from his neck. "He'll revive fast enough when we douse him clean in the stream. The scout has stew waiting, and sleep without dreams will do much to mend lost resilience."

"Oh, Ath," groaned Jieret. He stood up, wobbly at the knees with Arithon's wrapped weight in his arms. "That's if we survive the spate of raw language. The one thing this prince hates like fire is being handled like an invalid."

"Well, that will just provide more incentive." Traithe's grin was pure mischief. "If he wants us to stop, he'll just have to rebuild his strength."

In fact, Arithon succumbed before they had extracted him from the rock pool. Dried and swathed in the drover's cloak, he slept without moving throughout the late afternoon. As evening fell, he roused long enough to taste the stewed venison shared out in the bowls Traithe kept at hand for his spellcrafting. Twice, Jieret's reflexes righted the container that slipped from his liege's slack fingers. No scalding invective marked either incident. When Arithon slipped off into sleep once again, Traithe scribed a healing glyph over his forehead and snapped for Earl Jieret to stop pacing.

"Worry serves nothing. What we're seeing is nervous exhaustion." Like echo, he fielded a sleepy croak from the raven, gone to roost to the night chorus of frogs in the marsh. "I know, little brother, you, too," he agreed in tart sympathy. Then, to Jieret, who hovered uncertain with his hands whitely clenched to the tang of his broadsword, he added, "Keep watch. If I'm right, your liege will rouse in the darkest hours before dawn. He'll want to talk, and share the need for understanding companionship."

Settled to keep watch, while the studded patterns of summer constellations wheeled through the gaps in the oak leaves, Jieret oiled his knife sheaths. He compared stories with the scout, then helped to tie new fletching onto worn arrows. While Dakar dirtied his hands scraping the deer pelt, Felirin tested his new art of storytelling, until midnight saw all but the Sorcerer settled to rest.

"I haven't apologized, or thanked you properly for your help," Jieret said, his hands empty at last and folded against the stained leather of his baldric. "You've helped to restore a number of great gifts, among them the heart of my people. Like these scouts of Maenol's, we could see a harsh future as long as the Alliance keeps building. The headhunter campaigns from Etarra take their toll, but we can face anything, hopeful."

Traithe lifted his hat and raked back loose hair, the scar at his crown a jagged dark knot that belied his mild stance in the darkness. "The world will spin differently, because of tonight. All things are connected, as Arithon knows, since he was raised to think like a sorcerer. He still tries to honor his grandfather's teaching. That's why his failures strike hardest. You did well in your handling. Few could have made him attentive after the sorrows that took place at Riverton."

"He is as my brother, more than my liege," Jieret admitted, then blushed for a feeling he had never dared mention.

Traithe arose, tactful, to leave him in privacy for the hour when his prince must stir out of dreams and ask for account of Caolle's dying. The ending was two-edged, that the stay of victory for Tysan's clansmen had been won with no chance for a last word exchanged in reconciliation or parting.

Arithon's branding memory would still be of the sword thrust that had felled the friend who had righted the damage the Koriathain had set in his design.

"He will live with the gifts," Earl Jieret promised. "Though I swear I'd fret less if I had to bash the wind out of him, making the point stick with my fists."

The Sorcerer laughed. "You wear Caolle's stamp alongside of your father's. He will live on, for all that." Traithe gathered his satchel and snapped crippled fingers for his raven, which glided down from its roost in the treetops. It alighted, feathers folded like knives as it croaked testy inquiry from the threadbare perch of his shoulder.

"Fare you well, Earl Jieret. Wish your prince my regards." Then in short, limping steps, the Sorcerer turned away, to be far from Mainmere by morning.

Left alone with his thoughts, Earl Jieret listened, while the night celebrated its chorus of crickets and sheltered the rustles of foraging mice. The forest breathed life. Water and wind braided together in counterpoint. The agile bats swooped like manic shuttles, weaving their unseen strands on the loom of creation. Oddly content that his fresh loss of Caolle could be shared, he almost missed the first stir of movement as Arithon roused in the drover's cloak.

The first words came spare with the acerbic, dry wit he remembered. "You've got me tied like an infant in swaddling. Damned lucky I don't have a killing need to piss."

Jieret settled back against the bole of an oak, his fringed buckskins blurring his angular form in the darkness. "If you did, we'd make wagers on how long you would take to fall sound asleep with your breeks down."

Arithon snorted. His hands moved, restored to a semblance of dexterity as he freed the tucked cloak and flexed his constricted shoulders. Painfully gaunt, he paused to examine the shirt someone had given to cover his nakedness. "Make sure you say which scout I should thank."

"You don't like charity?" Jieret dared a grin behind his raised wrist. "What you wore was scarcely fit for a rag to oil the edge of a weapon."

Arithon said nothing, the tenor of his quiet like a test.

"The shirt was mine," Jieret admitted. "Though you could have guessed that by the pitiful fact we had to hack a handspan off the cuffs."

"And the shoulders fall down to my elbows, I know. Caolle always said I was too slight to bear weapons, and I just broke my pact. I wasn't going to be first to pick trouble."

Jieret swallowed.

The crickets filled in as Arithon shifted, then with tenacious effort, pushed his frame upright. Depleted as he was, his spirit was drawn wire. "Never mind the fool etiquette between prince and *caithdein*. As your oathbound brother, I'm sorry. Caolle was the right arm I never deserved. I'm grieved to have taken him from you."

"He took himself," Jieret said, truthful, and the difficult words of a sudden came easily as he described the altercation caused by his bull-headed past war captain on the subject of his prince's protection. "Did you know, he tossed the younger men who volunteered into the river to make his point? The irascible bastard said if they couldn't best him at wrestling, they weren't fit to keep guard on the slop in your chamber pot."

"How like him!" Turned pensive, Arithon also found the question spilled gently, without the barbed lash he had dreaded. "How did he die? You made me a bargain to buy my return, and by Ath, you'll need to deliver."

Under the kindly mantle of summer foliage, Jieret shared the tears and the triumphs that had won back the launched vessels from Riverton.

"So whose spell crystal have I inherited as my legacy?" Arithon asked at due length.

"You couldn't guess?" Earl Jieret reached into the loosened breast of his jerkin and tugged a fine silver chain over his riot of red hair. "Caolle never did things by the half measure. He's left you his last power of revenge upon First Senior Lirenda."

Arithon choked, hands pressed to his lips, while his shoulders spasmed with dammed-back delight and wild laughter. "Oh, Dharkaron's sweet Spear! That's too rich." He extended a thin arm and accepted the gift. Caught starlight in the crystalline facets flashed like the forerunning bolt of a tempest. His remonstrance held humor as he closed his marked fist, silver links snagged like a looped strand of tinsel between his irreverent fingers. "You know such an object should be veiled in silk?"

"So ask a townsman," Jieret said, piqued. "If the bitch finds her nerves pricked, that's her just deserts for trying to play us like string puppets."

But if Arithon shared the release in snide humor, his grave countenance showed no breaking sign. He seemed queerly grieved, head tilted a listening angle to one side, while the chain magnified the running fit of trembling that had reft the peace from his hands. "Is my lyranthe nearby?"

Jieret straightened, astounded by his urgency. "She's safe with the saddle packs. Why?"

Moved by Arithon's sudden, sweet smile of relief, he arose without question and fetched the priceless, wrapped bundle that had almost been lost in the disastrous flight out of Riverton. When the fine instrument was restored to the hands of the bard, Arithon laid the quartz crystal at his feet. He caressed the carved wood, musician to his core, and rapt with the call of his muse as he struck and fine-tuned each neglected, silver-wound string.

Then he launched into a haunting, free melody.

The cadence and the harmonies were like nothing before, speaking in lyric of sorrow and joy caught enraptured in a fired, double helix. Earl Jieret wept. The notes spilled and soared, each one an exquisite needle of inflection too fine to endure, and each measure an unfettered, tingling ecstasy bridged over desolate emptiness.

In the gloom of the trees, the scout stirred and gasped. Felirin awoke, raised his head, and crumpled, his maimed hands clasped to still the demand of a mourning he could not bear to release lest he damage the sheer majesty of the spell.

Of the thralled listeners embraced by the Masterbard's talent that night, only Dakar the Mad Prophet came to suspect the melody was not wrought for Caolle; nor yet for the tragedy of a free singer's burned hands; nor even to commemorate the survival of a most severe trial of s'Ffalenn conscience. The phrasing, stamped into empathic clarity, was Arithon's tuned response to the cry of a solitary spirit imprisoned in the lattice of a Koriani spell crystal.

Catalyst

Lirenda dreamed of a man and a melody, and awoke with tear-flooded eyes.

For one second, two, the sweeping immediate, razor-edged memory held her fast across the transition. Still, she could hear the rippling, sweet peal of struck notes. Plangent, silvered strings spoke their appeal just for her, a cry to flood joy through every unfulfilled cranny in her heart.

Weeping as a creature possessed, she suffered through the jarring reorientation of finding herself bereft, alone, and jostled in the rolling discomfort of a blue-water ocean passage. As her elbow struck an uncompromising edge of adzed wood, and the pull of the oars thumped in vibration to the beat of the coxswain's drum, she recalled her true place aboard Prince Lysaer's royal galley. That awareness revived her mazed will. The beguiling cascade of lyranthe notes lost their hold, snapped away like a net of burst thread.

She sat up, mired in a salt-musty snarl of damp linens. Protective as a provoked lioness, she let trained perception dissect the shreds of impression that even now slipped through her memory. At once, she picked out the familiar trace resonance of her personal crystal. She knew then. Her chain-lightning leap into fury kindled a startling sting: *the dream had ridden on the carrier tie between herself and her lost quartz.* By the aching wound opened by that one-shot bolt of compassion, then the pang of regret that was hers, inflicted as the harmony tangled and dispelled, she could surmise the hand of the meddler.

Her fleeting recall yielded the vision of shadowed green eyes. She still *felt* the deft empathy which had combed through the haunted depths of her mind, grasping after impressions to reclothe in music.

She knew; and her rage brimmed over and outran all restraint. Arithon s'Ffalenn had come to inherit possession of her personal spell crystal. Her life-tie to the quartz lattice had betrayed her, let him bare every weakness she possessed.

Her frustration found no outlet aboard Lysaer's galley. Alone in her cabin, surrounded by sleeping crown officers and men-at-arms sworn to the Alliance, she could not share confidence with anyone. The tedious, rolling beat of pulled oars offset nothing but the thrum of sea winds, and the hissed wash of cloven wavecrests. The dense heat of summer languished belowdecks and bathed her in trickles of sweat.

The repaired royal fleet rowed the last leg of the crossing from Corith to the mainland. But denied vital access to the channel of her crystal, Lirenda remained as blind to event as the common seaman on deck. She could do nothing but throw off stifling bedclothes and lie in her close, lampless berth, awaiting the moment when the masthead lookout sighted first land beneath the louring towers of seasonal thunder squalls.

Lirenda slept again just past dawn. Drugged by heat and the circling mill of her frustration, she suffered no dreams. This time no music came to haunt her. She emerged from a drowning, black well of oblivion to the filtered light of late afternoon. Clear over the groan of working timbers, she heard the running thump of sailors' bare feet over the decking above her. She clawed clinging tangles of ebony hair off the damp skin of her collarbones. Fighting groggy senses, she arose to refresh herself.

While she dressed in her meticulous layers of silk skirts and gauze-thin mantle of office, the activity on deck reached the fever-pitch anticipation provoked by an imminent landfall. She gathered from the bursts of excited talk and the flying strings of orders from the ship's officers that the peppery little navigator had not failed with his charts. He had led the fleet safely in to Orlest on the southwest shore of Tysan.

Swathed in her wind-fluttered, violet silk, Lirenda swept up the companionway. She displaced two off-duty oarsmen to garner a view at the rambade. The stroke of the crew on the benches below seemed enlivened. While the tumult of anticipation quickened about her, the late weeks at sea seemed an interval removed, time sealed in a pocket of salt-scented tranquillity. The breeze led the change. It brought smells of smoke and fish grease from the shoreside cook-fires, mingled into the sour, muddy reek of tidal marshes. Shoaling waters between ship and shingle heaved in striated tones of green enamel. Gulls flew, dipped gold in the late-day sun, which slashed through clouds strewn like feathers. The headland itself lay slatted in shadow, citrine as new ale where the marsh grasses spread tasseled seed heads.

During the burning, dry months of high summer, when the storms threw their rains off the coast, the tidal estuaries of south Tysan were worked for deposits of salt. Amid the fringed reeds at slack water, women raked crusted cakes into piles, while half-grown children sewed the glittering harvest into burlap for transport.

Past the low ground, flocks of goats grazed the stepped, rocky bluffs, raised like rucked baize above the path where a herdboy raced to warn the town of the arriving fleet.

Lirenda knew Orlest as a galleymen's haven. Here, captains put in to replenish provisions on their coast-hopping runs between the Riverton inlet and the rich ports past Hanshire.

As the oarsmen muscled the flagship against the chop of ebb tide, the town hove into view, tucked in a fold of the shoreline. Impressed in haze, and bounded in front by the scarred pilings of the traders' wharf, the crescent-shaped settlement was ruled by the running swell off Mainmere Bay. The low-lying houses were built upon stilts against the floods whipped in by offshore storms. Trapped heat rippled the sprawl of limed fishing shacks, their humped roofs thatched with cut reeds, and netted down with pendulous stone weights. Beside their unassuming stolidity, Sailhands' Alley stood out like a gaudy twist of silk, with its signboard array of brothels and wineshops.

The town also hosted a seasonal fishing fleet. While Lysaer's galleys steered a bending course through the cork floats of vacant moorings, word of their arrival ran ahead. Doors banged and craftshops emptied. A burgeoning crowd lined the docks as the flagship drove in, sunwheel banners streaming.

As the oarsmen's stroke sheared her patched hull shoreward, from rail and rambade, one could pick out the pristine white tunics of oathsworn Alliance guardsmen cutting an agitated swath through the gawkers like the mismatched gleam of thrown ice.

"Something's afoot," the watch officer remarked, creased eyes trained ashore. "Or why would a contingent of royal men-at-arms be billeted in force at Orlest?"

The steersman chimed in, "They would come to hold news for his Grace."

A likely enough guess; Orlest or Tideport were the logical sites to await an inbound fleet from Min Pierens.

Lirenda tapped manicured fingers on the rail, raked over by rabid frustration. Her curtailed powers would not let her access lane auguries at a glance, and the ignominy burned. The possibility for upset could not be dismissed: her misjudgment over Caolle's life may well have allowed Arithon s'Ffalenn to seize bold advantage on the continent.

She must have unwittingly mused her irritation out loud.

"But of course, the enemy would not stand idle through the summer." The reply intruded a pace from her shoulder; Lysaer s'Ilessid had apparently crept up through her moment of self-absorbed brooding.

He also had dressed for the landfall. Offset by the delicate sheen of her silk, his presence lost none of its magnificence. His impeccable, trimmed hair shone as burnished as filigree, and his pearls were cold fire in the sunlight. He was not smiling.

Anyone less than a Koriani observer would have missed his subtle satisfaction, as he added, "Did you truly believe the Shadow Master could be driven to unchecked flight without unpleasant repercussions?"

Lirenda's expression was fine marble veneer, impenetrable and aloof. A mere hour ago, she could have agreed without any sense of conflict. Now self-betrayed, subverted through access to her undefended quartz, she found herself battling phantoms. A masterfully tailored line of melody tugged her emotions on wild tangents, as if the imprinted perception of Arithon's intent gave the lie to his half brother's conviction.

Discomfited by Lysaer's probing interest, Lirenda returned a stare like chipped amber. "Why jab in pretense?" Her impulse for vengeance sparked out as small malice. "New discord but serves you. Bring down the Master of Shadow, by all means. Should I do less than applaud the picked course of your destiny?"

Lysaer laughed in that forthright honesty which effortlessly recaptured the heart. "Lady, your barbs are magnificent, but misplaced. Let us weigh the ill tidings before we presume to salvage the fruits of disaster."

Yet as the royal galley tied up at the wharf, no deft planning, nor calculated strategy of advance handling could smooth over the tumult which awaited the Prince of the Light.

Full night lay over the harbor, heavy as syrup with trapped warmth. Between the summer flicker of heat lightning, the rippled waters lapped like dark tarnish against the pilings, spindled with reflections from the torch pans set alight at the quayside. Amid that cast tangle of jittering light, Lysaer s'Ilessid stepped ashore.

The bystanders gathered to greet his return roared with one voice at first sight of him. Man, woman, and child, they surged against the men-at-arms who pressed to clear space for his egress. The prince took such mannerless enthusiasm in stride. All white silk and fitted elegance, he left the gangway, unhurried. As he passed down the wharf, his path became flanked by a wall of grasping, outthrust hands. The boldest strained against the cordon of soldiers, striving to touch his person for shared fortune, or to pluck at his glittering garments for a ribbon or lace to treasure as a memento.

Lirenda paced the prince one step behind, daunted by the sheer volume of noise, and by the relentless needy scramble of the crowd. The wharf narrowed past the jut of the ship's chandlery, with its stacked hogsheds of salt pork and beef. Royal guardsmen jostled a clear path with difficulty. The enchantress found herself unable to break away, even to lend polite semblance of privacy when the royal courier stepped to the fore.

He carried urgent news for Avenor's prince, a personal message too dire to withhold. "Your Grace, there's been tragedy. Best hear now, and quickly."

Caught in unwanted proximity, Lirenda shared the formal language of state which informed that his bewitchingly beautiful wife, Princess Talith, had passed the Wheel three months ago.

"By her own hand, your Lord Seneschal pronounced." Heads turned. The cheering near at hand faltered; still the messenger had to shout to make himself heard through the clamor. "Her Grace fell to her end. Succumbed to despair for her childless state and jumped from a high tower window."

Despite his matchless instinct for statecraft, Lysaer s'Ilessid missed stride.

For that given instant, he was no savior, no prince, no shining example to his people, but only a man, stunned by an unexpected, dark anguish. Grief exposed his humanity with leveling force. He faltered, stopped short. The flare of the firepans etched him in unmerciful light, each tremor of shock magnified by his jeweled studs and stitched seed pearls.

The sight of him humbled by wounding mortality struck Lirenda with inexplicable force.

She lost her own breath at the devastated speed with which his sustained strength came unraveled. The draw of his charisma had claimed her, unwitting, his dedicated campaign against the Master of Shadow became a mainstay she required to buoy her tripped sense of balance.

As a hapless observer, she felt strangely bereft; as if perfect quartz cracked like glass under polishing, or clouds on a whim had transformed into lead, to crush the green earth with blind force.

Lysaer seemed oblivious to the presence of an audience. Eyes closed, his ethereal majesty transformed to unalloyed sorrow, he murmured aloud in his anguish, "My dear, my dear! If not for the machinations of the enemy, I should never have strayed from your side."

The First Senior moved on blind instinct. She would offer her mantle, try any inadequate, stopgap gesture to shield his shattered poise from the insatiable maw of public curiosity.

Yet fast as she reacted, another pushed past and reached the s'Ilessid prince ahead of her.

This one wore the sweat-stained leathers of a courier who had transferred from post horse to post horse with small break for rest or refreshment. The chalky dust of the flats lined tired features, and his person wore the smell of hot horses and urgency.

He caught Lysaer's hand and dropped onto one knee. "Great lord, forgive me. I bring unpleasant tidings."

The Prince of the Light raised his head, eyes open and direct, if suspiciously bright. "Speak," he bade the man. "No tragedy of mine is so great that I cannot respond for my people."

Then he waited in all of his shattered splendor for a second round of ill news.

Lirenda stood near enough to overhear the fact that forty of Hanshire's finest men-at-arms had pursued Arithon s'Ffalenn into a cloudy veil of magecraft.

"That event happened some time ago. It's not canny, to have escaped official notice this long. But the first courier sent to Avenor was waylaid by a freak accident. His report was delayed for two months." The dazed messenger tipped his face up to the prince, torn into terrified appeal. "Search parties have swept the flats east to west, until the worst can't be doubted. The whole company of forty has disappeared, and left not a trace on the landscape."

Lysaer met the entreaty head-on, the shimmer of the tears he would not shed apparent to his circle of observers. "My loss, and my people's loss is not so different." Even in grief, his acute sense of kindness prevailed. "Had you kin among the missing?"

The messenger looked devastated. "A brother."

He received the hand of the prince on his shoulder. "Then we sorrow together, as we act side by side." Lysaer summoned a voice like grained iron. "There are widows in Hanshire this day who are bereaved by the loss of a mate, as I am. For them, you will go now and arrange mounts for myself and twenty-five of my personal guard. Find a guide who knows the countryside. Tell him he may ask any sum he desires from my treasury if he will show us the place on the flats where this happened."

When the original courier in Avenor's city colors elbowed his way in to protest, the prince quelled his concern with hammered steadiness. "There are no remains to attend, I trust?" Since his lady's death had occurred in the spring, he scarcely waited for affirmation that Talith's body had long since been cremated. "Then the ceremony to celebrate my personal regard for her can certainly bide a bit longer."

Lysaer made a painful effort to collect himself. Surrounded by darkness, beyond reach of the sultry glow from the firepans, his white tunic and jewels made him seem etched in light, a being set apart from the weathered squalor of the galley wharf. The dichotomy of his humanity hurt to behold as he raised his torn voice to explain. "I shall not return to Avenor until I have expended every effort to redeem this lost Hanshire company from the spellcraft which has spirited them from us."

The bystanders overheard. Struck by his purposeful denial of fresh loss, several women were moved to tears. First one man, then another began raggedly to chant, "*Lysaer of the Light!*" until the entire crowd at the waterfront had taken up the cry.

All at once, the night reechoed with a synchronous frenzy of admiration. The awe of the multitude expressed palpable excitement, that the Prince of the Light should give himself to their need before his own deeply personal sorrow.

His gold head a glittering beacon against the looming bulk of the warehouses, Lysaer s'Ilessid beckoned to the standing officer of his royal retinue. "Ready the best and the steadiest of my guardsmen." Over the tumult, his edged tone was the drawn sword, that would cut in fulfillment of its purpose. "We ride at speed for the Middlecross ferry!"

Very suddenly, Lirenda became the only stilled point in the maelstrom, as purposeful activity erupted around her.

Men-at-arms came forward to depart for the flats, and servants ran to gather clothing and supplies for the journey. While the fleet captains

501

who had managed the sea campaign at Corith were reorganized for return to Avenor, the Koriani First Senior believed herself forgotten. But where an ordinary man might have overlooked her insignificance, the Prince of the Light turned about.

He took her hand in his own and eased her small difficulty with the inspired attention to detail that marked his brilliance as a leader. "You wish to be elsewhere."

"I've been too long away from my order." Lirenda took an inadvertent step back, shaken by the impact of his caring.

Her trained senses perceived far too clearly. Lysaer's eyes were dark from the shock of his princess's death. Nor was his grip steady. Ridden by an all-too-visible anguish, the marred grace of his features reflected a transcendent need which drew on the heart like a magnet.

Even in weakness, his presence turned lives.

Yet again, Lirenda killed her surge of instinctive response. Swept by a sharp, reckless longing to cast off all ties and follow this prince in defense, she sampled firsthand the pull which caused men to leave home and swear service for life. Her Koriani discipline was scarcely enough to stand down the temptation, and recall the stakes of the sacrifice.

Belatedly she noticed that Lysaer was speaking, his offer an invitation to accompany his royal retinue as far as the landing at Middlecross.

"Weren't you bound for the Koriani sisterhouse in Capewell?" The diamonds at his collar flicked like held stars as he raised her fingers in a gesture of warmth and inquiry. "I presume you'd rather cross the inlet by ferry than ride the long way round through Riverton."

His selfless solicitude struck a chord of reciprocal concern. "Listen, you must know," Lirenda burst out in unpremeditated warning. "Those men-at-arms from Hanshire very likely entangled themselves in the bounds of a Paravian grimward. If you persist in seeking what became of them, you ride into unimaginable danger."

"They were lost on my orders in pursuit of the Spinner of Darkness." Lysaer's affirmation was clear-cut dedication over the rhythmical adulation of the crowd. "None of them will be abandoned for the sake of my safety. Your place is to accept my offer of escort as far as Middleton. There our ways part. Leave the fate and disposition of my people to me. You must serve your own order and bear my message on to your Prime."

Under the lucent weight of Lysaer's gaze, Lirenda knew no logical reason why she should feel humbled or shamed. Regal chivalry should not have overwhelmed pride. Bound into his debt by his dedicated sincerity, she could not shake the illusion that she was the lesser power. Though her poise stayed unbroken, all her wisdom and accomplishment as First Senior seemed diminished before his true grace as she accepted the gift of his kindness.

Checks and Balance

The hour that Arithon's sloop *Talliarthe* makes sail to cross Mainmere channel to Havish, a clan messenger departs for the sisterhouse in Capewell, in his hand a packet addressed to Morriel Prime which bears Rathain's leopard seal: the content, with Arithon's cordial regards, holds the First Senior's purloined spell crystal and cryptic promise that the debt has been duly discharged for Caolle's death. . . .

In the central chamber of the dragon skull at the vortex of the grimward, the Sorcerer Asandir leans on the shoulder of his black horse; near blind with fatigue, exhausting his last thread of depleted concentration, he frames the clear memory of the focus circle set into the dungeon of Althain Tower. . . .

In the mires of Mogg's Fen, Luhaine carries tidings to the *caithdein* of Tysan, that Arithon is safe across the channel to Torwent, and three brigs crewed by clansmen guard Mainmere Narrows to bear the refugee families into sanctuary under High King Eldir's justice; and amid tears and sorrow for those too late to spare, Maenol makes painful disposition that henceforward, every surviving clan bloodline will maintain a secure branch on the protection of foreign soil. . . .

XIV. Passages

The handpicked company which rode out with the Prince of the Light pressed straight on through the night. They traveled light and without fanfare for speed, with only one bannerman to announce the royal presence. The muggy, moist heat of the flatlands clung like syrup over the land. Darkness rang loud with the clicks of singing insects. The men behind the torch-bearing outriders mopped tearing eyes from streamed trailers of oily smoke. They held their formation in columns two abreast and trusted their horses to negotiate the hard-packed alkaline footing.

They thundered down to the sea inlet as fast as the posthouses could supply their urgent demand for remounts.

On that hour, the sheltered cove by the ferry wharf lay wrapped in woolly fog, the herring gulls wheeling and crying unseen against the filtered, rose blush of dawn. While horseboys still tousled from sleep in the loft led off their blown mounts, the serving girls from the ferryhouse brought them a meal of bacon, hot bread, and steamed fish. Men grown slack from their long weeks at sea cursed their new saddle blisters and stretched the kinks from their legs.

"Damnfool waste of effort, all this rush," a fresh recruit groused to a pair of weathered veterans who lounged by the tied boats at the waterfront. Experience had long since taught them not to waste themselves fretting. They listened, noncommittal, working their way through hard cheese and buttered biscuit.

While the incoming tide slapped at the bollards, their less experienced colleague nattered on. "Those riders from Hanshire have been lost for months. Whatever dark sorcery led them astray, they're probably dead. If not, what's the difference? Another day, or a week are unlikely to matter." Engrossed in self-pity, he failed to notice his companions had stiffened and stopped eating in disquiet. "If you ask me, we tire men and horses in a cross-country race to no purpose."

Seemingly out of nowhere, hard fingers locked onto the whiner's shoulder and jerked him face about toward the innyard.

"No man oathsworn to fight the shadow at my side shirks his given duty to his fellows," cracked Lysaer s'Ilessid. The pale white of his tunic melding into the mist, he had moved up unseen.

The grief of his past night's loss still marked him. Yet even through exhaustion and the incandescent fire of just anger, he noticed the ferryman's youngest toddler, wandered in his wake from the guesthouse. He knelt in the dust. "Go, child. The morning's too fine to spoil with shouting when you can pick shells from the beach."

As the girl wandered off, he straightened, confronted the miscreant, and resumed his lashing reprimand. "I will have it known beyond question that anyone needing help against the works of evil sorcery shall receive what they ask. Assistance will reach them with all the speed that crown resource can muster. My will on this matter shall brook no challenge. For today's lack of diligence, consider yourself released from your oath of service to the Light."

The recruit began a shocked protest.

Lysaer s'Ilessid cut him off. "Don't trouble to speak. I won't hear excuses." His blue eyes as inexorable as arctic ice, he insisted, "There can be no faint hearts in my ranks. As we shoulder the coming war against darkness, every man must stand ready to give his life *without question*."

"Mercy, bright lord." The young man fell to his knees, unmanned and broken to pleading. "Don't cast me out of your service!"

Lysaer snapped his fingers. The royal guard's captain stepped in on smart cue and ripped the sunwheel badge from the sleeve of the disgraced recruit's tunic.

"Leave us," commanded the Prince of the Light. "Stay clear of our crossing. The rest of this company has a task to accomplish in defense of this land and its people." He turned his back, let his icy regard sweep the rest of the company. "Believe this! Any man who looks back will be dismissed as well. Before threat of sorcery, we must harbor no weakness. Veer from our commitment for any man's faults, and the victory can never be ours."

Set against an ebb tide, the ferry passage to Middlecross required a half day to complete. The landing was accomplished amidst heat and haze in the close, summer fetor of a port town. While a dithering harbormaster recovered from receiving the royal party unwarned, Lirenda went her separate way and arranged passage by galley to Capewell.

The Prince of the Light saw her off with smooth courtesy, then made his presence felt among the town council through the due process of royal requisition. His small company prevailed against gathering crowds and deafening cries of adulation. On demand, his captain procured the fittest, fresh horses. Under the limp folds of the sunwheel banner, the two dozen mounted and rode out, watched by awed merchants and idle children, and by sailhands staggering drunk from the taverns who wandered upon the commotion. The prince's guard left behind a furor of fresh hope, and rumor that would spread east and north by the trade couriers.

Under sparse clouds like melted enamel, they left the trade road and crossed into the flats with a local guide to lead them. Across the windswept leagues of tilled farmland, past barking dogs and the stares of herders and goodwives, they pressed lathered horses. Four men were left when remounts ran short, and the day bled away toward sunset. Angled light stabbed flecks in the mica which crusted the striated rock. In ragged order, the company clattered across barren crests and dried gullies. They churned, slapping midges, through the mud of the sinkholes where the fog was first to gather, then camped by the glow of a three-quarter moon veiled under bridal-lace mist.

Astride once more in the half-light of dawn, the sea fogs like smoke about them, they passed the last inhabited farmstead; then its outlying sheep stanks of tumbledown stone, crusted in moss and gray lichen. Except for chinking bits and the creak of saddle leather, the riders might have been ghosts. They poured through the cross-stitched fronds of the willow thickets and exchanged no chatter at all.

Prince Lysaer led, his gleaming gold hair and scintillant jewels unearthly against the bald slabs of striated granite which scabbed that desolate setting.

The men at his back had outworn their will to raise spirits through railing banter. While the fogs rolled and shredded, and hazed sun speared down and raised trickling sweat under padded gambeson and helm, they dared set no words to their dread. No mind among them could grapple the horrors they might be required to face.

Somewhere ahead, forty competent soldiers had been swallowed alive by fell magic. The ones who rode now in sworn duty to try rescue owned no better protection than steel swords and their obdurate faith in the Light.

For Lysaer s'Ilessid himself, the bleak landscape left unpleasant, slack hours to think. His aching grief for Talith's loss became a torment of wretched persistence. As though the mainstay to his intellect had splintered like glass, pain left its branding reminder. Circling memories reopened old scars. The cycle of betrayal and abandon begun by his s'Ahelas mother now magnified and replayed, until he wished he was numb to all passion.

The friend who might have shared his hour of mourning lay dead, slain along with the war host massacred by the dark on the field at Dier Kenton Vale.

Nor could the Prince of the Light claim the luxury of solitude, even with the onset of night. The warren of scrub willow where the field troop made camp afforded no privacy for grief. Lysaer spoke and ate where necessity demanded. Duty bound to the needs of his men, he lay wakeful and watched the summer constellations melt slowly into the mist. The hour saw him more alone than he had ever been since the hour of his birth. Isolated by his royal rank, and by the cause that he shouldered to amend the defenseless plight of humanity, he still could not hide from himself.

Around him, no sound but the dry scrape of crickets; the plink of seeping water from a rock spring could not lull him to the forgetful oblivion of sleep. Nor could he silence his rampaging hurt.

Once, his marriage to a single woman had threatened to seduce him from his oathsworn obligation to bring down the Master of Shadow. Now Talith was gone. Temptation removed, he had not gained relief. Death had not brought him one iota of freedom from the drawing agony of her allure, which had dreadfully threatened to snap his integrity and undermine all his high principles. He felt newly lost. No grand cause could bridge the terrible vacancy love had left torn through his heart.

The only fire that remained to be fanned was his hatred for Arithon s'Ffalenn.

The Shadow Master's cleverness had manipulated Princess Talith to betrayal. In the months of her abduction, his accursed, scheming wiles had orchestrated her estrangement. Lysaer s'Ilessid endured the chill fact that he owned nothing dear in the world on which to build a bright future. Empty himself, royal justice demanded he not shirk his responsibility for the needs of his people. His life had meaning only if he delivered their destiny from the manipulative powers of the mage-born.

Yet even the comfort of resolve left him hollow.

Lysaer locked his teeth against flooding, bitter rage as the scourge of his faithless mother's s'Ahelas farsight mocked him to gritty self-honesty. At least for tonight, he could not mask the lie: he shouldered the challenge of the grimward for raw need, that the rooted aversion he held for all sorcery might drown out the pain of his loss.

Dawn saw him the first man arisen from his blankets. He still led the company through the baked heat of high morning. Starburst reflections jumped off the mica from the flood of sun overhead. Where bare rock was covered, the horses plowed chest high through topaz tassels of goldenrod and saw grass. Their hooves thudded over sod matted with gorse and bracken in the gullies which still hoarded moisture.

The land seemed empty, a circle of silence sealed under limitless sky. Then, with no warning, the horses took alarm. They snorted, necks rigid, their tails and ears raised, as if some uncanny presence raised distrust. No effort would settle them. Spur and rein, and feats of skilled horsemanship failed to restore their willing temperament.

"We'll dismount." Lysaer vaulted off his skittering mount, then waved for the hook-nosed local shepherd who served as guide to approach for immediate consultation. "Are we near the place where the men disappeared?"

"Your Grace, no." The man rammed the cork in the neck of his skin flask, mopped his dripping mustache, and glanced uneasily over both shoulders. "That site lies another day's ride to the east."

Down the ranks, a man slapped a fly. The report caused the guide to start out of his skin. "We should leave here. Animals are wiser to danger than we."

"I didn't come this far to run at the first breath of trouble." Lysaer raised his head, squinting against the glare of full noon. The strained quiet extended, while around him, the breeze stilled and died. Men shuddered with odd chills and gooseflesh. An insidious need stole over the mind to turn tail and beat swift retreat.

Chin up, eyes forward, his dust-caked surcoat straight on trim shoulders, Lysaer s'Ilessid masked the icy, first onset of fear. Only his stance of unmalleable determination kept the men steadfast at his heels.

A horse stamped. On a choking intake of breath, the local guide whirled and ran, thrashing a headlong course through the brush in blind panic to take himself elsewhere.

"Steady, keep sharp!" barked the captain. "Docked pay for any man who breaks from his place in the ranks!"

Suddenly the air gained an unsettled density, unsubtle and heavy as quartz. Sunlight fell magnified in unexplainable brilliance, as though the sky itself had turned refractive. The stabbed reflections off mail shirts and metallic gear caught in queer, actinic sparkles that befuddled clear vision. Then all natural sense of direction dissolved.

"By the light, we're being witched!" the bannerman gasped, shaken.

Lysaer touched the man's shoulder with quelling strength. "Be still." In reckless defiance, he raised his fist high and issued his own challenge in pure light.

The bolt seared aloft like the quenching shriek of hot steel. Its dazzling radiance slammed into resistance and summoned a veil of blank fog. Gray wisps eddied and curled, first as disorganized rags of vapor, then as a frothing, impenetrable veil which expanded to mask the known landscape.

To the men-at-arms rooted in trembling obedience, the surge of Lysaer's gift seemed to collide with an uncanny barrier of mage-force.

"Light save us!" the royal equerry cried through the murmur of another man's prayers.

The words rang flat and echoless with distance. Seared blind by the stifled, white radiance of his effort, Lysaer s'Ilessid fed the hard edge of his terror through the inborn channels of his talent. The more fight he raised, the more tightly he felt the unmalleable vortex of force twine like wire about his person. He sensed the connection. On the shaken verge of panic, he burned his gift like balefire, determined to rout the magecraft which bore down as if he had been chained as its target.

Visceral fear ripped through him.

Then the veil which masked mortal sight from the infinite tore across and shattered into light. The beacon this time *was not* of his making; his birth mastery could not grapple or bind it.

He beheld no land, no rock, *no live body*. Around him and through rang the dance of pure energy that fired the chord of Ath's mystery. A fist of dauntless power embraced him. He could not move, could not think, *only be*, melded as one with the forces which pealed to unbearable crescendo and Named him out of the void.

A cry like a shard of clear crystal lanced his mind.

"Lysaer, Prince of the Light, deliver me safe from the darkness!"

For one sustained second, ephemeral as moonlight on snow, or the whisper of thermals through a hawk's wing, the whole substance of displaced reality seemed to pivot and spin on its balance.

Then a peal of thunder cracked the luminescent air. Vibrations slapped his person with ranging force, tearing earth and sky back into solidified existence.

The land had not changed. Clear sun shone down, untrammeled by strange mists. Shocked speechless and scarcely able to stand upright, Lysaer s'Ilessid saw that his company of guards had been thrown to a man from their feet.

For a disjointed moment, they remained in stunned fear, flinching and paralyzed from reaction. Then a breeze stroked the weed tassels. A wren sang. The day resurged in all its diverse normality, while shocked men rubbed flash-blinded eyes. They groped after dropped weapons. A stupefied handful of seconds crept by before any of them noticed the miracle.

A dust-coated, haunted captain at arms was sprawled weeping at Lysaer's feet.

The prince blinked. He could not place the man's wiry, dark hair, nor the bloody gash raked down his forearm. The filthy, torn blazon on his surcoat was no sunwheel, but a sable stag on a scarlet shield.

His own captain was first to exclaim from the sidelines. "Hanshire? Sulfin Evend?" The name raised a babble of incredulous shouting.

"Look! Ath, it's him!"

"One of those who was taken by dark sorcery!"

"Behold! Did you see? *My Lord Prince of the Light has recovered the lost company's commander from the well of oblivion!*"

Lysaer took firm grip on his rattled nerves. Plunged into shocked chill, still half-unmoored and consumed by his struggle to dismiss the chord of grand mystery which had touched him, he fell back on reflexive inspiration. He caught the prostrate man's pitifully thin shoulder and raised him in a brother's embrace.

Then he studied the face, a square-jawed stranger's.

His racing heart rejected the implication, though to his bones, *he knew*. The powers which had redeemed the lost captain were none of his own. His memory of their uncanny strangeness pried at logic, undid belief, to the massive upset of clear principle.

Denial remained. If sorcery *was* wrought from the heart of life's source, if music and grand harmony and clean balance framed its powers, then Lysaer rocked on the edge of the abyss. All that he strove to accomplish in the world became unveiled as a misguided illusion.

511

"No." Lysaer shut his eyes, his two hands locked and shaking. Conflicted by self-honesty and devastated pride, he ached through a moment of absolute crisis, before he recalled his own truth: *the adepts of Ath's brotherhood once sought to sway him the same way*. They had used such diabolically crafted illusion to distort his perception, and blind honor, and convince him that Arithon s'Ffalenn was born innocent.

Indeed, what better way to seduce a mortal will from right action than to cloak perfect evil in a seamless, evocative beauty?

Around him, his dedicated company were clamoring for attention. He heard words, felt the heat of their worshipful astonishment. Sulfin Evend was speaking of his sojourn through terror, of seeing his small troop of men torn and savaged by monsters drawn from the First Age. He described landscapes cloaked in ice which had changed into mountains, or chasms of boiling rock between one man's step and the next. "Of all who followed in pursuit of the Shadow Master, I was the last left alive."

"Fellow, you're bleeding," the royal captain interjected. "Let's see that arm." At his reprimand, the equerry was sent to fetch bandages from a saddlebag.

"There was a Sorcerer," Sulfin Evend gasped, while a man knelt and cut away the clotted shreds of his sleeve to bare his untended wound. "He wore dark robes. While the rocks of Sithaer itself boiled and burned and ran molten about me, he came and forced me to walk down the throat of a dragon's skull. I fought him. He told me to cease struggling, that resistance was wasted. Then he flung me into the dark."

"Ugly, but just scrapes," the royal captain informed, his examination complete. "You're lucky the mess hasn't festered." He accepted the dollop of poultice paste the remiss equerry had mixed from stored remedies and a waterskin.

While his gashes were dressed, the victim insistently pursued his story, trembling from shock and amazement at his deliverance. "I knew I would be imprisoned in that place for all time. In my hour of despair I called on the Name of the Prince of the Light, and was heard!" He turned shining, worshipful eyes upon the blond-haired scion of s'Ilessid who stood a half step removed from his honor guard. "Praise your Grace! The blessed powers of Light have triumphed over darkness, and I stand before you alive."

The instant the bandage was secure on his arm, he pushed through the men and knelt once again at the feet of Lysaer s'Ilessid. "I have seen the truth. You are sent by divine mission to deliver us from darkness."

Surrounded by the worshipful circle of his men, the prince understood he must keep the pretense of manhood and react. If not, he risked being forced to explain how narrowly he had escaped an insidious and subtle attack of enemy subterfuge.

He laid his crossed hands upon Sulfin Evend's bent head. Unable to imagine how a man could stay sane through a harrowing ordeal wrought of sorcery, he chose utmost tact and said gently, "You need not still serve."

The Hanshire captain's fervent response became the balm which cemented cracked faith, and distanced the grief of Talith's passing.

"My lord prince, I would walk through Sithaer yet again to join in your battle against darkness!" Sulfin Evend tipped up his transformed, avid face. "Your Grace of the Light, let me ride at the forefront of your troops, that the spirit you have saved from the pit of evil should inspire others to stand strong."

Touched to relief, that a man of such fiber wished to carry his sunwheel banner against the legions of Shadow before him, Lysaer s'Ilessid raised the wiry Hanshire captain to stand erect at his side.

"You shall command the host of my field army." His royal admiration was no less than sincere as his choice squared battered shoulders under the singed tatters of his Hanshire surcoat. "The cause of humanity stands strengthened this day by the priceless gift of your courage. Your mettle is proven, Sulfin Evend. Your name shall resound unforgotten throughout history. No braver heart in all of Athera could spearhead the honor of the Light!"

Weeks after Lysaer's new Commander of Armies received his investiture at Avenor, the focus circle beneath Althain Tower captured light and then blazed into an actinic coruscation of raised power as a spelled tracer crossed the veil. A template of slipped time interlocked and aligned. Hurled through that storm's eye by the much delayed impetus of his homecoming, Asandir set foot on firm stone and staggered.

The Warden stood waiting by the center of the pattern; Sethvir caught his colleague's weak-kneed, failing weight before he measured his length.

"Blessed Ath," Asandir whispered. "I'd hoped you might meet me."

Around him, the restive flare of raised lane force sparkled and churned like a river flood sucked into whirlpool. Its brilliant intensity all at once shattered thought. His eyes would not focus. The laced mesh his own powers had called into being hazed into a blur, and his knees buckled under him after all. Despite the help of the Warden's staunch shoulder, Asandir understood in dismay he was not going to stave off collapse.

The dwindled reserves he tapped for clear speech became unimaginably precious. "The Major Balance is served." He paused to control a spasming shudder. "The Hanshire captain has been sent through alive."

"I know. He crossed back six weeks ago." Matter-of-fact before the shocking, hot touch of Asandir's clothing, Sethvir shifted his grip. "Don't speak." He clapped out a spark of conflagration with his palm, felt the stout weave of cloth and worn leather tatter away into ash. "I'm here. You don't have to fight to stay standing anymore."

With utmost gentle care, he eased his colleague's rangy frame onto the cool, grounding stone of the floor. One quelling word scribed a rune on the air. In response, the excited flare of stressed power dispersed. The focus patterns dimmed and subsided back into their dancing blue glimmer of quiescence.

"The second lane's left in chaos," Asandir murmured, eyes squeezed tight shut. The coiled tension in his body did not let go, as if his contact with dense matter, or even the currentless mild air caused him a sourceless pain. "The upset will have to be remedied quickly."

Between the spin of his unruly senses, he could not ignore the snagging ache of vibration thrown into disharmony. The unbalanced backlash shocked through the earth's lanes like a damping spill of poison. The black stone which channeled that energy beneath Althain belled in shared dissonance as the wayward, reverse polarity of the grimward strained distortions through the weakened geometry of the wardspells demarking its boundary in Korias. The world's natural weather would suffer in resonance if the magnetic turbulence was not curbed and sealed separate.

"Never mind." Sethvir's murmured assurance pattered echoes off the veined agate floor and glanced in multiplied whispers from the ceiling vaults. "Other hands will correct the imbalance this time. You're in no shape to do so yourself."

Asandir felt his senses slip, unraveling on a hurtling plunge toward chaos. He smelled metal and rust. Still dazed by deliverance from the reek of dead bone and charred rock, the dusky fragrance of sagebrush and meadow grass which clung to Sethvir's robes half unmoored him. The grateful, euphoric dizziness of knowing he was safe threatened his balance worst of all.

"I'm unfit to stand up," he allowed at last. His words fell away into distance like shot arrows. "You know the problem can't wait."

He forced his eyes open. Around him, the tower's white-marble walls fractured into light. His awareness remained vised in an uncontrolled flood of mage-sight, until thought and vision lost their form like run wax. The enveloping, lapping tingle of lane force strayed from the earth's tuned chord of identity and degenerated into spats of insensate static. "A magnetic disturbance on that scale is almost certain to—"

"You cannot concern yourself," Sethvir interrupted. "Not now."

"I must. Who else can you send?" Unable to separate which suffering was his, and which the ripped pulse of the world's discord, Asandir belabored the frayed rags of discipline to recoup a sure hold on his faculties.

"Be still!" The Warden's remonstrance clove his will like jarred iron. "Let me."

Through the jangled membrane of his skin, Asandir felt Sethvir's sensitive fingers. Touch came and went with the lightness of moth wings, testing, then mapping the vortices of fusion where his biological body engaged with the more subtle frequencies of spirit. His colleague's ministrations shored up flagging stamina, soothing with sympathetic infusions of fine energy; even so, Asandir felt the reverberation of each release drill through the marrow of his bones.

"Don't call Kharadmon." His strained eyes stayed open. The shocked, widened pupils were rimmed at the edge, the ephemeral, veiled silver of thin ice paned over turbulent water. "Especially now. The star ward must never be left unguarded for an instant."

"No," Sethvir agreed. He spun a thought like loomed silk. A circle of mystic seals gleamed above his cupped palms. He blew them to a cloud of indigo and silver, then let their essence purl like poured water over Asandir's crown, where they sank into the weave of his tangled, dusty hair. "Luhaine will come."

In a parallel response to that promised reassurance, Asandir sensed a needle of thought align with the pattern underneath him. Traced by that delicate key of vibration, the focus blazed active. Like the dislodged grain of sand which presaged a rockslide, lane forces resounded on Sethvir's command and sent forth his summons for assistance.

"Fires and light!" Asandir winced. "The Prime Matriarch herself must sit up and take notice of that."

Sethvir's concern cracked into a puckish glimmer of devilment. "She's meant to." He spread ink-stained hands and quelled his colleague's move to arise with a shockingly small stir of effort. "Luhaine's been riding herd on Morriel's councils since her plot to snatch Arithon came to light. A call sent through earth will bridge her wards fastest. Let go. Rest now. I daresay the world will continue to turn without your hand on its axis."

Asandir groaned through a dull burn of agony. He never intended to give way. But the coiling smokes of oblivion he grappled stole through his weakened defenses. Darkness slipped in on ghost feet and trampled the glimmering last spark of his protest.

The Warden of Althain rocked back on his heels. Lapped in the warm summer fragrance of herbs, and maroon robes like old, fusty parchment, he drew a long, calming breath. The patience he borrowed from stone itself could no longer stem his sharpened state of anxiety.

"For mercy and the world, we cannot keep on like this." Eyes shut through the moment he required to steady himself, he thanked every power in creation for Arithon s'Ffalenn's resolve to renew his offshore search for the Paravians. Each hour that the Shadow Master spent provisioning his brigantine at Innish seeded the potential for another disaster. The Mistwraith's curse had embedded too deeply since the great war in Vastmark. Lysaer's grand cause now commanded too widespread an influence, and simple evasions would no longer serve. This time no less than a Fellowship Sorcerer had nearly been lost in the breach.

Again, Sethvir ran distressed fingertips over his colleague's limp flesh.

Cinder burns had branded livid trails of blisters across Asandir's craggy features. Couched in cavernous bone, the pinched, closed eyes seemed to battle the drawn veil of sleep.

"You pushed your limit far too dangerously close," Sethvir admonished the Sorcerer who lay slack at his knees. Shaken by pity, he cupped his hands over cheekbone and jaw. His feather touch traced the lean, corded neck, then trailed over a chest that wore too little flesh over its vaulting of ribs. He paused, repeated his survey, then frowned and moved on, over the abdomen, and down the full length of long legs.

Then he arose and set to work.

Asandir never moved. The chamber beneath Althain seemed a capsule of stillness as Sethvir removed his soft shoes. Through the expedient decision to rechannel lane force as a restorative, the afflicted Sorcerer scarcely seemed to keep breathing.

Head tipped askance, Sethvir weighed his task through the extended spectrum of mage-sight. Refined perception unveiled the streaming cloud of the aura, and the energy knitted in layered octaves of transmission over the skin. Each bandwidth received his remorseless survey.

The damage he mapped made him ache with shared sorrow. A mage of Asandir's strength and stature should celebrate his existence wrapped in a mantle of pure light. His raiment of spirit *was* the limitless power of creation, maintained into flawless balance. The axis of his being should shine as a beacon, his shimmering vitality stitched like tamed lightning through the tapestry of sinew beneath. For a Fellowship Sorcerer, self-renewal became reflex. The infinite whole sustained his existence, channeled and tuned to harmonic alignment that flowed with each breath and surged to the rhythm of each heartbeat.

Instead, Sethvir beheld a fabric rubbed threadbare as old muslin. Where the weave should have blazed with energetic life, he saw dull voids, their edges dimmed to a fuzzy, splotched gray, etched like dark tarnish on lead. Where the energy vortices tangled, he reached through his mage-sense, raising the resonance and stroking out blockage. He coaxed each stressed channel, and whispered phrases of compassionate encouragement to the inner will, which would comprehend frequency and sound. No effort was spared. Past the blinds of unconsciousness, Asandir's senses still functioned. The mind would record, and the body respond, and rally the life force for healing.

Sethvir tuned with his breath, then used specific harmonic tones, released with ritual intent. His ordered precision called sparkling light to bridge and then settle the gapped paths of each stress-torn meridian. Nor were his hands still, all the while. He tapped through resistance, threaded current in bright bands through a body he knew like a brother's.

Sealed in timeless concentration, his work seemed a moment displaced from the far-distant past. Throughout their Second Age trials against drake spawn, he had accomplished the same service many times, as Asandir had done likewise for him.

Yet when three hours of meticulous labor failed to seal over the deficit which opened stray gaps in the flux, Sethvir straightened. He sighed and faced the damaging fact that Asandir needed more than rest and quiet. His prolonged manipulation of the entropic forces inside the grimward had shifted the polarities in his body. Those subtle interfaces grown too damaged to clear must be combed back into alignment by magnetics.

Sethvir arose. With remarkable strength for his wiry stature, he grasped Asandir's slackened wrists and arrayed his muscled frame into line with the north and south axis of the pattern. The large, craftsman's hands he placed palm upward on the intercepting arcs where the circles for sun, moon, and the twelve mariner's stars straddled the east and west meridian. He removed the scorched leather of Asandir's boots, stripped off the soiled hose underneath. Bare heels were arranged on the southernmost angles of the grand hexagon which connected the sixfold arcs of the earth circle.

"Forgive," he apologized. "The bath that you long for will just have to wait." Through a monologue of trivia, the Warden of Althain combed the smoke-stained, tangled hair with his fingers. He smoothed the stressed wrinkles from singed leather and cloth, and loosened the ties of laces and corded silk belt.

"Lie easy. You won't be abandoned," he whispered, hands flat on Asandir's forehead.

Then he rose and poured all his worry into haste.

Upstairs in his stillroom, Sethvir scoured his cupboards, fingers flying. He bundled dried leaves of sage and sweetgrass and cedar. Each herb was separately tied in specific laced patterns of dyed string. Returned to the focus, he set his offerings in the sockets of the carved gryphons which crouched in stilled vigil at the compass points. He shaved birch and oak bark from two faggots filched from his woodpile and leaved them into a spill. Then he blew golden runes into the crumbled lumps of copal resin snatched from his jar in the library. When all was laid ready, he faced north. His single, rolling word of command called a spark from the earth's vibrant consciousness.

For a long-drawn moment, plant fragrances mingled with the old stone of the chamber. Then a seed of white flame arose from the spill and winnowed smoke like living blue silk. Sethvir held the kindled bark aloft. He spoke an appeal, received a permission, then turned east and called a wild spark from the mantle of air, and bid each sconce by Name to ignite.

The stone gryphons crouched, crowned in the south's cleansing fire.

As if tuned to resonance by ordinary flame, the pattern whispered and bloomed to a coruscation of golden light.

Barefoot, Sethvir walked the pattern's outer circle. He blew out the wood spill and scribed phrases of runes in a knitted, running line of streamed smoke. Where the written hoop closed, he positioned himself on the key figure, invoked mastery, and stepped his mind's vibration into attunement with the majestic chord of the third lane.

Again he invoked a release; then he asked a second permission. The pattern sang back, embracing his being through contact with his bare soles and charging the smoke runes to a glowing royal purple. Ringed in bands of unconditional, free conjury, Althain's Warden spread his arms wide. His blessing and invocation called power from sun, moon, and stars, and raised each grand circle of the focus to capture its counterpart reflection.

One moment, he paused to give thanks. Then he appealed, and received third and final permission, which granted his use of raised power to heal.

In careful stages, he mediated the balance, tamed and downstepped the whorled vortex of magnetic energy which belted the central axis of the pattern. In spare, precise steps he aligned the subtle currents to match the damaged imprint of Asandir's aura. His work was meticulous. A misstep would trigger failure, or a backlash to fuse havoc down to the heart-core of the earth. The contact points of entry must be utterly precise, each line mathematically correct. No angle must jar. The ranging harmonics of each thread of power must sing exactly on key, the energy colors of each step in conjury matched to the individual.

Time passed. The patterning built, then glimmered with resonant harmony. Mage-sight revealed the comatose Sorcerer cocooned in a geometric lattice of pure light.

Sethvir squinted through the balefire glare of his handiwork. Made wise through his earth sense, he knew the planet's energies could heal all that lived under sky, given time to allow their quiet influence.

But to a grievously shorthanded Fellowship, idleness was not an affordable option. As Sethvir completed the last step to fine-tune the outer band of energies, a waft of chill air flapped his robe against the spiked bone of his ankles.

He paused, caught his streaming beard in two tufts, and accorded the invasive breeze a glance like the tart nip of hoarfrost. "You took your sweet time arriving."

"Well, your summons was thoughtlessly inopportune." Luhaine huffed into a spin across the chamber. "The Koriani Prime Matriarch's trouble enough without you upsetting her complacency."

"She's just about paralyzed," Sethvir corrected, while escaped strands of hair slashed his ears, and streamed smoke from the sconces made his eyes water. "She's been battened in silk quilts and healers since the hour she wakened without the strength to stand up."

Luhaine disagreed. "Her temper's a volcano waiting to blow." Tight, spinning eddies kicked trails through the fug as the spirit whirled again and plowed on in lugubrious pique. "You knew her First Senior's in detention at Capewell? Yes? Then I scarcely need mention the mischief that's certain to brew the moment she's called in to give her formal accounting. You'll have to agree the next round of intrigue will go all the worse for no watchdog on Morriel then."

Sethvir braced his feet against Luhaine's errant tempest, still clutching beard, while his eyes shone the vacant, flat blue of polished turquoise. "Whatever the Koriathain are plotting must wait upon Asandir's need."

Luhaine ceased his petulant prowl in the cavernous vicinity of the stairwell. "Very well. A few minutes won't hurt."

Sethvir cocked his head, all his faculties disconcertingly aligned on the present. "When you left," he said, concise, "Morriel was teaching a green initiate the selective process for expunging the dross of an unwanted vibration without detuning a quartz-crystal matrix."

Luhaine was not mollified. "Which tidbit happens to bear directly on why Asandir needs assistance at all." In a blasting, crisp sibilance of arctic air, he exploded. "You'd think, having blinded the advantage of his mage-sight, the Teir's'Ffalenn could refrain from twisting the snake's tail *this once!*"

Sethvir's brows rose. He opened clenched hands. The cascade of freed beard spilled down his chest like wool dropped fresh from its carding. "You speak of Prince Arithon's gracious return of Lirenda's personal spell crystal?"

"I refer to the specific disharmonies in her quartz that he retuned with compassionate melody, yes." Luhaine shrank to a pinpoint of cold and lit on the snout of a gargoyle. "Morriel knows we left Dakar to guard him, but a spellbinder's wards are not an infallible protection."

To stave off the chill, Sethvir retrieved his bushkins, and frowned at a spot worn long past salvage with a patch. "We are grown too few to manage our burdens, and since we can't borrow our spellbinder back, you're going to be gone more than minutes." He eased his tired footwear over baby pink toes, chin tipped toward the prone form arrayed in the pattern. "Asandir can't be left to heal unattended. Traithe's south in Havish, finishing the wards on the coast for King Eldir. Who's left but me to ride out and rebalance the damaged seal over that grimward?"

A spirit obsessed with tight focus, Luhaine paused at last and seized the gist. "Ath spare us from ruin! *How long was Asandir in there?*"

Sethvir declined comment. The intricate conjury drawn and sealed through live lane force offered a grim enough testament: Asandir's sacrifice had detained him to the bitter limit of survival. His perilous victory had stabilized the unruly fabric of the haunt's dream long enough to spare one more foolhardy human from the throes of a fatal predicament. Now came the cruel cost: the grimward's tangential polarities had drained his regenerative faculties beyond the point where he could recover on his own.

"I couldn't have done that," Luhaine said outright. "Never mind the fact I don't possess a body." Blunted now to respect like scraped bedrock, he admitted, "Prince Arithon's life is essential to see the Black Rose Prophecy completed. But to take on such risk for the sake of a misguided captain at arms was an act of softhearted insanity."

For the penalty extended beyond individual infirmity; the Fellowship's resources were already taxed beyond salvage. Luhaine could not shoulder the task which faced Sethvir. Stripped of mortal flesh, the fine energies of his spirit would become misaligned and erased upon contact with the raging, dire forces ringed inside the spelled bounds of a grimward.

Too fussy a perfectionist to stay passive in a crisis, the discorporate Sorcerer abandoned his perch on the gargoyle. He drifted over the pattern of the focus, and gave Sethvir's work his critical inspection. Where he perceived nuance beyond reach of an entity encumbered by flesh, he came and went as a stiletto point of light, fretting a chain of minute adjustments to the energies already laid down. Luhaine concluded on a note of grudging admiration. "What has been gained for that one life, but a dangerous, misguided incentive? You know Sulfin Evend has sworn to become all Lysaer ever asked of a warrior priest."

"Balance," Sethvir snapped. His unwonted shortness revealed his own depth of misery as he padded toward the lower stairwell. Under the vaulted archway, he turned, his beard ends and hair wisped into frost cobwebs against the blank shadow beyond. "When Asandir wakens, he's to rest. Make sure he does if you have to barricade the doors to contain him."

"Borrow his horse, then," Luhaine suggested. "You won't keep him, otherwise." The eddy of his presence settled and rearranged, surrounding his colleague's battered form in a mantle of radiance that blazed sympathy in contradiction to his dour, ending comment. "Stubborn as old granite, and pernicious when crossed. Well you are!" Luhaine insisted, as though Asandir had spoken in defense.

Sethvir hid his smile behind his crooked fist and ducked out, while Luhaine lectured the unconscious colleague he tended. "You've shown the bad grace and poor manners to walk through my being before, when I tried making sensible comments on your health."

Judgment

Swathed in quilts sewn with sigils of vitality chain-stitched in silver thread, and propped upright against goose-down pillows like piled snowdrifts, Morriel ruled the Koriani Order from an enormous, carved bed at Capewell. Reduced to a skeleton swathed in blanched skin, she held the reins of her power close to her breast, her eyes still like fathomless beads of chipped jet. Her speech was sparing, each word precise as engraving.

She was attended night and day, served in her fragile state of infirmity by no less than the sisterhouse peeress, her matched pair of pages, and a young girl initiate of exceptional talent, brought across Tysan in whirlwind haste from her first initiation at Cainford.

On the same afternoon Sethvir mounted his colleague's black stallion and rode out of Althain Tower, Morriel had a circle of seventh-rank Seniors immersed in deep trance at her bedside. Behind heavy, drawn drapes, the medicinal air wore expectancy like a brewing storm. Twelve candles burned upon silver stands arrayed in a perfect arc. Each enchantress was linked to a distant seer, tied by gifted sight to the free lane force that ranged in bands across Athera.

No draft flickered the beeswax candles. No shimmer teased the embroidery. The women held still as figures in wax. Their tranced talents activated an array of quartz-crystal balls, pocketed in a half-circle formation amid the rose-pattern quilts tucked over the Prime's crippled knees.

The Koriani Matriarch probed into the orbs like the listening spider slung in the strands of her web. One of these showed the dark horse and the rider, standing knee high in gold meadow grass. A maggot white smile turned the crone's bloodless lips as that particular scrying unfolded.

She did not miss the fleeting moment when the crystal appeared to cloud over. Satisfaction twitched a ghost imprint of amusement across her emaciated face. "Watch closely," she instructed the mollified young girl who attended the scrying at her elbow.

The initiate leaned nearer. Her braided blond hair trailed across the heaped bedclothes, and lush, rosebud lips loosed a sigh of awestruck wonder.

Inside the crystal, almost too faint to catch, a starred pulse of light flicked and vanished. A waving expanse of empty gorse remained, while a barred hawk arose and soared on spread wings. It circled the flinty spire of the tower, then banked and sheared in a graceful glide above the road which carved through the greener hills to the south.

"Hah!" The Koriani Prime gave a cackle of reedy delight. "I'd hoped so!" A withered stiff finger signed a rune of thanksgiving in the coppery light of the candles. "Events progress in fair form. Althain's Warden has no choice but to engage the Great Circle at Isaer."

With his tower's main focus pattern fully engaged to stabilize Asandir's life signs, the lane force at that site could not be retuned for transport. Nor could an unstable grimward be accessed as a homing point for the Sorcerer in transit.

Reedy with satisfaction, Morriel finished her thought. "We can safely presume Sethvir will cross by magecraft from Isaer to the Second Age ruin at Mainmere. He'll be forced to ride the Taerlin road." A round distance of a hundred and fifty leagues gave due time to plan without Fellowship interference.

The child initiate raised a round, freckled face, still written across with amazement. "Can the Fellowship Sorcerers really shapeshift?"

"Dear, no." Morriel fixed her with lightless, fierce eyes hooded under domed lids and milk lashes. "Sethvir is a master illusionist." She tapped the scrying crystal which imaged the flying hawk with the yellowed tip of a fingernail. "The travelers he encounters on his way will not see him. Even those with clairvoyance will believe they were brushed by no more than the shadow of a bird."

She trailed off, words lapsed into the labored hiss of forced breath. For long moments, the sealed, airless quiet of the room absorbed her stifled frustration. The Great Waystone offered the power to cut through Sethvir's ploys of illusion. Yet Morriel dared not attempt mastery of its matrix in her current depleted condition.

The mere effort of speech left her prostrate. Eyes shut, her hands curled on the coverlet like the wind-frozen claws of a sparrow, she needed long minutes to ease her heartbeat enough to dismiss the Senior circle and the twelve remote scryers. The quartz spheres she kept arrayed on the quilt. Each was now attuned to track the deflections that events imprinted on the earth's lane force. The sealed crystals would continue to reflect their sequence of distant events until natural attrition disunified the linking sigils.

With Sethvir's departure, no development held precedence ahead of the snag in affairs arrived home to roost at the Capewell sisterhouse.

Cut off from her access to the Great Waystone, Morriel had withheld her most critical business until the Fellowship watchdog, Luhaine, had been recalled to Althain Tower. Each passing minute became precious. Morriel hoarded her dwindled stamina while the last of the Seniors filed out in a whispery rustle of silk.

The door latch clicked shut.

"Veil yourself," Morriel ordered the sisterhouse peeress. Amid musky stillness and the cat-footed shadows cast by the slow-burning candles, the shattering impact of her next command came with unprecedented lack of formality. "The hour has come to pass judgment. You shall stand as the order's Ceremonial Inquisitor, and act as my voice through the coming closed trial."

The stout peeress started, then inclined her head. "Your will, matriarch." Her round, suet face turned prim with austerity as she bustled to the armoire to don the black robes of high office. Despite her stiff posture and clipped movement, she held no qualms over her assigned role; justice would be served for those acts of disharmony which had disrupted the serenity of her sisterhouse.

The wide-eyed young initiate remained seated in stunned shock by the bedside. The ritual about to commence was older than Koriani residence on Athera. Afraid her presence may have been summarily forgotten, she shrank, while one of the blond pages unpacked the elaborate silver-bordered layers of the inquisitor's veils. When Morriel's dry fingers closed over her elbow, she jerked with a soft, breathy cry.

"Bide, girl." The Prime's peremptory whisper seemed the scrape of glass beads through old dust. "You will stay on as a witness here."

To the statue-still page boy at her right hand, she delivered a whipcrack instruction. "Fetch me the box with the Skyron focus. Then go and inform the sisterhouse warden that the hour has come for the accused to stand before me and answer for her misconduct."

* * *

Upon receipt of her summons, First Senior Lirenda arose from her willow embroidery frame. She tidied her gold thread with unshaken hands. The needle she left pressed into drum-tight silk, like a fallen ray of light speared through darkness.

She could only hope the desperate strain did not show as she gave the page boy her acquiescence. Apparently without hurry, she removed her purple mantle from the clothes chest. Its folds sleeked her shoulders like poured Cheivalt wine, and spilled with extravagant grace over the shining cuffs of her matched bracelets, and her eight-banded robe of high office.

She had been Koriani First Senior for fifty-six years. Prepared in every detail for this audience, clear relief all but shook her, that the unbearable days of strained waiting had finally come to an end. She had not lost her heart or her spirit. Ignominy had not overtaken her courage and let her lapse into endless, pleading petitions for her Prime's intercession.

Yet the confidence born of her grip on main strength bled away as she arrived at Morriel's chamber.

The page boy swung open the strapped oaken door. "Madam," he bade her. "Enter."

Darkness as stilled as a panther's tread awaited over the threshold. The air within breathed of close-kept secrets and a dusty perfume of dried lavender. For as long as living memory, the Koriani Prime had preferred the night for her significant meetings. When council could not be avoided in daylight, she ordered her chambers kept dark. The curtains were sewn of black damask and velvet. The dagged valance was looped on silver rings, each cast in the sigil for eternity, the triple-coiled snake trapped forever in the act of swallowing its own tail. The sulfurous, candlelit well by the bedstead seemed sealed in an ironclad silence.

Lirenda loosened her fingers before they impressed sweaty marks on her immaculate silk. She, who had feared nearly nothing in life, almost lost the will to step forward.

Discipline saved her. Unbending in pride, she clamped down on raw dread and assumed the paper-thin semblance of dignity.

She advanced and acknowledged Morriel's presence, a meeting of eyes like crossed sword blades. Then she sank in traditional obeisance. "Your will, matriarch."

The Prime returned no verbal greeting. A presence swathed in violet veils, she seemed a wire puppet embodied in cloth, with a bleached death's-head skull, and the folds of loose garments pinned in place with set diamonds. Seconds dragged by. The Prime spoke no word of acknowledgment. Apprehension sliced a dagger of ice through the pit of Lirenda's stomach. While the pause stretched into an engulfing stillness, the page barred the door at her back.

Three others were present by Morriel's behest, one an untried girl with flaxen-fair braids, and another a grown woman wearing a blank-faced, idiot's stare. Lirenda took a moment to discern the forehead tattoo which signified an initiate who had failed in her vow of obedience. A deeper chill shocked her as she recognized the emptied creature's face. There stood the young initiate who had failed in her sworn charge to hold the circle of Morriel's grand conjury. The traditional penalty allowed no appeal. She would serve out her days as a mindless slave, her identity stripped through the power of the vows sworn through the Prime's master crystal.

Morriel would have her cruel reason for demanding the witless one's presence. Lirenda had not thought; had never imagined that she might be tested for the selfsame transgression.

This was no audience for private reprimand, but a closed-trial chamber. Subject to the Koriani Matriarch's sole judgment, Lirenda understood her defense might become her last chance for cognizant thought.

A darker veiled shadow embedded in the gloom to the right of Morriel's bedside called for the accused to stand before her Prime to be examined.

Lirenda arose. The unaccustomed, bitter taste of humility closed her throat as she gave the time-honored reply. "I stand before my betters to serve."

She had taken her privilege and authority for granted. Now the sharp drop in status among her own kind left her frightened and rudderless as the Prime laid unsteady, bird-claw hands on the ironbound coffer held by her second page boy. Her whisper invoked the release of the seals. Each protection gave way with a whine like parted wire, and points of burst light stabbed the dimness.

As Morriel raised the strapped lid, the young girl who cowered by the bedside rubbed forearms raised into gooseflesh. Lirenda knew well her chills were no phantom. The Skyron stone's presence was inimical as a predator, its etheric web steeped in old malice. Over the centuries while the Great Waystone had been held in Sethvir's custody at Althain Tower, the smaller aquamarine had carried the burden of the order's heaviest rituals. Years and hard use had left its channels surly with overload. That imbalance could never be rectified; not without losing the stored records of a thousand vows of service chained like steel-bolted ice through its heart.

As the knifing hostility of the unveiled jewel settled over the chamber, Lirenda's dread became overwhelming. Her palms broke into clammy sweat. The witless woman's stare drilled into her face, while from the chair that formerly had been hers, a green novice witnessed her fallen status with enormous cornflower eyes. Since by rigid tradition, the order's Prime Matriarch never addressed an oathbreaker, the Ceremonial Inquisitor intoned the opening accusation.

"Enchantress Lirenda, you stand before your Prime to answer for willful acts and disobedience against your vow of Koriani service." The matronly peeress smoothed the silver-bordered edge of her veil in prim self-importance and listed the formal charges. "You are accused of crossing a sealed ward without cause, and disrupting an act of grand conjury."

Lirenda bristled. After weeks of smothered pride in Prince Lysaer's company, and the ignominy of losing the crystal that accessed her trained talents, the moment's grinding weight of humility threatened her last grip on control.

Then Morriel signaled her readiness with a flick of a twig-thin finger. "Begin."

The Skyron stone lay unveiled in its coffer, its surface cold and glittering blue as the faceted heart of a glacier.

"Enchantress Lirenda, by your vow of obedience, you are asked to stare into the crystal's matrix," the Ceremonial Inquisitor commanded. "Lower your defenses. Surrender your mind for this inquest, that your innocence or guilt be established beyond any shadow of doubt."

Lirenda snapped at that moment. "Merciful Ath! This charge of oathbreaking is a mockery." Her protest slammed through the quiet like a shattering fist forced through lead. "As First Senior of the Koriathain, the authority was rightfully mine to use as I saw fit. I was summoned to Capewell because my Prime Matriarch had suffered a state of collapse. *Certainly, I broke no vow of initiation through my decision to enter the observatory!* If a personal shortcoming flawed my subsequent choices, that lapse is the one I must atone for. I demand a hearing in private. I will answer to my Prime for her broken conjury. Whether I forfeit free will for impertinence, *I refuse to submit to examination for a transgression I did not commit!*"

Behind silver-edged muslin, the Ceremonial Inquisitor huffed a breath for scathing rebuttal.

Yet the jerk of the Prime's skeletal forefinger froze her silent. Jet-dark eyes sheared across sullen gloom. Lirenda felt their angry weight bore into her, through her, reading and weighing; testing her down to the naked pith of the fear beneath her defenses.

She scarcely dared tremble. Her overpowering terror must surely rip through, unstring her last pride and see her weep. She could not call back the ultimatum just issued. Unmasked by the threat of the Skyron crystal, shamed before three indifferent witnesses, she could only endure, while sweat rolled down the channel of her back and soaked ragged stains in her silk.

No one spoke. Against the patched play of shadows, the few tall candles cast tips of sulfurous light. Splashed like disjointed fragments of dream, the quartz spheres on the counterpane flashed impressions of ordinary events recapped from distant sites on the continent: *a flying hawk, a dark-haired shepherd child, a leaping trout in a stream. In Tysan, a master shipwright inspected a load of new wood. In Havish, the royal midwife confirmed a queen's pregnancy. In Shand, a fat spellbinder paced down the Innish wharf to meet a dory off an inbound brig.*

Wrenched by longing for the warmth of carefree sunlight, Lirenda felt as if she might suffocate. She battled the urge to fall to her knees in abject, begging appeal.

Then Morriel Prime stirred to a hiss of silk coverlets and pronounced, "This closed trial is over." Diamonds spat glints like snap-frozen rainfall as she turned her head and excused the Ceremonial Inquisitor. "You are dismissed. As you leave, take the witless one with you."

The sisterhouse peeress slipped her veils with a disapproving bustle of industry. "Matriarch," she ventured, "should the junior initiate not be bidden to leave also?"

The Prime's sharpness fell like storm-cracked wood. "I may not walk, but I've not lost my faculties! No. The girl stays. The matter at hand concerns her most closely."

Emphatic enough warning, Lirenda understood. Morriel would not keep an untried initiate at hand, except as a successor in training. Lirenda needed to sit, but that comfort was denied her. Minutes passed, while her knees shook, and the peeress vented her vengeful, small cruelty by spending a maliciously long interval to smooth her mussed clothing and remove the half-wit from the chamber.

The final clank as the page boy reset the bar saved Lirenda from involuntary collapse. Now, when shaken nerves left her weakened, the Prime Matriarch pressed ahead with a scalpel's dispassion.

"You have claimed your right to autonomous responsibility. That is well." Eyes dark as death stayed pinned straight ahead. The bleached-paper finger of one hand stirred to point. "Had you not spoken, madam, your worth to me would have become less than nothing. At the ninth hour, you've dared the initiative to claim your mistake. For that, you have won small reprieve. I wait to be shown whether you can satisfy the balance and master the means to redeem yourself."

Lirenda swallowed. Through firsthand, hardened experience she sensed that no forward step would be easy. Morriel Prime would not volunteer her any grace of kindly assistance. Whatever petition the stakes would allow, the deposed First Senior understood she must assemble her case for herself. All the steel in her character was scarcely sufficient to let her ignore the puppyish, staring young girl. Battling a wildfire surge of resentment, she treated with the Prime as if the ongoing audience had been offered in perfect privacy.

"I let personal feelings interfere with clear judgment." Admission was painful. The darkness, the candles, the inimical bite of the Skyron crystal's aura abraded her cornered resolve to survive and reclaim her lost grace. "Give me trial by recompense. I would atone for the imperfections in my character, and see your trust in my competence restored."

Morriel's hooded stare pinned with a vulture's intensity. "Trust in your competence is the least of the issue. Your lapse will bring damaging consequences. In cold fact, the ramifications could prove more dire than you possibly imagine."

Lirenda ventured nothing.

"Oh yes," Morriel went on. Her stilled, folded fingers stirred to insectile life and fussed at a fold in the coverlet. "What you name a *mistake* may well cost the Koriani Order its unbroken thread of continuance."

"I can't see how," Lirenda burst out, unable to mask disbelief. "Arithon s'Ffalenn by himself could scarcely threaten the might of the entire sisterhood."

"You think not?" Morriel glared back, inimical. "He is the world's cipher to checkrein the Fellowship. We need him for that. Without him, we risk my succession itself. I have scried proof. Left at liberty, the course of the Shadow Master's destiny holds full potential to destroy us."

"I couldn't know!" Lirenda cried, crumbled in devastation. "My misjudgment back at Riverton stemmed from Caolle's life, and he was no more than the prince's sworn liegeman."

"Damage resulted." A hooded cobra nestled in bed linens, the Matriarch spat words in contempt. "You will have heard that my lower limbs are paralyzed. I cannot set another web of grand conjury from the confines of a sedan chair! At this time, active use of the Great Waystone presents too strenuous an ordeal. I must have complete rest to recover my strength just to pass on the secret of its mastery!"

No need for a tedious review of the obvious; Lirenda knew well enough. Without the Great Waystone, the full transfer of prime power could never be passed on intact.

Morriel resumed on the rags of a stertorous rage. "Since my vigor was lost for the sake of your folly, you are left to recoup the ground lost by your feckless action."

Lirenda stepped back, numbed as though the last air in existence had been forcibly reft from her lungs.

"Yes." Morriel snapped off a nod. "I see that you grasp my implications in full." She took perverse malice in her fallen First Senior's discomfiture. "If you are *ever* to wield my authority, then you must accomplish this feat before I die. Until then, you are not my named successor. You may claim neither honors nor title within the Koriani Order. Neither will your status improve until the hour that you place the Prince of Rathain in my hands as a living captive."

"Capture Arithon s'Ffalenn!" Lirenda shrank before the sweeping audacity of the demand. "Merciful Ath! That would set me alone against the might of the Fellowship Sorcerers!" She had lost her quartz jewel. Without its focus to amplify the inborn resonance of her talent, the simplest ward of protection lay outside of her reach. The plea wrenched from her and fell smothered against the hangings which masked out the daylight. "You have handed me a virtual death sentence, or worse, an impossible penance to break the mind and heart."

"You wish to walk in my shoes and sit the high seat of prime power?" Morriel laughed in bloodless castigation. "Then you will strive and not fail. Or all I have accomplished in your years of privileged study has been a waste of my effort."

Lirenda struggled to dam hopeless tears. "My jewel was lost to the Shadow Master's henchmen," she whispered in crushing humility.

"Prince Arithon returned it by courier, long since!" Morriel beckoned to the girl, who startled up from riveted fascination as if her round cheek had been slapped. "Show her."

The self-conscious initiate fumbled open the drawstrings of the silk remedy pouch in her lap. Her childish fingers removed the shining, white crystal on its original braided chain.

Lirenda's heart turned over. Before thought, she raised a yearning hand to touch the crystal's shining facets and reestablish rapport with its presence. Yet even as her being cried out for the link of her lost quartz's resonance, the impact of change stepped between. Fickle memory recaptured a living line of melody that stormed her mind, snapped her last hold on emotion, and broke her down in regret.

Under the Prime Matriarch's critical review, Lirenda burned into a **blush**. Tears she could no longer contain brimmed over and traced **salty ribbons** down her cheeks. "The stone was tampered with." Her voice emerged like an overcranked string, stressed past its usual smooth alto.

"Obviously so." Morriel's colorless lips twitched in distaste. "When the girl here masters the art of selective resonance, your crystal may be returned to you cleansed of its meddlesome influence. Until then, other enchantresses must supply the power you lack. My writ will command them."

A finger flicked in permission let the young initiate veil Lirenda's confiscated quartz. Morriel bided with eternity's patience while the girl's stubby fingers tripped over ties and strings. When the remedy bag was meticulously secured, she bade, "Be my hands, child."

Under the Prime's cryptic instruction, the initiate delved among the quilts. One quartz sphere was selected from the array left tuned by the scryers on lane watch. As the girl timidly cupped its chill weight, Lirenda glimpsed the mirrored image of the nondescript shepherd child. Only now, the boy's barefoot play had been joined by a Koriani enchantress whose loose hair gleamed auburn in the bleaching kiss of strong sunlight.

"Start there," Morriel said, then motioned for the girl to surrender the seeing crystal to Lirenda. "Consult the one of ours who knows your quarry's habits best."

Another quartz sphere was added to the first. This showed a southcoast wharf, where a fair-haired young woman stood in sailhand's garb, engaged in an energetic conversation with a slovenly fat man recognizable as the Mad Prophet. Lirenda had no more time to note details before the crystal changed hands to the leveling tone of Morriel Prime's summary.

"The Shadow Master himself is laired up at Innish in the attic of a merchant's mansion. He has not been well. The pair you observe through the lane's eye are his keepers as of this hour. Study them to keep track of his movements."

Then the penultimate word, cast in dismissal and sentence. "In three days' time, Sethvir will enter the Paravian Circle at Isaer," the Prime decreed, her wasted posture insistent. "While the Warden engages his power for spell transit to Mainmere, his earth-sense will be temporarily suspended by the chord of raised lane force. You will come to me then, and deliver the details of your plot to take Arithon. Mercy upon you if a sound plan of action has not been drawn up by that hour."

End Game

Shivering and clammy in the aftershock of dread, Lirenda sought refuge in a window seat ablaze with afternoon sunlight. The courtyard view outside, with its tubs of laden dwarf pear trees, seemed displaced from her fractured reality. A high-flying cloud cover combed to fine floss warned of a weather change to come. Yet even the oppressive summer heat through the glass could not offset the chills of Morriel Prime's final sentence. Nor had the curious, pitying stares from the peers she no longer outranked been easy to pass off with indifference.

Her world felt as if the foundations had crumbled, with herself like blown ash, cast adrift.

Lirenda shut her eyes. Her porcelain skin still burned ruddy with shame. Each step she had taken had been remarked, even by the impertinent laundry girls who dragged their wicker hampers of soiled linens from the sisterhouse nursery.

The gossip was unkind. The event of a first senior's downfall was certain to titillate for an uncomfortable interval to come.

Lirenda refused to retreat in self-pity. Chin raised, nerves stinging, she combed out, rebraided, and coiled the jet-satin length of her hair. Grooming helped steady her. If the small, shabby chamber with its lye-scoured floor reflected her sharp drop in station, at least she was given her privacy. While her hands slowly ceased their helpless shaking, she arose, slipped on a fresh robe, and laid a ritual fire in the grate. She regretted her need to muffle the daylight behind curtains, but she needed full darkness to work.

Her birch fire caught and flowered. She fed the new flame with aromatic herbs whose virtues heightened clairvoyance. A lick of gold light touched her offering. The fragrance of moonflower arose, mingled with the stinging pungency of tobacco ground and soaked in an infusion of tienelle blossom. Blue smoke scrolled through the closed chamber and flowed in vagrant script toward the rafters. The one chair, the bare clothes chest, and the straw-ticked cot in the corner came and went amid a sienna pavane of dense shadow.

The fumes thickened, a raw burn on the tender membranes of nose and throat. Lirenda welcomed their acridity, let the familiar expansive lift whirl her to sensitized awareness. Her natural affinity for flame resurged through her, a taproot of current awaiting the expression of her will. Like an addict starved for the intoxicating rush of spelled power, she chose the quartz sphere tuned into the sixth lane, which tracked events at the merchant household at Innish where Arithon s'Ffalenn took his refuge.

The reflection within still depicted the flamboyant blond woman, changed from sea slops into a blouse with silk ribbons. She sat now at the scrubbed planks of a kitchen table, tanned arms crossed amid the crumpled-up folds of a shirt tossed down for mending. Lirenda showed no surprise at the scene. The Shadow Master himself was notoriously hard to track. Mage-trained since childhood, he well knew to keep his mind stilled. Since lane force deflected to emotional vibrations, in his case the Koriani scryers were most often left to map the affairs of his more volatile associates.

The girl under cold scrutiny in the quartz appeared to be immersed in scathing argument with a pallid woman who shook a wooden spoon. Flour flew like wafted pollen when the girl tried to placate by setting a hand on the woman's wrist. The effort raised a startled, wide glance, then redoubled the tirade.

Lirenda cupped the crystal sphere in cool hands. The shell rims of her lids veiled amber eyes against the play of caught flame. The stone warmed, lined in light. While the resonance of its energies ran in parallel with her thought, the enchantress invoked three seals of mastery. A lifetime of discipline let her fuse her awareness. Linked to the quartz through her inborn affinity for fire, she embraced the tuned synergy and accessed the stone.

Her body seemed to lighten, and the room fell away. Lirenda breathed in the pungent smoke of the herbs until the closed barrier of her mind gave rise to white clarity. Her conscious awareness let go in a rush and merged with the scene in the quartz . . .

* * *

Leagues distant in Shand, Feylind crashed down her rope-callused fist. The plank jumped. Cheap crockery bowls bought used from the market flounced in response, and fine flour puffed from the meal just sifted for bread dough. "*Lysaer?* Sail ships? That's a laugh to stun a live jackfish!"

She wrinkled her tanned, peeling nose. Azure eyes flashed in pure scorn at her mother, who stood with thin hands clenched to the spoon as if plain wood could ward off a tempest.

Feylind gave her timid rebuttal no space. "Tysan's prince might say his new fleet's the best thing afloat, but Arithon's crews call it the royal shambles. It is, too! Look at the mess they made of their first engagement. The Shadow Master's men were boarded in chains, and they needed no more than the onset of night to upset Lysaer's sailing orders."

Jinesse rubbed her nose with the back of her wrist in transparent need to mask a wince. That news had reached Innish. The unflattering details spoke of three vessels taken on their maiden voyage by the same pack of convicts they had been dispatched to escort into slavery.

Feylind pounced again, unrelenting. "So, you did hear." She flipped back her straw braid and shot to her feet, restless already with four landlocked walls and the cozy domesticity of bread making. On their hooks by the hob, the polished copper kettles tracked her reflection in a wave of rippling energy. "Bet no one's bragging of the prize the Alliance lost at Corith, either. Ten royal galleys were assigned to safeguard her. Every last one got their keels chewed. Took those crews half the summer to make simple repairs and limp home. You say I'd do better under officers like those? Sithaer's coupling furies, mother! Their sort can't tell a hawser from what hangs cringing limp in their breeks!"

"Young lady!" Jinesse shouted, her china-frail features flushed into a delicate pink. "This is no ship's deck. Remember your manners as you were brought up in this house!"

The girl twitched her shoulder in an insolent shrug, the blouse she had donned in token femininity worn untucked above button-front breeches and sailhand's boots with brass buckles. "I speak the damned truth. You want me to sign on an Alliance ship? That's a frank surprise, since the Master of Shadow himself has been given shelter in your attic."

A cavernous silence filled the kitchen.

For drawn, disastrous seconds, the coal glow from the oven smudged sulfur light over the cracked and oil-stained flagstones. Outside the high window, disjointed with life, the clatter of hooves heralded the noon change of watch, and the cry of a vendor spiraled from the tent stalls of the shanty market.

Then tension broke with the bang of a squall line as Feylind swore her annoyance. "Fiends and Dharkaron's black bollocks!" Her expostulation tangled with Jinesse's mortified explosion, pitched through the arched door behind her.

"Fiark! Come here this instant!" Incensed to dauntless, maternal rage, she snatched her skirts up in fluttery fingers. Her banty-hen march to the hallway collided with a solid young man in neat town clothes.

Fiark eased her balance, straightened the pleats of his clerk's broadcloth doublet, then turned slate-colored eyes in smoking reproof upon his more volatile twin sister. "She wasn't meant to know."

"Ath's two-eyed vengeance!" Feylind swore. One breath ahead of her mother's renewed diatribe, she added, "I'm sorry, Fiark."

"Arithon! Here?" Jinesse closed in again to confront her son, a bristling head shorter than he. "This is your doing?"

Her shrill incredulity clashed outright with Fiark's nettled betrayal. "Feylind, you pest! How did you find out? The secret was never let loose in the stews at the dockside."

From snatched refuge behind the bread bowl, hands gripped on glazed crockery as if she might press-gang the first solid object in defense, Feylind flashed a grin of pure devilment. "I met Dakar at the landing."

Then the doorway darkened again. A voice with more gravel than Fiark's rolled over Jinesse's imprecations. "The spellbinder would have been honest to claim the invitation was mine."

Jinesse spun about, her nettled agitation displaced against the genteel shabbiness of the kitchen. "Tharrick!" Her thin fist smacked his chest. Slight as a straw wisp before the towering bulk of her husband, who wore the studded leather brigandine and cuffed bracers of a gentleman's guard captain, she nonetheless managed to prevail. "You did *what*?"

Fresh from a street fight in front of his employer's warehouse, Tharrick seemed caught aback that his morning round of scrapping had extended beneath his own roof. "I gave Arithon s'Ffalenn my leave to stay in the textile loft." He squared his shoulders, brows raised. "As I should have, considering the debt that I owe him."

Jinesse stiffened, her back ramrod straight beneath her limp muslin as she flew at him like a gnat. "You owe that man nothing, least of all charity."

535

Tharrick caught his wife's flying fists and restrained her before she tore her thin skin on his wrist studs. "Easy." His mercenary's stature made even the kitchen's high southland ceilings seem cramped. "Not for love or fury will I share your dislike of Rathain's prince."

Jinesse glared at him, breathing too fast, her limbs in his grasp as pliant and slim as cut withies. The whorled scars which disfigured his arms above the top edge of his bracers spoke with more eloquence than language: she could never forget the hot-tempered men in Prince Arithon's service who had put her husband to torture with hot irons during his absence.

"I sorely provoked them, but that scarcely matters," Tharrick soothed in the face of her smoking silence. He dared conflagration and kissed her knuckles one by one. As if she had softened, he let her go, then eased the leg which had stiffened and sat himself at the plank table. "Come on, girl," he invited Feylind. "We might as well suffer the wife's disapproval together."

When his stepdaughter relented and settled beside him, he flung a brawny arm across her young shoulders, as much to hold her down as he gave the subject his definitive dismissal. "You can't run him out, anyway, Jinesse. His Grace of Rathain has already left."

"What?" Feylind struggled to rise, spitting outrage like a doused cat. "He can't have! Dakar would have told him I was just back in port!" Still wildly grappling against Tharrick's restraint, she appealed to her twin. "Arithon would scarcely go without taking me along."

Sober in his tailored doublet, Fiark returned his level regard, coupled with implacable silence.

"Well, then, how dare he?" Feylind's features gained a violent, fresh flush. She strained hard against Tharrick's imprisoning arm. Slight as she was, ship life had muscled her. The man grunted. Jostled as though he battled a tiger, he braced his fist against the trestle, which rocked to their locked clash of wills.

Jinesse's protest went unnoticed as Feylind continued to howl. "His Grace can't leave me stranded on a merchant brig for another pig-rutting year!" While her mother resignedly dove past to rescue the bread dough, Fiark backed from the fray to spare his neat clothing a cross-fire dusting of flour.

"Damn him thrice over, and fiends plague his rigging for his slippery, finagling tongue!" Feylind snarled past the leather and studs of her stepfather's chest. "The Shadow Master *knows* how I hate those brigs with their wallowing round bottoms." A rebellious kick caught the trestle, which swayed with alarming violence. She snapped, "Sithaer's howling haunts, Tharrick! Will you damned well let me get up?"

536

The stepfather shot her twin a questioning glance, his forearm locked and unrelenting.

"Let her go," Fiark said from the scullery doorway. "Force has never stopped her before, and she keeps a mean grudge when she's furious."

On Tharrick's release, Feylind uncoiled from the bench and bolted before anyone but her twin sensed the tears behind her fierce anger. Her flying footsteps dwindled through the doorway and tapped over the scuffed floor tiles which adorned the run-down grace of the sea-quarter houses of Innish.

Lacking the spitfire heat of her presence, the workaday kitchen seemed suddenly airless and dead. Jinesse rubbed the stuck wisps of hair from her temples. Pale against the age-darkened paneling, she breathed in the mingled scent of beeswax and stale cooking, then sat in defeat beside Tharrick. "That girl could so easily come to a bad end, and for what? Arithon s'Ffalenn needs none of her help. She's headstrong and wild, and no one's good sense has the impact to mold her opinions."

Since Tharrick had no sound consolation to offer, he gathered his wife's tired shoulders to his side and caressed a smear of flour from her cheek.

"Let her be." Fiark moved the chipped bread bowl to the drain-board, puffed away the few stray flecks on his sleeves, then lent his good-natured advice. "Doesn't anyone notice? Feylind takes care of herself. She listens to Arithon. We'll just have to trust his sound planning will keep her out of harm's way."

Tharrick raised craggy brows, his eyes on his stepson grown piercing. "Better speak if you know something you haven't told us."

Fiark's subtle, secretive nod burst his restraint and exposed a conspirator's grin. "Arithon's own planning. You'll see."

Moments later, an earsplitting scream slapped echoes back down the corridor. Jinesse startled. From mercenary's instinct, Tharrick reached for the broadsword he forgot he always left at the armory.

When the cry changed pitch into shattering joy, Fiark took pity on his mother's confusion. "The Master of Shadow left her a letter."

Above the approaching patter of Feylind's swift feet, and another pealing crow which set tremors through the crockery on the shelves, Fiark answered Tharrick's puzzled inquiry. "Rathain's prince has bound us over clear title to the merchant brig, *Evenstar*. She's mine to ship cargoes, and Feylind's to captain. So I much doubt my sister will curse round-bottomed tubs after this. In fact, I'll lay silver her share of the vessel never gets sold to meet her woman's need for a dowry."

Now Jinesse straightened with surprising distress. "How long does he plan to be gone?"

Tharrick stared, amazed. "Then you're not glad he's left?"

"He was a friend," Jinesse stated in perfect aplomb. She shot up and paced to the small copper sink and splashed water over her face. "I just don't approve of his Grace's activities where the safety of my daughter's concerned. Now answer my question. When does he come back?"

Tharrick's honest features showed a disconcerted unease. "Never." His attentive regard held upon his wife's back as he qualified with soft sympathy. "Arithon made his will plain in absolute terms. He would hear no plans to renew ties on this continent for the rest of his natural life."

Far removed to the northwest, amid the firelit heat of her cramped room in Capewell, Enchantress Lirenda swore as she cleared her mind from the vivid scene in the quartz sphere. "Damn him! Fiends curse him for a conniving, clever bastard!"

No s'Ffalenn prince since Torbrand had ever welcomed anyone's prying; Arithon's unearthly, clever machinations made her problem by lengths more difficult.

Lirenda closed her eyes, the fine tendrils of hair at her temples licked to her flushed, sweating face. She put off her disgruntled longing for the comforts of a cool, scented bath. The knot held her tied. While her future swung in the balance, her quarry was no longer conveniently ill, languishing in cosseted vulnerability at Innish.

Again, Arithon had escaped to the open sea, where the lane scryers held no chance in creation of finding a trace of his movements.

Neither could she devise any way to predict the erratic, close secrecy of those landfalls he chose to arrange. If Morriel Prime expected a plan by the time Sethvir reached Isaer Circle, three days remained to deliver. The last avenue of inspiration was the quartz sphere which reflected the baked downs at Araethura, where the ostracized initiate Elaira sat in the hot dirt, drawing stick figures of animals beside a tattered shepherd urchin.

Stabbed by pinprick resentment for the carefree innocence of their play, Lirenda took up the scene reflected in the crystal's stone heart. The dry days that foreran the ending of summer touched the downs to a sea of gold grass. Woman and child shared the antique glaze of buttery, late-day sunlight. The herder's boy seemed an ordinary enough creature, his bare feet rimmed with powdery dust, and his sturdy wrists thrust out of ragged cuffs where growth had overtaken his wardrobe.

Elaira shared a like-minded untidiness. Her knuckles were briar scraped from foraging herbs, and her blouse of a faded, mulberry-dyed cotton clashed with the jarring, hard fire of her wind-tangled auburn hair.

Lirenda surveyed the exchange, secure within her groomed elegance. Her kohl-lined lids slitted with contempt that verged upon boredom until the child chanced to look up.

Through fronding black hair, his eyes were the identical, piercing green of any royal-born scion of s'Ffalenn. His expression of innocent entreaty gouged up the unbidden association: woke the echo of a grown prince's compassion with the opening force of a thunderbolt.

Lirenda froze with stopped breath.

In the quartz, trapped unguarded in the same moment, Elaira's tanned face recorded her unwitting and identical response: a flash-point surge of tender emotion, brought to light on the wings of a memory.

For the span of one fated second, the displaced First Senior felt as if the whole universe had rocked and resettled in her hand.

Then logic reasserted. The penciled arch of Lirenda's brow smoothed. Clear thought reengaged and stamped back the unbridled contamination of wild fancy. A high-order senior and a street-orphaned field herbalist held nothing at all in common. Resentment remained, that Elaira's headstrong fascination with Prince Arithon's character had been the original catalyst to bring Morriel's disfavor on them both.

Lirenda tapped an impatient nail against the crystal. Inspiration bent her thoughts to exquisite, fine malice. How better to amend a shared fall from grace than to see Elaira swept into the center of the plot to take down Arithon s'Ffalenn?

In the quiet, sealed room, wrapped in the musk of her heat-sodden silk, Lirenda sat straight. The quartz sphere itself seemed to kindle with fire as inspiration unfolded into a hard plan of action. Through Elaira, sure means could be formulated to match Morriel's demand. Satisfaction curved Lirenda's coral lips, then widened to a smile as sensuous and sure as the stalking crouch of a panther.

If Arithon s'Ffalenn could not be bought with gold, or tracked with spells, or snared into captivity through dark lures of compulsive magic, he still had one weakness for which he would hold no rear-guard defenses. The s'Ffalenn royal gift of compassion could not be gainsaid. He must come to the net of his own accord if the stakes were aligned, and the bait for her trap was an innocent.

Intervals

In the overfurnished sitting room of a cottage at Innish, Felirin the Scarlet winces and casts his lyranthe aside, resigned that his fire-scarred hands can no longer play for his living; nor is he aware of any observer until Halliron's spinster daughter addresses him from the doorway: "Never mind. This house cries out for the retired bard it never came to shelter. I would be pleased if you would consent to make your permanent home here with me. . . ."

At Avenor, faced across the pearl-inlaid lacquer of a table in a fashionable tavern, Mearn s'Brydion pours fine brandy for a drunken palace scribe, and presses the inveigling question he has waited like a snake to present: "Never mind principle. For the Light, I'd pay gold to congratulate the stout man who sent his letter to Etarra, betraying the Shadow Master's interests at the Riverton shipyard. . . ."

When the Paravian focus circle inside the Second Age ruin at Mainmere flares active to receive the spell-turned energies of Sethvir's crossing, Morriel Prime rules on the proposal Lirenda presents at Capewell: "Your plan to take Arithon has one severe drawback, and that, the fifteen-year span to achieve his final defeat. Yet the premise is sound. The quarry will succumb. You have my permission. Proceed. . . ."

GLOSSARY

AL'DUIN—deceased father of Halliron Masterbard.

    pronounced: al-dwin

    root meaning: *al*—over; *duinne*—hand

ALESTRON—city located in Midhalla, Melhalla. Ruled by the Duke Bransian, Teir's'Brydion, and his three brothers. This city did not fall to merchant townsmen in the Third Age uprising that threw down the high kings, but is still ruled by its clanblood heirs.

    pronounced: ah-less-tron

    root meaning: *alesstair*—stubborn; *an*—one

ALITHIEL—one of twelve Blades of Isaer, forged by centaur Ffereton s'Darian in the First Age from metal taken from a meteorite. Passed through Paravian possession, acquired the secondary name Dael-Farenn, or Kingmaker, since its owners tended to succeed the end of a royal line. Eventually was awarded to Kamridian s'Ffalenn for his valor in defense of the princess Taliennse, early Second Age. Currently in the possession of Arithon.

    pronounced: ah-lith-ee-el

    root meaning: *alith*—star; *iel*—light/ray

ALLAND—principality located in southeastern Shand. Ruled by the High Earl Teir's'Taleyn, *caithdein* of Shand by appointment. Current heir to the title is Erlien.

    pronounced: all-and

    root meaning: *a'lind*—pine glen

ALTHAIN TOWER—spire built at the edge of the Bittern Desert, beginning of the Second Age, to house records of Paravian histories. Third Age, became repository for the archives of all five royal houses of men after rebellion, overseen by Sethvir, Warden of Althain and Fellowship Sorcerer.

    pronounced: al—like "all," thain—to rhyme with "main"

    root meaning: *alt*—last; *thein*—tower, sanctuary

        original Paravian pronunciation: alt-thein (thein as in "the end")

AMROTH—kingdom on West Gate splinter world, Dascen Elur, ruled by s'Ilessid descendants of the prince exiled through the Worldsend Gate at the time of the rebellion, Third Age just after the Mistwraith's conquest.

    pronounced: am-roth—to rhyme with "sloth"

    root meaning: *am*—state of being; *roth*—brother "brotherhood"

AN'ALT—Paravian name for the rune symbolizing infinity.

    pronounced: an-allt

    root meaning: *an*—one/first; *alt*—end/last

ARAETHURA—grass plains in southwest Rathain; principality of the same name in that location. Largely inhabited by Riathan Paravians in the Second Age. Third Age, used as pastureland by widely scattered nomadic shepherds.

    pronounced: ar-eye-thoo-rah

    root meaning: *araeth*—grass; *era*—place, land

ARITHON—son of Avar, Prince of Rathain, 1,504th Teir's'Ffalenn after founder of the line, Torbrand in Third Age Year One. Also Master of Shadow, the Bane of Desh-thiere, and Halliron Masterbard's successor.

    pronounced: ar-i-thon—almost rhymes with "marathon"

    root meaning: *arithon*—fate-forger; one who is visionary

ARWENT—river in Araethura, Rathain, that flows from Daenfal Lake, through Halwythwood to empty into Instrell Bay

    pronounced: are-went

    root meaning: *arwient*—swiftest

ASANDIR—Fellowship Sorcerer. Secondary name, Kingmaker, since his hand crowned every High King of Men to rule in the Age of Men (Third Age). After the Mistwraith's conquest, he acted as field agent for the Fellowship's doings across the continent. Also called Fiend-quencher, for his reputation for quelling iyats; Storm-breaker, and Change-bringer for past actions in late Second Age, when Men first arrived upon Athera.

    pronounced: ah-san-deer

    root meaning: *asan*—heart; *dir*—stone "heartrock"

ATAINIA—northeastern principality of Tysan.

    pronounced: ah-tay-nee-ah

    root meaning: *itain*—the third; *ia*—suffix for "third domain" original Paravian, *itainia*

ATCHAZ—city located in Alland, Shand. Famed for its silk.

    pronounced: at-chas

    root meaning: *atchias*—silk

ATH CREATOR—prime vibration, force behind all life.

    pronounced: ath—to rhyme with "math"

    root meaning: *ath*—prime, first (as opposed to *an*, one)

ATHERA—name for the world which holds the Five High Kingdoms; four Worldsend Gates; original home of the Paravian races.

    pronounced: ath-air-ah

    root meaning: *ath*—prime force; *era*—place "Ath's world"

ATHIR—Second Age ruin of a Paravian stronghold, located in Ithilt, Rathain. Site of a seventh lane power focus.

    pronounced: ath-ear

    root meaning: *ath*—prime; *i'er*—the line/edge

ATHLIEN PARAVIANS—sunchildren. Small race of semimortals, pixielike, but possessed of great wisdom/keepers of the grand mystery.

    pronounced: ath-lee-en

    root meaning: *ath*—prime force; *lien*—to love "Ath-beloved"

AVENOR—Second Age ruin of a Paravian stronghold. Traditional seat of the s'Ilessid high kings. Restored to habitation in Third Age 5644. Became the ruling seat of the Alliance of Light in Third Age 5648. Located in Korias, Tysan.

    pronounced: ah-ven-or

    root meaning: *avie*—stag; *norh*—grove

BITTERN DESERT—waste located in Atainia, Tysan, north of Althain Tower. Site of a First Age battle between the great drakes and the Seardluin, permanently destroyed by dragonfire.

    pronounced: like bitter

    root meaning: to sear or char

BLACK ROSE PROPHECY—made by Dakar the Mad Prophet in Third Age 5637 at Althain Tower. Forecasts Davien the Betrayer's repentance, and the reunification of the Fellowship of Seven as tied to Arithon s'Ffalenn's voluntary resumption of Rathain's crown rule.

BRANSIAN s'BRYDION—Teir's'Brydion, ruling Duke of Alestron.

    pronounced: bran-see-an

    root meaning: *brand*—temper; *s'i'an*—suffix denoting "of the one"/the one with temper

BWIN EVOC s'LORNMEIN—founder of the line that became High Kings of Havish since Third Age Year One. The attribute he passed on by means of the Fellowship's geas was temperance.

    pronounced: bwin—to rhyme with "twin," ee-vahk—as in "evocative," lorn as in English equivalent, mein—to rhyme with "main"

    root meaning: *bwin*—firm; *evoc*—choice

CAINCYR ISLAND—islet located in the archipelago at Min Pierens, in the Westland Sea.

    pronounced: cain-seer

    root meaning: *caincyr*—sailfish

CAINFORD—city located in Taerlin, Tysan.

    pronounced: cay-in-ford

    root meaning: *caen*—vale; ford—not from the Paravian "ford at the vale"

CAITH-AL-CAEN—vale where Riathan Paravians (unicorns) celebrated equinox and solstice to renew the *athael*, or life-destiny of the world. Also the place where the Ilitharis Paravians first Named the winter stars—or encompassed their vibrational essence into language. Corrupted by the end of the Third Age to Castlecain.

    pronounced: cay-ith-al-cay-en, musical lilt, emphasis on second and last syllables; rising note on first two, falling note on last two

    root meaning: *caith*—shadow; *al*—over; *caen*—vale "vale of shadow" link with prime power. An old Paravian colloquialism for unicorn.

CAITHDEIN—Paravian name for a high king's first counselor; also, the one who would stand as regent, or steward, in the absence of the crowned ruler.

    pronounced: kay-ith-day-in

    root meaning: *caith*—shadow; *d'ein*—behind the chair "shadow behind the throne"

CAITHWOOD—forest located in Taerlin, southeast principality of Tysan.

    pronounced: kay-ith-wood

    root meaning: *caith*—shadow "shadowed wood"

CALUM KINCAID—the individual who invented the great weapon which destroyed the worlds of humanity, and caused the refugee faction, including the Koriathain, to seek sanctuary on Athera.

    pronounced: calum kin-cade

    root meaning not from the Paravian

CAMRIS—north-central principality of Tysan. Original ruling seat was the city of Erdane.

    pronounced: Kam-ris, the i as in "chris"

    root meaning: *caim*—cross; *ris*—way "crossroad"

CAOLLE—past war captain of the clans of Deshir, Rathain. First raised by, and then served under, Lord Steiven, Earl of the North and *caithdein* of Rathain. Planned the campaign at Vastmark and Dier Kenton Vale for the Master of Shadow. Currently in Jieret Red-beard's service, and feal liegeman to Arithon of Rathain.

    pronounced: kay-all-e, with the "e" nearly subliminal

    root meaning: *caille*—stubborn

CAPEWELL—city located on the south shore of Korias, Tysan. Home of a major Koriani sisterhouse.

CARIADWIN—ship stolen from the royal shipyard at Riverton, by Cattrick's conspiracy with Prince Arithon.

    pronounced: care-ee-add-win

    root meaning: *ciaria*—swallow; *dwin*—tail

CARITHWYR—principality consisting primarily of a grassland in Havish, once the province of the Riathan Paravians. A unicorn birthing ground. Currently used by man for grain and cattle; area name has become equated with fine hides.

    pronounced: car-ith-ear

    root meaning: *ci'arithiren*—forgers of the ultimate link with prime power. An old Paravian colloquialism for unicorn.

CATTRICK—master joiner hired to run the royal shipyard at Riverton; once in Arithon's employ at Merior by the Sea.

    pronounced: cat-rick

    root meaning: *ciattiaric*—a knot tied of withies that has the magical property of confusing enemies

CEREBELD—Avenor's Lord Examiner, whose given task is to hunt out and try those who practice dark spellcraft.

    pronounced: cara-belld

    root meaning: *ciarabeld*—ashes

CHEIVALT—coastal city south of Ostermere in Carithwyr, Havish. Known for its elegance and refined lifestyle.

    pronounced: shay-vault

    root meaning: *chiavalden*—a rare yellow flower which grows by the seaside

CILADIS THE LOST—Fellowship Sorcerer who left the continent in Third Age 3462 in search of the Paravian races after their disappearance following the rebellion.

pronounced: kill-ah-dis

root meaning: *cael*—leaf; *adeis*—whisper, compound; cael'adeis colloquialism for "gentleness that abides"

CILDORN—city famed for carpets and weaving, located in Deshir,
Rathain. Originally a Paravian holdfast, situated on a node of the third
lane.

pronounced: kill-dorn

root meaning: *cieal*—thread; *dorn*—net "tapestry"

CORITH—island west of Havish coast, in Westland Sea. Site of a drake
lair, and a ruined First Age foundation. Here, the council of Paravians
met during siege, and dragons dreamed the summoning of the Fellowship Sorcerers. First site to see sunlight upon Desh-thiere's defeat.

pronounced: kor-ith

root meaning: *cori*—ships, vessels; *itha*—five for the five harbors which
the old city overlooked

DAELION FATEMASTER—"entity" formed by set of mortal beliefs,
which determine the fate of the spirit after death. If Ath is the prime
vibration, or life force, Daelion is what governs the manifestation of free
will.

pronounced: day-el-ee-on

root meaning: *dael*—king or lord; *i'on*—of fate

DAELION's WHEEL—cycle of life and the crossing point which is the
transition into death.

pronounced: day-el-ee-on

root meaning: *dael*—king or lord; *i'on*—of fate

DAKAR THE MAD PROPHET—apprentice to Fellowship Sorcerer,
Asandir, during the Third Age following the Conquest of the Mistwraith. Given to spurious prophecies, it was Dakar who forecast the fall
of the Kings of Havish in time for the Fellowship to save the heir. He
made the Prophecy of West Gate, which forecast the Mistwraith's bane,
and also the Black Rose Prophecy, which called for reunification of the
Fellowship. At this time, assigned to defense of Arithon, Prince of
Rathain.

pronounced: dah-kar

root meaning: *dakiar*—clumsy

DANIA—wife of Rathain's former regent, Steiven s'Valerient. Died by
the hand of Pesquil's headhunters in the Battle of Strakewood. Jieret Red-
beard's mother.

pronounced: dan-ee-ah

root meaning: *deinia*—sparrow

DAON RAMON BARRENS—central principality of Rathain. Site where
Riathan Paravians (unicorns) bred and raised their young. Barrens was
not appended to the name until the years following the Mistwraith's conquest, when the River Severnir was diverted at the source by a task force
under Etarran jurisdiction.

pronounced: day-on-rah-mon

root meaning: *daon*—gold; *ramon*—hills/downs

DASCEN ELUR—splinter world off West Gate; primarily ocean with isolated archipelagoes. Includes kingdoms of Rauven, Amroth, and Karthan. Where three exiled high kings' heirs took refuge in the years following the great uprising. Birthplace of Lysaer and Arithon.

pronounced: das-en el-ur

root meaning: *dascen*—ocean; *e'lier*—small land

DAVIEN THE BETRAYER—Fellowship Sorcerer responsible for provoking the great uprising that resulted in the fall of the high kings after Desh-thiere's conquest. Rendered discorporate by the Fellowship's judgment in Third Age 5129. Exiled since, by personal choice. Davien's works included the Five Centuries Fountain near Mearth on the splinter world of the Red Desert through West Gate; the shaft at Rockfell Pit, used by the Sorcerers to imprison harmful entities; the Stair on Rockfell Peak; and also, Kewar Tunnel in the Mathorn Mountains.

pronounced: dah-vee-en

root meaning: *dahvi*—fool, mistake; *an*—one "mistaken one"

DAWR—grandmother of Duke Bransian of Alestron, and his brother, Mearn s'Brydion.

pronounced: dour

root meaning: *dwyiar*—vinegar wine

DESH-THIERE—Mistwraith that invaded Athera from the splinter worlds through South Gate in Third Age 4993. Access cut off by Fellowship Sorcerer, Traithe. Battled and contained in West Shand for twenty-five years, until the rebellion splintered the peace, and the high kings were forced to withdraw from the defense lines to attend their disrupted kingdoms. Confined through the combined powers of Lysaer s'Ilessid's gift of light and Arithon s'Ffalenn's gift of shadow. Currently imprisoned in a warded flask in Rockfell Pit.

pronounced: desh-thee-air-e (last "e" mostly subliminal)

root meaning: *desh*—mist; *thiere*—ghost or wraith

DESHIR—northwestern principality of Rathain.

pronounced: desh-eer

root meaning: *deshir*—misty

DHARKARON AVENGER—called Ath's Avenging Angel in legend. Drives a chariot drawn by five horses to convey the guilty to Sithaer. Dharkaron as defined by the adepts of Ath's Brotherhood is that dark thread mortal men weave with Ath, the prime vibration, that creates self-punishment, or the root of guilt.

pronounced dark-air-on

root meaning: *dhar*—evil; *khiaron*—one who stands in judgment

DIEGAN—once Lord Commander of Etarra's garrison; given over by his mayor to serve as Lysaer s'Ilessid's Lord Commander at Avenor. Titular commander of the war host sent against the Deshans to defeat the Master of Shadow at Tal Quorin; high commander of the war host mustered at

Werpoint. Also brother of Lady Talith. Died of a clan arrow in the Battle of Dier Kenton Vale in Vastmark, Third Age 5647.

    pronounced: dee-gan

    root meaning: *diegan*—trinket a dandy might wear/ornament

DIER KENTON VALE—valley located in the principality of Vastmark, Shand, where the war host thirty-five thousand strong, under command of Lysaer s'Ilessid, fought and lost to the Master of Shadow in Third Age 5647. The main body of the forces of light were decimated in one day by a shale slide. The remainder were harried by a small force of Vastmark shepherds under Caolle, who served as Arithon's war captain.

    pronounced: deer ken-ton

    root meaning: *dien'kendion*—a jewel with a severe flaw that may result
        in shearing or cracking

EILISH—Lord Minister of the Royal Treasury, Avenor.

    pronounced: eye-lish

    root meaning: *eyalish*—fussy

ELAIRA—initiate enchantress of the Koriathain. Originally a street child, taken on in Morvain for Koriani rearing.

    pronounced: ee-layer-ah

    root meaning: *e*—prefix, diminutive for small; *laere*—grace

ELDIR s'LORNMEIN—King of Havish and last surviving scion of s'Lornmein royal line. Raised as a wool-dyer until the Fellowship Sorcerers crowned him at Ostermere in Third Age 5643 following the defeat of the Mistwraith.

    pronounced: el-deer

    root meaning: *eldir*—to ponder, to consider, to weigh

ELSSINE—city located on the coast of Alland, Shand, famed for stone quarries used for ships' ballast.

    pronounced: el-seen

    root meaning: *elssien*—small pit

ELTAIR BAY—large bay off Cildein Ocean and east coast of Rathain; where River Severnir was diverted following the Mistwraith's conquest.

    pronounced: el-tay-er

    root meaning: *al'tieri*—of steel/a shortening of original Paravian
        name *dascen al'tieri*, which meant "ocean of steel," which
        referred to the color of the waves

ERDANE—old Paravian city, later taken over by Men. Seat of old princes of Camris until Desh-thiere's conquest and rebellion.

    pronounced: er-day-na with the last syllable almost subliminal

    root meaning: *er'deinia*—long walls

ERLIEN s'TALEYN—High Earl of Alland; *caithdein* of Shand, chieftain of the forest clansmen of Selkwood.

    pronounced: er-lee-an stall-ay-en

root meaning: *aierlyan*—bear; *tal*—branch; *an*—one/first "of first one branch"

ETARRA—trade city built across the Mathorn Pass by townsfolk after the revolt that cast down Ithamon and the High Kings of Rathain. Nest of corruption and intrigue, and policy maker for the North.

    pronounced: ee-tar-ah

    root meaning: *e*—prefix for small; *taria*—knots

EVENSTAR—first brig stolen from Riverton's royal shipyard by Cattrick's conspiracy with Prince Arithon.

FALGAIRE—coastal city on Instrell Bay, located in Araethura, Rathain, famed for its crystal and glassworks.

    pronounced: fall-gair—to rhyme with "air"

    root meaning: *fal'mier*—to sparkle or glitter

FALWOOD—forest located in West Shand.

    pronounced: fall-wood

    root meaning: *fal*—tree

FATE's WHEEL—see Daelion's Wheel.

FEITHAN—wife of Jieret s'Valerient, Earl of the North, and *caithdein* of Rathain.

    pronounced: faith-an

    root meaning: *feiathen*—ivy

FELIRIN—minstrel known as the Scarlet Bard; a past acquaintance of Prince Arithon.

    pronounced: fell-eer-in

    root meaning: *fel*—red; *lyron*—singer

FELLOWSHIP OF SEVEN—Sorcerers sworn to uphold the Law of the Major Balance, and to foster enlightened thought in Athera. Originators and keepers of the compact made with the Paravian races that allowed Men to settle on Athera.

FENLANDERS—the marsh dwellers who inhabit Mogg's Fen, descended from renegade townsmen, outlaws, or townborn supporters of the clans who were displaced during the rebellion.

FEYLIND—daughter of Jinesse; twin sister of Fiark; born in Merior by the Sea, and currently serving apprenticeship as a navigator under Arithon s'Ffalenn.

    pronounced: fay-lind

    root meaning: *faelind'an*—outspoken one/noisy one

FFEREDON-LI—ancient Paravian word for a healer, literally translated "bringer of grace"; still in use in the dialect of Araethura.

    pronounced: fair-eh-dun lee

    root meaning: *ffaraton*—maker; *li*—exalted grace

FIARK—son of Jinesse; twin brother of Feylind; born in Merior by the Sea, currently employed as a factor by an Innish merchant.

    pronounced: fee-ark

    root meaning: *fyerk*—to throw or toss

FIONN ARETH CAID'AN—shepherd child born in Third Age 5647; fated by prophecy to leave home and play a role in the Wars of Light and Shadow.

pronounced: fee-on-are-eth cayed-ahn

root meaning: *fionne arith caid an*—one who brings choice

FIRST AGE—marked by the arrival of the Paravian Races as Ath's gift to heal the marring of creation by the great drakes.

GACE STEWARD—Royal Steward of Avenor.

pronounced: gace—to rhyme with "race"

root meaning: *gyce*—weasel

GARTH's POND—small brackish pond in Merior by the Sea, on the Scimlade peninsula off Alland, Shand.

pronounced: garth—to rhyme with "hearth"

root meaning not from the Paravian

GREAT WAYSTONE—amethyst crystal, spherical in shape, once the grand power focus of the Koriani Order; lost during the great uprising, and finally recovered from Fellowship custody by First Senior Lirenda in Third Age 5647.

GREAT WEST ROAD—trade route which crosses Tysan from Karfael on the west coast, to Castle Point on Instrell Bay.

GRIMWARD—a circle of dire spells of Paravian making that seal and isolate forces that have the potential for unimaginable destruction. With the disappearance of the old races, the defenses are maintained by embodied Sorcerers of the Fellowship of Seven. There are seventeen separate sites listed at Althain Tower.

HALDUIN s'ILESSID—founder of the line that became High Kings of Tysan since Third Age Year One. The attribute he passed on, by means of the Fellowship's geas, was justice.

pronounced: hal-dwin

root meaning: *hal*—white; *duinne*—hand

HALLIRON MASTERBARD—native of Innish, Shand. Masterbard of Athera during the Third Age; inherited the accolade from his teacher Murchiel in the year 5597. Son of Al'Duin. Husband of Deartha. Arithon's master and mentor. Died from an injury inflicted by the Mayor of Jaelot in the year 5644.

pronounced: hal-eer-on

root meaning: *hal*—white; *lyron*—singer

HALWYTHWOOD—forest located in Araethura, Rathain.

pronounced: hall-with-wood

root meaning: *hal*—white; *wythe*—vista

HANSHIRE—port city on Westland Sea, coast of Korias, Tysan; reigning official Lord Mayor Garde; opposed to royal rule at the time of Avenor's restoration.

pronounced: han-sheer

root meaning: *hansh*—sand; *era*—place

HARRADENE—Lord Commander of Etarra's army at the time of the muster at Werpoint, still in power after Vastmark campaign.

pronounced: har-a-deen

root meaning: *harradien*—large mule

HAVENS—an inlet on the northeastern shore of Vastmark, Shand.

HAVISH—one of the Five High Kingdoms of Athera, as defined by the charters of the Fellowship of Seven. Ruled by Eldir s'Lornmein. Sigil: gold hawk on red field.

pronounced: hav-ish

root meaning: *havieshe*—hawk

HIGHSCARP—city on the coast of the Bay of Eltair, located in Daon Ramon, Rathain.

IANFAR s'GANNLEY—cousin and heir designate of Lord Maenol s'Gannley, *caithdein* of Tysan.

pronounced: ee-an-far s gan-lee

root meaning: *ianfiar*—birch tree

ILITHARIS PARAVIANS—centaurs, one of three semimortal old races; disappeared at the time of the Mistwraith's conquest. They were the guardians of the earth's mysteries.

pronounced: i-li-thar-is

root meaning: *i'lith'eans*—the keeper/preserver of mystery

ILSWATER—both a lake bordering the principalities of Korias and Taerlin; and the river which carries the water trade route from Caithwood to Riverton.

pronounced: ills-water

root meaning: *iel*—light

INNISH—city located on the southcoast of Shand at the delta of the River Ippash. Birthplace of Halliron Masterbard. Formerly known as "the Jewel of Shand," this was the site of the high king's winter court, prior to the time of the uprising.

pronounced: in-ish

root meaning: *inniesh*—a jewel with a pastel tint

INSTRELL BAY—body of water off the Gulf of Stormwell, that separates principality of Atainia, Tysan, from Deshir, Rathain.

pronounced: in-strell

root meaning: *arin'streal*—strong wind

ISAER—city located at the crossroads of the Great West Road in Atainia, Tysan. Also a power focus, built during the First Age, in Atainia, Tysan, to source the defense-works at the Paravian keep of the same name.

pronounced: i-say-er

root meaning: *i'saer*—the circle

ITHAMON—Second Age Paravian stronghold, and a Third Age ruin; built on a fifth lane power-node in Daon Ramon Barrens, Rathain, and inhabited until the year of the uprising. Site of the Compass Point Towers, or Sun Towers. Became the seat of the High Kings of Rathain during the Third Age and in year 5638 was the site where Princes Lysaer s'Ilessid and Arithon s'Ffalenn battled the Mistwraith to confinement.

pronounced: ith-a-mon

root meaning: *itha*—five; *mon*—needle, spire

IYAN—deaf-mute servant of Morriel Prime.

pronounced: ee-an

root meaning: *i'on*—fate

IYAT—energy sprite native to Athera, not visible to the eye, manifests in a poltergeist fashion by taking temporary possession of objects. Feeds upon natural energy sources: fire, breaking waves, lightning.

pronounced: ee-at

root meaning: *iyat*—to break

JAELOT—city located on the coast of Eltair Bay at the southern border of the Kingdom of Rathain. Once a Second Age power site, with a focus circle. Now a merchant city with a reputation for extreme snobbery and bad taste. Also the site where Arithon s'Ffalenn played his eulogy for Hall-iron Masterbard, which raised the powers of the Paravian focus circle beneath the mayor's palace. The forces of the mysteries and resonant harmonics caused damage to city buildings, watchkeeps, and walls, which has since been repaired.

pronounced: jay-lot

root meaning: *jielot*—affectation

JEYNSA—daughter of Jieret s'Valerient and Feithan, born Third Age 5653.

pronounced: jay-in-sa

root meaning: garnet

JIERET s'VALERIENT—Earl of the North, clan chief of Deshir; *caithdein* of Rathain, sworn liegeman of Prince Arithon s'Ffalenn. Also son and heir of Lord Steiven. Blood pacted to Arithon by sorcerer's oath prior to battle of Strakewood Forest. Came to be known by headhunters as Jieret Red-beard.

pronounced: jeer-et

root meaning: *jieret*—thorn

JINESSE—widow of a fisherman, mother of the twins Fiark and Feylind; formerly an inhabitant of Merior by the Sea. Remarried and now resides in Innish.

pronounced: gin-ess

root meaning: *jienesse*—to be washed out or pale; a wisp

JYCE—scout in Lord Maenol s'Gannley's band noted for his hearing.

pronounced: like ice with a J

root meaning: *jiess*—hare

KAMRIDIAN s'FFALENN—Crowned High King of Rathain, a tragic figure who died of his conscience under the fated influence of the Kewar Caverns, built by Davien the Betrayer into the Mathorn Mountains.

pronounced: cam-rid-ee-an

root meaning: *kaim'riadien*—thread cut shorter

KARFAEL—trader town on the coast of the Westland Sea, in Tysan. Built by townsmen as a trade port after the fall of the High Kings of Tysan. Prior to Desh-thiere's conquest, the site was kept clear of buildings to allow the second lane forces to flow untrammeled across the focus site at Avenor.

pronounced: kar-fay-el

root meaning: *kar'i'ffael*—literal translation "twist the dark"/colloquialism for "intrigue"

KARMAK—plain located in the northern portion of the principality of Camris, Tysan. Site of numerous First Age battles where Paravian forces opposed Khadrim packs that bred in volcanic sites in the northern Tornir Peaks.

pronounced: kar-mack

root meaning: *karmak*—wolf

KATHTAIRR—landmass in the southern ocean, across the world from Paravia.

pronounced: kath-tear

root meaning: *kait-th'era*—empty place

KEI—birthname for Jeynsa s'Valerient.

pronounced: kay

root meaning: *ka'i*—the girl

KELLIS—clan elder and Duchess of Mainmere.

pronounced: kell-iss

root meaning: *kiel'liess*—balm of grief

KHADRIM—drake-spawned creatures, flying, fire-breathing reptiles that were the scourge of the Second Age. By the Third Age, they had been driven back and confined in the Sorcerers' Preserve in the volcanic peaks in north Tysan.

pronounced: kaa-drim

root meaning: *khadrim*—dragon

KHARADMON—Sorcerer of the Fellowship of Seven; discorporate since rise of Khadrim and Seardluin leveled Paravian city at Ithamon in Second Age 3651. It was by Kharadmon's intervention that the survivors of the attack were sent to safety by means of transfer from the fifth lane power focus. Currently constructing the star ward to guard against invasion of wraiths from Marek.

pronounced: kah-rad-mun

root meaning: *kar'riad en mon*—phrase translates to mean "twisted thread on the needle" or colloquialism for "a knot in the works"

KHETIENN—name for a brigantine owned by Arithon; also a small spotted wildcat native to Daon Ramon Barrens that became the s'Ffalenn royal sigil.

pronounced: key-et-ee-en

root meaning: *kietienn*—small leopard

KORIANI—possessive form of the word "Koriathain"; see entry.

    pronounced: kor-ee-ah-nee

KORIAS—southwestern principality of Tysan.

    pronounced: kor-ee-as

    root meaning: *cor*—ship, vessel; *i'esh*—nest, haven

KORIATHAIN—order of enchantresses ruled by a circle of Seniors, under the power of one Prime Enchantress. They draw their talent from the orphaned children they raise, or from daughters dedicated to service by their parents. Initiation rite involves a vow of consent that ties the spirit to a power crystal keyed to the Prime's control.

    pronounced: kor-ee-ah-thain—to rhyme with "main"

    root meaning: *koriath*—order; *ain*—belonging to

KOSHLIN—influential trade minister from Erdane, renowned for his hatred of the clans, and for his support of the headhunters' leagues.

    pronounced: kosh-lynn

    root meaning: *kioshlin*—opaque

LANSHIRE—northwestern principality of Havish. Name taken from wastes at Scarpdale, site of First Age battles with Seardluin that seared the soil to a slag waste.

    pronounced: lahn-sheer-e (last "e" is nearly subliminal)

    root meaning: *lan'hansh'era*—place of hot sands

LAW OF THE MAJOR BALANCE—founding order of the powers of the Fellowship of Seven, as written by the Paravians. The primary tenet is that no force of nature should be used without consent, or against the will of another living being.

LIRENDA—First Senior Enchantress to the Prime, Koriani order; Morriel's intended successor.

    pronounced: leer-end-ah

    root meaning: *lyron*—singer; *di-ia*—a dissonance (the hyphen denotes a glottal stop)

LORN—town on the northcoast of Atainia, Tysan.

    pronounced: lorn

    root meaning: *loern*—an Atherian fish

LUHAINE—Sorcerer of the Fellowship of Seven—discorporate since the fall of Telmandir. Luhaine's body was pulled down by the mob while he was in ward trance, covering the escape of the royal heir to Havish.

    pronounced: loo-hay-ne

    root meaning: *luirhainon*—defender

LYRANTHE—instrument played by the bards of Athera. Strung with fourteen strings, tuned to seven tones (doubled). Two courses are "drone strings" set to octaves. Five are melody strings, the lower three courses being octaves, the upper two, in unison.

    pronounced: leer-anth-e (last "e" being nearly subliminal)

    root meaning: *lyr*—song, *anthe*—box

LYSAER s'ILLESSID—prince of Tysan, 1497th in succession after Halduin, founder of the line in Third Age Year One. Gifted at birth with control of Light, and Bane of Desh-Thiere.

pronounced: lie-say-er

root meaning: *lia*—blond, yellow or light, *saer*—circle

MAENALLE s'GANNLEY—former steward and *caithdein* of Tysan; put on trial for outlawry and theft on the trade roads; executed by Lysaer s'Ilessid at Isaer, Third Age 5645.

pronounced: may-nahl-e (last "e" is nearly subliminal)

root meaning: *maeni*—to fall, disrupt; *alli*—to save or preserve colloquial translation: "to patch together"

MAENOL—heir, after Maenalle s'Gannley, steward and *caithdein* of Tysan.

pronounced: may-nall

root meaning: *maeni'alli*—"to patch together"

MAINMERE—town at the head of the Valenford River, located in the principality of Taerlin, Tysan. Built by townsmen on a site originally kept clear to free the second lane focus in the ruins farther south.

pronounced: main-meer-e ("e" is subliminal)

root meaning: *maeni*—to fall, interrupt; *miere*—reflection, colloquial translation: "disrupt continuity"

MATHORN MOUNTAINS—range that bisects the Kingdom of Rathain east to west.

pronounced: math-orn

root meaning: *mathien*—massive

MATHORN ROAD—way passing to the south of the Mathorn Mountains, leading to the trade city of Etarra from the west.

pronounced: math-orn

root meaning: *mathien*—massive

MEARN s'BRYDION—youngest brother of Duke Bransian of Alestron. Ducal emissary to Lysaer s'Ilessid's Alliance of Light.

pronounced: may-arn

root meaning: *mierne*—to flit

MELHALLA—High Kingdom of Athera once ruled by the line of s'Ellestrion. The last prince died in the crossing of the Red Desert.

pronounced: mel-hall-ah

root meaning: *maelhallia*—grand meadows/plain—also word for an open space of any sort.

MELOR RIVER—located in the principality of Korias, Tysan. Its mouth forms the harbor for the port town of West End.

pronounced: mel-or

root meaning: *maeliur*—fish

MERIOR BY THE SEA—small seaside fishing village on the Scimlade peninsula in Alland, Shand. Once the temporary site of Arithon's shipyard.

pronounced: mare-ee-or

root meaning: *merioren*—cottages

MIDDLECROSS—town on the shores of Riverton Narrows, in Korias, Tysan.

MIN PIERENS—archipelago to the west of the Kingdom of West Shand, in the Westland Sea.
>   pronounced: min—to rhyme with "pin," pierre-ins
>   root meaning: *min*—purple; *pierens*—shoreline

MINCRESS—port town on Stormwell Gulf, in Camris, Tysan.
>   pronounced: min-cress
>   root meaning: *min*—purple; *crias*—inlet

MINDERL BAY—body of water behind Crescent Isle off the east coast of Rathain.
>   pronounced: mind-earl
>   root meaning: *minderl*—anvil

MIRALT HEAD—port city in northern Camris, Tysan.
>   pronounced: meer-alt
>   root meaning: *m'ier*—shore; *alt*—last

MOGG's FEN—marsh located in Korias, Tysan.
>   pronounced: mog's fen
>   root meaning: *miog*—cattail

MORNOS—city on the westshore of Lithmere, Havish.
>   pronounced: more-nose
>   root meaning: *moarnosh*—a coffer, specifically where a greedy person would hoard valuables.

MORRIEL—Prime Enchantress of the Koriathain since the Third Age 4212.
>   pronounced: more-real
>   root meaning: *moar*—greed; *riel*—silver

MORVAIN—city located in the principality of Araethura, Rathain, on the coast of Instrell Bay. Elaira's birthplace.
>   pronounced: more-vain
>   root meaning: *morvain*—swindlers' market

NARMS—city on the coast of Instrell Bay, built as a craft center by Men in the early Third Age. Best known for dyeworks.
>   pronounced: narms—to rhyme with "charms"
>   root meaning: *narms*—color

NORTHERLY—remote fishing and fur trappers' village on the northern point of Tysan.

NORTHSTRAIT—narrows between the mainland spur of northern Tysan, and the Trow Islands.

ORLAN—pass through the Thaldein Mountains, also location of the Camris clans' west outpost, in Camris, Tysan. Known for barbarian raids.
>   pronounced: or-lan
>   root meaning: *irlan*—ledge

ORLEST—galleymen's port on the coast of Korias, Tysan; also known for its salt harvest.

pronounced: or-lest

root meaning: *iorlest*—salt

ORVANDIR—principality located in northeastern Shand.

pronounced: or-van-deer

root meaning: *orvein*—crumbled; *dir*—stone

OSTERMERE—harbor and trade city, once smugglers' haven, located in Carithwyr, Havish; current seat of Eldir, King of Havish.

pronounced: os-tur-mere

root meaning: *ostier*—brick; *miere*—reflection

PARAVIAN—name for the three old races that inhabited Athera before Men. Including the centaurs, the sunchildren, and the unicorns, these races never die unless mishap befalls them; they are the world's channel, or direct connection to Ath Creator.

pronounced: par-ai-vee-ans

root meaning: *para*—great; *i'on*—fate or "great mystery"

PERDITH—city located on the eastshore in East Halla, Melhalla; known for its armorers.

pronounced: per-dith

root meaning: *pirdith*—anvil

PESQUIL—Mayor of the Northern League of Headhunters, at the time of the battle of Strakewood Forest. His strategies caused the Deshir clans the most punishing losses. Died of a clan vengeance arrow during the crossing of Valleygap in Third Age 5646.

pronounced: pes-quil like "pest-quill"

root meaning not from the Paravian

QUARN—town on the trade road that crosses Caithwood in Taerlin, Tysan.

pronounced: kwarn

root meaning: *quarin*—ravine, canyon

QUEN—deceased half-wit who once served as door guard and servant to the Prime Enchantress of the Koriathain, Morriel.

pronounced: cue-en

root meaning: *quenient*—witless

QUINOLD—Lord Chancellor of Avenor, and a member of Lysaer s'Ilessid's inner cabal.

pronounced: kwin-old

root meaning: *quen*—one who is narrow-minded

RADMOORE DOWNS—meadowlands in Midhalla, Melhalla.

pronounced: rad-more

root meaning: *riad*—thread; *mour*—carpet, rug

RATHAIN—High Kingdom of Athera ruled by descendants of Torbrand s'Ffalenn since Third Age Year One. Sigil: black-and-silver leopard on green field.

pronounced: rath-ayn

root meaning: *roth*—brother; *thein*—tower, sanctuary

RAUVEN TOWER—home of the s'Ahelas mages who brought up Arithon s'Ffalenn and trained him to the ways of power. Located on the splinter world, Dascen Elur, through West Gate.

pronounced: raw-ven

root meaning: *rauven*—invocation

RIATHAN PARAVIANS—unicorns, the purest and most direct connection to Ath Creator; the prime vibration channels directly through the horn.

pronounced: ree-ah-than

root meaning: *ria*—to touch; *ath*—prime life force; *ri'athon*—one who touches divinity

RIVERTON—trade town at the mouth of the Ilswater river, in Korias, Tysan; site of Lysaer's royal shipyard.

ROCKBAY HARBOR—body of water above Southstrait that divides Shand from West Shand.

ROCKFELL PIT—deep shaft cut into Rockfell Peak, used to imprison harmful entities throughout all three ages. Located in the principality of West Halla, Melhalla; became the warded prison for Desh-thiere.

pronounced: rock-fell

root meaning not from the Paravian

ROCKFELL VALE—valley below Rockfell Peak, located in principality of West Halla, Melhalla.

pronounced: rockfell vale

root meaning not from the Paravian

s'AHELAS—family name for the royal line appointed by the Fellowship Sorcerers in Third Age Year One to rule the High Kingdom of Shand. Gifted geas: farsight.

pronounced: s'ah-hell-as

root meaning: *ahelas*—mage-gifted

SANPASHIR—desert waste on the southcoast of Shand.

pronounced: sahn-pash-eer

root meaning: *san*—black or dark; *pash'era*—place of grit or gravel

SANSHEVAS—town located on the southcoast of Alland, Kingdom of Shand.

pronounced: san-shev-as

root meaning: *san*—black; *sheivas*—flint

s'BRYDION—ruling line of the Dukes of Alestron. The only old blood clansmen to maintain rule of their city through the uprising that defeated the rule of the high kings.

pronounced: s'bride-ee-on

root meaning: *baridien*—tenacity

SEARDLUIN—drake-spawned, vicious, intelligent, catlike predators that roved in packs whose hierarchy was arranged for ruthless and

efficient slaughter of other living things. By the middle of the Second **Age, they had** been battled to extinction.

    pronounced: seerd-lwin

    root meaning: *seard*—bearded; *luin*—feline

SECOND AGE—Marked by the arrival of the Fellowship of Seven at Crater Lake, their called purpose to fight the drake spawn.

SELKWOOD—forest located in Alland, Shand.

    pronounced: sellk-wood

    root meaning: *selk*—pattern

SETHVIR—Sorcerer of the Fellowship of Seven, served as Warden of Althain since the disappearance of the Paravians in the Third Age after the Mistwraith's conquest.

    pronounced: seth-veer

    root meaning: *seth*—fact; *vaer*—keep

SEVERNIR—river that once ran across the central part of Daon Ramon Barrens, Rathain. Diverted at the source after the Mistwraith's conquest, to run east into Eltair Bay.

    pronounced: se-ver-neer

    root meaning: *sevaer*—to travel; *nir*—south

s'FFALENN—family name for the royal line appointed by the Fellowship Sorcerers in Third Age Year One to rule the High Kingdom of Rathain. Gifted geas: compassion/empathy.

    pronounced: s-fal-en

    root meaning: *ffael*—dark, *an*—one

s'GANNLEY—family name for the line of Earls of the West, who stood as *caithdeinen* and stewards for the High Kings of Tysan.

    pronounced: s-gan-lee

    root meaning: *gaen*—to guide; *li*—exalted, or in harmony

SHADOWBANE—gold talisman coin struck at Avenor, bearing Lysaer's head, and a bane against darkness. Thrown out as largesse each day at noon in the square by the royal palace.

SHAND—High Kingdom on the southeast corner of the Paravian continent, originally ruled by the line of s'Ahelas. Device is falcon on a crescent moon, backed by purple-and-gold chevrons.

    pronounced: shand—as in "hand"

    root meaning: *shayn* or *shiand*—two/pair

SHANDIAN—refers to nationality, being of the Kingdom of Shand.

    pronounced: shand-ee-an

    root meaning: *shand*—two

SHAYN—Paravian rune for two.

    pronounced: shane

    root meaning: *shayn*—two

SHIEN—joint captain of Avenor's field troops, who maintained the home garrison while Lord Diegan marched to Vastmark.

    pronounced: she-en

    root meaning: *shien*—cord

s'ILESSID—family name for the royal line appointed by the Fellowship Sorcerers in Third Age Year One to rule the High Kingdom of Tysan. Gifted geas: justice.

    pronounced: s-ill-ess-id

    root meaning: *liessiad*—balance

SITHAER—mythological equivalent of hell, halls of Dharkaron Avenger's judgment; according to Ath's adepts, that state of being where the prime vibration is not recognized.

    pronounced: sith-air

    root meaning: *sid*—lost; *thiere*—wraith/spirit

SKANNT—headhunter captain, served under Pesquil.

    pronounced: scant

    root meaning: *sciant*—a lean, hard-run hound of mixed breeding

SKYRON FOCUS—large aquamarine focus stone, used by the Koriani Senior Circle for their major magic after the loss of the Great Waystone during the rebellion.

    pronounced: sky-run

    root meaning: *skyron*—colloquialism for shackle; *s'kyr'i'on*—literally "sorrowful fate"

s'LORNMEIN—family name for the royal line appointed by the Fellowship Sorcerers in Third Age Year One to rule the High Kingdom of Havish. Gifted geas: temperance.

    pronounced: s-lorn-main

    root meaning: *liernmein*—to center, or restrain, or bring into balance

SORCERERS' PRESERVE—warded territory located by Teal's Gap in Tornir Peaks in Tysan where the Khadrim are kept confined by Fellowship magic.

SOUTHSHIRE—southcoast port town located in Alland, Kingdom of Shand; known for its shipbuilding and orange groves.

STEIVEN—Earl of the North, *caithdein* and regent to the High Kingdom of Rathain at the time of Arithon Teir's'Ffalenn's return. Chieftain of the Deshans until his death in the battle of Strakewood Forest. Jieret Redbeard's father.

    pronounced: stay-vin

    root meaning: *steiven*—stag

STORMWELL—Gulf of Stormwell, body of water off the northcoast of Tysan.

STRAKEWOOD—forest in the principality of Deshir, Rathain; site of the battle of Strakewood Forest.

    pronounced: strayk-wood, similar to "stray wood"

    root meaning: *streik*—to quicken, to seed

SULFIN EVEND—Hanshire guard captain who leads a company of Men in pursuit of Arithon s'Ffalenn.

    pronounced: sool-finn ev-end

    root meaning: *suilfinn eiavend*—colloquialism, "diamond mind"—one who is persistent

SUNCHILDREN—translated term for Athlien Paravians.

SUNWHEEL—blazon of the Alliance of Light, consisting of a gold geometric on a white field.

s'VALERIENT—family name for the Earls of the North, regents and *caithdeinen* for the High Kings of Rathain.

    pronounced: val-er-ee-ent

    root meaning: *val*—straight; *erient*—spear

TAERLIN—southeastern principality of Kingdom of Tysan. Also a lake of that name, Taerlin Waters in the southern spur of Tornir Peaks. Halliron teaches Arithon a ballad of that name, which is of Paravian origin, and which commemorates the First Age slaughter of unicorn herd by Khadrim.

    pronounced: tay-er-lin

    root meaning: *taer*—calm; *lien*—to love

TAL QUORIN—river formed by the confluence of watershed on the southern side of Strakewood, principality of Deshir, Rathain, where traps were laid for Etarra's army in the battle of Strakewood Forest.

    pronounced: tal quar-in

    root meaning: *tal*—branch; *quorin*—canyons

TAL's CROSSING—town at the branch in the trade road that leads to Etarra and south, and northeastward to North Ward.

    pronounced: tal—to rhyme with "pal"

    root meaning: *tal*—branch

TALITH—Lord Diegan's sister; wife of Lysaer s'Ilessid.

    pronounced: tal-ith—to rhyme with "gal with"

    root meaning: *tal*—branch; *lith*—to keep/nurture

TALLIARTHE—name given to Arithon's pleasure sloop by Feylind; in Paravian myth, a sea sprite who spirits away maidens who stray too near to the tidemark at twilight.

    pronounced: tal-ee-arth

    root meaning: *tal*—branch; *li*—exalted, in harmony; *araithe*—to disperse or to send

TEIR—title fixed to a name denoting heirship. Feminine form is TEIREN.

    pronounced: tay-er

    root meaning: *teir's*—"successor to power"

TELLISEC—guild minister of Tysan, and one of Lysaer's inner cabal.

    pronounced: tell-i-sec

    root meaning: *tellisec*—a small spider

TELMANDIR—ruined city that once was the seat of the High Kings of Havish. Located in the principality of Lithmere, Havish.

    pronounced: tell-man-deer

    root meaning: *telman'en*—leaning; *dir*—rock

TELZEN—city on the coast of Alland, Shand, renowned for its lumber and saw millworks.

    pronounced: tell-zen

    root meaning: *tielsen*—to saw wood

THALDEINS—mountain range that borders the principality of Camris, Tysan, to the east. Site of the Camris clans' west outpost. Site of the raid at the Pass of Orlan.

    pronounced: thall-dayn

    root meaning: *thal*—head; *dein*—bird

THARRICK—former captain of the guard in the city of Alestron assigned charge of the duke's secret armory; now married to Jinesse and working as a gentleman mercenary guard at Innish.

    pronounced: thar-rick

    root meaning: *thierik*—unkind twist of fate

THIRD AGE—marked by the Fellowship's sealing of the compact with the Paravian races, and the arrival of Men to Athera.

THIRDMARK—seaside city on the shores of Rockbay Harbor at the northern edge of Vastmark, in Shand.

TIDEPORT—trade port on the south shore of Korias, Kingdom of Tysan.

TIENDAR—Paravian word invoking the tie between spirit and flesh.

    pronounced: tee-en-dar

    root meaning: *tiendar*—spirit tie

TIENELLE—high-altitude herb valued by mages for its mind-expanding properties. Highly toxic. No antidote. The leaves, dried and smoked, are most potent. To weaken its powerful side effects and allow safer access to its vision, Koriani enchantresses boil the flowers, then soak tobacco leaves with the brew.

    pronounced: tee-an-ell-e ("e" mostly subliminal)

    root meaning: *tien*—dream; *iel*—light/ray

TIRANS—trade city in East Halla, Melhalla.

    pronounced: tee-rans

    root meaning: *tier*—to hold fast, to keep, to covet

TORBRAND s'FFALENN—founder of the s'Ffalenn line appointed by the Fellowship of Seven to rule the High Kingdom of Rathain in Third Age Year One.

    pronounced: tor-brand

    root meaning: *tor*—sharp, keen; *brand*—temper

TORNIR PEAKS—mountain range on western border of the principality of Camris, Tysan. Northern half is actively volcanic, and there the last surviving packs of Khadrim are kept under ward.

    pronounced: tor-neer

    root meaning: *tor*—sharp, keen; *nier*—tooth

TORWENT—smuggler's haven and fishing town in Lanshire, Havish.

    pronounced: tore-went

    root meaning: *tor*—sharp; *wient*—bend

TRAITHE—Sorcerer of the Fellowship of Seven. Solely responsible for the closing of South Gate to deny further entry to the Mistwraith. Traithe lost most of his faculties in the process, and was left with a limp. Since it is not known whether he can make the transfer into discorporate existence with his powers impaired, he has retained his physical body.

    pronounced: tray-the

    root meaning: *traithe*—gentleness

TROW ISLANDS—archipelago at the far side of Northstrait in Tysan.

    pronounced: trow—to rhyme with how

    root meaning: *turow*—crab

TYSAN—one of the Five High Kingdoms of Athera, as defined by the charters of the Fellowship of Seven. Ruled by the s'Ilessid royal line. Sigil: gold star on blue field.

    pronounced: tie-san

    root meaning: *tiasen*—rich

VALENDALE—river arising in the Pass of Orlan in the Thaldein Mountains, in the principality of Atainia, Tysan.

    pronounced: val-en-dale

    root meaning: *valen*—braided; *dale*—foam

VALENFORD—city located in Taerlin, Tysan.

    pronounced: val-en-ford

    root meaning: *valen*—braided

VASTMARK—principality located in southwestern Shand. Highly mountainous and not served by trade roads. Its coasts are renowned for shipwrecks. Inhabited by nomadic shepherds and wyverns, non-fire-breathing, smaller relatives of Khadrim. Site of the grand massacre of Lysaer's war host in Third Age 5647.

    pronounced: vast-mark

    root meaning: *vhast*—bare; *mheark*—valley

VERRAIN—spellbinder, trained by Luhaine; stood as Guardian of Mirthlvain when the Fellowship of Seven was left shorthanded after the conquest of the Mistwraith.

    pronounced: ver-rain

    root meaning: *ver*—keep; *ria*—touch; *an*—one; original Paravian: ver
      ria'an

VHALZEIN—city located in West Shand, shore of Rockbay Harbor on the border by Havish.

    pronounced: val-zeen

    root meaning: from drakish, *vhchalsckeen*—white sands

VORRICE—Lord High Examiner of Avenor; charged with trying and executing cases of dark magecraft.

    pronounced: vor-iss

    root meaning: *vorisse*—to lay waste by fire

WARD—a guarding spell.

WARDEN OF ALTHAIN—alternative title for the Fellowship Sorcerer, Sethvir.

WENJ—servant at an inn along the coast road in Tysan that borders the Korias flats.

    pronounced: wenge

    root meaning: *wenje*—beetle

WERPOINT—fishing town and outpost on the northeast coast of Fallowmere, Rathain. Musterpoint for Lysaer's war host.

    pronounced: were-point

    root meaning: *wyr*—all/sum

WEST GATE PROPHECY—prophecy made by Dakar the Mad Prophet in Third Age 5061, which forecast the return of royal talent through the West Gate, and the bane of Desh-thiere and a return to untrammeled sunlight.

WESTCLIFF—port city located on the coast of Carithwyr, Kingdom of Havish.

WESTFEN—fishing town on the coast of Deshir, Kingdom of Rathain.

WESTWOOD—forest located in Camris, Tysan, north of the Great West Road.

WORLDSEND GATES—set at the four compass points of the continent of Paravia. These were spelled portals constructed by the Fellowship of Seven at the dawn of the Third Age, and were done in connection with the obligations created by their compact with the Paravian races which allowed men to settle on Athera.

Magician
Raymond E. Feist

New Revised Edition

Raymond E. Feist has prepared a new, revised edition, to incorporate over 15,000 words of text omitted from previous editions so that, in his own words, 'it is essentially the book I would have written had I the skills I possess today'.

At Crydee, a frontier outpost in the tranquil Kingdom of the Isles, an orphan boy, Pug is apprenticed to a master magician – and the destinies of two worlds are changed forever. Suddenly the peace of the Kingdom is destroyed as mysterious alien invaders swarm through the land. Pug is swept up into the conflict but for him and his warrior friend, Tomas, an odyssey into the unknown has only just begun. Tomas will inherit a legacy of savage power from an ancient civilisation. Pug's destiny is to lead him through a rift in the fabric of space and time to the mastery of the unimaginable powers of a strange new magic...

'Epic scope . . . fast-moving action . . . vivid imagination'
Washington Post

'Tons of intrigue and action' *Publishers Weekly*

ISBN 0 586 21783 3